HE CLOSED HIS HAND OVER HERS
and for an instant held her fingers hard. "Don't
be afraid," he whispered. "You're meant to feel
the way you do. You're made for it. You're just
finding out what it's like to live. But you're
going to learn a lot more. I'm going to teach
you."

With thrilling immediacy, Frances Parkinson Keyes cap-
tures the essence of New Orleans' famous French Quarter
and its sophisticated Southern aristocracy. Crescent Carnival, spanning the tangled lives and loves of three genera-
tions, is a dramatic tale of star-crossed lovers and a luxurious
portrait of the antebellum South.

"... written with brilliance
and verve ... a marked success."
—CATHOLIC WORLD

Crescent Carnival

BY FRANCES PARKINSON KEYES

A CREST REPRINT

CREST
BOOK

FAWCETT PUBLICATIONS, INC., GREENWICH, CONN.
MEMBER OF AMERICAN BOOK PUBLISHERS COUNCIL, INC.

With gratitude and affection
TO ALL THE FRIENDS
whose kindness and co-operation
made possible the creation of this novel

A Crest Book published by arrangement with Julian Messner, Inc.

PRINTING HISTORY
Published by Julian Messner, Inc.—13 printings
A selection of the Literary Guild

Third Crest printing, September 1965

Crest Books are published by Fawcett World Library,
67 West 44th Street, New York, New York 10036
Printed in the United States of America.

Author's Note

NEVER HAVE I written a book for which I felt the credit was so little due to myself.

The initial suggestion that I should write a book with a Louisiana background came from my friend, Clarence Bussey Hewes, who is a native of Jeanerette, though I met him first in Peking and afterwards in Berlin, when he was functioning with distinction in the American Foreign Service and I was ranging the world in my capacity as a journalist. Later, when he and I both became more or less settled in Washington, he urged me to go to New Orleans for Carnival, saying that he was sure, once I had seen this spectacle, I would not be able to help writing about it. His first idea was that I should produce a work of non-fiction on the Huey Long regime, its causes and its consequences. I told him very frankly that I was sure someone else would eventually do this much better than I possibly could, and my prophecy has since been fulfilled through the appearance of *Louisiana Hayride,* a book which has received well-merited acclaim for its thoroughness, accuracy and readability, by Harnett T. Kane, a staff writer of the *New Orleans Item.* But at the very first Carnival Ball which I attended—for Bussey did persuade me to go to New Orleans in 1940, supplementing a visit which I had made there of my own accord in 1933—the idea for a novel rushed to the forefront of my consciousness. It took me nearly two years to clear a crowded calendar sufficiently to spend the necessary months of writing and research there. But at last I succeeded in doing so, and I owe the pleasant period I have just passed in the Carnival City to Bussey Hewes' persistence. Whether the public will benefit by this as much as I have, it is much too soon to say. But personally, I cannot sufficiently express my appreciation for the privilege I have had.

Bussey, you had a wonderful idea. The next time you have another as good, tell me about that, too, won't you?

I realized from the beginning that I could not capture the atmosphere or correlate the facts for such a story as I had in mind, without a great deal of kindly, wise and expert assistance. Indeed, I think I might have lacked the courage to embark on an undertaking of such magnitude, if I had not had the assurance, before I left home, from my friend Dorothy Selden Spencer—herself an Orleanian and a former Carnival Queen—that she would help me in every way she could. A great many persons make a remark of this sort merely to be pleasant; Dorothy made it because she meant it. It was she who found quarters for me in one of the loveliest and most characteristic of New Orleans' old houses —the so-called "Claiborne Cottage," once the property of the family which gave Louisiana its first governor and now the home of Mr. and Mrs. Henri Mortimer Favrot. It was she who, Sunday after Sunday, invited groups of her friends to meet me in her own delightful home on Coliseum Street, presenting the tale of my necessities to them in such an irresistibly charming way that they could not decline to offer their services and invite me to their homes also. It was she who listened patiently, while I read every word of my first draft to her, pointing out anachronisms and mistakes, suggesting additions and deletions, scolding, denouncing, laughing, crying, praising, rewarding.

Dear Dorothy, words are so inadequate to express my indebtedness to you! No one knows better than you how frequently I fail in what I am trying to describe and interpret. But what my thanks lack in suavity, they possess in sincerity. Accept them as they are, remembering that I would make them more eloquent and more moving if I only could. It is the gift to do so that is lacking, not the reason nor the will.

What Dorothy Spencer did to help me visualize the social scene, both past and present, of New Orleans, Hermann Deutsch did to help me visualize the political scene and the fair, unfamiliar countryside. He is, himself, a peerless political writer, whose articles in the *Saturday Evening Post* have been universally accepted as the ultimate in authenticity, and whose contributions to the *New Orleans Item*, on which he was long a staff writer and of which he is now associate editor, are equally distinguished. This is so generally known that it hardly needs repeating, except for the pleasure and pride that it gives me personally to hail him as a collaborator. But it is, perhaps, less generally known that he is an inveterate fisherman and hunter and that, as such, he has come to know the remote reaches of the state, which I might never have discovered for myself in the course of an urban sojourn. I could, of course, have written some kind of book on Louisiana without his help; but I could not have written *this* book on Louisiana without his help.

Hermann, I have constantly thought, while we have been working together, of the captain, decorated for conspicuous gallantry, who protested that he did not deserve a medal, because all he had done was to stand on the bridge and give a few orders! I have been happy in learning from you how certain parts of this story should be written.

Besides these three, there are countless other persons whose helpfulness, lesser in scope, has been equally great in kindliness and effectiveness. The reader, gentle or otherwise, will probably guess that both Bois Fleuri and Splendida, like the Virginia plantations of my earlier novels, have their prototypes in reality, and also that I have taken my usual liberties in combining the characteristics of places that are actually far apart. Bois Fleuri is the name of a plantation, belonging to Mr. and Mrs. Alfred Grima, which is actually located at Covington and which has none of the characteristics of the imaginary one in my book; it is through Mrs. Grima's kind permission that I have been enabled to designate my fictional plantation, which in some respects resembles an historic property by another name really located in the vicinity of St. Martinville, by an appellation which seems to me exceptionally charming. In the second case the name is imaginary, but I have also done a good deal of combining and adapting. I am indebted to Mrs. George Wood Pigman, nee Dorothy Hébert, whose grandfather, John Andrews of Virginia, commissioned the great architect, Gallier, to build the real Splendida, for lending me the original plans of this palatial house and for telling me a great deal about its early history, with permission to retell this in fictionized form. And I am indebted to Dr. R. E. Lewis, the owner of Afton Villa, near St. Francisville, for graciously consenting to the poetic license to which I have resorted in transplanting his beautiful gardens and grounds so that they might seem to surround a palace located on the Mississippi! Mr. Favrot's drawing, which precedes Part V of the novel, and Miss Wendt's drawing, which precedes Part IX, were both sketched from a photograph Mrs. Pigman loaned me. Similarly, the drawing of the courtyard in the French Quarter, which precedes Part II, was made possible through the kindness of Colonel and Mrs. Kemper Williams, who now own the property of which it is a part; the drawing of the house with the iron galleries, which precedes Part III, through the kindness of Mrs. Alexander C. O'Donnell, who owns the one in the Garden District from which this sketch was made; the drawing of the "shotgun" house, which precedes Part VI, through the kindness of Mr. and Mrs. Gray Richardson and Mrs. George Hardee, who own twin houses of this type; and the drawing which precedes Part VIII, through the kindness of Mr. and Mrs. Mortimer Favrot, who permitted me to use their house, in which, I, myself, have so long been a guest, as a characteristic example of a "raised cottage."

Speaking of drawings, it is a satisfaction to announce that all those in the book have been done by New Orleans artists. Miss Margaret Wendt, a graduate of the Newcomb School of Design, originated the design for the jacket and drew the end papers and the illustrations preceding Parts I, III, VII and IX. The drawings preceding Parts II, IV, V, VI and VIII, all representing different, typical styles of Louisiana architecture, were done by Mortimer Favrot, himself an architect of note. (Incidentally, the end-paper design was adapted from the one used in the first edition of the Carnival song, *If Ever I Cease to Love*, as rendered in the burlesque, *Bluebeard*, by Miss Lydia Thompson, and given official recognition by the Grand Duke Alexis.) Even the lettering on on the jacket is Orleanian in origin; it is adapted from that on an ornate title page of *Jewell's Crescent City Illustrated*, a magazine which enjoyed great local vogue during the period of the earlier part of my story. This title page and permission for its adaptation were given me by Mr. and Mrs. Albert Lieutaud, the proprietors of the charming print shop on Royal Street, which now occupies the space that was once the carriage entrance to the "Lenoirs'" residence, leading into the courtyard now belonging to the Kemper Williamses.

My friend, Ralph Nicholson, president and publisher of

the *New Orleans Item,* has been most co-operative in his attitude regarding the research I have needed to do among the files of this paper and those of the *Tribune,* which was formerly published by the same organization. Special mention should be made of the excellent feature articles by Burdette Huggins and Frances Bryson, describing the Carnival of 1941, which appeared in this paper and on which I have drawn freely. Officials of the *Times-Picayune* have also assisted me by making available volumes of old newspapers in the *Times-Picayune-New Orleans States* Library, which include those of the *Daily Picayune* and the *New Orleans Times Democrat,* formerly published by this organization. In "Clippings and Correspondence" and elsewhere in the novel where a quotation is allegedly taken from one of these papers, this has actually been done in most instances, the only changes being the substitution of fictional names for real ones, or the addition of fictional names, and the occasional addition or deletion of a line needed to bring actual text in conformity with fictional text. However, in a few cases, like the description of the Pacifici Ball and the "Lenoir" wedding, for example, the more extensive adaptation indicated has been made. The story of "Maggie the Mule" which appears on page 300 of the novel was adapted from one written by Alex Melancon and published under the title of "Too Good for Her Own Good" in the *Times-Picayune-New Orleans States* on January 25, 1942. I am indebted both to Mr. Melancon and the *Times-Picayune-New Orleans States* for permission to use it myself. The announcement credited to the *Boston Transcript* for April 22, 1905 is entirely imaginary, but follows the form used at that period in this fine old paper, which, unfortunately, is no longer published.

I have followed my usual practice of calling outstanding historical characters by their real names and of giving names characteristic of the region to my fictional characters. The name of Shoog really belongs to the matchless cicerone at Afton Villa, the beautiful home of Dr. R. E. Lewis aforementioned; many of the sayings and characteristics attributed to her namesake in my story are actually hers, and it is through her kind permission and that of Dr. Lewis that I have been permitted to use her name and adapt her descriptions and actions and to represent her as living at my imaginary Splendida. If in any other instance, however, some fictional character resembles a real one, with the same or similar name, this is wholly accidental, and I apologize in advance. The special assignment to do recruiting through the bayous and swamps, ascribed in this novel to Raoul Bienvenu, was given by the Navy Department to Captain Robert Mouton, U. S. M. C., of Lafayette, a former Congressman from the Third District. I am happy in numbering many friends among the members of his distinguished family, and he, himself, has been kind enough to permit me to adapt a description of this commission to fictional requirements. But there is no personal resemblance between him and my imaginary character.

On the whole, historical events have been followed and local customs described as faithfully as possible. A few minor liberties have been taken. I have telescoped some events, in order to bring them closer together, and slightly changed the dates of a few others. For instance, the Firemen's Parade, which was so long an important feature in New Orleans life, always took place in March; I have set it forward to December. The last great epidemic of bubonic plague took place in 1914 and not in 1913. The year 1891 was one of the few when the Twelfth Night Revellers held no celebration. The famous feud between Comus and Proteus actually reached its culmination in 1899 and not in 1891, and, of course, the rival Captains were not named Andrew Breckenridge and Adrien Lenoir. This crisis is graphically described by Perry Young in the chapter entitled "Gaul and Saxon Clash" of his invaluable book, *The Mystik Krewe.* It has also been graphically described to me by the family of the real Comus Captain! The viewpoint on the nature and duration of the war, attributed to Drew in the last chapter, was inspired by Anne O'Hare McCormick's statement appearing in the *New York Times* on August 1, 1942.

Charpentier's opera, *Louise,* was sung in New York three times during the 1940-41 season of the Metropolitan, but the title role was taken each time by Miss Grace Moore. Massenet's *Manon* was sung in New Orleans on April 22, 1941, but the title role was taken by Miss Jarmila Novotna. It is, however, true that Mary Garden's first big chance came in the manner described, and that the program of entertaining, indicated as having been planned for Stella Fontaine, is typical of those arranged in the Crescent City for visiting stars.

Among the many other books which I have read or re-read with profit and delight, while working on my own, have been: *Louisiana Hayride*, by Harnett Kane, already mentioned; *Lanterns on the Levee*, by William A. Percy; *The French Quarter*, by Herbert Asbury; *With This Ring*, by Mignon Eberhardt; *Wild Is the River*, by Louis Bromfield; *Saratoga Trunk*, by Edna Ferber; *Chita*, by Lafcadio Hearn; *Stubborn Roots*, by Elma Godchaux; *Old New Orleans*, by Frances and Edward Larocque Tinker; *New Orleans* and *Memories of a Southern Woman of Letters*, by Grace King; *Old Creole Days*, by George Cable; *Madame Toussaint's Wedding Day*, by Thad St. Martin; *Acadian Reminiscences*, by Felix Voorhies; *New Orleans: Its Old Houses, Shops and Public Buildings*, by Nathaniel Courtlandt Curtis; *Old Louisiana*, by Lyle Saxon; *The Ursulines in New Orleans*, anonymous; *White Pillars*, by J. Frazer Smith; *New Orleans and Its Living Past*, by Clarence John Laughlin and David L. Cohn; *New Orleans and Its Environs*, by Italo William Ricciuti; *New Orleans City Guide*, American Guide Series; *Louisiana State Guide*, American Guide Series*; *Vieux Carré Guide*, by G. William Nott. Besides the helpful information that I have found in these, I have also gleaned a great deal from old scrapbooks and photograph albums especially those which have been kindly put at my disposal by Mrs. T. N. Gilmore, Miss Emma W. Glenny and Mrs. William A. Porteus.

There are several versions of most of the Creole and Cajun songs, as well as of the French songs and the Negro songs which I have quoted. The versions I have used, when there was a choice, are those taken from *The Louisiana State Guide* and *Bayou Ballads*, the latter a compilation by Mina Monroe. Negro stories have come to me from so many different sources that I could not possibly acknowledge them all separately, but I am indebted for some of the best to Mrs. Florence Bussey McGowen, Bussey Hewes' aunt, and Honorable Edward J. Gay. Mr. Harry B. Hewes of Jeanerette, Bussey's father, and Mr. and Mrs. Frederick J. Nehrbass of Lafayette are others who have helped me greatly in a

---

* It was in this book that I first ran across the words of the Negro songs, *Git it a-Going Emma T.* and *Say You Didn't Want Me*, and this discovery helped me to identify them later with the region I was describing.

general way, and their hospitality to me has been lavish and delightful. The ghost story of the wailing baby, attributed to Splendida, actually belongs to The Myrtles, near St. Francisville. I heard it told there myself, and it is also told in *The Louisiana State Guide* (page 514). The story of the little old lady in black, who leaves her carriage and walks down the avenue of oaks, actually belongs to Oak Allee, and was told me, with permission to adapt it, by the present owner of that beautiful plantation, Mrs. Andrew Stewart.

Since the original of Splendida is now in a state of deserted decay, I naturally have not been able to stay there, though I have gone there again and again, both in sunshine and in storm, both by daylight and by moonlight, feeling, as I lingered among its splendid ruins, as I have never felt elsewhere except among the ruins of the Acropolis; for here, too, is some of "the glory that was Greece," transplanted to the shores of the Mississippi River, which, for me, long ago ceased to be a sight and became an experience. But there are many other plantation houses, where I have been hospitably received, which have helped me to understand the sort of life that still goes on in them in spite of the "death and destruction" which the ruthless river so often carries with it. Among these, I must mention Acadia, St. Louis, Rienzi, Oak Allee, Burnside, Nottoways and Southdown.

Bertha Baker, who, under my direction, helped with the research through newspaper files, and also in the Howard Library, the Cabildo and other places where we sought for authentic records, deserves a public expression of thanks for the faithfulness and thoroughness with which she did her work. So does Jean Darling, who typed the entire manuscript as I read it aloud to her from the pencilled draft, which still represents, as it always has, my own wearisome way of writing a story.

The term, Creole, is so often inaccurately interpreted that I feel it is best to avert any possible misinterpretation of the word as it is used in this book. *Webster's Dictionary* defines it thus: "In the United States, a white person descended from the French or Spanish settlers of Louisiana and the Gulf States, and preserving their characteristic speech and culture." Mr. Lionel Durel, Professor of French at Tulane University in New Orleans, goes further, and defines a Creole as the white descendant of any Continental colonizer in the region, among whom there were also numerous Germans and some Italians. Either of these interpretations may be accepted as correct. Under no circumstances, however, is the term, Creole, used in the Southern States to denote a person with any colored blood, though this is sometimes done in the West Indies, and Webster authorizes it as a subsidiary usage, provided the word is not capitalized. The interpretation throughout this novel is that a Creole is a white person.

And now the story is finished. It has ceased to be mine. It becomes the public's. I hope the public will treat it kindly and, above all, that it will remember what I have already said so imperfectly but so feelingly: that it is a Louisiana story, the writing of which was made possible through the kindness and co-operation of many Louisianians to one lone Virginian, who came to their state to find a story and found friends as well.

F.P.K.

St. Charles Hotel, New Orleans, Louisiana—January-February, 1940.
Pine Grove Farm, North Haverhill, New Hampshire—September-October, 1941.
"Tradition" — Alexandria, Virginia — November-December, 1941.
5824 St. Charles Avenue, New Orleans, Louisiana—January-August, 1942.
Pine Grove Farm, North Haverhill, New Hampshire—September-October, 1942.

Contents

PART I

As It Drew to an End

January, 1940

CHAPTER 1

"MY DEAR, did you ever see such a spectacular parade in your life? I've heard that the Queen's costume cost one thousand dollars, without counting flowers and ornaments and presents, of course, and the Maids' five hundred apiece."

"*One* thousand! I should think it might easily have been two or three! It's perfectly gorgeous. Stella wears it well, too —she has the figure to set it off and the face to go with it. Really, I think she is the prettiest girl in New Orleans. And for once, beauty doesn't seem to be only skin-deep. She has a lovely disposition, too."

"Mathilde, she's acted mighty obstinate about this young Cajun lawyer from Abbeville, who's in the State Senate. Raoul Bienvenu, is that his name?"

"Yes. But I admire Stella for sticking to her guns, and I hear he is one of the most promising young politicians in the state. He's almost certain to go to Congress next fall, on the crest of this reform wave."

"Well, he is absolutely different from the type her family thought she would want to marry. I hear her grandmother is especially cut up over it."

"She would be. But I still admire Stella's spirit. And just look at her now! Isn't she a sight to remember all your life?"

The two friends, Barbara Emery and Mathilde Villeré, were sitting in the front row of the seats behind the balcony boxes in the Municipal Auditorium of New Orleans, where the Pacifici were holding their Fiftieth Anniversary Celebration. Of all the balls held since the Carnival Season was launched by the Twelfth Night Revellers, none had begun to create the excitement or arouse the curiosity that surrounded this one. Several of the "Krewes" were considered much more exclusive; half a dozen, at least, had a larger membership and more money at their command. But the Pacifici had managed to capture the attention, both of the "proletariat," which did not even expect to attend the ball, and could only read about it afterwards in the papers, and of the carefully culled guests whose names appeared on the invitation list. Many a maiden belonging to the sacred inner circle, who had hitherto turned up her pretty nose at anything except a card for the "call-out section," was only too glad to sit in the balcony this time; many an outsider who had hitherto scoffed—partly from ignorance and partly from envy—at the Carnival's system as farcical foolishness, was fascinated by the prospect of penetrating to its mysteries through the magic doors which the Pacifici graciously held open at last. This was partly because it was rumored that the "design," the theme of which was a well-guarded secret, would surpass in splendor and originality anything that had ever been seen in the Crescent City before; but it was still more largely because it was known that the Grand March would present a spectacle surpassing any in the annals of New Orleans since the first Carnival was celebrated in 1827. For on this unique occasion, Mrs. Marcel Fontaine, who as Estelle Lenoir had been the Queen of the Pacifici at their first ball, fifty years earlier, was to lead the march, escorted by that proud and perennial beau, Arthur Leroy. In their wake were to follow no less than forty of the fifty belles who had reigned as Queens of the Pacifici since the foundation of the Society. Many of them, who had retained their figures to a surprising degree, were wearing the regal robes in which they had made their first appearance, as Mrs. Fontaine herself was doing; while at the end of the procession, Stella Fontaine, Mrs. Fontaine's granddaughter and namesake, was scheduled to appear in all her glory, as Queen of the current ball.

As far as the weather was concerned, the evening had begun inauspiciously: it had been bitterly cold in New Orleans for more than a fortnight—so cold that many of the pipes, laid on the surface of the ground with characteristic optimism regarding the possibility of such abnormal temperatures, had inopportunely burst. The families consequently inconvenienced, whose houses were inadequately heated at best, had declined to take refuge with their more fortunately situated relatives, and had bravely, though a little bitterly, stood their ground, huddled together in two or three rooms. But so much overcrowding had not improved the harmony of the groups occupying such close quarters, and the sleet and rain through which they drove to the Municipal Auditorium on the night of the Pacifici Ball assumed the aspects of a final insult added to prolonged injury by the weatherman. The throng pressing around the entrance to the Auditorium was so dense that it was almost impossible to bring cars close to the curb; the beautiful dresses bought especially for the occasion would be splashed or soiled before their wearers were inside the doors. This was true even of the conventional ball gown, which, in the year of grace, 1940, fell full to the floor and was almost impossible to hold up adequately, because of its width; but it was truer still of the regal costumes worn by the female participants in the Court. They had already dressed at the establishment where they had bought their costumes; there was not the same luxurious provision made for them as for the Pacifici, only one retiring room, which was primarily the Queen's, being reserved for them. The Pacifici, themselves, like the members of other societies, were each assigned a room in which to dress and undress, mask and unmask, on the night of their great celebration, and with a Negro "porter" to act as valet.

Once inside the Auditorium, however, frayed feminine tempers began to improve. To be sure, there were the usual scattered murmurs that not only had the weather never been like this in the old days, but that no bare modern building, like the Municipal Auditorium, could possibly give the atmosphere for any ball, however gorgeous, which the old French Opera House had automatically supplied when it furnished the setting for such festivities.

But for the most part the spectators forgot the inadequate *décor* of the Auditorium when the curtain was slowly withdrawn and the stage disclosed. The Pacifici had outdone all their previous successful efforts in preparing their present

design. It had been inspired by a line from Browning, which
Senator Lodge had quoted, with appropriate connotations,
during the Washington Disarmament Conference of 1921.
Andrew Breckenridge, who was now a leading spirit among
the Pacifici, had visited his kinsman, old Senator Breckenridge, that winter, and had heard Henry Cabot Lodge make
the famous speech which no less a personage than Lord
Balfour had pronounced "admirable in its clarity and perfect
in its literary form." For some strange reason Andrew, who
had not been a scholarly youth by any means, had remembered the remarks made by Lodge—"The islands of the
Southwestern Pacific are—far more numerous than is generally realized. They are so dense that we might describe
them in the words of Browning as

> '. . . sprinkled isles
> Lily on lily, that o'erlace the sea.' "

Now the delighted Carnival audience had good reason to
be grateful for Andrew's unexpectedly retentive memory, on
which he had drawn for the benefit of his Society and the
pleasure of its guests. The stage had become a shimmering
sea, and scattered over it were large and lovely lilies, which
rose ethereally in pale shades of pink and cream, above the
glossy pads, floating over the shining surface that supported them. Slowly and provocatively, to the sound of the
softest music, the delicate petals opened, disclosing fairylike figures. Motionless until their charms, in immobility,
could be fully viewed, the figures then stepped lightly over
the petals, which had unfolded until they now formed only a
fragile overlay for the pads. Joining their white hands, the
fairies began to dance, their gauzy draperies billowing
around their beautiful bodies. The illusion that their flexible
feet touched nothing more solid than foam was never lost.
Rainbow-colored bubbles, tossed into the air, could not have
been frailer or more ephemeral. Finally, in the same airy
way in which they had come together, the fairies parted.
Once more, for an exquisite instant, they stood on their separate pads, a vision of grace and enchantment. Then the
prostrate petals began to enfold them again, slowly and
provocatively, as they had previously opened to reveal them.
The curtain swept swiftly across the stage, shutting away the
shimmering sea from which only large and lovely lilies rose.

The Auditorium echoed with spontaneous applause. Only

here and there some spectator sat spellbound, still too dazzled by the splendor of the vanished scene and the magic of
the fairy dance to move or clap. Barbara Emery, bringing
her palms together with such vigor that a small slit appeared at the seam of one of her spotless white gloves,
looked in astonishment at her friend. There was something
tense about Mathilde's stillness; she seemed overwhelmed.
Barbara nudged her playfully with her elbow.

"Wake up, Mathilde! The show's over—that part of it at
least. But the best of it is still ahead of us. Don't pass out
on me at this point."

"I won't pass out on you. But I am stunned. And it's so
inadequate to say that it is beautiful beyond belief. Barbara—did you know Andrew Breckenridge had it in him to
think up anything as exquisite as that?"

"No, I didn't. I've just thought of him the way most of
us do, I guess, as a mighty attractive wastrel, who might have
been a great architect, as your brother Ursin could tell you.
He's in Drew's office, isn't he, holding down the fort while
Drew never goes near it himself? It's disgraceful! Drew
might have been a great leader too, with his prestige and his
money and his charm. Almost anyone could tell you that.
But he never does anything worthwhile. He spends every
minute he can steal with——"

"Hush! You know you mustn't talk like that in a public
place, Babs! Why his relatives and—and hers are probably
sitting all around us."

Mathilde had emerged, anxiously, from her trance. But
the glance with which she swept her surroundings revealed
nothing to cause her alarm. A space divided the row of
seats where the two girls were installed from the boxes
fringing the balcony, reserved for especially privileged ladies,
so there was no one directly in front of them to overhear.
On one side of them were strangers—a woman with an
eager, interested face, to whom her escort, a blasé-looking
man whom Mathilde vaguely recognized as a Louisianian
seldom in his native state any more, was explaining Carnival
customs with far less enthusiasm than his listener revealed.
The lady was probably a New Yorker, Mathilde decided,
visiting New Orleans for the first time; her clothes were
smart rather than elegant, her manner sprightly rather than
suave. Doubtless, Walter Avery—that, Mathilde remembered
tardily, was the blasé escort's name—had met her in the

North, and had suggested to his sister Charlotte, because of courtesies he desired to return, that she might like to come to the Crescent City. But he would not tell a stranger scandal; whatever he thought of Andrew Breckenridge himself, he would keep it secret, outside of his own clan. That was the code, and it was a good one, Mathilde thought, with satisfaction and pride because she shared it herself. Besides, the unknown lady did not look as if she were the sort who would care for scandal anyway; her face, though intelligent, had a fresh, almost ingenuous appearance, and it was very kind. The girls were safe enough on that side, in spite of their indiscreet whispers.

They were safe on the other side, too. Mathilde knew the elderly couple there, Mr. and Mrs. Matthew Shannon, very well indeed; in fact they were kin to Barbara. But they were both so deaf that they followed ordinary conversation with difficulty, not only for themselves but also for the persons who were addressing them. They could not possibly have heard anything that was said in an undertone.

The rear was also safe. Mr. and Mrs. Charles Cutler were sitting immediately behind them, and the conversation centered on just one topic, as it always did wherever Mrs. Cutler went nowadays. She was the leader in the Women's Movement, which owed its very existence to her resolve that the corrupt political machine of Louisiana should, as she somewhat forcefully expressed it, "be smashed to smithereens." Josephine Cutler was an admirable and earnest woman, and she had genuine ability coupled with great driving power. She had accomplished wonders, both in awaking general public opinion to the disgrace and danger of "the cesspool which had swallowed up statesmanship," and in dislodging conservative gentlewomen from their aloof position, where politics were concerned. But some of her friends could not help wishing that she would occasionally relax and enjoy herself, and permit them to do the same, when they were in her company. She was growing grimmer and grimmer; she was becoming more and more exclusively the zealot.

"I'm so glad the Grand March has started," one of her guests was saying to her now. "Of course the design was beautiful—the most artistic I've ever seen—but it doesn't begin to give me the thrill that I get in watching that magnificent old lady at one end of the procession and her lovely granddaughter at the other. Don't you feel the same way about it, Josephine?"

"I know it's the present fashion never to refer to Mrs. Marcel Fontaine except as 'that magnificent old lady,' " Josephine responded fiercely. "But she hasn't given me a particle of support in my campaign against the forces of evil —not a particle. Oh yes, a check! But she ought to lend her house for patriotic parlor meetings; there isn't another in this city so well suited for them! She ought to be out addressing groups herself, too, rounding up voters, influencing public opinion. With her prestige, there's no end to what she could accomplish. But she's more interested in the fact that she's kept her figure and her fortune intact than she is in the fact that we're in the clutches of an infamous dictatorship!"

"She is a lovely-looking woman, Josephine," Charles Cutler ventured to remark. "Seventy, isn't she? And look at the way she carries herself! She's slim as a reed and straight as an arrow still. There isn't a girl of twenty in the Auditorium tonight, including her own granddaughter, who couldn't take pointers from her— You know I've always thought old age was the real test," he went on, turning to Mrs. John Beal, the guest his wife had answered with such fierceness. "Now any girl can be pretty—well, almost any girl. And with all the beauty 'shoppes" and fancy toilet preparations there are on the market, I'd say there was no reason why a woman shouldn't put up a mighty good imitation of youthful charm to the age of fifty or thereabouts. After that, it takes more than a permanent wave and a special shade of lipstick—not to mention a careful diet!—to keep or make the female of the species easy on the eye. About that time everything she's done and been begins to show, right through all the make-up she can put on and all the foundation garments she can squeeze herself into. If she's been lazy or intemperate or selfish or mean or vicious, the marks of it are all there, for everyone to see. But Mrs. Fontaine meets the acid test. She's an incomparable example of all we mean when we speak of a lady as a 'perfect Southern gentlewoman.' "

"She's an aristocrat, and shows it, if that's what you're trying to say," Josephine Cutler remarked contemptuously. "The kind that never cared what happened to the rest of the world as long as she and her own family were comfortable and secure and important. Oh, of course she's *charitable,* in that condescending way that draws a line between equals and inferiors. If she'd brought up that spineless son of hers, Olivier, to do his duty, he'd have gone into politics, and carried on the great traditions of our earliest governors and senators. But, oh no! she had a tradition of her own. In her heyday *gentlemen* weren't mixing in anything that might turn out to be muddy. So they lived in leisure and luxury on inherited money, and married simpering little fools like Bessie Rose Renier, who wouldn't have known a ballot box from a footstool!"

"Josephine, my dear, I'm afraid we're disturbing some of the other spectators. I've noticed Miss Villeré, who's sitting in front of us, turning around several times."

The first time that Mathilde turned around, it had been to reassure herself, which she had instantly done, when she discovered the identity of the group behind her. She doubted whether Mrs. Cutler, in her present preoccupation, even knew that Andrew Breckenridge was having the most scandalous affair of his arresting career, or with whom. In fact, she would not have put it past Mrs. Cutler, should such tidings come to her ears, to go straight to Andrew with the request that he use his influence with his inamorata to vote for Sam Jones, the "reform" candidate that the Women's Council was backing for governor against Earl Long, the heir and brother of the late unlamented "Kingfish," who for so long had held the destinies of the state in his hands. Now that she was perfectly sure the whispers she and Barbara had exchanged would have no disastrous results, Mathilde did indeed wish that Mrs. Cutler would stop talking politics and permit her to enjoy the progress of the Grand March undisturbed; so it was true that her later glances had been designed to convey this impression to Mrs. Cutler, as that lady's husband suspected. But Mrs. Cutler was not to be diverted. Having indignantly dismissed the Fontaines from her mind, in spite of the fact that the incomparable grandmother and granddaughter were riveting the attention of everyone else in the Auditorium at the moment, she turned to attack her own guest, Mrs. John Beal.

"Esther, there's another person who isn't giving me the support she should, and that's your daughter, Julia. I've been trying to get a chance to speak to you about it, but I've been so rushed that I couldn't. I might as well do it now."

Mrs. Beal sighed softly. "I've tried my best to interest

Julia in the cause, Josephine, and I can't," she said sadly.
"I'd have been glad to do it for my own sake as well as yours
—you know I believe in it, too. But she's withdrawing more
and more from society. I'm beginning to be sorry John and
I opposed her desire to become a nun. She hasn't accepted a
single invitation to Carnival, and she had some very nice
ones. Instead, she's serving—in a lay capacity, of course—
at the Convent of the Poor Clares. You know they always
ask for volunteers among the ladies of the parish, because
there aren't enough nuns in the community to maintain
the three-day vigil in its entirety without help. They suspend
a small oak tablet, to which a piece of paper is attached, from
one of their front pews and——"

"Oh yes, I know all about the Poor Clares and their vigil
and their tablet! 'Beginning Sunday, the fourth, and continuing through Monday and Tuesday, Carnival Day, the
Blessed Sacrament will be exposed all day to make repara-
tion for the insults offered to Almighty God during the
Carnival Season. *Will the ladies be able to take the same time
every day?*' Then comes the list of half-hour intervals, made
out in the same way that they appear on a pad in an important executive's office: '9-9:30, Mrs. Jones. 9:30-10,
Mrs. Smith. 10-10:30, Mrs. Brown'—and so on. I suppose
the present reading of the pad is '10:30-11, Miss Beal.' Or
does she take one of the terribly early hours, in order to be
doubly uncomfortable? I should think you'd put an end to
such foolishness, Esther. I would, if Julia were my daughter.
The pious ladies and the Poor Clares would both be a good
deal better employed if they were out working for the cause
than they are shut up in that stuffy little chapel, praying!"

Mrs. Beal pressed her lips together for a moment before she answered, and her pleasant face flushed. "You
haven't a daughter, Josephine," she said at last, speaking
mildly but with a certain finality. "If you had, I believe
you'd realize it isn't always as easy to control one as you
seem to think. And even when a mother can do so, she
isn't always sure, afterwards, that she acted wisely. I've just
reminded you of that, indirectly, by saying I was beginning
to be sorry John and I opposed Julia's wish to become a
nun. Mrs. Fontaine wasn't able to do that much, successfully,
in the case of her only daughter. Think of Marie Céleste!"

"I don't want to think of her," Mrs. Cutler said harshly.
"And I don't want to see you let Julia get out of hand

either. If she had a serious suitor, she'd recover from these cloisteral notions of hers fast enough. Is it true she had a crush, as they say, on Andrew Breckenridge? And that he wasn't responsive? I can understand that might hurt her pride. But after all, he isn't the only personable man in New Orleans, by any means."

Though Mrs. Beal made no answer, Mrs. Cutler laughed, and Mathilde Villeré turned around to look at her again. This was partly because her attention was arrested when the name of Andrew Breckenridge was mentioned after all, but it was more especially because she really was beginning to feel annoyed that Mrs. Cutler's faultfinding went on and on. She wanted to enjoy undisturbed the pageantry unfolding below her.

The Queens, past and present, had finished their triumphant processional around the hall, and all those except Mrs. Marcel Fontaine and her granddaughter had taken prominent seats on either side of the Auditorium; they could be advantageously seen, both from the balcony and from the call-out section below it. Their costumes, covering a range of fifty years, served as a picturesque and varied reminder of period creations: the balloon sleeves of the "gay nineties," the "straight fronts" and hobble skirts of the new century, the flat, hip-length bodices and scant knee-length draperies of the post-war period—doubly fantastic when a court train was attached to them—all these and many other styles, dearer because dead, were amply represented. Mathilde reflected that none of them equalled in grace and elegance the superb green and silver costume which Stella was wearing. For a moment she wondered, whimsically, whether every girl felt the same about the current mode, whatever it was, and then decided that this was probable, illogical as it seemed; though surely no one could be so tasteless as to feel that the dress worn by Mrs. Baldwin, who had been Queen of the Pacifici in 1921, could compare with the one Stella had on.

Mathilde was thankful that her friend had not reigned at a time when her small, supple waist and budding breasts would alike have been concealed in the craze for a "boyish build" that had prevailed for so long. She had been right in reminding Barbara that even a costume as gorgeous as Stella's would have lost half its effect if the Queen had not been the happy possessor of a face and figure to set it off.

Her carriage, too, had almost as much dignity as her grand-mother's. Her glittering crown of brilliants and mock emer-alds, with pendant earrings and an elaborate necklace to match, did not seem to oppress her. Her dazzling train, for all its actual weight, hung freely from the transparent, jewel-studded ruff to which it was attached; she held her jewelled sceptre lightly in her white-gloved hands, bending her slim wrists with ease in spite of their encircling bracelets. But there was nothing fixed about her smile, nothing stiff about her bearing, for all her composure. Her progress was marked by the graciousness of her greetings, and by the spontaneity with which she inclined her head to acknowledge the applause that showered her. She was equally happy in her acknowledg-ment of the tribute paid her when she was finally ensconced on her magnificent throne, beside the King of the Pacifici. Her buoyancy was unaffected by the length of the ceremonial, and by her own automatic exclusion from the dancing, which had now begun. As each couple advanced solemnly to-wards her, she put something gay and personal into her own salutation. The praises which had been heaped on her earlier in the evening increased in volume and number now.

In the call-out section, under the balcony and back of the space cleared for dancing, the customary bedlam had begun to reign. The black-coated committeemen were roaring out names: "Miss Blanche Duval—Miss Penelope Phillips—Mrs. Joseph Courtney—Mrs. Harold Latimer—*Mrs. Duval! Mrs. Courtney!*" The girls and women, whose ears were already cocked for the welcome summons, were sliding from their seats, wedging their way in front of the rows of their less fortunate companions—who, unheralded, were perforce await-ing a later call with what patience they might—and hastening down the aisles to the edge of the dance floor, where the maskers awaited them. Singled out by the gentlemen, whose heavy masks concealed—or at all events were supposed to conceal—their own identity from their chosen partners, and proffered a courtly arm sheathed in a gorgeous sleeve, the happy ladies proceeded to pay their respects to the King and Queen, to dance while the music lasted, and to stroll around during the intermission, exchanging greetings with their friends. Finally they returned to their seats, triumphantly bearing with them the favors extracted from the silken sacks slung over the maskers' arms and presented at the moment of parting. Before there was time to unwrap these, the committeemen were calling out names again: "Miss Lapeyre—Mrs. Richard Craig—Miss Helen Scott—Miss Betty Heyward—*Mrs. Craig!*" The sliding, the wedging, the rushing, the coupling, had begun all over.

By the time three or four dances had come to a close, the girls who had not yet been called out commenced to feel self-conscious and nervous. Patty Forrestal, who was one of the shyest of the Season's debutantes, sat miserably in her seat, the pink palms of her small hands growing more and more moist, the smile on her pleasant mouth more and more forced, each time she rose to let Evelyn Baird, who was placed beside her, pass by her. Patty was not surprised that Evelyn, who was the acknowledged belle of the young married set, should be summoned in every call-out, and she was not jealous of her, either, because it was not in Patty's kind heart to be jealous of anyone. But she could not help wishing, not that she could go instead of Evelyn, but that she could go, too. She felt very guilty, even at this much envy, and she tried to quiet her conscience by speaking to Evelyn, whom she knew slightly and admired intensely, during the very brief interludes when Evelyn's attention was not otherwise engaged.

"Did you go to the Boston Club to see the parade today, Mrs. Baird?"

"Yes. But unfortunately Harold went to drink gin fizzes. He had to be put to bed upstairs before the afternoon was over. So I can't say it was a great success, from my point of view."

Mrs. Baird did not speak disagreeably, but she did speak rather contemptuously, and Patty winced. It was very sad and very unfortunate, of course, that Mr. Baird, who was otherwise so attractive, should be so intemperate. But after all, it was only recently that he had carried his failing far enough to be condemned by public opinion; probably a little earlier he could have been controlled or even cured by a different attitude. And however that might be, Patty could not help feeling that his wife should have stood up for him in any case, that she should not have spoken about him in that contemptuous tone to a young girl, especially a young girl who was not an intimate friend. It would have been so simple for her to say, "Yes, I saw the parade. I hope you did, too. It was very striking, wasn't it?" That, and nothing more. Evelyn did not need to mention Harold at all.

As Evelyn, her name resounding through the Auditorium, slid by her for the fifth time, Patty looked down on the pile of presents with which her neighbor's seat was heaped, trying harder than ever to still the envy stirring in her breast. Evelyn had hardly bothered to look at her favors—indeed, she had hardly been given time to do so. But Patty could catch glimpses of all sorts of pretty trifles, emerging from shredded paper and soft cotton, where the fancy wrappings had parted and the colored ribbons fallen away. Patty thought she could have been completely happy if she could have taken home just one small bottle of perfume, or one pretty compact, with her that night. To be sure, she never used perfume, because she liked lavender water better, and her preferred make-up consisted only of a little powder to keep her nose from looking shiny. But it was the principle of the thing. Of course, if you were not invited to sit in the call-out section at all, that was different. Patty had seen Barbara Emery and Mathilde Villeré sitting together in the front row of the balcony, without even a male escort, and still looking completely contented, as she would have been, herself, under the same circumstances. She had no illusions about her looks. She was aware that she did not know how to make the most of her good points—her bright hair and her fresh skin and her clear eyes—and that she had grown so fast that she had not had time to adjust herself to her height or to put on weight enough to go with it. She lacked grace and composure and chic and every other attribute, like gaiety and nonchalance and pertness, which went into the making of the successful debutante. But she had finished school so young that there seemed nothing for her to do but come out, though she was barely seventeen—at least her parents and her brothers and her innumerable male cousins all seemed to think so, and Patty had been ashamed to confess that she would much rather have gone to college. More and more New Orleans girls were going to college before they came out, especially if they had not studied in Europe, as Stella Fontaine had done. Europe was now out of the question, of course, on account of the war; but college was still feasible for many girls. Not for Patty, however. There was not much money to spare, after paying for the boys' school; and besides, her brothers and cousins, who did not think much of her mind, would have hooted at such a suggestion, just as they would be sure to hoot at her now, if she went home without any favors. If you did sit in the call-out section, and everyone knew it, you should have something to show for it. Patty hoped the people around her did not pity her. She could stand anything but that.

Evelyn was coming back again, sliding into her seat with that ease in which Patty was so woefully lacking. She looked lovelier than ever—a little flushed—but that was becoming to her—more becoming than the coolness and indifference she had shown so far; a little natural pink in her cheeks did not detract from the smooth, scarlet line of her lips, though she, herself, seemed to think so, for she always left her camellia-colored skin untouched, and there was no denying its effectiveness with her black hair. The favor she was carrying this time was in a small box, and she began to untie it carefully, instead of tossing it casually aside, as she had done with all the others. Patty did not mean to watch her while she undid the little package, but it was hard for her to keep her eyes off Evelyn, who was so beautiful and whom she admired so much. Involuntarily, she turned her head, just as Evelyn was cramming a glittering ornament of some sort back into a satin-lined velvet box.

Still involuntarily, Patty drew a deep breath as she turned her head away, and, feeling guiltier than ever, began to argue with herself. Probably the ornament she had seen was just an inexpensive bit of costume jewelry, such as any masker might give to any, or several, of his partners. There were such wonderful imitations of precious stones nowadays, which could be bought for a song, that a gift of that sort meant nothing any more. Or if the brilliants were real, after all, probably the masker with whom Evelyn had been dancing was a near relative, a brother or a cousin or an uncle, who was very rich. Patty could not remember, offhand, any such person in the Denis family to which Evelyn, herself, belonged, or even in the Baird family into which she had married. But Patty was sure that there must be one. That is, unless the brilliants were imitation. Resolutely, she tried to think about something else, and to a surprising degree, she succeeded.

Evelyn, who was dancing again, was for once the less composed of the two. She raised her beautiful face close to the mask of the man who held her so easily, yet so closely, and wh spered to him.

"You must be losing your mind. What am I going to say to Harold when he sees that favor?"

"Lovely lady, your words are completely incomprehensible to me. My mind does not amount to much, I know, but it never was clearer than at this happy moment. And what is the mysterious object which you fear may rouse Harold's wrath, when he sees it?"

"Please don't pretend. You know. The bracelet you gave me in the last dance."

"One of my fellow members of the Pacifici must have been sadly indiscreet. Your secret is safe enough with me. But I did not have the honor of the last dance with you. It was the one before the last. You, yourself. must be confused, loveliest of ladies. I had the last dance with Blanche Duval."

"I said, please don't pretend," Evelyn repeated a trifle more insistently. "The little Forrestal girl—Patty, is that her name?—has the seat beside mine in the call-out section. She hasn't moved from it either! And I am almost sure she saw the bracelet when I opened the box. She's kept staring at me. She'll probably tattle all over town, too."

"Pat Forrestal? Tattle?" the masker said scornfully. "She'd bite out her tongue first. If there ever was a trustworthy kid, it's Pat. Just take a good look at her eyes, the next time she stares at you, as you call it. They're big and brown and beautiful. But they're better than all that. They're honest. I'm sorry she's having such a thin time. Perhaps——"

"Well, what could you expect? I never saw anything beautiful about her, and this is the first time I've heard of anyone else who did. She's the gawkiest creature I ever saw. It must have been one of her flock of brothers and cousins, or someone else uninspiring like that, who invited her here tonight. She not only isn't a glamor girl—she's actually been a complete flop as a deb. Now, I suppose, the relative responsible for her presence. whoever it is, has forgotten all about her, and won't remember her until he's danced with everyone he really wants to, if he does at all. But as I was saying, Drew, I can't imagine——"

"Since you received a favor that displeased you, why didn't you bring it with you, when you were called out the next time, so that you could try to return it, if you thought you identified the masker who gave it to you?"

"I was so flustered I didn't think of it. But if you'll come to the house about four tomorrow—no, I think we'd better say three-thirty—I'll give it back to you then. That is, I'll talk the matter over with you. Because, you see, Harold's getting terribly suspicious and——"

"Lovely lady, I am more desolated than I can say. But I must go straight from the ball to my plantation. In fact, for all practical purposes, I have been at the plantation for two days already. You may tell Harold that, if it will simplify things for you."

"It wouldn't at all. He suspects you, but at least he doesn't suspect me of having more than one lov——"

The masker bent his head, as if to catch her words more closely, but so swiftly that he succeeded in smothering the last of these before it was wholly spoken. His own voice sank to a whisper.

"Speaking of discretion——" he murmured with a touch of sarcasm. "Ah—is this really the end of the intermission? What a pity! But, after all, I hope I may look forward to seeing you—somewhere—when I return from the country."

"Somewhere—when you return from the country! But, Drew, there are still any number of dances, and——"

There was not time to say any more. They had already reached the fringe of seats, and the masker, plunging his hand into his sack, had extracted a package wrapped in silver paper and tied with golden ribbon, which he handed to his partner as he bowed his farewell to her. It was a large package, so large that Evelyn knew, without taking the trouble to undo it, that it contained nothing which was either incriminating or valuable. She put it in the crook of her elbow and swept forward up the aisle, her rose taffeta robe-de-style, ornamented with garlands of golden flowers, rustling about her as she moved. Patty Forrestal, whose own dress was made of plain white crepe, drew back to let her pass. But Patty did not look at her this time, or speak to her. The girl's eyes were downcast, and her lips were set in a straight line. She did not even glance up when the committeemen began their raucous chorus. It was only when Evelyn, who, inexplicably, was still sitting in her own seat, gave Patty a slight nudge, that she started.

"Can't you hear that man? He's shouted 'Miss Patricia Forrestal' half a dozen times!"

Patty rose, incredulous. Then she went down the aisle very

slowly, because she still could not believe it was true that she had been called out after all. But it was obviously she whom the masker standing at the edge of the dance floor was awaiting, for the other girls whose names had been called were already crossing towards the stage, to salute the King and Queen and Mrs. Marcel Fontaine, who was holding a court of her own on a dias placed just below the one where her granddaughter was enthroned. The masker gave Patty his arm ceremoniously.

"I am very much honored to have you for a partner, Miss Forrestal," he said in a grave way.

She vaguely recognized the voice without being able to place it. It was agreeable and cultured, but it lacked something characteristic of the cadences of the deep South. The unknown masker had not lived in Louisiana all his life, Patty decided instantly, though perhaps his accent owed its alteration only to a Northern education or an extended European sojourn. Not many of the boys Patty knew had gone to Harvard or Yale or Princeton, and fewer still had gone to Oxford or to the Sorbonne. However, there were one or two. She tried, hastily, to think who they were, but before she had run through the brief list, she decided that the masker, who continued to talk to her as he led her towards the throne, was not a contemporary of hers, in any case. He was older than her usual companions, perhaps as old as thirty, and much more polished in his manner.

"—I hope you are enjoying the ball," he was saying, still gravely, and Patty became aware that she had missed some other remark, which had preceded this one, because she had stupidly allowed herself to grow absorbed in the question of his identity instead of listening more intently to his conversation.

"Well—that is, yes, I am, very much—now," she answered inadequately, and knowing only too well how inadequately, added hastily, "I think Stella's the most beautiful Queen of the Season, so far, don't you?"

"There can be no doubt of it. Still, I don't think she personifies the old saying, '*Pulchra mater, pulchrior filia*'—or rather an adaptation of it—for, in this case, it is actually a grandmother instead of a mother, isn't it, who is the more beautiful of the two? If Estelle Lenoir and I had been young at the same time I am sure I would have slaughtered every other male in sight, to get her."

"Marcel Fontaine did have very formidable competition, didn't he? I know Grandfather said something— Would you mind very much if we went and spoke to Mrs. Baldwin before we began to dance? I've been watching her from where I sat, and she hasn't had anywhere nearly as much attention as most of the former Queens. It isn't strange, I know—she isn't nearly as pretty as many of them. But I can't help believing she must have felt neglected, and she isn't well. There's a thyroid complication, or something of the sort. That's why she's so clumsy, and I think she's sensitive about that, too, for she isn't a bit lazy or greedy either, and I know she thinks people suppose she must be."

"I'm delighted that you wish to speak to Mrs. Baldwin. She's a grand old girl—one of my favorites. But I'm afraid, now you've reminded me, that I'm one of the many miscreants who's neglected her this evening."

Mrs. Baldwin was delighted with their attention, and later, when they approached the throne and Mrs. Fontaine's own special seat of honor, they were again greeted with great cordiality, for the Queen was one of Pat's best friends, and she spent a great deal of time in the fine old house on Prytania Street, where Stella lived with her grandmother. The clammy feeling in the palms of Pat's hands, the chill around her heart, were all gone now; the sense of neglect and inadequacy was gone, too. Happiness and warmth had begun to stream through her, with returning self-confidence. But it was not until she began to dance that a strange new sensation of exaltation and excitement, such as she had never felt before, flooded her being. Her partner led her easily, so that following him was an effortless delight. But it was much more than that. The clasp in which he held her, though conventional enough, was so close that it soon ceased to be impersonal. The strength in the arm around her waist and the firmness of the hand that held her own did more than support her physically; they uplifted her emotionally also. For this man had not only grace and strength, he had magnetism, too. It flowed around her, encompassing her, until it became as inescapable as the tangible pressure of his embrace. Gradually she grew aware of conflict permeating her gladness. Her feet seemed to spring from the ground, as they followed his steps, but her limbs lost all independence of movement, in achieving harmony with his. Suddenly she desired to feel the force of his breast against hers, and, as if he instantly knew this, he drew her still closer and held her locked to his heart. If the caress with which he released her had not been a lingering one, giving her time to steady herself, during his gradual withdrawal, she might have fallen, so wholly had she achieved unison with him.

"I am sorry that the music has stopped," he said gently. The regret, like the tenderness in his voice, sounded very real; but Pat had needed the reminder, for she was still dazed. It took her a moment to realize that the mysterious tie between herself and this strange masker was severed.

"I hope that you will dance with me again, later in the evening," he went on. "Meanwhile, will you accept a favor as a slight token of my gratitude for the gladness you have given me?"

He pressed her hand again as he closed her fingers around the package he had placed between them. They trembled as she untied it, walking up the aisle with steps that no longer sprang from the ground, now that they were no longer following his, but that lagged a little instead. It was not until she was seated again that she lifted the lid from a small velvet box lined with satin. Inside, sunk in a narrow groove, lay a bracelet of brilliants, a counterpart of the one which half an hour before—or was it half a lifetime?—she had seen Evelyn Baird thrusting secretively back among its wrappings.

The bracelet had an immediate and twofold effect on Patricia Forrestal.

In the first place, it took a load of dismay and disturbance from her mind; if the unknown masker was giving two such bracelets away, to different women, in the course of the same evening, then naturally, they must be paste. There was no earthly reason why Evelyn Baird should not have received such a gift, and the fact that she, Pat, had seen it in Evelyn's possession, had no significance whatsoever. In like measure, there was no reason why she might not also receive such a gift—except that she had never dared to dream that anyone would wish to give her anything so exquisite. The fact that someone did—and that someone like the paragon with whom she had just danced—lifted her spirits again to the pitch where he had first raised them. She clasped the bracelet proudly around her wrist to admire it and exult in it, when she heard one of the committeemen calling out her name again.

She hastened forward, half hoping and half fearing that she would find herself once more confronted by the mysterious masker who had given her the bracelet. She was relieved rather than disappointed when she was speedily caught up by another masker. It was too soon to repeat the experience she had just been through. She wanted, and needed, time to adjust herself to it, and, joyously, she was convinced that her former partner had been aware of this, and that he would not claim her again too soon, though that he would do so eventually, she did not doubt for a moment. She thought that in her present partner she recognized, from his build and bearing, her kinsman, Gail Rutledge; and as soon as he spoke to her, she found that she had not been mistaken.

"I'm mighty sorry I couldn't dance with you sooner, Pat. I got all tangled up."

"It doesn't matter at all." (It didn't any more. The one measure she had danced was worth all the others she had missed.)

"I'm through with my duty dances now. I can look after you the rest of the evening." (But you won't have to, she thought. Someone else is going to do that. He'll be back in a few minutes. He's only biding his time.) "You're sure you're not sore with me, Pat?"

"Yes, I am sure. Don't be silly, Gail."

"Because I think a lot of you. I'd feel terrible if I thought you didn't know that."

"But I do know it." (Only that didn't matter either, any more—that cousinly kind of attachment that Gail had for her. She possessed something better now, at least the beginning of something better.)

"Well, you don't need to be so damn cool about it. I'll bet you are sore, after all."

"I'm not sore, but you bore me, Gail, when you act like this. Let's not talk at all. Let's just dance."

Andrew Breckenridge came out of his dressing room and stood for a moment just beyond the threshold of the door which Sam, his Negro porter, had obsequiously opened for him. Andrew demanded, and received, superlative service; but at the end of the evening he tipped with a lavishness unap-

proached by any other member of the "Krewe." The broad
grin on Sam's face was proof positive of his master's prodigality. Like all the rest, Andrew had drunk his share of
champagne before the masking began, and he had also made
way with considerable liquid refreshment while Sam had
been engaged in delivering him from his ten-pound mask
and correspondingly heavy armor. But he did not need to be
"poured into a taxi," as the current phrase ran, now that the
ball was over. (Not that Andrew customarily rode in taxis,
under any circumstances. He owned a Cadillac coupé,
which Louis, his manservant, drove for him when he went
out in the evening, and at all other times when doing so
himself would have been a nuisance to him.) He was still
cold sober, which was more than could be said for most of
the men emerging from the dressing rooms adjacent to his.
Andrew, pausing on his threshold, looked at them with an
expression which would have been close to contempt, if it
had not been so essentially charming and courteous. He
secretly despised the man who could not hold his liquor,
in the same measure that he despised a man who kissed
and told. No intrigue in which he had ever engaged had
been discovered through betrayal on his part; it was always
the eventual indiscretion of the recipient of his ardent
though undependable attention who had given herself
away, usually through anger or desperation. Though what
was going to happen, now that he had bestowed one of the
pair of diamond bracelets which he had bought for Evelyn
Baird on Patricia Forrestal instead, was certainly a provocative
question——

Smiling slightly as he thought of the complications which
might arise, he drew back towards the door again, to make
room for the other members of the "Krewes" who were already leaving. His careful courtesy was wasted on the men
stumbling past him, leaning on their porters, or linking
their arms with boon companions. When the door of the
dressing room opposite his own was flung open, however,
and Gail Rutledge came out of it, Andrew saw that there
was at least one uninebriated member of the Pacifici besides
himself. But Gail was not only obviously sober. He was also
obviously angry. He slammed the door of his dressing room
after him, instead of permitting his porter to close it quietly
for him, and then he wrenched it open again, to fling back
an inadequate roll of dollar bills, with only a hasty mutter

of thanks for services rendered. When he faced around and started towards the exit, Andrew spoke to him with amusement, which he took less pains to conceal then he had his contempt for the others.

"Hello there, Gail," he said. "What's eating you?"

Gail, still muttering, made an unintelligible reply and hurried down the corridor. Without any apparent effort or haste, Andrew caught up with him.

"You don't look like a man who has found the evening an unmitigated success," he remarked. "I thought it was very pleasant, myself— Have you got a car here? If you haven't, why don't you let me give you a lift—and a nightcap along the way, if you'd like it?"

"I don't need a lift or a nightcap either. I can walk, and I've had more than enough liquor for one evening already, like everyone else."

"You wouldn't insinuate that I was drunk, would you, Gail?" Andrew inquired agreeably.

"I wasn't trying to insinuate anything. You can take it or leave it, just as you like."

Gail Rutledge had never been distinguished for good manners, but it was not like him to be churlish. Andrew, who was seldom surprised at anything, looked at him in mild, though untroubled astonishment.

"You didn't have a falling out with your ladylove, by any chance, did you, Gail?" he inquired.

"I haven't got a ladylove, as you call it. But I'd like damn well to know what's come over my cousin Pat Forrestal. If you happen to hear, you might pass on the news to me—and then go to hell!"

The angry boy flung himself out of sight, swallowed up by the darkness and the rain beyond the blaze of lights encircling the porte-cochere. Louis, with the uncanny intuition he always revealed, was waiting at the entrance, in the Cadillac coupé, as if he had divined the exact moment when his master would pass through the door of the Auditorium. Simultaneously, the doorman, himself, hastened forward. Andrew Breckenridge got into his car and rode easily away, the little smile of half-concealed contempt still playing around his lips, but a light which was neither amused nor contemptuous shining in his eyes.

It was very cold in the chapel of the Poor Clares. Julia

Beal, kneeling before the oaken altar surmounted by a Calvary and adorned with twin angels on either side of the tabernacle, felt chilled through and through—so chilled that she wondered if the chattering of her teeth would not soon be audible. She was stiff, too—so stiff that she knew that she would not be able to rise without help, when her half-hour vigil was over. Half an hour—that was a short time, really. She was ashamed to own how long it had seemed to her. She bent her aching neck, and tried to pray with redoubled fervor.

"Jesus, most amiable—have mercy upon us.
Jesus most admirable—have mercy upon us."

She felt a light touch on her shoulder and turned, startled, for the nun who came to relieve her never touched her. She merely knelt, quietly, beside her, stretching out a hand to help her rise, when this was obviously needed. It was always a nun who relieved Julia, because she was the only lay woman who was willing to share in the vigil during the desolate hour just before dawn. But when she turned, startled, she saw that it was her father who had touched her arm, and that the nun, whose coming she awaited, was also there, ready to take her place. John Beal, who was wearing a coat with the collar turned up, over his evening clothes, put his hand under his daughter's elbow and supported her as she arose. She was grateful for his support and for his presence, more grateful than she would have been willing to admit. They went out of the chapel together, and she saw that the rain was still falling in sheets. Her father held an umbrella for her as they descended the stone steps and got into the waiting car, which John Beal was driving himself.

"Is the Queen's Supper over?" Julia asked wearily, for the sake of saying something. She was afraid that, if she did not say anything, her father would guess how tired she was.

"Yes. Your mother wanted to go to it. I didn't suppose she'd care even to stay to see the end of the ball. Though I don't think she had a particularly good time. Josephine Cutler sat beside her, and she kept badgering your mother about this committee she's formed to defeat Earl Long. She's very much displeased because you've been so unresponsive to her overtures, Julia."

Julia ignored the indirect reprimand. "I suppose you saw lots of other people we know."

"Well, Mathilde Villeré and Barbara Emery sat right in front of us. I always thought they were very pleasant girls. They came out the same year you did, I believe."

"Yes, but I don't often see them any more—did you notice who seemed to be getting the most call-outs, or were you too far off to see?"

"No, we could see very well. Evelyn Baird was greatly in evidence, as she always is—at least during the first part of the evening. After that I didn't notice her so much. But she looked radiant and triumphant when she was on the floor. You know what a way she has of seeming to eclipse other women around her."

"Yes, I know."

Her father touched her arm again. "I'm sorry, Julia."

"It's all right, Father. There's nothing you or anyone else can do about it."

"I wonder—a rather strange thing happened. After the first third of the ball was over, I didn't see so much of Evelyn. But I noticed the masker she'd been with before that, dancing a good deal with another girl. You'd never guess who it was."

"Then suppose you tell me."

"It was that Forrestal youngster. I can't even think of her first name. I didn't know she was old enough to go to balls."

"You don't mean Pat?"

"Yes, that's it. Pat Forrestal. Andrew Breckenridge danced most of the evening with little Pat Forrestal. Not that she's so little any more. She's quite a tall girl. But she's young—she's very young. Much too young to——"

"To have her heart broken? I doubt it, if she has been dancing with Drew. But if I were only thinking of him—I'd a thousand times rather it were Pat than Evelyn, Father."

Mrs. Marcel Fontaine was very tired. No one, seeing her in the Auditorium, could possibly have guessed it. The sweetness of her smile, the straightness of her carriage, the spontaneity of her greetings—all these had remained unchanged throughout the evening. But now that she was back in her own room at last, she did not need to pretend any longer. She lay back, gratefully, on her chaise longue, sipping the cocoa which Julie, the granddaughter of the woman who had been her maid when she was a girl, had brought her, and from time to time looking thoughtfully at herself in the hand mirror, framed with brilliants, which she picked up from the little table where it lay within easy reach. While she was doing this, Julie removed first her jewels and then her shoes, and brushed out her snow-white, abundant hair. Julie had already unfastened her dress, enveloping her in a cashmere wrapper, daintily featherstitched and scalloped. Later, one by one, came off the silk stockings, the petticoats to which Mrs. Fontaine had always clung, the corsets with stiff boning and strong lacing, which had been so hard to find on the market until a transient fancy for them had brought them briefly back into the mode. Finally, when Julie held out the old-fashioned nightdress to slip over her mistress's head, Mrs. Fontaine, with the swiftness of long-established practice, stepped out of her last undergarments, shielded by the fine lawn that, at the same moment, dropped to encase her from throat to ankle. Then she lay down again, this time in the vast bed of carved rosewood with rose-colored draperies, where, half a century before, Marcel Fontaine had installed her as his bride.

"Thank you, Julie. You may go now. I don't need anything more. But I wish you'd knock on Miss Stella's door as you go past. If she's still awake, I'd like to speak to her."

"Yes, Madame, she's still awake. I heard her moving around there, singing to herself, like she does. I'll tell her you want to see her, Miss Estelle."

The French maid went slowly across the floor and down the corridor. Mrs. Fontaine closed her eyes, trying to rest them. The glare in the Auditorium had been very trying. But she opened them again when she heard a quick step outstripping the slow one, and looked up to see her granddaughter standing beside her, entrancingly if scantily clad in pink chiffon banded with lace.

"You wanted me, Grannie dear?"

"Only to hear you say once more that you were happy, *chère,* before you bade me good night."

"It gave me a great thrill to be at the end of that procession you were leading, Grannie, with all those other grand girls in between us, if that's what you mean. And to know you were sitting on a dais of your own, even if I couldn't see you there, while I was on my throne."

Mrs. Fontaine sighed faintly. "I hoped you'd say more than that, Stella. I hoped you'd tell me that now you've come

back to New Orleans, now that you have taken up the pleasant thread of your life here and entered into our time-honored celebration yourself, you'd be content to stay here."

"I can't say that, Grannie, even to please you. I'll have to
live in Abbeville for a while, you know that, because Raoul's
practice is there. That is, unless he's elected to Congress almost as soon as we're married. After all, the primaries are
in July and we're going to announce our engagement Easter
Sunday, and get married in June. Just as you promised we
might, if I did all the things you wanted me to do first. And
I *have* done them, haven't I?"

Mrs. Fontaine sighed again. "Yes, *chère,* you have done
them. But June isn't here yet. It's months off. And a great
deal can happen before then."

"Nothing can happen before then that can keep me from
marrying Raoul. Except his death—or mine. You wouldn't
want me to die would you, Grannie?"

"Heaven forbid!"

"There, you see! I don't think you'd be so cruel as to wish
Raoul would die either, even though he isn't the man you
chose for me."

"No, I wish no harm to anyone, Stella. But sometimes I
cannot help wishing that I might die, myself."

"Now you're going to make me feel badly, Grannie, talking like that! Why it wasn't I that was the belle of the ball
tonight, it was you! You're the most admired—and the most
beloved—woman in New Orleans. Doesn't life seem worth
living to you when you know that?"

"No, *chère.* Because you are unwilling to carry on the
tradition I have tried to save. If I felt sure you would do
that, I would live content for a few years more, and then die
content, but as it is——"

"You'd rather have me marry a man I don't love than the
one I do, for the sake of a tradition?"

"You're putting it very baldly, Stella."

"But I've put it truthfully, haven't I? If I'd told you tonight that I was going to marry Drew Breckenridge, instead
of Raoul Bienvenu, in June, you wouldn't have talked to me
about wanting to die, would you, Grannie?"

"No, Stella. I would have said that I still have a great
deal to live for."

The girl drew up a little brocaded footstool, and sat down

beside the bed, taking her grandmother's hand. "Grannie dear," she said gently, "you keep telling me we've come to the end of an era, and you always say it sadly, as if you thought the new era, if there's going to be one, couldn't possibly be as fine and joyous and constructive as the one that's over. I don't see why it shouldn't. I don't see why you shouldn't feel that Raoul and I can have just as much to live for, in 1940, as you and grandfather had in 1890. I don't see why you shouldn't want us to be happy in our own way, just as you were happy in your own way, and why you can't stop repining because it isn't the same way. Did you carry on your grandmother's tradition? Or did you make one of your own? Tell me truthfully, Grannie, the way I've tried to talk to you!"

Mrs. Fontaine sighed once more, more deeply than she had before, and tried to shake her head. But she was uncertain whether she actually succeeded in doing so or not. Her weariness had become an abyss, engulfing her; even so slight a movement as that now seemed beyond her strength. What was worse, faintness had begun to sweep over her, in waves. She grasped the purport of what Stella was saying to her, but she did not hear the separate words distinctly; and her own voice did not sound natural to her as she tried to answer.

"Not tonight, Stella. I'm too tired to talk to you tonight. — Some other time— And you must be tired, too— Give me a kiss, and then scamper off to bed— Sweet dreams, *chère*."

"The same to you, Grannie! You can dream about the past while I am dreaming about the future— Then we'll both be happy! That is, I'll be happy if you won't talk to me any more about dying—or even think about it— You won't, will you?"

"No, *chère*. I'll just dream happily about the past, as you suggest."

She felt Stella's light kiss on her brow, and, for an instant, the clasp of the girl's strong young arms, encircling her frail shoulders. She heard the springing step again, and the gentle closing of one door after another. When everything was still, she picked up the jewelled mirror which she had continued to keep beside her, after laying it down, and looked into it once more. But, though she still saw her own face in it, this was no longer as it was now, but as it had been fifty years before, and another face was framed with it. She went on looking at it, for a long time, uncertain not only where reality ended and mirage began, but where the present merged with the past——

PART II

As It Began

"Frenchtown," November, 1890–
January, 1891

CHAPTER 2

WHEN ESTELLE LENOIR was a very little girl, her grandmother, whom she dearly loved, made her a bright little dress, trimmed with bells around the bottom of the short scalloped skirt, and sewed bells around the edge of her broad-brimmed hat. Together with a mask, the bright dress and the broad hat constituted a costume for Estelle to wear to Carnival, and after Grand'mère had made her these gay little garments and she had worn them, Estelle always loved Carnival and the preparations for it. But she grew up without daring to dream that some day she, herself, would be the Queen of one of the Carnival Balls. She did not believe it even when she heard that Monsieur Leroux, who held the fate of all potential queens firmly in his adroit hands, had spoken formally to her father, asking if he could conveniently be received on a certain day at a certain hour in the Lenoirs' house on Royal Street.

She could hardly believe it even after the ritual champagne had been bought, and the silver ice bucket polished till it shone like a mirror, and the one placed inside the other, beside a plate of little frosted cakes, on the center table in the *salon*, under the crystal chandelier, there to await the arrival of Monsieur Leroux. She went into the *salon* and looked at these symbols of hospitality, and she was still filled with incredulity mingled with awe. The mirror above the console table, standing between the two front windows which were .draped with lovely lace and looped brocade, and the twin mirror, standing above the console table between the two doors leading into the dining room, made them all seem doubly splendid and significant. So did the appearance of her grandmother, who had retired to the second story, for Monsieur Lenoir would receive Monsieur Leroux alone, according to custom. Nevertheless, Madame Lenoir *mère* had put on her fine lace cap trimmed with lavender bows, instead of the one made of sheer batiste, banded simply in black, as became the cap of a widow, which Grand'mère wore on all except the greatest occasions. Estelle's father and mother were impressive, too—Madame Lenoir—who had gone upstairs with Grand'mère—in garnet grosgrain with ornaments to match, and Monsieur Lenoir in a Prince Albert coat and gray striped trousers. But Estelle knew it was the little lavender bows on Grand'mère's cap that meant the most—those and the flowers in the vases on either side of the gilt clock, which stood under a dome of glass on the mantelpiece. The vases were made of Sèvres porcelain, and were very beautiful in themselves. Indeed, Estelle could not remember that she had ever seen flowers in them before, except at the funerals of her grandfather and of her little brother, and at the wedding of her young aunt, who had lived with them, and on the day when she herself had made her first Communion. So she knew that this day was another landmark in the history of the family, as those had been, though still she could not believe it.

While she was surveying the champagne and the flowers, her father came into the *salon* and kissed her gravely on the brow, and told her that she must retire, because Monsieur Leroux must not see her, either. But she did not go upstairs, as her grandmother and her mother had done. She went into the dining room, closing the door tightly behind her. She knew that the conversation between her father and Monsieur Leroux would be carried on in whispers, and that she was not supposed to hear it, officially. But there was an unwritten law that she might take a chair, and place it as near as possible to the closed door, and listen. Listening like that was not like ordinary eavesdropping, because this was not an ordinary occasion. But for the moment there was nothing to which she could listen, because Monsieur Leroux had not arrived yet. So she sat still and continued to think how unbelievable it was that anything of this sort should be happening to her.

She had led a happy life, but on the whole it had been a rather quiet one, set in a rather prim pattern, aside from New Year's Eve and Twelfth Night and Mardi Gras and other infrequent occasions which had been the exception to the general rule. She had seen her parents' intimate friends briefly when they came to the house, but she had never been permitted to appear at one of her mother's formal receptions. She had gone to the day school conducted by the Ursulines, never taking the short walk alone, but going back and forth between Royal Street and Esplanade, accompanied by Julie, the erect, middle-aged Parisian, who was invariably clad in black silk and wore small gold earrings as her only ornament, and who acted in the triple capacity of personal attendant on Madame Lenoir, governess to Estelle, and supervisor of all the colored servants in the Lenoir establishment. It was an establishment which looked comparatively modest when viewed from the outside, on Royal Street, for the house stood in the middle of a block and had a blank narrow façade; but it opened up to amazing proportions around a paved courtyard which could not be seen from the street at all. In the center of this courtyard stood a lantern on a high stand, made after the manner of an old-fashioned street lamp, and this lantern was always lighted at night, just as the street lamps were, because the rays it shed were needed to illumine so large a courtyard. There were closed galleries with green jalousies, which led into the living quarters on either side of it, and open galleries at either end, those furthest from the street leading to the stable and kitchen and offices, and those nearest the street to the dining room, which, in turn, led into the *salon*. Magnolias and azaleas and bamboo, growing in earthen pots, were scattered about the courtyard, softening its severity, and it was cool and quiet there, no matter how hot and noisy it was on Royal Street. Much of the life of the household flowed through it, and Julie saw to it that everything was as well-ordered there as it was indoors.

Besides going to school, Estelle took a singing lesson at home every Tuesday, and every Thursday she took a piano lesson. Usually, on Friday evenings, she joined a group of young people, who were the sons and daughters of her parents' friends, for dancing, under strict chaperonage, at the home of some member of the group. There was no dancing master present on these occasions, as there always had been in the more affluent days before the War between the States; some of the families could well have afforded one, but others could not, and it was out of consideration for the latter that none was employed. The older cousins and brothers and sisters taught the younger ones, and they learned to dance very quickly and easily, because dancing was in their blood.

Estelle enjoyed these weekly dances, especially when they were held at the Fontaines' house, which was more elegant and spacious than any other where she visited, though it was not ostentatious and immense, like the houses which the Anglo-Saxon "newcomers" had built for themselves. The Fontaines' house, which was located on Bayou St. John instead of in the heart of the city, was encircled by a garden inclosed by a picket fence, and similar pickets appeared as a railing for the upper gallery, which was supported by slender wooden columns, whereas the columns of the lower galleries were made of sturdy stone. The galleries surrounded the house on both stories, adding importantly to its size; and inside, the rooms, though they were not designed for display, were furnished very handsomely and opened expansively into each other. They never seemed crowded, but they were always agreeably filled, for the Fontaines lived a less exclusive life than the Lenoirs. They were wealthy and hospitable and had quantities of company, which, in addition to their own family, kept the house very gay. There were four boys: Auguste, who was planning to be a priest, and Octave, who was bold and boisterous, and Marcel, who was livelier than Auguste but quieter than Octave and nicer than either, and Narcisse, who was still only a child. There were also two girls: Aurore, a great beauty who was already grown-up, and Clarisse, who was Estelle's own age and her best friend.

They were never happier than when they were sharing each other's pleasures. In the spring their favorite diversion was gathering violets, which grew in great profusion along the bayou. They decorated all the rooms in the Fontaines' house with these, and under the housekeeper's direction, they also made them into a special kind of syrup, which was consumed only on the greatest occasions, and attained not a little local renown. Sometimes Marcel helped them gather the violets, and often he and Napier Rutledge, a friend of his who lived near-by, took them sailing on Lake Pontchartrain. Madame Fontaine was still young and lively, and she enjoyed acting as chaperone on all these occasions. There was never any trouble about that. She, herself, had been one of ten children, very strictly raised, and she was determined that her own children, and their friends, should have more freedom and enjoyment than she had had.

After her mother died and her elder sister married, her father had put her at the head of his table, opposite himself, and had obliged her to sit there every night, in full evening dress, in a chair without a back, making agreeable conversation with her eight brothers, four of whom flanked the table on either side. She was never allowed to say that she did not feel well, or to shirk in any way. Her father felt that this discipline would be good training for her future career as a hostess, and if he were not pleased with the way she entered the dining room and left it, or the way she seated herself at table and rose from it, he made her repeat all these procedures over and over again, until he was satisfied. Madame Fontaine told the children about this in such a vivid way that it made Estelle ache and shiver to think of her, as a young girl, sitting in her comfortless chair in a cold room, or walking back and forth, trying to please her father. Estelle was thankful that this kind and lively lady, whom she liked very much, could do as she pleased now.

Between Marcel and Clarisse, Estelle always had a good time on Bayou St. John, but still, neither the dances nor the violet gathering nor the sailing gave her the thrill that she experienced every time that she went to the opera. Her parents had a *loge grillée* instead of an open *baignoire*, on account of Grand'mère's mourning; since Grand-père was dead, Grand'mère would be in mourning all the rest of her life, and so she did not appear at festive functions, outside the family. But once in a great while she went to the opera, sitting in the extreme rear of the *loge grillée*. On these occasions the grille was always closed, and there was no visiting back and forth with the Fontaines, who had one of the beautiful big proscenium boxes, and with other congenial friends; these friends all understood that Grand'mère wished to remain in retirement, and did not intrude, even to pay their dinner calls, which were so convenient to make in this way,

and which, under ordinary circumstances, were considered
highly acceptable.

Estelle, sitting tense behind the closed door of the dining
room, grasping a little metal hand warmer, containing a tiny
lump of charcoal, in her cold fingers, felt a rush of gratitude,
coursing like a warm flood through her chilled body, for all
the beautiful music she had heard from the *loge grillée*.
From the time she was quite a little girl, Saturdays and Sundays were the red-letter days in her weeks, for then she went
to the matinees, and she counted off, on her calendar, all the
lesser days that led to these.

The greatest experience of all, however, had been the voyage aboard the *Nantes* in 1887, when the Lenoirs, returning to
New Orleans after one of their biennial trips to Europe,
found that the eighty members of the French opera troupe
were their fellow passengers. Throughout the voyage, this
troupe rehearsed the repertoire for the coming winter, and
the five-thousand-ton vessel resounded with melody from
morning till night. There were three hundred and fifty Italian
emigrants on board, as well, and from their cramped and
crowded quarters below deck came never-ending echoes of
all the arias that the artistes sang. The passage was an unusually rough one, but there was no day so stormy and no
night so dark that it was not beatified and enlightened by
song. Estelle thought she had learned the meaning of music
when she sat secluded in the *loge grillée*. Now that she heard
it ringing out across the endless expanse of the ocean, in un-
confined majesty, her soul swelled with its splendor.

Madame Lenoir cautioned her daughter, when they embarked at Bordeaux, that one did not make friends of professional singers, but before they were halfway across the Atlantic, she, herself, was speaking very civilly to Mademoiselle
de Rinkly, the first falcon, and Mademoiselle Hervey, the
light soprano; and she ceased to reprove Estelle, when she
saw the girl chatting gaily with Madame Raphaël, Madame
Garelli and other outstanding performers. There was something about the sea that stimulated friendliness. Even Madame
Lenoir admitted this, though she never put it into words; but
Monsieur Lenoir freely admitted his unexpected liking for
Monsieur Berger, the first tenor, Monsieur Claverie, the first
baritone, Monsieur Desnoyers, the first bass, and Monsieur
L'Enfant, the leader of the orchestra. The days were so full
of delight that no one wanted them to come to an end; but

after all, the climax of the voyage was one of such splendor that all regrets were engulfed in the excitement of this grand finale.

The instant the news that the *Nantes* had crossed the bar reached New Orleans by telegraph, about noon on November seventh, a party of gentlemen boarded a tug and went down the river to meet the steamer. The tug had been placed at the disposal of Mr. Frederic Mauge, the Director of the Opera Company, by Captain Wood, and stocked with the finest wines and rarest viands. It had the reputation of being "a very fast mover," and its run was almost too short to suit its privileged guests; their high spirits were apparent as it approached the "gigantic vessel"—the designation given the *Nantes* by the journalists who had been permitted to accompany the French Consul, the port officials, and other dignitaries. The emigrants, thronging the lower deck in their gay peasant costumes, gave unchecked expression to their sympathetic delight as the distinguished guests came gaily swarming up the gangplank, waving their tall hats and shouting salutations as they mounted. Estelle, standing by an upper railing at her father's side, also exclaimed with pleasure as she recognized family friends among the visitors. It was interesting to hear Commandant Arthur, whom she liked immensely, talking to the strange young journalist who said he represented the *Picayune:* the *Nantes* had reached the upper quarantine station at three the previous afternoon, the genial, swarthy Captain was saying, and he had feared there might be a prolonged delay there; but the physicians in charge of the station had decided simply to fumigate the effects of the Italian emigrants and disinfect the ship.

By the time the Captain had finished giving this information, and the representative of the press had finished jotting it down, a steward had approached Commandant Arthur, and, saluting respectfully, announced that preparations for the banquet had been completed, and that this could begin at any time. By the spreading light of the setting sun, Estelle saw that a canvas canopy had been stretched over a large portion of the deck, and that a great table, beautifully adorned with fruit and flowers, had been spread there. Her mother thought she was too young to assist at such a fete, and her father, who had infinite respect for his wife's opinion, hesitated; for one dreadful moment Estelle had a vision of herself, supping forlornly in the deserted dining saloon, while

everyone else was feasting on the transfigured deck. It was
Grand'mère who interceded for her, and Estelle, flanked
on either side by her parents, was seated exultantly at the ban-
queting table, where she could look at the lovely singers, and
the distinguished gentlemen who had made up the gay party
on the tug; she could eat her share of the splendid supper,
and listen to the speeches and share in the toasting which
went on and on. Good feeling ran so high and became so
general that even the press received a toast.

Then, how could Mademoiselle de Rinkly, or Monsieur
Berger, or any of the other members of the troupe refuse to
confer a favor, when so many had been heaped on them?
Céleste Aïda and *La Donna é Mobile* and the *Anvil Chorus*
rang out as the *Nantes* slid further and further up the river.
The spreading crimson of the sun had vanished long before.
But the stars had come out, and a crescent moon repeated in
the sky the form of the curving stream which was outlined on
either side by twinkling lights. It was eleven o'clock when the
Nantes finally eased into her berth by the wharf at the foot of
St. Mary's Street. There at the dock the Lenoirs' carriage was
awaiting them, and two private wagons, besides, to convey
their luggage without delay to the Royal Street house, and
their servants as well as their relatives were mingled in the
great crowd, waiting to see the ship come in—the customs
officers, the established merchants and bankers, the young
men about town, the vendors of lottery tickets, the octoroons
who rented *chambres garnies*. The arrival of the troupe meant
trade as well as diversion, for the Season lasted at least six
months, and the artistes lived well and became a part of the
community. Those who could afford it generally chose to put
up at Antoine's, for there they had the benefit of incomparable meals as well as elegant quarters; but for all that, they
were scattered from one end of Frenchtown to the other,
and the Vieux Carré, never dull or drab, quickened to
greater gaiety and a livelier pace, with their arrival——

Yes, Estelle said to herself, cocking her ear again in vain
for the awaited sound of Monsieur Leroux, there had never
been a performance at the Opera House, or any series of
performances, equal to those rehearsals she had heard on
board the *Nantes*, and the singing at that beautiful banquet
served at sundown, with which they had come to an end.
Neither had there ever been a voyage which she held in such
enthralled remembrance as that one, and she loved the *Nantes*

as she loved no other ship; but as far as that went, she held in great affection all the ships of the French Line that put in at New Orleans—the *Paris*, the *Havre*, the *Marseille*, the *Bordeaux*, the *Dupuy-de-L'Orne*. She had travelled on them all, and, in spite of the restrictions with which she was surrounded, knew them from stem to stern as well as she knew the "round" boats, on which she went to visit her relatives along Bayou Teche and in St. Martinville. Every other summer, she and her parents and her grandmother went to France, and though there was only that one magical voyage when they had the entire Opera Troupe for fellow-passengers, there were often other celebrities, and almost always a group from their own circle, carefully chosen beforehand, so that it seemed like one great family party. They all sat at the Captain's table, for he would never have dreamed of permitting them to be anywhere else, any more than he would have dreamed of failing to call at the homes of all his patrons, to pay his respects, when his ship came into the port of the Crescent City at other seasons of the year.

The groups honored by the Captain's hospitality were all very gay and happy together, eating and drinking of the best, and playing deck games and parlor games all the way across the Atlantic—a long journey, for the ship always stopped at Martinique and often at Cuba, before landing them safely in France, after several weeks of delight. Then the circle was severed, temporarily, for some of its members went to Gascony, and some to Limousin and some to Touraine and some to Dunkirk. The Lenoirs, themselves, went to Normandy, visiting their relatives, the de Hauterives and the de Gruys, who lived near Lisieux, and remaining at their ancestral *manoir* until it was almost time to return to Louisiana. They then went to Paris, where they rejoined their Creole friends, for all these had now come there, too, in order that the ladies might replenish their wardrobes, and the gentlemen lay in stocks of fine wines, and buy beautiful furniture for the *salons* and boudoirs of their wives and daughters, and handsome leather-bound books for their own libraries. The reunion was always a glad one and the voyage home equally joyous. And when they got as far as Havana, they invariably found that other friends had come out from New Orleans to meet them, and make the final days aboard ship the gayest of all.

Because of these biennial trips to France, Estelle had seen

Havana and Fort-de-France and Caen many times, before she had seen any city in the United States except New Orleans. Indeed, the Lenoirs did very little travelling around, outside of Louisiana, except that during the alternate summers they took a cottage at Bay St. Louis across the border, in Mississippi. In the wintertime they always stayed close to their own home and their own quarter, "Le Vieux Carré," or "Frenchtown," as it was called by the newcomers who lived in the Garden District, between Jackson Avenue and Louisiana Avenue, and Camp Street and St. Charles Avenue— Yes, Estelle knew very little about the United States and its Anglo-Saxon inhabitants, she reflected, still listening for the murmur of voices and clinking of glasses beyond the closed drawing-room door. But it was only lately that she had become aware of this, still more recently that she had been troubled by it. She could remember the first time very well.

Her father took her to the races as well as to the opera, driving the family carriage himself to the spring meetings of the Jockey Club, and seeing that she was well enveloped in a linen duster before they started. She loved the old track, laid out on the grounds of the still older Riding and Driving Club, which had now ceased to exist, shaded, along the infield, by a grove of live oaks, oldest of all. It was a good track as well as an old one, where the foremost breeders and sportsmen of the country had been proud to race their best horses. Wade Hampton and Andrew Jackson had both been outstanding figures in the early days of New Orleans racing, and people still talked of the great race between Lexington and Lecomte in 1853. Recently Castaway II, of the Berwyck Stables, owned by the ex-mayor of Albany, Mr. Nolan, and ridden by "The Dutchman," as the famous jockey, Taral, was always called, had caused a furor by defeating Keevena, the favorite, for the Pickwick Club stakes. Now, everyone was discussing the six-furlong dash, in which Mr. Williams' Carlton had defeated Brown & Company's Lida L. Mr. Brown was sure his entry had been carried out at the head of the stretch, so that Carlton might come on and win; he offered to run Carlton the same race over again any day that week, for a thousand dollars a side. Feeling ran high, and might have run higher still, if a newcomer, Supremus, a superb black stallion, had not appeared almost unheralded in the field, and diverted public attention, by unexpectedly beating the favorite by a nose under the wire.

"Whose horse is he, Papa?" Estelle asked, excitedly, when the tumult began to subside, and she could make herself heard. "The program only lists him as coming from the Splendida Stables, just as Forever is listed from the Avondale Stables, and Hardee from the Lone Star Stables. Of course I know that Vattell and Florine belong to that rich Mr. Vanderbilt of New York, because his stables carry his own name. But Splendida—that is very mystifying, isn't it? I know nothing about Supremus. No one has told me."

"It appears that he is the property of a young man named Andrew Breckenridge, whose family originally came from Kentucky. His father was enormously wealthy and inordinately fond of sports. I believe the son is less wealthy, being also inordinately fond of sports, and not so prudent in other respects as his father. Breckenridge *père*—or it may have been the grandfather—built a private race track for special occasions at Splendida, which is his plantation in Iberville Parish, and I understand that the son keeps it constantly in use. But I am not certain. I met the elder Breckenridge, at large gatherings, once or twice. But I cannot really say that I was acquainted with him. He was away a great deal, and the son has his same restless habits. We never visited."

"And you don't know the son at all, Papa?"

"No, not at all. He has only just returned from an extended stay abroad." Monsieur Lenoir leaned forward, and tapped the shoulder of his friend, Monsieur Castaigne, who was sitting in front of him. "Estelle interests herself in this new constellation on the horizon," he said playfully. "One star to another, I suppose. Do you know anything about the young Breckenridge, Aristide?"

"*C'est un jeune Américain*," Monsieur Castaigne answered, in a tone of voice that was not reassuring, much less encouraging. Estelle thought that the air with which he regarded her was tinged with anxiety. Monsieur Castaigne had always been very kind to her, from the time she was a child, regularly laying in a stock of nougat from which to supply her in case she backed the wrong horse, and felt disappointed. But there was nothing the matter with her spirits now, though she had lost to Supremus, like everyone else.

"But *cher Monsieur*, so are you! So am I! We are all Americans in New Orleans now. We have been for nearly ninety years! Or so my teachers tell me."

"Oh, as to that!" Monsieur Castaigne shrugged his shoulders and spread out his hands, looking more distressed than ever, as if he suspected the Ursulines of spreading misinformation. *"Eh bien,"* he said grudgingly, "I understand that Spendida is now the most magnificent plantation house in Louisiana—if it may be called a house. It is more like a palace, with Corinthian pillars forty feet high on the façade and series of lesser ones in the entrance hall and drawing rooms, according to reports. You know the American taste for display and extravagance, Adrien. This young Breckenridge spends much of his time in his pretentious palace. But I have seen him here and there, of course. He goes about a great deal, and he has a way of making himself conspicuous. However, I do not really know him. Our families never visit."

Estelle sighed and decided to make some inquiry on her own initiative. But she could not do so immediately. A bell was ringing; another race was beginning. Hardee had been picked to win, but the odds veered around until Lady Blackburn was the first choice. She was a medium-sized, trimly built filly, who had been raised at Belle Meade, where the disgruntled Mr. Brown had bought her as a yearling; when she won the first three-year-old stake of the year, handily, in fair time, Mr. Brown's spirits rose, and nothing further was said about Carlton and Lida L. The weather was perfect, the track fast, and the fields the best of the year; everyone was agreed that the finest features of the winter sport had been retained, and indeed, that in some ways, the races showed marked improvement. The contests were more lively, the betting heavier and brisker; there were ten bookmakers in the ring now instead of six, and the crowd was enormous. Though no ladies were admitted to the grandstand unaccompanied by gentlemen, members of the new Louisiana Jockey Club were entitled to free admission for the ladies they escorted, and the loveliest girls in New Orleans, as well as its worthiest citizens, swelled the crowd. The title of Baron von Mysenbug gave an extra touch of distinction to the list of the Reception Committee members, and such local celebrities as Mr. Charnock, Mr. Wallace, Mr. Slidell, and Mr. Violett were all in attendance. There were three coaching parties and a jam of carriages. It was a red-letter day in New Orleans racing.

Estelle, surreptitiously munching the nougat which Monsieur Castaigne had given her, according to his time-honored custom, shared in the general enthusiasm and decided she could well wait to satisfy her personal curiosity. But the next evening, when she went to one of the periodic dancing parties at the Fontaines', she created an opportunity to ask Clarisse whether, by any chance, she had met Mr. Breckenridge, *le jeune Américain* who owned Supremus and had a private race track on his plantation, Splendida, in Iberville Parish.

"Yes, I have met him," Clarisse answered surprisedly. "He was presented to Aurore at the Bal des Roses, and the following Sunday, as she and I were leaving the cathedral, he happened to be emerging from the park. He bowed, and I think Aurore paused a little. At all events, he advanced and saluted us, and Aurore presented him to me before Uncle Théophile, who had taken us to Mass that morning, could stop her. You know poor Uncle Théophile is lame, so he did not instantly catch up with us. But when he did, he scowled and muttered and hurried us along, and I have not seen young Mr. Breckenridge since." Clarisse paused, and sighed softly. "I must confess to you, however, dear Estelle, that I should like to see more of him. Really, he is charming. Such manners! Such a figure! Such eyes! Such a voice! Besides, I hear that he not only holds races at his plantation, but gives balls there, which are as splendid as the place itself, and that, so they say, is superb. It is rumored that the draperies in the drawing room alone cost five thousand dollars, and there is a Sèvres service for a hundred, which is only one of many priceless sets of porcelain. Tablecloths sixty-five feet long and Sheffield trays with love scenes on the borders that are rather—well, rather— Oh, you understand, Estelle! Sixty magnificent apartments, if you count the housekeeper's apartment and the servants' waiting rooms; then there is a gentlemen's bathing room on the main floor and a ladies' dressing room on the second floor, which are absolutely *le dernier cri* in the way of appointments. Young Mr. Breckenridge also owns a property on Prytania Street, a big white house with galleries of black ironwork, like black lace overlaying a white satin dress. This house has a ballroom as large as the one at Splendida, and a great adjacent stable, connected by galleries to the wing. It is a superb establishment."

"And does he live in such a superb establishment all alone? Is he a bachelor?"

"No, he is a widower, but Aurore says he has been 'taking second notice' for some time now. He has a small son nicknamed 'Breck,' a beautiful bold-faced little boy about six years old. I have seen this child out with his mammy, from whom he constantly runs away, and whom he teases most unmercifully; but just the same he is much more engaging than Narcisse was at his age." Clarisse spoke scornfully, after the manner of an elder sister who has been forced to endure a great deal from a younger brother. "His mammy sits gossiping with her friends on one of those crosswise seats that go over the gutters, and whenever Breck gets into trouble, he runs and hides his head in her apron, and then looks up at her with the most winning smile you ever saw in your life. It is simply irresistible! Of course, this little boy is with his father, but I understand that, otherwise, young Mr. Breckenridge lives quite alone, at both his superb establishments, except for the innumerable guests whom he has constantly about him."

"I am surprised that he should spend so much time at the races and give such elaborate balls. You would suppose he would still be in deep mourning."

"You talk as if he had been guilty of what our Negroes insist the Bible tells widows and widowers to do without fail—'Look around at de grave an' pick out de nex' one!' Remember, a gentleman has not the same incentive to wear black as a lady. What can he put on that could compare in charm and coquettishness with a widow's veil? And he would never think of draping a baby carriage in crepe unless a female relative reminded him this should be done. Besides, it really is true that Americans are out of mourning in no time at all—generally at the end of two or three years. And I believe this poor young lady of whom we speak has been dead nearly four. She died when her second baby was born —a little girl— You know that sometimes—" The conversation of Clarisse became inaccurately but gloatingly obstetrical as she dwelt on the horrors of childbirth.

"This lady was a connection of the Rutledges, who now live near us on the bayou, and who have told me about her," Clarisse went on. "Her name was Anne Forrestal. She was also related to the Forstalls—in fact, their name used to be spelled the same way hers was, before that branch of the family moved from England to France and then to Martinique. They have told me about her, too. Apparently she was very lovely. I have heard that every morning before she was awake, her husband went out in the garden and plucked a fresh rose which he laid, still wet with dew, on her breakfast tray. I have also heard that in other ways he was not so attentive, indeed that he—" Again the voice of the young gossip sank to a horrified though delighted whisper. "The Forstalls cannot overlook this. But Anne Forrestal forgave him everything because of the beautiful roses."

"I suppose they might make her forget a great deal," Estelle remarked thoughtfully. "Every morning, did you say, Clarisse?" She had hardly listened to the parts that were whispered, because the rest intrigued her so much more. "I wish I could meet Mr. Breckenridge, myself. He must be charming, as you say. And I wish I could see the house that makes one think of a white satin dress, overlaid with black lace. Of course we do not often go into the Garden District, but——"

"Oh, as to that, neither do we! And I cannot expect to know Mr. Breckenridge well, even though he was invited to the Bal des Roses, and is received, because of his wife, by the Rutledges, who are entirely *comme il faut*, although not of our circle. But it is not as if the Forstall connection still existed. Without it, of course our families would never visit."

"Well, and why not?" Estelle heard herself saying, surprisingly. Afterwards she was a little ashamed of her outburst. But she felt she could not stand that phrase again. Never visit, indeed! *Eh bien,* she was like Clarisse in one way—she could think of many things worse than visiting in the family of a charming young man whose eyes and figure and manner left nothing to be desired, whose habits included the plucking of dewy roses, and who, moreover, owned blooded horses and private race tracks and maintained two magnificent establishments where he gave splendid balls. But in another way, she was unlike Clarisse—whom she privately considered a rather unimaginative girl—because she was not afraid to express her thoughts, and because young Mr. Breckenridge's reputed wildness, and the consequent disapproval of the Forstall family, did not seem to her very important. And though she had never manoeuvred before, to do anything that was not part of the prim, pleasant pattern which Grand'mère and Papa and Maman had so carefully planned for her, she manoeuvred now until she met "Andy" Breckenridge herself—and promptly fell in love with him.

The actual meeting took less ingenuity than she had feared it might. Young Mr. Breckenridge seemed to be ubiquitous, and, as Monsieur Castaigne said, he had a way of making himself conspicuous wherever he went. After six o'clock in the afternoon, he always wore full evening dress, and his fellow callers who appeared in Prince Alberts and cutaways, not to mention ordinary business suits, at ladies' receptions and other informal social gatherings, soon realized how far they were outshone. It was rumored that Mr. Breckenridge went regularly to London to buy his clothes, just as so many Creole ladies went regularly to Paris, and not a few young gentlemen of fashion experienced pangs of jealousy and resolved to save their surplus for similar expeditions; meanwhile a small, exclusive clique was formed for the avowed purpose of copying Mr. Breckenridge's garments and habits in New Orleans.

Still, no one succeeded in making as dramatic an entry to a drawing room as he did, or in focussing public attention so generally upon himself. Most persons, who went to Antoine's for midnight supper after the opera, contented themselves with toasting the stars and other celebrities from where they, themselves, sat, but young Mr. Breckenridge went straight to their tables, if he were not actually entertaining them in the first place, which was frequently the case.

Everything else he did showed the same sort of spirit. When Dr. and Mrs. John Beal gave a wagonette party, on the third day of the spring races, which was the last word in exclusive elegance, nobody noticed it after young Mr. Breckenridge came dashing up in his tallyho, which was described in the local press as "a bower of beauty on wheels." When a family group made a Sunday excursion to the Spanish fort and settled sedately down for a leisurely meal at Tranchini's Restaurant, the decorum of the day was upset by the boisterous arrival of young Mr. Breckenridge and his boon companions, who pre-empted the best table and galvanized the waiters into a state of exclusive attention. When Napier Rutledge asked a few friends to go for a sail on Lake Pontchartrain, in his catboat, young Mr. Breckenridge steamed away on his glittering yacht, serving a handsome luncheon on deck to a group who had been assembled to meet his cousin from Kentucky, who was a Member of Congress. When Mr. and Mrs. Edward Cutler issued invitations for a progressive euchre, nearly all the recipients declined on the ground of a previous engagement to dine with Mr. Breckenridge at the Jockey Club, and the favors, the decorations and the entertainment at this dinner were the talk of the town for days.

The families with whom Mr. Breckenridge did not exchange visits daily diminished in number, and those who were pleased to receive him and flattered to be received by him in return increased in like measure. The day was bound to come when he and Estelle, who had seen each other with mutually increasing interest over and over again, went to the same party, and Mr. Breckenridge lost no time in getting himself presented to her.

The occasion was a soiree of private theatricals, given by Madame Félix Denis, who had a playhouse de luxe called the Rose Lawn Theatre situated in a corner of the spacious grounds encircling her residence, more elegant and complete than any local professional theatre. It seated three hundred and fifty persons easily, and the hostess, in arranging to fill it to capacity, had inevitably included on her list all the presentable young men about town; she could not draw the line between those the more conservative among her friends would approve of and those of whom they would not approve, with the same rigidity she would have used if she had been giving a dinner, or even a small reception. She had also included most of the young girls who had not yet made their debut, but who would soon be doing so, in the cases where she had asked their parents and their older brothers and sisters. Andrew Breckenridge came into the former category and Clarisse Fontaine into the latter. When she learned of this, Estelle, who had also been invited, persuaded Monsieur and Madame Lenoir to take her with them to the fete of Madame Félix Denis.

She had little difficulty in doing so, for the very reason that it was the first time she had ever importuned them; and she sat so demurely at their side, as long as the play lasted, that they exchanged glances meaning that they admitted to each other that they had made no mistake in giving the girl so innocent a pleasure, since she had set her heart on it. But they had hardly reached the aisle, after the performance, when they began to change their minds.

Octave Fontaine, of whom they disapproved but whom they could not ignore, since they had known him since childhood, bore down on them, accompanied by two other young men, one fair and slight, the other dark and strong. Having greeted the Lenoirs himself, in his usual free fashion, Octave begged leave to present his neighbor, Napier Rutledge, and Napier's great friend, Mr. Andrew Breckenridge.

The acknowledgment of this presentation was as brief as courtesy permitted. Indeed, Monsieur and Madame Lenoir almost immediately indicated that they must seek other friends whom they had promised to meet in the dining room, where a sumptuous supper was already being served. Octave's bold manner became suddenly more respectful.

"Would you and your friends not excuse Estelle, Madame? Some of the younger guests have made up a little group of their own, and Aurore hoped you would let Estelle join it. She sent me to ask. We got separated for a minute, but she is just beside the door. See, Clarisse and Marcel are with her."

Again Monsieur and Madame Lenoir exchanged glances. After all, Aurore would be there with the younger girls, and Marcel could be trusted to keep his brother in order and his brother's acquaintances at a suitable distance.

"Very well, Octave. Of course none of you will leave the dining room, where Monsieur Lenoir and I will be with our own friends. And we shall count on you and Aurore to see that Estelle rejoins us within twenty minutes."

"It is understood, Madame. Thank you a thousand times."

Octave drew back to permit Monsieur and Madame Lenoir to precede the others up the aisle. Young Mr. Breckenridge had offered Estelle his arm, and she had taken it, before her parents realized that he, and not Marcel, was destined for her escort.

Looking up to measure his height above her own, she regarded him covertly but carefully. He was even handsomer, seen at her side, than viewed from a distance. Everything about him was brilliant—his white teeth, his dark brows, his crisp hair, his bright color; but this brilliance was as different from the flashiness which repelled her in Octave as it was from the restraint which annoyed her in Napier. He had the bluest eyes she had ever seen and it was these, even more than the clear red and white of his skin, and the strength of his build, that made him outstanding in a group of Creoles. His eyes delighted her, but they dazzled her, too. He moved with grace as well as freedom, and carried himself as if he were completely at ease in a world which he had molded to suit himself, and supremely satisfied with life and all that it held for him. His laugh had a warm ring to it. Estelle suspected that he was laughing a little at her, but the suspicion did not trouble her; it entranced her.

"So you're the young lady who called me *le jeune Américain?*"

"Pardon, Monsieur. It was not I who called you that. It was my father's friend, Monsieur Castaigne."

"And doesn't Monsieur Castaigne know that, willy-nilly, he's an American now, too?"

"I reminded him of that, Monsieur."

"How very wise of you! But I need a reminder that you are."

"Why, Monsieur?"

"Because American girls are accessible, and you're guarded like the Grail. Frenchtown must be the last surviving patriarchate. Do you ever move without your parents' permission?"

"Yes, Monsieur."

"Then suppose I give you a lesson in American ways. Let's not go into the dining room. Let's stay in the garden instead."

"I gave my word, Monsieur."

For a moment he hesitated. Then he spoke less lightly.

"In that case, of course you must keep it. This is the direction, I think."

After that, they talked only of trivialities. In the midst of such a crowd, and of so much noise, confusion and excitement, they could do nothing else and nothing more. But before the twenty minutes were up, young Mr. Breckenridge had managed to whisper a question.

"What is the next gathering to which you are going?"

"I am not sure that I shall go to any others this spring. But there is a chance——"

"Yes? Tell me quickly!"

"Madame O'Brien and Madame Villeré are giving a pink and green tea together at Madame O'Brien's house next Wednesday. Madame Fontaine is permitting Clarisse to go because Aurore is going, as she did in the case of this soiree. Possibly, for the same reason, Maman might let me assist, also."

"But that is a party for ladies only, I understand."

"Yes, for the first part of the evening, while tea is being served. Those of us who have been invited to help with this are asked to wear white dotted muslin and lace, and our hostess is furnishing us with pink and green India silk aprons, and porcelain trays with ribbons run through the latticed edges, to fasten around our necks."

"Very sylvan and sweet, I should say."

"I am not sure that I follow you, Monsieur. But I understand that later in the evening, after our duties are done, young gentlemen are coming in to dance with us. It has just been decided to include them in the festivities, as a reward. I am certain you will receive a card."

"If I do not, I shall naturally assume that it was lost in the mail. And I shall depend on you to save me the first waltz."

"Oh, Monsieur! I am not even sure yet, as I said, that I can go."

"Don't talk like that. Of course you can go, if you make up your mind to it. And of course you will save me the waltz. Promise!"

"But Monsieur, how can I do that?"

"Nothing could be simpler. Merely say, 'I promise,' and I shall be satisfied. I know already that you keep your word."

She still did not know how she had managed to do so, or for that matter how she had persuaded her parents to permit her to go, for the second time, to a party, before she had made her debut. But unwittingly, Madame O'Brien and Madame Villeré allied themselves with her by separately telling Madame Lenoir that there was no one whom the costume they had chosen for their young assistants would become as it would her daughter; and after Madame Lenoir had repeated this twice to her husband and her mother-in-law, the matter was as good as settled. At the appointed time, Estelle, clad in her dotted swiss and her rosy apron, and balancing her porcelain tray on its ribbons, stood under the trailing ropes of smilax which swung from the crystal chandelier overhead to the four corners of the "fairylike bower" into which the O'Brien's dining room had been transformed. Two hours later, she stepped through the ivy-twined doorway into the garlanded gallery, straight to the waiting arms of Andrew Breckenridge, and waltzed with him, listening, with mingled fear and fascination, to the words which were muffled by the strains of the *Beautiful Blue Danube*.

"Did you ever fall in love, Miss Lenoir?"

"No, Monsieur."

"Are you sure?"

"Yes, Monsieur."

"I'm not. I think you're doing it right now. At least I hope so."

"Oh, Monsieur! Why should you say such a thing?"

"Because I'm certainly falling in love with you. Head over heels. I'm going to propose to you properly as soon as I can find a secluded spot."

But even the resourcefulness of young Mr. Breckenridge was unequal to finding a secluded spot at the pink and green tea of Madame O'Brien and Madame Villeré. The "fairylike bower," ethereal though it seemed, was constructed with a view to observing all the conventions; and at the end of the first waltz, Madame Lenoir, to whom nothing had been said about dancing, in the course of the conversations about the dotted-swiss costumes, signalled to Estelle that it was time to go home. She relented, to the extent of permitting her daughter to remain for a schottische, which came next on the program, with Marcel. After that she was inexorable, however, not only on the subject of remaining any longer at the pink and green tea, but also on the subject of any further parties that spring.

But in spite of the well-guarded seclusion into which Estelle was so unwillingly thrust back, she knew, beyond any shadow of a doubt, that young Mr. Breckenridge had been right when he said she had fallen in love with him, and she longed, more than she had longed for anything else in the world, to believe that he had told her the truth when he said he had fallen in love with her.

She did not tell anyone what had happened to her. Indeed, she tried not to think about it too much, because she and Grand'mère and Papa and Maman were all so close together, in spirit as well as in body, that she was afraid they might divine what was passing in her mind, if she dwelt on it very much. And in spite of all her care, she must have betrayed herself. For it was only a few days after that fateful dance with Andy Breckenridge, one time when she was in bed with a slight migraine, that her mother came and sat beside her and told her something very astonishing.

"Are you feeling better, my darling? Ah, that is well— It was repose you needed, in your own tranquil room, nothing else. And now that your head no longer aches, I have something to tell you which I believe will please you very much."

"Yes, Maman?"

"Your grandmother and your father and I have decided to permit you to make your debut this coming winter, instead of winter after next. You have grown to such a great girl that it seems pointless to prevent you from becoming a young lady any longer. To be sure, you are slightly under the usual age. But soon you will have completed your course at the Ursulines, with great credit, and though we have sometimes thought that we should give you a year's schooling in France after that, we have decided against this, because we cannot bear the prospect of separation from you. If we could remain abroad with you, that would be different. But your father cannot leave his clients and his courts, and it goes without saying that his mother and I cannot be parted from him. Therefore the year in France must be foregone, though of course we shall go this summer as usual—in fact, we may be able to leave earlier than usual. And then, as I have said——"

Madame Lenoir paused, as if awaiting some comment from her daughter. Estelle made none, because, instead of being immensely pleased at the prospect of her impending entrance into society, as her mother had anticipated, and as, indeed, she, herself, had always anticipated, she was vaguely disturbed. She felt that there was more behind this sudden change of program than was revealed, and that it might be untoward.

"Of course, since we have not planned for it in advance, it will not be possible for you to have an elaborate debut," Madame Lenoir said, and paused again. Estelle thought she was probably thinking of her own debut, when for weeks and weeks before the great ball was given, she and her mother and sisters and all the Provosty cousins had spent their time making little paper frills to encircle the hundreds of candles used in the superb chandelier, so that the wax from them should not drip down on the dancers; or possibly of the magnificent gesture of tearing down the walls between two of the homes in the Pontalba block on St. Peter Street, with the ready consent of the friend occupying the one adjacent to the Provostys'—because Grand-père Provosty decided that his own was not large enough to do justice to his daughter's debut.

"A ball would be out of the question unless we took money from the sum we are setting aside for your dot, and that, naturally, would be unthinkable, especially as the moment is not far distant when you may need it." She stressed these words slightly and paused again, but Estelle, who continued to lie silently back on her pillow and look at her mother with large anxious eyes, did not avail herself of the opportunity to speak. "On the opening night of the opera, however, you will sit in the front of the loge, beside me, with your bouquets piled all around you. The grille will be drawn back and even your grandmother will appear, though of course she will remain in the background. Your father will sit beside her. All our friends will come to greet you and extend their good wishes. It should be a very happy occasion for you."

It was on this premise that Estelle was taken to Europe, earlier in the season than usual, as her mother had predicted —indeed, as soon as she had finished her course at the Ursulines and before she had contrived to talk with Andy Breckenridge again except in the midst of a crowd. She was a very fortunate girl because she was to make her debut under such auspicious circumstances; it would be a very happy occasion for her. She told herself this, over and over again, during the course of the summer, and she felt very guilty because she did not succeed in convincing herself that she *was* most fortunate, or that her debut would be supremely joyous. The European sojourn was really very pleasant and eventful, for the Lenoirs travelled about more than ever before, and stayed for a longer time in Paris. Estelle saw beautiful parts of Spain and Greece, where previously she had never been, and the creation of the dress for her debut was entrusted to Worth, whose establishment she had hitherto visited only when she accompanied her mother for fittings. But she was conscious of a lacking thrill which should have pierced her when she stood in front of the long mirror in her bedroom, just before she started for the opera, and again surveyed the exquisite model which had been packed with such care that not even a ruffle was rumpled when it was lifted from its tissue-paper wrappings. The tulle of which the dress was made was faintly tinged with pink and formed into dozens of crisp little frills, caught up, here and there, with pale rosebuds. The wreath for her hair and the bouquet she was to carry matched these; so did her satin slippers and her little painted fan. They were all extremely becoming and extremely suitable. Estelle realized how skillfully the dress was fashioned to bring out the best points in her figure. Moreover, the coloring of her costume was perfect for her, giving the tinge of rose to her cheeks which they lacked, for all the creaminess of the skin which blended so exquisitely with her hazel eyes and nut-brown hair. She had never been told that she was pretty, except by Andrew Breckenridge, and she feared he was prejudiced. But she knew now, indubitably, that she was very close to being beautiful. And still she was not wholly happy.

The first arrangement of the wreath did not satisfy Madame Lenoir, who had supervised very detail of Estelle's meticulous toilette, at which Julie was also assisting. She, herself, adjusted the wreath more effectively in the shining masses of Estelle's hair, which waved softly over her ears from a white part in the center, and was gathered into a great knot at the nape of her neck. Then, seeing that the girl's fingers were trembling so uncontrollably that she could not pull on her white glacé gloves, much less button them, she took her daughter's unresisting hands and helped her, adroitly.

"*Voyons*," she said soothingly. "You must not have a *crise de nerfs* at this moment, *chère*. Your appearance is very creditable, and now that your family has taken every precaution to see that this should be so, you in turn must repay us by proving that your deportment leaves nothing to be desired. What is there about the situation which should cause you to tremble like this? You have only to sit in the loge, as you have always done; the fact that you will be more in evidence than heretofore should make no difference in your bearing. Is this not so?"

"Yes, Maman. But suppose something untoward *should* happen——"

"Nothing will happen," Madame Lenoir said calmly. "But if you are determined to mar your pleasure, and mine, by imagining impossibilities—why then, I can only say, that if anything untoward should happen, you will completely ignore it, you will act as if everything were progressing as usual. That is what any lady would naturally do under the circumstances. Surely I do not need to give you lessons, at this late day, in the conduct which is becoming to a gentlewoman, after having devoted my life to this for nearly eighteen years!" Then, speaking more gently, she added, "My darling, you are all that I could desire for a daughter. It is because I have such confidence in you that I urge you to have confidence in yourself. Come, we must not keep your grandmother and your father waiting any longer. The carriage should be at the door by this time. I will help you to hold up your skirts as we go down the stairs, so that there may be no danger that they will become soiled."

At first Estelle was inclined to believe that her mother was right, that her own fears had been groundless. She had dreaded the drive down Bourbon Street, as ceremonial, in its own way, as the drive through the parkway to Buckingham Palace, and as inescapable for the local debutante destined to carry on a great tradition. But the crowd was less critical than a London crowd, and kindlier. As the shining carriage, in which she rode, rolled away, the horses which drew it stepping high, Estelle sensed that the men standing in little groups at the street corners, who stared in the carriage windows and nudged each other, were essentially respectful, that there were few smirks hidden behind their smiles, and no veiled insults in their complimentary comments. The old ladies who came hurrying out on the galleries, clutching their little gray shawls around them to protect them from the cold, were retrieving a precious fragment of their own lost youth, as they waved and chattered, and the children who stood on the edge of the banquettes, clapping their hands and cheering, were saluting with the same impersonal zest and vigor that they would have shown for any passing show that pleased them.

Because she knew all this, Estelle was braced and not intimidated as she rode along. They had left the house in good season, so they were early in arriving at the opera; she had plenty of time to install herself in her central chair, unhurriedly, and to give the finishing touches to the bouquets, already tastefully arranged around the velvet-covered railing of the loge. With her mother beside her, and her father and her grandmother established in the rear, she had a sense of reinforcement. Her mother's gracious greetings to the acquaintances who passed by on their way to their own loges, her father's courtly bows to the friends in the proscenium boxes, even the rustle and the accustomed scent of her grandmother's silks—all these were reassuring. So was the brilliant picture made by the *corbeille*, for every box and stall in this great horseshoe was occupied, and many of them contained girls, who, like herself, were being brought out in beautiful dresses, decked with jewels and surrounded by flowers. Most of them were smiling and chatting gaily; they did not seem in the least nervous; and since this was so, why should she? She remembered hearing it said that the sight of the French Opera House filled to overflowing with the most beautiful of all women—the Creoles of Louisiana—exquisitely and elaborately turned out, was even more dazzling to a stranger in New Orleans than the most splendid stage spectacle, and that many came hundreds of miles in order to see it. Surely she should be proud and pleased, as her parents had assumed, to be part of such a superb sight!

Her formless fears began to flutter away. And when the overture commenced, and the amphitheatre was darkened, she almost forgot, in the melodious gloom, so friendly and so familiar, that she was making her debut. When the curtain went up, she forgot it completely, at least for the moment. The opera was *La Traviata*, one of her favorites. She had sighed and sobbed over the ill-fated Violetta many times, but always with a resurgent absorption in the romantic tragedy of the story. Even when the actress impersonating Violetta weighed upwards of two hundred pounds, robbing her lingering death from "consumption" of all illusionary enchantment for others, Estelle shed tears over it. During the first scene, so swiftly paced, so splendidly dramatic, she was always intoxicated afresh.

It was not until the curtain had gone down, and the entr'acte had begun, that she returned to reality as embodied by her own share of the evening's entertainment. She had laid her fan and her bouquet carefully in her lap, so that she might be free to applaud the singers as they came forward to acknowledge the acclaim which greeted them. She was still clapping, still softly crying "Bravo!" and "Encore!" when she became aware that the *baignoires* and boxes were emptying, and that the customary promenading and exchange of visits had begun. The Fontaines were the first to stop before the *loge grillée*. They were there in full force, from the lean and aged uncle, who lived with them, just as Grand'mère lived with the Lenoirs, to little Narcisse, who was attending an evening performance for the first time, and looking very smug and satisfied with himself. All had sent her bouquets, and Narcisse proudly pointed to his, telling her he had selected it himself; in thanking the little boy, and in praising his taste, Estelle forgot to be self-conscious. It was easy to express her gratitude to decrepit old uncle Théophile also—he was the one impoverished member of the affluent family, and when he bought a bouquet, Estelle knew that he went without something else to do so. Having talked without effort to Narcisse and Uncle Théophile, Estelle talked without effort to the others also. She forgot her awe of Auguste, her aversion for Octave; she found Marcel unusually appealing.

But she had hardly spoken to Marcel, when she saw another attractive young gentleman, dressed in the height of fashion, approaching the loge, and stopped suddenly, her new-found poise abruptly shattered, her heart beating fast, as she recognized Andy Breckenridge. She had not seen him since her return from France; Clarisse had told her he was in England. Dread and delight seized her simultaneously. Now, unconsciously, she made an impulsive gesture. In doing so, she swept all the flowers that lay fragrantly piled in front of her, from the velvet-padded railing of the loge to the floor of the aisle.

The Fontaines had the quick grace of their class and kind. But before any of them had succeeded in stooping, Andy Breckenridge, with incredible swiftness, had retrieved the fallen flowers and was deftly replacing them where they had been before. Only those in the most immediate neighborhood of the loge could possibly have observed the accident.

"Good evening, Mesdames. Good evening, Monsieur. A very pleasing performance, is it not? It seems to me that Bovet is in an especially good voice tonight, and Dynah Duquesne is really lovely to look at," young Mr. Breckenridge was saying, agreeably. "But I rather dread the next act—the heavy father always affects me adversely, he is such a hypocrite, and I think most of the members of the *corps de ballet* must be grandmothers."

He spoke excellent French, idiomatic and fluent, which was always a point in favor of "Americans" from the Creole point of view; and as far as his salutation of her parents and her grandmother went, Estelle knew that his manner left nothing to be desired. But when he turned to her, it lacked the subdued respect with which a gentleman with polish and perception traditionally spoke to a young girl. It was jesting, almost bantering in tone. "Mademoiselle, you reverse the normal order of things. It is I who should be casting flowers at your feet. I should never have dared to hope for such an attention."

"Monsieur, my daughter regrets the unfortunate accident in the same measure that I do," Monsieur Lenoir said icily. "But it is unworthy of you to designate it as an attention."

"I am a very unworthy young man, Monsieur," Andy Breckenridge replied, his voice, though now slightly satirical, still unsubdued. His answer had come instantly; there had been no pause indicating constraint and contrition, such as a correct youth generally allowed to elapse when rebuked by his elders. "Nevertheless, the Fates have always been kind to me, though never so kind as now—I have restored all your flowers to you, Mademoiselle," he went on, turning to Estelle again. "As a reward, will you not return one rosebud to me? It would be a great favor."

"My daughter does not bestow favors, Monsieur, least of all outside her own circle," Monsieur Lenoir remarked, even more icily than before. "It occurs to me that you must have made an error. No doubt you thought that we shared this loge, instead of occupying it exclusively, with friends of yours, whom you expected to find here and who must be anxiously awaiting your arrival."

"My life has been full of errors," young Mr. Breckenridge said with a sigh, which did not sound especially sad. "But believe me, Monsieur, I made no mistake this time. I shall try to convince you of this, on some later and more appropriate occasion. But for the moment it would ill beseem me to monopolize the conversation when there are so many others who are waiting to offer their good wishes to Mademoiselle. Monsieur, *mes compliments*. Mesdames, *mes homages*."

He was gone as suddenly as he had come, his figure obscured by the crowd which by this time was surging in every direction, his voice swallowed up in the chatter and laughter, the swish of silk, the tread of feet, the opening and shutting of doors. But somehow, his presence seemed to linger, as it always did long after he had actually disappeared.

Estelle, her hands shaking uncontrollably again, forced herself to sit very still, holding her head high and looking straight in front of her. Even in this terrible moment, she did not forget her mother's admonition: she must not fail her family; she must act as if nothing had gone wrong, no matter if the very skies, instead of a few flowers, seemed to fall. She thought of the day of her first Communion, when she had been consumed with fear lest the lighted candle she carried might set fire to her veil. She had held it unsteadily, for her hands had shaken in the same way then that they did now, but somehow she had found the strength to be silent in the midst of her fear, and, though the tulle of which her veil was made kept floating close to the flame, she had never flinched. If she had succeeded then, surely she could succeed now. She remembered the tiny pocket that Grand'mère had sewed into the belt of her first Communion dress. It had held her offering and her handkerchief, too. The thought of this little pocket, so secret, yet so practical, had given her a sense of security. She wished she had something comparable to think of now, but she had not. Worth did not sew pockets in the waistbands of his creations. Well, she must manage without. She did not try to speak, because she was afraid that if she did, her trembling tone would indicate her terrible inner agitation, but nothing in her bearing betrayed this. And she had her reward. For presently she heard Marcel, who was still standing in front of the loge, with his Uncle Théophile, hovering behind him and his arm around his little brother, Narcisse, speaking to her father, temperately and wisely and kindly.

"Monsieur, may I venture to beg that you do not misinterpret the manner of my very good friend, Andrew Breckenridge? I have seen much of him at the Rutledges, who are Americans also, and who now have come to live near us on Bayou St. John. *C'est un très brave garçon*—he is really an excellent fellow. I do not know a keener sportsman or a better card player, and he has many gentler graces, too. Aurore assures me that he dances divinely, whatever that may mean, and that all the young blades about town are endeavoring to copy his special steps. He was not insolent or impertinent of intent. But he loves to jest, and he cannot resist the allure of a *double-entendre*."

"I understand he cannot resist the lure of the lottery either," Monsieur Lenoir answered with stiffness, though less icily than before. It was impossible for anyone to be icy with Marcel.

"Then he shares a characteristic of many of our foremost citizens, does he not, Monsieur? And believe me, he regards you and Madame with great respect, while as for Estelle—" He broke off, turning from Monsieur Lenoir to his daughter, not boldly, as the young Mr. Breckenridge had done, but in the quiet way so rightfully regarded as correct. "*Regarde*, Estelle," he said, using the familiar form in which they had addressed each other from childhood. "Monsieur Leroux is looking at you through his opera glasses. See, he has beckoned to one of his lieutenants. Why, this is very exciting! I am sure that he must have been struck, as we all were, with your suitability for a Queen, the minute he saw you sitting here, surrounded by your flowers— With the permission of all of you, we should like to come into the loge for a few moments, my uncle and my little brother and I. It would be a privilege for us to watch with you the growing appreciation of Monsieur Leroux."

This had happened more than a month before, and during the interval, the name of young Mr. Breckenridge had never been pronounced by her father and mother in Estelle's presence, except when one of his frequent invitations was declined, as it always was on the ground of a previous engagement. She realized her parents must be aware that she saw him almost everywhere she went, since he was now even more generally in evidence than he had been the previous spring; but they could not forbid her to speak to him, or charge her to avoid him, without seeming to cast reflections on the hostesses at whose houses these inevitable encounters took place. She knew, however, that the frequent conversations, seemingly so casual, which condemned the lottery scandal, were intended to remind her of his close connection with this. Estelle noticed that no one suggested that she should do her devotional reading or practice on the piano, when these conversations were taking place, as either her grandmother or her mother was very apt to do when something far more agreeable was under discussion; and she was also tacitly encouraged to listen when her parents and their friends spoke of the police order closing gambling houses and the arrest of the voodoo doctor, James Alexander, in the midst of an orgy on Roman Street, which the young bloods of the town had watched, if they had not actually joined. Hitherto, she had always been dismissed when any subject not strictly suitable for a young girl happened to come up, and she had not failed to grasp the significance of all this: by the adroit inference that young Mr. Breckenridge was connected, directly or indirectly, with every scandal in the city, they hoped to arouse antagonism to him. They might have spared themselves their pains, for she was sure he was maligned, and their hopes were vain—as vain as the hope that in her preoccupation with the approaching Carnival, she would forget young Mr. Breckenridge entirely, if her own participation in the festivities were sufficiently dazzling and sufficiently intensive. For though he had never found a "secluded spot in which he could propose to her properly"— which she now knew meant a place where he could kiss her unobserved—in the well-chaperoned circles where they moved, he had managed to whisper over and over again that he loved her, and had tried to wring from her the admission that she loved him in return. Since this was so, what could Carnival offer that would be half so thrilling and so precious, and how could anything her parents might do hereafter prevail against what Andrew Breckenridge had already done?

And now Monsieur Leroux was actually in the drawing room, talking to Monsieur Lenoir in hushed and solemn tones, which were appropriate for so portentous an occasion. Estelle had been conscious of the murmuring of voices and the clinking of glasses, for which she had so long waited in vain, for some moments now. But though she had not stirred from her seat near the tightly closed door, she had not been able to hear a single sentence in its entirety. She had caught only an occasional *"Cela va sans dire"* or a *"Bien entendu"* from Monsieur Leroux and the long-drawn-out exclamation which her father gave when he was supremely satisfied about something. "Ah-hah—Ah-hah—Ah-hah—Ah-hah!" It went something like that, but not exactly. "Ah-hah—Ah-hah!" she said under her breath. Then she heard the voices, no longer hushed and solemn, coming from the *salon*, but ringing and hearty, coming from the hall. A moment later the front door opened and shut, and then her father returned, approaching the dining room. She rose respectfully to meet him.

"Eh bien, ma fille," Monsieur Lenoir said, with unconcealed gratification. "I have some very important news for

you. It seems that our good friend, Monsieur Leroux, was most favorably impressed with your appearance on the opening night of the opera, and by your bearing even more than your looks. He was kind enough to say that he had seldom seen such a young girl with so much dignity, and that his lieutenants shared this impression. Happily, he did not observe the little contretemps of which we do not need to speak at the present moment. This means, however, that Monsieur Leroux, who is beginning to show his age, is not quite so observant as he fancies himself, and not that a certain other person, who shall be nameless, behaved with suitable discretion." Estelle saw that her father was still determined not to mention Andrew Breckenridge by name, but she was not deceived by his silence any more than she was deceived by his jocularity. "As I was saying, Monsieur Leroux has been favorably impressed, indeed to the point where he has done us both the honor of asking me if I would permit you to preside as the Queen of a Carnival Ball."

"Oh, Papa!" said Estelle faintly.

"I can understand that you are agitated. But, *chère,* you must not permit yourself to be concerned. There is no occasion for concern." Monsieur Lenoir took Estelle's hand and patted it, his pride and pleasure shining in his eyes. "*Tout s'arrangera*—everything will arrange itself," he went on. "Let us go upstairs together, and share the good news with your mother and grandmother. You will see that they will relieve you of all responsibility in regard to this festival, as they did in regard to your debut. Of course it will only be one of many. You will probably be designated as a Maid at one or more other balls, besides becoming the Queen of the Pacifici. This will mean preparation also."

"Yes, Papa," Estelle said, a little less faintly. She knew that there was not as much responsibility connected with the role of a Maid as there was for the reign of a Queen, and the prospect did not overawe her so much. Indeed, she had more or less taken it for granted that she would be one of the Maids at the Proteus Ball, since her father was the Captain of this outstanding Creole "Krewe."

"And you will attend all the others," Monsieur Lenoir went on, quite as if he were imparting surprising information to Estelle, who had been dreaming of doing this very thing for years. But she did not interrupt him, partly because she had never done anything so disrespectful in her life, and partly because she enjoyed hearing enumerated all the details of the delights which awaited her, quite as much as her father enjoyed recounting them. "All those, that is to say, in which persons of our social standing participate. I do not need to tell you that there are some in which they do not."

"No, Papa," Estelle answered. She spoke quite truthfully and quite successfully concealed, in speaking, the regret which she could not wholly stifle, in her secret thoughts. She felt quite sure that young Mr. Breckenridge would participate in some, and indeed most, of the balls which her father dismissed with such condescension, and therefore she would have liked to attend them, too.

"After the Twelfth Night Revels there will be a little lull, aside from the regular debutante activities. That is as well, for it will give you an opportunity for partial repose before the final period which is so crowded. And crowded it is indeed! I understand the Pacifici have settled on a date a full week at least before Mardi Gras. Then comes the Momus Ball the Thursday before, and considering the prominence of her father in the Louisiana Club, I think there is no doubt that your charming young acquaintance, Mademoiselle Amélie Aldigé, will be the unanimous choice for the Momus Queen. This will give that occasion a special interest for you. Next comes the Carnival German the Friday before Mardi Gras and both the Proteus Ball and the Rex Ball on Mardi Gras itself! There are rumors that Comus is intending to stage a spectacular return, after a decade of inactivity, but I place no credence in that. Even with the arrogance that has always characterized him, he could hardly expect to displace Proteus on the date now accepted as ours, and to relegate us to an earlier and less important one."

"Hardly, Papa," Estelle agreed. But in her heart she was less certain. She had been hearing rumors about the newly-elected Captain of Comus which made her uneasy, when it came to a question of disregarding possible displays of arrogance.

"The balls in themselves would suffice to keep you occupied and diverted," Monsieur Lenoir went on, with unfounded complacency. "But then, of course, there are all the other spectacles and entertainments besides. I think I can promise you that you will be included in the group which will go down the harbor to greet Rex on his arrival. It happens that the substantial citizen who has been chosen to represent that merry monarch in this year's festivities is a very old friend of mine. He is not only a man of wealth—*cela va sans dire!* —but he is also a person of considerable culture. I believe that his reign will be characterized by taste as well as lavishness."

"How very nice!" Estelle murmured, approvingly.

"Yes, it is gratifying. The many strangers who come here during Carnival to see a great spectacle and share in a traditional fete should not secure a false impression. It has been rightly said that Carnival is the voice of a people determined to be gay always. But to be gay is not to be vulgar, and masking and merrymaking need not be common or commercialized in order to reveal spontaneous high spirits. Remember that, *ma fille.*"

"I shall, Papa."

"I believe the Mexican warship, *Zaragossa*, is to be included in the flotilla this year," Monsieur Lenoir went on, reverting to the arrival of Rex, now that he thought his little homily had produced the right effect, "and that the *Galveston* has been designated as the royal yacht. When the King appears on deck, and the orchestra begins to play *If Ever I Cease to Love,* I see no reason why you should not participate in the singing, if you would care to do so. After all, it was adopted as the Carnival Song because it was so pleasing to an imperial grand duke, and it has since been recognized as a sort of royal anthem. Your voice is really very pleasing, thanks to the excellent training you have received. Though of course I should not ordinarily expect you to permit anyone to hear it outside of your own and your friends' homes, I think the reception of Rex is so *ex*traordinary an occasion that you may, with propriety, do so."

Estelle had heard other rumors to the effect that the predilection of Grand Duke Alexis for the song in question was based on his unconcealed admiration for a certain Miss Lydia Thompson, rather than on any special sentiment for New Orleans' supreme celebration. It was whispered, even in the hearing of young girls, that it was because the lovely Lydia's rendition of the ditty from the burlesque, *Bluebeard,* had so entranced the imperial visitor, that he had singled it out for distinction, and that if Carnival had not come along just then he would have found some other way of making it prominent. However, he had occasioned the first Rex parade and inspired the Grand March which Carnival immortal-ized, when he opportunely visited New Orleans in '72, in the course of his Grand American Tour, and Estelle was entirely receptive to the idea of designating his favorite—and his favorite's!—song as a "royal anthem," if such a designation would give her the long-coveted opportunity of singing in public herself.

"I shall be very glad to sing on such an occasion, Papa," she said demurely. "Of course I shall be careful to do so softly."

"Of course, of course, *chère*. I have complete confidence in your discretion. I know you would never make yourself conspicuous, as Aurore Fontaine has such an unfortunate habit of doing. I understand that last year she was actually recognized at the Sazerac Bar on Mardi Gras, she went there so inadequately masked."

"But ladies are admitted to the Sazerac Bar on that day, aren't they, Papa?"

"*Women* are admitted," Monsieur Lenoir said a little grimly. Then fearing that perhaps he had been too severe, he added, "Not that we should be over-critical of Aurore, herself. She is a charming girl, and though I am afraid her parents are not always careful enough of the company they permit her to keep, that is their lack of judgment, not hers. I am sure I do not need to warn *you, chère,* that I do not wish you to go to the Sazerac Bar, or to tell you that no escort whom I should approve would ever suggest it. But you will be at the Boston Club on Mardi Gras, which does welcome ladies, on that one day of the year, as you know. You will see the Queen of Carnival seated on the balcony, surrounded by her Maids, when Rex rides past in all his glory on his chariot, and lifts his goblet, toasting her to the tune of *If Ever I Cease to Love*. In fact—though it is still too soon to say for certain, and I tell you this in the strictest secrecy— you will probably be *among* the Maids surrounding her. Let us venture to assume that this will be the case. In that event you will follow her when the President of the Club comes out onto the balcony to escort her inside, in order that she may preside at the festival luncheon prepared in her honor. And what a beautiful sight that table is, decorated with the Carnival colors and surrounded by a bevy of beauty! You have been satisfied, so far, to celebrate Carnival by romping around in a simple little bell-trimmed dress that your grandmother made for you. You have no idea what enjoyment awaits you now that you are no longer a child, but officially recognized as a young lady belonging to one of the best families in New Orleans."

"I did not half realize it before you began to talk to me, Papa. But you are making it all very vivid to me now."

"Seen from the balcony of the Boston Club, what a pageant the parades become!" Monsieur Lenoir went on, warming to his subject. "The eager crowds thronging the immense width of Canal Street, until it seems as if half the world must be assembled in New Orleans! The great floats, released at last from their 'dens,' redecorated, reanimated, after their long confinement! Who is there, never having seen them, that would guess cloth and paint, paste and gilt, could produce so fairylike an effect? Or that mere men, lawyers and merchants, bankers and brokers, could indeed assume the legendary aspect of the noble figures whom they impersonate for a day or a night? Rolling along, tossing out gifts as they go, they bring back the days when knighthood was in flower and it was the privilege of princes to distribute largesse."

"But the gifts never have any real value, do they, Papa?"

"No, they are merely baubles—beads and bangles, whistles and balls and such like. That is, unless one intended for some other purpose is thrown out by accident! There is the story of a man who tossed down a string of pearls which he had intended to present as a favor that night—to his wife, of course. It was never recovered, and some carousing bystander was undeservedly enriched."

"Perhaps it was some poor girl, Papa, who would never have had a pretty necklace if it had not been for such an accident."

"Perhaps. But in that case, if she recognized its value, she should have advertised it in the 'Lost and Found Column' and been suitably, though modestly, rewarded for her honesty. If she did not know its value, its possession would have meant nothing to her."

"Except for the enjoyment of beauty, aside from value."

"Yes. Yes. That is something. But a prudent person does not lose sight of value in the pursuit of beauty. Remember that, too, Estelle."

"Yes, Papa."

"Not that I expect you to let the thought absorb you on Mardi Gras," he continued indulgently. "I expect that the flowers, and the champagne, and the pretty dresses, and the manifold attentions and favors you will receive may turn your head a little then. It is to be expected. These and the police escort and the red carpet spread out for the Queen and her Maids to walk on. Is there any young girl whose heart does not flutter at the sight of a red carpet? I hardly believe so. There will be one for the Queen of Proteus and her Maids at the Boston Club, and in that Court I think I may safely say you will surely appear. And there will be one spread out, on purpose for you, at the Grand Opera House the night you reign as Queen of the Pacifici—a red carpet, and a special dressing room, daintily decorated, at the end of its expanse, where you will stay while you await the signal from the chairman who will escort you to the Captain of the Ball. That is a further detail over which you must not concern yourself. He is another very old friend. He will guide you and advise you. It would not be possible for you to be in better hands."

"I am very glad, Papa."

"Of course there will be other privileges and other pleasures besides those I have mentioned. But I must not fatigue you in advance, however delightfully, by dwelling on them too long at this moment," Monsieur Lenoir concluded, patting Estelle's hand again. "Besides, as I have said, I know your mother and your grandmother are awaiting us, and we should go to them without further delay. Naturally you understand that you are not to mention to anyone the special mark of favor that has been revealed to you by Monsieur Leroux' visit. Indeed, you are not supposed to know anything about it, until you receive the scroll and the roses which will reach you on the morning of Christmas Day, by special messenger. But it is best that I should confide in you, for two reasons: first, that you may be properly prepared, and second, that you may dismiss all matters of lesser import from your mind. I cannot think, for instance, that you will be interested, any more, in receiving those floral offerings which have been coming to you, anonymously, every morning for the past month. I shall tell Julie that she need not trouble herself to take them up to your room any more. I will see that they are sent to the Maison Hospitalière and St. Vincent's Orphanage. You will be having many other flowers, more worthy of you, from now on. For I understand that this 'Krewe' over which you are to reign proposes to do everything in the most lavish way. It is a new one. So you, my dear, as its first Queen, must set the standard for all the other Queens who are to follow after you."

CHAPTER 3

"To me, Lolette, there is nothing so shocking about the situation as the fact that even ladies have felt obliged to emerge from their genteel seclusion in the proper province of the home to give it attention. I understand from Madame Villeré that this League which has been formed now has branches in all the parishes of Louisiana, and that the parent branch, here in New Orleans, numbers seven hundred members. She also tells me that the president of this daring organization, Mrs. William Preston Johnson, is actually a personage whom we Creoles may regard with respect and follow with readiness."

"I believe that is true, *ma mère*. I think I, myself, have told you it is rumored that her disciples are fired with such zeal, in their determination to stamp out the evil which threatens to engulf us, that one of them offered her only valuable piece of jewelry, a gold watch, to be sold by the finance committee for the benefit of the anti-lottery fund."

Estelle, who was sitting by the window sewing, sighed softly. Except for her morning Reading Club, to which she had been with Clarisse that day, she had been free from engagements outside the family, for the first time in a long while, and her mother had suggested that she should profit by the temporary lull to resume her neglected needlework. She rather enjoyed stitching away on the delicate lawn, that was shaping itself into a chemise, as she rolled the edges before she whipped on the lace, and ran the fine tucks and seams. But she was beginning to be bored by the conversation. The story of the watch was a favorite of the younger Madame Lenoir. If she had told it once, she had told it at least a dozen times. Her mother-in-law, after listening to it with earnest approval, invariably reminded her, at the end of her recital, that they must also remember the Archbishop's ban, forbidding that lottery tickets should be blessed, as they always had been, in more degenerate times. She did so now and Estelle sighed again.

Monsieur Lenoir constantly cited the Archbishop, too, in family conversation, adding that even Protestant clergymen were showing themselves alive to the danger and disgrace in which Louisiana stood, citing line by line, the declaration of the Reverend Carradine that "if asked to name the agencies of immorality in the land, after mentioning Mormonism and impurity and intemperance, we would not have declared the giant evil until we had named the Louisiana State Lottery."

Monsieur Lenoir had read this aloud, with the same repetitious monotony and in the same sombre tones which his wife used in telling the story of the watch. He was even more prone, when Monsieur Denis and Monsieur Castaigne and other male friends, members of the Anti-Lottery League, were visiting him, to speak of the dramatic plea made by Monsieur Charles Parlange at the Anti-Lottery Democratic Convention, which had taken place in Baton Rouge in August, while the Lenoirs were in Europe. Judge White had made a motion empowering Monsieur Parlange to address the Convention in French, and this motion had been passed without a single dissenting voice. Then Monsieur Parlange had risen and burst into an impassioned speech.

"Etes-vous prêts à vendre pour de l'argent, à une demi-douzaine d'hommes dont un seul a osé dire son nom, la noble prérogative d'êtres vos propres maîtres? N'oubliez-vous pas que depuis le jour où le canon du Fort Sumter a ébranlé ce continent aucun Etat de l'Union Américaine ne s'est trouvé en présence d'une situation aussi menaçante que celle de la Louisiane aujourd'hui?"

"It is true, it is all too true, Aristide," Monsieur Lenoir always said, shaking his head as he spoke. "The situation is indeed menacing to a degree unparalleled in our history. No man who is not utterly depraved can fail to be roused. The lottery magnates who have been thronging Baton Rouge are pouring out money in an endless stream, and are undaunted even when they are caught bribing the Legislature. Their atrocities in 1868 and 1879 were child's play compared to the carnival of crime and debauchery that has been staged this time."

"Alas! You are right as usual, Adrien," Monsieur Castaigne always replied at this juncture. "They have subsidized everything money could buy—newspapers, barrooms, restaurants, houses of pros——"

Monsieur Denis, who was a rather silent man, and who, up to then, had contented himself with nodding, coughed at this juncture, and Monsieur Castaigne never finished the word that began with "pros," in Estelle's hearing; so she was left guessing what it might mean while Monsieur Castaigne continued with heat. "They have systematically peered into every man's history to find some scandal with which to blackmail him, and often, alas! they have been successful. And when they have won a man to their side by fair means or foul, they have set a 'death-watch' on him. Two or three of their henchmen have surrounded him day and night so that no one else could communicate with him. Sometimes these victims repent, but too late. You know the sad story, Adrien, of that senator who shall be nameless and who was the last man needed for a Lottery victory. He had previously been with us, he had signed the anti-lottery pledge. But he was ill and impoverished; he was harassed with the nightmare that he no longer would be able to support his family. He voted to submit the question to the people, and then sank into his seat in the Senate, burying his face in his hands in shame. I hear that he now lies ill at the Hotel Dieu here in New Orleans. I should be willing to wager that if he dies, a very substantial sum, in cash, will be found among his effects."

Monsieur Lenoir and his friends did, indeed, all know the story, but that did not prevent them from telling it, over and over again. Estelle was growing extremely tired of all this repetition. Personally, she had been thrilled at hearing, from young Mr. Breckenridge, that one of the proponents of the Lottery, who lay at death's door, had volunteered, with his wife's knowledge and approval, to go to the Senate on a stretcher, upon learning that his vote was needed to override the Governor's veto. That was heroic, she thought, and young Mr. Breckenridge heartily agreed with her; but when she ventured to say so, in the family circle, she was severely reprimanded. The fatal illness, it appeared, had been caused by delirium tremens brought on by excesses during the celebration of impending victory by the forces of evil; an explanation of the nature of this condition was coupled with the comment that it was only men of the type who might succumb that supported the Lottery. She resented increasingly the reflection which this remark, together with all the correlative talk, was meant to cast on the character of Andrew Breckenridge. He still remained unnamed in the discussions of the Lenoirs and their intimates; but she knew he was in the forefront of those "magnates" who were accused of subsidy, bribery, crime and debauchery. The day had now come when she was determined to listen no longer. She folded her sewing into a neat little square and rose resolutely.

"Pardon, Maman, is it not time we were starting for the St. Charles? Three o'clock, Tante Toinette said, I think."

It was Madame Lenoir's turn to sigh, though she did so even more guardedly than her daughter. Her husband's cousins, the de Gruys, who were down from St. Martinville to do their winter shopping, had always been thorns in her side. Like most people living on Bayou Teche, they were very independent in their ways—the very retention of the "de" in their names years after everyone in New Orleans had dropped it, except on wedding invitations and death notices, went to show that! They never could be persuaded to stay with the Lenoirs, or any of their other connections, when they came to New Orleans, nor would they bring servants and carriages with them, and put up in style at the Hotel St. Louis, where the galleried apartments surrounding the courtyard were the last word in secluded elegance. During Carnival time they made their headquarters on the "round boat" by which they had travelled, and which remained conveniently tied up at the end of Canal Street until it shoved off on its return trip; at other times they "descended" to the St. Charles Hotel, occupying ordinary rooms there. Monsieur and Madame Lenoir dined with them there, under protest, and only because if they did not, the de Gruys would not dine with them in Royal Street either. But Grand'mère never did, and since, naturally, she could not be left to dine alone, Estelle's parents were glad of a pretext for sending their daughter home. The less she was seen in "American" hotels, the better they liked it.

It was unfortunate, however, that Madame de Gruy should take such offense when Julie accompanied Madame Lenoir and Estelle to the St. Charles, for the purpose of taking the girl back to Royal Street after she had made the conventional call on her aunt, while her mother remained with her Tante Toinette, awaiting the arrival of her father from the office. Madame de Gruy had once asked Madame Lenoir in a very spirited way, whether the presence of a maid indicated that Estelle was ashamed to be seen on the streets with her country cousins, or whether Estelle's parents did not realize how much older and more experienced Allain and Myrthé were than their own daughter. Allain and Myrthé were both good-looking, and, since Allain was already thirty and Myrthé uncomfortably close to it, they had indubitably reached an age which, coupled with their relationship, constituted valid chaperonage. For all her *savoirenfaire,* Madame Lenoir could not find a way of tactfully telling her husband's relative that it was not a question of either appearance or age which was involved, but of essential suitability, as she understood this. She misprized the de Gruys on general principles, as she considered them lacking in fine feelings no less than finished manners, and she specifically doubted their discretion.

There was, however, no pretext on which she could avoid the impending visit herself, or exclude her daughter from the earlier part of it. She rose, with her usual composure, and after seeing that Madame Lenoir *mère* had everything she could require during her own absence, said au revoir to her mother-in-law affectionately and respectfully. Then she left the *salon* to change from a house dress into a walking dress, and to complete her costume with the addition of a sealskin cape and muff, as the day was chilly. She felt justly satisfied with her own appearance, and she looked at Estelle, whose cape and muff were made of beaver instead of sealskin, with approval as they started out. The furs were among the novelties which they had brought back with them from Paris that fall, but the weather had been so unseasonably mild that they had not had a chance to wear them before. Madame Lenoir was not sorry that they should do so for the first time when calling on Madame de Gruy.

"You have hardly mentioned the debutante luncheon and tea to which you went yesterday, *chère,*" Madame Lenoir observed, as they walked along towards Canal Street. "Really you are becoming more and more silent all the time! And you used to be such a chatterbox! Your grandmother and your father have also remarked this. You said they were pleasant parties, but that was all. Were they in no way distinctive?"

"No, they were much like all the other parties and very much like each other. For a luncheon centerpiece, a lyre of pink rosebuds and ferns, and at tea, a large old-fashioned kettle of pink and white roses. On both occasions the table was crossed with broad pink ribbons that ended with a large bow at each corner, and lighted with pink candles shaded with rose-colored silk, and on both occasions the mantels and cabinets were massed with flowers to match the center-pieces. Even the debutantes' names were outlined in pink and white roses around the centerpiece. I am getting a little tired of so many pink ribbons and so many shaded candles and so many massed flowers. It is not even possible to have an entertainment for General Lee's daughter without calling it a rose party and giving each guest a pink petal from a Robert E. Lee Rose, with a bit of poetry written on it by the host-ess. I should like to see a different color for a change. I am beginning to believe that debutantes are supposed to breathe freely only in a rose-scented atmosphere and to see every-thing *en couleur de rose.*"

It was seldom that Estelle spoke either so fully or so crit-ically. Her mother looked at her with thoughtful attention.

"I hear the party last night was much more original," Estelle went on. "You remember, the one you declined for me on the ground of a previous engagement. I know you thought the tea would last much longer than it did, and that this would prevent me from going to the german, also. But it seems there was an interval between the two—they were planned that way on purpose, so that the guests could go to both. Clarisse told me this morning that the favors were particularly lavish—fancy aprons, fans, tambourines, pins, flower-balls, helmets, blotters and Japanese match holders. Mr. Breckenridge and Mr. Rutledge were the two leaders, and they were very successful; they introduced a number of intricate and fancy figures, all new. Mr. Breckenridge, him-self, originated the most attractive and picturesque of the evening. It was called the 'Bridal Figure,' and the girls were all given snowy veils made of illusion. Clarisse said they re-ceived so many compliments on their bewitching appearance that she was sure this figure will prove the most popular of the winter."

"I did not understand that this german was a debutante party, Estelle, or that Clarisse was going to it. I distinctly understood Madame Fontaine to say that it was Aurore who was invited, but that she doubted very much if she would attend."

"Aurore is a liar," Estelle said coldly. "She has been to

every party Mr. Breckenridge has given this winter, and then she has boasted about it afterwards. Madame Fontaine is proud of the fact, too, whatever she may say. She would have been tremendously pleased if Mr. Breckenridge had asked her to act as hostess for him, instead of Madame Denis. Mr. Breckenridge never gives debutante parties. He thinks they are dull. But he includes a few debutantes on his list each time. This time he included Clarisse. And me, as you know."

Madame Lenoir continued to look at her daughter with increasing attention. There was an expression to the girl's mouth that she had never seen before that day, but, now she thought of it, she remembered that Estelle had looked both sulky and sullen as she sat sewing by the window, instead of amiable and composed, as a lady should. Now Madame Lenoir resolved to tell her husband, that very evening, that there was even more cause for alarm than they had feared.

"Clarisse says she is sure Mr. Breckenridge will call on you and Papa before long, and ask you to name a date when I do not have a previous engagement," Estelle went on. "Any date, no matter how far ahead. After Carnival even. She says he must realize that it is unthinkable for any girl, however popular, to have as many engagements as I do. Aurore, who is the greatest belle in New Orleans, does not have half so many as you claim for me, Clarisse said. She is very curious, Maman, about these engagements of mine."

"There is no reason why you should satisfy the curiosity of Clarisse, Estelle. And no reason why she should attribute such insolent intentions to Mr. Breckenridge unless he is actually guilty of them. I can hardly believe that his presumption would be as great as she hints, for all his audacity. But we shall have to discuss this some other time, for here we are at the St. Charles. And I shall have to retract what I said about your silence. You have done a great deal of indiscreet talking yourself, and I am very far from pleased with some of your remarks. I hope you will behave better while we are calling on your aunt."

Madame Lenoir's hopes were fulfilled. Estelle's deportment, in the course of the call, left nothing to be desired. She sat quietly by while her mother and her Tante Toinette discussed the weather, the fashions, the undependability of their servants, the state of their own health, and—in an undertone which Myrthé covered, at a sign from her mother, by chattering loudly about something else—the delicate condition of a young relative who lived on Bayou Teche near New Iberia. Throughout the discussion, Estelle responded pleasantly and amiably whenever she was addressed, but did not speak unless she was, though her expression remained uniformly alert and agreeable. It was only when Madame Lenoir began to tell Madame de Gruy the story of the gold watch, which had been sacrificed to swell the anti-lottery fund, that Madame Lenoir thought she detected signs of restlessness in her daughter; and at that moment Allain de Gruy came in and respectfully informed his aunt that he and Myrthé were going to take a short walk before it grew dark and hoped she would permit Estelle to join them. Of course they would see her safely back to Royal Street before they returned to the hotel themselves——

Estelle rose with exactly the right attitude of deference to her mother's wishes and reluctance to leave her aunt, mingled with alacrity in following her cousin's suggestion. Madame Lenoir watched her leave the room with such pride that, momentarily, she forgot both her earlier dissatisfaction with her daughter and her deep-rooted distrust of Allain and Myrthé de Gruy. Her complacency was peculiarly ill-timed. The cousins were hardly outside the door, when Allain turned to Estelle with a startling proposal.

"Myrthé and I weren't really intending to take a walk. We meant to go to the four-o'clock drawing of the Lottery. Wouldn't you like to come with us?"

"Do you really mean it? Could you really take me?"

"Of course. What could be simpler?"

He saw Estelle's face light up when he first spoke, and now she was already rushing forward at his side, her eagerness unconcealed. He did not fully grasp the cause of her extraordinary enthusiasm, but this made no special difference. He offered an arm to each girl, and went gaily forward.

The hotel lobby was thronged with vendors, many of them women, who were making last-minute sales. They stopped every passer-by, thrusting their long strips of tickets in his face and shrilly shouting their wares. Outside, the crowd was even more dense. The cousins had hard work wedging their way through it, and crossing first the banquette and then the street. But they did not have far to go. The lottery building stood almost directly across from the St. Charles Hotel, its opaque windows giving it an air of gloom and secretiveness. As the cousins entered the courtyard, and passed by the shallow pool where a wicked-looking alligator lay sprawled at the base of a skimpy fountain, blinking malignly, Myrthé shuddered and crossed herself.

"*La sale bête!*" she muttered. "This must be the monster to which the poor of the city cast their helpless children to placate the Goddess of Fortune. Even the shadow it casts is evil. Are you not frightened, Estelle?"

Timid as she was, Estelle had hardly noticed the alligator, for her attention was otherwise engaged. A door at the further end of the courtyard had opened just as they reached the fountain, and two men, absorbed in each other's conversation, paused on the threshold to continue their talk. One of them was a heavy, elderly man, with grizzled hair and a commanding carriage; the other was young and graceful, and his manner towards his superior was mocking rather than deferential. Yet the magnate, whom Estelle thought she recognized as the famous Mr. Howard, seemed to be taking no offense. The discussion was intense, but it was not violent, and after a moment or two, the large gray-haired man laughed in a way that showed he was assenting agreeably to something the other had said, and turned back into the building. The young man, laughing too, came down the steps alone, swinging an elegant cane, and putting on a shining hat. He lifted this instantly again, as he caught sight of the two girls beside the pool. Then he stopped short, with an exclamation of pleased astonishment.

"Miss Lenoir! What a delightful surprise! This is the last place I should ever have expected to see you. Myrthé, you minx! Why didn't you let me know that you were here? I thought it was next week you were coming to New Orleans. Allain, my dear fellow, how are you?"

Estelle, who had known young Mr. Breckenridge instantly, stood silently apart while her cousins fell upon him with cries of delight. She had not even heard before that they knew him; now it appeared that they were on terms of intimacy with him, that they had been to stay with him at Splendida, and that he in turn had visited them on Bayou Teche. The de Gruys raised sugar on an extensive scale; so, it appeared, did young Mr. Breckenridge, whose gainful pursuits, in Estelle's mind, had hitherto been limited to the race track and the Lottery. She had not thought of him previously as a planter. She would have been still more impressed if Allain had been more generally considered a "serious person," capable of measuring the attainments of others in a judicial way. Even so, she felt happier than she had in a long time. Surely her parents could not hold out forever against a man who, as it presently appeared, had raised a crop consisting of ninety acres of plant and fifty acres of stubble cane that year, not to mention a hundred and sixty acres of corn and considerable cotton——

"Look here, de Gruy, we mustn't stand here talking shop all the afternoon. Myrthé may enjoy it, but it must be terribly dull for Miss Lenoir. Remember her father's a lawyer, not a planter, and, so far, she has never had a chance to talk to any other man, for more than two minutes at a time. She can't be expected to take a breathless interest in crops. We must open up some more exhilarating channel of conversation for her. Where were you bound for, when I met you?"

"We were on our way to see the Lottery drawing."

"Oh, but that isn't here, you know, this afternoon! It's only the insignificant daily drawings that are held in the Lottery Building itself. The monthly drawings all take place in the Academy of Music—grand extraordinary drawings in June and December, and grand single-number drawings the other ten months. Don't you read the advertisements we squander such sums to put in the papers?"

He unfolded the paper he was carrying under his arm, turned the pages, and refolded it for them to read. They clustered around him to do so.

UNPRECEDENTED ATTRACTION!
OVER TWO MILLIONS DISTRIBUTED
L. S. L.
LOUISIANA STATE LOTTERY COMPANY

Incorporated by the Legislature for Educational and Charitable purposes, and its franchise made a part of the present State Constitution in 1879, by an overwhelming popular vote.

To Continue Until January 1, 1895.

Its Grand Extraordinary Drawings take place Semi-Annually (June and December) and its Grand Singular-Number Drawings take place in each of the other ten months in the year, and are all drawn in public at the Academy of Music, New Orleans, La.

"I reckon I missed the place. I was so dazzled by the figures," Allain said jocosely, pointing to a paragraph further down. But Estelle was reading straight through the advertisement with avidity.

Famed for Twenty Years for Integrity of Its
Drawings and Prompt Payment of Prizes Attested as follows:

"We do hereby certify that we supervise the arrangements for all the Monthly and Semiannual Drawings of the Louisiana State Lottery Co., and in person manage and control the Drawings themselves, and that the same are conducted with honesty, fairness, and in good faith toward all parties, and we authorize the Company to use this certificate, with facsimiles of our signatures attached, in its advertisements."

G. T. Beauregard
J. T. Early
Commissioners.

We, the undersigned Banks and Bankers, will pay all Prizes drawn in the Louisiana State Lotteries, which may be presented at our counters.

R. M. Walmsley, Prest. La. Nat. Bank
P. Lanaux, Prest. State Nat. Bank
A. Baldwin, Prest. N. O. Nat. Bank
Carl Kohn, Prest. Union Nat. Bank.

GRAND MONTHLY DRAWING

will take place at the Academy of Music, New Orleans
TUESDAY, DEC. 16, 1890
CAPITAL PRIZE $600,000.
100,000 Numbers in the Wheel

LIST OF PRIZES:

1 Prize of	$600,000 is	.... $	600,000
1 Prize of	200,000 is	....	200,000
1 Prize of	100,000 is	....	100,000
1 Prize of	50,000 is	....	50,000
2 Prizes of	20,000 are	....	40,000
5 Prizes of	10,000 are	....	50,000
10 Prizes of	5,000 are	....	50,000
25 Prizes of	2,000 are	....	50,000
100 Prizes of	800 are	....	80,000
200 Prizes of	600 are	....	120,000
500 Prizes of	400 are	....	200,000

Approximation Prizes

100 Prizes of	1,000 are	....	100,000
100 Prizes of	800 are	....	80,000
100 Prizes of	400 are	....	40,000

Terminal Prizes

999 Prizes of	200 are	....	199,800
999 Prizes of	200 are	....	199,800
3,144 Prizes amounting to		....	$2,159,600

PRICE OF TICKETS

Whole Tickets at Forty Dollars
Halves $20; Quarters $10; Eighths $5;
Twentieths $2; Fortieths $1.
Club Rates, 55 Fractional Tickets at $1 for $50

Special Rates to Agents
Agents Wanted Everywhere

IMPORTANT

How to Send Money
Remit Currency by Express at our Expense
Not Less Than Five Dollars.

Address M. A. Dauphin,
New Orleans

Give full address and make signature plain.
We Pay All Charges On Orders Of Five Dollars And Upwards.

Congress having passed laws prohibiting the use of the mails to All Lotteries, we use the Express Companies in answering correspondents and sending Lists of Prizes. Official List of Prizes can be obtained from the Local Agents by all holders of tickets.

ATTENTION: The present Charter of the Louisiana State Lottery Company which is part of the Constitution of the State, and by decision of the Supreme Court of the United States is an inviolable contract between the State and the Lottery Company, will remain in force under any circumstances *Five Years Longer, Until 1895.*

The Louisiana Legislature, which adjourned July 10th, voted by two-thirds majority in each house to let the people decide at an election whether the Lottery shall continue from 1895 until 1919. The general impression is that *The People Will Favor Continuance.*

"All through?" Mr. Breckenridge inquired with a smile, refolding the paper and putting it back under his arm. "You see this is one of the two greatest days of the year. I'm on my way to the Academy now myself, and I'd be charmed to have you share my box. We can go over immediately. Unless you'll come in for a minute, and see my office here first."

"Do you have an office of your own, you showy son of a gun?"

"Nothing like a little privacy, you know, Allain, for almost any kind of a transaction. As long as you're here, you'd better see where I do my best to make a living. You'll be surprised, Miss Lenoir. It doesn't look in the least like a den of iniquity. Just a pretty little parlor."

He led them into the building through a large crowded public room with a counter at one end, where a bevy of frantic clerks were striving to serve the heterogeneous throng that pressed in upon them. Mingled with the tough-looking men, many of them roisterers in an advanced stage of intoxication, and hoodlums, who were evidently strangers to soap and water, there were some pathetic specimens of humanity—frail-looking creatures, who looked like down-at-the-heel musicians, shabby young clerks, seedy old derelicts and drug addicts in a state of complete daze; there were also persons who appeared to be substantial citizens and numerous fashionable young men about town. There were women there, too—a pretty young widow in deep mourning, a country woman with a large, flapping sun-bonnet and a market basket over her arm, a buxom matron with two children tugging at her skirts and another at her breast, some dark, brightly painted girls clad with startling immodesty. Estelle had never seen such a motley. It was bewildering, it was alarming, it was revolting; at the same time it was unexpectedly thrilling.

"This way, Miss Lenoir. Won't you take my arm? I think I'd better get you out of this. I don't want you to be crushed."

She put her fingers lightly on his sleeve. The contact sent a current of unfamiliar feeling coursing through her; the effect was like an electric shock. Unexpectedly, involuntarily, she pressed his arm. He looked down at her with an expression of such unmasked fervor that she tried, belatedly, to draw away. But he was too quick for her. He took his free hand and for an instant held her fingers hard.

"Do that again," he whispered insistently. "Press my arm, I mean. Don't be afraid. You're meant to feel the way you do. You're made for it. You're just finding out what it's like to live. But you're going to learn a lot more. I'm going to teach you."

He had led them, while he was whispering to her, down a narrow, dingy corridor towards an inconspicuous door which he undid with a latch key. There was certainly nothing sinister about the appearance of the room into which he ushered them. A cheerful fire was burning brightly on the grate, and a bronze clock stood between matching candelabra on the mantelpiece, under a Troye painting. There were fine old maps on the walls, and in the middle of the room an oval table, with comfortable chairs companionably grouped around it. Myrthé clasped her hands in admiration as she looked about her.

"Andy, how charming! Whoever would guess that there was a room like this tucked away beyond the courtyard where that wicked alligator lies basking, and the noisy, smelly office, where all those dreadful people are milling around! But I am sure none of the other directors has quarters comparable to this! You have such impeccable taste! Every place you inhabit reveals it! Oh, Estelle, if Aunt Lolotte would only let you go to Splendida! You simply cannot imagine its magnificence!"

"I still hope that Miss Lenoir will see Splendida some day," Andrew Breckenridge said smoothly. "But don't raise her hopes too high, Myrthé. I really think you were more impressed with the running water than with anything else. Probably you didn't know, Miss Lenoir, that Splendida was the first plantation house in Louisiana to have modern plumbing, or care much, if you did. But Myrthé was so fascinated with it that I was afraid she might turn into an undine. I'm thinking of building a swimming pool on purpose for her, before she visits me again, so that I can see more of her, if she has definitely decided that water is her natural element. She spent half her time locked away from me in the ladies' bathing room."

"*Dressing room*, Andy! You know you made a great point of telling me that the room downstairs, for the gentlemen, was a *bathing* room, but that we must be careful to refer to

ours, upstairs, as a dressing room, because ladies were never
supposed to openly discuss such a subject as bathing! And
here you are doing it yourself, to Estelle of all persons! Why
she is so modest that she wouldn't so much as speak of stockings, in mixed company!"

"Oh, yes, she would. Give her a little time, and she'll talk
about all sorts of things. But don't hurry her too much. And
don't forget that modesty isn't as unbecoming as you'd like to
make out."

Estelle, blushing furiously, looked at Andrew Breckenridge
with gratitude, from under her lowered lids. Myrthé, unre-
buked, rattled gaily on.

"Oh, I know you think everything about her is perfect, just
as it is! Really, Estelle, he is very much *épris*. I could tell
that from the way he talked about you the last time I saw
him. But he has put you on such a pedestal that it makes me
feel quite uncomfortable and inferior. Hearing him say 'Miss
Lenoir," for instance, in that hushed, respectful way. Why
on earth shouldn't he call you Estelle, if he calls me Myrthé?"

"There isn't any reason, Myrthé, if he'd like to. I should
be very pleased to have him."

Estelle could hardly believe her own ears as she spoke.
But ever since she had heard him talking so familiarly with
her cousin, she had been longing to hear him say Estelle. He
did it now, in tones as full of feeling as his look and his
touch had been a few minutes earlier.

"I've kept hoping for a long time you'd say that. Of course
I've been thinking of you as Estelle ever since I met you. It's
such a lovely name and it's so suited to you, but remember
it's a poor rule that doesn't work both ways. You must stop
thinking of me as young Mr. Breckenridge and begin thinking
of me as Andy. You must call me that."

Their eyes met, full of undisguised attraction towards each
other. It was Andy, more mindful of Estelle's cousins than
she was herself, in that ecstatic moment, who was the first to
look away, before Allain had a chance to break in with gibes
and ribaldry.

"I said you mustn't be hurried, Estelle, and yet I'm afraid
I'll have to hurry you after all. That is, if you really want to
go to the drawing."

"But of course we want to go to the drawing. That's what
we're out for. You're right, Andy, it's getting late. Come on,
lead us to this box of yours."

Allain spoke before Estelle could answer, grabbing up his hat and bolting towards the door, as if determined to make up for lost time. Now that he had been reminded it was growing late, he wanted to rush along the corridor, through the courtyard and up the street. The Academy of Music was a scant two blocks away, so they had only a short distance to go; but if it had been miles, he could not have shown more impatience. Andy finally laid a restraining arm on his, and spoke to him agreeably but warningly.

"Don't rush so, Allain. There's really plenty of time. Everyone is staring at you and there's no use in attracting unnecessary attention to the young ladies. It doesn't matter whether we get to the Academy for the first drawing or not. There'll be hundreds of them. Of course my box is reserved for me, and fortunately I haven't asked anyone else to share it this afternoon, because Mr. Howard had detained me on matters of business. I'm sorry there are no *loges grillées,* as there are at the Opera House. But if Myrthé and Estelle sit in the rear, I don't think they'll be recognized. No one will be expecting to see Estelle, considering her father's attitude both to me and to the Lottery. And very often people only see what they're looking for. Besides, your friends aren't the sort who come to drawings."

They were inside the Academy building now, and Andy was guiding them around the foyer as he spoke. He bowed, courteously, to several men as he went along, but he did not stop at all, and he walked in such a way as to seem more or less detached from Estelle and her cousins. It was only when they reached the box, which an attendant sprang forward with alacrity to open from the rear, that he came close to Estelle and surreptitiously pressed her hand again as she went in.

"Sit here, Estelle. You'll be more comfortable here than you would further front. And I'm sure you can see all right. You there, Myrthé. Well, here we are. Take a good look around you and then tell me what you think of it."

He must have known she would be too overwhelmed to answer him instantly, Estelle thought wildly, as she tried to quiet the turmoil of her impressions and steady her dazzled vision. When Allain had spoken of going to a Lottery Drawing, she had imagined nothing like this. There had been no clear picture in her mind, but still she had supposed it would be held in some unpretentious hall with comparative quiet, comparative privacy. Instead, she found herself in a huge auditorium with two balconies above the boxes, and a crowded floor, stretching in endless rows of seats towards the orchestra pit. A dozen or more musicians were ensconced there, looking somewhat lost in the space that provided for many more. But the stage gave a still greater impression of vastness. The long, full curtains were drawn back on either side, disclosing statues in railed niches, which added to its effect of grandeur. The formal backdrop could hardly be seen, it was so far to the rear. Three glittering chandeliers, one in the center and one on either side, hung from its unseen, remote rafters; they cast an unrelieved glare on the group of men, presumably officials of the Lottery Company, who sat scattered about beneath them, and upon the two imposing figures standing beside the wheels on either side of the stage.

One of these figures was familiar to Estelle. She knew it was General Pierre Gustave Toutant-Beauregard, who was a near neighbor of the Lenoirs, and who had been a good friend of her father's before they had quarrelled over the Lottery: a quiet, rather sad-looking man, his iron-gray hair parted on the side and worn in long waves over the ears, his small mustache and pointed goatee, reminiscent of the third Napoleon, his presence, one of outstanding dignity and distinction despite his slender build. The other man, wearing a row of medals on his full-dress Confederate uniform, was very tall, but he stooped a little, which detracted from his military bearing. He was also very bald; and as if to make up for the lack of hair on his head, a patriarchal white beard flowed down over his chest, almost to his waist. His eyes were his most arresting feature. Even at the distance from which she looked at them, Estelle could see that they were keen and piercing, that they missed no detail of what was happening anywhere within their range of vision. Estelle leaned towards Andy, who was already bending over her, awaiting her first whisper.

"Is that General Early by the big wheel?"

"Yes. He looks like a Mormon Elder, doesn't he?"

"I don't know. I never saw a Mormon Elder. But I'd never try to do anything I didn't want him to know. I'm sure he sees everything. I like General Beauregard better."

"Because you think he doesn't see so much?"

"No, not just for that, but he's different somehow. I can't

explain unless it's that I feel he is a Creole, like myself, and that General Early———"

"Is an American like me?"

"Andy, don't you ever stop teasing?"

"You brought that on yourself."

"I know I did, but you must forgive me. Don't make fun of me now. Explain to me. I don't understand how those wheels work."

"The big wheel is made with a glass disk on either side of it, enclosing it. I don't know whether you can see them from here, but they form the receptacle for the little rubber tubes that hold the slips of paper with the lottery numbers printed on them. There are a hundred thousand of those. The small wheel is made in just about the same way, but that has only three thousand odd tubes in it."

"Why should there be that number, specifically?"

"The general plan calls for the distribution of three thousand four hundred and thirty-four prizes. But there are not quite that many prize tubes, because a number of 'terminal' and 'approximation' prizes has to be deducted from them."

"But if there are a hundred thousand numbers and only three thousand prizes, then only one person in every thirty-three will get a prize!"

"You're a good mathematician, Estelle, better than I'd have expected. I've heard that Creoles don't like to bother with figures."

"No, but Andy—that means more than thirty persons lose for everyone that wins!"

"Right again. Go to the head of the class."

"And all the others—why all the others must lose and lose and lose!"

"For heavens sake, Estelle! you sound like Uncle Adrien! Don't sit there and moan and moralize! Watch the stage! Another drawing is going to begin. We must have just missed one. Now we'll see something!"

Allain spoke excitedly. Estelle, pressing her lips together, leaned forward and promptly forgot her distress in her own excitement. A little boy, decently but meanly dressed, had been led onto the stage and guided to a place near the big wheel over which General Early was presiding. At first Estelle could not understand the child's apparent helplessness or the vacant expression on his face. Then she realized what the matter was, and caught her breath.

"Can't the poor little boy see, Andy? Is—is he blind?"

"Yes. He's been brought in from the Orphan Asylum. You'll see his companion at the small wheel in a minute. These blind boys always draw the numbers from the wheels. That does away with the last chance of cheating. Look! There's a slide in the glass for them to put their hands in."

A powerful Negro had begun to turn the crank of the big wheel. It spun around, dizzily, slowed down, came to a stop. The little blind boy lifted his hand, fumbled among the tubes, and drew one from the glass container. At a sign from General Early, one of the men sitting on the stage came forward, took the tube from the child's hand, and extracting the rolled slip, held it up for the audience to see as he announced the number 5 3 8 4 6. Instantly afterwards, the other blind boy drew a tube from the smaller wheel and handed it to a man whom General Beauregard had signalled.

"Prize of a thousand dollars!" the second man cried out, showing the slip he held to the audience in his turn.

There was hardly a ripple of interest. The winning number had not been held by anyone in the audience, and a thousand dollars was a picayune sum, compared to the vast ones still to be distributed. It was only a moment before a buzz of aimless talk filled the auditorium again; some of the boxes emptied and others became crowded. Estelle had a moment of panic lest callers might come to Andy's, and that then inevitably presentations would take place. As if he divined her dread, he leaned towards her again.

"I told the attendant I couldn't see anyone this afternoon. That's not unusual; it's well known that I don't like to be bothered at a drawing. He's to take messages, and I'll attend to them tomorrow, at the office."

"You think of everything, Andy."

"I don't think of anything or anyone but you nowadays. But I want to see you alone. I want——"

"Hush! Myrthé will hear you. And see, there's going to be another drawing!"

The second one was even less exciting than the first. The "number wheel," at the blind child's touch, yielded up a tube containing a slip stamped 9 0 0 1 8. The "prize wheel," in its turn, designated this as representing only two hundred dollars' worth of booty. A series of revolutions brought similarly disappointing results. Then suddenly a fifty-thousand-dollar prize was announced. The winning number was held by a woman sitting in the orchestra section, who leapt up, shrieking with joy. Pandemonium broke loose all around her. She swiftly became hysterical, and was led out of the auditorium, supported by two strong men, and shrieking as she went. The tumult was so great that General Beauregard had to signal for order, at first gently, then with increasing severity. Allain and Myrthé were both on their feet, clapping and shouting with the others. Andy had to repress them both. But first, under cover of the prevailing excitement, he had managed to seize Estelle's hand again and squeeze it between his until she cried out faintly.

"You're hurting me, Andy!"

"I didn't mean to. Don't take it away."

"I must. Someone will see us."

"No one can, as long as Myrthé and Allain are standing up. I'll let go, when they sit down again."

Another arid stretch followed the frantic outburst. Allain, determined to witness the drawing of the capital prize, sat doggedly through the dull period, with more patience than either his sister or his cousin had ever seen him show. But Estelle was beginning to be gnawingly conscious of the passage of time.

"I'm afraid we ought to go. Grand'mère will expect me for dinner at six."

"Then we will have to go. It's nearly that now. And we've got a quarter of a mile to walk."

"Oh, wait for one more number! A few minutes aren't going to matter."

They waited, and the next drawing was unexhilarating also. Estelle began to betray nervousness.

"Allain, you promised Maman that you'd see me safely home. It isn't fair of you to make me wait like this."

"You'd be just as thrilled as I would if you could see someone in this audience get that capital prize."

"Yes, but there isn't a chance in a million that I would. Think of all the different places the tickets are sold! Someone in a little distant village may get the capital prize. Or someone in San Francisco or Detroit, Charleston—Boston even. Andy says more tickets are sold in Boston than in almost any other city."

"Maybe. But there's always the chance that a bright young fellow from St. Martinville might be the lucky man."

"Why Allain! Have you bought a ticket yourself? Where did you ever get so much money?"

Estelle had never had a sum as large as forty dollars in her possession. She was amazed that Allain could command such wealth.

"Oh, I manage to put by a little here and a little there."

"You mean you've done it more than once?"

"Of course. I do it right along."

"And did you ever win anything?"

"No. But I shall some day."

"Does Aunt Alzire know?"

"Look here, Estelle, you're asking an awful lot of questions. As a matter of fact, she doesn't. Now do keep still for a change and watch the stage."

Again they waited, and this time they were, in a measure, rewarded. A hundred-thousand-dollar prize was drawn, and a man in the upper gallery rose to roar out that it was his. In the midst of the demonstration that followed the second favor from Lady Luck in their midst, Andy rose, held open the door for the girls, and propelled the protesting Allain out of the box. The attendant locked the door after them, handed a sheaf of messages to Andy with a bow, and looked after them with curiosity, but in silence, as they went hastily through the foyer. The next instant they were out on the street again, and the clean, cold air was blowing freshly in their faces. The great adventure was over.

As they went down the steps, Myrthé managed to slip her arm through Andy's, leaving Estelle to follow with Allain. It was, after all, the logical arrangement, and one that was impossible to reverse without forcing the situation. But Estelle resented the unconcealed triumph with which Myrthé looked back at her.

"Did you see anyone there that you knew, Estelle?"

"No, not a soul. I can't be thankful enough. It would have been terrible if I had, wouldn't it? And some acquaintance may have seen me. That would be fatal."

The audacity of what she had done had begun to dawn on her. In her first impetuous assent to her cousin's suggestion, she had entirely disregarded the possible consequences of her rash act. Now the realization of what they might be suddenly overwhelmed her.

"Not necessarily. You can't be boiled alive in oil, you know, for going to a lottery drawing, even if you are found out. After all, this is a very liberal-minded city. If you don't believe me, read the crime columns in the *Daily Picayune*. Beg pardon, in *L'Abeille*. There are more murders and robberies to the block than any place I ever heard of, and most of them go unpunished. So I believe your peccadillo will, too. I did read the other night of a young lady who had died from eating poisoned sherbet. Perhaps her parents put the poison in it to punish her; but I'd be more inclined to think they'd try to poison importunate suitors than their own daughter."

It was Andy who spoke this time, looking back over his shoulder in his turn. Estelle knew that his mockery was meant to bolster her courage. But she was not at ease with him when he spoke in this way, as he so often did. His manner was too alien, at such times, to that with which the other men whom she knew had accustomed her—deferent, soothing, and so full of flattery that she was oblivious of the condescension mingled with their compliments. Andy loved to tease, and no one, not even herself, was immune from his raillery. Suddenly she longed to be safe at home with her grandmother, out of this noisy street, and away from these unhallowed companions, before her indiscretion was discovered. Of course she wanted to see Andy alone, to hear him make the long-postponed proposal— Or was she, after all, ready for that yet? She revelled in the secret knowledge that he loved her; she longed to listen to the fateful words he was so eager to pronounce; but would she be able to bear the violence of an embrace; could she yield her untouched lips to kisses which might smart and sting? She still recoiled from the thought of such a surrender. Until she overcame this reluctance, it was perhaps best, after all, that she should not be alone with Andy. A tender caress —she would feel differently about that. She thrilled to the touch of his hand when he took her fingers in his, to the pressure of his arm when they waltzed together. But she had no delusions. For all her inexperience, she instinctively knew that his long-suppressed love-making, once unleashed, would be irresistibly intense— She had already had a sample that afternoon of what she might expect.

"Andy's right. You're so thoroughly cowed you don't see how silly it is to let Tante Lolotte browbeat you. If you broke loose once in a while, instead of always acting the dutiful daughter, she wouldn't be so blind to the signs of the times, and she'd let up on you a little. Why not try it out now, since you've made such a good start already? It's practically dinner time. Let's stop in at Antoine's and sample this new dish of his everyone is raving about. Oysters Rockefeller, is that what they call it?"

"Oh, Allain, you know we couldn't go to Antoine's without a chaperone! Any number of people I know *would* be there!"

"If Myrthé isn't enough of a *vieille fille* now to be a chaperone, she never will be," her brother said brutally. "Don't you agree with me, Andy, that there'd be no time like the present for Estelle to break loose?"

"I should like nothing better than to introduce you to Oysters Rockefeller, served with a bottle of the best Chablis and followed by several other *spécialités de la maison*," Andy said smilingly. "But I fear I can't subscribe to your estimate of your sister as a chaperone, Allain. She is about the same age as Mademoiselle Aurore Fontaine, isn't she? She might create the same sort of a furor; I've been noticing a marked resemblance between them." Estelle glanced covertly at Andy, recognizing more of his mockery. She had told her mother the truth when she said that Aurore was now the undisputed belle of New Orleans, and Myrthé resembled her about as much as one of the characteristic little lamps of the Cajuns resembled the crystal chandelier of the Creoles. But Myrthé was simpering with satisfaction, and even Allain was obviously gratified. "With this in mind, I hesitate to take such a risk. But you must decide, of course, as the man of the family," Andy went on.

"Possibly you could find a quiet corner upstairs, or a private room," Allain suggested, loath to forego the oysters and the Chablis, but beginning to sense difficulties.

"There are no quiet corners at Antoine's. They're all crowded, as they deserve to be," Andrew replied. "As for a private room—wouldn't you prefer to take one after the theatre some night soon, at some less correct restaurant and—forgive me Mademoiselle de Gruy—forgive me, Mademoiselle Lenoir—in some other company? Of course, I should be enchanted to dine with your sister and your cousin, though I fear I should get confused trying to talk to them both at once and to look at them both simultaneously. But perhaps you would find it more—exhilarating, shall we say? —to have supper with ladies to whom you're not related.

Two charming members of the French Opera Troupe, perhaps. I know a number of them quite well, and we shouldn't have any trouble in making a selection."

"That's a very good idea of yours, Andy. I'll take you up on it."

Estelle saw Allain wink at Andy, and noticed a sinister little smile lurking around Andy's lips. She was disgusted with her cousin, but she was overwhelmingly grateful to Andy. How tactfully he had handled a situation which had already embarrassed her, and which might well have ended by compromising her! How adroitly he had catered to Myrthé's vanity and Allain's grossness! In her appreciation of what he had done, she forgot that her eyes should always be downcast when she addressed a young man, and looked up at him with a shining expression.

"It's a wonderful idea. But I think the best idea of all would be to take me home now, don't you, before Grand'-mère begins to wonder what's happened to me? Anyway, we can't stand here indefinitely at the corner of St. Louis Street. We're blocking the banquette."

She did not let Myrthé get ahead of her a second time. She slipped her own arm through Andy's and hurried forward so that her cousins could not hear her when she whispered to him.

"I cried all last night, I was so disappointed at missing your german."

"Well, don't cry over a missed german. Or spilt milk either. If you're scolded about the lottery drawing, say that you couldn't help going. Say that Allain de Gruy started to make a scene in the lobby of the St. Charles when you said you wouldn't go, and that, afterwards, he asked me to join your party over your protests."

"But it wouldn't be true!"

"It's near enough the truth to get by. Don't stop to argue with me. They'll catch up with us in a minute. Listen! I can't stand seeing you in a crowd at pink parties any longer. Tell me where I can meet you and talk to you alone."

"I don't know. I can't think. I wish I could. I'm tired of pink parties, too."

"Couldn't you slip away to church?"

"I might. I'll try. I'll let you know——"

Myrthé and Allain were already upon them. Allain laughed boisterously.

"You're not running away with my cousin, are you, Andy?"

"Of course I am. I'm going to kidnap her and hold her for ransom. There's a boat leaving for Mexico tonight. Didn't you see me trying to head towards the river?"

"It did look that way. But here we are right at Tante Lolotte's house."

Estelle had been wondering, as they rushed along, what she should do when they reached the front door. It would be crudely inhospitable not to ask her cousins to come in. Yet she could not do that without asking Andy also, and she knew that all his efforts to pay his respects to her parents had been rebuffed. To be sure, her grandmother would receive him with icy politeness; but after he had gone, his presence in their midst would require explanation; where and how did she happen to meet him; why had he joined her? The visit to the Lottery drawing would inevitably be disclosed. And there was still just a chance that it might be kept secret——

As if to take the decision out of her hands, the door flew open while she was still hesitating, and the gaunt figure of Julie appeared in the opening, her black dress silhouetted against the inner light, her little gold earrings gleaming. Completely ignoring the presence of the others, she spoke to Estelle in tones of unmitigated rebuke.

"Madame *Mère* has been waiting for you for more than half an hour, Mademoiselle. Would you be good enough to come in at once, before the dinner is entirely burnt up?"

Estelle said good-bye, and went into the house alone, still feeling the firm pressure of Andy's fingers, still hearing the lilt to his voice, as he bent over her whispering, "The Cathedral. Five o'clock. Tomorrow afternoon." Julie was muttering, too, something about "common Cajuns" and "coarse Americans," under her breath; but Estelle paid no attention to her or to the unveiled hints from Allain and Myrthé that they expected to stay for supper. She disregarded Julie's ill-humor, deciding to deal with it later, and she did not care whether her cousins were offended or not. She went into the drawing room, and did a very bold thing; she told her grandmother where she had been and with whom. If she slanted the story a little, in line with Andy's suggestion, she could hardly be blamed for that; at least she herself felt no qualms of conscience because she had done so. She listened respectfully to her grandmother's reproof, and

promised that she would never, never permit herself to be
led so far astray again if Grand'mère would only be merci-
ful, and regard her confession as confidential. Then she sat
contentedly making plans to meet Andy in church the next
day, while she and Madame Lenoir *mère* talked about the
coming Carnival, to their mutual satisfaction.

CHAPTER 4

IT WAS very cold in the Cathedral and very dark. The
place smelt of stale incense and unwashed congregations.
When Andy Breckenridge pushed open one of the soiled
leather doors, a bevy of ragged, dirty guides immediately
sprang forward and leapt upon him. They wanted to show
him the painting on the ceiling and tell him about the width
of the nave, and in return for these services, they wanted
liberal remuneration. As a quick glance sufficed to show
him that Estelle was nowhere to be seen, Andy permitted
the guides to drag him from pillar to post while reciting
their story in a whining singsong. Then he gave them each
five dollars.

"Thank you very much for showing me the Cathedral,"
he said politely. "But don't forget, the next time you see me
here, that you have shown it to me. I'm willing to jog your
memory, every now and then, but I'll take the initiative
about that. If you try to do it, there won't be any more
largesse. Now run along."

Although this was by no means the first time he had met
a young lady by secret appointment, he had never done so
in a church before. He rather expected that Estelle would
wait for him to join her by one of the confessionals or one
of the holy water basins; people were passing to and fro in
front of those all the time, and a chance meeting would
never be noticed in the obscurity. But she was not there
and she did not come. After he had paced futilely up and
down for several moments with growing impatience, he realized that there was something familiar about a kneeling
figure in one of the rear pews, otherwise unoccupied, and
that no other worshippers were anywhere near it. He walked
over to the pew in question, looked at the kneeling figure

more closely, and slid in beside it. The veiled lady went on telling her beads with rapt intentness. But Andy could see her delicate profile underneath the soft chiffon, and he was sure there was only one girl in the world who moved her slim hands with such unstudied but consummate grace. He slid closer and whispered to her.

"Why didn't you give me a hint where you'd be? I was about ready to chew nails in my fury, I was so sure you hadn't come. I don't know the technique of this sort of thing. You'll have to teach me."

Estelle finished her decade without a sign that she had heard him. Then she slipped the rosary back over her wrist, and whispered.

"Don't scold me, Andy. I don't know any more about the technique of all this than you do. I don't believe I know as much. But it seemed natural to pray while I waited for you. Wasn't that all right?"

"Well, it seemed to me as if you prayed a good while. But it's all right now that you've stopped."

"Why, I haven't stopped! I've got to begin right away, before anyone notices. And in a few minutes I've got to go home."

"I don't see how this is going to do us much good then."

"I didn't say that it would. I never dared to hope that it would. But you asked me if I wouldn't meet you in church, and I have. That shows I wanted to do what you asked me, Andy. I don't see how I can meet you at this time of day again, though. It's just the time all the parties are going on. I had terribly hard work getting away. I had to lie and lie, and now I'm very much frightened that we'll be caught."

He could see her lips quivering underneath her veil, her hands trembling, as she slid the rosary forward between her fingers again. He tried to speak to her more gently.

"Would there be any better place, or any better time?"

"I can't think of any other place at all. A better time would be at early Mass."

"And what time is that?"

"The first one is at five o'clock."

Andy gave a slight groan which ended in a smothered laugh. Estelle looked towards him in alarm, forgetting her first fear that they might be seen, in a new fear that they might be heard.

"Forgive me, darling. I didn't mean to do that. But there

is something humorous in the idea that I'd be willing to get up at five o'clock in the morning for anybody. Three-thirty, rather. After all, I do have to shave and dress, and it takes me at least an hour to get here from Prytania Street. Of course the answer to that is that I won't go to bed at all. At least until after this Mass of yours."

"It isn't my Mass. It's everybody's Mass. And there is another at five-thirty and another at six. But six is too late to be safe."

"It's always better to be safe than sorry. Five o'clock it is then. But if I get here and don't find you at that hour, I will certainly be the maddest man in New Orleans. My rage this afternoon won't be a circumstance to it."

"I don't know that I can come every morning, Andy. But being Advent makes it easier. And then of course I can make a Christmas Novena."

"What's that?"

"Why, Andy, don't you know? A novena is a nine days' devotion said as a preparation for some particular feast, or in order to obtain some special favor. The Christmas Novena is the oldest one of which we have any certain knowledge and I think its special meaning is the most beautiful of all. It commemorates the nine months before Our Blessed Lady gave birth to the Christ Child."

"I see," Andy Breckenridge said gravely, the laughter all gone from his voice.

"Only I don't know that I could be happy, Andy, if I made this Novena a pretext for seeing you. I know it isn't right for me to meet you at all and——"

"I don't agree with you. As long as we can't meet the way we've both tried to meet and want to meet, I believe it's right for us to meet any way and anywhere we can. But I don't want you to be unhappy about anything we do together."

"Well—I'll come to Mass, day after tomorrow, anyway, at five. I'll try to be in this same pew. Don't talk to me any more now, Andy."

"I won't. But I'll be here day after tomorrow at five, too."

As usual, they were at the same party the next evening. Andy, who was becoming more and more adroit in such matters, managed to steer Estelle far enough away from the other dancers to ask her a brief question.

"Won't you be exhausted if you try to go to church, after this, with only an hour or two of sleep?"

"No. I think perhaps I can go back to sleep again after Mass. Anyway, I want to go to it. Things are more favorable than I dared to hope they'd be, Andy. Julie has a very bad cold, with fever. I don't think she'll be about much before Christmastime. And Grand'mère and Maman and Papa all seem to be a good deal impressed because I want to observe Advent so scrupulously. But they've talked it over, and decided that it's all right for me to go to early Mass alone. I don't think they want to discourage devoutness; and yet I don't think that any one of them wants to get up at five any more than you do."

Andy grinned. "You mean half past three."

"Well, of course it wouldn't be half past three for them, we live such a short distance from the Cathedral. But still it would be rather early."

"You put it mildly, my dear. Well, I only hope Julie develops double pneumonia."

"Andy, how can you be so cruel?"

She did not really think he was cruel. She smiled as she asked the question, and she voiced no objection when he stayed beside her throughout Mass, or when he remained by her side as she left the pew and walked down the aisle, though she did speak to him reprovingly about something else.

"It would be more respectful, Andy, if you should genuflect."

"All right, I will the next time, if you want me to."

She dipped her fingers in the holy water basin and held them out to him. He caught at them eagerly but uncomprehendingly.

"No! No!" she exclaimed, drawing them away again and looking anxiously around her. But her fears were groundless. There were very few people in the church, and the scattered scrubwomen and clerks who had come to this early service were all hurrying away to their own heavy toil and humdrum tasks, without paying the slightest attention to what anyone else was doing. "When holy water is passed from one person to another, it is not just a special sign of affection, though it is that, too," Estelle went on. "It also carries a special blessing with it. You should have accepted it and crossed yourself with it."

"Oh, I see! Give me some more then and I will."

The street lamps were flickering wanly, but the stars were still shining brightly when they went out of the church side by side. There was enough light for Andy to see that Estelle was very pale. He drew her arm through his, almost abruptly.

"Look here, this is too much for you, just as I knew it would be. Did you have anything to eat before you started out?"

"No, of course not, but——"

"Of course *not!* Of course you should have. You're coming across to the French Market with me this minute for coffee and doughnuts."

"Oh, Andy, I can't do that! Someone might see us."

"Someone! The teamsters and farmers the café was really started for! The poor people bringing in their produce from the country, half frozen and half famished by the time they get it here. And the scrubwomen and the clerks we've seen in church. Nobody else at this hour. It's too late for the partygoers and too early for anyone else. And even if it weren't, I'm not going to have you fainting away on my hands. You look half frozen and half famished yourself! I'm going to put my arm around you while we walk across the square, to keep you warm and to support you."

"Andy, you mustn't!"

"If you don't stop objecting to everything I say and do, I'll kiss you right here on the street before we go another step. That'll teach you I'm not to be trifled with. Just take a good look at the old bronze general, up there on horseback, and think what he'd do, under the same circumstances. I'm sure he never let a lady go uncared-for, from all I've heard. Look here, Estelle, I meant what I said—about the coffee and about the kissing, too, if you didn't come along."

The coffee did bring some color into her cheeks. But she hardly tasted her doughnut, and she was unresponsive while Andy talked to her as he devoured his own and called out for another. He realized afresh how extremely sensitive she was, how careful he must be not to harass her or hasten her. He was sure she was capable of great and lasting love, but she would never love easily or lightly. He said nothing more to her about kissing, and he did not try to touch her again. Instead, he began to speak of impersonal things, pushing back the thick white cups from which they had been drinking, and leaning forward across the small marble-topped table. Had she ever really seen Frenchtown, he asked her? Oh, he knew she went around there every day. But he was sure she'd never looked at all the things he'd like to show her. He didn't know anyone who lived there that did—or heard all the stories he'd like to tell her—for instance—in all the times that she'd been to Mass at the Cathedral, had she ever walked through the alley back of it to Father Anthony's garden? No? Well, someday they would go there together and sit under the palm tree and eat dates while he told her the legend about it. He was sure that, when she looked up at the tree, she would believe the legend.

"What is the legend, Andy? You can tell it to me now. And then—perhaps—someday—we can go and sit under the palm."

"The legend is that Père Antoine and Emile Jardain, who were very great friends, were preparing for the priesthood together, when they both fell in love with the same girl. That is the sort of situation which is apt to lead to complications, Estelle. You'll be careful to see that no one besides myself falls in love with you, won't you?"

"I—Andy, don't be so absurd. Go on with your story."

"Well, the girl, whose name I don't know, eloped with Emile, though I haven't the slightest doubt that Antoine was the better man. Girls aren't much good at sizing up men, alas!"

"Andy, if you don't go on with the story, I'll have to leave without hearing the end of it."

"Why, the end of it was sad. That's another frequent occurrence when a girl marries the wrong man. Emile deserted his wife, and when she was on her death bed, she sent her baby to Père Antoine. He did the best he could for it, but after all, he wasn't its physical father, as he should have been; he was only a priest, so the baby died, too, and Père Antoine planted a palm to mark its grave. The palm flourished, even though the baby didn't. It's tall and beautiful and it bears delicious dates."

"And has the garden always been a holy place, Andy?"

Andy smiled. "Hardly. Probably that's why you've never been told more about it. Nearly all the duels that were fought over the girls who graced the quadroon balls took place there. The gay young bloods didn't wait to go out to the duelling oaks the morning after the ball, when two of them wanted the same enchantress. They settled the question as to who should have her then and there. And the survivor got her. To the victor belonged the spoils. That's as it should be and always has been."

"But those weren't—well, they weren't nice young men, were they, Andy?"

"I'm not sure what you'd call a nice young man. Someone like Marcel Fontaine, I suppose, whose morals are good, as men's morals go, and whose manners are perfect, but who haven't enough magnetism to make you tingle with it fifteen minutes, or enough force to knock over a flowerpot."

"Andy, you mustn't talk that way about my friends."

"Sorry. But you invited it with your juvenile question about nice young men. Now I think some of the elder Fontaines might have been perfectly capable of fighting a duel in Père Antoine's garden. In fact——"

"In fact what, Andy?"

"In fact, I have a suspicion that one of them did. But that's neither here nor there. We've said enough about the Fontaines, anyway. Let's say something about Andy Breckenridge and Estelle Lenoir for a change."

He went on talking, ordering more coffee and sprinkling sugar liberally, from the large shaker on the table, onto the fresh doughnuts the white-aproned waiter had brought them. When they had finished their second serving, they left the French Market and went back across Jackson Square. The stars were dimmer now, but there was a mystic quality to the crepuscule, which lent enchantment to the long rectangles of the Pontalba, on either side of them, and to the façade of the Cathedral and the portals of the Cabildo in front of them. Andy called Estelle's attention to the supernal beauty before they turned up Chartres Street. It would be better to go up that than Royal, Estelle said. Early as it still was, some of the servants would be starting out to market by this time, with their big baskets over their arms, and all those who worked in the immediate vicinity of her home knew her both by sight and by name. When she and Andy reached St. Louis Street, she would slip across the block alone. Andy nodded, understandingly, and when she saw that he was not going to make difficulties about the last block, which she thought it better to traverse by herself, she did not try to hurry. She let him stop again to tell her more stories, this time about the Napoleon house, and the bitter, thwarted little man who had once been great and for whom his faithful followers had prepared it. After that, they stopped a third time, so that he could buy her some *tout-chauds* from a huge Negress who was just setting up her little stand for the day, and whose puffy rice cakes were still hot from the oven. The *tout-chauds* were a happy thought; Estelle ate them with more appetite than she had the doughnuts and Andy was very pleased.

Dawn had begun to break as they sauntered up Chartres Street. The stars were gone, and the grayness that had succeeded it. The sky was streaked with faint ribbons of rose. Some of the shutters were already open at the shop windows. As they passed a grilled doorway of a courtyard, the sound of singing floated out to them. Estelle stopped of her own accord and spontaneously laid her fingers on Andy's arm.

"Listen!" she said. "That must be Mademoiselle Valgalier singing! She's succeeded Mademoiselle de Rinkly, you know, as first falcon at the opera. And Mademoiselle de Rinkly used to sing that song every morning on the *Nantes*, while she was dressing. She had the cabin next to mine, and I used to lie in my berth and listen to her. I've always loved the music from *Carmen* better than almost any other, I think. That's the *Habañera*, you know. Let's stop and listen to it now."

They drew back on the banquette to let the passers-by go on. Then Andy had a better idea. He tried the grilled gate and found it unlocked. They stepped into the courtyard. The glorious song came pouring out to meet them, from an upper window.

> *"L'amour est enfant de bohème,*
> *Il n'a jamais, jamais connu de loi,*
> *Si tu ne m'aimes pas, je t'aime;*
> *Si je t'aime, prends garde à toi!"*

"*Prends garde à toi!*" Andy echoed warningly, as the last note died away. "You'd better beware, Estelle. For I do love you. And it's true that love's never known any laws."

He put a finger under her chin, and tilted this up, so that she would have to look at him. But he did it gently, and the merriment of his manner mitigated its intensity. He had his reward.

"Andy," Estelle said shyly, "I want to tell you something. But I don't dare."

"You must dare. Because I want you to tell me."

"Whatever it is?"

"Yes, of course. There's nothing you could possibly want to tell me that I wouldn't want to hear."

"I'm afraid you'll think I'm very silly, and perhaps you'll think I'm very unladylike."

Andy laughed. He had two kinds of laughter, one that Estelle loved and one that frightened her a little. This was the kind she loved.

"You're never silly," he said. "You're sweet. And you couldn't be unladylike if you tried. Ladies are born, not made. The quality doesn't necessarily have anything to do with the background and surroundings that are generally considered genteel either. But never mind about that. Tell me what's on your mind that you're afraid I'll think is silly and unladylike and that I assure you I won't."

"I love music, and——"

"Yes, I gathered that much. Go on."

"I'd like to sing myself."

"Well, bless your heart! Why don't you then?"

"I do. At home. And once in a while at the Fontaines' house. Marcel's always saying he likes to hear me, though I don't think the others care much about it. And I don't wonder at all. I haven't much voice, really. Besides, I've never been taught how to use it, or the music to anything but a few foolish little songs."

"I know the type. But you could learn how to use your voice so you'd make the most of what you do have. And someone could teach you other songs."

"Ye-es, I suppose so. But it wouldn't do me much good, even if I did get that far. Because I'd like to sing a great deal, at all sort of times, in all sorts of places. Wherever I happened to be, whenever I felt like it. The way Valgalier sings, for instance. On shipboard, in a courtyard, at—at an Opera House. When I was dressing in the morning, or surrounded with friends in the evening. Or when the people around me were actually strangers. For their pleasure as well as my own."

"Well, I'll be darned!"

"I told you I was afraid to tell you. I told you that you'd think I was silly and unladylike."

"But I don't. I think it's a wonderful idea. I think you would give a great many people pleasure. I think you ought to go right ahead and try to do it."

"Why, Andy, you know how Maman and Papa would feel if they knew I wanted to do anything like that! And Grand'-mère—it might be fatal to Grand'mère, at her age, if she found out! It makes her uneasy just to suspect that I'd like to sing more than I do now. She often comes into the *salon* when I'm at the piano and asks me if I'm going to stay there all day."

"Well, the next time she does that, why don't you say, very pleasantly but still very firmly, 'Yes, Grand'mère, all day and perhaps all night, too?' "

"I couldn't do that, Andy."

"There's just one thing about you that worries me, Estelle, and it's that there are so many things you think you can't do. You ought to go on the principle that there's nothing you can't do."

He held open the grilled gate for her, smiling so beguilingly that, though her heart fluttered at the sight of him, standing there and looking lovingly down at her, it was again with happiness and not with alarm. He went on talking to her as if he knew this.

"Therefore I'm taking it for granted that you can meet me at Mass tomorrow morning. And that after Mass you'll take coffee with me at the French Market again, and that this time you'll eat your doughnut, too. And that after that we'll walk up Chartres Street together and buy *tout-chauds* and linger in a courtyard listening to a song and continuing this very interesting conversation about your own promising musical career."

"I really think we'd better say day after tomorrow, Andy. Please don't ask me to try to do it every day. It is hard and I do get tired. I didn't sleep at all last night after the dance. I didn't dare let myself go to sleep, for fear I wouldn't wake up in time to meet you, for of course there wasn't anyone to wake me up. Tomorrow I'll be tireder still. Because there's another dance tonight, as you know. And this noon I have to go to Monsieur Fontaine's office to watch the Firemen's Parade. He and Madame Fontaine are giving a large luncheon there."

"By George, this is the day of the Firemen's Parade, isn't it! That means that I won't be seeing you at the dance tonight.

I'll have to go to the banquet at Washington Artillery Hall given by Perseverance Number Thirteen."

"I didn't know you belonged to Perseverance Number Thirteen, Andy! Octave Fontaine belongs to Creole Number Nine and he's going to march. That's why his family are having this party. I've never liked Octave very well, so I wasn't especially interested in seeing the parade, just on his account. But now that I know you'll be in it——"

"Oh, I'll be in it! I seem to get into a little of everything. And this is the fifty-second anniversary of 'good work in a noble cause' for old Perseverance. So I don't doubt the banquet will be supplied with good cheer of both the solid and the liquid variety in unusually large quantities. And I seem to remember that after the banquet the Company's expected to go in a body to Bidwell's Academy of Music. Mrs. Bidwell's invited us to see Charlotte Thompson in her own version of *Jane Eyre*. I'd be a little more enthusiastic if I knew just what her own version of Brontë was. I'm slightly skeptical about feminine intuition when it comes to interpretation of the classics. I think I may sneak away to one of the fancy-dress balls instead. Perhaps to Creole Number Nine, where Octave Fontaine will be. What have you got against him? He isn't a bad fellow. I like him better than any of his brothers."

"Oh, I don't! I'm a little in awe of Auguste, but of course it is proper that I should be, since he is studying for the priesthood. But Narcisse is a sweet child, and Marcel is always so courteous and considerate."

"I'm afraid I forgot about the sweet child. I don't instinctively think of them as males until they get to be a little older than he is. And I'm not at all in awe of Auguste. He plays the best game of poker of any Creole I've ever met. There's nothing the matter with Marcel. But when you've said that, you've said all there is to say."

"I've just told you, he's unusually courteous and considerate."

"You talk as if those were qualities. In his case, they're only habits. I'd like to get you away from all those smooth Creoles. It would be fun if I could take you to one of the fancy-dress balls tonight."

"But you know I couldn't do that!"

"Yes, for once I'm willing to grant there might be obstacles. Besides, even if it could be managed, those Firemen's

Balls get pretty rowdy. I was just joking. I wouldn't really choose one as the setting for a sweetheart who was born a lady. Good-bye, darling. Day after tomorrow then, at the same ungodly hour."

It seemed rather futile to Estelle to be going to Monsieur Charles Fontaine's office, on the corner of Gravier and Camp Streets, when she could have seen the parade equally well from one of the windows of her own home. It was to follow its accustomed route up Camp to Calliope, to St. Charles, to First, to Magazine, to Julia, to St. Charles, to Canal, to Esplanade, to Dauphine, to Elysian Fields, to Levee, to Esplanade, to Royal and to Canal, where it would finally be dismissed. But when she reminded her mother of this, and said that she was sleepy, and that she would rather peek at the parade from behind the shutters and then lie down for a little while after lunch, Madame Lenoir spoke to her reprovingly.

"I hope that none of the Spanish Creoles whom you have been meeting lately have intrigued you with the idea of taking siestas, Estelle. I assure you there is nothing French in such an indolent custom. None of the girls in my own circle ever thought of lying down in the daytime, no matter how late they had been out dancing, or how early they had gone to Mass. Besides, the feasibility of watching the parade pass by here has nothing to do with the case at all. We have already accepted the Fontaines' kind invitation, and the acceptance of any invitation should be regarded as final, unless there is a death in the immediate family, or possibly very serious illness of a contagious character. I was sure I had taught you that long ago."

"You did, Maman. And I did not mean to imply that I wished to take a siesta every day. It was only——"

"We will not say anything more about it, *ma fille.*"

On general principles, Estelle rather enjoyed going to Monsieur Fontaine's office, which she had done several times before. It interested her to see the clerks, clad in all-enveloping linen dusters, who stood in front of the long tables in the outer rooms, sampling the spot cotton. Marcel, who was already a junior in his father's brokerage firm, had shown her how this was tested. She knew that the Egyptian cotton had the longest fibre, but that Sea Island cotton was also very good indeed. She enjoyed the feeling of soft fluffy masses in her own hands; she liked to pick the samples up, to try to imitate the motions of the clerks and pass sage judgments on the qualities, as they did. Usually she paused in the outer offices long enough to do so. But today she was not in the mood. The clerks, who knew her by name as well as by sight, and who all liked her very much, were disappointed, though she did not neglect to bow to them pleasantly. They raised their eyebrows and looked at each other in a knowing way after she had gone on to Monsieur Fontaine's private sanctum, and one of them even went so far as to speak about her under his breath to the clerk who stood next to him.

"The wind is in the east today, eh, Paul? It doesn't bode well for Monsieur Marcel."

"If you ask me, René, I think the wind is blowing down the river from White Castle, or thereabouts, and sweeping everything before it. But that may be only idle gossip."

"Without doubt, without doubt."

It was fortunate that Estelle, not to mention her mother, was oblivious of this conversation. While it was still going on, she had greeted her host and hostess with deference, and the younger Fontaines—who, with the exception of Octave, were all there—with less formality, and had permitted Marcel to install her in a chair, and bring her a glass of wine and a plate laden with the delicacies that Nellie Murray, the famous colored cateress, had sent in for the occasion. The Rutledges were also there, and though they were the only "Americans," several outstanding Creole families were present, with sons and daughters of about Estelle's age, who were good friends of hers. She knew that she ought to be enjoying their company, as she usually did. But she did not join in their chit-chat, and after taking a few sips of wine and one or two mouthfuls of *daube glacée*, she set down her glass and pushed back her plate.

"What's the matter, Estelle? Isn't there anything that you like? Could I get you something else?"

There was Marcel, at her elbow again, though she had thought that Cléon Gautier seemed to have him well in hand. She gave her plate another little push, and then caught her mother's reproving eye upon her, reminding her that this was very rude. She flushed, feeling tears close to the surface. But she tried to answer Marcel with appreciation.

"It's all delicious. But I have a slight headache today. I think perhaps I'd better not try to eat. I'd like a *petit noir* very much though, Marcel."

"Of course. I'm so sorry, Estelle, that you have a headache."

He was solicitude itself. She saw him go to his mother, and heard him say that Estelle must have a comfortable chair to sit in, while the parade was going on, like the older guests, and not be left to perch or stand anywhere, like the rest of her contemporaries. His mother nodded, looked at Estelle with sympathetic affection, and placed the young girl beside herself. Marcel, who had apparently forgotten all about Cléon Gautier by this time, stood between the two chairs, leaning over each in turn.

"What perfect weather! Uncle Théophile calls it a day fit for the gods! It's almost as warm as summer, in the sun."

Estelle, who had not felt really warm, except around her heart, since she left the Cathedral, did not succeed in responding very adequately to Marcel's comments on the weather. But he persevered with his own glad remarks, undaunted by her lukewarm attitude.

"The bunting is pretty, isn't it, Estelle, floating from that building across the street? I really think there is more on that one than on any of the others, though they are all well decorated. And I always enjoy seeing such a display of flags."

He paused, and Estelle, now aware that her mother's eye was again upon her, murmured almost inaudibly that she also enjoyed such a sight.

"Look down at the banquettes! I do not think I ever saw them so crowded! And all the windows and galleries are crowded, too! I read in *L'Abeille* this morning that we might expect fewer decorations than usual, but that there would be a larger number of men at the ropes. I believe there are to be at least three thousand in line, and it is estimated that there will be nearly a hundred thousand spectators. Everyone must enjoy seeing a Firemen's Parade, I think."

Estelle, following his glance, admitted that the crowds did, indeed, seem to be larger than usual, and that such numbers were impressive.

"Don't you agree with me that this parade is one of the most amusing sights we have in New Orleans, Estelle? Almost as amusing as Carnival! Those great bouquets the firemen carry, for instance, made out of cabbages stuck full of cigars! None of the Carnival baubles has as much originality as that! Octave had nine cigars that had been given him, stuck in his cabbage, when he left Bayou St. John."

Estelle, wondering how many Andy had in his, and feeling sure there must be at least a dozen, murmured that nine cigars were a great many and that Marcel must be very proud of Octave's popularity.

"Yes, it is gratifying. Listen, Estelle! Can't you hear the music? A fine band, isn't it? I think the parade will be swinging into sight any moment now."

She was glad of an excuse to crane her neck and watch for it, without feeling obliged to murmur platitudes any longer, though she was willing to grant that the parade undoubtedly would be very fine. This was the fifty-fifth anniversary of the Brigade's foundation, and she knew that "the gallant foes of the fiery element," as the press described them, would make the most of the opportunity thus offered them, for putting on their gaudy uniforms and marching out in full force. As far as she was concerned, there was only one participant in the parade whom she really wanted to see, but she did not know at what point Perseverance Number Thirteen would appear, so she was determined to keep a sharp lookout from the beginning. As a secondary consideration, she remembered that she must also watch closely for Creole Number Nine, so that she would not fail to applaud loudly when Octave, carrying his cabbage riddled with nine cigars, swung impudently past. But all her genuine interest was centered in Andy.

The music had been coming nearer and nearer while she listened and watched. Now she could see the Grand Marshal, whose name was Mr. David Hennessy, swinging into sight, surrounded by his eighteen aides. They were followed by a cortege of carriages containing the Honorable I. N. Marks, President of the Firemen's Charitable Association, and various dignitaries who held high office in it. They were, for the most part, very substantial citizens, literally as well as figuratively, and Estelle could well imagine that they would be more comfortable sitting on cushioned seats than riding on horseback or marching on foot. They waved their silk hats and bowed right and left to the populace, which responded with polite applause; but it was not until the Companies themselves came along that the cheering and clapping became really spontaneous.

Volunteer Number One, captioned with the motto "Perseverance and Industry Overcome All Obstacles," was the first Company to follow the cortege. There were sixty men in line, proudly carrying "bouquets" and streamers, and the Company's prize horses, Pete Fabacher, and H. B. Whelage, were decked out in red satin saddles and silver-corded bridles. Still, the spectators were slightly disappointed, for the engine, though beautifully burnished, had not been decorated, and this was contrary to the best traditions. But the crowds were unstinted in their demonstrations when Métairie Number Four, proclaiming itself "Ready for Duty," followed after Volunteer Number One. The President of this gallant Company had recently passed away, and the scheme of decoration was selected to commemorate this sad event. From the center of the chemical rose a pyramid of black velvet, relieved by pansies and immortelles, while surmounting it was a white dove with outspread wings, which held in its beak a black ribbon bearing the inscription "In Memory of Our President." A crayon portrait of the deceased leader, festooned with crepe, completed the ensemble. Everyone in the Fontaine's party agreed that this was a very touching tribute, and several of the ladies present, whose mourning, like that of Madame Lenoir *mère*, was perpetual, produced black-bordered handkerchiefs, and murmured that they were too much moved to applaud.

But their spirits rose when Mississippi Number Two hove into sight. This Company had modestly chosen "The Nations" for its subject. No mere cornucopia adorned the smokestack in this instance; the Goddess of Liberty surmounted it, holding the American flag high in one hand, and in her other, holding the American shield to protect her bosom. Germany, England, Spain and Russia, all gorgeously personified, acted as her bodyguard. France stood at the driver's seat with the tricolor in her hand and the red cap of the Revolutionists on her head. Mexico with her eagle and her serpent watched at the rear of the bunker. Small statues of various other nations were placed on the brackets, and even the wheels of the engine were painted with the shields of still others. Mississippi Number Two had indeed surpassed itself and all its competitors. The applause became uproarious.

Estelle joined in this half-heartedly. She was afraid that, at this rate, the enthusiasm of the crowd might spend itself before Perseverance Number Thirteen came along. As other spectacles met her eyes, this fear increased, but, like so many of her other fears, this proved unfounded.

Perseverance Number Thirteen, with a motto of "Rough and Ready," struck a wholly new note, and one in which she was sure Andy had had a voice. An enormous floral horseshoe surmounted a white pyramid with heavy gilt and silver trimmings, a horseshoe only slightly smaller, supporting the numerals "13," towered above the driver's seat, and there were miniature horseshoes on all the brackets. The horses, themselves, were decked out with such gorgeousness that the trappings of those which had passed with Volunteer Number One, half an hour earlier, seemed tame and tawdry by comparison. There were gold and silver chimes on their saddles, and as they pranced along, the chimes rang out in tuneful harmony. Three of the horses—Josh Lippman, Captain John Fitzpatrick and Chris Bertheson—were led by jockeys flamboyantly dressed; but Andy, himself, was astride the fourth, striking the chimes with a little silver hammer, so that they rang out more loudly and more melodiously than all the rest put together. His reins were pushed back over his wrist, while he played the chimes; every now and then, still holding his silver hammer, he reached down into a saddlebag, drew out a fistful of tiny horseshoes and tossed them right and left, high and low; with his free hand, he waved his hat in circles over his head. The winter sunshine fell on his crisp hair, his white teeth gleamed between his laughing lips, and even from the distance at which she beheld him, Estelle could see the sparkle in his blue eyes. Voices from the crowd rose to hail him on every side.

"Hey, there, Andy!"—"Toss us one of your horseshoes for good luck!"—"Howarya, Andy!"—"I hope you have the luck of the Irish yourself!"—*"Bravo, mon vieux!"*—"Breckenridge's best, I'd say!"—*"La, la, le petit choux!"*—"Say, what about a bunch of lottery tickets or a change!"—"I'm still betting on Supremus, Andy!"—"I'm still betting on *you!*" Everyone knew him, from the smallest child on the edge of the banquette, to the oldest man in the highest window. And all of them, apparently, followed him and exulted in him and adored him. How could her parents be so blind to the qualities that held thousands spellbound, Estelle asked herself? And how could she have doubted for one instant that, however arresting the spectacle that someone else presented, Andy would find a way to surpass it?

"That was original, wasn't it?" she heard Marcel saying pleasantly. "Andy is indeed a splendid showman. I am certain he would have made a fortune on the stage. To be sure, he has a fortune anyway. But he could have been actormanager and property designer, too, all at the same time. Don't you think so, Estelle?"

"Yes, I believe he could," she said faintly. Her mother was watching her again, and she knew that it was not safe to speak of Andy, hardly safe to think of him, while Madame Lenoir was observing her with such attention.

"But Creole Number Nine has a very original design, too," Marcel went on. "It's even more of a tribute to Octave than the horseshoes were to Andy. You wait and see."

She did not have long to wait. Creole Number Nine, proclaiming "Union, Justice and Confidence," followed closely in the wake of Perseverance Number Thirteen, and she instantly recognized the source of Marcel's pride in a *"fontaine lumineuse,"* surrounded by a circle of lesser fountains, all luminous also. There was real beauty to this design; obviously it has been created with feeling and care as well as taste. Estelle had a sudden inspiration.

"It was you, wasn't it, Marcel, who thought of a *'fontaine lumineuse?'* It's such a beautiful thought—a 'fountain of light.' It seems more like one of your thoughts than one of Octave's. But he's benefiting by it." She saw the joy that suffused Marcel's face as she spoke, and something impelled her to go on speaking, to be just, as well as generous. "It's even more beautiful than the horseshoes, Marcel," she said. "It's the most beautiful design in the whole parade."

The Parade had come to an end. The Fontaines' guests, with renewed expressions of appreciation, had begun to disperse. Estelle, looking surreptitiously at the small watch, which was tucked inside her tight belt, at the end of a long chain, saw that she would have barely time, before her duties began, to get to the first of the rosy teas at which she was supposed to assist, and after that, she would have to go home and dress for the dance to which Andy was not going, because he was attending the banquet at Washington Artillery Hall and going afterwards to Bidwell's Academy of Music, if he did not play hooky and go to a rowdy fancy-dress ball instead. With sudden courage, she decided that she would not go to a tame and tepid party either. She would go home and sleep and sleep and sleep. But there was Marcel, still at her elbow, still courteous and considerate, as she had told Andy, and almost pathetically eager to please her.

"Clarisse and I are going to the Provostys', Estelle," he said. "Maman is going, too. Why don't you come with us? Madame Lenoir has just told me that she is a little tired— that she is going home at once."

"I'm a little tired myself. I'll ask Maman to take me with her. I want to go home, too. I don't see why I ever said I'd assist at the Provostys' tea in the first place," Estelle answered. She knew that she sounded cross, now that her outburst of generosity was over, and she was aware that was something a lady should never do. (But what was it Andy had said? That ladies were born, not made? Then why this effort all the time, if she were bound to be one anyway?) "I'm very tired," she went on, growing bolder with every word she spoke. "It's enough to make any girl tired, assisting at all the teas that I have. Besides, I went to five o'clock Mass this morning. I like to go to early Mass. It's so quiet and peaceful. There's no one around to bother me. I'm tired of seeing the same people over and over again, at church and everywhere else. I'm going to avoid them by going to early Mass for the present and taking siestas in the middle of the day. I'm going to make the Christmas Novena, too. I really don't believe you'll see me at any more parties, Marcel, during Advent."

CHAPTER 5

ESTELLE, WHO had been to midnight Mass and consequently had not gone to bed until nearly two o'clock, was still asleep when Julie knocked on her door Christmas morning. It was not until Julie rapped for the third time that Estelle answered, drowsily and reluctantly, suppressing her inclination to nestle deeper down under the bedclothes, and forcing herself to sit upright instead. Julie entered with an air of great importance, carrying a box over a yard long,

with a roll of parchment placed significantly on top of it.
When Julie had removed the lid, several dozen American
Beauty roses were revealed, so large that they were top-
heavy on their long, sturdy stems. The scroll, temporarily
laid aside, which Julie next unfurled for Estelle to see, was
inscribed with an impressive salutation:

> Oceanus,
> King of the Pacifici,
> Sends Greetings to
> Estelle Lenoir
> and
> issues his royal edict.
> As the King decreeth, so shall it be.
> You are appointed Royal
> Consort to His Majesty the King
> to perform such duties as may
> be required of you on the night
> of February third.
> See that you fail not in this, your royal duty.
> Oceanus

Estelle read through this scroll twice, while Julie busied
herself by lighting a fire and pulling back the curtains. Then
she re-rolled it and laid it down quietly on the bedside table.

"You had better put the flowers in water at once, Julie.
They are very handsome, and we must not allow them to
wilt. Then you may take them to Madame. I am sure she will
wish to see them."

"Mademoiselle does not desire to keep them here?" Julie
inquired, betraying her surprise.

"They are too large to look well in this small bedroom.
And their perfume is very strong. I'm afraid, if I kept them
here, I would have a headache."

"Just as Mademoiselle says. But before I take away the
flowers, I must give her the other presents that came for her
this morning."

It was Estelle's turn to look surprised. New Year's and
not Christmas was the day for exchanging gifts. She had
never received a Christmas present in her life. Now Julie
placed two packages, one large and square, the other small
and narrow, but both beautifully done up, on the bed beside
her.

"What do you suppose they can be, Julie?"

"Doubtless Mademoiselle will see when she opens them," suggested Julie practically.

"Yes, of course. But which would you open first?"

"Oh, the large one by all means, since Mademoiselle asks my opinion."

They removed the gay ribbons and the soft wrappings together. Then Estelle, herself, lifted the cover of the large square box. Inside, she could see, at first, only masses of lightly shredded paper. Parting this cautiously, she lifted from it, one by one, the five pieces of turquoise-colored glass, ringed with gilt and beautifully painted with pink and white lilies, that made up an exquisite toilet set: two small vases, a covered jar, somewhat larger, and two tall decanters. The flowers to go in the vases, the powder and puff for which the jar was designed, and the perfume to fill the decanters, were all there, too, separately and carefully enclosed. At the bottom of the jar lay a scented envelope, sealed with a crested wafer. Estelle broke the seal slowly and read the card inside.

Joyeux Noël. Toujours à toi. Marcel.

Estelle replaced the card in the envelope and began setting the pieces of turquoise-colored glass inside the scroll on the bedside table. Then seeing that this was not large enough to hold them all safely, she removed those she had placed there, and handed them all to Julie instead.

"I think that perhaps it would be best to put these on the mantel, Julie. They are probably very valuable. We must not permit them to get broken."

"Mademoiselle does not intend to use them on her dressing stand?"

"Perhaps. But not at once. That is covered with other objects now. These ornaments would have to be properly arranged before they could be put to use. Besides, you know I am very fond of the porcelain scent bottle shaped like a little lady that Monsieur Pécot gave me for lagniappe the last time Grand'mère bought a barrel of toilet water from him. I would rather go on using her."

It was evident that Julie did not approve of this preference for the mantelpiece as a setting for the turquoise-colored glass, but Estelle ignored the obvious reluctance with which the maid started to install it there, and herself began to open the other package. It contained the most magnificent fan that Estelle had ever seen. It was apparently made of gold, for it glittered as she held it, and a slight metallic sound came from it as she moved it; but it was impossible to tell, for it was almost completely covered with painting in rich and various colors. There were flowers and figures on the sticks as well as on the spread, and the design was equally elaborate on both sides. One picture showed a queen seated on a throne, with courtiers standing around her and a suppliant kneeling before her; the other represented a regal wedding. A tiny mirror framed in jewels was set in the stick at either end, and the pivot on which the sticks turned was a precious stone. A fan-shaped card, painted in miniature, to suggest the decoration of the real fan, dangled from this at the end of a tasselled cord; and the superscription which this card carried, unconcealed by any envelope, leapt boldly out in heavy black handwriting to meet the girl's startled eyes.

Dearest Estelle:

I am afraid you broke the fan which you dropped at the opera when you overturned your bouquets. I hope this may serve to replace it. I am daring to take it for granted that you do not subscribe to the old plantation superstition that a fan should never be offered or accepted as a gift because it cools friendship, perhaps because I myself believe that much more often it fans friendship into flame. However, before that point is reached I do hope that this one will give you the necessary coolness to answer me the next time I address you. You are beautiful when you blush, but I like the sound of your voice, too. I shall find an opportunity to hear it again very soon, and I dare to hope that your lovely lips will form the word 'Yes' in answer to the question I shall ask you.

Unworthily your servant, but undauntedly your suitor,
Andrew Breckenridge.

Estelle closed the fan hurriedly. The little metallic sound that it gave forth was almost like the quick tinkle from a music box; she felt it must be stilled before it betrayed itself. She stuffed it back into the velvet case that had contained it, snapping down the cover, and avoiding the searching gaze of Julie, who looked at her, tight-lipped, but undeceived, while she did so; then she rose with haste. She divined that her mother would come to her room before long, and she was determined that she would be out of bed before Madame

Lenoir tapped at her door. She had always felt that if she had not been supine when her mother came to tell her about her debut, she would not have submitted so tamely to all the plans that had been made for her. But she could not interrupt Madame Lenoir in the middle of a discourse given by this lady, and her prostrate position affected her spirits as well as her person. She thrust her feet into bedshoes, and slipped into her chemise under cover of her nightgown, with the rapidity of long practice. But she had hardly begun to clasp her rigid little corset, when the knock she had been expecting smote lightly against the door, and Madame Lenoir entered her daughter's chamber.

"Bon jour et joyeux Noël, ma fille," she said, coming forward and kissing the girl on the brow. "You are a little late with your toilette, are you not? Though that is no excuse for performing it in a haphazard way. Is it possible that you are putting on your stays without having them relaced? Julie, you may go. And if I ever find you so negligent again, I shall assign one of the Negro servants to wait on Mademoiselle. Since old Eugénie claims to have been a queen in her own country, she may understand the requirements of a young lady better than you do."

As she spoke, Madame Lenoir untied the lacings, which were knotted at the waistline, and began to loosen them both above that point and below it. Involuntarily, Estelle drew a deep breath. She knew that the respite this loosening gave her was only momentary, and she tried to profit by the last lovely moment of freedom. The next instant she felt the pressure over her hips and diaphragm, as Madame Lenoir began to draw the strings together.

"Oh please! You are hurting me, Maman!" she said pleadingly.

"Nonsense! You may have an instant's discomfort, because I shall have to work fast, if you are to be properly clothed before noon, and therefore I cannot take time to do this gradually. But once the corset is adjusted, you will accustom yourself to its position, as usual. And perhaps your temporary discomfort may be salutary. I hope you will remember it the next time you are tempted to lie so late in bed, or to dress in so slovenly a fashion."

The lower part of the girl's torso now being closely confined, Madame Lenoir began to work above the waistline. As

Estelle's diaphragm became more and more compressed, her breasts, small as these were, swelled above it.

"Maman, dear Maman, you have never laced me like this! You have said yourself that tight lacing has gone out of fashion."

"I have never before seen you when you so obviously required tight lacing. And as to its being outmoded, I referred only to the clumsy American practice of fastening the strings to a bedpost and walking away from this. That is entirely different from the proper adjustment of stays. What is the use of buying them from the first *corsetière* in Paris if you put them on with no more care than you would a scarf?"

"I will be more careful in the future, Maman, I will indeed. But——"

"Stop talking to me, if you please, Estelle, and hold your breath. I am about to retie the strings in the middle, and first it will be necessary to pull them much harder than I have done so far. This is not only in order to insure snugness at the waist, which should, of course, be small; it is also to create the appropriate curves on either side of it. A girl of eighteen whose figure still shows so little sign of femininity must watch herself carefully—or if she does not do it for herself, her mother must do it for her."

If Estelle had not known that Madame Lenoir loved her dearly, if she had not believed her to be uniformly kind and gentle, she would have thought there was deliberate cruelty in the tugging that accompanied these words, and in the final wrench which brought the two sides of the corset together over her quivering spine. Never had she worn her stays before without an open space there, several inches in width; now they met like pincers that crushed before they imprisoned. She had grown giddy and faint, and besides the pain which she felt all over her body, there was another, of which she had never been conscious, which kept striking deep in her vitals. Tears which she could no longer control overflowed from her eyes and smothered sobs choked her. A handkerchief would have helped, but she had none about her, and she could not seem to move. She stood helplessly before her mother, clad in her fine chemise and her cruel corset, both of which had become symbols, the first of the delicate luxury in which she was lapped, the second of the unyielding code to which she must conform.

"There, there, you will be all right in a minute," Madame

Lenoir said, speaking more gently now that she had accomplished her purpose. "Since it is already so late, we may as well sit down and chat, while you compose yourself before you go on with your dressing." She held up a pretty peignoir for her daughter to put on, and wrapped it carefully around her. "So the significant scroll, so long awaited, has at last been delivered to you," she went on. "Are you not going to offer to show it to me? After all, I came here on purpose to see it."

"It is on the bedside table. I will get it for you."

"No, no, remain where you are. You are still looking a little pale. I will get it myself." Madame Lenoir crossed the room with a gliding motion, and having unfurled the scroll, read it carefully, for she understood English well, though she could never be persuaded to speak it. "That is indeed charming, is it not?" she said, refolding the scroll and replacing it. "You are overjoyed with it, Estelle, are you not?"

"Yes, Maman."

"And what are those beautiful ornaments that I see on the mantelpiece?"

"They came to me with a card from Marcel. I suppose that I should put them on the dressing table. But I have had no time to clear it yet."

"Oh, yes, Marcel!" Madame Lenoir said in so matter of fact a way that Estelle looked at her with fresh amazement. "I thought it was possible that Marcel might send you a little gift," her mother went on smoothly. "This is perhaps somewhat too costly, for a first offering. But I am sure he did not mean to exceed the limits of good taste."

"You don't think the ornaments are in good taste, Maman?"

"Oh, artistically they are perfect. I meant conventionally. But after all, you have been friends from childhood, and now— What sort of a card came with Marcel's gift, Estelle?"

"Do you wish to see that, too?"

"But certainly I wish to see that, too. What a question!"

Estelle had forgotten about Marcel's card when she opened the box containing the painted fan. But she knew it was somewhere between the sheets. As far as that went, so was the fan box. In her fear lest her mother might begin searching for Marcel's card and, in so doing, discover Andrew's, she disregarded her pain, and sprang towards the bed.

"I must have mislaid it after I read it. I was stupid not to remember that naturally you would wish to see it, too. I should have placed it carefully with the ornaments. But I am sure I can find it quickly. Yes, here it is."

She handed it to her mother unhesitatingly. Madame Lenoir looked at her with increasing attention.

"You cannot have attached much importance to it, *ma fille,* since you mislaid it so easily. Yet it came with a very beautiful and valuable present—the first of its kind you have ever received from a young man. And this message should mean a great deal to you, Estelle."

"Yes, of course. I am very fond of Marcel."

"And he is devoted to you. '*Toujours à toi*'—forever thine. Those are words, *ma fille,* that many a young man utters lightly. But it has not been so in this case. You are the one love of Marcel Fontaine's life, and he has given unmistakable evidence of his feeling. This is perhaps a good moment to tell you that last Saturday, when you went to confession, he came here by appointment, accompanied by his father, to ask for your hand in marriage."

This time, when Estelle sprang up, she forgot her previous pain completely, because the pain with which she was now pierced was so much more deadly. She cried out in anguish.

"Oh, but Maman! Surely you did not say yes!"

"It was not I who answered, Estelle. It was your father, of course. But naturally he said yes. How could he have replied otherwise? It has been his fondest hope, as it has been that of Monsieur Fontaine, that some day you and Marcel would marry. I may add that it has also been the careful plan of both. And now the plan had come to fruition. Not that there will be any immediate and formal announcement. Monsieur Fontaine and your father are agreed that, under all the circumstances, this should be deferred until after Easter. It would not be best, during the Carnival, that you should be known as betrothed. And, *bien entendu,* one does not announce a betrothal during Lent. But at Eastertime this will be done in proper form. Meanwhile, Marcel, who has consented with good grace to the delay, will be entitled to some of the privileges of a fiancé. He will make you gifts from time to time, though he will give you no jewelry at present. He will call on you regularly, and you will receive him alone, except that your father and I, or your grandmother, will always sit in the next room with the door ajar. He will kiss your hand upon arrival and departure, and after the betrothal is official, your brow. I do not need to warn you that you should permit no further advance, for Marcel would not attempt them. He is a gentleman, and he regards you with all the respect due his future bride."

"But Maman, you never told me of these careful plans and these fond hopes! I did not know Papa wished me to marry Marcel, or that Marcel himself desired it! I have thought no more of him than of Auguste or of Octave!"

"How can that be true, Estelle? You know that Auguste is studying for holy orders— Surely you never would have allowed your thoughts to stray towards one destined to be a priest! And you must have divined, though naturally it is never discussed, that Octave is not a young man of good habits, that no loving father would give his cherished daughter to Octave in marriage. But Marcel is free and his character is exemplary. Can you suppose that your father and I would have permitted you and him to be so much together if marriage were not in our minds?"

"I have only seen Marcel more than any other young man because he is the brother of Clarisse, and Clarisse is my best friend!"

"And Clarisse would not have become your best friend, or you hers, if your parents and hers had not supposed that you would marry one of her brothers. Your father and I would have arranged that your best friend belonged to some other family, and very properly hers would have done the same. But there is no occasion for all this discussion, which even savors of argument. I am as much astonished as I am displeased that you should appear to question your parents' judgment, or the judgment of your fiancé's parents. Surely you know that we all have our children's welfare at heart! And surely you also know that in our maturity and with our experience we can decide better than they what will bring them happiness. Is this not so, Estelle?"

"Yes, Maman. But——"

"There are no 'buts,' *ma fille*. The matter is settled, and your compliance to our wishes should be permeated with joy because we have so safeguarded you. Yet this does not seem to be the case. What most amazes me is that you should seem to shrink from the thought of bestowing your hand on Marcel. He is young, he is charming, he is well-born, he is rich. And he is kindness, itself—think of his attitude to his aged uncle and his little brother, and judge for yourself what his attitude would be towards a beloved woman. What more could you ask for?"

"It is that I had not thought of Marcel as my fiancé. I had only thought of him as the brother of Clarisse."

"You are fortunate in the prospect of thinking of him differently from now on. Suppose you were destined to marry a man who was mean or ugly! A man who was very old! In my day, a girl of sixteen, whom I knew well, was married to her great-uncle, in order that the fortune might be preserved intact in the family. There was a special dispensation from the Holy Father, and official permission was granted by the President of France, where the ceremony took place. But the married pair returned to New Orleans afterwards, and the bride was always an ornament to society, charming and gay, yet wholly discreet, and solicitude, itself, in her attitude towards her aged husband. I fear, *ma fille,* that you lack the great qualities of resignation and docility which characterized my friend, although I should have expected some reluctance if I had proposed marrying you to a man old enough to be your grandfather, or to one who lacked refinement and compassion." She leaned forward, looking at Estelle so impellingly that the girl was forced to meet her eyes. "You cringed and winced and wept when I hurt you a little, just now, lacing your corset," she said scornfully. "Do you know that a great many men are cruel to their wives? Sometimes brides are beaten—sometimes they are maltreated in other ways. Do not tempt us to give you to one with whom your life might be one of prolonged pain, by hesitating to accept the husband who has been chosen for you with such care."

Horror submerged the pain which struck deeper and deeper into Estelle's being. Her mother rose, triumphantly.

"I am sure that no such harsh measures will be indicated," she said, her voice kind, almost playful, again. "But I think that while I am here you had better show me the other card which you 'mislaid.' No doubt you forgot it in your excitement over the scroll and the roses, and the beautiful gift from Marcel. But am I mistaken in thinking I saw Julie bringing you a third package? Ah, I see that I am not! Here it is, among the bedclothes, just as I thought it might be!"

She had plunged her hand between the sheets and drawn out the fan box. Estelle gave a little cry to which Madame Lenoir paid no attention. Instead, she calmly unfurled the fan, inspected the signature of a famous artist, which was entwined with the painted roses, and which had entirely escaped Estelle's attention, and then slowly perused the letter from Andrew Breckenridge.

"On second thought, it seems impossible that you could have forgotten this," she said evenly. "Therefore I am forced to the reluctant conclusion that you must have deliberately concealed it. Am I wrong?"

"Yes, Maman. At least partly. I did not conceal it deliberately. I merely left it where you found it, when I began to dress. Since then, there has been no favorable opportunity to put it elsewhere."

She spoke with the sudden boldness of despair, looking her mother full in the face at last. If Madame Lenoir appreciated the extent of her daughter's courage, she gave no sign of this as she continued her inflexible questioning.

"And I suppose you found no favorable opportunity to speak of it either?"

"No, Maman."

"So that if I had left your room without extracting it from its hiding-place, you would not have spoken of it at all?"

"No, Maman."

"Does your conscience not smite you for such secretiveness?"

"No, Maman. Because I knew if you found this present you would take it away from me, and I wanted to keep it. I thought I might have at least a fan as a keepsake from— someone I like very much." She paused so briefly that her mother did not have time to interrupt her before she went on. "Last spring, as soon as you and Papa guessed that I liked Mr. Breckenridge, you took me away from New Orleans. When he appeared at our *loge*, Papa curtly dismissed him. When he sent me flowers, they were given away. When he came to call, he was told it was not your day at home, though he must have heard the voices of other visitors in the *salon*. When he went to Papa's *bureau*, the purpose of his mission was misinterpreted, much more deliberately than I hid my fan. He was told by a clerk that Papa could not take any more clients at present. And he went not to solicit legal advice or protection, but to ask for my hand—at the *bureau* because he could not get into the house! A month before Marcel thought of doing so! And he was not even granted the courtesy of an interview! To all intents and purposes the door was slammed in his face! And I was never told that he had asked for me. I was allowed to infer that his attentions were unworthy, that he was trifling with my affections. When all this is true, how can you reproach me for trying to conceal a fan, and for planning to answer a letter that vitally concerns my happiness?"

She stopped at last, her temerity exhausted with her breath. But by this time she was careless of the consequences. In her desperation, she felt it no longer mattered what happened; and she was even conscious of a rush of thankfulness that she had found the courage to speak from her soul, at least once, before she was silenced forever. She did not know what her mother would do to her next; but she understood now that the lacing had been a lesson, and that if she did not heed it, she might expect far more painful punishment—perhaps in the form at which her mother had hinted, through marriage to a man who would mistreat her. She was so sure that worse was in store for her, that she drew no comfort from her mother's quietness; and the corroding suspicion that her grandmother, on whose mercy she had thrown herself, had violated her confidence and thus precipitated her betrothal, began to gnaw its way into her tortured mind. She had trusted Grand'mère more than anyone else in the world, and if her grandmother had so betrayed her, who was there to whom she could turn?

"It appears you have been deceiving us for some time, since you know all this," Madame Lenoir was saying, in the same even way she had spoken before. "Your father and I have assumed we could trust you to talk of nothing but trivialities, and to do even that most briefly, when circumstances you could not control compelled you to meet, at other houses, a person we would not admit to our own. I see our trust was misplaced. You must have been meeting him by stealth and talking to him without modesty or reserve. But I will add to your store of knowledge, and possibly you will then have the sense to see that what you have so improperly gleaned for yourself is worthless, since it is incomplete. Your father is not so wholly without heart as you seem to suppose he has suddenly become, though why you should imagine he would be lacking in tenderness, when all your life he has given you fostering care, I cannot imagine. I will not speak of myself, or of your dear grandmother, though your ingratitude has wounded us to the quick— When your father saw you were attracted to this young man, and realized moreover that Mr. Breckenridge was determined to pursue you, in spite of the parental opposition which would have discouraged a person of finer feeling, he made inquiries. He learned, as he expected to do, that Mr. Breckenridge was a heretic, or to put it more plainly and truthfully, an unbeliever. How could any young girl, reared in the true faith, hope for happiness with a man who would make a mock of religion? Your father also learned that Mr. Breckenridge, for all his show of wealth, has squandered the greater part of his fortune in riotous living. He is deeply in debt, his property is mortgaged to the hilt, and his notorious connection with the Lottery represents a desperate attempt to recoup his fallen fortunes. How could any young girl, reared in security and luxury, be happy with a man who would not, and indeed could not, prudently provide for her? Furthermore, your father learned that the unfortunate young woman, nee Anne Forrestal, who, with her baby girl, died in childbirth, was utterly miserable as the wife of this profligate. It appears that she was a lady, though an American, a Christian, though a non-Catholic, and in all respects a devoted mother and dutiful wife. Yet her worthless spouse neglected her in order to spend his time with loose-living companions."

"I do not believe it. He gave her a fresh rose every morning. I know that for a fact. No man who was thoughtful enough to do that would neglect or abuse his wife!"

"He gave her a fresh rose every morning!" Madame Lenoir echoed with increased contempt. "And you imagine this proves he did not neglect or abuse her! I see that your ignorance is even more abysmal than I supposed, your lack of judgment even more appalling! It is indeed fortunate that you have parents to protect you from this wolf in sheep's clothing. When I told you that some men were merciless, my words were primarily inspired by the reports which had reached me of his inhumanity. As I have already told you, it has not been our plan to let you suffer at the hands of any man; but even if the worst came to the worst, you may be sure that we would at least choose a Frenchman. He might be cruel, but he would not be brutal. I shall see, and so will your father, that you are saved from yourself. But I realize, in the light of the conversation we have just had, so disillusioning to a fond mother, that we shall need to redouble our precautions, in order to do so."

Madame Lenoir had continued to hold the fan all the time

she was talking. Now she replaced it carefully in its box, folding Andrew's note around it.

"I will see that this letter is answered and this gift returned," she said, moving towards the door with her usual smooth gliding motion. "You need not concern yourself any more about either one. I am leaving you, *ma fille*, to finish your toilette by yourself. Now that you are properly laced, you should be able to make short work of it. I shall expect to see you in the *salon* at noon exactly. Marcel will be here, with his parents, to greet you on the stroke of twelve."

CHAPTER 6

IN ONE of the small drawers of Estelle's ornamental but unserviceable secretary were a few sheets of lace-edged paper, similar to the sort that was greatly in vogue for valentines. This paper was not intended for ordinary use; it was kept in a decorated carton and scrupulously saved, with a layer of tissue between each sheet, for a very special purpose. Every year, on the vigil of Epiphany, Estelle wrote a little note on this paper addressed to her mother, carefully copying it from the ruled notebook on which she had first drafted it. The note, couched in terms of respectful devotion, began and ended with an expression of this sentiment; but the main part of it was devoted to an outline of her good resolution for the coming year.

As the last day of 1890 drew to an end, Estelle sat down at the secretary and conscientiously tried to perform this accustomed task. She had just come from confession, and her mood, under these circumstances, would normally have been both tranquil and exalted. Since Christmas, she had never succeeded in slipping out to church alone, and she guessed that her mother suspected that clandestine meetings might have been taking place in the Cathedral, for Estelle had been closely guarded whenever she went there, as well as everywhere else. But frustrated as she felt, because those sweet, secret rendezvous with Andy had been intercepted, her religion meant a great deal to her, and she was genuinely fond of her confessor, who was a family friend besides being a spiritual advisor. She also had great confidence in him. Their mutual affection dated from a day, shortly after her first Communion, which she had made at the age of ten, when she had entered the confessional somewhat hesitantly because prolonged reflection had not sufficed to recall to her mind even the most venial sin which she had committed since she last received absolution. Fully aware that the purpose of confession was to confess, she had continued to rack her brain up to the very moment of entering the church. Then she remembered seeing one of the maids, shedding bitter tears as she stood on the landing of the back stairs, with her head on the shoulder of another servant, and muttering broken words between her sobs. The words in themselves meant nothing to Estelle, but they were obviously indicative of repentance and despair. She decided to echo them, feeling sure they would fill in the gap that so deeply concerned her, and breathed a sigh of relief, well satisfied with her resourcefulness.

"Bless me, Father, for I have sinned," she said glibly, getting down on her knees, and pattering out the rest of the accustomed formula, *"J'ai péché, j'ai beaucoup péché. Je suis enceinte."*

She heard a slight rustle on the further side of the grille, as if the priest were moving about in his seat. Afterwards, she thought the curtain was raised a little, but she was not sure, because her head was bent over her clasped hands. She left the Cathedral in a state of continued satisfaction, deciding that henceforth, when she did not know what else to confess, she would always announce herself *enceinte,* and the next morning she went to Communion without a quiver. On the following Monday, however, when she returned from school, she heard Père Maillard, whose voice she recognized and admired, talking with her father as she passed by the *salon* on her way upstairs, and the remarks he was making were followed by a subdued chuckle. He remained to dinner with them, *en famille,* and off and on through the meal, she caught him regarding her with covert amusement. Later, when she was in bed, her mother came and explained rather sketchily the true meaning of what Estelle had mistakenly said, and why Rosalie had been ashamed and frightened, when she confided in Henriette that she was going to have a baby. Out of the vagueness, one fact emerged clearly: Père Maillard had been comprehending and kind; he had understood Estelle's dilemma, and the motive for her desperate and innocent little lie. He was not shocked; he was only faintly amused and quietly touched. He had known that she should be enlightened and not rebuked, and he had made her mother see this also. She had loved him and trusted him from that time on.

Would he understand now, she wondered, if she unburdened her heavy and aching heart? Could he help her to heal it? Could he show her the way, not only to celestial but to temporal salvation? She resolved to put him to the proof, at least. But that morning, she learned that Père Maillard was seriously ill, and that consequently a substitute, who was a stranger, would take his place in the confessional. Her distress over the misfortune which had befallen her friend was by no means disinterested, though she did her best to make it so; and knowing that there was a stranger on the other side of the grille, she spoke in a stereotyped way: she had been inattentive at Mass; she had neglected her morning prayers; she had given way to anger; she had been guilty of a trifling deception. She did not know of any mortal sin which she had committed since her last confession, but she was heartily sorry for the venial sins she had enumerated, and for all the sins of her past life——

"What was the trifling deception of which you were guilty, my daughter?" she heard the voice on the other side of the grille saying, surprisingly.

For a moment she was too startled to answer. She had taken it for granted that her confession would be received as automatically as it had been uttered. She tried to collect herself.

"I concealed a letter, and a gift that came with it, from my mother. But later she saw them both."

"Because you repented of your deception and showed them to her voluntarily?"

"No, *mon père*. Because she extracted them from their hiding-place, and confronted me with them."

"Ah— There was then some reason why you should not have received them?"

"My mother thought so, *mon père*."

"And have you begged your mother's pardon, and God's, for your unfilial behavior, doubly deplorable since it was coupled with deception?"

"No, *mon père*."

"And still you tell me that you have been guilty of no mortal sin since your last confession! Was the writer of this letter and the donor of this gift someone of whom your parents disapprove? A suitor whom they discouraged, perhaps?"

"Yes, *mon père*. They claim he is not a Catholic or even a Christian. They say he is a gambler and a spendthrift, and bring other grave charges against his character. But I cannot believe that all this is true. And even if it were, I should love him just the same."

There was a short silence. Then the unseen priest spoke severely. "Be very sure, my daughter, that your parents would bring no such charges unjustly. They have good reason to forbid you to listen to such a man. The attitude of the Church would be the same, only more rigid. It discourages all mixed marriages, as you know. When there is a question of a marriage between a good Catholic and an individual who cannot even be called a Christian, it discountenances it altogether. You must put this man entirely out of your mind, and you must never voluntarily see him again. You must also beg your mother's forgiveness without delay. For your penance, say five Our Fathers and ten Hail Marys before you leave the Cathedral, and every night and morning for the next week, double the number of your usual devotions. You may now make your act of contrition——"

As Estelle sat at her secretary, overlaid with the sheets of lace-edged paper on which she had still written nothing, after staring at them for nearly an hour, she decided that she must be the wickedest girl in the world. She had made her act of contrition and said her other prayers as fast as possible, hurrying out of the Cathedral and up Royal Street as if she feared that the priest who had spoken to her so severely might overtake her and lay a detaining hand on her shoulder, preparatory to imposing further penance. And now that she was safely in her own room at last, with the ideal means of seeking forgiveness before her, in the shape of the traditional lace-edged paper, she had not the least desire to take advantage of it. She did not feel repentant. She felt revengeful. She wished she could make her mother suffer, in the same measure that she had suffered, herself; and more than anything else in the world, she wished that she could see Andrew Breckenridge alone. The longer she sat and stared at the lace-edged paper, the more uncontrollable this desire became. At last she could stand it no longer. She seized a sheet, and began to write, not to her mother, but to her suitor.

Dear Andy:

My mother found your note and your present and took them away from me. She said she would acknowledge the note when she returned the fan. I do not know what she said to you when she did so. But I wish I could have a chance to say something to you myself, very privately, If you can think of any way that I could, please tell me.

Trustfully yours,
Estelle Lenoir

P. S. I hope you will not think that this paper looks silly. It is the only kind I have, of my own. I am supposed to write good resolutions on it, and give it to my mother. But the one resolution I have at present is that I am going to see you alone, if I possibly can.

She folded the paper, thrust it defiantly into an envelope and sealed it. Then she looked desperately around her. She had forgotten that she was unsupplied with stamps and that, unless she could manage to steal one from some other secretary in the house, she would have no way of sending the letter; she would have to wait until she saw Andy Breckenridge, and contrive to slip the letter into his hand then.

It had long been the custom for the young people who belonged to the same dancing class to celebrate New Year's Eve together, with more freedom and merriment than they were allowed to enjoy at any other time except during Carnival. They went up and down Canal Street in gay little groups, tooting whistles, shaking rattles and blowing horns; this was all part of *Réveillon* and they kept it up until they were hoarse and tired. Afterwards they forgathered at the Fontaines' house for a steaming gumbo and some well-spiked punch, and saw the New Year in together, dancing and playing games until it was time to go for five-o'clock Mass. This was a younger, less sophisticated circle than the one in which Andy moved; Estelle knew there was no reason why he should suddenly and pointlessly be included in it, and, as she had feared, he was not present at the *Réveillon*.

The next day, her mother and grandmother kept open house, as all Creole ladies of importance did on New Year's Day; Estelle assisted at their receptions, now that she had made her debut; but Andy was not among the thirty or forty young men about town who called to pay their respects and drink punch. She did not blame him for not coming to her home again, when he had been so uncivilly rebuffed, and, for the next few days, every sort of circumstance seemed to prevent her from seeing him. Desperately she began to realize that the first big ball of the year, which was given by the Twelfth Night Revellers, and which was still several days distant, would probably provide the first chance, and she could not even be certain of that. She supposed Andy must belong to the Revellers, but considering the secrecy surrounding the membership of all "Krewes," there was no way that she could be sure. She could only count off the hours, with her heart in her breast, hoping against hope.

Her desperation was intensified by the attitude of Marcel, whom she saw constantly during the same interval. His attachment to her was so singlehearted that she reproached herself for not being touched by it; but there were unmistakable signs that his tenderness was beginning to be permeated with ardor, and that he was impatiently awaiting an opportunity to give tangible proof of this. So far, as her mother had foretold, he had kissed only her hand and her brow, but his lips showed a tendency to stray. She knew the day would come when she could not prevent their closing down on hers, but she was determined this should not happen before Andy had set his own seal upon her.

Somehow she staved Marcel off until Twelfth Night, when they went, as usual, to the Fontaines' house for the burning of the Christmas greens. The Lenoirs, themselves, had never decorated their house for Christmas or set up a tree, but the Fontaines, on the other hand, always did both, and surrounded the bonfire with traditional gaiety. They always had a king's cake, too, not a make-believe cake, like the one that was the *pièce de résistance* at the Twelfth Night Ball, but a real cake, made by López, the famous confectioner, which was a delight to eye and palate alike. They ate it for *goûter*, like a real French family, washing it down with champagne, and gathering their friends around them.

When the Lenoirs arrived at the Fontaines' for this celebration, Marcel urged Estelle to come out in the garden and have a last look at the heaped-up greens with him, before they all went out together to set them on fire. When Estelle hung back, it was actually Madame Lenoir, herself, who made a sign to her that she should go. They were hardly out of their elders' sight, when Marcel put his arm around Estelle.

"Je veux t'embrasser," he said pleadingly. *"Voyons, chère—donne-moi un petit baiser."*

Andy, given a similar opportunity, would never have asked, as Estelle was well aware, and she would have revelled in his passionate assertiveness. But instead of melting before Marcel's restrained entreaty, she instantly stiffened.

"Don't talk like that," she said, almost sharply. "You know you're not supposed to kiss me until the engagement is official."

"Not officially. But this would be unofficial. Your parents know how I feel, and they don't resent it. Do you suppose they would have let me come out here with you if they had?"

"Doesn't it make any difference to you whether I resent it or not?"

"But, Estelle, why should you? When we love each other so much? When we're going to be married so soon?"

"I never said I loved you. And I'll never marry you if you act like this."

She broke away from him, and rushed back towards the house. He had hard work catching up with her before she reached the door, and his expression betrayed his hurt bewilderment. Madame Lenoir looked at Estelle questioningly.

"You have returned very quickly, *ma fille,"* she said.

"It does not take long to look at a few dead greens," Estelle said in a cold voice, and walked over to the corner where Clarisse was standing, leaving Marcel behind her.

Ordinarily she stayed on for dinner with the Fontaines, after the burning of the greens, but this time she went back to Royal Street with her parents, in order to dress for the Twelfth Night Ball. There was no time to spare for explanations. The Fontaines called for her early, so that she and Clarisse and Aurore would not fail to secure seats in the front of the call-out section together. It seemed strange to be placed in the open orchestra instead of the sheltered loge, and to see the *fauteuils* all cleared away there and the floor, rising with a sort of swell as it approached the stage, covered with white canvas. Aurore, who had been going to balls for three years now, warned Clarisse and Estelle beforehand about this rise, telling them it was hard to surmount gracefully. She had also warned them that they should be sure to wear brand-new slippers, and their most elaborate petticoats, because, in lifting their skirts to dance over the rise, they would show their footwear and their lingerie more than usual. She spoke with the condescendingly helpful air of the full-fledged young lady addressing inexperienced debutantes. But Estelle was far too preoccupied to worry about the rise, or about slippers and petticoats. She thought she would suffocate with suspense if she did not soon discover whether Andy was there or not; she felt as if the little note lying between her breasts would burn her if it stayed hidden any longer.

At last the King took his place on the throne in the middle of the stage, and the Dukes, dressed like chefs, in enveloping white aprons and tall fluted caps, accompanied by their small cousins and brothers similarly clad, wheeled the great papier-mâché King's Cake out into the middle of the cleared space and capered gaily around it. They were joined in a rush by the other maskers, and then they romped across the floor, beckoning to the debutantes sitting in the call-out section to join them. Presently the girls and the Revellers were all clustering around the cake together, and the maskers were thrusting their hands into it and drawing out miniature cake boxes, which they offered to their partners. In the majority of instances, they did this rather casually. It was only in the cases of the marked boxes, which they knew contained beans, that they encouraged the debutantes to open up the little square cartons and poke through their contents. The one supremely lucky girl, who found a golden bean in her cake, would be the Queen; the six, only less lucky, who found silver beans, would be the Maids.

It was a foregone conclusion that Clarisse would get the golden bean, because of Monsieur Fontaine's seniority in the Revellers, and the many services he had rendered the "Krewe": but the year before there had been an unfortunate contretemps; a marked box had been handed by mistake to the wrong girl, and an awkward moment ensued, while the Captain explained, with much embarrassment, that she must surrender the golden bean to the predestined Queen. Though she had finally given in, she had been first mutinous and then vindictive, and all the rest of the evening she had made sarcastic remarks about pre-arrangement and favoritism and pull. The gaiety of the entire group had been dampened because she was such a spoilsport, and Estelle, who had heard numberless accounts of the debacle, trembled lest Clarisse should be subjected to a similar experience. She actually forgot her own heartbreaking excitement for the moment, as she watched Clarisse undo her little cardboard box, while her attendant Duke bent solicitously over her. When she heard Clarisse give a little squeal of joy, and saw her hold up the long golden chain, with the small gold bean which was the symbol of her sovereignty dangling from it, she, herself, gave a deep sigh of relief; and for the next few moments she watched breathlessly, while Clarisse was led to her throne beside the King's, the thrones jointly surmounted by a revolving cake, lighted with candles, and while masked dominos emerged from behind the curtains to attach a court train to the Queen's shoulders, set a glittering crown on her head and hand her a ceremonial sheaf of flowers. Estelle knew that these dominos were really only dressmakers and their attendants, whose part in the proceedings was carefully charted beforehand, like all the rest; just the same, she was thrilled and awed to see them hovering mysteriously around Clarisse, their identity concealed, their ministrations spotlighted. When she finally took her eyes off Clarisse for a moment, it was to glance stealthily down at her *décolletage* to see if the note was still safe, and then to look eagerly around the orchestra, trying to recognize Andy's familiar figure beneath a grotesque disguise.

"You had better open your own box, Mademoiselle. You may have a pleasant surprise."

With a startled exclamation, she looked up at the chef standing beside her. He had bowed without speaking in handing her box to her, and she had taken it inattentively. Now she realized that all the time she had been desperately looking for Andy, he had been close at hand, and that her misery might have been abridged by ten or fifteen minutes, if she had only been more alert. It took a second reminder from him, this time in the form of a gentle warning, to keep her from trying to draw him aside and talking with him confidentially then and there. A few weeks earlier, the receipt of a silver bean, designating her as a Maid in the Queen's Court, would have filled her with delight. Now it only meant the postponement of the time when she could pour out her heart to Andy. She thought the Grand March would never come to an end, that she would never be through with the necessary bowing and smiling, first in one direction, and then in another, as she followed in the wake of the Queen with the other Maids and their escorts. But finally, the formal ranks broke, the King and Queen returned

to their thrones, and dancing became general. Andy's arm
was around her waist at last, his hand holding hers, his
head bent to listen to her. She raised her face and began to
whisper breathlessly.

"I haven't been able to meet you. Julie's been sent with
me when I've gone to confession, and all the rest of the
time I've been watched."

"I saw Julie, and I knew something must have happened.
What was it?"

"I can't tell you now. I wrote you a letter but I couldn't
send it because I didn't have a stamp."

"What's become of it?"

"I've carried it around with me ever since, hoping I'd see
you some time. And I haven't. But I've got it with me tonight. Do you think I could slip it to you without being
seen?"

"Of course. When I give you your favor at the end of
this dance, hand it to me."

"I'll have to get it out first, and I don't know how I can
manage. It's—it's inside my dress."

"Your brooch is undone, Mademoiselle. The one fastening the lace in the front of your bodice. We had better stop
dancing, so that you can reclasp it— There, you see how
simple that was. Do you always make mountains out of
molehills, Estelle?"

"They look like mountains to me, Andy. It's only when
you're with me that they flatten out."

"Then you must be with me more, and live in level country, like the country around Splendida, for instance. Oh—
Is that the end? I thank you a thousand times, Mademoiselle,
for the honor of this dance. Will you accept this trifling
favor from me?"

The "trifling favor," when she undid it, proved to be a
mirror framed in brilliants. The silver handle and the border
encircling the brilliants were both beautifully chased; but the
silver back was smooth, bearing only her monogram and the
date. As she looked ecstatically down at her own reflection,
she suddenly remembered a painting by Titian of Laura de'
Dianti, which she had seen in Paris, and of which, so she
had heard, Andy had an early and valuable copy. It represented a beautiful woman holding a mirror as she arranged
her long, auburn tresses, while a man, seen dimly in the
background, leaned over her shoulder looking into the mirror,

too, so that his face might be framed with hers. As Estelle gazed into her own mirror, she knew that Andy had been thinking of this painting when he bought the favor for her, and with a strange shiver of foreboding also knew that never, as long as she lived, would she fail to see him, mirrored beside her in imagination, when she saw herself——

"Didn't you hear your name called, *chère?* And are you so entranced with one favor that you don't want another?"

She sprang to her feet, flushing furiously. For the second time that evening she had been taken unawares, and this time her surprise was shot through with the sensation of great guilt. She had forgotten entirely about Marcel in her preoccupation with Andy; and now here was Marcel, himself, only flimsily disguised, waiting for her, puzzled by this preoccupation, probably even a little piqued by it. She tried to make amends by chattering with forced gaiety.

"It's a beautiful ball, isn't it? Doesn't Clarisse look lovely? Aurore told us the Queen of the Revellers couldn't compare with other Queens, because her robes weren't bought beforehand from Schweitzer, on purpose, and because she didn't have a chance to practice bowing and sceptre-waving. But I think that's silly. Just see how gracious and easy she acts."

"She does look lovely. But even in all her regal robes, she can't compare with you, *chère.*"

"Nonsense! It *is* too bad the Maids' dresses can't match, under the circumstances. That spoils half the effect—Narcisse was one of the little chefs, wasn't he? I was sure I recognized him. He must have been delighted to be chosen."

"*Chère,* I don't want to talk about Clarisse or Aurore or Narcisse, or any other member of the Fontaine family. I want to talk about you."

"There isn't anything to say about me. I'm not important."

"Oh, yes, you are! You're supremely important. That is, to me. When I see you, looking so lovely as a Maid, I can't help thinking how much more beautiful you'll be as a bride."

The Duke, whom she had belatedly recognized as Andy, was dancing very near them with Aurore. Estelle was almost certain that he must have overheard, for he made a sudden movement, as ungraceful as it was uncharacteristic; the next instant he and his partner were out of step. He recovered himself immediately and went on dancing, in his usual smooth way. But he kept very close to Estelle and

Marcel until the dance was finished; Marcel could not whisper any further endearment; and when Andy came quickly to claim her, the instant the next dance began, his resentment blazed out at her.

"If I hear Marcel Fontaine calling you *chère* again, or rambling on about beautiful brides, I'll call him out and make short work of him. I could carve him up like a chicken."

"Please, Andy! It— You mustn't mind what Marcel says. You mustn't even think about quarrelling with him. If you've read my note, by now you know——"

"Yes, I've read your note. I hope you're in earnest. Are you? Would you really be willing to come to a place where you could see me alone? Not at church, where there may be spies lurking in every corner, where I can't speak aloud, where I can't touch you——"

"I'll go anywhere. I'll come to your house if there's no other place."

He knew this was the urgency of complete desperation. He drew her more closely to him, and spoke to her with tenderness such as she had never heard before.

"Darling, you won't have to do that. Though I'll never forget that you offered. But there is another place. That is, I own another house besides the one you're thinking of— the big white one with the black balconies on Prytania Street. This other house is a little one, on Kerlerec Street, not far from where you live. It won't take you all day to get there and back, as it would if you tried to go to the other. It's a little 'shotgun house.' You'll find it very easily."

"I'll find it somehow. Is—is it empty? How'll I get in it?"

"No, it isn't empty. I wouldn't ask you to meet me in an empty house, darling, unless there really wasn't any other way. But there is. A very old lady lives in this house. I bought it for her. She's a relative of Anne's. It was Anne asked me to buy it."

"Anne?"

"Yes. Anne was my wife, you know. A long time ago, before I knew you. You're not jealous of her, are you, dear?"

"No. At least I don't think so. Did you love her very much?"

"Yes, I loved her. But you don't need to be jealous of her. It wasn't like this. We were both children. It was her first love affair, and mine too, of that kind."

"This is my first love affair, Andy."

"Yes, darling, I know. But I'm older now. That'll help us both. I understand women better; I know more about love. I loved Anne liked a boy, but I love you like a man. I appreciate you more than I did her; I can make you happier than I did her; I can take better care of you. I didn't know enough to take care of her. I was warned that she wasn't well, but I didn't believe it because I'm so strong myself. I've never been sick in my life. I didn't understand. I was impatient when she was sick, and I was blind to so many of her good qualities. There were so many things that she wanted me to do that I didn't do, that I didn't even bother about trying to do, or that I teased her about doing. When we were travelling through France on our honeymoon, she wanted to order a set of Limoges china decorated with flowers and I insisted it must be decorated with birds. So birds were painted in the center of the plates, with wreaths of flowers on the edges. I always hated that set of china. I smashed every dish in it after she died. Of course, it's just a trivial thing, but it shows you what I mean. About the way I treated her, that is. I did buy this little house though, just because Anne asked me to. I've always been glad. I'm gladder than ever now."

"Will the little old lady let me in?"

"No, I'll let you in. You won't even see her unless you want to. She lies down a great deal. She isn't strong. She'll be lying down, in the back of the house, when you get there. I'll tell her I had to see someone privately, that I thought of her house. She'll be glad to have me use it. Tell me when you can come, darling, and I'll be there."

It was true, Estelle had no trouble in finding the house. It stood out in a row of similar small houses, easily identified as the one which would belong to Andy, because, while the others were drab and unkempt, this one had freshly-painted white clapboards and green shutters, and fronted a neat little lawn encircled with Louis Philippe roses. The neighborhood was respectable, but it was shabby, except for this one house. After descending from the one-mule tramcar, and looking up and down the block, Estelle had walked to it unhesitatingly.

She had never been in a tramcar before, and she had found it a rather gruelling experience. She tried to tell herself that this was only because she had not recovered, after suffering so terribly from the fear that she would not be able to fulfill her purpose of walking straight out of her parents' house and going to Andy's. When she had not been able to slip away to church, when she had not been able even to steal a stamp, how could she hope to succeed this time? If Andy had not told her that he would wait all day for her, if necessary, so that the feeling of haste had not been piled upon her feeling of fear, she might never have managed it. But since she was able to begin, early in the morning, to watch for her chance, she had found it: before Madame Lenoir *mère* had waked from the short nap that she took every day, and after Monsieur Lenoir had gone to his office, while Julie was out doing an errand and when Eugénie had called Madame Lenoir to act in a small household emergency, Estelle dove out of the door and was swallowed up by the crowds on Royal Street.

She took the one-mule tramcar at Bourbon Street. It was small and smelly and cold, and seated beside Estelle was a strange little old woman, with her head muffled up, who kept muttering *"Façons américaines! Cochon américaines!"* The mutterings of the old woman reminded Estelle that Andy was an "American," and that he had American ways, though she was still unconvinced that any of these were evil, much less bestial. Resolutely she tried not to listen, since listening put such thoughts into her head, though it was hard to help it. That was another reason why the ride had been such a trying experience. But when she got out of the tramcar and saw the trim, fresh-looking little house, rising reassuringly before her, she felt much better.

She still braced herself, however, with a queer little quiver that was half dread and half delight, for the moment of meeting with Andy. She knew that now he would kiss her, that she could not stop or soften his embrace, because, in telling him that she would meet him anywhere, even at his own house, she had given him the right to infer that she was ready to accept any sort of kiss which he chose to give her. As she opened the little gate, and went up the short walk, her feet began to falter, and when she reached the tiny gallery, she tried to turn back. But then it was too late. Andy opened the door and drew her in——

It was a long time before she told him. At first she could not talk, because of the kisses, and even after he had stopped kissing her, he stood holding her, until she stopped trembling and, herself, stood quietly, resting against his heart. And then, because it was so lovely to stand like that, with all her dread gone and all her delight increased a thousandfold, she could not bear to mar her joy or his by telling him. If he had not questioned her, she might have left him, after all, without doing so.

"You haven't told me yet, darling, why you felt you had to talk to me."

"I will presently. But let me get accustomed to—all this first. And let me look around me. It's such a dear little house. I think it's the sweetest house I ever saw."

Her eyes rested, with gratitude and appreciation, on the tasteful restraint of the little drawing room. It was simply, almost sparingly furnished, but everything in it was perfect, from the wide smooth boards of the floor to the exquisite rosette in the ceiling. The draperies and upholstery were a fresh color of green, the chairs and secretary made of well-rubbed maple; a fire burned brightly behind burnished andirons. The whole effect was not only one of harmony, but of cleanliness and coziness. Instead of being intimidated or repelled by her surroundings, as she had expected to be, she was reassured by them.

"Was it Anne who planned this room, or was it the little old lady?"

"They did it together. I'm glad you like it. Would it interest you to see the rest of the house?"

"I'd love to. And—the little old lady, too, if she wouldn't mind meeting me."

"She'd love to meet you. I didn't want to be the one to suggest it, but I think it would be a very good thing if you and she did meet. Then you could always say you came to see her, if you found you needed to say something. You may be very sure she'd back you up. Of course you'd still have to explain why you rushed off impulsively alone. But we can worry about that later."

With his arm around her, he led her through the little house. There were two bedrooms back of the drawing room, and further back still a dining room and a kitchen. Each room was directly in the rear of the one in front of it, in the peculiar "shotgun" fashion, and each was furnished in the same exquisite and quiet taste as the little drawing room. In the second of the two bedrooms they found the old lady, lying on the sofa in front of the fire, with a soft white shawl around her shoulders and soft white knitting in her hands. Her hair was softer and whiter still. She looked up at Estelle with an expression of such kindness and understanding in her face that the girl did not instantly realize she was blind.

"This is my sweetheart, Estelle, of whom I told you, Aunt Rachel," Andy said, guiding the old woman's delicate blue-veined hands towards the girl's.

"I am glad you came to see me, my child, glad that Andy brought you. He has put so much pleasure into my life that I cannot thank him enough. I hope he will bring you again."

"Of course I shall, Aunt Rachel. Unless I decide to save myself the trouble of bringing her back and forth by keeping her here for good and all."

"You know how welcome she would be, my dear boy, whichever you decide to do."

"What do you think of my suggestion?" Andy asked, when he and Estelle had gone back to the drawing room. He pulled a love seat up in front of the fire, and sat down on it beside her, his arm still around her. He looked happier and younger than she had ever seen him. His joy in her presence was obviously so complete that he had forgotten everything else.

"It was a sweet suggestion. But I can't come back, Andy. And of course I can't stay. You knew that when you said it."

"I don't see why not. Aunt Rachel would take wonderful care of you. But perhaps I'll understand better when you tell me why you came at all."

"It's so hard, Andy."

"Nothing is going to be hard any more."

"But it is. It's very hard. It's hard to say. It'll be much harder to do. Andy—I'm going to be married."

"Of course you are. You're going to marry me. But that won't be hard for you. It'll be like this. You were afraid to have me kiss you. Come now, confess! You were terribly afraid. And now you're not any more. You're all ready to have me kiss you again. Dying to have me. Like this——"

Once more it was a long time before she could speak. But now she knew she must not put it off any longer. His kisses were harder now, and when she tried to draw away from him, he held her fast.

"I'm not going to marry you, Andy. I can't. I'm going to marry Marcel. I've got to. When he called me *chère* and described me as his bride, it wasn't just Carnival jesting. He had a right to."

"Marry Marcel! You're crazy! What do you mean, telling me you've got to?"

He released her so abruptly that she struck the back of the love seat before she could steady herself. Her voice shook, as well as her body, when she answered.

"I mean, it's all arranged. His father and mine arranged it a month ago. They've been planning it for years. Maman told me about it on Christmas Day."

"Do you want to marry Marcel?"

"Oh, Andy, you know I'd rather die than marry anyone except you!"

"If you feel that way about it, you won't do it. No matter what's been planned, no matter what's been arranged. If you love me like that you will die before you'll let anyone force you into marrying another man. If you want to marry me enough, you'll let the whole world crash to pieces without stopping you from doing it."

"I do love you like that. I do want to marry you. But I'm afraid. Are you angry with me, Andy, for being afraid?"

"Angry! Of course I'm angry. I am also very sorry and rather surprised. I didn't think, after you offered to come here, that you were the sort of girl who would let fear stand in her way, if she really wanted to marry anyone. What are you afraid of?"

"Everything."

"That's a rather sweeping statement. If you'll be a little more explicit, I can tell you whether your fears are well-grounded or not. Probably they don't amount to anything. I've told you before that you're always making mountains out of molehills."

"I don't want to be unjust. I don't want to say anything that will hurt your feelings."

Andrew Breckenridge laughed. His manner was mocking now, not tender any longer, and she had always quailed before his mocking moods. Even so, his raillery had invariably been lighthearted before, and now there was a deeper note in it, one that sounded almost harsh. Estelle was bewildered by his unaccustomed brusqueness; it made her position much harder than it had been already.

"Don't worry about being unjust. You probably couldn't say anything so severe that I wouldn't deserve it. And you certainly couldn't hurt my feelings. They're perfectly bullet-proof."

"My father and mother are very much opposed to your suit."

Andy laughed again, still more mockingly than before. "My dear child, you astound me! I thought they were eagerly endeavoring to secure me for a son-in-law. Certainly everything about their conduct points to such avidity."

"I can't talk to you, Andy, if you act like this. I shan't even try."

"How do you want me to act?"

"The way you did when I first came in. As if you loved me. Not as if you were contemptuous of me, because I'm afraid."

"I'm trying to convince you there's nothing to be afraid of. I thought perhaps a little wholesome ridicule might do it. But I apologize for seeming quite so scornful. Probably I wouldn't have been, if your parents' attitude hadn't annoyed me more than I like to admit. To tell you the truth, it's made me very angry. They've done everything in their power to humiliate me and discredit me, but it isn't fair to take out my resentment on you. I'll try to be a little more lover-like. Only, if I am, don't tell me that frightens you, too, just when I was flattering myself you were learning to enjoy it."

He smiled, in his usual winning way, and put his arm around her again. She did not repulse him, but neither did she return his caress. Indeed, this time she seemed almost oblivious of it. He saw that she must tell him everything that was on her mind, and that he must make this easier for her, and not harder, as he had been doing, before she would respond to another embrace. He spoke more gently.

"Let's face the fact that your mother and father don't want you to marry me, Estelle. It's unfortunate, but it isn't alarming. At least, it shouldn't be. A great many people have married in spite of parental opposition. We can, if you care enough."

"How? My confessor is opposed to you also. He has told me I shouldn't marry you. The banns could never be published. The Archbishop would prevent it."

"We don't have to be married by a priest, darling, after the banns have been proclaimed three times from the pulpit. I could get a license very quietly, and we can be married, immediately afterwards, by a Protestant clergyman, or even by a justice of the peace, with only a couple of witnesses. It's done all the time. It's perfectly legal. And after it's done, there's no way of undoing it, except by divorce."

"But it isn't sacramental. You know, Andy, that I couldn't get married like that."

"I don't see why not. We could get married over again, later on, by a priest, if that would make you feel any better. I've told you that it would be easy, if you cared enough, and it would be. But of course if you are going to make all sorts of objections——"

"Are you really a heretic, Andy? I mean, not just a Protestant, but an unbeliever?"

"I suppose so. Yes, that's what I am—an unbeliever. I don't believe in anything—not even your love, when you show me how little it amounts to."

He was speaking satirically again. He withdrew his hand from her waist, and folded his arms, looking at her with far greater scorn than before. But this time she did not seem to notice it.

"That's one of the things they told me about you," she said sadly. "That you were an agnostic, that I couldn't be happy with you because you'd make a mock of my religion, as you do of so many other things. And I didn't believe them. Now I see that what they said was true."

"So you're beginning to think that perhaps some of the other charges were also true?"

"Yes, Andy. I wish I weren't. I wish I didn't have to. But I do."

"If you'll tell me what they are, I'll let you know."

"They said you were practically penniless."

"Well, had you thought of marrying me for my money?"

"Oh, Andy, of course not! How can you say anything so unkind. But if you're deeply in debt, and still go on squandering more and more money, the way you do all the time, what would we live on, after a few years? I wouldn't have any dot, if I eloped with you. I'd be dependent on you. Besides, there's your little son to think of. You've got to provide for him."

"You needn't worry about Breck," Andy said, with a sharp

ring of pride in his voice. "He's a tough little devil. He'll be able to look out for himself, whatever happens. Not that his mother's people wouldn't take care of him, if worst came to worst. But it never will, with Breck. He's got more guts than I have. And more sense. He'll never make ducks and drakes of a great fortune— There's some money left, though, at that—enough to take care of you decently, even if you are 'dependent' on me. We could live in a house like this, for instance, if we really had to. That wouldn't take much."

"No, but——"

"But when you said it was the sweetest house you ever saw, you didn't mean to have me take you so seriously? Well, I suppose I ought not to blame you—too much. But don't blame me, either, when I tell you that I wouldn't touch a cent of your dot if you had one, after the way your parents have acted. I'll have money enough again before long, though. Supremus is bound to win again sometime, and I can't lose on every other horse I breed or back and in every card game I play forever. The tide's bound to turn, sooner or later. Besides, there's my Lottery stock. That's sound enough."

"But, Andy, wouldn't it be wicked to live on money that you made in that way, even if you could keep on making it?"

"Wicked! Look here, Estelle. Suppose you try to see things straight." He took hold of her again, not gently this time, but roughly, seizing her arms at the elbows and gripping them hard. "So it's wicked to live on the Lottery, is it? That's what you've been told? That's what you're holding against me! And did anyone tell you that Lottery capital keeps the cotton mills turning and the sugar cane grinding? That it contributes hundreds of thousands of dollars to flood relief? That it supports the Opera House, where you and all your fine French friends are so fond of going, and so proud of being seen? That it maintains the hospital you go to when you're sick and controls the supply of water you drink while you're alive, and the cemetery where you'll be buried after you're dead? If you don't believe me, ask any other man you like. He may beat about the bush, but in the end he'll have to tell you the truth, the way I have. But it is true. The only difference between me and the other men who pretend to be so righteous is that they're whited sepulchers and I'm not!

Why, the greatest surgeon and the most brilliant social leader this city ever had manoeuvred the Lottery into the Constitution of 1879, and left his estate nothing but Lottery stock when he died!"

He released her abruptly, sprang to his feet, and strode across the room. Estelle sat very still, her fear mounting by leaps and bounds. Her head was bent, and through the tears that hung on her lashes, she could see the red marks on her arm, where Andy's fingers had rested. She did not think he had meant to hurt her; she believed that in his excitement and resentment, he had dug deeper than he knew. But as she saw what he had done, and felt the pain he had caused, she forgot the Lottery entirely, and thought, involuntarily, only of what her mother had said—"When I told you some men were merciless, my words were primarily inspired by the reports that had reached me of his inhumanity— Sometimes brides are beaten: sometimes they are maltreated in other ways—" What were those "other ways" to which she had referred so mysteriously? Estelle had been trying to imagine, with terrified fascination, ever since her mother had hinted at the horrors to which an innocent victim might be subjected. Now she wondered if the treatment she had just received, trivial as the hurt was in itself, might not be a warning of what lay in store for her if Andy were really angered, or if she tempted him too much and trusted him too far.

She rose, silently, and tried to reach the door without making any noise. But her step, light as it was, sounded against the carpet, and her dress rustled as she moved forward. Andrew turned abruptly and confronted her.

"So you're going?" he said, with more harshness than she had ever heard. "You can't take a chance— You can't stand the truth. Well, I might have known it. You think your marriage will be a sacrament if you walk up the center aisle of the Cathedral, on your father's arm, dressed in satin and veiled in lace, even if you don't love the man that's waiting for you beside the priest? You think your future will be safe if this man's bargained with your father for a marriage settlement the way he would with a trainer for a race horse, and has the money salted away in government bonds! You think righteousness and respectability are synonymous, and that neither can flourish in the fetid atmosphere of the Lottery! You poor, weak, silly little fool! Don't you know there's more to life than being a Carnival Queen, and announcing your engagement at a luncheon with lilies of the valley strewn over a lace tablecloth, and having the champagne glasses at your wedding tied with gauze bows! If you'd stay here with me, now that you've screwed up the courage to come, if you never went back to that pretty prison you call a home, and those pious people who are your keepers, you'd find out your mistake and thank God on your knees that you had."

"Andy, you're unjust; you're terribly unjust. You know those aren't the things that matter. But there are other things that do, and——"

"Being a dutiful daughter, for instance? As if that mattered half so much as being a happy wife! There's only one thing that matters at this moment and that's our love. If you deny that, we're both lost."

He stepped swiftly in front of the door and held out his arms. "Come here," he commanded. "Come here, of your own free will, and say, 'Andy, I do love you. I'll prove it to you. I will stay with you. I won't let anything stop me or delay our marriage. I don't care about the tawdry glitter of the Carnival, or the empty pomp of a fashionable wedding, or anything else that I'd give up to be your wife. I'm not afraid of obstacles or scandal or disaster. I'm not afraid of what you'll take from me or of what you'll do to me. I want you for my lover. I'll have you for my husband. Not just for richer; for poorer, too. Not just for better; for worse, too. Not just in health; in sickness, too. Till death do us part.' Say it, darling. Say it. I swear you'll never be sorry. I swear you'll live gloriously, whether you live safely or not. I swear I'll never act like a boor or a beast again, or make a mock of your religion. If I could believe in you, I might even believe in God. I'd be so touched by your trust that it would make a man out of me. Not just a braggart and a spendthrift and a rake, the way I've been so far. But a real man, that you'd be proud of. That even your parents would be proud of by and by. Give me a chance, darling, a fighting chance. Then I'll pull through and come up on top. For you—with you—as my wife!"

For a moment she faltered. If her mind had not been so subtly impoisoned, if she had not been so long fed with fear, she might have gone to him, she might have saved them both. But she was not strong enough to shake off the shackles that held her. She sobbed and shook her head.

"I can't, Andy," she said brokenly. "I do love you. I will love you all my life. But I don't dare. I can't take the risks. And I mustn't stay here. I oughtn't to have come at all. I've got to go now, before anyone finds me in your house. Please open the door and let me out."

PART III

Clippings and Correspondence

1891–1905

CHAPTER 7

The Daily Picayune, February 4, 1891

THE PACIFICI
DESCENDANTS OF SEA GOD OCEANUS APPEAR TO WELCOME REX

INAUGURAL BALL AND TABLEAUX OF THE ORDER REPRESENTING GREAT OUTER SEA ENCIRCLING THE EARTH

VIVID PORTRAYAL OF CORTEZ GAZING ON THE PACIFIC
FOLLOWED BY MAGNIFICENT REPRESENTATION OF MYTHOLOGICAL STORY OF OCEANUS, TETHYS AND THEIR DAUGHTERS THE OCEANIDS

AT THE GRAND OPERA HOUSE

Not only has his Gracious Majesty, Rex, Carnival King of New Orleans, won the love and allegiance of a democratic people, but his fame has reached far back into the past and the descendants of a famous god and

159

goddess are the first this year to celebrate Rex's annual visit to his favorite Capital City.

The Grand Opera House presented a beautiful appearance last night. The vestibules and stairway were decorated with shrubbery and evergreen garlands, and from the central chandeliers hung floral Pacifici emblems.

When the drop curtain rolled up last night, there was an eloquent silence and then a deafening burst of applause, for before the delighted eyes of the audience were seen the outlines of a dark mountain mantled in tropical verdure, and beyond it a shimmering sea, glittering in the sunshine. At first only a single human being could be discerned on this exotic scene—the figure of a warrior clad in armor, standing on the summit of the mountain, shielding his eyes with his hand as he gazed out on the limitless expanse of water. Then as the light shifted to reveal more of the mountainside, other figures were disclosed, similarly clad and similarly startled. The fascinated audience did not need to glance down at the quotation from Keats, printed in green and silver on their programs. Nevertheless, for the benefit of our readers whose memories may need jogging, we give it herewith:

> "Or like stout Cortez when with eagle eyes
> He star'd at the Pacific—and all his men
> Look'd at each other with a wild surmise—
> Silent, upon a peak in Darien."

Before the applause died out, the stage was darkened, and when light stole over it again, dim and eerie at first, but gradually growing radiant, the Spanish soldiers had disappeared. On the shores of the sea, more shimmering than ever, appeared the great king Oceanus and his consort Tethys, clad in royal robes and seated upon silver thrones. Around the base of these thrones were a number of immense shells, which, dropping down, disclosed the forms of the loveliest maidens among the Oceanids, daughters of the royal couple, reclining on dolphins of bright metal. Then one by one, amidst the waves, other Oceanids appeared, attired in close-fitting garments covered with parti-colored scales which glistened beneath their streaming hair. Emerging from the billowy deep, they joined their sisters in paying obeisance to their parents. Then, clasping hands, all danced around the throne together.

Afterwards, the sky grew dark, while lightning played upon the peak of Darien. The flashes became more vivid, and the distant thunder rumbled, growing louder and louder. The Oceanids knelt upon the sand, bowing their heads in reverence and awe. A mighty burst of thunder shook the throne, the ocean rolled in from the sides, and a sheet of water fell from the skies, transforming the scene into a roaring, tossing sea, which swallowed up the Queen and all her daughters, leaving the King solitary upon his tottering throne.

At this point the curtain fell, amidst tumultuous applause, but soon it rose again, and the entire personnel of the two tableaux, headed by the King and followed by Cortez escorting the Queen and the Spanish soldiers escorting the Oceanids, marched around the stage. At the conclusion of the march, the violin orchestra, which had been constantly playing sweet music, rendered *Hail Columbia,* and Oceanus, Cortez, and the latter's lieutenants, approaching one of the stage boxes led out the Queen of the evening and her three Maids of Honor. The Queen, Miss Estelle Lenoir, wore a trailing sea-green moire dress made with shoulder puffs, and trimmed over the entire front with delicate lace, embroidered in pearls and diamonds. The Maids, Miss Violet Beal, Miss Sophie Baird and Miss Odile Gauthier, wore green gauze dresses trimmed with sequins.

The Pacifici are to be congratulated upon their first appearance, which was generally pronounced one of the finest sets of tableaux ever witnessed here, and upon their Queen, Miss Estelle Lenoir, one of the most lovely young ladies, who has ever reigned over a Carnival Ball.

The Daily Picayune, February 10, 1891

REX BEGINS A MERRY REIGN
A TRIUMPHAL ENTRY
REX AND HIS COURT
ARRIVE ON THE ROYAL FLEET

The city is in the midst of one of the gayest and most successful Carnivals that have been feted in the Crescent City. Rex's arrival yesterday was a grand and imposing event. Thousands of visitors from all parts of this vast republic fraternized with the hospitable and ever-welcoming citizens of New Orleans, and formed no small proportion of the tens of thousands of loyal subjects, who spent their overwrought enthusiasm in continuous cheering while the brave pageantry of noble courtiers and princely personages, all in glittering costumes, passed through the streets, followed by the flower of martial manhood in elegant accouterments.

No more propitious weather could have been desired. A steady, invigorating breeze, tempered to the proper degree by the warm rays of the sun, shining through the spotless cerulean expanse, invited even the most sedate of people to be outdoors and breathe the pure air of the balmy southern clime.

Rex had the entire allegiance of every citizen of high or low degree, merchant prince, petty tradesman or humble denizen. From almost every balcony the royal colors were displayed, and all loyal subjects wore boutonnieres of purple, blue and gold. Public edifices, newspaper offices and the shipping threw to the caresses of the toying winds the cherished flags and banners and pennants of His Gracious Majesty.

His Majesty's royal yacht *Galveston* and flotilla yesterday entered, in triumphal array, the harbor of the Crescent City. Rex, the glorious, the ever-young, the all-beloved, arrived during the afternoon, and was greeted and welcomed with every demonstration of respect and affection. Every vessel in the harbor displayed, besides its national flag, the colors of the benign potentate. Cannons roared, crafts of all descriptions gave shrill, prolonged sounds of welcome; the people, assembled by thousands and thousands on the wharves and landings, cheered and cheered again and again.

A distinguished party of ladies and gentlemen had the extreme pleasure and high honor of greeting His Majesty in the cabin of honor. Among them were Mr. and Mrs. Charles Fontaine, Miss Aurore Fontaine, Miss Clarisse Fontaine, Mr. Marcel Fontaine, Mr. and Mrs. Adrien Lenoir, Miss Estelle Lenoir, Mr. and Mrs.

Horace Rutledge and Mr. Andrew Breckenridge.* The fortunate and liege dukes, marquises, counts, duchesses and marchionesses and countesses who attended the King were sworn to the deepest secrecy not to reveal by outward sign or indiscreet outcries of joy, the august presence.

At noon a delicious lunch was served. The King's health was pledged in sparkling wine of the vintages of Champagne. After lunch, the King retired to his royal cabin, where he was assisted by the Lord High Chamberlain and the officers of his suite in donning the royal robes and crown.

His Majesty next appeared on deck, surrounded by the peers of the realm, and attended by the Earl Marshal and the Lord High Chamberlain. The royal orchestra struck, with allegro movement, notes of the royal anthem, *If Ever I Cease to Love,* and cheer upon cheer rent the air. The escorting warship *Zaragossa* then fired a royal salute of twenty-one guns.

The flag of the King was hoisted at the fore of the royal yacht, and the cutter *Forward* fired a royal salute of twenty-one guns. Then the royal fleet prepared to move. The *Galveston,* closely followed by the *Zaragossa,* streamed downstream. The rest of the fleet closed in behind the royal flagship, with ceaseless din and tooting of steam whistles.

The royal yacht landed at the Canal Street ferry pontoon at two o'clock, and was escorted while landing by the tugs *W. G. Wilmot* and *B. D. Wood.* The King, accompanied by his courtiers, and escorted by the Admiral, the Fleet Captain and the Captain and officers of the royal yacht, disembarked and walked to his carriage, in waiting at the landing, just beyond the ferry-house.

By a path, cut through the dense mass of eager, delirious, joyful subjects that were massed on the wharves by tens and tens of thousands, His Majesty reached his royal carriage and prepared to make his triumphal entry into his beloved Crescent City.

---

* N. B. The editor has here deleted a certain number of names of no interest to the average reader.

Letter from Marcel Fontaine of New Orleans
to
His Friend, Napier Rutledge,
A Senior at the University of Virginia

Ash Wednesday, 1891

Dear Nap:

You'll probably be surprised to get a letter from me written today, because if you've given your friends at home a thought, I'm certain it's been to visualize them sleeping off the effects of Mardi Gras, except for the few who've kept awake long enough to stagger out to church and have their foreheads smeared with penitential ashes. Your mental picture would be fairly correct, too. But as it happens, yesterday's events affected me pretty closely, in a personal way, and I'd rather write you about them myself than to have you hear about them indirectly. So here goes.

You know that it's five years since Comus has been active in any way, and during this time Proteus has appropriated the night of Mardi Gras for its parade. It seems to me perfectly natural that Proteus should have come to feel that its greatest rival had forfeited its prerogatives, because of this inactivity, and that's the viewpoint of all the friends with whom I've talked. But Comus is as arrogant as ever in spite of his long retirement from the Carnival scene. Apparently he thought that no one would ever dream of questioning his preeminent position, for he didn't even take the trouble to explain that he had decided to stage a come-back, or suggest any kind of co-ordination. The result was that last evening the glare of torches appeared in two different sections of the city simultaneously, signifying that two parades were on their way to Canal Street at the same time!

Comus actually got his floats out a little sooner of the two, and might have had time to get around Canal Street before we arrived, except that he had two breakdowns, and that delayed him a good deal. The result was that we arrived first, and our pageant was halfway up the Canal Street route by the time Comus reached it. But in spite of this head-start, there, for the first time in history, were two parades advancing at the same time, each detracting from the effect of the other! And parades at that, promoted and produced by the greatest rivals among the Krewes, because one is so predominantly American and the other so predominantly

Creole! Parades, moreover, headed by the two bitterest enemies in the city! Yes, here's my biggest piece of news: Of course you've known for a long time that Monsieur Adrien Lenoir is the venerated Captain of Proteus. But I doubt whether you've heard that Andy Breckenridge is the new Captain of Comus. Of course it's almost unheard-of for so young a man to be elected to such a position. But Andy Breckenridge gets everything—or almost everything—that he goes out after, and he's got that, since you've been away at college.

Well, as you know, it's usual for a parade to move first on the downtown side of Canal Street, as far as Claiborne Avenue or thereabouts, and then swing back on the uptown side to Bourbon Street, and make the turn there. This was the rule that we were following, because Proteus was going to receive his Queen and his guests at the French Opera House. Comus, who was going to hold his Ball at the Grand Opera House, followed the same initial route, but quite a way behind, because of those breakdowns I've mentioned. So when the head of our parade reached Bourbon Street, on the return, just half of the Mystic Krewe had reached that point. Of course, this was no part of our plan, but neither was it any part of our plan to hold up our parade and retard the opening of our Ball. So we started across the neutral ground headed straight for the middle of the Comus display.

The instant the Comus Captain—that is, Andy Breckenridge—saw that a collision was about to occur, if something was not done about it and done very quickly, he came galloping up, all beplumed and bemantled, and there in the middle of the neutral ground he came face to face—as much as you can under a mask—with our Captain—that is, Monsieur Adrien Lenoir—also all beplumed and bemantled. Neither had the slightest intention of giving way, not only because each was fully convinced that his parade was entitled to precedence, and because he represented the supreme authority of his own Society, which he could not permit to have publicly flouted, but also each has the bitterest hatred for the other that I've ever seen a Latin show for an Anglo-Saxon and vice versa. So it won't surprise you to learn that presently the air was blue with their fulminations against each other, and though it has since been denied that they went so far as to draw their swords, I personally believe that they did. At all events, I wouldn't dare to put down on paper what they called each other for fear that this letter wouldn't get through the mails. Suffice it to say that Monsieur Lenoir vehemently declared he had the right of way by virtue of his route, that nothing would induce him to halt his parade, that Comus should have foreseen the disgraceful situation which had arisen and avoided it, and that he proposed to lead his procession on. And all the time he was declaiming, Andrew Breckenridge kept shouting "Over my dead body!" with a string of oaths that would make your hair stand on end.

We all thought we were about to find out, through actual experience, what happens if an irresistible force meets an immovable body, when a domino dashed down from the banquette and snatched the reins out of Monsieur Lenoir's hands, making his horse rear and almost unseating him. With our leader disabled in this way, our parade naturally had to stop, and instantly Andy Breckenridge pushed up a shout and gave a high sign, galloping forward again at the head of the Comus floats, which lumbered along after him. The police came scurrying up, and put the domino under arrest, too late to do any good, because by that time it was also too late to save Proteus from humiliation. We had to wait until the way to Bourbon Street was clear.

I don't need to tell you that nobody believes this dramatic intervention was accidental. There is a very strong suspicion that the domino was none other than Allain de Gruy, one of the few Creoles who belongs to Comus as well as Proteus and who was consequently prepared for trouble. We believe that he posted himself on Canal Street on purpose to watch developments and spring to the rescue if Andy needed him. He was led off to the police station, but his arrest was nothing but a farce, for he was released in time to join Comus when the unloading began at the Grand Opera House. There's another strong suspicion that Andy Breckenridge has a great way with the police.

Of course there was a good deal of gloom at the Proteus Ball, because we all realized that, having once given way, we could never prevent Comus from taking over Mardi Gras evening hereafter, and that we should have to content ourselves with Monday night instead. What is worse still, the episode marks a public triumph of the Americans over the Creoles from which we'll never recover. But personally I got a good deal of pleasure out of the Ball anyway, for Clarisse and Estelle were both Maids and both looked so lovely that

I swelled with pride whenever I looked at them. And this brings me to the personal part of my story.

I know it is no secret to you that I have been deeply in love with Estelle for a long time; but because I was pledged to secrecy, I have not told you that shortly before Christmas I formally asked for her hand. Her parents were good enough to respond favorably to my suit, but said that the formal announcement of the betrothal must not be made until Easter. However, Andy Breckenridge has been actively pressing a most unwelcome suit in the same quarter; Monsieur and Madame Lenoir have been seeking a pretext to publicly discountenance this; and I have been watching my chance to call one to their attention. So this morning, after church, I went straight to their house, and boldly said that in view of what happened last night, I felt the engagement should be made known at once, and that the date of the wedding should be advanced from June to Easter. I am happy to tell you that they agreed with me. By the time this letter reaches you, all New Orleans will be ringing with my good news. And I had the inestimable joy of seeing my dearest Estelle alone today for nearly an hour and of revealing my love for her more fully than I have ever been able to do heretofore. She is still very shy and strange with me, which is natural, and her lovely modesty and sweet reserve make me worship her the more. I believe, too, that the knowledge of Andy's suit has harassed and depressed her. Needless to say, she had never countenanced it, much less encouraged it; but still I think it must be the source of her sadness, and I am sure that when we are married she will instantly forget the trouble he has caused her. Then her natural spirits will revive and she will be completely happy herself besides making me the happiest of men. It is hard to think that six weeks must elapse before I can claim her completely. But these will pass, surely though slowly, and then with what joy I shall receive her as my bride.

Of course, my dear Nap, I shall count on you to be one of my groomsmen. Fortunately your spring vacation should make this service easily possible for you. And I am thankful that since you will be graduating in June, we will never be separated for long again, but see each other daily in the future, as we used to in the past.

Ever your friend,
Marcel Fontaine

The Daily Picayune, April 2, 1891
(Society Section)

The marriage of Miss Estelle Lenoir and Mr. Marcel Fontaine was celebrated yesterday evening at the Cathedral of St. Louis, his Excellency, the Archbishop of New Orleans, assisted by the Reverend Father Maillard, performing the impressive nuptial service of the Catholic Church. The Cathedral was exquisitely decorated, all the beautiful adornments of Eastertide being used, with the addition of several handsome floral designs. About the chancel were placed palms and graceful potted plants. The altar was embellished with white roses, and handsome brass candelabra held lighted waxen tapers. Above the chancel rail were twined garlands of rosebuds, and banked at the base of the rail were pink and white roses. Suspended over the bridal couple was a huge marriage bell of white rosebuds, and two balls of roses on which were perched white fluttering doves. To the strains of *Tannhäuser* the bridal party entered. First were the ushers, who also acted as groomsmen: Mr. Octave Fontaine, Mr. Allain de Gruy, Mr. Napier Rutledge, Mr. Patrick O'Brien, Mr. Félix Denis Jr., Mr. Jules Provosty and Mr. Numa Castaigne. Then the bridesmaids: Miss Aurore Fontaine, Miss Clarisse Fontaine, Miss Myrthé de Gruy, Miss Charlotte Provosty, Miss Henriette de Hauterive, Miss Cléon Gauthier and Miss Odile Cénas. Master Narcisse Fontaine acted as page. The bride, who has been acclaimed as one of the most beautiful debutantes of the Season, wore a magnificent gown of heavy white brocade, an importation from Paris, trimmed across the front with superb flounces of rose point, caught with clusters of lilies of the valley, her chosen flower. The veil, also of rose point, fell in graceful folds from her queenly head to the end of the long train, and was held in place by a spray of diamonds, the bridal gift of the groom. She carried an exquisite bunch of lilies of the valley, tied with broad ribbons of moire. The bridesmaids wore picturesque gowns of crepe de Chine in rainbow colors, draped in embroidered chiffon. Each carried flowers distinctive in color: Duchesse de Brabant roses, Henriettes, American

Beauties, Maréchal Niels and daisies, tied with multi-colored moire ribbons, and these, with jewelled pins, were the gift of the groom. During the ceremony the organist played softly *Träumerei*, and after the blessing, in solemn and impressive tones, had been pronounced by the Archbishop, the bridal party left the Cathedral to the strains of *Aïda*.

The ceremony was followed by a reception, limited to the bridal party and the immediate relatives of the two families, which was held at the home of the bride's parents, Mr. and Mrs. Adrien Lenoir, on Royal Street. The house was artistically decorated with flowers and many superb floral offerings sent by friends. Much pleasurable excitement was caused by the fact that when the bride went upstairs to change into her travelling costume, the bridal bouquet was caught by Miss Aurore Fontaine, the elder sister of the groom, an incomparable beauty and an outstanding belle. Many were the conjectures as to what this happy omen might portend in the way of another wedding in the Fontaine family not too distantly in the future.

The bridal couple left on *The New Camellia* for a short wedding trip. The bride, who is much beloved, and has been a great favorite during her short social reign, made her debut at the opening of the Opera Season last October. She was a Maid at the Twelfth Night Revels, in the Court of Proteus and in the Court of Rex and Queen at the Inaugural Ball of the New Order of the Pacifici. She was the recipient of many costly presents, including silver, diamonds, paintings, bric-a-brac and cut glass.

Letter from Madame Adrien Lenoir of New Orleans
to
Her Cousin, Madame Pierre de Gruy of St. Martinville

September 10, 1891
My Dear Alzire:
I am writing belatedly, yet gratefully, to thank you for your letter of condolence, composed in a spirit of such touching sympathy, as soon as you learned of the great loss my husband and I had sustained through the death of his

dear mother. We recognized the complicated situation in your own immediate family which prevented you from assisting at the funeral, and appreciated the respect which caused you to have a Requiem Mass said for the repose of my poor mother-in-law's soul. Indeed, she was in all regards a woman of such unparalleled excellence that I cannot believe it would be the design of the good God to detain her long in purgatory!

Since my husband has already sent you all the formal notices relative to the obsequies, I shall not weary you with a further detailed description of these. Regarding my mother-in-law's last illness, I am thankful to say that it was brief and comparatively painless, being due almost entirely to the inescapable infirmities of old age. Her greatest suffering was caused by delusions. She was under the anguished impression that she had wronged Estelle irreparably in some obscure way, and done her great harm. As you know, she always treated the child, who was the apple of her eye, with incomparable loving-kindness, and therefore these tortured imaginings had not the slightest foundation in reality. We tried the experiment of bringing Estelle into her presence, hoping this would serve to calm her, but it seemed only to excite her the more. She wept bitterly, imploring Estelle to forgive her, and seeking reassurance as to the child's happiness. Unfortunately, Estelle was incapable of giving her grandmother much comfort. She seemed unable to act naturally in my mother-in-law's presence. For the most part she was very silent, and when she did speak, it was only in set phrases which had been suggested to her. Once, when we urged her to embrace her grandmother, she grew deathly white and shortly afterwards fell in a dead faint. She is already enceinte, and her condition, while not alarming, has from the first been far from satisfactory. So we did not press her again, for fear of marking her infant.

You will understand that our anxiety about Estelle, coupled with our grief for the loss of our mother, has greatly saddened my husband's life and my own, especially when I tell you that our concern for our only daughter is not limited to solicitude about her health. We are beginning to fear that the Fontaine family is not, after all, the one we should have chosen for an alliance. The first reason for this is because the behavior of the second son, Octave, is becoming more and more of an open scandal. Probably you never knew that his Uncle Théophile, in his youth, maintained a mistress, whom he met at a quadroon ball, quite in the stereotyped fashion of that degenerate day. The affair was handled with great discretion, and, though Théophile squandered his patrimony upon this young person, and remained a bachelor for her sake, his behavior was on the whole discreet, and his family was never disgraced by it. His mistress has been dead a long time, and their only child, a little girl, was sent to France for her education, and remained there, in good hands. But recently Théophile, who is failing fast, insisted that he must see her before he died, and to quiet him she was brought back to this country, since he was too feeble to undertake the voyage across the Atlantic. The matter was delicately handled, but unfortunately, through some mischance, Octave saw the girl and fell desperately in love with her. No considerations of either propriety or advantage have had the slightest weight with him, and Théophile, who is certainly in his dotage, has aided and abetted him in the shameful cause. Théophile has now left his brother's house, where he has had shelter and maintenance for many years, and has gone to the one where Octave, who recently received a small legacy from a relative of his mother's, has installed this octoroon, his own cousin.

I should not relate this scandalous history to you, if all New Orleans were not already rocking with it, so that you would be sure to hear it sooner or later in any case, in an exaggerated form, though the actual facts are certainly bad enough. The Fontaines have shown a great deal of bravado about the matter, which my husband and I feel ill beseems them; and though we assume that Octave has been reprimanded, his parents' home has not been closed to him, so that he goes to Bayou St. John whenever he chooses and Estelle is forced to see him there. I may add that she also meets him elsewhere, for he has not been wholly ostracized by what passes for good society, though how such behavior can be countenanced is something we shall never comprehend. Even his brother Auguste, now on the verge of taking holy orders, is still seen from time to time in his company.

All this is indeed sad to relate, but, alas! my dear Alzire, I have further tidings of misfortune, though perhaps these will not move you as much as I might wish, considering your own attitude towards a matter about which we have differed. But here are the facts: Within a day or two of the time you receive this letter, the betrothal of both my son-in-law's sisters will be simultaneously announced. The younger, Clarisse, has, with her parents' full knowledge and consent, engaged herself to a young man named Napier Rutledge, who lives near the Fontaines on Bayou St. John. I know of nothing actually derogatory to this young man; but he is a rather colorless American, much preoccupied with yachting, and his parents, comparative outsiders, who have amused themselves by turning the old Spanish Customs House into a residence of sorts, seem to have no more serious purpose in life than this act of restoration. Certainly I should never have believed that the Fontaines would consider Napier Rutledge in the light of a possible parti *for their younger daughter, who is really very pretty and charming; yet they act as if they were delighted at the match; and their viewpoint in this regard, astonishing as it has been to us, has not begun to give us the pained surprise caused by their behavior concerning the betrothal of their elder daughter, Aurore, the greatest beauty and belle in New Orleans, to that notorious sportsman, Andrew Breckenridge. It can be no secret to you, since you have permitted your own son and daughter to cultivate an acquaintance with him—an act of leniency which my husband and I shall never understand—that this ostentatious rake was an aspirant for Estelle's hand and that his suit was suppressed with the severity which such impudence deserved. The Fontaines themselves are well aware of his aggressive conduct—indeed they made it a pretext for pressing the courtship of their son Marcel, with many expressions indicating that they were as much scandalized by young Mr. Breckenridge as we were. Yet Marcel and Estelle returned from their wedding journey to find him an habitué of the Fontaines' house, and the match between him and Aurore already as good as made! It appears that we had been somewhat mistaken in assuming that Mr. Breckenridge was on the verge of bankruptcy; if you will permit me to say so, I think you might have been more enlightening regarding the state of his plantation, which, so it seems, is highly productive. Moreover, he has had another successful season at the races, where the progeny of his first winner, Supremus, have now begun to appear; and his connection with the Lottery, where he is the right-hand man of Mr. Morris and Mr. Howard, has proven more profitable than ever this year. When we attempted to protest to the Fontaines over the incon-*

sistency of the course they were pursuing with Aurore, they somewhat satirically informed us that since we were mistaken regarding the financial status of Mr. Breckenridge, we might well have misjudged him in other ways also; and that however this may be, they were not in the least ashamed of any of the sources of their future son-in-law's wealth, since the fortune itself was so substantial and since their daughter was so radiantly happy. I should not myself have applied the word radiant to Aurore; arrogant would better describe it. She acts as if she had carried off the greatest prize in the South, and talks insolently of her plans for playing the chatelaine at Splendida, and for becoming the most outstanding hostess in New Orleans. She also makes a parade of her unbridled infatuation for her fiancé, unseemly to the last degree in a girl of good family and good breeding. His manner, which has always been mocking, has now become insufferable, and it offends me even to think of him.

The two sisters are to be married, in the very near future, at a double marriage ceremony, which the Fontaines evidently intend shall surpass in splendor even the Durance wedding of which you still like to talk on the Teche. To be sure I have not heard of their sending to China for a shipload of spiders, but probably that is only because there is no mile-long avenue of trees leading up to their house, where these spiders might be released to weave webs, which the servants in turn could spray with gold and silver dust. But I do not doubt in the least that the Fontaines will contrive to dazzle their guests with some similar spectacle, and that the invités will be as numerous and as overawed as those at the Durance wedding. And I hear that the prospective bridegroom has invited no less than forty persons to stay at his home during the festivities. It fills me with grief to think that our best Creole customs, so restrained and so dignified, are fast becoming contaminated with vulgar display, that we can no longer trust even our oldest and most valued friends to carry on our own hallowed traditions and to spurn those of showy outsiders. Greatly as I deplore the delicacy of Estelle's health, I cannot be altogether regretful that her condition, not to mention her mourning, will preclude her from appearing at this function, about which all New Orleans will soon be chattering as if it were the most important event in the world. I do not doubt that even the scandal about Octave will be swallowed up in the general *gloating over this forthcoming spectacle, so unseemly in the sight of a person with refined tastes.*

This long letter can hardly give you pleasure in any part, my dear Alzire, and I am certain that you realize that I write it with pain. But I feel I owe you an explanation, as well as an apology, for my long silence. And I feel, too, that you will understand our depression and anxiety, and support us with your sympathy.

Always affectionately your cousin,
Charlotte Lenoir-Provosty

The Daily Picayune, January 28, 1892

The most notable social event of the season was the magnificent ball given on Wednesday evening by Mr. and Mrs. Andrew Breckenridge, as a housewarming on their return from their honeymoon. Probably no other private residence in New Orleans can compare with the artistic finishing of the interior of their princely home. Each room is a masterpiece and the work of foreign artists. The drawing room, a magnificent apartment, is finished in white and gold, with panels of cream satin, and springing from the side walls are numberless French gilt sconces holding waxen candles, whose myriad lights bring out to the greatest advantage the tints in the room of porcelain-like daintiness. The ceiling, which is a work of art, represents the graceful figure of a beautiful woman reclining at full length, and sporting about her, holding garlands of pale pink roses, are dimpled cupids, who are lifelike in their infantile loveliness. Mr. and Mrs. Breckenridge received their guests in this superb apartment. The dining room and library were thrown into one, and used for dancing. The dining room whose appointments and furnishings are in oak, in early English style, is a magnificent room of large dimensions. The library is finished in mahogany, into which panels of tapestry are set, above the bookshelves that line the walls. The entire appointments of the house are of the most artistic description. In addition, the entire lower floor, which was used for dancing and receiving, was converted into a floral bower by the aid of graceful palms and plants, garlands of smilax and superb orchids and tulips and delicate lace-like maidenhair fern, which were grouped in every available space. A magnificent supper room was built for the occasion, and beautifully tinted in pink and white; seven or eight immense chandeliers lighted the beautiful room, where one hundred and fifty guests were seated at once. Flowers of various kinds adorned the tables.

The ladies of the receiving party were presented with clusters of flowers of different kinds, including carnations, lilies of the valley, tulips, calla lilies, roses and hyacinths, tied with white ribbons. Mrs. Breckenridge was very handsomely growned in gold brocaded satin made in Empire style, trimmed with point lace. A tiara and necklace and brooch of diamonds finished the superb costume of the gracious and lovely hostess. Her sister, Mrs. Napier Rutledge, also a recent bride, was exquisitely gowned in pink satin, trimmed with gold, and looked exceedingly handsome. Their mother, Mrs. Charles Fontaine, was superbly dressed in sapphire blue and pearl-colored brocade, trimmed in point lace, and wore diamond ornaments. Much regret was expressed over the absence, owing to illness, of Mrs. Marcel Fontaine, nee Estelle Lenoir, another recent bride and a sister-in-law of the hostess.

The Daily Picayune, February 2, 1892

CLEVELAND IN TOWN

THE EX-PRESIDENT REACHES NEW ORLEANS ON HIS RETURN FROM IBERIA

ENTERTAINED AT THE PICKWICK CLUB AND BY MR. ANDREW BRECKENRIDGE

THE NEW YORK STATESMAN TAKES A LOOK AT THE GARDEN DISTRICT

HE SHAKES HANDS WITH A FEW THOUSANDS AT THE CITY HALL

Ex-President Grover Cleveland arrived yesterday and was the city's guest. Ten days ago he passed through the city with Mr. Charles B. Jefferson to spend a short vacation in hunting and fishing around Mr. Joseph Jefferson's orange grove near New Iberia.

Last Thursday, Mr. Cleveland wound up his hunting, after making quite *a record on ducks*, and after a day's rest, on Saturday he visited the famous Petite Anse Island and the Avery salt mines. Naturally he found warm hospitality at the Averys', and he proved a genial and unassuming guest and an agreeable companion.

Sunday morning he reached New Iberia and was met by a large delegation of citizens and ladies. He was pressed to accept a hearty invitation to visit the rooms of the Iberia Exchange and hold an informal reception. After an hour's handshaking, he was driven to the residence of Mr. Allain de Gruy, one of the loveliest in the little city, and there received another taste of Louisiana hospitality.

At seven-thirty o'clock the train reached New Orleans. A detail of police kept the road clear, while Mr. Cleveland and Mr. Charles B. Jefferson entered a phaeton and drove off.

The vehicle went out Esplanade to Royal and thence out Canal Street to the Pickwick Club. There the gentlemen who came to the city with him met him and formed a Breakfast Party. Shortly after ten o'clock, Mr. Cleveland reached the St. Charles Hotel, and Mr. Andrew Breckenridge and ex-Senator B. F. Jones paid him a social visit. Both say that politics was not mentioned. Mr. Breckenridge had a carriage, with driver and footman in livery, in waiting, and the ex-President accepted an invitation for a drive. Mr. Cleveland saw the Garden District at its best, with flowers in bloom in the gardens, and the handsome mansions forming bright pictures in the sunlight. At one o'clock there was a luncheon at the residence of Mr. Breckenridge. It was, of course, an elegant affair, in decorations and in menu, and Mr. Cleveland had the pleasure of meeting some lovely Southern women, among them the charming wife of his host and her sister, Mrs. Napier Rutledge.

The New Orleans Item, April 2, 1892

LOTTERY DOOMED!

Election of Murphy J. Foster to the governorship on April 19th seals the doom of the Louisiana Lottery, that incubus that has fastened its tentacles into the public life of this state. It will avail the baffled supporters of Governor McEnery little to raise the cry of "Fraud!" which they have unsuccessfully sought to establish ever since the nominating convention and the primary election of last month. Final compilation of the returns as we have been printing them in the columns of the ITEM show that Mr. Foster received 79,388 votes, and Mr. McEnery but 47,037. The few votes accorded the Republican tickets were too insignificant to affect the result.

The doom of the Lottery was really sealed when Governor Nicholls heroically refused to affix his signature to a bill which would have perpetuated this monstrosity, in a stirring message, asserting, "I could not permit one of my hands to degrade what I sacrificed the other to uphold;" and when that grand old indomitable crusader for righteousness, Rev. Dr. Palmer, delivered before a mass meeting this winter the most stirring oration ever heard here, directed solely against the Louisiana State Lottery.

This vote must not be construed by any as a reflection upon Samuel Douglas McEnery; that would be as stupid as the lament of the defeated lotteryites who backed his candidacy, and who now wail that Mr. Foster's triumph was a blow to white supremacy, on a par with the shameful deeds of Madison Wells and H. C. Warmoth during the depths of our degradation by carpetbaggers.

The Daily Picayune, September 8, 1892

CHAMPION CORBETT

THE CALIFORNIAN SHATTERS THE LONG-TIME IDOL OF THE RING
AND
LAYS JOHN L. SULLIVAN LOW IN THE TWENTY-FIRST ROUND

BOTH MEN MAKE A FAIR, MANLY FIGHT

BUT CORBETT'S SCIENCE OUTLAWS SULLIVAN'S STRENGTH

THE OLD CHAMPION'S RUSHES LACK THEIR DREADED FORCE, AND HIS YOUNGER RIVAL SCORES A DECIDED AND A POPULAR VICTORY

AN IMMENSE THRONG

THE LARGEST CROWD THAT EVER GATHERED TO WITNESS A PRIZE FIGHT

MR. ANDREW BRECKENRIDGE SPONSORS EVENT

Nobody would have thought, a few years ago, that the ordinary everyday man in the average walk of life would surrender $15 for a 90-minute seat on a rough pine board elevated in mid-air, with all the attendant discomfort of being elbowed to rib-aching soreness, and far enough away to reduce the central objects of attraction to miniature dimensions. And yet such was the case last night at the Olympic Club on the ground floor, as well as in the attic observatory, but neither of these respective portions of the immense amphitheatre was filled to its fullest capacity.

* * * (Detailed description of the fight omitted here) . . .

At eleven o'clock, Corbett and his retinue forced their way through a wildly cheering crowd and, entering their carriages, still accompanied by the faithful, wildly joyous and most envied members of the police force, started for the Southern Athletic Club, where a reception had been prepared.

Later, a smaller reception was given at the residence of Mr. Andrew Breckenridge, to whom much of the success of the evening may be considered due, since he was largely instrumental in bringing the fight to New Orleans.

The Daily Picayune, May 21, 1893

ROWING RACES

ANNUAL REGATTA OF THE ST. JOHN ROWING CLUB

The St. John Rowing Club, the oldest organization of its kind in the city, yesterday celebrated its twenty-first anniversary by a boat race and dance, and, as is its usual happy custom, gave much enjoyment to the large number of invited guests. At four o'clock the spacious veranda of the club and the tiers of seats on the left were crowded with eager expectants. There were the fathers and mothers of the heroes who were to pull, the white and pink and blue dressed sisters and sweethearts, chattering and happy; there were the looking-on members, rigged out in their white flannel suits and jaunty caps, and, last of all, the poor, ordinary, plainly-dressed mortals not fortunate enough to be members of the Club. Most of the ladies had pretty paper roses in their hats. It is a curious fact that ladies always wear paper roses in their hats when they go to boat races.

The race course was to stakes half a mile out and back again. The first on the program was a wherry race, Napier Rutledge in the *Undine,* Marcel Fontaine in the *Oceanid,* and Félix Denis Jr. in the *Charmer.* Rutledge took the lead at the start with a long easy stroke. He was the first to turn the halfway stake, and passed the house stake two lengths ahead of the second man. Time: Rutledge 9:50, Fontaine 10:02, Denis 10:30.

The Picayune Bureau

Baton Rouge, La., July 12, 1894

The legislature, during the session just closed, has passed the following joint resolutions proposing amendments to the constitution.

HOUSE BILLS

By Mr. Ware—No. 424: An act to suppress lotteries, to prohibit and punish the promotion, setting up or drawing of any lottery; to prohibit and punish the sale of lottery tickets or the bonds or shares of stock of any lottery company; to prohibit and punish the advertisement of any lottery.

The Daily Picayune, November 7, 1894

CARDINAL GIBBONS
ON A VISIT TO HIS OLD NEW ORLEANS HOME
SPEAKS OF THE RAPID ADVANCEMENT
OF THE SOUTH

ENTERTAINED AT BRECKENRIDGE HOME

On Wednesday, Mr. and Mrs. Andrew Breckenridge entertained at a very brilliant dinner in honor of His Eminence, Cardinal Gibbons. The table was exquisitely arranged with crimson roses and brevardia and with maidenhair ferns. Candelabras holding crimson, waxen candles adorned the board and added much to the brilliancy and effectiveness of the beautiful cardinal decorations. Corsage bouquets of crimson brevardia and maidenhair ferns, tied with broad cardinal ribbons, were presented to each lady.

Among the guests of Mr. and Mrs. Breckenridge were His Excellency the Archbishop of New Orleans: the Reverend Auguste Fontaine, brother of the hostess: her parents, Mr. and Mrs. Charles Fontaine: her sister and brother-in-law, Mr. and Mrs. Napier Rutledge.

"I am very much impressed with the great improvement in the material condition of the South since the War," said Cardinal Gibbons, in speaking of his visit to New Orleans. "The city shows signs of improvement in spite of the heavy municipal debt under which it is struggling due to corruption and mismanagement. The abolition of the Louisiana Lottery seems to be regarded by all parties as a blessing to the city. People here recognize that the income which the State of Louisiana received from the lottery was in the end paid by its citizens."

The Daily Picayune, April 21, 1896

SARAH BERNHARDT IN A GREAT ROLE
"IZEYL" AT THE GRAND OPERA HOUSE
TRAGEDIENNE ENTERTAINED BY MR. AND
MRS. ANDREW BRECKENRIDGE

Last evening the Grand Opera House was filled with a large and enthusiastic audience, who had gathered in that dainty playhouse to welcome the great French actress. So many of the Creoles who never go to any of the American theatres make it a point to go and see her and feast on the melody of the French tongue as spoken by the "divine Sarah".

The audience was a large and fashionable one, and numbered all the cultured and intellectual people of New Orleans, who wanted to see the great tragedienne. In the audience were noted Mr. and Mrs. Andrew Breckenridge, who entertained in honor of the great tragedienne at Antoine's after the performance, Mr. and Mrs. Napier Rutledge, Mr. and Mrs. Charles Fontaine and Mr. Narcisse Fontaine, Señor Don Luiz de Alpiente and Señora Doña Inés de Alpiente and their daughter, Señorita Carmen de Alpiente, and many others. It is understood that the divine Sarah has expressed a desire to see an alligator hunt and that Mr. Breckenridge is arranging the details of this to meet her pleasure. Meanwhile he has presented her with one of these extraordinary creatures, in order to satisfy another wish that she has made known, to have one for a pet.

The Daily Picayune, July 7, 1898

A FRIGHTFUL DISASTER AT SEA
THE FRENCH STEAMER LA BOURGOGNE COLLIDED WITH AN ENGLISH VESSEL AND SOON AFTERWARD SANK WITH OVER 500 PASSENGERS AND CREW

LESS THAN 200 WERE SAVED, AND THE SURVIVORS TELL A TERRIBLE STORY OF THE BATTLE FOR LIFE ABOARD THE SHIP, IN THE BOATS AND ON RAFTS

THE CREW THREW WOMEN AND CHILDREN INTO THE SEA TO SAVE THEMSELVES

PASSENGERS STABBED AND BEATEN BY THE CREW—PROMINENT ORLEANIANS AMONG

THE LOST, INCLUDING
MR. AND MRS. ANDREW BRECKENRIDGE AND
THEIR TWO LITTLE DAUGHTERS
MRS. JULES ALDIGE AND MEMBERS OF HER
PROMINENT FAMILY
AND OTHER UNFORTUNATE CITIZENS, WHOSE
FATE SPREAD MOURNING THROUGHOUT
THE METROPOLIS

A thrill of horror and of pity pervaded this city yester-day, when the news of the sinking of the transatlantic steamer *La Bourgogne* was received, and the information spread that six hundred souls had found a watery grave, in less than a quarter of an hour after the terrible collision with the English vessel *Cromatyshire*, the details of which are given in the telegraphic columns of *The Picayune*.

The feeling of commiseration at the appalling fate of so many hapless people was intensified when it was learned that a number of residents of New Orleans were aboard, and that, in all probability, they had been lost.

As it was stated that of the two hundred saved the large majority were steerage passengers and members of the crew, and that only one woman had survived the awful calamity, there was not much hope left as to the rescue of any of the first-class passengers.

There was grief impossible to describe in many a home yesterday, and sorrowful indeed was the mission of the reporter of *The Picayune*, as he went from one stricken household to the other.

Through the loss of their elder daughter, nee Aurore Fontaine, their prominent son-in-law, Andrew Breck-enridge, and their two little granddaughters, Pauline and Angèle, the Fontaine family has been cruelly bereaved. This family is among the best-known and most respected in the city. The Fontaines have figured for years very prominently in social, financial and commercial circles. Mr. Charles Fontaine, the head of the family, is one of the most solid financiers of this city, and as a cotton broker, does business on a very large scale. His wife was nee Louise de la Vergne. Their sons and daughters are related by marriage to some of the best families of New Orleans, their younger daughter, nee Clarisse Fontaine being now Mrs. Napier Rutledge, and their son, Marcel, having married Miss Estelle Lenoir, the daughter of Mr. and Mrs. Adrien Lenoir. Their eldest son, Auguste, is now pastor of the Church of Our Lady of Mercies. The engagement of their youngest son, Narcisse, a prominent young attorney, to Miss Carmen de Alpiente has recently been announced.

Mr. and Mrs. Breckenridge left New Orleans about ten days ago with the former's son by a previous marriage, Andrew Breckenridge Jr., and their two little daughters. Their first destination was New York City, where they took passage aboard the *Bourgogne* to enjoy their annual Continental tour. Andrew Breckenridge Jr. attended to the embarkment of his parents and sisters, but did not accompany them, as he planned to spend the summer in New England with relatives of his own mother. He is expected to arrive in this city today or tomorrow.

Mr. Andrew Breckenridge was long an outstanding figure in New Orleans. He was the owner of the magnificent plantation Splendida, in Iberville Parish, where he maintained a fine stud, stable and race track, and where he raised Supremus and other horses which brought him fame as a breeder and sportsman. He also owned a fine property on Prytania Street, which, since his marriage to the former Aurore Fontaine, was a brilliant social center. Through his first wife, the late Anne Forrestal, he was connected with both the Northern and Southern branches of that prominent family. He was a member of the Jockey Club, the Southern Yacht Club and the Boston Club. His loss will be deeply and sincerely mourned. The loss of his charming wife will also be greatly deplored in the social circles in which she shone, and there is added grief at the demise of the lovely little daughters of this prominent young couple.

The Daily Picayune, July 9, 1898

At the entrance of the Breckenridge family residence, on Prytania Street, a flowing black crepe tells of the mourning and desolation of a solitary youth, bereft of his father, and the passer-by reverently stops and reads the sad lines printed on the black-bordered notice:

DIED AT SEA
JULY 4, 1898
ANDREW BRECKENRIDGE
AURORE FONTAINE BRECKENRIDGE
PAULINE BRECKENRIDGE
ANGELE BRECKENRIDGE

Letter from Andrew Breckenridge Jr. of Boston
to
Mrs. Marcel Fontaine of New Orleans

September 10, 1898

Dear Aunt Estelle:

I hate to think how ungrateful I must seem to you for all your kindness to me. I guess I must be an awful coward. But somehow it's been just impossible for me to sit down and write a letter that had anything to do with Father. It's been bad enough, not being able to help thinking about him, whatever I've kept doing during the day, or dreaming about him at night, no matter how hard I've tried to wear myself out so that I'd sleep from sheer exhaustion. But it hasn't been any use. He's been in my mind all the time. You know what an awfully alive *person he was anyway. You hardly knew anyone else was in the room, if he was there, and even in a big crowd, he stood out. That is, he did to me, and I guess you know what I mean even if you didn't feel the same way about him. Well, I still keep looking up, expecting to see him, and quite often I wake up calling him, and in both cases it makes me feel pretty badly after I find it's been no use. So to deliberately do something that would seem to bring him nearer than ever, for a few minutes, when I know I'll never see him again, has been just beyond me, that's all. I do hope you'll understand.*

I guess I wouldn't feel so badly about his death, if I didn't still believe it needn't have happened, if there'd been any order or discipline on the Bourgogne, *or even the most elementary sort of humanity among the sailors and steerage passengers; or if I could be sure he hadn't suffered or—suffocated. That's the worst, I keep thinking he probably choked to death, and that he knew he hadn't been able to save Aunt Aurore and Pauline and Angèle. If I knew he'd perished gloriously after seeing them to safety, there'd at least be some consolation in that.*

But I guess you know most of this already, and it must make you feel badly, too, for I know you always admired the French Line and felt that some of your happiest memories were connected with it. I'll never forget the stories you've told me about that trip on the Nantes when the whole Opera Company was on board and you had such a wonderful time. So I don't know why I write you this way, except that now I've started I can't stop. I want to go on and on because it's a relief after all to put words on paper. And I know you will understand, because you are such an understanding person. I really think I should have gone crazy when I came back to New Orleans after the shipwreck if it hadn't been for you. I don't think I could have stood all those Requiem Masses, and the smothering crepe everyone had on and the empty house and the formal visits of condolence and the endless discussions about a suitable memorial stone. I like the Fontaine family very much, and every single member of it has always been as kind as possible to me, and has treated me just as affectionately as my little half sisters and has tried to make me feel as if I belonged. But I never have felt that way, though I've tried, too, because I didn't want to seem unappreciative. Sometimes I have felt sort of half way as if I belonged to you, or might have, if I'd had a fair chance. But of course you're not a Fontaine except by marriage, any more than I am except because of my father's marriage. I hope you won't think I'm fresh to say what I have, because that's not the way I mean it. Naturally I can't remember my own mother at all, but I think from what I've heard she must have been something like you, very gentle and sweet and loving, and I think if Father had only married you instead of Aunt Aurore, I would feel now as if I belonged to somebody. I admired my stepmother a whole lot and she was good fun and it would almost knock you over to look at her when she was dressed up to go to a party, but I didn't really love her, and do you know I believe that down deep in his heart Father didn't either? I think he loved somebody else. He as good as told me so once, as much as he could without being disloyal to Aunt Aurore, which of course he never was. But I don't know how many times he said he hoped I'd be very happy when I got married, that I mustn't do it just to put on a bold front and prevent anyone from guessing how much I'd been hurt, and that I mustn't let anything stop me if I was sure I loved the right girl, and that she loved me. And at the same time he kept telling me I must always be very gentle with girls because they did not stand up well under treatment that seemed to them harsh, even when boys and men did not mean to be rough and would not have hurt them for the world. I think I am very fortunate to have had a father who talked to me like that, especially now that I have lost him and have no one to confide in any more.

There is one other person besides yourself in New Orleans towards whom I feel especially grateful and that is Uncle Octave. Of course I know he is considered the black sheep of the Fontaine family and I know why. That is another thing Father explained to me. But Uncle Octave came and stayed with me several nights when otherwise I would have been all alone in that dreadful, empty house, and finally I told him I was very grateful for his company and didn't want to be deprived of it, but that I was afraid he must be missing his home and family. So I asked him if he wouldn't like to have me spend a night at his house instead. He seemed to be very much touched and pleased, and I went there. It's a very nice little house, and the lady he lives with is very nice, too. She talks nothing but French and she looks and acts like a Frenchwoman, rather like an Arlésienne. She has a little girl named Laure, who is just about the age my sister Pauline was and made me think of her a lot, except that Laure is even prettier than Pauline. She is one of the prettiest little girls I ever saw in my life. There was a picture on the wall of a really beautiful girl, with long, soft black waving hair and big, black eyes, dressed in a very low green satin bodice and a white ruffled skirt. There was something about this picture that made me look at it all the time without meaning to or even wanting to, and finally Laure's mother told me that it was her mother. After I saw it I understood better about poor old Uncle Théophile. Well, anyway, Laure came and climbed up in my lap just the way Pauline used to, and went to sleep there, and her mother let me carry her into her room and

*put her down on her little white bed, and then she half
waked up and kissed me good night. It all made me feel
very strange and sad, and if I could ever do anything for
Laure, I should like to.*

*Now I will just tell you what I expect to do next, and
then I will close. My own mother's family, here in Boston,
has been very kind to me, and though I don't feel that I
really belong to them any more than to the Fontaines (in
their case because of not associating them with anyone who
has been real to me) I have decided to do what they want
me to just now, which is to enter Groton this fall and prepare for Harvard there. It will all be so different from the
sort of life I would have had with Father that perhaps it
will help me to forget him. I'll come back to New Orleans
someday, and I'm not going to sell the house there or anything like that; but it reminds me too much of Father to
try to live in it now, or to make any definite plans when
I will. Aunt Clarisse writes me that she thinks Roscoe and
his wife seem to be doing very well as caretakers, so I've
told her I'd like to have them stay on and she's promised
to find good places for the other servants, and I know you
will help her with this if it should be necessary. Of course
I couldn't have a better foreman at Splendida than Marcy
Yates and he's told me I can depend on him to keep things
running just as Father would have liked. I guess he will
really do better without having me around asking him questions and bothering him and trying to boss him. But I care
a lot about the plantation, even more than I do about New
Orleans, so it may not be so very long after all before I
get back there, for a while anyway.*

*I shall miss you very much and your cute kids, too, for
I really think they are the cunningest children I ever saw,
Marie Céleste especially, though Olivier is also a very cute
kid. It just tickles me to death to see Marie Céleste
dance and hear her sing her little Creole songs. At least it
used to, and of course someday it will again. I hope you
won't forget me and that if you aren't too busy you will
write me once in a while, because I do think a lot of you
and when I do come back it will be because I want to see
you and those cute kids of yours.*

*Please remember me very kindly to your parents and Uncle
Marcel, who have always been very good to me, too, and*

*give Olivier a big hug and Marie Céleste a sweet kiss for
me.*

Affectionately and gratefully yours,
Andrew Breckenridge Jr.

*I wrote the Jr. before I thought. I still keep doing it
from force of habit, but I won't rub it out because that
would make such a smudge. I can't think of myself as the
only Andrew Breckenridge. I'll always think of my father
that way, unless sometime I should have a son just like
him, which of course is what I hope for more than anything else in the world. But even if I should marry as young
as he was when he married my mother, that couldn't be
for eight years yet, and that's a long way off.*

Breck

Boston Transcript, Saturday Evening, April 29, 1905
(Society Section)

Mr. and Mrs. George Hemingway Forbes, of Beacon
Hill and Nahant, announce the engagement of their
daughter, Miss Anna Lyman Forbes, to Mr. Andrew
Breckenridge of New Orleans.

Miss Forbes graduated from Miss Winsor's School in
1902, and made her debut the following year. She is a
member of the Sewing Circle and the Vincent Club. She
is allied to many of the most prominent families in
Boston, her paternal grandmother having been Miss
Penelope Hemingway before her marriage, and her
mother, Miss Gertrude Lyman. Mr. Forbes is the President of the well-known banking firm of Forbes, Dexter
& Forbes, and Treasurer of the Union Club.

Mr. Breckenridge, who is a senior at Harvard, prepared for college at Groton. He is a member of the
A.D. and Hasty Pudding Clubs. He is a "Three Letter"
man having made both the 'Varsity football team and
the 'Varsity hockey team, and being now Captain of the
'Varsity Crew. Since the death of his father in 1898, he
has made his home with Mr. and Mrs. Richard T. Forrestal, of Commonwealth Avenue and Dedham, relatives
of his mother, the late Anne Forrestal Breckenridge.

Through his mother, Mr. Breckenridge is also related to the Southern branch of the Forrestal family residing in New Orleans, as well as to the Rutledges and many other prominent Orleanian families. Through his father, he is related to Senator Breckenridge of Kentucky, and by marriage, to the Fontaines of New Orleans, his late stepmother having been the daughter of Mrs. Charles Fontaine of that city, and the sister of the Reverend Auguste Fontaine, Mr. Marcel Fontaine, Mr. Narcisse Fontaine and Mrs. Napier Rutledge, nee Clarisse Fontaine. It is expected that a large Southern contingent will be present at the wedding, which will take place at Trinity Church in June, immediately after Mr. Breckenridge's graduation from Harvard.

After taking a wedding trip around the world, the young couple will reside in Milton, as Mr. Breckenridge expects to enter his father-in-law's firm. He retains his interests and his property in Louisiana, but has no immediate plans for returning there for any length of time.

Kendall's *History of New Orleans*, page 500

The lottery continued to do business with New Orleans as its headquarters until the expiration of its charter. But it worked under constantly increasing difficulties. In 1895, Congress passed another act, by which the interstate transportation of lottery tickets or other publications was prohibited. The management of the company was advised by counsel that this act was unconstitutional, and for some years it appears they continued to send their tickets throughout the country through the express company. In the meantime it was casting around for a new home. Mexico was at first considered, the government there having legalized lotteries by instituting a tax on them; but Honduras ultimately received the doubtful honor of the choice. The change of domicile was effected in 1895. Thereafter the company was known as the Honduras National Lottery. But the mere fact that its legal residence was abroad did not prevent it from doing the greater part of its business in the United States. . . .

When, as a result of a decision of the supreme court

in 1903 the express companies were closed to the use of the lottery, the company adopted the practice of sending its tickets as personal baggage, and thus avoided the transmission of them by common carrier. Thereafter the tickets were printed at a printing office in Wilmington, Del., which ostensibly was doing a legitimate business. . . . At Mobile the approximation and terminal prizes—which were numerous and important—were figured out. At Mobile, also, were printed the lists of prizes, which, when completed, were shipped by express under assumed names to the agents throughout the country.

The attention of the authorities was eventually called to the printing office in Wilmington during a printers' strike. . . . The place was raided, several lottery officials were discovered, and 21 printers and pressmen were taken into custody. The prosecution of the parties now known to be behind the business in the United States was arranged, but came to an abrupt termination when the defendants in the Mobile cases, through their attorney, announced their willingness to plead guilty and accept punishment. The maximum fines were imposed; the printing establishments at Mobile and Wilmington were closed up, and the paraphernalia and records of the business were surrendered to the government. This result was attained in June, 1907. With that date the history of the Louisiana Lottery, as far as New Orleans and the United States is concerned, came to an end.

PART IV

The Garden District

Spring, 1913

CHAPTER 8

ANNA FORBES BRECKENRIDGE of Boston, whose husband, christened Andrew for his father, but universally known as Breck, had belatedly brought her to New Orleans, was conscientiously but critically returning the first calls that had been made on her.

She was a tall, clean-cut young woman with gray eyes, neatly braided hair and fresh healthy color, and she looked well in the tailored suit and sailor hat that she had bought, along with numerous similar outfits, at the best shop on Boylston Street, before starting South. She distrusted shopping facilities in New Orleans on general principles, and besides, she always liked to be well prepared beforehand. She was walking from her own house to Mrs. Marcel Fontaine's, where she intended to start that afternoon, for only a few blocks divided the two, and she believed in exercise. She always wore sensible shoes. She walked well and rode well, she played excellent golf and still better tennis, and she had won cups in several swimming contests. It did not look to her as if she would get as much of this sort of thing as she would like, in New Orleans. Most of the young women she had met so far went to each other's houses in the morning with their sewing, and listened while one of their number read aloud from some classical work, instead of getting

out into the open air. Anna understood French, because she
had been to a very good school in Switzerland for two years,
after she had gone to Miss Carroll's and before she had
gone to Miss Winsor's, besides taking special courses at the
Sorbonne later on and travelling extensively on the Continent.
But this did not mean that she thought the reading of
Molière's plays, by a self-conscious amateur, provided a
stimulating morning pastime, nor did she find the noisy
bridge games, with which the girls who sewed in the morning
whiled away their afternoons, any more satisfactory. They
all took lessons from a Miss Evie Noble, and daily practiced
what she taught them; then once a week they met for a
party in the studio of Miss Noble's great friend, Mrs. George
Whitney, who was large-hearted and loved to entertain. In
Anna's eyes, the studio was the most astonishing apartment,
supported by golden baroque columns and adorned with tapestries, paintings, vases, brasses and bas-reliefs. Anna was
told with bated breath that the prizes awarded at the end
of the year would be simply magnificent, running even to
lamp shades, breakfast sets and petit point handbags. Anna
thought it would be much simpler to go out and buy such
things for oneself, in the course of a single shopping trip
and in accordance with one's own taste, than to spend countless afternoons in the stuffy studio striving to win them by
the uncertain means of the bridge table. But when she said
this to Miss Evie Noble's devotees, they stared at her for a
moment, and then picked up their cards again and went on
chattering.

Anna was glad to have escaped from this uncongenial atmosphere on the polite pretext of calling, and as it was
exercise upon which she was primarily now intent, she missed
much of the beauty which flowered along her way as she
went up Prytania Street. The camellias were at the height of
their bloom; every yard she passed was flanked with luxuriant bushes laden with glossy green leaves and flowers of
waxen perfection. The sweet olive was blossoming, too, its
fragrance intensified by a recent rain; and yellow jasmine,
yellow tulips and Lady Banksia Roses united in producing an
effect of widespread glory which Anna barely glimpsed,
though she saw, with disapproval, the open gutters, the un-
paved streets and the crumbling pavements. The Fontaine
house was imposingly situated, on a corner, and the grounds
with which it was surrounded were spacious and shady.

Architecturally, it was not unlike that house to which Breck had brought her, with unconcealed pride. But instead of being white with black galleries, which even Anna admitted was an effective combination, it was painted in a deep shade of dull cream, galleries and all, which happened to be one of the colors for which she did not care. Inside, it bore comparison even less favorably, in her opinion; Breck's house was admittedly furnished in an outmoded way, but everything in it was the best of its period, and it had been kept unusually clear of clutter, and open to light. Here, there was too much of everything and it was too ponderous and too inclosed to suit her taste. Heavy draperies hung at the windows, heavy carpets lay on the floor, and heavy sofas and armchairs were grouped in immovable state around a massive center table. Anna, awaiting the arrival of her hostess, felt that a woman living in such surroundings must inevitably be stifled and shrouded.

Although there had been no undue delay in answering her ring at the doorbell, this had not received the instantaneous attention which Anna demanded, and received, in her own house; and the colored butler, instead of wearing formal morning clothes, appeared in a white coat which had a slightly frayed collar and a missing button. He was cheerful and cordial, and assured her, as he ushered her into the dim drawing room, that Miss Estelle would be glad to see her— that she would be right down; but that had been a quarter of an hour before, and Anna had still seen no sign of her hostess. How could these Orleanians be so slack about their servants —and about everything—she asked herself scornfully. A woman who could afford to live in a house of such pretentiousness, could certainly afford to pay her butler well, and this being the case, she should certainly insist that he should perform his duties in a meticulous way, meticulously clad. And she, herself, should be more punctilious; either she should say she was not receiving, or she should put in an appearance within five minutes of her visitor's arrival. But it was not either straitened circumstances or ignorance of the conventions that ailed these Southern women; it was simply a congenital indifference to order and efficiency and to domestic and social detail.

Outside, the sun was shining brightly, but none of its devastating rays penetrated the brocade draperies overlaying the lace curtains at the long windows; and though the cheery butler had switched on some of the lights when Anna entered the drawing room, all the lamps were enveloped in silk shades, finished with long beaded fringe. The only real radiance in the room was focussed on a large painting, hanging at one end of it, and illumined, in the best professional manner, by bright bulbs arranged in a series within a brass casing. Anna glanced at the painting, found it unexpectedly arresting, and continued to look at it with increasing attention.

It was the life-size portrait of a young and beautiful woman with her two children, which, for all its artificiality of pose, setting and costumes, had a certain distinction and considerable charm. It was ridiculous, Anna said to herself, to portray a young mother laden with jewels and attired in full evening dress, such as she would wear only to a ball, when depicting a domestic scene. Yet this was what the artist had done with great effect. He had painted her wearing a long, circular skirt and square-cut bodice finished with cap sleeves, all made of *point appliqué,* the *décolletage* edged with a network of brilliants; and furthermore, she had on pearl earrings, a pearl dog collar with diamond bars, a string of pearls with a pear-shaped pendant, and a diamond chain finished with a large square-cut gem. Really, it looked as if the sitter and the painter had conspired to see how much lace and how many pearls it would be possible to get into one picture! The overdressed lady was seated on an ornately carved sofa, upholstered in petit point, and here redundancy was again revealed, for the sofa was placed against a background of tapestry, a length of brocade was draped over it, and a large Chinese vase filled with azaleas towered behind it. A little boy, with his dark hair parted in the middle and carefully slicked down on either side, was represented standing with one of his painfully clean hands resting on the arm of the sofa, above the brocade, and the other on the ornate carving which constituted its back. His collar was high and stiff, his tightly knotted necktie white, his suit a spotless navy blue; he looked much too good and much too immaculate to be true. A little girl was the most natural figure of the three; she was curled up comfortably on the sofa beside her mother, dressed in simple white muslin, wearing a large pink bow on the top of her hair and a turquoise and pendant heart for ornaments. But the artist had not been able to resist the temptation of drawing all her hair down over one shoulder, so that its full luxuriance would show; it fell in shining bronze-colored masses, well below her waist. The little girl was very like her mother, but there were indications that in time she might be the more beautiful of the two. Her clear hazel eyes were even larger, and her features more exquisitely proportioned. From her expression, she seemed to have found the process of having her portrait painted a serious matter. She looked a little overawed. But back of the surface gravity lurked intrinsic lightheartedness. Her mother's expression, on the other hand, was so essentially sad that it was evident the artist had been able to beguile her into only the most superficial sort of animation.

Anna was so engrossed in her study of this portrait that she did not hear her hostess coming down the stairs and through the hall into the drawing room. She turned, slightly startled, to see that she was no longer alone.

"This is Anna Breckenridge, Mrs. Fontaine," she said, ashamed of her embarrassment, and speaking swiftly to cover it. "I've been admiring your portrait while I waited for you. This is you, isn't it? But I really don't need to ask. It's a wonderful likeness!"

"My husband thought so, when Alexander painted it, ten years ago," Mrs. Fontaine answered. "He also liked it lighted in this way, and therefore I have continued to keep it just as he placed it. But I am afraid I have changed a good deal since then. Are you sure you see some resemblance, still?" She spoke with such a decided French accent that her visitor found it hard to believe her speech was without affectation, but her smile had great sweetness, and she went on talking with the utmost cordiality. "It is good of you to return my call so promptly. I was extremely sorry to find you out when I came to see you, and now I am truly sorry to have kept you waiting, with nothing better to do than to gaze at my likeness. But my maid had not finished dressing my hair when you arrived. She is a very good *coiffeuse*—or at least I think so!—but she is not a rapid one, and it distresses her to be interrupted or hurried. She has been with me a long time and I cannot bear to make her unhappy. So I hope you will excuse me."

Of course, this was the sort of woman who would habitually have her hair dressed for her, Anna reflected, looking at the puffs and coils surmounting her hostess's head, as she accepted Mrs. Fontaine's small, heavily ringed hand. The puffs and coils were soft and becoming; they were, indeed, ar-

ranged with consummate art, and there was not a single white
hair among them. But they bore out the general air of artificiality which Anna found so trying. No doubt Mrs. Fontaine was naturally slender; still, no woman of her age would
normally have a waist of such a small size, and the slight
rigidity in her otherwise graceful bearing, as well as the
molded way in which her clothes fitted her, bore out the impression that an unyielding corset underlay her exquisitely
cut dress. She was wearing very deep mourning; but its
severity was relieved by the triple strands of pearls which
hung around her neck and the creaminess of the skin on
which they rested, which had the extreme softness that sometimes comes, instead of wrinkles, at middle age, to delicately
nurtured women, when there is enough flesh beneath it to
sheath their exquisitely formed bones. Her eyes lacked the
radiant quality of youth, but there was a gentle lambency
about them which was so appealing that Anna suspected they
might have had even more allure than an earlier brilliancy, if
they had not been so sad. The smile which lent such sweetness to the lips did not seem to touch them at all.

"We are all delighted in this neighborhood that you and
Breck are opening up your house," Mrs. Fontaine continued,
as Anna remarked that the delay had not mattered at all, in a
tone of voice betraying that she really thought it was inexcusable. "It has stood vacant so many years, and it used to be
the center of the most delightful life in New Orleans. Of
course it will be again, now that you are its chatelaine. You
New Englanders are so very capable and cosmopolitan that
you set an example to us indolent Creoles, which I am afraid
we need very much." She spoke with such charming candor
that Anna realized that the compliment and the disparagement were both sincere, and that there had been no hidden
sting to her words. "And we are even more delighted to have
you here, *chère*, than to see the house open. Breck has made
us wait a long time for the privilege of welcoming his beautiful Boston bride."

"I'm afraid I don't answer to that description, Mrs. Fontaine. You're the first person who has ever called me beautiful—except Breck, of course, in his moments of aberration,
but he doesn't have those any longer. And with a child seven
years old, I certainly can't consider myself a bride."

"Is your little boy really as old as that! What do you call
him?"

"Drew. I don't care for nicknames myself. But Breck said it was impossible to call a new-born infant Andrew, it had such a solemn sound! And he insisted there never could be but one Andy— He simply worshipped his father, though I've never quite understood why he should! Anyway, Drew seemed to suit the baby better, and somehow it stuck."

A shadow, so deep that it looked almost like a disfigurement, passed over Mrs. Fontaine's face. For a moment her finely formed features were incomprehensibly blurred, and her lips, like her eyes, became tense with tragedy. She did not instantly answer, and when she did, her voice had hardened, her accent was more marked than before, and she asked a wholly conventional question.

"He is your only child, I believe. Or am I mistaken?"

"No, he's quite enough. Breck had all sorts of wild ideas at first about a large family, but I never shared them. And Drew was an instrument baby—I believe my muscles were too taut because I had played so much tennis. Anyway, I wasn't sorry when my doctor said I shouldn't have another baby for at least three years. By that time, Breck was more reasonable. You know how men are."

In assuming the airs of one worldly woman addressing another who would inevitably share her views, Anna felt that she was paying Mrs. Fontaine a compliment. Her hostess answered with startling simplicity.

"I'm afraid I have had less opportunity of observing them than you have. But I can sympathize with your suffering. I also had a rather hard time when my son was born, though not because of playing too much tennis. It will probably surprise you to learn that I have never played a game of tennis in my life. And doubtless it will surprise you still more to hear that I did not have a doctor for my accouchements."

"You didn't have a doctor!"

"No. My husband was solicitude itself, and gave me a beautiful bracelet with *'Dieu te garde'* outlined in diamonds on a wide enamelled band. But though he was very generous and had modern views in many ways, he never outgrew the aversion of most Creoles to having any other man brought into close contact with their wives, even for the most impersonal and humanitarian of reasons. I needed to have God guard me, for I had only a midwife with me at the time of my children's birth. She did not mean to be unkind, but she had grown callous in her profession, and I know now that she was not very skillful. Besides, I had no idea how to take care of myself beforehand. And of course there was no question of anaesthetics. That was a long time ago, however. Olivier is twenty-one now, and Marie Céleste seventeen. I believe that since their arrival matters have been made much easier for young mothers everywhere, and the viewpoint about male doctors, even among Creoles, has changed. In any case, it all seems worth while afterwards, does it not? And I assure you that the second experience is not only much less painful, but much more rewarding than the first." She smiled again, and went on quickly, as if to rob her words of any implied rebuke, "When you see my little daughter, you will understand why I feel as I do. Of course I am proud to be the mother of a son, as any woman is, and I adore my big boy. But Olivier has never seemed as close to me as Marie Céleste."

"Your son has been away to preparatory school and to college, I presume?" Anna said politely.

"No. He went first to the Jesuit School and then to Tulane, here in New Orleans. But now he has a miniature establishment of his own. I know a young man likes to feel independent— Our ancestors recognized this when they built their *garçonnières*. As there is nothing of the sort on this place, I have turned a small property which I own on Kerlerec Street over to him. It is a pretty little house, really quite perfect in its way. I am sure Olivier would be delighted to have me bring you and your husband to take coffee there with him sometime, and you might enjoy seeing it. Are you familiar with our term 'shotgun' in architecture?"

"No. But it sounds very dangerous."

"Then the term is misleading," Mrs. Fontaine said. "I believe they were first called shotgun houses because they are built long and narrow with all the rooms in a straight row, one behind the other, and a shot fired in the front room could go straight through all the others. There were a good many shots fired in those days, but the houses are quiet enough now. A blind old lady of whom I was very fond used to live in this particular house. When she died, she left it to me. I have not given it to Olivier; I have only loaned it to him. Perhaps when I am a very old lady myself, I shall go and live there. Meanwhile, until Céleste is married, I naturally should not think of moving. When she makes her debut, we shall be glad of this large house for entertaining."

"She isn't out yet, then?"

"No. She is coming out next year. So then we shall be very gay again. It will seem strange after my long seclusion. A series of deaths came close together in my family, and after my father died, my mother left her house and moved to mine. She stayed here for the rest of her own life; and she did not care to go out at all, or to see anyone. Then there were three years when I never went downstairs."

"Three years!" Anna echoed in amazement. "Did you have an accident?"

"No. I have always been remarkably well, all things considered, though I have not much endurance. But my husband was a chronic invalid for a long time, and he did not like to have me leave him."

"You never went downstairs for three years because your husband was an invalid!"

"Does that seem strange to you, *chère?* I hope you do not mind having me call you *chère,* since we are to be friends and neighbors. . . ." Anna did not like the term, which she considered a colloquialism when robbed of the possessive pronoun, but she permitted it to pass by, accepting it tacitly, and Mrs. Fontaine continued, "I assure you that no Creole of my acquaintance would have dreamed of doing otherwise. But I sometimes think it was very hard on the children. If this house had been a little gayer, perhaps Olivier would not have demanded one of his own, quite so soon; and if Céleste could have had young friends about her, she would not have been quite so hungry for companionship. But it is too late to think of all that now, and there is going to be a change, which perhaps you will help me to bring about. You might even persuade me to alter some of my household arrangements, as my more up-to-date friends have kept urging me to do for a long time. Everything in this house is exactly as it was when my husband bought it for me, furnished, twenty-two years ago."

The arrival of coffee and cakes checked another outburst of amazement from Anna. She had been wondering, for some moments, why she had been offered no refreshments of any sort, and she had been making mental comparisons, by no means for the first time, between the rapidity with which these automatically appeared, in her own house, and the slowness of service in a Southern ménage. She hated Creole coffee, especially in the afternoon, and she also disliked sticky sweets of any sort; she could not understand why, after all this time, it never seemed to dawn on an Orleanian that a Northerner would prefer China tea and cucumber sandwiches. But she made a pretense of sipping the strong brew and of crumbling the frosted cake, deciding to tell Breck, as soon as she reached home, that she intended to set an example in the neighborhood which she hoped the old-timers would have sense enough to follow.

Mrs. Fontaine, though oblivious of her visitor's plans for her improvement, did sense something of Anna's surprise at the statement she had been making when the coffee was brought into the room. "The Fontaines were almost the first Creoles to come to the Garden District," she explained. "My husband wanted to give me a house of my own for a wedding present, and since his sister, Aurore, came to live so near here, when she married your father-in-law, he felt it was most fortunate that this one was put on the market about the same time. Did you notice the iron fence as you entered, with its pattern of corn and wheat? The bride of the first owner came from the Middle West, and her husband designed that fence for her himself. He said if she lived surrounded with her native products, he was sure she would never be lonely. And I hear that she never was—that it was a very happy marriage. But unfortunately it was a childless one. When she died, he did not care to live here by himself. He put it on the market, just as it was, and moved away."

"I didn't notice the fence. I was looking at the open gutters. I am sure they must be very unhealthful— But didn't you want your own furniture—weren't you interested in fixing up a house yourself?"

"I was very young, *chère*—only eighteen. I think I was rather glad to accept it as it stood, without any further effort. I was tired after assembling my trousseau and going through the ordeal of a big wedding. And then there were all the visits. In those days a Creole bride and groom went to stay with every relative of each family, all the way up and down the Mississippi River, not to mention St. Martinville and the rest of the Teche Country. Some of the Fontaine relatives I had never seen before and I found it very exhausting, always to be formally dressed in my stiff new clothes, straight through the heat of the summer, and always to be seated at table for large, elaborate meals, in the midst of strangers. I had reason to expect that my little son was already on his way, by June—and I had the usual feeling of languor and aversion to food during that period. No—I was so thankful, when my husband brought me here in the fall, to think that we could be in a house by ourselves at last, that I am afraid I did not think about furniture at all. I am afraid I was very indolent and very indifferent."

"But hadn't you been by yourselves any of the time until then? Didn't you have any honeymoon, or any wedding trip?"

Mrs. Fontaine smiled again. "It was quite a trip, *chère*, going up and down the rivers and the bayous in those days. The steamer *Teche* took nearly a week to make the trip between here and St. Martinville, and the *Danube*—the Bayou Goula tri-weekly packet—made no better time, and it was only on Saturdays that it went as far as Plaquemine. The *Laura Lee* that went to Baton Rouge and beyond was larger and faster; but all the steamers reserved the right to pass a landing that looked unsafe, and at the last moment you might be carried past your destination or prevented from embarking for it."

"But how could a landing be unsafe?"

"Because there were no docks or wharfs, as you would understand these, at the smaller places; the landings were only natural ones made by the river; and if the banks were very steep or very insecure, or overflowing, there might well be danger. At the way-landings, when a trip was made at night, bonfires were built as a signal that passengers were waiting. It always seemed like an adventure to leave a plantation house for a landing, accompanied by a little Negro carrying a bundle of kindling wood over his shoulder, and then, after the flames were flaring up, to stand watching them and listening for the faint long whistle that told you your blaze had been seen from afar off."

"It does sound romantic; but rather undependable."

"Exactly, *chère*. And that is characteristic of this country, as you will soon find out. But the plantation houses were very luxurious and the river trips were not uncomfortable. The food was surprisingly good, and the quarters adequate. The larger boats even had so-called bridal suites, because so many wedding journeys were made on them. In the evening there was always singing and card playing, and when space permitted there was dancing, too. And the days never dragged. The scenery along the shore changed all the time, and some of it was very beautiful. And the loading and unloading of the cargo at the different landings was bustling and exciting."

"But weren't the boats hot and smelly? Weren't you always in a crowd when you were travelling on them and making those visits to plantation houses? Did you and your husband ever get off by yourselves at all?"

"No. We went first for three days to Claiborne Cottage at Covington, driving there after we had taken the *New Camellia* from Milneburg to Mandeville. Milneburg was only a few miles from New Orleans, and we made the first part of the trip in a funny little train called Smoky Mary. But Claiborne Cottage was a resort hotel. We knew a great many people there, too, and we were in their midst all the time. So I told you the truth when I said that this house was the first place where I found any real peace and quiet after my marriage. Except for the little old church in St. Martinville. I have always loved that little church. You must go and see it for yourself sometime, *chère*, for it is one of the loveliest sights in all Louisiana. The little square panes in the windows are made of stained glass in beautiful bright colors, like sapphires and rubies and topazes, and in the sanctuary are the escutcheons of all the founders of the town, suspended on the stone walls surrounding the altar—the de Blancs, the Ernervilles, the Duchamps de Chastaignes, the Pelletiers, the de la Houssayes, the de Hauterives, the de Clouettes. I may have forgotten one or two, but all these I remember, and they have a noble look and a noble sound, and what is more important still, a noble meaning, for they belonged to men and women who were really great and really brave. The pews in this little church are large and square, and have the present owners' names on them on little slides. There are a great many families named Bienvenu in St. Martinville and I used to seek out one of their pews and kneel down in it because I hoped that I was *bienvenue*—really welcome—there also in the sight of God. When the feeling that I was came over me, I grew tranquil, and went back in peace to the plantation where I was visiting. But of course even a church is not the same as her own house for a woman. When I reached here, I could order all the blinds closed and go back to bed, after I had seen my husband off to his office, and stay there in the cool darkness until it was time for him to come home in the evening. I was increasingly ill as the summer wore on, and I do not know what I should have done without this respite. Perhaps it was because of my weariness and my illness that I did not pay more attention to furniture and things of that sort. But I am afraid, as I said before, that I was very indolent and very indifferent, and I think now, that I should have made more of an effort."

Anna was inclined to agree with her hostess. She could not imagine a young girl so spineless that she would permit herself to be saddled with a huge cumbersome house fully furnished with Victorian monstrosities, for no better reason than that her husband desired to make her a showy wedding present, and at the same time accommodate himself in the vicinity of his elder sister's establishment. For that matter, she could not imagine permitting herself to be led off on a series of tedious, exacting family visits labelled as a wedding journey, or going at first to a resort hotel where she and her bridegroom would be followed by nods and winks and snickerings wherever they went. She would have supposed that Mrs. Fontaine, who seemed extremely sensitive in spite of her cultivated composure, would have found such an experience a far more gruelling trial than a large wedding; and suddenly, as she looked at her hostess, she realized that it had been, that marriage had meant an ordeal to this tranquil, mature woman from the very beginning, and that passing years had never accustomed her to a cross which she had borne with fortitude and resignation. Anna was not given to gratitude, as far as Breck was concerned, for she shared the general viewpoint of the Forbes family, that she had conferred a great favor on him by marrying him. But as she sat sipping her bitter coffee and crumbling her frosted cake, she thought, involuntarily, of the tranquil lake to which he had taken her when they were first married, of the stillness that had surrounded her and the sweet smell of the fir trees enclosing the little lodge where they stayed, so safeguarded and so secret.

She was roused from her reminiscences by the sound of Breck's voice in the hallway. For the second time that afternoon she was startled, for it seemed to her almost as if she had called him and he had answered. What he was saying to the butler was trivial enough: only that he was Mr. Breck grown up, that he understood that Mrs. Breckenridge was calling on Mrs. Fontaine, and that he had come, hoping for an opportunity to pay his respects also. But, as usual, his voice rang out in such a way that his words took on the semblance of an import they did not really possess. Before the butler could draw back the heavy portieres and announce him formally, he had entered the drawing room and was halfway across the floor. Though a stranger might have hesitated to classify him as a Southerner, anyone who had known his father would have recognized him instantly as the son of Andy Breckenridge. The coloring was almost identical, except that Breck's was less vivid. The build, too, was the same, except that Breck's was slighter. He gave less the effect of force and more the effect of finish. The refinement and reserve of his mother had entered into his make-up, essentially, though almost imperceptibly. The tragedy which had shadowed his life when he was still too young to stand it, though old enough to be shattered by it, had left its mark, too; so had the cultural restraint of his upbringing and education. But in spite of all this, his entrance was characterized by the complete ease and evident joyousness of the guest assured of his welcome in a place where he had always been happy.

"Hello, Anna!" he said pleasantly. "Aunt Estelle, you don't mind having me barge in like this, do you? I suddenly felt I couldn't wait to see you for another minute. I was terribly disappointed that you were in Europe the last time I came home, just before I was married. And you know I've always told you that the best part about getting back to New Orleans, for me, would be getting back to you."

He took the hand that Mrs. Fontaine extended, and without awkwardness or hesitation, leaned over and kissed it, before he put his arm around her shoulder and kissed her on both cheeks. Anna, who had never seen an American kiss a lady's hand before, stared at him, wondering if there would be any end to the surprises of the afternoon.

"You look just the way you always did," he went on swiftly, drawing the least cumbersome of the chairs in the set circle nearer to Mrs. Fontaine, and sitting down, having accepted with alacrity a cup of coffee and a little cake. "The house looks just the same, too. I'm so thankful that it does. I was scared to death for fear you might have spoiled it by changing it in some way. Or that you might have changed yourself."

"It's always pleasant for a woman of forty to hear that she has not changed, even though she is undeceived by such flattery," Mr. Fontaine said smilingly. Anna had noticed the extreme gentleness with which she spoke, from the beginning; but now a still tenderer tone had crept into her voice. "I shall be more truthful than you, however, and say that I do see a change in you."

"Not underneath," Breck hastened to assure her. "Did you ever hear of Thomas Bailey Aldrich, Aunt Estelle? He lived here when he was a boy, for a little while, though that was a long time ago. He's always been identified with New England as an author, but he himself used to say that he wasn't Boston sterling, only Boston plated. That's like me, I guess— My, but this coffee is good, Aunt Estelle! But these little cups don't hold more than one gulp. Could I have some more? And what about that cherry bounce, or whatever you call it that you used to serve in the afternoon, too? Does that still exist, and could I have some?"

"Of course, *cher*. Please ring the bell that is behind you. I am so glad that you still like our Creole coffee. Strangers don't, always— Emile, bring some cordial to Monsieur and do not forget to put it on the tray again when he is here."

"That's the idea! But, Aunt Estelle, I'm not a stranger. The fact that I've been uprooted for fifteen years is only more or less incidental. I like everything about New Orleans. I got no end of a kick, just out of walking over, from my house to yours. I met a scissors man as I came along, and a chimney sweep with a tall hat on the back of his head. I felt like slapping them both on the back and saying, 'Hello, old fellah, are you really still here, just like you used to be? Or are you too good to be true?' And then joining in with their song."

"If you felt like doing it, I'm rather surprised that you refrained," Anna said, somewhat acidly. "You're pretty apt to follow those wild ideas of yours through."

"Well, give me credit for more self-control than you thought I had, then. But I tell you I do love to see the coalmen riding around, on the top of their little wagons, and the fat old laundresses waddling along, with their fluffy white wash bouncing up and down in the baskets they carry on their heads. You'd think the clothes would fall out, wouldn't you? But they never seem to. Those baskets look just as steady as ever. Later on I suppose the fig women will be along and the blackberry women too. Will they, Aunt Estelle? Singing their songs, too?"

"As surely as summer itself comes, *cher*."

"I'll be watching for them— And do you know I think my kid, Drew, is going to get just as much of a kick out of everything here as I do. He's taken to New Orleans like a duck to water, and he's stopped barking his poor little head off since we got him away from the Back Bay breezes. I'm having hard work to make him stop calling a banquette a sidewalk and a gallery a porch. But he'll learn. I bribed him this afternoon. I sold all the old bottles in the cellar to a vendor that came along and gave him the money. And I bought a whole cartload of violets and narcissi from another vendor for you, Anna. I put them in the pantry sink."

"Flowers that are sold in the street like that are always seconds, Breck. They never last."

"In Boston! Because they freeze. They last in New Orleans. Or if they don't, you can always buy more. So what difference does it make?"

"You mustn't mind Breck, Mrs. Fontaine. This is the way he always runs on. And the way he always spends money. He never thinks it makes any difference how much, any more than he thinks it makes any difference if flowers don't last."

"Narcissi and violets don't cost much."

"That's what you say about everything. And you end by spending thousands."

Mrs. Fontaine was about to create the tactful diversion for which the discussion had obviously begun to call, when the drawing-room curtains parted again, and another young man came into the room, this time entirely unannounced. This must be Olivier, Anna said to herself instantly. Like Mrs. Fontaine, he was dressed in deep and handsome mourning, which was extraordinarily becoming to him; the finely cut black cloth and stiff snowy linen set off his slender figure and swarthy skin to great advantage, and harmonized with his brown eyes and glossy hair. He was considerably darker than his mother, and weakness, rather than gentleness, characterized his otherwise attractive face; nevertheless, there was a marked resemblance between them. The indicated presentation had hardly taken place before Anna decided that she did not like him. The rather cursory glance which he cast in her direction gave her the uncomfortable feeling that, mentally, he had undressed her, and finding the results unstimulating, had put her out of his mind. She felt at one and the same time insulted and piqued. His attitude to Breck was somewhat more courteous, but it was patently casual. He kissed his mother deferentially, drew a small stool up in front of her, and having seated himself on it and opened a cigarette case, began to talk to her in French. It was only after a sign from her, which did not escape Anna's attention, that he tardily offered the cigarette case to their visitors, and shifted, with a slight stiffening of manner, into rather stilted English.

"I'm afraid we're interrupting a family conference, Breck. And it is high time we left in any case. I had planned to make six calls today, and this is only the first. You've delayed me, bursting in as you did."

"My dear Anna, I beg of you not to go. Please, *cher*, sit down again. My son always visits me at this hour. But we are delighted when others share his visit, are we not, Olivier? Besides, I am expecting Marie Céleste at any minute. She and I will both be bitterly disappointed if you do not wait to see her."

"I'm coming now, Mamma. I am just taking off my hat. Please ask our visitors to stay! I do want very much to see them."

The voice did not seem to come from the hallway this time; it sounded further off, as if the speaker had come in from a side door, and was advancing from the rear. There was a sound of light footsteps—snatches of a gay little song. Then the gloomy stretches reaching from one dim drawing room to another were suddenly illumined as a young girl came down them. She was dressed entirely in white, her bronze-colored curls cascaded over her shoulders, and her arms were full of flowers. Like her brother, she went directly to her mother and kissed her, less deferentially than he had, but with more spontaneity. Then she turned swiftly towards Anna, holding out her blossoming armful.

"I heard you were here, when I came in from school," she said. "So I went to the garden and picked these for you. No— Please take them all! They'll look so pretty in your lovely house. I'll come and help you arrange them, if it's too much trouble for you to do it alone. But we must save out one to pin on your dress. See, like this! It brightens the whole costume. And I'll take just one other—" She put the flowers into Anna's hesitant hands, extracting a single camellia from the masses she had tumbled together, ranging in color from deep purplish crimson to waxen white. The one she chose had a faint warm tinge to it. Turning again, she held it up to Breck.

"For you," she said, finishing her sentence. "This is my favorite. I thought perhaps you'd wear it as an emblem that we're going to be friends."

"I can't think of anything I'd rather do," Breck answered.

CHAPTER 9

ANNA BRECKENRIDGE liked a substantial breakfast, and she never took it in her room. She had always considered taking *café au lait* in bed a "filthy French custom" and had not hesitated to so designate it, even when visiting in Norman châteaux; now she designated the early morning *petit noir* of the Creoles in the same way. When she was abroad, she went through a constant struggle to secure grapefruit, Shredded Wheat, cream and hot buttered toast made of wholewheat bread, in downstairs dining rooms, early in the morning. When she was at home, she ate all these foodstuffs, along with various others, at a meticulously set table, at eight o'clock on weekdays and nine o'clock on Sundays. Neither her husband nor her servants had ever succeeded in swerving her from this rule, and even when she was recovering from one of her rare illnesses, the first meal she ate downstairs was always breakfast.

When she and Breck moved to New Orleans, because Breck's doctor insisted that he must spend the early spring in a milder climate, after a hard bout with pneumonia, she remained persistently blind to the benefits of the "balcony," as she continued to call the upper gallery, in spite of Breck's suggestion that it might serve as a happy compromise between his tastes and hers. She believed in setting a good example for children, she retorted, and she proposed to show Drew, from the beginning, that he could not get into slovenly Southern ways. So day after day she sat erect behind her shining coffee service, clad in a trim, immaculate tailored dress, with Breck facing her across the well-arranged flowers, and Drew between them, drinking milk from a polished silver cup, and eating oatmeal from a polished silver porringer. Upstairs the sunlight slanted over the empty gallery, while the branches of the magnolia trees swayed slightly over it in the spring breeze.

She was still going through her mail, the morning after her call on Mrs. Fontaine, when the butler brought her a light, brittle package, with a note tucked into the white ribbon with which it was tied. Anna opened the package and frowned slightly as she surveyed its contents, a small bundle of pale, crooked roots tied neatly together, that gave forth a faint scent. Clearing a space between herself and Drew, she laid the little bundle down, and read the note, first to herself and then aloud.

My dear Anna:

I like to picture you putting the old Breckenridge house into beautiful order, so I am sending you some of our native vetivert, to lay on the shelves of your armoires and in the drawers of your dressing tables, as we do in Louisiana.

My son and daughter and I all enjoyed the visit you and Breck made us so much that we are eager to see more of you, and we should like to mark our emergence from first mourning by giving a dinner in your honor, if you will permit us. I have been making out a tentative list, and it has occurred to me that I might ask the John Beals and the Edouard Denises, both because I believe you would find them congenial in themselves, and because they have children about the same age as your little son, who might prove to be pleasant playmates for him. John Beal's father was a very famous physician, especially noted for his research on the cause and cure of yellow fever, and the son, also a doctor, is already making a name for himself. Mr. Denis comes from a famous old French banking family, and is carrying on that tradition. I should naturally include your husband's connections through his stepmother, who are also mine by marriage, and if there is anyone of whom I have not thought, whom you would especially like to meet, I hope you will let me know. I think a company of eighteen or twenty would be agreeable, and any night next week which would meet your convenience, would suit me also. Céleste will stop in on her way from school this afternoon to receive your answer, which I hope may be favorable.

With cordial greeting to Breck and yourself, and a kiss for your little son,

> *Believe me, my dear Anna,*
>> *Affectionately yours,*
>>> *Estelle Lenoir-Fontaine.*

"Gosh, but that's nice of her!" Breck exclaimed heartily. "She is a peach, isn't she, Anna? Imagine thinking of sending you something to put in your bureau drawers, and lightening her mourning on purpose to give us a dinner and provide playmates for Drew. I call that pretty darned thoughtful."

"I wish you wouldn't keep saying gosh and darn in front of Drew," Anna remarked reprovingly. "He's beginning to imitate you—I heard him say both yesterday— So these funny little sticks are a local form of sachet! I'm really interested to find out. I've noticed this same odor, coming from the clothes of some of the women I've met, but I thought it was Southern perspiration. Of course we all know that daily baths aren't a matter of routine here, and———"

Breck put back his head and laughed unrestrainedly. "Southern perspiration!" he echoed, rubbing his hands over his chin in a way he had when he was especially amused. "That's priceless, Anna. You couldn't have got off anything half as good as that if you'd been making a special effort! But I wouldn't repeat it among your new-found friends, if I were you. As a matter of fact, I think they probably take just as many baths as you do, though they may not go in for cold showers early in the morning. And I think probably their ancestors took more than yours did. The climate's more conducive to it, in the first place— Bathing must have been an endurance test in New England before there was any central heating. And in the second place, there were always plenty of slaves to carry the tubs around before there was any modern plumbing. Why I can remember an old servant of ours, who still persisted in going from room to room at night, asking the ladies if they didn't want their feet washed, because she'd been trained to do that as a young girl."

"Their *feet!* As if having their feet washed would mean they were thoroughly clean!"

"It was a good old Biblical custom," Breck said quietly. Then, as if to soften the implied rebuke, he added more lightly, "And there were hat tubs and hip tubs and sitz tubs and heaven knows what all besides. Probably people took care of the different parts of their anatomy at different times in the day. You can see how it would work out. If they began with a hat tub the first thing in the morning, it would be natural to get to a foot tub by night. As I've said, they had plenty of water brought to them."

"It's repugnant to me to think of human beings doing all that fetching and carrying," Anna said coldly.

Breck knew that he had annoyed her, first by laughing at her mistake over the "Southern perspiration" and then by his Biblical allusion. He changed the subject. "You'd enjoy this dinner Mrs. Fontaine suggests, wouldn't you, dear?"

"I hope so. I haven't enjoyed anything I've been to yet very much. The women don't talk about anything except bridge and babies, and the girls don't talk about anything except their beaux. Oh, yes they do. They all talk about who was Queen last year, and who's going to be Queen next, and why so-and-so didn't even get to be a Maid, and whoever thought that whosis would be chosen for Rex. You'd think Carnival was the only thing on earth that really mattered to them."

"I guess it does matter a good deal. It always has somehow. It's in their blood. I suppose that cute girl we saw yesterday will be a Queen next year."

"If you mean Marie Céleste Fontaine, of course she will. I'm sure her family has been scheming for it ever since she was born. But why do you call her cute? Honestly, Breck! How do you expect Drew to talk any kind of English if you use such incorrect expressions. You know as well as I do what cute really means."

"Well, what do you want me to call her? A knockout? That's what she was all right. She really did just about knock me over when she came walking down through those long, gloomy rooms, in her white dress, with her hair tumbling over her shoulders, and her flowers in her hands."

"I thought it was rather theatrical. I've seen any number of Ophelias make just such entrances. I expected to hear her say, 'There's rosemary, that's for remembrance;—and there is pansies, that's for thoughts.' As a matter of fact I couldn't understand a word of what she did say. Her enunciation must be very poor."

"It wasn't the enunciation. I'm afraid your nice Swiss French isn't equal to the Cajun patois. That was *Z'Amour Marianne,* one of the bayou ballads, that she was singing. Those are the local equivalents to spirituals. Only instead of being all about religion, they're all about love. A great improvement, I call it."

He rose, pushing back his seat. At the same time, Drew wriggled down from the pillows that built up his chair.

"I want to go out and play, Mother. I'm tired of staying here."

"Sit still, Drew. Mother hasn't finished her breakfast yet. It's very rude to get up before Mother's finished."

"Daddy did."

Anna sighed and looked towards her husband, in a way that left no possible doubt as to what she thought of his bad example. She hoped such a glance would be sufficient. Breck was generally very courteous. But for some reason, he seemed out of hand that morning.

"For God's sake, Anna! The poor kid can't sit here all day! We've been at the table nearly an hour already. Let him get out and stretch his legs. You believe in exercise."

"Very well, Drew. Since your father thinks you need exercise, I will excuse you. But be sure to put on your rubbers. And tell Nana to take her sewing outside, where she can watch you." Then, as the child rushed through the door, without waiting for her to change her mind, she gathered up the despised vetivert and her correspondence, including Mrs. Fontaine's note, and rising in her turn, walked over to her husband's side. "So you wish me to accept this dinner invitation?" she asked.

"Yes, I do. But I wish you wouldn't talk in such a martyred way, as if it would be a great ordeal which you're willing to undergo because you're a model wife, and your consent would constitute a concession to me. You ought to get some pleasure out of going yourself."

"I've told you already that I'm bored beyond words by everyone I've met in New Orleans so far. Now if I could only meet some politically-minded women somewhere near my own age, who are interested in equal suffrage and prohibition, and some men who acted as if they understood the meaning of the word initiative——"

She paused, to let the last part of her sentence sink in. She was, of course, striking indirectly at Breck as she spoke. But involuntarily her mind reverted to the handsome, insolent young Creole she had met for the first time the day before. There was a man, she felt sure, who had never lifted a hand for himself or done a day's work in his life, who had been waited on by inches from his birth. She thought she would like to see him with those stiff, spotless cuffs of his rolled up, and those slim, shapely hands covered with some sort of grime. She thought she would like to see his sleek, black hair disarranged, and lines of weariness in his smooth, sneering face. What supreme effrontery he had shown in his attitude towards her, acting as if she hardly existed, as if she were not worth a glance or a civil word! She, Anna Forbes of Boston, a blueblood of the Brahmins and the greatest heiress on the Back Bay, besides!

"I'm afraid prohibition isn't very popular in New Orleans. But perhaps you might find someone who would go in for suffrage with you," Breck was saying, cutting across her unwelcome train of thought. "Anna—I don't know whether you'd approve or not—but I've sometimes thought I'd like to go in for politics myself."

"*You!* Whatever gave you such an absurd idea?"

"I don't know. I've been thinking about it, that's all— Does it really seem so absurd?"

"Of course it does— What sort of politics?"

"Well, I might begin by trying for the State Legislature. From a country district. We could establish residence at Splendida. Then if I did happen to be any good, later on I could run for Congress."

"And what would you live on all this time?"

Breck reddened. "I don't suppose it would cost us any more to live while I was doing that than it does now."

"Of course it would. You'd have to make campaign contributions and travel around seeing your constituents and entertain all sorts of undesirable persons. It would cost a great deal of money. And in the end it would all be thrown away."

"Well, we've got plenty of money—between us. We might just as well throw it away on that as on anything else."

"Aren't you ever going to be ashamed of living on other people's money, Breck? Aren't you ever going to make a serious effort to earn some of your own?"

"I'm not ashamed of living on the money my father left me."

"Your stepmother's money!"

"Part of it. But that was his, too, when he left it to me," Breck said stubbornly. "And it's mine now. I've never asked you for any of yours, Anna. And the only reason we use so much is because you always go in so vigorously for keeping everything up and improving everything and having the best of everything and doing everything in the best way. I'd be willing to live a lot more simply, I'd let most of these details you fuss over slide. In fact I think life would be ever so much pleasanter and easier if we did. But I promised to let you travel your own way, and keep house your own way and bring up Drew your own way." He looked out towards the lawn, where his small son, joyously exercising his freedom, was digging up a flower bed with a little spade. "I don't know whether I did right or not, but anyway I promised, and I've tried to keep my word. I couldn't do anything to make money while we were taking a trip around the world, and that was what you wanted to do when we were first married, or when I was laid up with pneumonia and its aftereffects, as I have been twice now. And I admit I didn't show up so well as a bond salesman for a select Boston office. But now that we've come down here—now that I'm home again at last, I would like to try. You may not believe it, but I would. I want to get out to Splendida just as soon as you feel you have this house well enough settled to leave it. There was a lot of money made at Splendida in the old days."

"With slave labor!" Anna said scornfully.

"Well, yes, at first. But Splendida pulled through the War between the States better than most plantations. None of the animals on the place was lost. They were all driven into the big basement and hidden there, in safety. It pulled through the reconstruction era remarkably well, too, without slave labor."

"With considerable help from the race track and the Lottery."

"Listen, Anna—are you just trying to be disagreeable? Because, of course, if you are, you can. But there are nearly five thousand acres of land at Splendida, and it's as good as any land in this state, very choice and high and perfectly drained. About a third of it is woodland, but the rest of it is under cultivation and it's very fertile. There's no reason why it shouldn't yield good crops, and it does, corn and cotton and sugar, all three. But I believe it could yield better crops still, and more different kinds. I'd like to see if I couldn't make it. Why, there's getting to be quite an industry for moss, the kind that hangs on the trees. It used to be considered just a pretty parasite. But now it's often dried and used for filling in fairly good mattresses and upholstery. Lots of people like moss mattresses better than any other kind. Then there are some swamp lands and cypress tracts about five miles away that belong to me, too, and they're almost inexhaustible because they're still all covered with virgin timber. We've never cut the cypress off our swamps, as so many planters have had to do because they got into a tight place. The only time it's ever been touched was when the house was built. All the beams and floors in that were made of our own wood—from pride, not from necessity. And there's a refinery on the plantation, as well as a race track. There's a steam sawmill, too, and a large frame cooperage, and a big warehouse near the riverbank, to store sugar waiting for shipment and receive goods from the plantation. These buildings are all old, but they're sound, and it wouldn't cost much to bring them up to date. You'd enjoy helping me improve the place. It's just the kind of thing you like to do. I can just see you modernizing the hospital and putting plumbing in the Negro cabins—there are twenty of those, all double, with brick chimneys and little galleries, besides the overseer's house, which is made of wood and has eight rooms in it, and a supplementary brick house, only a little smaller, that can be put to almost any kind of purpose. You'll probably think up a mighty good one right away that never even occurred to me. Come down there with me, anyhow, and look the place over. You may get a pleasant surprise."

He put his arm around her and rubbed his cheek softly against hers. Like rubbing his chin with his hand, it was a habit of his, and when they were engaged, she had found it very winning. "Just wait until you've seen the grounds by moonlight," he said softly. "There's something magical about them—the live oaks draped with moss and the cape jasmine and the magnolia fuscata. Of course there's hardly a plantation house in the deep South that hasn't a splendid avenue of trees leading up to it, but at Splendida there's so much more than an avenue—acres and acres of beautiful woodland inside the entrance gate, and then great stretches of smooth lawn, wide and free and spacious, with statues scattered through the spaces that look like graceful ghosts, when you see them from a distance, half hidden in the greenery. And in the garden there's a pool where you look down and see your own face framed with lilies, and a little arbor where lovers have always plighted their troth. There's a cemetery, too, with beautiful raised tombs in it made of mellow carved marble, like the sarcophagi you see abroad. It's flanked with a memorial chalice that I put there, and it's inclosed with white flowers, and white blossoming trees. The snowdrops must be out by now, and the flowering quince, and the white flag—I really think that's the prettiest of all. In the wintertime when the carpet grass is touched with frost, it turns a sort of dusty pink that almost matches the house, and when you see all this in the sunset, it all seems part of the same rosy dream. The frost's gone now, so you'll have to wait till next winter for that and until next fall to see the sugar cane all royal purple, ready for grinding, and the cotton puffing out in big white balls. But everything else is at its very loveliest. Let's go down there next Sunday, Anna, and see it. Let's stop bickering with each other and hurting each other, the way we've been doing lately, and make love to each other again, in the moonlight."

Anna did not repulse him. She stood still, letting him rub his face against her cheek and clasp her waist closely with his arm. But for the second time that morning, the image of Olivier Fontaine rose insolently before her. If he went with her into this free and lovely garden, instead of seeing her in the stilted setting of his mother's drawing room, he might visualize her as she secretly longed to be seen—a chaste Diana, remote and imperious, but still a goddess, still desirable. Then he would not turn away from her slightingly; he would pursue her, vainly but eagerly— The vision became less and less unwelcome the longer she dwelt on it.

"Stop— You mustn't," she said, her thought of Olivier directing the words she spoke to Breck. Her voice was so unexpectedly warm that her husband was puzzled— If his caress really annoyed her, why did she talk to him in that way? Yet it was not like Anna to be coquettish— Wisely he waited a minute, and then, as she still had not withdrawn from him, he sensed that in some way she had been emotionally stirred and kissed her. She put her arms around his neck and clung to him briefly.

"There," she said at last, drawing away from him, but without brusqueness. "There— We really must stop, Breck. Think how silly we would feel if one of the servants came in and saw us— That was what I meant when I asked you not to. But you can be very sweet, you know, when you're in the mood— It's hard to say no to you. And you have made me see that garden, or at least to feel that I'd like to. I'd be glad to go down there with you some Sunday soon; perhaps, later on, when the place is in running order, we can ask a few of your friends down for a week end, and return their courtesies to us in that way. I'll write a note to Mrs. Fontaine suggesting the fifteenth for the dinner—shall I? And don't be worried—I'll thank her for the 'Southern perspiration' at the same time."

He opened the door for her and they went out together, smiling at each other, both pleased that a morning which had threatened to be tempestuous had, after all, turned out so pleasantly. Anna went to her desk and wrote to Mrs. Fontaine, still thinking of Olivier in the moonlight at Splendida. It was fortunate for her already stimulated state of mind that she did not guess her husband was thinking, quite as involuntarily, of Marie Céleste in the same setting.

CHAPTER 10

EVEN ANNA was ready to admit that, from the viewpoint of both appointment and gastronomy, Mrs. Fontaine's dinner left nothing to be desired. She was especially impressed with the enormous epergne which served as the central decoration for the table, formed like a miniature tree, with seven small silver cups concealed in the silver branches, overflowing with mimosa, narcissi and cyclamen, silver deer reclining at the base of the silver trunk, and silver rabbits pursuing each other around the miniature lake—a mirror spread with maidenhair—which encircled the whole. But the matching goblets and service plates of *repoussé* silver, the Sèvres plates ornamented with the court beauties of France, the *point de Venise* cloth and lace-edged napkins, all came in for their share of admiration.

In a general way, Breck also realized that all these things were valuable and beautiful, and he was gratified because Anna appreciated them; but his enthusiasm was far more stimulated by the crawfish bisque, the grilled pompano, the noble saddle of mutton and the incomparable wines, than by the sportive deer and simpering queens. He found Mrs. Fontaine, at whose right he sat, very "easy to look at." This was all he said to Anna afterwards, in attempting to describe her. But without analyzing the effect she gave, he knew that she was the type of woman whose fascination was ageless and on whom no man would ever look uncharmed. The candle-light enhanced her soft and delicate beauty; her sheer black dress lay in graceful folds over her white breasts and fell, in flowing lengths, away from her white arms. She was wearing quantities of diamonds, set in black onyx, and they sparkled whenever she moved her white fingers, her flexible wrists, or her slender throat; the rise and fall of her bosom were accentuated by them. She carried her forty years so lightly as to make them seem unbelievable; time, in touching her, had given her only increasing gentleness and increasing quietude.

Glancing from the mother to the daughter, he was aware of the same enchanting qualities. Céleste was again a vision in white; and though her shining hair was now piled high on her gracefully set head, this, somehow, made her look younger than ever, almost like a little girl "dressing up." She was seated halfway down the table, between two of her cousins, and it was only occasionally that she flashed him an arch, joyous glance. But he found himself waiting to catch her eye and acknowledge her friendly indication that he had been quickly accepted by the charmed circle to which she belonged. He recognized the breeding, style, and *savoir-faire* of the other women around him and enjoyed their company; but none of them had the irresistible allure of which he was becoming increasingly conscious in both Estelle Fontaine and Marie Céleste.

How was Anna making out with Olivier, he wondered idly, from time to time? Like most male Anglo-Saxons, though greatly admiring Latin women, he failed to find any fascination in Latin men, feeling that they lacked both mental and physical virility, and that the immaculate appearance they presented was only a sort of surface cleanliness, just as their beautiful manners were an undependable indication of basic decency in their attitude towards women. He would not have put it past Olivier, whose linen actually glistened, to wear the same underclothes for a week, and he doubted whether the handsome Creole could pull his own weight in any kind of a boat, while convinced that he would make an intrigue out of any situation, if he desired to do so. Breck felt rather sorry that Anna should be subjected to the society of such a spineless fop as the son of his peerless hostess seemed to be; and he was pleased with what seemed to him very good grace on his wife's part, under the circumstances. She looked very handsome herself, in her severe satin and well-set sapphires, with her fresh natural color, erect carriage, and smooth hair; and she was obviously making herself agreeable without apparent condescension, both to her host and to young Doctor Beal, who sat on her other side. Breck was proud of her personally, and prouder still to see how outstanding she was in such a distinguished setting. But he looked at Céleste oftener than he did at Anna, and as soon as possible after dinner, he sought her out, and stayed with her most of the time until Anna rose to give the signal for their departure.

"You had a good time, didn't you?" he said heartily, as they started home together through the fragrant darkness. (Even when she was in full evening dress, Anna did not overlook the merits of exercise, so they had not gone to the dinner in their car.) "I was a little worried about you at first, with that frog. But he came out of the daze, or whatever it was he was in the other day, pretty well, didn't he? Not that I'd say that he was hail-fellow-well-met, at that."

"Don't call him a frog, Breck. It's silly and vulgar to talk the way you do. I wish you'd stop. There's really a good deal of elegance to Olivier Fontaine's manner. And he's sophisticated, too, in his way. Not that he's particularly well-informed on the questions and events of the day. But then nobody here seems to know what's going on anywhere else in the world."

"Perhaps they don't want to be bothered with it. They've got a pretty nice world of their own."

"It's a very slow-moving one. Do you realize we were at the dinner table over two hours? The service was so slow that I began to think something must have broken down in the kitchen. But a dinner of eight courses is ridiculous anyway, and you know what I think of having six different kinds of alcoholic beverages."

"You aren't suggesting that Mrs. Fontaine impresses you as a dipsomaniac are you, Anna?" Breck asked jocosely.

"Don't be absurd. She is a museum piece though, isn't she? She took me upstairs while the cigars and port were going around, and she has just the sort of room you'd expect —rosewood furniture, a half tester lined with tufted satin on a huge carved bed with front posts that slide down into the legs, but can be raised as props for mosquito netting, and everything else in keeping— Even a marble-topped washstand with a rose-wreathed porcelain toilet set, though there's a perfectly good connecting bathroom. I did see one beautiful thing, though, on the dressing table—an oval-shaped silver hand mirror, set with brilliants— What's the matter Breck?"

"Nothing. It sounds like a Carnival favor. How is it marked?"

"Only with her initials and a date. January 6th, 1891, I think it was."

"The date of the Twelfth Night Revels!"

"Perhaps so. I haven't got these queer celebrations of theirs straightened out in my mind yet, and the only favors I ever saw were the silly little things we used to get at germans. But I believe I might be converted to Carnival, if you gave me anything like that mirror." She paused, giving Breck an opportunity for an appropriate response, but as he made none, she went on, "Well, as I was saying, I do think Mrs. Fontaine is a museum piece. Did I tell you that she said the other day she never went downstairs for three years, while her husband was sick? And now, when she does go out, it's in the same brougham and with the same horses that he bought for her, and the same coachman that he engaged for her. She doesn't even own an automobile, much less drive one! Olivier has a car of his own; but Céleste goes back and forth to school in a carriage, and a maid goes with her. How can a girl even learn to be independent if she's brought up like that? Now a nice brisk walk, morning and afternoon——"

"I have a notion Céleste won't ever need to be independent. I imagine someone will always be glad to look out for her."

"Yes, but think of the effect on *her*. You know perfectly well, Breck, that in this day and age girls ought to be self-reliant."

Breck made no immediate answer. He was still thinking about the oval mirror, framed in brilliants, that Anna had seen on Mrs. Fontaine's dressing table. In going through his father's papers, after Andy Breckenridge's death, he had seen a drawing for just such a design as she described, together with a jeweler's estimate, which came to a staggering sum. He knew a good deal about his father's prodigal habits, which Anna so often accused him of inheriting, and he also knew that a costly gift, tendered as a Carnival favor, did not necessarily have a special significance. But something restrained him from saying, "I'll have the mirror copied for you; nothing could be easier," when Anna, who rarely suggested or even welcomed presents, had hinted so broadly that here at last was one she coveted. He could not risk the questions that she would be sure to ask. He did not want her to know that it was his father who had given that mirror to Mrs. Fontaine, when she was still Estelle Lenoir, but already engaged to the man whom she married a little later, and that it had been cherished for more than twenty years. He was both bewildered and troubled because he knew it himself.

"I thought John Beal and his wife were very pleasant, didn't you?" he asked at length, rousing himself from his reflection and forcing himself to speak. "It's nice to know a reliable doctor personally. The Bairds and the Denises are nice, too. I understand the Bairds have a boy, Harold, just about Drew's age, and that the Beals and the Denises both have girls a little younger. Julia and Evelyn their names are, I think. None of them lives far from here. It'll be easy for the kids to get together."

"I thought you wanted to go to Splendida right away, and get ready for a house party."

"Well, we can ask them for the house party. Goodness knows there's enough room. The kids can play down there this spring and here after we get back in the fall. I don't see that there's anything complicated about that."

"I didn't know you had such a big party in mind. I thought you meant to ask just the Fontaines, and perhaps one extra man, so that we'd have an even number."

"I didn't have it all arithmetically arranged. But I do think it would be nice to have one couple with a child, or children, for Drew's sake. He's alone a lot. It's healthy for a youngster to have other kids to play with."

Anna had a moment of concern lest Breck might be about to reopen the question of an increase in their family, which, for some time, she had considered closed forever, and she feared that she had made a mistake in mentioning the mirror, which he might use as a bribe. However, to her relief, he did not pursue the subject, and she went on serenely, herself.

"Let's have the Beals then. As you say, it gives you a comfortable feeling to be in close touch with a good doctor and they seem very sensible. Probably their little girls will be very well brought up. I didn't care so much for the Bairds, and boys are so destructive—it's bad enough to have one of our own tearing everything to pieces around the house, without inviting trouble by getting in another."

"I didn't ask you to invite trouble. I asked you to invite the kid."

"Really, Breck, you do keep on saying the silliest things! Now I'll tell you who was the most interesting woman at the dinner, in my opinion. You haven't even mentioned her, but of course that's exactly like a man. Her husband evidently doesn't amount to much; but she's the first person I've met in New Orleans who seems to have some public spirit and some civic consciousness. I had quite a nice little talk with her and I found that she's just as interested in equal suffrage as I am. She said that there isn't a state in the Union where politics need purification more than they do here. Why, she told me that there's actually a definite area set aside in the French Quarter as a red-light district, and that prostitution flourishes under the protection of the police. It takes in thirty-eight blocks altogether. Isn't that appalling?"

"It's supposed to be one of the great sights of the South. Visitors come from far and wide to go down the line."

"Breck, it's bad enough to have you slangy and silly without having you ribald, too. If you're going to take that attitude about the most revolting evil in the world, I won't try to talk to you any more about it. But I've asked Mrs. Cutler to lunch with me day after tomorrow, so that we can continue our conversation. She says there are things she can tell me in confidence that will make my blood run cold. I hesitated to ask you to go out for fear you'd accuse me of shoving you aside. After what you just said though, I don't believe you'd mind having lunch at the Union Club, or whatever it's called."

"I wouldn't advise you to call it that publicly, in New Orleans, or anywhere else in the South for that matter. It's the Boston Club. But it wasn't named for your birthplace. It was named for a nice quiet gambling game called boston. That's how my grandfather happened to get the house we're living in—one of his cronies at the Boston Club lost it to him in the course of a genial evening. I'm perfectly willing to lunch there, as often as you like—especially when Mrs. Cutler's lunching with you. But I wouldn't voluntarily contribute to anything, Anna, that would make your blood run any colder than it does already. It might reach the freezing point."

Breck had left the Fontaines' house with the comfortable feeling characteristic of the average normal man who has dined well, in congenial company, and who has found any one or more women unusually charming, without finding any one of them excessively disturbing. But during the short walk home, he had become increasingly irritated. Everything Anna said seemed to rub him the wrong way. They finished their walk in silence, with resentfulness on her part, annoyance on his. When he reached for his latchkey, she put out a detaining hand.

"Please ring, Breck. I've told Roscoe that he must stay on duty until we get in. I can't stand this habit Southern servants have of scurrying off to their own little shanties the minute their work is done—if you can call it being done! I expect him to come to the door, whatever hour we get home."

Without answering, Breck pressed the doorbell. There was no response. He rang three times, with the same result. Then he looked at Anna inquiringly.

"He's either gone home, after all, or else he's so sound asleep that he'll never hear us. Do you want me to go on ringing all night, or are you willing that I should open the door myself, so that we can get to bed?"

"I'm willing that you should open the door, of course. But I expect you to discharge Roscoe the first thing in the morning."

"He wouldn't understand what I was talking about. He was born at Splendida, he's worked for the Breckenridges all his life. He just takes it for granted that he belongs. I'm not equal to disillusioning him. You'd better try it yourself, Anna."

Breck closed the door after them and bolted it. The night was so mild that he had gone to the dinner bareheaded and without an overcoat, and he was thankful that at least Anna could not reproach him for flinging down his topper and his white scarf and his Chesterfield on the hall settee, as he was very apt to do when there was no one at hand to take things from him, instead of hanging them up, neatly, himself. Then he moved towards the library, where the lights were still burning.

"I didn't look at the evening papers before we went out," he said. "I think that perhaps I'd better, before I go to bed, or you'll be telling me pretty soon that I don't know what's going on in the world any more than other Orleanians. Good night. I hope you get a good rest."

An hour later, he went out on the gallery and looked moodily, almost unseeingly, over the lawn towards the flowering shrubs and graceful trees. The fragrance of the sweet olive and the yellow jasmine came to him in waves, and the shadow of their branches, patterned by moonlight, lay dark over the bright grass. For a moment he stood still, hesitating. Then he walked down the path and into the deserted street.

He had no set purpose. He had not meant to go anywhere, when he stepped out on the gallery. He had not been able to put the jewelled mirror out of his mind. He had always wondered why he felt such extraordinary tenderness towards Mrs. Fontaine; now he began to wonder if the feeling might not be inherited. Phrases from a letter he had written years before and forgotten until now floated back into his consciousness: "Sometimes I've sort of felt halfway as if I belonged to you, or might have, if I'd had a fair chance. I admired my stepmother, but I didn't really love her, and I believe that down deep in his heart Father didn't either. I think he loved someone else. He as good as told me so once." If his father had loved Estelle Lenoir, it was inconceivable that she should not have returned his devotion; Andy Breckenridge had been irresistible. Then why had they never married? Why had they both married others, with whom they were not in love?

The luminous night gave no answer to his questions; and now that it had tempted him to wander out into its inescapable fragrance and beauty, he still lacked any sense of direction. But soon he realized that he was retracing his steps over the ground which he had crossed such a short time before. Almost before he knew it, he had reached the Fontaines' house again.

The front of it was in darkness. But lights still shone from some of the side windows, and the sound of music floated through them. He stopped and listened.

It was *Z'Amour Marianne*, the same song that Céleste had been singing when she came into the dim drawing room the day of his first call—the plaint of the poor planter whose sugar crop had been destroyed, and whose mercenary mistress was taunting him with its loss. The mocking melody floated out to meet Breck again now:

> "*Toutes mes cannes sont brulées, Marianne,*
> *Toutes mes cannes sont brulées, Marianne*
> *Toutes mes cannes sont brulées,*
> *Ma récolte est flambée!*
> *Si cannes à vous brulées, Michiéla,*
> *Si cannes à vous brulées, Michiéla*
> *Si cannes à vous brulées,*
> *L'amour à vous flambé!*"

Breck opened and closed the garden gate quietly; afterwards, supporting himself against it, he took off first one shoe and then the other. He did not think he would make any noise when he trod on the soft grass, even if he had them on, but he wanted to be sure he was unheard. He crept cautiously forward over the lawn, skirting the house. When he reached the clump of shrubbery surrounding the music room, he stopped. He could see Céleste sitting at the piano, with the light from a tall lamp streaming down over her bronze-colored hair and her white neck and arms. The rest of the room was in darkness. He stepped back among the bamboos and waited.

He did not have to wait long. Céleste had finished singing *Z'Amour Marianne* while he was crossing the lawn, and then for a few moments she ran her fingers more or less aimlessly over the keys. Now she began to sing again, this time the West Indian lament of a Negro lover sympathizing with the grief felt by his quadroon sweetheart because her rival had supplanted her in the affections of her white master:

> "*Pov' piti' Momzel Zizi!*
> *Pov' piti' Momzel Zizi!*
> *Pov' piti' Momzel Zizi!*
> *Li gagnin bobo, bobo, bobo*
> *Li gagnin bobo dans coeur a li!*
> *Z'autres qu'a di moin ça yo bonheur;*
> *Et moin va di, ça yo peine;*
> *D'amour quand porte la chaine,*
> *Adieu, courri tout bonheur!*
>
> *Pov' piti' Momzel Zizi!*
> *Pov' piti' Momzel Zizi!*
> *Pov' piti' Momzel Zizi!*"

She went on from one of the old familiar love songs to another, *Ah Suzette, Chère—Clémentine—Suzanne, Suzanne, Suzanne, Jolie Femme!* Breck knew them all and revelled in them all. When he was a little boy, his mammy had sung them to him as she fed him and bathed him and rocked him to sleep. There had been others, too, more rollicking in character, and one, *En avant, Grenadiers!* with a swift military swing. He hoped that Céleste would interpolate that among the love songs, and she did. Unconsciously he began to hum it with her, and when he stopped, she stopped too, and for a moment there was a silence unbroken even by random chords. Then she began to sing again, and this time it was a song he had never heard:

> *"Je suis la délaissée*
> *Qui pleure nuit et jour*
> *Celui qui m'a trompée*
> *Etait mon seul amour.*
>
> *J'avais seize ans à peine*
> *Belle comme une fleur*
> *Il a fallu qu'il vienne*
> *Empoisonner mon coeur."*

The final notes trailed softly off into further silence. Céleste sat still for a moment. Then she rose, and with one hand resting lightly on the keys, inclined her head, as if bowing to an unseen audience. After making two of these little bows, she curtsied deeply, and when she straightened up again, she turned and walked slowly from the room, switching off the one remaining light that had shone over her, and leaving the place in darkness. Breck continued to stand quietly among the bamboos for a long time. But there was no further sound and no light coming from the house anywhere. He slipped on his shoes again, went out of the garden as noiselessly as he had entered it, and walked slowly down the street towards his own house. When he had closed and bolted the door for the second time, he went still more slowly up the stairs, and after a moment's hesitation, turned the knob of the door leading not into his own room, but into Drew's.

Anna had never been willing that the little boy should have a mammy. The professional nurse, who had assisted the famous specialist in bringing him into the world, had continued to care for him until he was nearly two; then he had been turned over to an equally clean, capable, and impersonal English "Nana." Nana still had charge of him, occupying a small room situated near to his large sunny nursery, but without an adjoining door, for Anna did not approve of having anyone sleep in the same room with a child, or in accustoming one to call constantly for drinks of water and other superfluities during the night. Breck was reasonably sure that if he went in and sat down by his little son, no one would be the wiser.

He was not mistaken. He drew up a chair to the side of the crib and seated himself cautiously. Enough light filtered into the room from the open window for him to see, dimly, and as his eyes became accustomed to the obscurity, he could make out the contour of Drew's dark, tousled head and red, rounded cheeks. He was clutching a toy animal, made of wood. Anna would not allow him to sleep with a woolly one, because she considered it unsanitary; but Breck, while admitting that the wooden one was more easily washed, often worried lest the little boy might be bruised by it in his sleep, though he had never said so, for fear that such an expression on his part might deprive the child of any kind of a pet, a live dog having been ruled out from the beginning. Now he could not resist the temptation of moving the toy animal slightly, so that the ridge of its back should not be pressed against Drew's chest. Gently as he touched it, the child stirred, sleepily, tightened his hold on the animal, and turned over. Breck bent down and kissed him.

"Don't worry, old man, I wasn't going to take it away from you," he whispered reassuringly, patting the child's back and drawing the covers more closely around him. Then in a still lower voice he muttered. "I hope you won't have to go on hugging wood forever, though. And I hope you'll have more sense than your father and your grandfather. I hope you won't marry while you're still a kid yourself. I hope you'll wait until you know what it's all about. No matter how you amuse yourself in the meantime. If I'm still alive when you're twenty-one, I'll see you don't lack for amusement. We'll do things together. We'll be pals. But I'll keep a shotgun handy for the female of the species. That is, the marrying kind——"

He fell asleep himself, with his arms still folded over Drew's crib. His dreams were very troubled. He thought he saw a young and lovely girl, whom he took at first for Estelle

Lenoir, gazing into a jewelled mirror, and a man, whom he took at first to be his father, looking over her shoulder, so that their joyous faces were framed together. But when he looked more closely, he suddenly realized that the girl was Marie Céleste, and that instead of being happy, she was crying bitterly, and that he was the man, and instead of being triumphant, he was thwarted. He waked, shivering, and went, still shivering, into his own room. He did not sleep any more that night.

CHAPTER 11

THE NEXT afternoon, when Breck returned from the Boston Club, he found Anna in an unusually amiable mood. She had talked severely to Roscoe, who had given her a plausible alibi for his absence, and who had promised her that he would never be so remiss again; she was sure she had impressed him with the fact that she would not tolerate any further slackness, and he had served luncheon impeccably; Mrs. Charles Cutler had complimented her on her butler. Her guest had also proved a godsend by telling her that it was perfectly possible to play golf in New Orleans; there was a very good course, it seemed, at the Bayou St. John Golf Club. Anna did not see why Breck had not mentioned this himself.

"I'm sorry, Anna. I honestly didn't think of it. No one was golf-conscious when I left here fourteen years ago, and I never thought of Bayou St. John except in connection with the Fontaine and Rutledge places. I'll be glad to go down there with you, whenever you like. I'm afraid I'll never be much good at golf myself. But I can visit with Aunt Clarisse and Uncle Napier while you play, and Drew can chase around the grounds. There are no children just his age there now, but Napier Junior and his wife, who've taken over the old customhouse, have a baby boy, Gail, and I believe the eldest daughter, Louise, is expecting, so there'll be another kid there before long— These Creoles marry young and they're usually pretty prolific. Drew probably would enjoy the baby, and, anyway, he'd enjoy the place— It's a happy hunting ground for youngsters as I well remember, myself. You might be interested in seeing Aunt Clarisse make some of her celebrated violet syrup, or even helping her with it, if you had time for that as well as golf. She's been putting it up for years and she's developed it to a fine art."

Anna was not especially intrigued with the idea of violet syrup, but she was still further mollified by Breck's co-operative attitude regarding Bayou St. John generally, and she continued to talk about her visit with Mrs. Cutler in a pleased way. Apparently the two young women had derived mutual satisfaction from their conference. Anna thought she understood the terrible local situation, as far as both suffrage and prostitution were concerned, fairly well now, she said; but she wanted to study and investigate it in detail before she took any definite action; when she had done this, a committee would be formed, of which Mrs. Cutler would be the chairman, but in which she, Anna, would actually be the ruling spirit. They had not decided on the name of this committee because it was rather hard to think of one that would not be confusing, in view of their dual purpose of securing votes for women and suppressing the red-light district. They had tried out one or two, and the trouble was that it was hard to tell from these which item was to be secured and which was to be suppressed. Well, Breck did not need to laugh—Perhaps they would end by forming two committees. Now that the cause of suffrage had been so stimulated by the triumphal march of "General" Rosalie Jones and her "army" from New York to Washington, and by the splendid sight which she presented, astride a white charger, at the head of her "troops," the moment was propitious to lift high the banner of women's rights, even in New Orleans. Breck forebore from mentioning the headlines which succeeded those—to which Anna proudly pointed—stating that "women's beauty, grace and art bewilder the Capital" and that "miles of fluttering femininity present entrancing suffrage appeal." There were others, to which Anna did not point, saying that three thousand women had fought their way up Pennsylvania Avenue, that troops from Fort Myer had been called out to restore order and take charge of demonstrations that were "little less than a riot," that more than two hundred persons were crushed or trampled and that large numbers of these had been taken to the Emergency Hospital. He was too pleased by the general turn events had taken to run the risk of upsetting anything now, and his reticence was rewarded. Presently Anna, bridling a little but still exuding satisfaction, went on that what she had started to say, when he interrupted her in such a ribald manner, was that she thought that this might be as good a time as any to go up to Splendida, because she could take with her the material Mrs. Cutler had given her, and study it there at her leisure. At the same time, she could supervise getting the place in order. She supposed it must be in deplorable condition, after so many years of neglect.

"I don't think it's been neglected, Anna. Marcy Yates, the overseer, is a very decent sort, intelligent and honest and industrious. He sends me regular statements and very careful accounts. The place has prospered all the time he's had complete responsibility for it, ever since my father's death. And the caretaker's a riot. Just wait until you see her. Her name is Shoog and she weighs about three hundred and fifty. But she gets around, at that."

"Shoog!"

"I suppose it must be an abbreviation for Sugar. I don't know. I never heard what her real name was, and she's been there ever since I can remember. She waddles around, prattling as she goes. She never stops talking except to catch her breath."

"She isn't very different from most of the women I've seen in the South then," Anna remarked sarcastically. "Does she do any work at all, between her waddling and her prattling?"

"Well, she makes the best pralines I ever ate. And somebody keeps the house aired and cleaned. Maybe she just supervises her little slavies. She's got a whole flock of dusky daughters, as I remember it. Anyway, I think you'll find the place in better order than you expect. If we go down to-morrow——"

"Marie Céleste Fontaine dropped in on her way home from school to invite us to have dinner tomorrow evening with Olivier and herself, and to go to see 'St. Joseph's altars' afterwards. She told me her mother was very broad-minded about letting her dine out in public like that. It seems it's the exception rather than the rule for young girls to do so here, even with a married couple and a member of her own family for chaperones. Antediluvian, isn't it? And she said this would be *Mi-Carême,* and that there was always a very interesting celebration. Did you ever hear of it?"

"Of course I have. We always used to make a tour of the Italian Quarter on St. Joseph's Evening, when I was a youngster, to see the altars. Well, that was darned thoughtful of her, wasn't it? Did you say we'd go?"

"Yes. Provided you wanted to. I was careful not to commit you to anything, Breck."

"But gosh, I'd like to be committed to anything that's as much fun as that is. And we could go up to Splendida the next day, or even the day after. I don't see why we couldn't be ready to have a house party a week from Sunday even then. Father used to have them all the time, at a moment's notice, or none at all."

"I don't like to do things that way. I like to make careful preparations. And I like to have a program and keep to it. But day after tomorrow will be all right in this case."

Breck had already had considerable experience with Anna's preparations and programs, and he was secretly somewhat surprised that her present schedule was sufficiently elastic to allow her to act so spontaneously as far as St. Joseph's altars were concerned; but he was also very much pleased, and his spirits continued to mount throughout the next twenty-four hours. By the time Olivier and Marie Céleste called for Anna and himself, in Olivier's elegant red-cushioned, white-bodied car, he was in holiday mood. This suffered a slight setback when Olivier automatically assisted Anna into the back seat beside Marie Céleste. Breck had taken it for granted that Anna would sit beside Olivier, leaving himself and Marie Céleste free to talk uninterruptedly about music and flowers and other things that interested her, all the way down town. He had forgotten that according to standardized etiquette, gentlemen invariably rode together in the front of an equipage and ladies in the back. But in spite of his disappointment, he made himself very agreeable to Olivier, encouraging him to talk about his own special interests, and asking him general questions about racing and other sports in and around New Orleans.

Olivier was not especially responsive. It appeared that he had not yet decided on a profession, though he might eventually try to follow in the footsteps of his Grandfather Lenoir by studying law. For the moment, he was taking a year off, as he had found the academic course which he finished at Tulane the previous spring very fatiguing. He was not especially interested in sports either. He rode, but he did not race or hunt; he did not care at all for yachting and swimming, though his cousins, the Rutledges, spent half their

time on the water and the other half in it, when they were
left to themselves. If Breck liked that sort of thing, Napier
Junior and his brother Charles would be only too delighted
to see that he got all he wanted of it.

Breck thanked Olivier, casually mentioned his own preference for horses, in spite of the rowing he had done at college, and tried his host out on politics, local and national,
without getting any further than he had on the other subjects. He was far too friendly and even tempered by nature to
be disposed towards a critical attitude, but he could not help
feeling increasingly that Olivier was shallow, and intract-
able despite his languor, perhaps as a result of having passed
his most formative years uncontrolled by his invalid father,
while indulged and adored by his gentle mother. Breck remembered hearing a middle-aged spinster, whose brother had
been showered with all the advantages she lacked, exclaim
with some feeling, "If I'm ever reincarnated, I don't care
whether I have riches or fame or position, or anything like
that. All I ask is to be born the only son of a Southern
mother!" In the case of the Fontaines, the daughter had certainly been adored and indulged as much as the son, but it
had affected her differently. She returned her mother's devotion, instead of profiting by it; and she had expanded and
developed, under fondness and fostering care, in the same
way that the flowers she loved so much expanded and developed in balmy air and bright sunshine. She was indeed a
true child of the Garden District. Breck turned and glanced
back at her now; she was talking artlessly and affectionately
to Anna; and if she were troubled by the lack of response
which she, in her turn, was receiving, she did not show it.

She continued to indicate and explain the points of interest
along the way; the monument in Margaret Place, which was
the first statue erected to a woman in the United States, and
that an unlettered woman who had been very poor and humble, keeping first a dairy and then a bakery, but showing such
loving-kindness towards little children and such wisdom in
their care, that her honored name had become a byword for
goodness and generosity; Céleste's other favorite among
monuments, the statue to General Lee in the Circle com-
memorating him, placed, as she said, "facing the North because he had never turned his back on it." The Post Office,
for which she did not care much, but which she thought Anna
might admire, because it had been built by a Boston archi-

tect, the celebrated Mr. Richardson. The St. Charles Hotel, originally designed by Gallier, the French architect whose work she admired more than she did Mr. Richardson's, and which was the place visiting celebrities generally stayed, now that the beautiful old St. Louis was so overrun with rats. The enormous width of Canal Street, which had once really been a canal, dividing the old part of the city from the new, and which had then become a fashionable residential avenue; it was too bad stores had taken it over now——

None of these sights, except Mr. Richardson's Post Office, seemed to impress Anna greatly, so Céleste turned to Carnival as a topic of conversation. It was a shame Breck and Anna had not reached New Orleans before Mardi Gras, everyone had had such a good time. Of course it had not been as exciting as the occasions when General "Joe" Wheeler and Miss Alice Roosevelt had been guests of the Boston Club, of which everyone still talked. But then, Carnival was always wonderful; everyone always had a good time, especially on Mardi Gras. And as she would be coming out herself next year, she would be able to do more for Anna then, so perhaps, after all, it was just as well that there had been a delay, and that the conditions under which she would have her first impressions could be doubly propitious. Céleste's mother was hoping that she would be chosen Queen of the Pacifici, because Mamma had been Queen at the first Ball they had ever had, and she cherished a special sentiment for their "Krewe." Secretly Céleste would much rather be Queen of Comus, and it was very seldom a girl was chosen for both, though such a thing had happened. But she would not mention her preference for the world, for fear of hurting Mamma's feelings. Mamma did not care so much for Comus, for some reason, although her great friend, Amélie Aldigé, who had been Queen of Momus the same year Mamma had been queen of the Pacifici, had been a Maid in the Comus Court.

Céleste was still talking to Anna about Carnival when Olivier brought his car smoothly to a stop in front of a small restaurant on Bourbon Street with the name, Galatoire, inconspicuously displayed in front of it. It had been opened only a few years before, he said: some Boston Club members had patronized it almost by chance when it was only a tiny, two-table café, hidden away on a side street, and finding it excellent, had underwritten its expansion; it was al-

ready considered one of the best in the Quarter. The drinks
and dishes that appeared as soon as the party was seated
made its reputation easy to understand; these were served
with a Gallic flourish by a mustachioed waiter, assisted by
a white-aproned *sommelier,* and it was not long before the
proprietor himself came forward to pay his respects, to inquire if everything was to his visitors' liking, and to ask
them to accept a drink on the house. Olivier was evidently
not only a good patron, in a financial sense, but a natural
gourmet, and as such, doubly welcome in a French establishment. Breck, though he recognized and enjoyed good food,
thought it was slightly silly to lay quite so much stress on
the temperature of a wine and the seasoning of a sauce, and
decided that he should have tried to talk to Olivier about
fresh flaked crab and Haut Sauterne instead of politics and
professions. But he continued to make himself thoroughly
agreeable, and Olivier, as the excellent fare began to take
effect, grew increasingly amiable himself. The little dinner
passed off triumphantly.

It would be easier to walk now than to keep getting in and
out of the car and parking it on the narrow streets, Olivier
explained, as they finally rose from the table. None of the
places they were going were far from Galatoire's or from
each other. As they stepped out into the street, he offered his
arm to Anna with a brief little bow; the lights were inadequate, he said, and the pavements very bad; would she honor
him by letting him assist her? She took the offered arm
rather self-consciously; but Marie Céleste slipped her warm
little hand spontaneously into Breck's, and curled her fingers
around his.

"We'll let Olivier lead, with Anna, and we'll follow," she
said. "Because Olivier knows the way and you don't, do you?
This is fun, isn't it?"

"I'll say it's fun. I'm having the time of my life."

He said this heartily. But the streets were certainly very
dark and also very dirty. They were filled with tattered and
filthy beggars, too, many of these hideously malformed, whining and worming their way through the crowds, and lying in
wait for the holidaymakers that came out of bars and restaurants. Breck felt his stomach turn over at the sight of some
of them, and tried to hurry Marie Céleste past them quickly,
so that she would not see as much as he did. The wretched
creatures were not only poverty-ridden, they were disease-

ridden, too; there were countless inebriates and drug addicts and perverts among them. He took one coin after another out of his pocket and tossed it in the direction of a mendicant to cut short his wail and forestall the hideous chance that any of them might put his foul hands on Marie Céleste and try to detain her. He had forgotten this blemishing aspect of New Orleans life, or he had been too young to notice it, before. He hoped Marie Céleste would not notice it now, though he knew that Anna would, and that she would speak to him about it the next day, almost as if he were responsible for it, if she did not actually make it a subject of conversation the next time they stopped. But glancing ahead, he could tell she was not talking about it at present. Even in the dim light he saw the animated expression of her face as she turned to Olivier, and in the midst of the confusion he could hear, with relief, the pleasant expression of her voice.

"We're almost to Montefiori's, the first place Olivier planned to stop," Céleste was saying. "It's a very good grocery store, opened since you left here. Mamma gets all her best cheeses from there. And the proprietor is very devout. He's gone to Mass every day for years, and believes he's under the special protection of St. Joseph. He always has a splendid display; I'm sure you'll admire it. We go into his shop first, and pass down a narrow aisle beside the counter. You'll see some porcelain vases, shaped like hands, as soon as you go in, with round holes in the palms. You must put a coin in one of those and make a wish. Then Montefiori or his wife or perhaps his daughter will give you a lucky bean to keep and tell you to take your choice between the lighted candles standing on the counter. You may call any one of them yours, though of course you leave it where it is. It will burn for nine hours, and after that your wish will come true."

"No matter what kind of a wish I make?"

"Well, of course you would not make an evil wish. Even a wicked man would not do that on St. Joseph's Eve. And I am sure you would not do so at any time."

She pressed his hand, warmly, as if to show her confidence in his character, and then detached her fingers from his, as he and she slid, single file, into the entrance of the grocery store. The narrow aisle was very crowded, and it was impossible for them to stand side by side any longer, or to move fast. But Breck could see the china hand of which Marie Céleste had spoken, shining in the flickering light of the candles that stood beyond them, and hear the sonorous voice of a powerful, swarthy man stationed behind the counter, who kept saying over and over again, in a deep monotone, "Put your offering in the hand of God. Put your offering in the hand of God. Take your bean and choose your candle and make your wish. Take your bean and choose your candle and make your wish."

Breck had given away so many coins to beggars that when he felt for another he could not find one. He took a dollar from his billfold, and creased it into as small a space as possible; but he had to stop and squeeze it before it would go into the round hole, and this held up the crowd. He knew that Anna would tell him later that he had made himself conspicuous, and he was truly sorry to have appeared showy. There were no tourists among the crowds, and very few persons who gave the effect of being in comfortable circumstances. Most of the people in the grocery store were obviously very poor, the men wearing soiled shirts open at the neck, the women with shawls over their heads and babies in their arms. There were groups of children, too, flocking together, and talking to each other excitedly in Italian. The children were putting only pennies in "the hand of God," the shirt-sleeved men and shawled women nickels and dimes. Breck was relieved when he saw a rapt-looking boy and girl, more prosperous in appearance than the others and obviously deeply in love, follow his example by folding a dollar bill and pushing it into the round hole, helping each other to do so.

"What do you suppose they are wishing?" Marie Céleste whispered to him.

"It isn't hard to guess. There's only one thing on earth that would be worth that much to them."

"But you put in a dollar, too!"

"Because I didn't have anything smaller left. But as far as that goes, how do you know I wasn't wishing for the same thing?"

"Because you couldn't be. Not if I understand what you mean. You're married already!"

"Well, don't worry about my wish. Tell me about yours."

"Oh, I couldn't do that! If I did, it wouldn't come true. It was just a silly little wish, anyhow. Come, we must get through this crowd and into the back room. Anna and Olivier are way ahead of us."

She pressed forward again, and then suddenly stopped, stifling a small cry. In her haste she had collided with a young girl coming from the opposite direction, and as she looked up, with a courteous murmur of apology, she saw that she was confronted with an image of herself. If she had been looking into her own mirror, the impression of a reflection could not have been more complete. The other girl was equally startled. They stared at each other, first a little frightened and then completely fascinated. But it was for only an instant. Almost immediately the man who was with the strange girl gently but impellingly drew her forward. Céleste, still staring after her double, saw the man's face also and cried out again.

"Why Uncle Octave!" she exclaimed. "Are you touring St. Joseph's altars, too? Won't you stop and join our party? You and—and——"

She had no idea how to finish her sentence. The identity of her double was still a deep mystery to her. This did not trouble her, as she took it for granted that her uncle would instantly enlighten her, and she was confident that the explanation would intrigue her. But he answered her almost brusquely, over his shoulder, still propelling the girl in front of him.

"Sorry, Céleste, but I've got to get along. I'm in a big hurry right now. Hello, Breck! Glad to see you again."

He was gone and the girl with him. Céleste looked hopefully up at Breck for the explanation her uncle had withheld.

"Breck, did you see that girl? I mean, did you see how much she looked like me? It was uncanny."

"I don't know. I've heard that we all have doubles in this world. Probably it's true. We just don't run into them often, that's all."

"But how did she happen to be with Uncle Octave? And why didn't he stop, at least long enough to introduce us to each other?"

"He probably was in a hurry, just as he said. Don't worry about it, Céleste. We ought to hurry ourselves, oughtn't we, to catch up with Anna and Olivier? You reminded me quite a while ago that they were way ahead of us. We don't want to get permanently separated from them."

Céleste was not satisfied, and for a moment more she showed it. But the occasion was too exhilarating for her to be downcast or distressed for long. The room back of the shop presented an even more extraordinary appearance than the shop, itself. It was papered entirely in religious chromos, gaudy in coloring and lurid in character, and it was almost completely filled with an enormous table, only a narrow passageway being left around it. At one end of the table was erected a small shrine, enclosing a statue of St. Joseph and encircled with lighted candles and china figurines. But the rest of the table was laden with dishes heaped high with foodstuffs. There were raw fruits and raw vegetables of every description, bundles of uncooked macaroni, pyramids of homemade dough, pistachio nuts and pecans. There were stuffed eggs and stuffed artichokes. There were crabs and crawfish and shrimps. There were great round loaves of bread and bread twisted into the form of staffs and crosses. There were small cakes stuffed with figs, and large cakes frosted with chocolate and inscribed with the name of St. Joseph. Breck joined in Céleste's delighted investigation of these remarkable delicacies; but Anna, who had never before seen so much food, of so many different kinds, on display all at once, was bothered and bewildered by it. Raising her voice, so that she could be heard above the din, she asked Olivier questions about it.

"I don't understand what all this means."

"Only that at *Mi-Carême*, the middle of Lent, it has long been customary to have a break in fasting and some sort of a celebration. The feast of St. Joseph comes at just the right time to connect the celebration with his name."

"But it's terribly extravagant to waste all this food!"

"The Italians save money for months beforehand to adorn St. Joseph's altars when the time comes. And the food won't be wasted. Tomorrow some little orphans, recommended by their teachers for good behavior and good scholarship, will be brought in by a priest and urged to eat all they want of it. After they've had their fill, the general public will be invited. Many a man will go away stuffed tomorrow, who's been hungry a long time."

"But that fish will be spoiled by morning in this heat! It has a strong smell already. And that dough will turn sour, and those bananas will get soft. I'm sure the orphans will all have ptomaine poisoning. It would be so much better to provide a proper fund for them, so that they'd have plain, wholesome food throughout the year, than to let them gorge themselves like that, just once, and suffer from malnutrition all the rest of the time. I can't see any sound sense to it, much less any true charity."

Olivier shrugged his shoulders slightly. He disliked the effort of arguing, under any circumstances, and he did not propose to be led into a serious discussion when he had gone out for an evening's enjoyment. His manner became detached, as it had been when Anna first met him, and his ennui was evident as he answered.

"If the celebration doesn't interest you, perhaps you would rather go home. After all, these displays are very much alike. When you've seen one, you've seen them all."

"Olivier, how can you say such a thing! They're not in the least alike. Angelo's, for instance, is as different as possible from Montefiori's. I'm sure Anna wants to go to Angelo's at least, and have some *spumone*, before we start home."

"Of course she does. And so do I— Come on, Anna, we're going to Angelo's. And then we should show her two or three of the smaller, simpler displays, too, don't you think so, Céleste?"

Anna was not at all pleased at the turn things had taken. She resented Olivier's obvious reluctance to concern himself seriously with her theories of philanthropy; but she resented just as much having a little chit like Céleste speak so confidently for her, and having her own husband close a question without consulting her. However, she was far from being ready to go home. She had really enjoyed the dinner at Galatoire's very much, and she was confident that before the evening was over she would extract still more enjoyment from the outing. She gave Breck a withering look, which he did not even see, and then she permitted Olivier to escort her expertly from the grocery store.

The Italian ice-cream parlor, where he guided them next, was, as Céleste had said, entirely different in character from Montefiori's. At this second stopping place, they were confronted by the altar erected in honor of St. Joseph as soon as they entered the door, the little tin tables, which ordinarily occupied the space, having been pushed close together at one side, together with a small stringed orchestra, which was literally pressed against the wall. The altar, which was surmounted by a canopy of azure silk and silver tissue, was decorated with large vases filled with Easter lilies, and was more elaborate in every way than the first one they had seen. The candles which illuminated it were very tall, tied with ribbons, and ornamented with various designs of flowers and figures in color; three were grouped together to represent the Trinity. A fine linen cloth, beautifully embroidered, covered the immense table where the various viands were spread forth, and these reached a degree of ornamentation that was staggering. Some of the cakes were in the shape of twinkling stars, others represented the Sacred Heart. The *pièce de résistance*, which stood at the front of the table, in the center, was an immense five-tiered cake, covered with dark yellow frosting of mysterious composition, and ornamented with bead-like bits of red and green candy. It was surmounted by a group of white marble statuettes, representing St. Joseph and the Virgin Mary with the Christ Child between them. Most of the people tumbling into the ice-cream parlor fell on their knees in front of this cake, before scrambling and seeking places at the crowded tin tables. Anna drew back in genuine revulsion of spirit.

"It's sacrilegious," she said shortly. "It's simply appalling —kneeling down to a cake!"

Breck knew by the tone of her voice that she was angry, and he had good reason to dread Anna's anger. She very seldom lost her temper; but when she did, all her characteristic self-control was engulfed in her rage. She became another person, violent, hysterical, irrational, and she was quite capable of making a public scene. But Céleste, who was unaware of this, was quite undisturbed. She tried to reason with Anna gently.

"Why, Anna, they are not kneeling down to a cake! They're kneeling before the Blessed Virgin and Her Most Chaste Spouse and Our Dear Lord, who are gracing their feast. It is natural and lovely for them to do so. It makes me want to do it myself."

Céleste had actually knelt herself before she had finished speaking, crossing herself and closing her eyes, entirely without self-consciousness. Anna could see her lips moving in prayer. In Boston, the only Catholics with whom she, herself, had ever come in contact were her mother's Irish servants, who upset the household by their propensity for going to early Mass, and the immigrants who swarmed along the "wrong" side of Beacon Hill, where there was a clinic in which she and her friends had spasmodically volunteered for work. It had been quite a fad at one time, but it had been short-lived. She had also heard her father speaking of all the most corrupt politicians in town as Catholics, in a way that allied their corruption with their religion. In a vague way, she knew that there were Catholic schools and Catholic colleges in the city, but she had never known anyone who went to these, and it had not occurred to her that a person who was indubitably an aristocrat might also be a Catholic; now it slowly dawned on her that not only Céleste, but Olivier, their mother, aunts, uncles and cousins, and, indeed, almost everyone she had met socially in New Orleans came into that startling category. It was a shock to her. It was also a shock to see Céleste kneeling down on a floor which Anna suspected was very dirty, amidst a crowd concerning whose lack of cleanliness there could be no possible question.

"Please get up, Céleste!" she said in a peremptory voice. Céleste shook her head, showing that she had heard Anna, but also showing that she did not intend to move until she had finished her spontaneous devotions in her own way. Anna and Breck and Olivier stood behind her, waiting for her to rise, Anna with rapidly mounting discomfiture, Olivier with indifference, and Breck with a strange, disturbing thrill. At last Céleste crossed herself again, rose with the same ease and grace that she had shown in kneeling, and looked eagerly about her.

"I prayed for the same thing I wished for," she said. "Now, I want some *spumone*. There's no place in New Orleans where it's as good as it is here. Do you suppose there's any possible chance of getting a table?"

"Of course we can get a table. There's an international method of persuasion that I've found infallible."

Though Breck's loose silver was gone, there were still plenty of dollars in his billfold. He extracted another of these, unobtrusively, and laid a detaining hand on the arm of a hurrying waiter, speaking to him in a low voice at the same time. The waiter instantly paused, and almost immediately afterwards a table miraculously became vacant. Céleste sat down and looked up at Breck with admiration.

"You did that beautifully," she said. "Thank you so much. Tell the waiter we all want *spumone*, won't you?"

Breck nodded. He was feeling inexplicably happy, but it was hard to make himself heard. Everyone in the room was talking, and the little orchestra was playing. Breck thought he recognized the tune as an aria from *Rigoletto*. Céleste evidently recognized it, too, for she began to hum it under her breath. Soon half the Italians in the room were humming, and before long several of them had begun to sing. Anna and Olivier were still standing, Anna because she thought her attitude might indicate her displeasure, Olivier because his code of civility would not permit him to sit down until she did. But Breck, forgetful of such a convention, slipped thoughtlessly into the chair beside Céleste as soon as he had given their order. Under cover of the music, she leaned over and whispered to him.

"You love music, just the way I do, don't you?" she asked.

"I don't know. I never thought much about it."

"But if you don't," she persisted, "what made you come back to the garden the other night and listen to my singing?"

He drew a deep breath and moved nearer to her. Against the edge of the chair, he could feel the warmth of her presence, close to his own.

"What made you go on singing?" he asked. "After you knew I was there?"

CHAPTER 12

ANNA'S "PROGRAM" called for departure from New Orleans on a Thursday at quarter before ten in the morning. This would enable her to see that everything was in order at the Prytania Street house before she left it, and still get to Splendida in time for dinner. She took Mehitabel, her own maid, Nana and Roscoe, sending Drew with them in the car that Rufus, the chauffeur, drove, instead of taking him in the one which she and Breck drove by turns. This suited neither the father nor the son, but it suited Anna, and as usual she had her way. Roscoe was also extremely depressed, for he had parted most unwillingly from Rose, the cook. But Anna, having learned with shocked surprise that the two had never been married "by the Book," was determined to separate them, though they had lived together with great faithfulness and contentment for twenty years since they first "took up."

She had considered leaving Roscoe behind, because, in spite of her lecture about remaining on duty to let Breck and herself into the house, no matter how late they were, and Roscoe's apparent repentance and vociferous promise to do better in the future than in the past, he had been derelict in his duty again when they returned from their tour of St. Joseph's altars. But expediency had triumphed over annoyance, for Roscoe, as a butler, was indispensable to her. But she punished him effectively by separating him from Rose, saying that she was sure that Shoog and her daughters, whom she had heard so greatly extolled, ought to be able to "manage" the cooking on the plantation. In doing this, she made another arrangement which suited no one except herself, but it troubled her no more in this case than in the other.

Breck had warned her beforehand that the river roads were rough, and that after a rain they were, indeed, often almost or quite impassable because of mud holes. He strongly recommended the *Boyce Local* or the *Ferriday Local*, of the Texas and Pacific Railroad, as a means of transportation which she would find much more comfortable than a motor car. And when she shuddered at the suggestion of a local, reminding him that as far as train travel was concerned she never considered anything except a Limited, but that she disliked all trains on general principles, he spoke of the river route. The steamer, *J. H. Menge,* of the Mississippi Packet Company, left New Orleans for Lutcher, Garyville and all way-landings every Monday and Thursday at five p. m.; the steamship *William Garig,* of the Carter Packet Company, left for Donaldsonville, Plaquemine, Baton Rouge and all way-landings every Wednesday at five p.m. Both offered good food and comfortable accommodations and made stops near Splendida. Granting that the romance of "Steamboat 'Round the Bend" was now partly a thing of the past, the Mississippi itself was a source of varying and inexhaustible delight. But he was obliged to confess, in answer to Anna's question, that there were no private bathrooms on either the *Menge* or the *Garig,* and she held out stubbornly for transportation by automobile. They would need the cars after they reached Splendida, she argued. Surely Breck would not show such bad management as to send them up there empty!

As long as there were no rains, Breck did not continue to argue with her, and she triumphantly pointed out to him, several times on the way, that they had not seen a single mud hole. But this was her first experience with Louisiana highways, and in spite of all that Breck had said, she was not prepared to find them as bad as they actually were. She was terribly shaken up, getting one unexpected jolt after another. Moreover, she and Breck had two blowouts along the way, which did not help matters, for he had to change tires unaided, and this was a long and wearisome process. They had been invited to stop for lunch at Rimini, the plantation home of the Alpientes, whose daughter, Carmen, had married Narcisse Fontaine, the lawyer of the family, and it was soon obvious that they would be late in arriving. This, Breck assured Anna, would not matter in the least; time had always meant even less to the Spaniards than to the French, and their Creole descendants had the same characteristics. But Anna fretted and fumed; she did not greatly care whether the Alpientes were inconvenienced, but she did not like an overdone meal, and above all she did not want her own schedule upset.

She was temporarily diverted from her irritation by the attractiveness of Rimini, which had been built by order of the Queen of Spain for one of her ladies in waiting, and which was a mellow and charming example of early colonial building in the deep South. Anna understood and appreciated fine architecture, and no distinctive feature of this remarkable specimen went unobserved: the graceful outer staircases, leading from the lower to the upper galleries, which both encircled the house; the contrasting columns, sturdy on the first story, slender on the second; the cruciform corridors dividing the great square rooms on the ground floor; the long hallway on the upper one; the fanlights over the panelled doors.

But the general atmosphere of leisurely culture and charm impressed her less. She was greatly irked at being obliged to sit, for over an hour, under the shade of the guardian oaks, while everyone except herself unhurriedly consumed mint juleps, and conversation was effortless and desultory. It was nearly half past two when luncheon was finally announced, and Doña de Alpiente, without apology or consciousness that any was needed, led the way into the dining room, where a groaning board awaited them. Another hour

was exhausted in consuming the prodigious meal that had
been prepared; and it was four o'clock when they finally
succeeded in making their adieus. By that time Anna was
almost visibly fuming.

Breck, who had been gratified by her appreciation of Rimini, architecturally speaking, suggested that they should stop
at one or two other interesting houses occupied by relatives
or old friends of his. But Anna was not receptive to these
suggestions; she said their schedule was too much upset
already; and a further delay at the Donaldsonville ferry,
where the levee banks were steep and the ferry boat filthy
and behindtime, angered her still more. In an effort to soothe
her, Breck called her attention to a beautiful red bird that
streaked past them like a scarlet arrow, and asked her if
she realized that they were not far from the "Audubon
Country" now. There were not quite as many birds around
Splendida as there were in the Felicianas, he said, or quite
so many houses where Audubon had painted family portraits
and company china, and tutored children, while eking out
a precarious livelihood for himself and his young wife. But
he, himself, owned a copy of the Elephant Edition—that is,
of course, they both owned it—and he was sure that Anna
would be entranced by the orioles strutting over the lawns
at Splendida, and the mockingbirds, which perched on the
chimneys, chattering to each other, so that it was almost impossible, if you were sitting near a fireplace, not to keep
looking up, expecting to see them hopping around on the
rug.

Breck was really making an earnest effort to be both
pleasant and informative, the greater because his conscience
was troubling him, as far as Anna was concerned. He had
not dwelt very much, mentally, on Marie Céleste's primary
attraction for him. Her appeal had seemed to him that of
a charming child, nothing more. But the effect of her singing
had been lasting and disturbing. That final song of hers—*Je
suis la délaissée*—he could not get it out of his mind. Of
course it was inconceivable that Marie Céleste, who was the
very embodiment of joy, should ever be sad or that anyone
so lovely should ever be abandoned. Certainly he, himself,
would be the last to deceive her or to "poison her heart." As
far as other details of the ditty went, she was well over
sixteen, nearly eighteen at least, but at that, it was too soon
for her to be saying that she had met and parted from the

one love of her life. All in all, it was rather a pointless
song for Céleste to sing and for him to heed, and he was
a fool to let it affect him as it had. But even as he told
himself this, the refrain sounded in his ears over and over
again, and the image of Céleste as she sang it rose before
his eyes.

The outing on St. Joseph's Eve had done nothing to obscure
this image. On the contrary, it had intensified this and
multiplied its aspects. Everything Céleste had said and done
that night had been so artless and winning: her eagerness
to show Anna the sights of the city, her frank avowal of her
Carnival aspirations, her trustfulness as she wished on her
candle, her spontaneity in prayer, the lack of self-consciousness with which she had risen from her knees to demand
spumone. There had been a simplicity and a sweetness about
all this that he had found unexpectedly alluring. And then
her answer, when he had asked her why she had gone on
singing after discovering his presence in the garden—"I
thought you wanted me to."—This candor, this compliance
to his will was utterly disarming.

Unquestionably, it was a very good thing that he was
leaving New Orleans for the time being. Céleste was too
young and too innocent to be affected herself, or to realize
how much she had affected him; but he could no longer
deceive himself into pretending that he was not very deeply
stirred. Well, he would discourage Anna from going ahead
with the plans for that projected visit; there was no use in
risking a still greater emotional upheaval. He had considerable self-control, but it was not indestructible. If only he
did not feel so alone, in every way that counted! If only
he had not always felt that way, ever since his father had
died! If only Anna had satisfied his craving for communion,
as he had felt so sure she would, before their marriage;
if only she had not been so critical as well as cold! He
would not have minded that they so soon ceased to be lovers,
could they have remained companions. That is, he did not
believe that he would have. But he kept thinking what a mate
Marie Céleste would make for a man, when she had learned
how to love. Yes, even from the beginning, for she would
welcome her bridegroom with touching joy, she would trustfully receive his caresses and tractably accept his control,
quickly becoming ardent herself, apt in the arts of love,
eager and able to return every evidence of his passion. Breck

seemed to see her, enthroned on her bridal bed, flushed and adorable and inviting. And with a larger vision, reaching down to the future, he saw her, after the years had laid their weight upon her and their first raptures were only a memory, a helpmate to her husband, her constancy and closeness still an eternal wellspring of joy and fulfillment for him——

"Breck, I've asked you the same question three times. Aren't you paying any attention to me at all?"

"I'm sorry, Anna. I didn't mean to be rude. I must have fallen into some kind of a brown study. What was it you wanted to know?"

"Something very strange happened the other night. At that grocery store, Montefiori, was that the name of it? I meant to speak about it at the time, but I got so upset about all that poisonous food, being fed to the poor little orphans, that I forgot. Then yesterday, I was absorbed in what Mrs. Cutler had told me, and——"

"Well, what *is* it?"

"I'm trying to tell you. You and Marie Céleste lagged behind Olivier and me, and we got separated."

"We didn't intentionally lag behind, but we did get separated from you. It's hard for a group to keep together in such a crowd."

"You don't need to talk as if I were accusing you of anything. I'm not. But I saw a girl that I thought was Céleste coming out as Olivier and I were going in. I couldn't understand how she could have got turned around so quickly and I was puzzled. I asked her how she'd done it. Then I saw that the man who was with her wasn't you, and I realized I'd made a mistake. But I certainly never saw two human beings look so much alike."

"Well?"

"Well, I want to know if you have any idea who she might be. I'm almost certain that Olivier and her escort knew each other. In fact, they bowed to each other, very briefly and coolly to be sure, but still they did bow. They didn't speak to each other though, or stop, and the girl didn't look at Olivier at all. She looked straight past him, as if he hadn't been there."

Breck shifted gears, quite unnecessarily it seemed to Anna. He did not answer.

"Don't you hear me now, Breck?"

"Yes, I hear you now. But I'm trying to think what to say to you."

"You know who the girl is then?"

"Yes, I know who the girl is. I saw her that night, too, and so did Marie Céleste. It gave her an awful shock, coming face to face with a double like that. Of course, I tried to pretend that it didn't signify anything. I said I'd heard we all had doubles. But I'd seen the girl before. I know all about her. And Marie Céleste knows nothing. I hope she'll never have to."

"But who *is* she?"

"She's Marie Céleste's own cousin, her Uncle Octave's daughter. Octave Fontaine was the man you saw with her."

"But if they're own cousins——"

"It's on the wrong side of the blanket, Anna. And that isn't the worst of it. The blanket isn't all wool and a yard wide, so to speak, or rather some black sheep got mixed up in it."

"You don't mean the girl is colored! Why, she can't be! She's as white as Céleste!"

Breck laughed, mirthlessly and briefly. "My simile was a bad one. When I spoke of black sheep, I was actually thinking of those in the Fontaine family—old Théophile, who met his mistress at a quadroon ball, and poor Octave, who fell in love with their octoroon daughter at first sight. Of course, he is her cousin, too. That girl you saw is one-sixteenth colored. It won't ever show in her hair or her skin or her eyes—not even in her fingernails, and they're the greatest giveaway. But she might as well be coal-black, for all the good her white blood will do her."

"Why, it's an outrage! It's a disgrace! Mrs. Cutler told me something about this sort of situation, but I didn't believe it. Breck, we must do something about that girl. We must ask her to our house."

"That would be about the cruelest thing you could do, in the long run. Don't try to cope with the color question, Anna, until you've solved the social evil. I admit that the two are more or less allied. But I think you've bitten off about as much as you can chew for the moment. Be reasonable. You know that bastards aren't received in Boston, if they're recognized as such—I suppose there are accidents, even on the Back Bay. Octave Fontaine and Camille Dupuy aren't married. Let it go at that, without dragging in the other factor.

They couldn't be married, according to the law of Louisiana and the law all over the South, for that matter. It isn't a question of the Napoleonic Code. As far as that goes, they could be married in France, but either Uncle Octave never thought of that, or he didn't care quite enough to go through with it. But if you've never heard of the principle of miscegenation, you'd better study that, after you get through with the rest of your research. You may change the law of the Medes and Persians yet. I wouldn't put it past you. But you'll never change the feeling of the South on that point."

Anna had been looking at him with unusual attention all the time he had been talking. Now, not disagreeably, but with unconcealed interest, she went on with her questioning.

"What's the girl's name? How did you happen to know her?"

"Her name is Laure. Laure Dupuy, of course. I saw her for the first time when she was a little girl. You know that my stepmother was Octave Fontaine's sister. After the wreck of the *Bourgogne* he was very kind to me, kinder than anyone except Aunt Estelle. He stayed with me night after night in my great empty house. So finally I suggested going to his house instead. Laure was about five years old. She came and sat in my lap and went to sleep there. I was glad to have her. She reminded me of the little half sister I'd lost. Not that she looked like Pauline. She always looked like Céleste. But she had ways like Pauline. They appealed to me very much."

"Did you ever see her again after that until last night?"

"Yes. I saw her when I came home just before you and I were married. Laure was thirteen then. The Marcel Fontaines were in Europe, so I didn't see them. But Octave Fontaine was here and I went to his house."

"Is that the only other time?"

"No, I saw her day before yesterday in the afternoon, as well as last night. I thought you and Mrs. Cutler wanted to have an uninterrupted talk, and I didn't have anything special to do, after lunch at the Boston Club, so I went down to Uncle Octave's house then. I know he's always glad to see me, and I'm very grateful to him. I always shall be. It doesn't do anybody any harm for me to go to his house, and I feel that I'm welcome. He didn't say anything about taking Laure to see St. Joseph's altars. If he had, I'd have tried to steer Céleste off, for fear the very thing might happen that did happen. Probably he took her just on the spur of the moment. There aren't many places he can take her and he's very fond of her. I'm sure he didn't dream of running into anyone he knew in that heterogeneous crowd."

"Probably he didn't. But, Breck, are you sure it's all right for you to go to his house, without me? Mightn't that be misunderstood?"

"I'm afraid I don't follow you, Anna."

"Mightn't he think that you were attracted by Laure still? Differently from the way you were attracted when she was a child? Mightn't she think so?"

"No, Anna, neither of them would think so. Neither of them would insult me that way. I shouldn't have supposed it would have entered your head to insult me that way either. If ever a man was faithful to his wife, I've been faithful to you."

"I know you have been, Breck. I've never doubted it. But still——"

"There aren't any 'buts.' Even if I weren't thinking of you, I'd still have Drew to think of. I'll never let him be shamed by his father. He's going to be proud of his father, the way I am of mine."

He was terribly angry, and his rage was no less intense because he recognized that it was both unreasonable and inconsistent. If Anna had charged him with being more than halfway in love with Marie Céleste, he would have had hard work defending himself convincingly, for the accusation would have been just. But because she suggested that he might be looking at Laure with desirous eyes, he was filled with righteous indignation, though he had no more right to covet one cousin than the other. It was so rare a thing for him to lose his temper, that Anna, in her turn, felt twinges of conscience and made a genuine effort to placate him. It was a long time before she succeeded. But eventually he quieted down and to change the subject, began to tell her something about the batture dwellers, the strange folk who lived on the land built up by the sediment from the Mississippi, outside of the levees on the very edge of the great river; miserable squatters with no fixed habitation, except scattered shacks on stilts, who wandered back and forth in droves, finding a foothold and a shelter as they could, subsisting largely on their precarious catch; inbred, lawless and illiterate, but for the most part surprisingly droll and light-hearted. Anna was interested in these people. She enlarged, as a result of the remarks Breck made about their poverty and ignorance, on some further statistics Mrs. Cutler had given her, showing that Louisiana had the lowest per capita income of almost any state in the Union, and one of the highest rates of illiteracy. She was still talking about this, bracing herself to take the bumps better, when Breck slowed down, turning, and she realized that they were approaching the entrance to Splendida.

At first it looked very much like many of the other entrances before which they had paused. There was the same wide, swinging gate, set between tall, solid posts, and beyond it, a long avenue paved with crushed oyster shells, dappled with fitful sunshine, and bordered by live oaks, which had Spanish moss, filmy and gray against the glossy green of their leaves, floating in long, tenuous streamers from their branches. But the avenue was not short and straight, with a pillared mansion, plainly visible from the entrance, looming up at the end of it. Instead, it curved away into the mysterious depths of a great grove, and she remembered how Breck had described it to her: "There's so much more than an avenue at Splendida. There are acres and acres of beautiful woodland, and then great stretches of smooth lawn before you get to the terraced garden." Well, now that they were winding through the woodland, on a road where you could see neither the end nor the beginning, she could understand why there had been such poignancy in his voice when he spoke of it. She had never been in a forest which gave her so strong a sensation of eeriness and enchantment—a forest where she would fear to stay, lest its sorcery might ensnare her, and yet, which she could not bear to leave lest its magic spell might be broken. When at last the clustering trees with their ghostly draperies became more and more scattered, and the "smooth stretches" of grass, velvety and verdant, came into view, the house also rose before her, glowing through the great trees, its fluted columns reaching towards the flawless sky. Never had she seen a dwelling place at one and the same time so majestic, yet so luminous. She gazed at it in unstinted admiration mingled with reluctant awe.

"I told you there wasn't another place like it in the world, Anna," Breck was saying. "Perhaps now you'll believe me."

She did not try to dispute him. He helped her out of the car, and they stood together looking silently up at the superb structure which towered before them in such grandeur. Splendida! If ever a place had deserved its name, this one did, Anna said to herself, and realized that she was saying it ungrudgingly, that she was gratified to the core of her being because she was the mistress and co-owner of such a domain. No matter what it cost, no matter how fantastic and reckless and ostentatious such a venture might be, she knew that she wanted to possess this place in her own way, to bring it within her control, to administer and even to expand it. As she put her foot on the first of the long flight of marble steps leading up to the doorway, she knew that this movement was symbolic, that she never would rest until she had surmounted not only the steps, but everything that was there——

The second car had come up the driveway, its wheels making a crunching sound as they passed over the oyster shells. Drew was out of the door with a bound, and eluding Nana, came rushing up to catapult himself against his father.

"That isn't a house, is it, Daddy? A real house, to live in? It doesn't look like one. It looks like—like——"

"Never mind what it looks like. Of course it's a house. It's *our* house. Come on in and see it with Daddy— That's all right, Nana. I'll look after Drew. You go around to the side with the others. There's a basement entrance on the right. You'll find you're expected and that everything is ready for you."

He went up the steps with his arm around his little son. He had to take them slowly, for they were high, and Drew could manage only one at a time. Anna had already reached the top long before they did and stood looking around her, the admiration and awe in her face deepening the longer she gazed. Breck was not sorry to see the expression; at last Anna was confronted with something of his offering on which she could not look with contempt. But he was gladder still to feel that he was taking Drew up those endless majestic steps leading to the house which was his heritage. In some happy hereafter, Splendida would belong to Drew, and Drew would rule it and reign in it as he himself had never been able to do. Not Drew's wife, though Drew would eventually have a wife, of course, for there must be a chatelaine for such a place as Splendida, and a mother for all the Breckenridges of the next generation. Drew would not have a solitary son, as he and his father had had, but a big brood of happy, hearty youngsters, riding their ponies through the grove, shooting their arrows at a target set out on the lawn, eating prodigiously at a long table, filling the great rooms with their laughter by day and sleeping soundly in their tester beds at night. Financially Anna would "provide" for Drew, so that his heritage would be safe. But he, Breck, would guide and admonish him so that when the boy did marry it would not be some fragile girl who could not survive childbirth, or some unsexed athlete, who could not or would not accept abundant maternity——

"We're sure glad to welcome you home again, Mr. Breck, and to see the Missus and the little boy, too." It was Marcy Yates, the overseer, who spoke. He was waiting in the portico to receive them, hailing them heartily, though respectfully. "It's Drew you call him, isn't it? My eye, if he ain't the spittin' image of his grandfather! I think he favors Mr. Andy even more than he does you, Mr. Breck. How are you, son? You'll be coming out with me in the morning to see the horses and the cows, won't you, as soon as the plantation bell rings?"

"Yes, please, Mr. Yates. That is, if Daddy does. I want to do everything the same way as Daddy."

"The spittin' image," Mr. Yates said again enthusiastically. "Well, I hope you will be minded to come with the youngster, and with me, Mr. Breck, all over the place. I've done the best I could, but every plantation needs its owner to look after it now and again, and it's been a right smart while since you've been here. You couldn't have come more timely, though. I've been thinking I might have to send for you."

Anna had given Yates a cool nod that recognized the overseer's presence without welcoming it. Then she had gone into the vestibule leading to the great pillared hall that ran straight through the main part of the house. Breck had looked forward to showing her the house himself—the drawing room, parlor, dining room and "piazza" (as Gallier had designated the dining-room gallery in his architectural drawings, and as the Breckenridges had continued to call it, contrary to Louisiana custom), and the famous "gentlemen's bathing room" which had created such a furor when the first plantation plumbing in the South was installed there in 1857. When she had inspected these he meant to take her out onto the "portico" (another favorite term of Gallier's which had been retained) on which all three rooms on the other side of the entrance hall opened, to see the view; and after that into the square "staircase hall," where he would make her stop and look up at the great multicolored window, which followed the circular staircase in both form and height. The light would be at its very loveliest there now, streaming in from the west, and there would be luminous rainbow-colored lozenges made by its reflection on the gleaming marble. He had meant to tell her the story of this jewel-like glass, similar to the small panes which surmounted the front door, and old and precious and beautiful like the glass in the quaint church at St. Martinville, which it so closely resembled; and then he had meant to take her still further back to the rear wing containing the mellow library where the Audubon books and the Shakespeare folios and the great mediaeval globes were kept, and to the "bachelor bedroom" beyond it, which had its own little gallery and had always had its own bathroom, too, where the original copper tub, encased in black walnut, and the original mottled marble washstand, also encased, still stood. He had meant to show her all sorts of pleasing little details and prized possessions along the way, too—the porcelain door knobs painted with flowers, the roses and camellias of tinted plaster which formed the frieze in the suite at the left of the entrance, the medicine cabinet with its separate spaces for bottles, mortar and pestle and its secret drawer for poisons in the rear, the inlaid mahogany box with separate compartments for green tea and black tea, and the bowl in the center for mixing these together.

And now Anna was rushing ahead to look at all these, avidly, without him, gloating in the knowledge that they were hers now, without making them a matter of mutual rejoicing, or acknowledging the obligation to him, which they represented. She would be upstairs, exploring the bedrooms and bathrooms, even the closets and the linen room, deciding where she would sleep, where he should sleep, where Drew should sleep, before he could catch up with her. For something deterred him from following her. Still standing with his arm around Drew, on the front portico, he had seen an expression of anxiety underlying the pleasure on the over-

seer's face, and had known he must find out the reason for
it before it went any further.

"I'm glad to be here myself, Yates," he said. "And I'm
sorry I couldn't come any sooner. But there wasn't any real
reason for me to do so, you've always taken such good care
of the place. Don't tell me there's anything wrong on the
plantation now?"

The overseer shifted his weight from one foot to the other,
and at the same time moved a blade of grass he had been
chewing from one side to the other of his mouth. Then he
spat the grass out altogether, over the balustrade, skillfully,
so that he would not defile the priceless marble of which it
was formed.

"No, sir, not to say wrong. But some of those smart-aleck
engineers that are in cahoots with the Levee Board up to
Baton Rouge was down here last week, and they started talking about moving the levee. I've been sort of worrying about
'em and looking for 'em, quite a spell now. The water's
been gnawing into the bank, a right smart space, and it's
been coming through in places, going on two years now. The
engineers said that they wouldn't have to make much of
a change, except to move the storehouse—set the entrance
gates back three or four hundred feet, or some such matter.
Of course with grounds the size of these, you'd hardly
notice the difference, and the storehouse needs repairing
anyway. It was one of the first things I was going to talk
to you about. But the entrance is right pretty, just like it is
now, and I don't like to think, sir, that Splendida would
ever be different anyway from what it's always been."

"It won't be," Breck said heartily. "If they try to change
it, it'll be over my dead body. When they come back here,
I'll go out to meet them with a pistol. That's been done
before, and it can be done again. Don't you worry, Yates.
The entrance won't be moved, or anything else at Splendida.
It's going to be kept, just the way it is now, for this boy
here."

"I hope you're right, Mr. Breck," Marcy Yates said bravely.
But as he spoke, he looked out past the portico and the
lawn and the grove, towards the distant levee, as if he
were listening to the sound of rushing waters.

PART V

Splendida Plantation

Spring, 1913

CHAPTER 13

BRECK WAS sleeping worse and worse, dreaming more and more. The deep quiet of the country, broken only by the small stirrings and chirpings of friendly little creatures, failed to soothe him, as he had kept telling himself beforehand that it would. The scent stealing in from the garden, the patches of moonlight patterning the floor of his room, the breeze that moved the white curtains, making them look like scarfs floating from the forms of disembodied spirits—their presence the more powerful because invisible—all these disturbed his rest during the first night he spent at Splendida. Without knowing exactly what it was that he dreaded, he kept watching for something he did not see, and listening for something he did not hear. He could not lie still, because when he did, he instinctively became more and more watchful and alert. He thrashed from one side of his bed to the other until it was completely disordered. Then he jumped up and tramped about the room, returning eventually to his rumpled sheets, misshapen pillow and displaced mattress, only because the enormous room had begun to seem more and more cage-like to him, the longer he paced back and forth in it. At last he took a strong sedative, and subsided into a stupor which had no relation to normal drowsiness, though he found some relief in the realization of approaching un-

257

consciousness. When he heard the clanging of a distant bell, he thought it was only part of another troubled dream. But when commotion began in the corridor directly beyond his room, and his door flew open, bringing this commotion straight to his bedside, he knew that he was again confronted with some unwelcome reality. Rousing himself reluctantly, he opened his eyes and sat up, just as Drew, bellowing with rage and indignantly pursued by Nana, hurled himself against his father.

"Let go of me, you old fuss!" he shouted in the direction of his nurse. "Daddy, we promised Mr. Yates. We told him that we would go out on the plantation when the bell rang. And now Nana won't let me."

"It's only six o'clock, Mr. Breckenridge, or just after. You know that Mrs. Breckenridge has always made a point of having Master Drew stay in bed until seven-thirty. I think that so far, sir, I've always been successful in carrying out her wishes. But this morning Master Drew is most disobedient, if you'll permit me to say so. Most unruly and boisterous. His conduct isn't at all becoming a little gentleman."

"It's probably my fault, Nana. I did promise Drew that he could go out with me when the plantation bell rang. I ought to have told you so last night. And I ought to have been up early enough myself to see that he was ready on time. Go back to the nursery with Nana, Drew, and get dressed. I'll meet you at the front door in ten minutes."

"I beg pardon, sir, but it takes at least half an hour for me to give Master Drew his bath and——"

"He can have his bath when he comes in for breakfast. And another tonight. And half a dozen in between times, for all I care. But if you can't see that he climbs into his clothes inside of ten minutes, I can. Perhaps you'd better bring them in here, and let me attend to him."

"Oh, Daddy, please do! If Nana takes me away, she *will* make me take a bath. And then I *will* be late, then I won't see our people starting out into the fields to hoe the sugar cane, the way Mr. Yates said I could."

"Well, cheer up. If you don't see them this morning, you'll see them plenty of mornings after this. But I think perhaps it would be better for you to get dressed here. Go ahead, Nana. Do what I told you to."

Still bristling with unconcealed indignation, the Englishwoman turned towards the door leading to the corridor and walked stiffly through it, closing it after her with precision. She had hardly done so when another door opened, this time the one which connected the two main bedrooms, and another reproachful figure appeared. Anna, in selecting her own quarters the evening before, had chosen the great southeast chamber over the drawing room, with adjacent semicircular dressing room, which surmounted the alcove downstairs. The size of this chamber, even without the dressing room, was such that half a dozen persons could easily have been accommodated in it, without getting in each other's way; but it contained only one bed, and though this was all of seven feet wide, its size made no difference to Anna. Even on her honeymoon, she had clung to the principle that it was unsanitary and unsuitable for two persons to share the same bed, and Breck had not argued the point with her for long; unless there were twin beds in the room Anna occupied, and of late occasionally even when there were, he betook himself to another. Upon their arrival at Splendida, he had not even suggested that he should use the apartment where his mother had forfeited her life in such wasteful anguish, and which his stepmother—reigning with unforgettable splendor in the suite across the hall, with his father—had always declined to use. Instead, he had automatically installed himself in the one back of Anna's. He was already sorry he had done so. If he had only had the sense to sleep at the other end of the house, Drew would have come to him there, and Anna would not have heard all this uproar. She would not now be standing accusingly on his threshold.

"Drew, what do you mean by coming to your father's room at this hour? Go back to Nana at once. Breck, I cannot understand why you countenance all this commotion!"

"I made a promise, Anna, and forgot it. But that doesn't mean I'm going to break it. I've told Drew I'd take him out when the plantation bell rang. I'm going to do it—this morning and every morning. It's the only way for him to learn what' going on around the place. I'm very sorry you were disturbed. I'm sure Drew is, too, and that he'll tell you so. But I'll see that it doesn't happen again. I'll sleep downstairs after this, in the rear wing. I've always liked the bedroom there, back of the library. Drew can have the other downstairs chamber. The dressing room that connects with it ought to be all right for Nana— It leads out on the north portico, and it's larger than any of the servants' quarters. If you don't approve of that arrangement, Drew and I can bunk together, in either of those suites. Perhaps that will be the best plan of all. He's getting pretty big to be tied to a nurse's apron strings."

Anna had begun the inevitable objection, when Nana grimly re-entered. She had taken time to put on her uniform and tidy her hair, and she no longer had that grotesquely dishevelled appearance she had presented when she so unceremoniously burst into her master's room a few minutes earlier, in pursuit of her charge. She was carrying Drew's small garments in a gingerly way over one arm, and with lips still tightly pressed together, she began to lay them one by one over the back of a chair. Breck took them from her brusquely.

"All right, Nana. That'll be all. Take off your pajamas, Drew. Unbutton the jacket first, just the way I'm unbuttoning mine. Then step right out of the trousers. Like this."

It would all have to be thrashed out again, later on, he knew, but Breck was in no mood to argue any more at the moment, and his method of bringing the discussion to a close was effective, at least temporarily. Nana's uniformed figure had hardly vanished through one door, before Anna's erect form, encased in a neat, featherstitched cashmere wrapper, had disappeared through the other. Breck, without saying anything about brushing the teeth or washing behind the ears, paused long enough to help Drew with the more inaccessible buttons as he flung himself into his own clothes. Then he lifted his small son to his shoulder and strode from the room himself.

"What do you say we slide down the banisters?" he inquired. "That would save time, and we *are* late you know."

"Gee, Daddy, that would be great!"

Their precipitous glide eliminated the stairway. The next instant Breck was drawing back the bolts from the door leading to the rear gallery, and as the door stuck, Drew helped his father tug at it until it yielded, abruptly, to their touch. Then they went through it and down another flight of steps into the arbor that divided the house from the garden—past the dairy—on towards the fields. Neither the scent of the flowers nor the song of the birds was disturbing any longer. Breck was unaware of them now. He was aware only of Drew, tearing along at his side, happy and triumphant.

From the double row of cabins to the south, Negroes were still filing out, the women with their heads wrapped in bright *tignons*, the men wearing patched shirts repeating the same gay colors, most of them singing, all of them carrying hoes in their hands. Some of the women had big golden hoops in their ears. The sunlight, suddenly streaming over the pale opalescence of dawn, settled on these hoops, turning them to radiant wire, and on the hoes, which began to shine like silver. The cane, knee-high already, shot up from the rich sooty earth in slender verdant spears. Drew rushed down into the furrows, tugging at Breck's hand, looking up into his face.

"May I touch the leaves, Daddy? May I stroke them with my fingers?"

"Yes, all you want to. But gently. Don't break them. And don't trample on them either. They've got to grow a lot yet. Watch where you're going."

"I am watching. I'm looking at everything."

The Negroes were close to them now. They stopped singing to nod and duck and grin; their teeth showed startlingly white between their full magenta-colored lips, and the whites of their eyes were amazing, too, as they rolled the glistening orbs from side to side. Drew was still a little strange with Negroes, for he had never seen any until he had come to New Orleans, and Roscoe and Rufus, to whom he had gradually grown accustomed, were both "high yellows," utterly alien in both build and bearing to these slow powerful people who seemed almost a part of the dark soil from which they derived their sustenance. For a moment he hung back a little, holding Breck's hand more tightly. Then seeing the smiles of the Negroes and sensing their friendliness, he began to smile, too, and to say hello, as they greeted first his father and then him by name. "Mornin', Mr. Breck. Mornin', Mr. Drew. Mornin', sah. Mornin', honey chile!" Marcy Yates came cantering up while the exchange of greetings was still going on.

"Well, sir, I see you didn't forget your promise. You got here 'before soon' as they say around here. It's a mighty pleasing sight to me, let me tell you, to see you, too."

"I did forget at that. Or rather, I overslept. It was Drew here who woke me up and reminded me."

"The spittin' image!" Marcy Yates exclaimed, this time without even adding of whom. Breck had a momentary pang, realizing that to the overseer, as to himself, the first Andrew Breckenridge had been a sort of god, and that though Yates was already admitting that someday Drew might stand in his grandfather's shoes, he, Breck, had never done so and never would. But he was too generous to be jealous, either of the dead man he had once worshipped, or of the living child whom he now worshipped still more. He looked at Drew proudly. The little boy was no longer clutching his father's fingers, but stroking the cane, while he kept his eyes on the Negroes, who had already begun to hoe and who had resumed their singing. The "top hand" had set the pace for the hoeing as he sang the first line of the chorus they all took up.

"Git it agoin', Emma T!"

There was a moment's silence, and then the rich husky voice of a woman wailed out.

"Po lil' Jesus!"

There was no apparent connection between Emma T. and poor little Jesus. However, the workers seemed to sense one, for presently all the hands had joined in the harmony and their hoes fell together as they reached the end of a row.

"Hail, Lawd!"

There was another pause, a little longer than the first, and then the leader began to chant again.

"They bound Him with a haltuh."

"Hail, Lawd!" rejoined the hands, their hoes lifted now.

"What makes them sing like that, Mr. Yates?" Drew asked curiously.

"It rests them, son. Leastwise that's what they say, and they do work better when they sing. So much better that the leader gets paid extra to keep them singing. He says it rests them and undoes the knots in their muscles."

"I don't see how. But I like to hear them. Don't you, Daddy?"

"Yes, I like it very much. I am glad you like to hear them sing, too, Drew."

He looked at his son attentively, as he did with greater

and greater frequency in these days. The child's face was very attractive, eager and alert and confident, so confident in fact that it already held a quality less like a little boy's unquestioning trustfulness than like a proud man's unassailable arrogance. Here again was the evidence of the image to which Yates kept referring. Breck stifled a sigh and looked out over the cane.

"That ought to be a good crop, Marcy."

"Yes, sir. The best we've ever had, unless we get a late frost or a twister. But there's no use meeting trouble halfway, until we have to— Do you want to stay here in the fields, son, till breakfast time, or would you like to come and look at the lambs?"

"Are there really lambs, Mr. Yates? Live ones?"

"Just as live as you are, son. There's one I've been thinking maybe you'd like for a cosset. I've been hand-feeding her myself ever since she was born. Bessie, I call her."

"What's a cosset, Mr. Yates?"

"A kind of pet. Just like a puppy or a kitten, you know."

"I haven't ever had a puppy or a kitten. Oh, Daddy, do you think Mother will let me have Bessie?"

Breck's face hardened. "Of course she'll let you have Bessie. And a puppy and some kittens, too, now that we're on the plantation. The country is a place for pets. That's why you haven't had one before, because we haven't been in the country. But I think perhaps we'd better wait until after breakfast before we go to find Bessie. We'll go to see all the animals then—the colts and the calves and the chickens. We'll go down to the cypress swamps, too, and up on the levee. We'll ride, like Mr. Yates."

"*We'll* ride!"

"Yes. Mr. Yates has a pony for you as well as a cosset. You'll be sore and lame tomorrow, but you mustn't mind that. Everyone gets sore and lame after riding for the first time, or after not doing it for a long while. I'll be sore and lame, too."

"I don't care how sore and lame I am, Daddy, if I can only ride. A pony, too— Oh, gosh! Will there be races here by and by, the way there used to be when your father was alive?"

"Of course there will be, and you'll ride in those. We'll look over the track, too, this morning, and see what condition that's in."

"Oh, Daddy, that'll be great. Gee, we're doing lots of things together, aren't we?"

There was no doubt of it, Drew was beginning to say Gee and Gosh, as Anna had predicted, and after he had been out among the hands for a few days, he would be saying worse. But Breck did not correct him, and decided that he would not reprove him later either. The child's happiness was so intense that he did not want it controlled or dampened in any way. He went back to the house, as he had left it, with his son's hand in his; but this time they went in a more leisurely way. Breck paused long enough to look in at the dim cool dairy and to point out the great cisterns where rain water was stored, explaining the process of separating to Drew, and asking him if he knew how many quarts there were in ten thousand gallons, the amount that the cisterns held. Well then, they would have to take time out for arithmetic lessons, he said, when Drew told his father that he did not; but he said it lightly as well as teasingly, and Drew was not worried for fear that he would be kept cooped up with books, either that day or any day in the near future. As they entered the house from the rear, they saw that Roscoe had set the table for breakfast on the "piazza" back of the dining room, but that places were laid for only two. Drew looked at his father questioningly, but Breck declined to be disturbed by the possible portentousness of Anna's absence.

"Come on into the 'gentlemen's bathing room', Drew," he said. "We'll scrub up there together. Then we'll dig into our food. I hope there are hot cakes and cuite."

"What's cuite?"

"A special kind of thick cane syrup, drawn just before it turns to sugar. You'll like it."

"Don't you think Mother would like it, too?"

"I doubt it. But Roscoe can take her some, anyway."

"Miss Breckenridge done had her breakfast, sah. She done have it at eight o'clock, same as usual. It's a quarter till nine now. She had grapefruit and oatmeal and——"

"All right, Roscoe, I know. I'm sorry we're late. But I'll explain to Mrs. Breckenridge later."

The servants had never said "Miss Anna" in speaking of his wife, or to her, and Breck knew that this was a bad sign. But it was another point he had decided was not worth an argument, especially as he knew that Anna herself would never grasp the full significance of the formal term which labelled her as an outsider. He ate his cakes and cuite with appetite, and permitted Drew to gorge himself unchecked. Then he lighted a cigarette, and after looking lazily out towards the landscape for a few minutes, rose, and strolled, still lazily, towards the rear gallery which led to the garden and fields, and from which the library and the "bachelor bedroom" in turn led, forming a wing by themselves. When he got as far as the square "staircase hall," he saw Anna, with Shoog standing beside her, and stopped to speak to her. The light from the great multicolored window was falling on her gray dress and pale hair, giving warmth and color to them. She looked cool and capable and unusually attractive. Momentarily he forgot his deep-seated annoyance with her.

"Drew and I are going to take a ride over the place," he said. "Don't you want to come with us?"

"No, thank you. I'm too tired to ride. I've had a very restless night, and then, as you know, I was rather rudely awakened this morning, after I finally had fallen asleep."

"I've told you already how sorry I am about that. But I also told you it won't happen again. I was just on my way to inspect the 'bachelor bedroom,' with a view of adapting it to my needs. Was there something special that disturbed you in the night?"

"Yes. I kept thinking I heard a baby crying."

"What!"

"Really, I could have sworn it was in the room with me."

Breck turned away. He had always known that Aurore Fontaine had not declined to occupy the state bedroom merely because it had been the conjugal chamber of her predecessor, or because Anne Forrestal had died in it. He knew that Aurore had believed, as every Negro on the place believed, that the room was haunted by the spirit of the child which had cost his mother's life, and which had wailed unceasingly during the few days that it had survived her. But he did not want to tell Anna about that superstition, which was only one of several on the place. There was, for instance, the legend of the little old lady clad in a black flounced dress and carrying a small black parasol, who alighted from her carriage at the entrance of the driveway and wandered among the oaks, trailing her dress after her and shielding her eyes with her parasol. And then the other, of the girl wearing a yellow plumed bonnet, who crept into the guest rooms whenever these were occupied by persons to whom she bore ill will, and lifted the mosquito netting from their beds, so that they would be badly bitten before morning, lingering long enough herself to peer down at them and make sure that the insects were already doing their deadly work. He felt sure that Anna would only deride such stories. Yet, after all, since she had been disturbed, it might do no harm to suggest a traditional remedy.

"If you hear the baby crying again, light a candle in the room. That's supposed to quiet it," he said cryptically. "But don't think about it any more now. Get into your habit and come out into the sunshine. It'll do you good."

"I can't imagine what you're talking about, Breck. A lighted candle! I never heard such nonsense! This wasn't a real baby. There isn't any baby in this house."

"No, unfortunately there isn't. And don't light the candle if you don't feel like it. That was just a suggestion. But come out, anyway."

"I'm afraid I haven't time to spend a morning riding for pleasure. I'm afraid there's a great deal I need to adjust and supervise, inside this immense house."

"I think you'll be interested in the plantation, Anna. We'll look over the stock and the outbuildings both, before we come back. It'll be a pleasant ride, I hope, but it won't be just *for* pleasure, if you get what I mean."

"I *understand* what you mean. And I intend to see the stock and the outbuildings later, of course. But if you're going to take over this rear wing, I must see that your belongings are moved. And I am willing that Drew and Nana should sleep downstairs for the present, at any rate, since you prefer that arrangement also. You know how much I dislike downstairs bedrooms myself. Though they're not as conspicuous here, I'm glad to say, as those we kept seeing in New Orleans. It seemed to me there, that in every other house we entered, a huge bedstead in the room on one side of the front door was the first thing that loomed up in front of us."

"Well, that's true enough. But you must admit they were very good-looking bedsteads. And Orleanians think more highly of beds, for all sorts of reasons, than you do."

I ought not to have said that, he told himself, before the words were out of his mouth. She really has made a concession, giving in about Drew, and she does dislike downstairs bedrooms, she always has. Why do I have to say something sarcastic and suggestive, the sort of thing that's most offensive to her? But then, why did she have to spoil a generous gesture by striking out at Orleanians? She was sarcastic herself, though heaven knew she was not suggestive. And her sarcasm so often led to one of those fits of uncontrolled anger, which he dreaded so greatly and with so much reason. It was all hopeless, it was all hideous, they were hurting each other more and more every day in spite of his resolutions that after they reached the plantation he would make such an effort to do better that he would succeed. Did husbands and wives always do that, after their first dazzling fever for each other had passed? He did not believe it, he would not believe it. Yet he had tried, he had kept on trying, and still it had all been futile, as far as he was concerned, though it had not all been his fault. Some of this almost unbearable antagonism and strain must be due to Anna. Once again, against his will, he saw the image of Marie Céleste, compliant and gentle, lovely and loving. If he had jested about beds with Marie Céleste, there would have been no sting to his satire, merely a provocative merriment; and though she might have been puzzled at first, because she failed to catch the innuendo, when she did understand she would have laughed with him, and perhaps made a shy little joke of her own. Only of course he would never have spoken on such a subject to Marie Céleste, or to anyone else in her presence. A man did not do that, with a girl like her. Unless he were married to her— And why on earth did he keep thinking, involuntarily, about Marie Céleste as if they were so intimate, so close to each other in every way, when actually they were almost strangers?

He emerged from his unhappy reverie with the realization that Drew was looking at him with puzzled eyes, that Anna had not deigned to answer him, and that Shoog was regarding her new mistress with something that closely resembled a sneer. The caretaker had been beaming the day before, when they arrived, her broad black face illumined with as much genuine joy as Marcy Yates' lean red one. Now when Shoog caught him glancing at her, she ceased to sneer, but the blankness of her expression was permeated with unmistakable mulishness. He knew that she resented Anna's attitude of interference and that she would resent it increasingly, if Anna persisted in a rigorous and tactless course of "supervision." Shoog prided herself on her reliability and efficiency, just as Yates did. She wanted the lady of the house to praise and approve, not to dissect and to criticize, and she had hopefully expected praise and approval. Now that her hopes were already dissipated, she might be hard to handle. Breck longed to put in a word which might placate her, but he knew if he tried he might merely make a bad matter worse, and he decided that one show of independence was enough for one day, in any case. So he fell back on his usual line of non-interference as the easiest way out of the difficulty.

"Well, I'm sorry you don't feel you can join us, but we'll have to be getting along, if we're going to cover the plantation before dinner time. Come on, Drew. Shoog, I know I can count on you to be very helpful to Mrs. Breckenridge."

He and Drew were gone for nearly three hours. When he came back into the house, he left the little boy, stiff and sore from his ride, as Breck had predicted, but wholly unsubdued, and playing rapturously on the lawn with Bessie, the cosset lamb. Breck sought out Anna, feeling vaguely contrite because the morning had been such a success without her, and resolved to make another effort towards harmony. He found her seated at a desk in the reception room, which she had already announced that she intended to use as her private study, and in which she had begun to rearrange the furniture in a manner more suited to serious occupancy. She was obviously busy with lists and ledgers, and looked up importantly, but, as he was relieved to observe, without any acrimony, when he entered. Shoog was nowhere to be seen.

"The time I've had!" Anna said, in a vexed voice, which, nevertheless, betrayed traces of satisfaction. "All that Negress wanted to do was to talk, just as I expected. She kept telling me stories about the place, and pointing out items of interest. She said it was such a 'pretty day' that it was too bad to stay indoors. She gave me no peace at all until I went out to the summerhouse with her, so that she could show me the seat where all the lovers have sat. She said it was there your father led Aurore Fontaine when he was 'taking second notice' and she came here to visit, that he 'gained' her right on that very settee. I don't know exactly what she meant by that, but I didn't like the sound of it at all."

"I suppose if she had said 'won' it would have sounded all right to you. I'm sorry to disappoint you, Anna, but I don't think it means a thing, except that she consented to marry him there. As far as I know, the Breckenridges haven't gone in for seducing the women they wanted for their wives, much less raping them. It's never been their technique."

There he was, doing it again, after he had resolved so firmly that he never would. But Anna was getting more and more insufferable, and sarcasm was his only defense against the wounds she inflicted. He could not stop her insults to his father, except by insulting her in return. She was too fully armored by blamelessness. Or was a wife who deliberately tried to make her husband unhappy really blameless, no matter how chaste in her behavior and how correct in her speech? He wondered——

"I think you're getting more and more vulgar all the time, Breck." Anna was retorting this time, and he was glad of it. If she had not spoken, he might have drifted off into another reverie, he might have made more involuntary comparisons between her and Marie Céleste. "This morning was bad enough, but now—really! As if I had said anything, or would, about seduction, or—or——"

"Rape?"

"I'm not going to repeat such a word. All I was trying to tell you was that from the summerhouse Shoog took me out to the garden and showed me the statues that are scattered all over the lawn. It seems that your grandather selected them in Europe, and that some of them represent the Seasons, and others the Continents, and so on. Shoog especially admires the one of 'Miss Flora, who comes from Rome and has quite a history!' "

Breck threw back his head and laughed, his anger suddenly swallowed up in welcome amusement. Anna continued to maintain the attitude ascribed to Queen Victoria on a similar occasion.

"I don't think it's so terribly funny— And next Shoog waddled over to the cemetery. That wasn't funny at all, it was ghoulish. I don't feel at all sure it's sanitary to have a burying ground so close to living quarters. I'll have to consult an expert. Possibly it ought to be moved." She saw the danger signals flying in Breck's face once more, but she went on as if she had not noticed them. "I finally got her back into the house again, with the greatest difficulty. As you know, that was where I wanted to stay in the first place. Then she stood in front of a picture representing a Swiss scene which represented the birthplace of 'Mr. William Tell.' Another of your grandfather's acquisitions, I believe. Anyway, it's an atrocity, and so are the statues. They should all be eliminated. You must tell Gates, or whatever his name is, to have them carted away."

"If you like we can try rearranging them, or setting them further back, later on. I'm open to conviction on that point, though I honestly believe you'd find, after they were gone, that you missed them. It's hard to explain, but they sort of belong, just like that picture of William Tell. I don't admire it any more than you do, but somehow it fits. And I should think there might be other things that needed doing before we worried too much about carting heavy marbles and paintings around."

"Well, there are, of course. A great many other things. Some of the rooms look as if they had been decorated on purpose to please the Daughters of the Confederacy. I never saw so many Civil War flags and photographs in my life. I suppose that a picture of Lee and a steel engraving of General Latané's funeral are inescapable— I've never seen a house south of the Mason and Dixon Line that didn't have them in the most prominent possible place. But when it comes to banners of every sort, and gory battle scenes, and Beauregard surrounded by his staff——"

"My grandfather was a member of that staff, Anna. Perhaps you didn't realize."

"No, I didn't. It's your father I've always associated with Beauregard. Not in relation to the Civil War though. In connection with the——"

"Yes, I know, the Lottery. Suppose we don't get started on that today. I don't suppose it would interest you, but General Beauregard really had quite a remarkable record in the War between the States, as we call it down here, and as a matter of fact, my grandfather did, too. But I can put all those 'flags and photographs' together in the rear wing, which I am about to occupy, if you like. I don't imagine you'll see them very often there."

"I think that's an excellent idea," Anna replied. Breck was not sure whether she was ignoring the sarcasm which had crept back into his voice, or whether she was unconscious of it. But it did not matter much. "I'll count on you to attend to that, then. But there are any number of other matters, as you say. You'd never think of such a detail, but I've found out that this house is never properly aired. I told Shoog to open the shutters in the drawing room and let the sunshine in. Of course I also wanted to see if the room was really clean. Do you know that she absolutely refused? She said that she'd kept the draperies from 'drapping to pieces' and the colors in the carpet from fading for nearly fifteen years, and she wasn't going to have all her work done for nothing now."

"The light is pretty strong, Anna, here in the South, and those curtains and floor coverings are old—old and very valuable. I remember hearing my stepmother say that the drawing room draperies alone cost five thousand dollars. They're—I suppose they're almost historic, in a way. No one will ever have any like them again. That era is gone. You appreciate beautiful things and their worth. I should think you'd be pleased because Shoog has taken such good care of the family things."

"I'm not pleased to have any servant tell me what I can do in my own house. I've had Roscoe fasten all the shutters back with nails. They're going to stay open from now on."

It was unreasonable, Breck knew, for him to wince when Anna spoke of Splendida as her own house. But he did. And it made him doubly uncomfortable to think that Shoog and Roscoe were probably discussing her order about the shutters in their quarters at that minute. But rather than retort or reason again, he said nothing.

"I'll admit that the house was cleaner than I expected," Anna went on, as if he deserved some reward for his reticence. "Aside from its gloominess, it's in very good order, really. I don't see why we shouldn't have company at any time. I've already written a note to Mrs. Fontaine telling her I hope she and Olivier and Marie Céleste will come down here over next week end. I've asked her to suggest another man I might invite, too, who'd be congenial. I thought of that young Walter Avery we've seen here and there. I understand he's in love with Céleste."

"In love with Céleste!"

"Yes. It seems ridiculous, of course, to think of a grown man being attracted to an undeveloped little school girl. But Southerners are very emotional, aren't they, as a rule? Even the more sensible type, like Walter Avery. I confess he's impressed me quite favorably. And I believe Creoles mature very young. Olivier Fontaine, for instance, acts and appears much older than twenty-one."

"His age doesn't matter. He doesn't appear like anything but a fop and an ass and he never will. I don't see how Aunt Estelle ever came to have such a son. I despise the very sight of him. I'm sorry you asked him down here. Or anyone, just yet, for that matter."

"Why, Breck, how inhospitable you sound! I thought you liked to have company!"

"I do, as a rule. But I'd like to get 'adjusted' here, as you call it, before we fill the house up. And I don't think my standard of hospitality is elastic enough to include much of Olivier Fontaine, at any time."

He rose, abruptly, and began to pace up and down the room. Anna was genuinely astonished at his attitude, and slightly disconcerted by it. She did not understand that she had upset Breck by telling him that Walter Avery was in love with Céleste, and that he was already so much in love with her himself that he shrank from the thought of having her come to his house as a guest, for fear of what might happen if she did. But the last thing Anna desired to do was to close the doors of Splendida to Olivier Fontaine. She had been thinking about him a good deal that morning—in the summerhouse, while Shoog was talking about the lovers who 'gained' their sweethearts there, in the garden where the walks were so sheltered and so still, in the stately drawing room which made such a superb setting for a woman like herself. Breck had said something, when they first talked of coming to Splendida, which had led her to believe he might try to make love to her again himself, and the idea had not been as displeasing to her as she had given him to believe. But the night before he had been silent and sleepy, and this morning he had rushed off with the overseer, after making a scene about Drew. There was nothing ardent in his attitude. However, Olivier was essentially ardent. She was certain of it. When he came he would pay her compliments, he would attempt liberties. It was delightful to think about, and dangerous, and, of course, very, very wicked. Anna prided herself that she had never done anything in the least wicked in all her life, and of course she did not intend to now. But she meant to have Olivier Fontaine come to Splendida and come soon. And she meant to make Breck tractable, as she had always made him. Only, since he seemed to be getting out of hand, she might have to try new tactics.

"The adjustment isn't going to take long, after all," she said quite pleasantly. "I told you the house was much cleaner than I expected. And very, very beautiful—the most beautiful house I've ever seen. I don't wonder you're proud of it, Breck, and that you love it so. I'm proud of it myself, already. And I'm sure I'm going to love it, too. Now that I've been over it thoroughly, I'd like to go out with you and see the plantation. We could go this afternoon, couldn't we, right after lunch? I haven't forgotten that you said it might interest me to put modern improvements in the cabins and in the hospital. I think it would, too. Anyway, I want to look them over. I've been doing some figuring, Breck. I haven't begun to spend my income these last two years. I'm prepared to lay out a very substantial sum on Splendida. When we've been around together, we can decide what ought to be done first, can't we?"

Breck went slowly up the path leading to the top of the levee.

The sun was setting, and along the ridge of the embankment, the cows that were pastured there were darkly silhouetted against the sky. The sound they made, as they cropped the juicy young grass, was the only one he could hear. The scene was one of great abundance and complete peace. When he reached the top of the levee himself, he could see a fisherman, throwing out a line over one of the still pools which the willows inclosed, on the batture beyond the embankment. Farther off, a group of squatters had pitched a tent, and smoke was curling upwards from the fire they had built. Farther yet, the great river flowed silently and swiftly to the sea. But its currents were concealed; its forces were confined. At this evening hour it was mighty but beneficent in all its aspects.

Breck sat down, gratefully drinking in the beauty all around him. This was his land, at one and the same time his heritage and his hope, to which for years he had yearned vainly to return. But now that he was here, his joy in it was riddled with complexity and foreboding. In his own heart there was none of the peace which permeated the countryside.

Not that Anna had angered or even annoyed him again. On

the contrary, he could not remember when he had seen her so amiable and so enthusiastic. She had chatted agreeably all through lunch, both to Drew and to himself. She had made no objection to the presence of the cosset lamb on the lawn, or to the suggestion of other possible pets which might be added to it. Her comments, as she had ridden over the plantation afterwards, had been both agreeable and intelligent. While praising the beauty of the place, she had revealed an understanding of its value, actual and potential. The renovations and repairs which she wholeheartedly agreed to underwrite were improvements which Breck himself had long desired to make, and which he had not been able, without her help, to afford. But it was her very eagerness to begin these without delay which precipitated his present problem. For of all the buildings on the plantation, there was none in such poor repair as the old warehouse by the river. It was here that Anna thought they should start their program of restoration and modernization. Normally, Breck would have agreed with her. But if the levee were moved back, then the warehouse would have to be moved, too. And in spite of all he could say or do, the decision regarding the levee would not, in the last analysis, rest with him. It would rest with the State Levee Board, acting upon the advice of the army engineers. At any moment it saw fit, the Levee Board could act. When it acted, the beauty which Anna had admired would be marred, and the value she had respected would be impaired and she would be angry. She would ask why anyone should ever have built, wastefully and pridefully, in a place of such danger. She would not understand that when the building had been done there was no prospect of peril, that no one could foresee or foretell when the river would change its course, devastating one of its banks to glut the other——

And what if, after all, the Board left them in peace, if through bravado or bribery or both, he could succeed in keeping the levee where it was, at least for the present? Such tactics had worked before, as he had reminded Marcy Yates. They might conceivably work again. Yes, and something else might happen, too, something that had also happened before. If the levee were not moved in time, if there were a flood and a crevasse, Splendida and all that it stood for might be engulfed and submerged, like many another plantation. He might have to choose between Anna's anger and all that it would do to his pride and his prestige, and the possible annihilation of everything he loved best in the world. Everything—but not everybody. He loved Drew better than he loved this legacy he had tried to safeguard for the child, and which, between them, Anna and he might secure for him yet. He loved—what was the use in denying it any longer?—Marie Céleste more still. If he lost everything else, but could gain her, what would the rest matter? If he could "gain" her—that was the word from which Anna had shrunk. But he did not shrink from it. In the midst of his misery, he exulted in it, and in all that it could mean and might mean——

But the misery still persisted. He had tried to avoid Anna's anger before, under circumstances similar to those with which he was battling now, and in the end the day of reckoning had been all the harder because of the postponement. He remembered all too well his purchase of the house in Boston where he and Anna had lived when they were first married. He had told her he had plenty of money to buy it; as a matter of fact, he had mortgaged it heavily. When the first payment on the mortgage was due, he had no ready money to meet it; but he took it for granted that the bank through which the financing had been done would be lenient. Unfortunately, the directors of the bank had a different viewpoint, and Anna overheard a telephone conversation, peremptory on the one side, confused on the other. Their first serious quarrel had come as a result of this involuntary eavesdropping. She had told him then, in the heat of anger, that if he ever deceived her like that again, she would leave him. Afterwards she had said that of course she did not mean that and he did not believe for a moment that she had. But the next time she said the same thing, she never retracted it, though there was no further reference to the matter.

He remembered that time very well, too. He had been tactfully told that his services as a bond salesman were superfluous to his father-in-law's firm. Instead of confessing this at once to Anna, he had continued to leave the house at the usual hour every morning, giving her the impression that he was going downtown, whereas, as a matter of fact, he merely wandered aimlessly over Beacon Hill and around Back Bay. He knew that someday, when he came home, he would find that Mr. Forbes, himself, had told her. And yet Breck could not pronounce the words which proclaimed his own inefficiency.

Episodes like these had occurred over and over again during the eight years of his marriage. But he had never learned to cope with them, as he knew his father would have managed to do, with a mixture of bluff, braggadocio and timely love-making. Rousing himself reluctantly, he now saw that it was really growing dark. The cows were not shining silhouettes any longer, they were only dim shapes. The fisherman was paddling softly towards the shore. The squatters were gathered around their fire, eating their supper. It was time that he went home himself—that he faced Anna across their own supper table. She had said, when they separated, that she wanted to get back to her desk for a little while before the last mail went out; there were certain supplies that she had to order for the warehouse right away. Breck had nodded, and thanked her, and said he thought, if she did not mind, he would stroll a while by the river. He would be back in time to see Drew before the child was tucked in for the night. They had parted harmoniously, and as far as Anna was concerned, happily. She was very much pleased with the results of her strategy. He had said nothing more about Olivier Fontaine.

When he came back to the house, he said nothing about the levee either. The letter, ordering supplies, went into the mail that night.

CHAPTER 14

ANNA'S FIRST gesture of hospitality towards the Fontaines met with an unexpected check. Olivier and Mrs. Fontaine—the latter speaking for both Céleste and herself—wrote her charming notes, expressing their deep regret at their inability to accept her invitation. But the fact remained that they did decline it. Now that Mrs. Fontaine had shaken off the shackles of her long seclusion, she was seeing more of her friends than she had in many years, and she was already pledged to several engagements for the period that Anna had indicated for a visit; in fact, she was entertaining, herself, in honor of Cardinal Gibbons, who was coming to New Orleans for the first time in several years. Formerly, as Breck would perhaps remember, it was at the Breckenridge house that His

Eminence had usually been received; but though she could not hope to achieve the dignity and distinction with which Aurore, her beautiful sister-in-law, had entertained him, she must do her best to carry on the family tradition. Of course Olivier must act as her host, and he was further committed to taking a prominent part in the civic celebration planned in honor of Harry Lauder and his company of Scotch bagpipers, and to attending the banquet which Governor Luther Hall was giving for the great comedian. Céleste, according to her mother, was so much occupied with her school, her singing lessons and her Lenten devotions, that she was finding it almost impossible to take part in as many of the "sub-deb" activities as Mrs. Fontaine herself would have been glad to see the girl enjoy. They had lived the life of mourning too long. Now she wanted her daughter to enjoy all the delightful diversions which were so readily available. She hoped that dear Anna would understand. Perhaps a little later, if the tempting invitation could be renewed——

Anna showed the letters from Olivier and his mother to Breck with expressions of regret that were genuine, and he saw that she was making an honest effort to keep from being resentful. Of course she would ask them again later, she said. Did he ' ' she might approach Mrs. Fontaine again in a fortnight. vould it be better to wait a month? In the meantime, what about asking the Beals? The Bairds, too, and the Denises, since he liked them so much. She supposed the children would be out of doors most of the time, and that did make a difference. She had never known Drew to be so little trouble, or to look so well. Did Breck really remember the Cardinal's visits at the Prytania Street house? Would they have been likely to entertain him themselves if they had stayed in town?

"Yes, I remember him very well. No one who ever saw him could possibly forget him. He was really a grand old boy, pleasant as could be, but with something stern underneath the surface and the most piercing eyes I ever saw. He made me feel as if he were looking straight through me, and as if he knew by instinct all the naughty things I'd ever done —which he probably was and did. But he joked and chatted with me in a very kind way at that. I was proud as punch, telling my cronies about it afterwards— No, I don't suppose he'd have come to our house this time. It's more natural, of course, that he should visit the leading Catholic families."

"Why, your father wasn't a Catholic!"

"No, but Aunt Aurore was. Her father was one of the leading laymen in Louisiana, and Uncle Auguste had made a name for himself, locally, in the Church even then. So of course the Fontaine family were entitled to entertain him, and Aunt Aurore had the most appropriate establishment for such an entertainment—at least they all felt that way about the Breckenridge house. And my father fitted into the picture perfectly. He was just as much at ease with Cardinal Gibbons as he was with John L. Sullivan, and they were both equally at ease with him. I remember that the cardinal and Father joked together, too. Father asked him if he really believed that the Pope was infallible, and a twinkle came into those piercing eyes of the Cardinal. Then he said, 'Well, my son, the last time I saw him, he called me Jibbons!' "

Anna smiled, appreciatively. Since she had discovered the excellent social standing of Catholicism in New Orleans her viewpoint regarding it had changed. "I really would like to meet him myself, Breck. Perhaps some other time when he's South—even if we couldn't have him at our house, I'm sure Mrs. Fontaine would be glad to include us on her list, if we were in town. She seemed extremely friendly, even if she did decline my invitation— You haven't told me yet what you think of inviting the Beals and the Bairds."

"Sure, go ahead. I'd be glad to have you."

"I'll get the letters right off. By the way, Marcy Yates told me this morning he had the bill of lading for the asbestos shingles and the steel supports I ordered for the storehouse. So it looks as if we could start repairs there almost immediately."

"Yes, it does. I'm very grateful to you, Anna. I appreciate your interest in the property very much."

"Well, I *am* interested. I think we ought to do something about the hospital next. I know you were only joking when you told me I'd try to put modern plumbing in all the cabins, but I really don't see why it shouldn't be put in the hospital, and why there shouldn't be some sheds with showers, one for the men and one for the women."

"They'd probably be tickled to death with the looks of them, whether they ever used them or not. Well, I must be getting along, Anna. Yates wanted me to have a look at some of the ditches this morning. It's important for them to be kept open, and it may be that we'll need to take two or three men away from the hoeing and set them to digging instead. I'll take Drew along with me. He's beginning to ride very well, and he's crazy about it."

Anna nodded, still smiling amiably. There was no doubt about it, she was softening visibly in the congenial atmosphere of Splendida. A little awkwardly, because it was so long since he had done such a thing spontaneously, Breck bent over and kissed her, first laying his cheek against hers in accordance with his old habit. She returned the kiss, almost shyly, like a girl, but she did not do so coldly or mechanically. Instead, she revealed more than receptivity to the caress and made no effort to shorten it. When Breck raised his head, she stretched out her hand, and took his, of her own accord.

"Breck," she said. "I've been thinking some more about what you said when we first went to New Orleans—about your entering politics, you know. I believe you were right and I was wrong. I believe it really would be a very good idea. I don't know the first steps you ought to take, in Louisiana, and perhaps you don't either. But of course you could easily find out. Probably you ought to make an effort to get around in the parish, meeting the men who are the local leaders and finding out about their problems and interests, first of all. After you have an idea of their general views, you'd know whether you could broach the subject of a possible candidacy. If they were receptive to the plan, I suppose you'd want to begin asking them to your house and going to theirs. Anything I can do to help entertain them— And perhaps you'd like to go up to Baton Rouge, too, and talk over your possible prospects with some of the politicians there. I'll go with you, if you wish. Or if it would be likely to antagonize people who might help you, having a woman around, at the beginning anyhow, I'll wait until a little later. By the way, I had a letter from Mrs. Cutler this morning. She thinks everything is going to come out well with the committee we're organizing. And she suggested that I might like to join one of those that are being formed in the new Civic Branch of the National Consumer's League. There was a meeting at Newcomb College a few days ago, and a Miss Gillean was elected President of the New Orleans Branch. Mrs. Cutler is one of the twelve vice-presidents. Of course you know what the Consumer's League is, Breck."

"I'm afraid I don't, Anna. But that doesn't mean it isn't a good thing. Tell me about it."

"I won't detain you by going into details now, when you want to go out and look at the ditches. I know those are important, too. I can talk to you about the League this evening. It's an organization devoted to bettering the working conditions of factory employees all over the country. Miss Gillean seems to have made a very moving little speech about it. Mrs. Cutler sent me a clipping from the *Item* with an extract from her speech. Here it is, right under my hand."

Anna handed the clipping to Breck. He accepted it politely, and ran through the column.

"The average woman shopper has it in her power to better factory conditions for little children all over the country, if she only knew it," he read. "All she has to do is simply to demand of her merchants that the ready-made clothes she buys have the National Consumer's League label sewed inside. The League's business is to grant labels to factories that are operated under humanitarian systems. Any factory has a right to ask for the National Consumer's League label. When it does, the League dispatches an agent to look over its premises. Then it grants the label, in case the board of health of a place and the state factory inspector report things in proper order. The label stands for four things: That a factory obeys the state law; that all the goods are made on its premises—not in tenement houses; that employees are not worked overtime, and that children under sixteen years are not employed in it."

"Sounds like a very worthy purpose," he said, handing back the clipping. "I'd like to have you tell me more about it this evening. And I think you'd probably enjoy serving on a local committee. I'm glad you've been asked to. And of course I'm tremendously pleased that you've changed your mind about that political bee I have in my bonnet. I'll get to work right away—locally, at first, as you say. Then later I'll go up to the Capital. I've been thinking of doing that anyhow. Well, so long, Anna, and thanks again, for everything."

He left her and went through the vestibule to the front portico and down the steps towards the lawn where Drew was playing with his lamb, trying to tell himself that there was nothing for him to worry about any more, that everything was going to come out all right after all. But he could not carry his self-deception through successfully. He knew that he ought not to have let Anna buy the asbestos shingles and the steel supports for the warehouse in the first place, and he certainly

ought not to let her go ahead with the repair work now that
these had arrived. He had not failed to perceive the bewilderment in Marcy Yates' honest face when the overseer heard
that the supplies were ordered, and he knew that sooner or
later he would have to let Yates know, directly or indirectly,
that he had been too cowardly to tell his wife the truth about
the state of the levee. Well, if he went to Baton Rouge in the
near future, he would make it a point to go to the headquarters of the Levee Board, and see what could be done; he
would have a reasonable excuse for the trip, now that Anna
had suggested it, and he certainly intended to take it before
she could change her mind again about his potential political
career. He might well be able to head off the arrival of the
army engineers on his land. And he would watch for a chance,
now that Anna was in such a mellow mood, to explain the
principle of the changing course of the river, and to assure
her that even if the Levee Board's final decision was adverse,
this had no really disastrous significance: they might actually
improve the entrance to the plantation, by changing it to suit
themselves; it would probably be cheaper in the end to tear
down the old storehouse, using the materials they took from it,
together with those she had bought, to build a new one on
a thoroughly safe foundation. But even as he told himself all
this, he knew he could not tell it to Anna. He knew that he
must accept her present state of mind as a reprieve and not
as a change. He knew that she would harden and withdraw
when she learned of this new evasion, this new cravenness on
his part. The day of reckoning would be doubly dreadful, not
only because he had postponed it, but because he had postponed it through fear of a woman's wrath and a woman's
tongue and a woman's power over him and his child.

The thought of this was enough to corrode his pleasure in
his altered political prospects. But he had a second reason
for feeling guilty that day. He, too, had received a letter in
the morning mail. Marie Céleste, instead of writing to Anna,
had written to him. The impulse which had caused her to do
this was natural and friendly, the letter itself, as innocent
as it was gay. And yet, when Anna had shown him her letters from Mrs. Fontaine and from Olivier, something had
prevented him from showing Céleste's letter to her. He had
not thought that Anna would be shocked, or offended, because Marie Céleste had written to him. She had too much
self-assurance to be readily jealous, or to take umbrage at

some trivial slight. But he had been afraid she would regard
Céleste's lighthearted missive as childish, that she might
deride its merry mixture of simple events and ingenuous
opinions as insignificant and silly. To him the letter was utterly charming, from start to finish, though it was slightly
disturbing in places; he could not bear the thought that anything so sweet should be submitted to satire. So he had been
silent, as if he were ashamed. He had smirched Céleste's
letter himself by his deliberate concealment of it. And now he
really was ashamed.

As Breck reached the bottom of the great flight of steps,
Drew came bounding over the grass to meet him. The hoped-
for increase in pets had become a reality. Besides the lamb,
which gambolled gracelessly but endearingly after Drew,
two puppies tumbled about at his heels and he carried a small
fuzzy kitten in his arms. He held the kitten up to his father.

"Stroke her, Daddy!" he said. "She's as soft as—as—I don't
know what. What else is there as soft as a kitten? A baby?"

"Yes. A baby's very soft, too. Differently from a kitten, of
course. It's a baby's skin that's soft and a kitten's fur."

"It's too bad we haven't a baby, too, Daddy."

"Yes, Drew, it is."

"Don't you think Mr. Yates would get us a baby, if we
asked him to?"

"No, Drew, I'm afraid he couldn't."

"Why not? He's got us everything else we've asked him
for."

"Yes, but now I guess he's reached his limit."

"I don't see why, Daddy."

"Drew, don't start saying *why* this morning."

"Why, Daddy? Why not this morning? Usually you aren't
cross when I ask you why."

"I'm not cross this morning, Drew. I don't feel like answering questions, that's all. There's a limit to the number of questions I can answer, just as there's a limit to the number of
things Mr. Yates can get for you. Here, take your kitten. I
want to read a letter."

"Aren't we going to see the ditches?"

"Yes. But I want to read this letter first."

He sat down on one of the decorative iron seats, elaborately wrought, and painted a glistening white, that were scattered at intervals over the lawn. Drew, cuddling the kitten

again, stood still, regarding him attentively and a little anxiously. It made Breck feel uncomfortable to open Marie Céleste's letter while confronted by his son's watchful gaze. But once he was on horseback, there would not be another chance until dinner time. He could not wait that long to re-read it.

Dear Breck:

Mamma has told me about the lovely invitation from you and Anna, and I know she and Olivier are writing Anna to tell you both how sorry we are that we cannot accept it. But I have decided to write you also, because I am afraid that Mamma and Olivier will not go into all the reasons for fear of boring you. I mean, all my reasons. Of course Mamma will tell Anna about the Cardinal and Olivier will tell her about Harry Lauder, but I am sure they will not tell her about the Style Show, and that is important, too. At least I think so, and I believe you would be interested in hearing about it.

It opened Monday and twenty-five stores are co-operating to put it on. There is an article in the Item *saying that more than a million dollars have been spent in bringing models and fabrics here. There are at least a hundred mannequins from London and Paris and Vienna, and some of them are very famous. I think the prettiest of all is the one that Henry Hutt uses as his model for magazine covers in his "Girlhood" series. She is what you would call a knockout.*

All last Saturday and Sunday the shop windows on Canal Street were covered with tarpaulins, while style experts worked behind these, setting up all sorts of wonderful things. Then suddenly there was a signal, and the tarpaulins were all whisked away, and everyone came crowding up to see what had been behind them. Of course there has been a great deal of friendly rivalry among the stores to see which would put on the best display, so all of them are marvelous. One store is showing the pure white crepe dress that was made for Mrs. John Jacob Astor's first mourning after her husband lost his life in the Titanic *disaster. (That was almost as bad as the Bourgogne, wasn't it? Except that on the* Titanic *everyone was brave; even the musicians kept on playing while the ship went down, and Mr. Astor helped his wife into a lifeboat and then stepped back himself, although it must have been dreadful for him to leave her and for her to have him, especially as she was expecting a baby.) The white dress did make a great impression on me, because it is so different from the terrible black crepe that everyone wears here, after there has been a death in the family, and so much more appropriate and lovely. I talked to Mamma about it, and she said she agreed with me. Before this she has not always approved when I have wanted to wear white myself for mourning, but now she says she understands. So Mrs. Astor's dress has made a great change in my life. I shall never have to wear that terrible black crepe again, no matter who dies. I shall always wear lovely white dresses.*

The manager of one of the other stores had an idea that is really just as good, in a different way: beginning tomorrow he is going to show a replica of the dress that Mrs. Woodrow Wilson wore at the Inaugural Ball on March 4th. I can hardly wait to see it, and of course I shall go straight down to Canal Street from school. An inauguration seems so much more personal if you see what the President's wife wore.

Mamma says that perhaps if Anna asks us again we can come to Splendida later on in the Spring, and I hope we can, because I have always heard so much about it and wanted so much to see it. But please hint to Anna that it would be easier for us to come after Lent. I go to church very faithfully during Lent and in Holy Week there isn't time to do much of anything except go to church, with the Tenebrae and the Three Hours' Service and all. And of course Holy Thursday is even fuller of church-going than Good Friday, itself, because on Holy Thursday my friends and I always visit nine churches together and make a liberal contribution at each, before we finally go to St. Roch's to pray for husbands. We feel sure that if our contributions have been generous, our prayers will be answered, and it is especially important that I should make the pilgrimage this year, because I am going to offer the same prayer that I did on St. Joseph's Eve after we got our lucky beans and before we had our spumone: I am going to pray for a husband exactly like you! Because, Breck, I really do think you are the nicest man I ever met in my life, and if I could only have someone just like you for a husband, I know I couldn't help living 'happily ever after.' Of course I realize that probably there couldn't be two people as nice as you in the world, but you told me yourself that everyone had a double, so I hope that is true in your case as well as mine.

Speaking of my double, Uncle Octave came to see Mamma the evening after you and Anna left New Orleans and they had a long talk together in the library. I didn't think much about it at the time, because Walter Avery was calling on me, and I was very much thrilled at having a caller of my own. Mamma has decided that I am old enough to do so, on week ends, when I do not have to study, and Walter came the very next evening after she told him this. I think Mamma intended to sit in the back parlor while he was there, but when Uncle Octave appeared, she said something to Walter about being sure she could trust him and went off with Uncle Octave to the library. And since then she seems to have abandoned the idea of sitting in the back parlor when I have company. At least she told me the next day that her parents were very conservative, and that when she was a young girl she was never allowed (she said 'allowed' first and then corrected herself and said 'supposed') to see any young man except in their presence until she was engaged to Papa, and that even then there was always someone in the next room. Afterwards she went on to say that she, herself, was not sure this was the best method, though she added hastily that I must not get the idea she was criticizing anything her parents had done, because she knew they loved her dearly and had her welfare at heart. It was really a wonderful talk that Mamma and I had together, Breck, and by and by she stopped speaking about Walter (and other young men) and calling customs, past and present, and said she thought I was old enough to hear a rather sad story and that she felt the time had come when she ought to tell it to me. She had hoped that it might never be necessary for her to do so, but after what had happened on St. Joseph's Eve, which Uncle Octave had told her about in the library, she was afraid it was. So then she told me about my double, Breck. There are some parts of this sad story that I still do not understand very well, and I should like to talk them over with you sometime, if you would let me. Because I could see that it made Mamma unhappy to talk about it too long, and when I tried to talk to Olivier about it, he was very short with me. This puzzled me, too, because I gather that he does sometimes go to Uncle Octave's house, so why shouldn't he be willing to talk about it? I wish I could go there myself, because after all

Laure is just as much my cousin as Charles Rutledge and Carmelita Fontaine, isn't she? But Mamma says no, that Olivier may go to Uncle Octave's house but that I may not, and I have never known her to be so firm about anything as she was about that.

There is another strange thing I might mention, and this is, I believe that Walter goes to Uncle Octave's house, too. He and Uncle Octave shook hands with each other quite cordially that evening they both came to call at the same time, and though I did not think anything about it at the moment, I did after Mamma talked to me. It came over me that it was not the first time they had met, that they had known each other before. But I have not said anything about this to Walter, as it does not seem to me the sort of thing that is natural to say to him (or to any other young man).

I have learned two new songs since you were here, the Valse Brune *and* Coeur de ma Mie, *and I am very eager to sing them to you. The words of* Coeur de ma Mie *intrigue me very much, especially where the lover speaks of his dear one's 'little, little heart' and also where he says* It is different with men. *I have not sung* La Délaissée *since you were here, listening in the garden, because I feel that is your song now.*

Now I have written you a very long letter, and I have done it in the study period that is supposed to be devoted to sacred history, so I am really feeling a little guilty. But just the same I have enjoyed writing it, and I should be very pleased if you should happen to answer it.

> *Affectionately yours,*
> *Marie Céleste de Fontaine*

Breck refolded Marie Céleste's letter, very slowly, and put it back in his pocket. Then he looked up and saw that Drew was still standing in front of him, squeezing and stroking his kitten, and staring at his father with solemn and troubled eyes. Breck jumped up and put his arm around the little boy.

"Come on," he said. "Set that ball of fluff down on the seat and get yourself a cap. We must be off to see those ditches before it gets any later."

CHAPTER 15

SPRING CAME sweeping up the river from the gulf and every day it brought more beauty with it, adding this to the beauty which already lay like a garment over the fields and forests of Splendida Plantation.

In the garden, the waxen camellia petals had begun to fall, but all around, the roses, infinitely warmer and sweeter, were beginning to bloom. The rosebushes grew as tall as trees, and it was not only the mansion that was surrounded with them; every Negro cabin on the place was transfigured by the butter-colored or shell-pink blossoms. Back of the bushes, the chinaberry trees, which had been brown and barren for so long, were bursting, rocket-like, into multiple green balls. Beds and walks were bordered with magenta-colored thrift, its riotous growth belying its prim name; and where the driveway met the highroad there were hedges of lilies. Where the shade of the trees encircling the garden lay deepest, there was a carpet of violets; everywhere else, the carpet was patterned with white clover, springing up abundantly in the green grass. In the morning light, when the dew was still on it, it seemed to be studded with jewels.

Drew, riding over these meadows or along the top of the levee at his father's side, hoped the pony's hoofs would not crush the clover, and that the stock would not consume it all. His concern did not have the same source as Marcy's, who told him that when the cows ate too much clover, they were sometimes sick. He was sorry about this, but he would have been sorrier still to see the clover disappear. Every morning when he went out he was relieved to find that there was still more than there had been the day before, and just as many tall purple thistles, too. In a way, the thistles were even prettier than the clover, but Drew soon found out that they were not pleasant to pick, and another source of relief was his pony's disinclination to eat them, for he would not have liked Sport to get thistles in his mouth. He had a more personal feeling for Sport than for the cows, and he did not mind so much seeing the mules eat the thistles, because he did not care so much for mules. He talked to Breck about them.

"Mules are queer animals, aren't they, Daddy? Sometimes, when you look at one, it seems as if you were seeing a horse, and then you look again, and it seems as if you were seeing a donkey. I can't make out why."

"I'll tell you why, Drew. It's because the mule has a mare for a mother and a donkey for a father. That's why it doesn't seem wholly like either one or the other to you. It's a hybrid."

"What's a hybrid, Daddy?"

"Why, I just told you that a mule is! But there are other kinds, too. A hybrid can be any sort of creature whose father and mother are different."

"Not just animals? Boys and girls, too?"

"It seems that way sometimes. But it isn't ever polite to speak about them as hybrids, even though you may think they are. Don't ever call anyone a hybrid, Drew."

"All right, Daddy I won't— Are mules queer in other ways?"

"Yes, they're sterile."

"What's sterile, Daddy?"

"They can't reproduce themselves. I mean they can't have young. A little colt grows up into a mare or a stallion, and by and by it can breed or sire more little colts. It's the same with other animals. Except mules."

"That's rather hard on the mules, isn't it, Daddy? Because everyone likes to have babies."

"I'll try to explain all these things to you little by little, Drew. Don't worry about the mules. I think they have very happy lives on plantations. And they're very useful to us, better suited to the work we have done than heavy horses. A horse has to be very large and powerful to do the same amount of work as a good strong sugar mule, and it costs a good deal more in the beginning. We have one mule here whose name is Maggie, and who can not only do the work of three horses, but of three other sugar mules. She's quite a character. You must get Yates to tell you about her sometime."

"You tell me now, Daddy."

"Well, it seems that she works faithfully and hard all day, hardest of all during the grinding season, when the work is heaviest, but at night she runs away. No one's ever found out how she manages to do it. The fence is very high around the yard where she's kept, and the gate's always securely locked. It doesn't seem as if she could possibly jump over the fence or push the gate open, but I guess she does. Because in the morning she's gone. Someone has to go out and seek her and bring her back. The hands say she's like a girl named Lute, who loves to go out a lot, too. They say that when her day's work's done she's 'got to walk de road.' Not that Maggie would get as far in doing that as Lute does."

"I don't know what you mean, Daddy."

"I don't mean anything. Now that's enough about mules for the present. We've got to get going if you want to come up onto the levee with me."

It was the levee that Drew loved the most, more than those rich smutty fields from which the sugar cane and cotton stalks were shooting higher and higher day by day, more than the gardens or the groves or the swampland. He revelled in feeling Sport struggle and scramble up the steep rocky path, and when he had reached the summit of the slope, he liked to let his pony rest while he watched the other animals grazing on one side of it, and looked out on the batture and the river on the other. There were colts, frisking beside their staid mothers or stooping to nuzzle them, calves nestling against each other, spry little kids and lambs, less cossetted than Bessie, leaping lightly over the clover, all pastured on the plantation side of the levee. Sometimes even a grunting sow, surrounded by small pink pigs, strayed as far as this, though swine, like poultry, was theoretically more confined. It was because he found the limits of the pens and runs and ponds less fascinating than the freedom and openness of the levee, that Drew cared less for porklings and chickens and goslings than he did for colts and calves, kids and lambs. Restraint of any kind had always been irksome to him, and now that he had tasted the delights of complete liberty for the first time, these had gone to his head.

He stayed on the levee for hours at a time. He learned the names of all the local steamers—the *Menge*, and the *Garig* which his mother had disdained, the *Gem* and the *Tom* and the *Omaha* as well. He also learned to tell the ocean-going steamers and the big river steamers from the bayou packets, not only by their size, but by their pilot houses. The steamers had glassed-in pilot houses, and great gilded devices swung between their smoke-stacks; the packets had little open cubicles. Then there were the stern-wheelers and the side-wheelers. He was thrilled by them all; he waited and watched for them to come swinging down the river or puffing up it. He kept a big red handkerchief stuffed in with the scraps of string and pencil stubs and pen-knives and stick candy in his pocket, ready to wave as the boats went by. He made friends with all the people he met—the fat colored women with their heads wrapped in *tignons*, the lean Italians with their faces screened by sunbonnets, the ragged galloping horsemen, the tumbling potbellied pickaninnies. The stray fishermen, sitting patiently under the feathery willows, or moving quietly about in their little boats, also fascinated him, as they did his father. Breck explained to him that the men fishing with lines in the little pools were out after crawfish, which their wives would make into gumbo and crawfish bisque by and by, but that the men by the river-side, facing the current, with strong black nets in their hands, were out after catfish and perch and sacaulaits, which their wives would fry.

"Sacaulait's a funny word, Daddy."

"It's a French word. *Sac-au-lait* means a bag of milk. The French settlers called the fish that because there was so much nourishment in them, and because there was such a white milky look to the meat. If you had a French governess, as your mother wanted you to, she would have taught you enough by this time so that you could have figured that out for yourself."

"But I don't need to have a governess to teach me things, or to try too hard to figure them out for myself when you're here to tell me. Couldn't we go fishing for crabs and sacaulaits ourselves?"

Breck laughed and said Drew would never keep still long enough to make a good fisherman. When the child persisted, Breck told him, carefully, as he would have told one of his own contemporaries, that there was not time to go fishing just now, because there was so much else to do on the plantation.

"You remember those ditches we had to clear so that they'd stay open. And there are some bridges over in the swamp that need repairing, and places where there aren't any bridges at all yet but where some ought to be built. I thought I'd take you to look those places over tomorrow if you'd like to go."

"Gosh, Daddy, you know I'd like to go!"

"All right, I'll take you. But don't talk to me about wasting time going fishing while bridges need to be built. We need to watch this levee you like so much pretty carefully at this time of the year, too. It isn't here just to look pretty, you know, or to give the stock extra grazing space. It's here to keep the river from overflowing the land. We must keep it mended. We can't risk a crevasse."

"What's a crevasse, Daddy?"

"It's a break in the levee. At least that's what it means in this part of the world. There are some other parts where it means a deep fissure in a glacier."

"What other parts of the world? What's a fissure? What's a glacier?"

"Look here, you human interrogation point, I think we'd better stick to Louisiana in our question and answer department, for now. I don't think we can take in the universe, all at once."

"All right, Daddy. But don't forget to tell me about the fissures and glaciers by and by. Has there ever been a crevasse near Splendida?"

Breck winced. "Yes, there was one last year. It did some damage, but that's very unusual. The river isn't likely to overflow our land and hurt our crops or any of us. The bayous above us and below us generally take care of the greater part of the overflow. And probably there won't be another in a long while. There never was one in your grandfather's time, or your great-grandfather's. Don't be afraid of a crevasse, Drew. Just see how peaceful it looks over there on the batture and how contented all those squatters and fishermen seem to be. If the river were rising, the batture wouldn't look like that and the batture dwellers would be fleeing."

"I'm not afraid of anything, Daddy. Why is the land out there called a batture?"

"There's a French word, *battre,* that means to beat. In the early days women used to take clothes out to the riverbank and beat them clean as they washed them, just as they still do in some parts of France. I believe I'd better get you a governess, after all. *Battre* is another word you'd have known if you'd had a governess."

"Oh, Daddy, please don't get me a governess! I'm sure she'd be an old whore!"

"If your mother heard you using that word, Drew, she'd tell Nana to mop out your moth with soap and water. Where did you hear it? Do you know what it means?"

"No, I don't know what it means exactly, except that it's

something that isn't very nice. I've heard the men say it lots of times. Even Mr. Yates called one of the girls a whore the other day—the pretty one who isn't black at all, and wears big gold earrings and long gold chains and red dresses on Sundays. I think it's the same one you said was like Maggie the mule, the one named Lute— What does 'whore' mean, Daddy?"

"Look out, Drew. I'm certainly going to get you that governess if you ask me any more questions today."

"I won't, Daddy. I promise I won't. I don't mean to ask too many questions. But I'm so interested."

That was it. He was so interested. Breck never looked down into his son's bold handsome little face that he did not see it lighted with eagerness and intentness. Drew was almost as much enthralled with the swamp as he was with the levee. The sight of the trees rising out of the water, of eagles perching on lofty limbs and niggergeese skimming over little lakes, delighted him in the same way as the sight of the young stock on the clover-grown slopes with the waving willows and rushing river beyond them. He laughed at an alligator that came waddling and squirming down to the water's edge. He quickly and gleefully killed a snake that darted across his path. He accepted the redbug bites that made great welts on the bare knees above his wool socks. He said nothing about being tired or hungry or hot all day, and he handled a hammer better than the ten-year-old Negro boys who went with the party. When Breck went to see him, according to custom, after Drew was tucked into bed that night, his heart was so overflowing in happy pride in his son that he volunteered to answer all the questions about glaciers and fissures that Drew wanted to ask him.

And it was not only when he was riding far afield that the child was happy. He responded with alacrity when Breck suggested that he might like to plant a vegetable garden himself, and presently had reason to be proud of his own small patch of corn, peas, onions, pumpkins and potatoes. This patch adjoined the strawberry beds, and two or three times he came into the house with a bad stomach-ache, the source of which was a mystery to Anna, and later, with a face smeared by a deeper red than his own natural high color. This was more obviously telltale in character. But he carried off both the agonizing cramps and the evidences of his guilt with his usual jaunty and irresistible air of bravado that carried its own guarantee of forgiveness with it, at least from his father.

On rainy days he watched the men intently while they poured molasses, shaved shingles, fashioned hoop poles and made hogsheads. He proved to be as handy with all tools as he had shown himself first with a hammer, and he was completely happy and thoroughly at home in the cooperage, the sawmill and the blacksmith shop. In the cotton fields he quickly learned to speak of tender young leaves "stringing the rows," and of chopping the young stalks "out to a stand." He soon subscribed to the belief that cotton should be planted during the full of the Easter moon, and that as for the rest, foodstuffs which grew above the ground should be planted when the moon was waxing, and foodstuffs which grew below the ground when it was waning. He picked up not only the good-natured profanity and quaint colloquialisms of the Negroes, but some of their proverbs and superstitions and songs. He startled Breck by saying one day, almost too aptly, "De dog that bites off his own tail, sets a bad example for de puppy." It was even more startling the day he began to hum under his breath:

"Say you know you didn't want me
The day you lay across ma bed,

You was drinkin' bad liquor
An' talkin' out of you' head.

But I'd rather see a coffin comin' to ma back do'
Than to heah you sayin' you don't want me no mo'."

"Good grief, Drew! Where did you pick that up?"

"I heard Lute singing it. You know, the pretty girl with the gold earrings. The one you said was like Maggie the mule and that Mr. Yates called a whore."

"Oh! Well, I wouldn't sing it any more if I were you."

"Why not, Daddy?"

"I just wouldn't, that's all."

"Is it because you think it's a better song for a big girl to sing than a little boy?"

"Maybe. Yes, I guess that's it. A girl like Lute, anyway."

"You mean a girl like Marie Céleste wouldn't sing it?"

"Lord no!— When did you hear Marie Céleste singing?"

"Why, lots of times! Nearly every day, while we were in New Orleans. Didn't you ever heard her sing, Daddy?"

"Yes, I've heard her sing."

"Didn't you *like* to hear her sing?"

"Yes, I liked it very much."

"Well, then——"

"Drew, I think you'd better go and hoe your garden. I saw there were a good many weeds in it when I was down there this morning. And don't stuff yourself on strawberries, either, while you're about it."

"All right, Daddy, I won't."

He went off, whistling cheerfully. Later on in the morning, Breck heard him singing Lute's song again. But evidently he had reverted to it quite unconsciously, and Breck decided that it was wiser not to make an issue of it, especially since, upon reflection, he realized that there was not much difference, basically, in the meaning of Céleste's song and of Lute's. Again he seemed to be standing in the shaded garden, listening:

> . . . *Je suis la délaissée*
> *Qui pleure nuit et jour*
> *Celui qui m'a trompée*
> *Etait mon seul amour.* . . .

"Have you written to Mrs. Fontaine again?" he asked Anna that night at supper.

"No, but I will. I'd be glad to. I've been waiting for you to speak about it again. I didn't think you were very enthusiastic when I suggested it the first time, or very sorry when the invitation was declined."

"I wasn't. But we're getting better organized now. And I thought our first week-end party was a great success, Anna. You handled everything beautifully. My stepmother was the most famous hostess of her day in Louisiana, but you could have given her cards and spades, last Sunday."

Anna actually flushed a little. He could not remember that he had ever seen her so pleased with his praise. She certainly deserved it. Guests would have had to be captious indeed not to be satisfied with the hospitality dispensed at Splendida, and neither the Beals, the Bairds nor the Denises had been disposed to be captious. Anna had made their visit the occasion of the first dinner to which she invited her neighbors living on near-by plantations, with whom she had already exchanged calls—the Gays of St. Louis, the Randolphs of Nottoway, the Héberts of Plaisance, the Allains of Australia, the Kochs and Aldigés of Belle Alliance and many others—so many, indeed, that one of the famous old tablecloths, sixty-five feet long, was taken from the armoire where it had long lain in vetivert, to grace the occasion. The Sèvres service, of which Clarisse Fontaine had also whispered excitedly to Estelle Lenoir when they were both girls, captivated by the legend of "young Mr. Breckenridge," was brought out also, and many other rarities—the two-lipped finger bowls, the goblets with the strange ring to them, the "satin-glass" china that was as "smooth as a ribbon." The feast itself was in every way worthy of its setting. The cook had received the traditional training at one of the best restaurants in New Orleans, and the turtle soup, the trout Marguerite, the roasted pigeons, and all that went with them, were the last word in perfection. The supplies in the Breckenridge cellar were inexhaustible. It had always contained casks of Bordeaux for daily consumption, Tokay and Madeira in five-gallon demijohns, champagne in wicker baskets. For a special occasion like this gala dinner there were bottles of all the best Châteaux, Veuve Cliquot of the rarest vintage, chartreuse and benedictine that gurgled richly as they dropped in green and golden streams from crystal decanters into tiny gilded glasses. Foodstuffs as well as beverages were laid by in the same inexhaustible quantities, for Breck had never broken with the tradition that his father and grandfather had upheld, in running the plantation, so far as possible, as it had been run before the War between the States. Besides all the fresh fish from the river and the new-killed meat and poultry which the place supplied, besides the crisp green vegetables and lucious red berries pouring in from the garden, there were ham and sausage and souse, corned beef and jerked beef in the smokehouse, and in the storehouse, sugar in hogsheads, apples in barrels, and pyramid after pyramid of Louisiana oranges. Anna had seen to it that the best of all these were represented on the festive board, taking an illogical pleasure in surpassing the display she had condemned at the Fontaine house.

This initial gesture of hospitality had been deeply appreciated and lavishly returned. During the visit of the guests from New Orleans at Splendida, the Randolphs had given a dance in their famous ballroom, where not only the walls and

pillars and ceiling but the very floor were a glistening white.
Not to be outdone, the Héberts had offered a Sunday "breakdown" which had lasted so long that everyone had gone
straight from there to Belle Alliance for mint juleps. Meantime the younger generation had been left at Splendida, in
charge of Nana, whose report to her mistress, when the latter returned with a slight headache and an unaccustomed
flush, late in the evening, struck almost the only jarring note
in the course of the house party. Julia, the Beals' little daughter, was a sweet child, Nana admitted. She had set quietly
playing with Drew's kitten most of the day, and had eaten
her lamb chop and spinach and baked potato like a little
lady, without spilling so much as a smitch on her bib. In
fact, her starched white dress was just as clean, when Nana
took it off, before her nap, as it had been when she came out
of her mother's room that morning. She had been lovely to
Nana too—so affectionate, so polite. But as for that Denis
child, Evelyn—well, there was no doing anything with her at
all. She was pert, she was plaguy, she was everywhere she
ought not to be and nowhere she should be; she had succes-
sively got into a mud puddle and a hornet's nest and a frosted
cake that was being saved for supper. She had tormented the
poor innocent little kitten that was sleeping so peacefully in
Julia's arms, and tied the puppies' tails together. When Drew
found this out, he had slapped her and called her a naughty
name. Nana did not like to pronounce this wicked word
herself, but she felt she ought to tell Mrs. Breckenridge that
it began with a W and ended with an E. Evelyn had slapped
back at Drew and bitten him, and pulled out quantities of his
hair—it was a mercy it grew so thick you wouldn't notice.
And then, after doing him much more damage than he had
done her, except by his repeated insults, she had screamed
to Harold, who had been quiet enough up to then, playing
with Drew's Meccano. Drew had hit her, she yelled, and was
hurting her more and more. So then Harold had come down
off the portico and fought with Drew. They both had black
eyes and bloody noses now, and they had called each other
names that were even worse than what Drew had called
Evelyn. Nana could not bring herself to pronounce even the
first and last letters of this. She did not see how little gentlemen ever picked up such language.

Anna might have taken the Englishwoman's recital more
to heart if it had not been for the headache she had by that

time, and if, aside from the children's ructions, the day had not been such a success. But she did speak to Breck about it, and ask him to reprove Drew when he went to "tell" his son good night. Breck was secretly very much amused, but he had tried to speak sternly to Drew, whose black eye was almost concealed by bedtime, because his face was so swollen all around it.

"You shouldn't pick a quarrel with a guest, Drew."

"I didn't, Daddy. They picked the quarrels with me. First Evelyn and then Harold."

"Well, it takes two to make a quarrel. You should have avoided getting actually involved."

"Don't you think a boy has a right to do something if a girl bites him, Daddy?"

"I suppose so. But he needn't slap her. And he needn't start cuffing another boy."

"I tell you I didn't start it, Daddy. You don't want me to run and hide, do you, when a blue-bellied bastard like Harold Baird socks me in the eye?"

"No, I don't want you to run away exactly. I don't want you to call him that either."

"Aren't you glad, really, Daddy, that I licked him? Because that's what I did. And I bet Evelyn won't forget what I did to her. I tied her right hand and her left foot together and toppled her over and put a handkerchief in her mouth, so that she couldn't scream. It served her right, too. Those poor little puppies!"

"I'm afraid Evelyn must have a cruel streak. But no matter what she did or what Harold did, you shouldn't have called them those names. I'll have to punish you if you go on using such bad language, Drew."

"I can't help it if you do. I do think Evelyn is a whore and I do think Harold is a blue-bellied bastard."

"You don't even know what those words mean. I'll tell you by and by. But until I do, I want you to promise me you won't use them."

"All right, Daddy, I do promise. When will you tell me? What do they mean?"

This episode had been the only contretemps, and as the parents of the visiting children had apparently taken it no more seriously than Breck, or at any rate, than Anna, no harm had come of it. But as Drew seemed to be perfectly contented now on the plantation without any playmates except the pets for which his devotion daily grew, Breck was inclined to agree with Anna that he could get along, at least for the present, without the interpolation of little girls who bit and little boys who bullied, on the otherwise peaceful scene. He also agreed with her that they, themselves, could have a second house party which would be even more successful than the first one, if there were no disturbing elements in it. But he had hardly expressed himself to this effect, after Anna had so cordially responded to his suggestion about the Fontaines, than he realized how inaccurate he had been through implying that this family would supply none. A dozen children, each twenty times worse than Evelyn and Harold put together, would not be half so disturbing to him as Marie Céleste, and he knew it. And still, after postponing and evading another encounter with her for weeks, he was actually precipitating one now.

He found all sorts of excuses for his action. If the invitation were not repeated, Mrs. Fontaine might think they had taken umbrage because she had declined the first one, and he was so sincerely devoted to his Aunt Estelle that he would deeply regret a misunderstanding on her part. Since Walter Avery was to be the sixth person in the party, he, himself, would not see much of Marie Céleste anyway, except at mealtimes—indeed it was probable that he would never see her alone at all. And in admitting to himself that he loved her, he had never had the presumption to assume that she loved him—indeed the very idea was fantastic. So what harm could his feeling do her in any case, since it was not reciprocated? Besides, he believed that this feeling was now very well under control, and there were all sorts of reasons why it should be. He was happier than he had been in a long time. He was living at last as he had always yearned to live, on his own land, among his own people; and as if it were not enough that this major desire was at last fulfilled, there were actually indications that the minor desire for political activity was no longer impossible of fulfillment either.

His first tentative overtures in the neighborhood had met with encouraging response. He was gratified to find that the local people seemed to like him, and—in a more practical sense—that, as a prominent planter on whom many were dependent, he could probably control about three hundred votes. Moreover, it was a propitious moment for a newcomer to break in because the old order had recently undergone a complete upheaval. The state, through the impetus of the Good Government League was in the throes of one of those periodical "reform movements" typical of the American way of life. The year before, Martin Behrman, the powerful mayor of New Orleans, had lost the strangle hold in which he had long gripped the state as well as the city. It had been his proud boast that he could swing any state election to suit himself, simply by "sending word down the line" twenty-four hours before it took place; and the conviction that to get anything done it was first necessary to "dicker with Behrman" was almost universal. But a sequence of unpredictable "breaks" had sent the "reform" candidate, Luther E. Hall, to Baton Rouge as governor. Now Hall had called a Constitutional Convention for the following fall. Breck's interest had been easily awakened, and the prospect of becoming a delegate to the Convention, which had been suggested to him as a logical first step, politically speaking, attracted him very much. One by one he was making the necessary moves indicated to turn the prospect into a certainty, and he was enjoying all the contacts and all the experiences connected with his novitiate.

What meant infinitely more, his companionship with his little son was deepening into closer and closer communion day by day; it was joyous, it was tender, it was full of harmony. Passionately as he had adored his own father, proudly as his father had regarded him, he knew that there had never been a bond between them that could compare with this. It would be the act of a madman as well as a criminal to jeopardize it.

And then there was Anna, herself—happier, too, than he had ever seen her—proud, yet grown gentler in proportion to her growing gladness. When he had first known her, she had seemed to embody the answer to all his questions, the goal of all his searching: her strength, her rectitude, even her slight severity—these were the qualities he needed to supplement those that he lacked. He had loved her sincerely, he had trusted her implicitly, he had respected her infinitely; he had not missed the spark of divine fire which she failed to kindle because no one else had ever kindled it either. He still trusted her and still respected her; there should be a chance that his love for her might revive under conditions at last beneficent for them both. He already recognized, with ungrudging admiration, the unexpected excellence of her supervision at

Splendida, and gave thanks, with wholehearted gratitude, for her equally unexpected enthusiasm and liberality. There was no longer any doubt that she could, and would, fill the position of a politician's wife with the same skill and the same showmanship that she had displayed in playing the part of a planter's wife; she would greatly enhance the importance and the distinction of any position he might be called upon to fill, and it was unquestionable that with her he might attain lofty places which without her he could not have reached. Now that his latent ambition was so thoroughly aroused, he had no mind to disregard Anna's value in the scheme of coming events. When she told him that Mrs. Fontaine had accepted her second invitation, and that Marie Céleste, Olivier and Walter Avery would all accompany her to Splendida, he told Anna he was very glad, and he told himself there was no reason why he should have made such a desperate effort to keep his voice calm while he said it.

Certainly there was no reason why he should have foreseen that Marie Céleste would hardly have entered his door, before he would again begin making comparisons between her and Anna which were to the latter's disadvantage. But by a curious coincidence, it happened that Céleste did exactly what he hoped Anna would do and which she had failed to do: instead of rushing on into the house without him, she stood at his side on the portico, while her mother and her brother went on ahead with Anna, looking up at the almost unbelievable height of the Corinthian columns with admiration and awe, until he asked her if she would not like to see the columns in the vestibule and the state suite, too, since they were almost as imposing; and once inside, she instinctively stopped to admire every feature and every object he had meant to point out to Anna, but which Anna had preferred to discover for herself. She paused first before the marble bust of a maiden holding a dove to her breast, carved in medallion form, below the mantelshelf in the drawing room; and then, raising her eyes, gazed steadfastly for a long time at the famous replica of Titian's Laura de' Dianti which hung above it. She lifted the stopper from the double-decker scent bottle designed to hold perfume above and toilet water below, and the lid from the opium jar with the red lacquer center and the border of turquoises. She ran her fingers over the mother-of-pearl inlay on the piano; and all the time she kept giving little exclamations of appreciation and delight, and telling Breck that he certainly had the most beautiful house in the world and the most wonderful things in it.

To be sure, Walter Avery, who had not gone ahead with the others, stayed close by her side, but momentarily, at least, she seemed oblivious of him; her interest was centered intensively on Breck's belongings, and everything that Breck was telling her about them. While he talked to her, he regarded Walter with covert attention but without animosity: an agreeable-looking, clean-cut young man, slightly stereotyped in style, but somehow none the less pleasing on that account. He was not in the least tongue-tied, but neither did he show any inclination to intrude. It was evident that he shared Marie Céleste's enthusiasm for their surroundings, in a general way, since the remarks he did make were hearty and intelligent; and if he were not as enthralled with every detail as she was, that was natural enough, for he would logically have a casual masculine viewpoint rather than a cultivated feminine estimate of the beautiful and the rare. Breck thought that Walter, for all his civility, would probably prefer to get out on the grounds than to linger indefinitely indoors; and feeling that his suggestion was singularly commendable, considering how happy he was himself under existing conditions, he eventually asked his guest whether this were not the case.

"I think Anna's expecting that we'll come out on the piazza for tea, after the ladies have been up to their rooms to take off their things. We're having a barbecue tonight, with extra guests in, so supper'll be late—we thought you and Céleste might enjoy that more than a formal dinner. Perhaps you would like to have a wash yourself— I'll show you where we've put you. But what about a little tennis after tea?"

"That would be fine. Will you and Mrs. Breckenridge take on Céleste and me?"

That would hardly work out, Breck thought, since it would leave Mrs. Fontaine alone; but he was actually less displeased than Olivier with the arrangement upon which they eventually agreed. This was that he, himself, should continue to sit on the piazza with Mrs. Fontaine, after Roscoe had taken the tea things away, and watch the game with her from there. Olivier did not care for tennis, and Breck did; but after all, that was beside the point. Even Olivier tacitly admitted that Breck must necessarily act the attentive host and that he, himself, must act the complacent guest. Looking very elegant

in his spotless flannel trousers and silk shirt, he went languidly out towards the court, where the others were already alertly awaiting him.

"I think it will be very dull for you to sit here and talk to
an old lady while all the other young people are playing,
Breck," Mrs. Fontaine protested. "Really I should enjoy a
little rest at this time. And to tell you the truth, I think Olivier
would, too. He is not as strong as he should be. His health
gives me a great deal of concern. Please go and take his
place after all!"

"I will, a little later, if you insist," he said. "But you can't
really believe I find it dull talking to you, and I don't know
where you get that old lady stuff. I've always loved to talk to
you. And lately I've especially been wanting to talk to you
about my little boy."

"He reminds me so much of you, Breck, at the same age.
I remember so well seeing you out with your black mammy,
who used to sit with her cronies on one of the little seats that
spanned the gutters in those days. You constantly ran away
from her and teased her in other ways, too. But she adored
you— Where is Drew all this time, by the way?"

"He's out with Marcy Yates, our overseer, and a very good
man. He never comes in until the plantation bell rings at
'quittin' time'. He's picking up the lore of the land—it
seems to sink in through the pores, at that age, the way a
foreign language does. Incidentally, he's picking up some
language, too—not foreign but fairly fancy—Anna's rather
worried about it. His favorite designation just now for any
female creature he doesn't like is one that Webster might pronounce 'no longer acceptable in refined circles.' I haven't been
able to explain to him just what it really means."

Mrs. Fontaine smiled indulgently. "I'll have to reassure
Anna by telling her that when I was ten, I told a startled
priest that I was *enceinte* because I didn't know what else
to confess, and I thought that sounded adequate, though I
didn't have any idea what it meant either. I'd heard one of
our servants sobbing out a similar confession, which put
the thought into my head. But the priest was very kind to
me, and very helpful. He taught me to understand. You can
do that with Drew, Breck, if you're patient and tactful and
candid and never set him a bad example yourself."

"Yes, I know I ought to be careful about that. And he's
having a grand time. He's crazy about this place."

"That pleases you, naturally."

"Yes, naturally—Aunt Estelle, I am very anxious to have him grow up in the South. I don't want him to be separated from his rightful heritage, the way I was."

"But my dear boy, why should you imagine he would be? You are settled here now for good, I hope. After a long absence, it is true. But better late than never."

"I hope and believe I'm settled here. Anna likes the plantation better than she expected to. And she approves a hankering for politics I've always had. But she's already talking about sending Drew to Groton, as if it were all settled. As a matter of fact, he was entered there the day he was born."

"I have heard of that quaint New England custom. And after Groton would come Harvard I suppose?"

"Yes, and all things being equal, a postgraduate course at Oxford or Cambridge. And of course numerous trips to Europe in the meantime. Anna's been talking of a winter in Tours, where the French is so good. She has friends who have a château near there."

"Those are all great advantages, Breck."

"Yes, but I don't want him weaned away."

"You weren't weaned away. But then perhaps you have a stronger character."

"Stronger than Drew's! You don't know what you're saying, Aunt Estelle! Drew is much more like my father than I am. Marcy calls him the 'spittin' image' and it's apt. I'm just a poor imitation."

"Your father didn't think so. He thought you were stronger than *he* was. He told me once that I mustn't worry about you, that you were a tough little devil. He said you'd be able to look out for yourself, whatever happened—that you'd never make ducks and drakes of a great fortune. He said you had more sense than he had and— were we referring to unrefined expressions?—more guts."

"My father said that! To *you!* Why, how did he happen to?"

"I was very fond of you, Breck, and I was concerned about you. Your father really was very extravagant, you know, and—and very carefree in his ways. I was afraid he might not provide for you properly. Something came up that caused him to speak to me about you. Of course this was before he married my sister-in-law. Naturally after that

I wasn't concerned about you any longer. I knew you'd have every possible care and safe-guard."

"But if my father talked to you like that it must have been because——"

He stopped himself just in time. It had been on the tip of his tongue to say, "It must have been because he expected to marry you. He wouldn't have done it otherwise." Again he thought of the jewelled mirror that Anna had seen lying on Mrs. Fontaine's dressing table, and the design for it that was locked away in his own desk. He wished he could tell her about this design, he wished he could ask her— but he knew that he must not until she, of her own accord, said more to him than she had ever said yet, even in those dreadful days after his father's death, when he had clung to her so desperately. She did say more now than she ever had before, but it was not what he had expected, or hoped for.

"He knew that I was very fond of you, Breck, as I have said. And I still am. I do not believe his confidence in you was misplaced. Or that mine will be either. I think that you have great sensibility and great courage and great endurance. Shall we use those words perhaps, instead of his? After all, they mean much the same. I'm very happy to know that you are living on our good land again, and that you want to serve your country in other ways as well. There is so much you can do for it, and for all of us. After you have first done your duty to your wife and child of course. I know you will never fail either of them. Or any of your friends who love and trust you either. Among whom I hope you will always remember to number me—and mine."

She rose and walked slowly over to the parapet. Breck moved forward and stood beside her, unable for the moment to speak. It was no longer a question of how much he knew, but of how much she knew. She had turned the tables on him so gently, yet so adroitly, that he was shocked to silence by her skill. For a moment they stood side by side, looking down on the tennis players and listening to the merry banter that rose from the court. Then she laid her hand lightly on his arm.

"I have had a very selfish purpose in coming to Splendida," she said softly. "Of course, I have always wanted to see it, as who does not? It is the fulfillment of every woman's dream of the palace which the fairy prince provides! But it is not merely of the palace that I have thought, for many years. It is of the little cemetery beyond the garden, perennially inclosed, so I am told, with white flowers. I believe your mother is buried there, Breck—your mother and the little sister who died as she was brought into the world. I am sure you visit it often because of them, and I should be glad to pay their tomb the tribute of a visit also. But besides, there is a memorial, is there not, where there could not be a tomb? A snowy chalice giving forth perpetual light? Every time I have been to visit my husband's mausoleum in Métairie I have passed the Aldigés' monument, and I have always paused before the great stone ship rising above the sculptured waves, with the cross surmounting it and the shipwrecked victims transformed into triumphant angels. I have looked at it in admiration and in supreme sympathy. But in doing so I have always thought— I have always hoped—that someday— Do you think that now, while no one would miss us———?"

Breck went through the staircase hall, patterned, as it always was at that hour, with rainbow-colored light, and down the steps of the rear gallery to the garden and beyond it, with Mrs. Fontaine's hand still resting on his arm. She was right. No one missed them while they tarried together in the place sacred to his father's memory.

CHAPTER 16

IT PROVED almost impossible for Breck to readjust himself after Mrs. Fontaine had gone to her room to rest. To be sure, he succeeded in playing the part of the genial host, taking Olivier's place on the tennis court, and thus freeing his debilitated guest to follow his mother's example. Céleste suggested that they should change partners, that Walter should play with Anna now; and whereas, up to that time, the players had been evenly matched, Anna's fine game offsetting Olivier's indifferent one, and Walter's expertness counterbalancing Céleste's inexperience, Breck and Céleste together were no match for Anna and Walter. To all appearances, Breck took his smashing defeat as lightheartedly as Céleste did; but this lightheartedness, genuine in her case, was only assumed in his. He did not feel cheerful about anything. Though there was a quality akin to relief in his acceptance of Anna's satisfaction over her easy victory, he did not really feel pleased at being publicly worsted by her in a test of skill and speed, and he was even less pleased at being so worsted by Walter Avery. Not that he attached undue importance to any game. But the chance identity of the persons who had beaten him was irritating, especially when he thought of it in connection with the identity of the person who had so adroitly circumvented him that afternoon. It was useless to tell himself that he was depressed by his visit to the cemetery, that he should not have stayed there so long, or talked so much about his father. He knew that the crux of his depression lay far less in that than in the fact that Marie Céleste's mother had divined the desire which he thought was in part concealed and in part smothered, and that nothing he did or thought or felt could be kept secret from her any longer.

He was sorry they had decided on a barbecue. Mrs. Fontaine would probably have enjoyed a formal dinner more after all. The entire pattern of her life having always been so confined and conventional, they should not have expected her to enjoy sitting outdoors on a rustic seat, and eating, with a solitary fork, a variety of smoky food piled high on a single dish. When it came to that, he did not believe Olivier would enjoy the barbecue either. He was sure Olivier was one of those rare creatures, upon whom other men always look with contempt, actually more at ease in evening clothes than in any other kind of garment. Olivier would undoubtedly have preferred getting into fine broadcloth and glossy linen and sitting down at a long table covered with a damask cloth and adorned with flowers, to wandering haphazardly among the trees in old clothes, hobnobbing here and there with other male guests and helping the servants supply the ladies with food. He and Anna had made a mistake in considering what Céleste and Walter would enjoy rather than what Mrs. Fontaine and Olivier would enjoy. Marie Céleste and Walter—Anna kept coupling their names and so did everyone else. Anyone would think, to hear Anna talk, that they were engaged already. And yet Anna, herself, had said that Marie Céleste was only a child, and Marie Céleste had said nothing at all that would indicate extraordinary interest in Walter.

Breck flung himself into his clothes, after a hasty shower, and spoke shortly to Drew when the little boy came in from the fields. What the dickens did he mean by being so late? He wasn't late, Drew protested, it was just the same time as usual. He looked at his father in the same troubled way as when he had stood holding his kitten, while Breck was reading Marie Céleste's letter. Couldn't he please stay up to the barbecue, he went on. He had never been to a barbecue, and Mr. Yates had been telling him all about them. Gee, he thought they must be great. Certainly not, Breck said, still speaking shortly; it wouldn't be getting under way for at least an hour yet, and there would be drinks and delays of various sorts before the barbecue actually began. Drew had better eat his supper right off and hustle away to bed before he got under foot. Well, would Daddy come to see him after he was in bed? There were so many things Drew wanted to ask him. Good Lord, no, Breck couldn't sit and answer questions when there would be twenty or thirty people waiting outside to see him; he should think Drew would know that much.

The child did not answer impudently; he turned and went away, holding his head unusually high, as if to indicate that he didn't care, and transiently Breck thought of Andy's comments about the danger of doing a thing just to show off, so that no one would know there was a hurt underneath. But there was no time to call Drew back then, even if his pride would have permitted it. The guests were beginning to arrive. Several of them were already clustered around the brick barbecue pit when Breck went out on the rear lawn. Both the lamb and the pig which had been roasted whole had been taken from the large iron skewers and laid, already sliced, on a wooden butcher block. A big bowl of highly flavored celery sauce stood between the platters arrayed on a long plank table, and Lute, the "high-yellow" girl, whom Drew had described with such innocent exactitude to his father, was engaged in toasting, over the hot coals, the bread designed to be eaten with the rich sauce and the smoky meat. She was wearing a uniform of sorts, but she had contrived to give it the same daring look as her customary red dress, and she had not taken off her jewelry. The great golden hoops dangled in a tantalizing way from her small amber-colored ears as she bent her head, and the long golden chain disappeared, still more tantalizingly, between her breasts as she bent her body. Olivier and one or two of the other male guests were taking the toast from her as she made it, and joking with her as they put it on one of the stacked plates after another, before spreading the meat and the sauce over it. Then Roscoe and Rufus passed the plates around. Rufus was apparently enjoying this; but Roscoe's normal cheerfulness seemed to be slightly overcast, and Breck gathered that the butler considered the piazza more suitable than the lawn for the entertainment of guests. He kept colliding with the shrubbery as he served, and each time he did so, he turned around, glared at the offending bush and addressed it rebukingly, as if in reproach of a human being. "What you tryin' to do to me dere?"— "Aimin' to tear off my close what Mr. Breck done give me new, is you?"— "Keep yo' thorns offen my pussun, you worm-eaten pest!"

Evidently Lute had been pressed into service to help the house servants, for some reason or other; perhaps because Roscoe had made his annoyance evident beforehand, or perhaps because the number of guests was unexpectedly large. Breck did not know and he could not object or inquire then. But he made a mental note that he must speak to Anna about it in the morning, and tell her that it must not happen again, no matter how short-handed she was, though he feared he would have some difficulty in convincing her that Lute's presence on the lawn was a mistake, not only because Anna never liked interference with her own arrangements, but because Lute's behavior was deceptively correct. Her replies to the guests' badinage were brief and respectful; her expression was restrained and demure. She raised her great dark eyes only once, and instantly lowered them again; but in that split second Breck saw their impudent challenge to Olivier. Though the barbecue, on the whole, was going much better than the host had expected, that brazen invitation and its nonchalant but unmistakable acceptance were in themselves enough to make him sure that his forebording of trouble in one quarter were only too well founded.

If Mrs. Fontaine noticed her son's moment of aberration, she gave no sign of having been disturbed. On the contrary, she appeared to enjoy the evening's entertainment tranquilly but unequivocally. She pronounced both the barbecued meats and the celery sauce soignée, and said she would never have believed that eating outdoors could have given her so much additional appetite. She found the service and setting most original, and her fellow guests delightful. All Breck's fears regarding her pleasure were charmingly quieted by her graciousness.

Marie Céleste threw herself into the spirit of the occasion with even greater zest. And when the feast itself was over and the Negroes who made up the choir in the colored church came from the quarters to sing, her delight in their performance was exuberant. They began with some spirituals which she had never heard before, though one of these, "I'm Going to Tell God All My Troubles," was very generally sung through the South. The other, "We'll Understand It Better By and By," was a local favorite, which the hands were accustomed to sing in the fields when they did not start their day's work with "Pore Lil Jesus." Céleste went close to the singers, so that she could follow the melody and hear the words:

> " 'By and by when the mo'ning comes,
>   When all the Saints of God be gatherin' home
>   We will tell the story of how we've overcome
>   And we'll understand it better by and by.
>
> Po' man come to the rich man's gate
>   Asked him for some crumbs but he drove him
>   away wid hate
>   He kneeled down to pray, fer the Lord to
>   show him the way
>   And we'll understand it better by and by.' "

When the darkies switched from spirituals to love songs, she was even more enchanted. After the guests had dispersed and the choir had gone back to their quarters, the last cadences dying away in the distance as the singers strolled along, Céleste seated herself at the inlaid piano in the parlor, running her fingers happily over the keys as the lines she had just learned poured joyously from her throat:

> " 'I'm a-thinkin' of you honey,
>   Thinkin' 'case I love you so,
>   And my heart keeps thumpin' and a-thumpin',
>   As I hoe down row after row'——

"Sing the chorus with me," she said, looking up at Breck, who had followed her into the parlor.

"I couldn't sing a note to save my life, Céleste."

"Nonsense! Of course you could. Everyone can sing. You too, Walter."

Walter had come into the parlor too now, Walter and Mrs. Fontaine and Anna. Only Olivier was missing. But in a minute Céleste had all the others singing with her:

> " 'Row after row, my baby,
> Row after row, my baby,
> Row after row, my baby,
> Row after row.' "

The feeling of festivity which the barbecue had evoked was prolonged for another hour and might have been sustained even longer if the consciousness of approaching bedtime had not brought about a discussion of the next day's schedule. It had not occurred to Anna, in making plans for the Fontaine's visit, that churchgoing should form a part of it. She, herself, regarded churchgoing respectfully, but incidentally, like most of the people she knew. Mrs. Fontaine's question concerning the hours of Mass at White Castle, and the time it would be most convenient for her hostess to send herself and her son and daughter there took Anna completely by surprise.

"Why, I'm afraid I don't know, Mrs. Fontaine. I'll be glad to find out, if you want me to. I suppose there must be a telephone at the rectory, or if there isn't, I can send Rufus to inquire. But I really don't believe you'd enjoy the service very much. The church at White Castle is just a little——"

"It doesn't matter whether Mass is said in a cathedral or a chapel, you know, Anna. It's always the same Sacrifice, and you can always feel the same Presence when the Miracle takes place."

It was Céleste who spoke so impetuously and, as it seemed to Anna, with such unnecessary intensity. Yes, decidedly, these Creoles were very emotional. And Céleste did not stop. She went on.

"What I really want to see most of all, while I'm here, is the little chapel near Bayou Goula—the one in the Italian settlement that's called 'the one-man church.' I believe they don't have Mass there regularly, though—only once a year, on

Assumption; so of course we have to go to church in White Castle, too. But I've heard that the local women go to this little chapel to pray, every afternoon, during May, in honor of the Virgin, and every afternoon, during June, in honor of the Sacred Heart. They ring the bell themselves, and gather there together, informally but very devoutly. It must be sweet to see them. Do you think we could go there tomorrow afternoon, Anna?"

"I'm afraid we couldn't, Céleste. You see, the Héberts——"

"Well, what about Monday? Could we go on Monday?"

"On Monday we've been invited out, too. By the Randolphs. To some queer sort of party that's called a fish fry. And Breck thinks we ought to go, because——"

"Oh, I'd love to go to a fish fry! I've always wanted to go to one. I think that's wonderful! Where is it going to be?"

"Why, it's going to be in a grove, somewhere on the Bayou Goula you just mentioned. I don't know just how far it is from the village. But perhaps, on your way back, if you like, you could go to this chapel. I'll try to find out more about that, too."

"I am sorry we are putting you to so much bother, *chère*. Mass, of course, is obligatory for us. But if it is too much trouble to arrange for the other visit——"

Privately, Anna did think it was a good deal of trouble. But at least Mrs. Fontaine was not so outspoken and so upsetting as she was beginning to find Céleste. It appeared that there was only one Mass at White Castle, because the priest in charge had to go elsewhere to celebrate others, and this was at a most inconvenient hour, just at breakfast time. However, Anna changed her orders to the cook, and spoke to Rufus about taking the Fontaines to the service. At the last minute, Walter Avery also appeared, and asked if there were room for him in the car; if there were, he would like to go, too, he said. Anna could not see any good reason why Walter Avery, who, as she knew, was not a Catholic, should go to Mass, even if he were in love with Céleste. Anna thought that if he wanted to marry her, he would do much better by taking a firm stand from the beginning, and making it clear to her that he did not propose to permit any proselyting. But she could not very well argue about this with Walter, at least not just then. She was obliged to say that yes, of course, there was plenty of room in the car. But she did argue with Breck, when he also appeared on the portico, quite evidently prepared to go to church, too.

"Why, Breck! I never knew you to suggest such a thing before!"

"The occasion hasn't ever arisen before. This is the first time we've had the honor of entertaining lovely ladies who are as devout as they are charming."

He went over to Mrs. Fontaine and kissed her, in the way he had a habit of doing, naturally and spontaneously, as if he were a favorite nephew or a cherished younger cousin. She returned his caress, in the same quiet and easy way. But to Anna's relief, she discouraged his proffered escort.

"Walter is going with us, *cher*. With him and Olivier both, Céleste and I will be amply accompanied. I beg of you not to upset Anna's arrangements, which unfortunately we have complicated so much already."

"Please don't feel that way, Mrs. Fontaine. Of course, I wish to have my guests accommodated, in every possible way. But it is true that the car will be a little crowded."

"It is perfectly possible to take two cars," Breck said almost brusquely. "I was planning to ask Aunt Estelle to let me drive her to church in my runabout, and then drive Céleste back."

"I do appreciate your thoughtfulness, Breck. But see, we are all practically in the big car together, already. We shall be back very soon, and shall look forward to seeing you at breakfast. *Au revoir.*"

Without being actually importunate, Breck could not insist any further. He watched the car out of sight, and then turned to Anna sulkily.

"Why did you make such a fuss about nothing? Didn't it occur to you that it would be courteous if either their host or hostess went with them? And since you didn't offer——"

"No, it never did occur to me to offer. I think you're the one who's making a great fuss about nothing. The schedule for the entire day has got to be changed now. We're going to be terribly late for breakfast."

Anna sounded sulky, too, which was unusual, since sharpness was much more characteristic of her. But she was decidedly out of sorts. She had been restless all night. The illusion that she heard a baby wailing had disturbed her again, as it had intermittently ever since she had been at Splendida,

and she had remained adamant about trying the experiment
of a lighted candle. Now she was thinking resentfully
about Olivier's appearance, which had been damaging to her
insistent self-assurance that he was the embodiment of masculine charm. He obviously had not shaved before starting
for church, and, like most very dark men under those circumstances, looked somewhat ruffiantly, but in a smutty
rather than in a romantic way. Even his usually sleek hair
was tousled, and the general effect he gave was one of un-
kemptness, almost of uncleanliness. Crossly, Anna wondered why you could nearly always tell, in looking at a fully
clothed man, how long it was since he had bathed all over;
you would suppose that if his face and hands were clean, the
rest would be his own secret. But this never seemed to be
the case. And as far as Olivier was concerned, his face and
hands did not look clean, either. The contrast between him
and Walter, who had obviously just sprung from a shower,
and who at all times had the fresh ingenuous look of a young
man whose habits were good, whose health was perfect,
and whose mentality was unremarkable, annoyed her very
much. So did the contrast between Olivier and Breck, whom
she had yet to see in a slovenly state, no matter what he was
doing or wearing. She was doubly aggrieved when he snapped
at her now.

"What difference does it make what time we have breakfast? We've got the whole day ahead of us, haven't we?"

"We have to be at the Héberts' at two, and we'll hardly
have finished one hearty meal before we'll be starting in on
another. It isn't wholesome or rational to eat that way. All
the best authorities say there ought to be at least four
hours——"

"Oh, for God's sake! Do stop thinking about schedules
for a little while! Or if you can't forget about them yourself,
at least let the rest of us do it."

He ran down the steps, and disappeared beyond the bulk
of the house. Before he had reached the dairy, Drew caught
up with him.

"Where are you going, Daddy? May I come with you?"

"I'm not going any special place. But you're welcome to
stay with me."

"I thought you were going to church."

"I thought so, too. But apparently the idea wasn't welcome
to anybody."

"Why don't you go to Shoog's church, Daddy? You would be welcome there. She says your father used to, every now and then, and she told me his people were awfully pleased when he did."

Breck slackened his pace and looked at his small son attentively.

"Why, I believe my father did go to Shoog's church every now and then," he said slowly. "I'd forgotten about it though."

"But you shouldn't forget things like that, should you, Daddy? Because they mean so much to other people. Your mother was very thoughtful, too, Shoog said. I don't mean the lady you called Aunt Aurore. I mean your own mother."

"What did Shoog tell you that my own mother did, Drew?"

"She said your own mother used to read aloud to their preacher, whose name was Uncle Zeno. On weekdays he worked in the fields, just like all the other hands, but Shoog said you could always pick him out a long way off, because the patches on his clothes were in such bright colors. But on Sundays he put on a nice black suit and tucked a big Bible under his arm, and took a walking stick and a tall hat and came up to the big house. Then he would stand by the front steps and wait patiently until your mother came out on the portico. She would sit down on the steps and take his Bible from him and read aloud to him out of it and tell him the meaning of what she had read. If she hadn't done that Uncle Zeno couldn't have preached. Because he couldn't read himself, and he wasn't very good at figuring out meanings. But he had a pretty good memory. After she had read and explained to him, he took the Bible back, and thanked her, and went on to the little church where the rest of the people were waiting for him. He walked up to the pulpit and laid the Bible down on it, and then, first of all, he said, 'I've come all this way to tell you some good news. Yes, my sisters and brothers, I got good news for you.' After that he told them as much as he could remember of what your mother had read to him and explained to him. Of course he gave out hymns, too. Shoog said his favorite was, *I'm on my way to heaven, and I don't want to stop. I don't want to be no stumbling block*. But mostly the service was made up of what your mother had helped Uncle Zeno to learn."

"I had no idea Shoog had been talking to you about my

mother, Drew. I can't remember her at all myself. You see I was only three years old when she died."

"But you can remember your father, can't you, Daddy?"

"Yes, I can remember him. He didn't die until I was fourteen. But I believe I'd have remembered him, even if I'd been only a little boy when it happened. I don't think anyone who knew him ever forgot him."

"I don't think anyone who knew you would ever forget you either, Daddy."

"Don't you, Drew? Well, I'm not going to die, that is, not until I am an old, old man, so we won't have a chance to find out. Let's not talk about it either. Would you like to go to Shoog's church with me this morning?"

"Gee, Daddy, wouldn't I just!"

The arrival of the father and son at the small colored church caused quite a pleasant stir. The service had already begun when they entered and tried to take their seats in the rear pew. But they were immediately led up to the front, in the course of a pause that was permeated with pride. Then the normal proceedings were resumed, and both Breck and Drew found them very arresting. The church was well filled. The elder women were wearing clean aprons, and bright *tignons* with hats perched on top of them, the younger ones sleazy silk dresses in bright colors. There was a similar contrast between the clothing of the men of different ages, the old steadies wearing neat though rusty black, the young bucks gaudy "store suits," tan shoes, and violent ties. None of them seemed to feel any impulsion to sit still or to keep silent for very long. Frequently several of them rose precipitately, and walked up and down the aisle, shouting and singing as they went. Even those who did not move kept applauding the words of the preacher and exclaiming, "Glory be to God! Bless the Lord!" Two of the "sisters" fainted away, and were borne outside, amidst much pleasurable excitement. When they revived and returned to the church, they were quite the center of attraction. After the sermon was over, the preacher called for a collection, and, having himself placed a plate on the table near the pulpit, stood watchfully by it. As the members of the congregation advanced to contribute, they swayed back and forth, singing as they went.

"It looks like a dance, doesn't it, Daddy?" Drew whispered to Breck, watching them with fascination.

"Yes, it does, something. But they don't think of it as dancing. It's natural for them to walk that way in church."

"I know it, Daddy. I like to see them, too."

Even more alertly than his white visitors, the preacher was watching his congregation. The few members of it who remained in their seats at this juncture did not escape his eagle eye. He called out to them, "Come on, sisters, and give some money to the Lord. Come on, brothers. Come all, come all." They results were eminently satisfactory. The collection plate was piled amazingly high before Breck put in a crisp five-dollar bill on top of it, and Drew, after considerable burrowing through his pockets, produced a dingy dime. The final hymn was sung with great fervor

> "In the weary land ma Savior am
> a-rockin'
> In the weary land, the weary land.
> You may talk about me as much as
> you please,
> But while you are a-talkin'
> I am bendin' my knees."

Breck and Drew stopped outside to speak to the people as they came out of the church. Breck was surprised to find how many of them Drew knew by name, how thoroughly at ease he seemed among them, and how greatly they delighted in him. As he and his father walked back to the big house, he told Breck more stories.

"Uncle Numy told me that when he was baptized he saw Jesus, right there under the water. Do you believe he really did, Daddy?"

"I suppose he must think he did, or he wouldn't have told you so. Which one was Uncle Numy?"

"He was the old, old man that sat in the front on the other side of the aisle from us. He's deaf. He kept leaning forward and kept trying to hear with his hand. Another old man who looks exactly like him sat beside him. He's deaf, too. His name is Uncle Ralgy. Uncle Numy and Uncle Ralgy are twins."

"Drew, you know more about these people already than I've ever forgotten."

"Well, it's interesting, Daddy, to find out about people,

don't you think so? Uncle Numy's real name is Pneumonia and Uncle Ralgy's real name is Neuralgia. I think that's very interesting."

"Good grief, Drew, I should think it was!"

"And their father was a twin, too. He's dead now, and so is his twin brother, but Uncle Numy told me all about them. His father's name was Abraham Lincoln and his uncle's name was Jefferson Davis. Their mother said she didn't like to show any par—part——"

"Partiality?"

"Yes, that was the word, Daddy. She didn't like to show any partiality when she named them."

"I think she was very successful in her efforts. Well, shall we go up on the piazza and see if there's any breakfast left?"

There was plenty of breakfast left, and though the other churchgoers had reached Splendida before Breck and Drew, everyone was still gathered companionately around the long table. Anna had recovered her equanimity under the candid expression of admiration which came from both Mrs. Fontaine and Céleste regarding the table's appointments. She had not forgotten the silver epergne with the miniature lake, the branching tree, the deer and the rabbits, which had adorned the dinner at the Fontaines'; and though she had been disappointed in finding nothing similar at Splendida, she had discovered a gigantic "Lazy Susan" made of embossed silver, with a deep bowl in the center, four large compartments at the sides, and containers for salt and pepper to give good measure. This was now gracing the Sunday breakfast, each compartment filled with a different delicacy; while a container for eggs, with compartments in the shape of charming figurines, stood beside it. Céleste had drawn this up to her and was amusing herself by naming the figurines.

"This is Anna," she said. "And this is Aurore, and this is—what was your mother's name, Breck?"

"Anne. The Breckenridges not only have the same names themselves, they marry girls who do."

"I think that's very nice. Well, this is Anne. And these two smaller ones are Pauline and Angèle. Now there's just one more, so I'm going to name her for myself. This is Céleste. Now they're all named! I like to give names to things, don't you?"

Breck, helping himself liberally to the contents of "Lazy

Susan," said that he did, very much, and that he was delighted with all the names she had given the figurines, particularly with Céleste. Anna thought it was very silly to name inanimate objects, but for once she neither expressed nor betrayed an unfavorable impression. Olivier had taken time to make a belated toilet before coming to the table, and looked sleek and immaculate again. He was enjoying his breakfast, and was making himself extremely agreeable. Anna thought that perhaps she had judged him rather too severely, earlier in the morning. After all, it must be very trying to get up to go to church without any breakfast. She had never heard of such a thing in Boston. Everyone she knew had fish balls and baked beans and brown bread and applesauce and doughnuts before starting out for Trinity or the Arlington Street Church. She was ready to admit that this must make a difference.

There was no blinking the fact, however, that breakfast was hardly over before it was time to start for the Héberts, and that she had neither appetite nor inclination for another big meal when they reached Plaisance. She did not like the interruption that occurred in the middle of dinner either. As everything was behindhand, Walter Avery was obliged to leave by the time they reached the roast, in order to take the afternoon "local" back to New Orleans. Breck insisted on driving him to the station, and Céleste insisted on going to see him off. This meant that Olivier, at an almost imperceptible sign from his mother, also went. It was terrible to have a table so disrupted, Anna thought, though Mrs. Hébert did not seem to find it in the least upsetting. The chairs that were still occupied were brought nearer together to make up for those that were vacant, and the tomato salad came on as if nothing had happened. By the time Breck and Céleste and Olivier got back, everyone else had almost finished eating strawberry ice cream. But the tomato salad was brought back again for the three truants and everyone sat at ease while they ate that in a leisurely way, and then the ice cream, with no more signs of haste. The afternoon was practically over by the time they rose from the table, and by the time coffee had been served there was barely enough light left to play croquet, which evidently no one had told Mrs. Hébert was now completely outmoded. Croquet went on until it was really dark, and this darkness gave Anna the pretext she had been eagerly await-

ing to give the signal to return to Splendida. She knew there
would be further adjustments to make there. No one could
possibly eat a big supper now. Instead, there would have to
be some kind of light, casual refreshments served about bedtime. But while she was brooding on this unwelcome change,
she realized that it might have advantages after all. As she
alighted from the motor car, she made a suggestion which
seemed to her most meritorious.

"I know you'd like to lie down for a little while, Mrs.
Fontaine. You must have found the day very exhausting. I'll
come to your room with you, to make sure you have everything you'd like, and I must speak to the servants, too, about
a late supper. It's fortunate they're good-natured about such
things. Afterwards I'd like to get a little exercise. We've been
rushing around so since you came, with church and all, that
Breck and I haven't had any chance to show Céleste and
Olivier the garden and grounds. You wouldn't feel deserted,
would you, or object, if we wandered around through them
for an hour or so? I really think they're more charming by
moonlight than in the day time."

"I can well imagine that they might be, *chère*. No, certainly I should not feel deserted. You are right, I am a little
tired. I should welcome a short rest before we meet again
later in the evening. And what possible objection could I
have to such a pleasant little excursion as you suggest? I
know that between them Breck and Olivier will take the
best possible care of you and of my little girl."

She's pretending to talk to Anna, Breck thought, as Mrs.
Fontaine left them; but she's really talking to me. She's tell-
ing me she's going to trust me not to wander away from
Olivier and Anna with Céleste. But she doesn't trust me
any too much, in spite of what she said last night. She
wouldn't let Céleste go to the station with me to see Walter
off, without signalling to Olivier to go along, too, so that
Céleste wouldn't be alone with me on the ride back to
Plaisance. This time she believes, with four of us together—
Well, I mustn't let her down. I've got to play up to her.
What the hell else can I do? Céleste's a guest in my house,
she's only seventeen years old, she's going out for a quiet
walk through the garden and grounds with her brother and
her host and his wife——

"Olivier," Anna was saying, "do you feel like walking
across the lawn with me to see 'Miss Flora of Rome'

that I told you about? The statue Shoog says 'has quite a history.' I know Breck doesn't care to go. He and I are always quarrelling about the statues on the plantation. Well, I don't mean quarrelling exactly, but you know the little altercations husbands and wives do have! It would be too bad to mar this lovely evening by anything of that sort."

"Of course I should be delighted to see the statue of Flora," Olivier replied politely. "It must be a very interesting work of art, from what you tell me about it."

"Oh, it is!" Céleste chimed in quickly. "I went to see it last evening, with Walter. He felt he needed exercise, just as you do now, Anna, and he insisted no one would miss us if we left the barbecue for a few minutes. I don't believe anyone did either."

"I did," interposed Breck.

"Oh, I'm very sorry! I wouldn't have gone if I had thought you would. But we had a very nice walk. Now I'm tired myself. I'm glad you think Breck'd better not go along with you to see the statues, Anna. Because I'd much rather sit in the arbor than do any more walking and of course I want someone to keep me company. Breck and I will wait here for you and Olivier until you come back."

Breck could see that Olivier hesitated. He was not sure whether it was because the Creole did not feel he ought to leave his sister, or because he really felt no impulsion to stroll in Anna's company. But whatever the cause of his objection, it was swiftly overruled. Anna laid her hand lightly on his arm, as if to show him the way along the garden path. Céleste sat down on the rustic seat in the arbor, and leaned her head back against the lattice. The moonlight patterned this against her hair, but the arbor itself was engulfed in shadow.

"What a nice place!" she said joyously. "Why haven't you shown it to me before, Breck?"

"Well, you know that, as Anna said, we've been rushing around so——"

"You haven't acted as if you *wanted* to show me anything, Breck. And I'd been looking forward to it all so! I thought you'd show me the grove and the pool and the rose garden."

"I can show you the pool now, if you like. That's very near here."

"No, I don't want to go now. I want to stay in the arbor.

Why don't you sit down, Breck? You look so restless, standing up like that!"

He sat down on the seat opposite her, with the dark width of the arbor between them.

"Do you mind if I smoke, Céleste?"

"No, of course not."

He lighted a cigarette, felt his hand shaking a little, hoped Céleste would not notice it. But apparently she was not thinking about the cigarette.

"You're not angry with me or anything, are you, Breck?"

"No, of course not. What makes you ask such a foolish question?"

"I'm sorry that it sounds foolish. But you see I thought we were such friends. You see I counted on having you take me——"

He threw the cigarette out of the arbor and leapt up. At the same instant Céleste rose and took a step towards him. The shifting light of the moon, suddenly illuminating the arbor, shone on her upturned face. As he caught hold of her arms he saw that she was looking lovingly up at him, without the slightest sign of fear in her shining eyes, or the slightest recoil from the embrace which was so imminent. She had counted on having him *take* her! Why, in God's name, had she chanced, in her innocence, on that special word? Desperately he asked himself this, and as he did so, he remembered the other word which had been used in referring to this same arbor, and what he and Anna had said to each other. "Shoog told me that your father 'gained' Aurore right on that very settee. I don't know just what she meant by it, but I didn't like the sound of ·it at all."— "I'm sorry to disappoint you, Anna, but I don't think it means a thing, except that she consented to marry him in there. As far as I know, the Breckenridges haven't gone in for seducing the women they wanted for their wives, much less raping them. It's never been their technique." Yes, but then they had been talking of men who were free to marry, to whose infinite yearning and deep desire honor had formed no impediment. *What if they had not been free?* What if Andy Breckenridge and Estelle Lenoir had met in this arbor where he and Céleste were standing now, after she had been given, against her will, to Marcel Fontaine, and he, with tragic bravado, had married Marcel's sister?

He tried to answer the question to suit his driving will. But he could not. He knew they had never met in the arbor, or anywhere else, because they knew they must not. He knew that even if they had, Estelle would have been wiser, as well as sadder, by that time, than this guileless girl who stood waiting for him to gather her into his arms. The evanescent moonlight was gone. They were again engulfed in mystic darkness permeated with relentless force. But he knew that he must turn away from the brimming cup that was offered him when it was already touching his lips. There was no ecstasy on earth that could atone for the crime he had come so close to committing.

"Céleste," he said gently. "Céleste—my dear little girl." He stopped, and she waited, patiently, for him to go on, without taking her eyes off his face. "I will take you to see the pool and the roses and the grove, sometime," he said. "You can't possibly want to have me do it as much as I want to do it myself. But not tonight. You said yourself you were tired, that you didn't want to walk any more. I think perhaps we ought to go out to meet Anna and Olivier, so that it won't seem to them as if we weren't welcoming them back. But that will be just a little way. They'll be crossing the lawn again at any minute. And then I think we should all go in and try to get some sleep. Because we're going to do so many things tomorrow. And we want to be fresh and ready to do them, don't we, and happy about it?"

CHAPTER 17

BRECK WENT, as usual, into the fields at six the next morning with Drew, returning to the house in time for breakfast. He found Anna alone on the piazza. Mrs. Fontaine had sent down word that she was still a little tired, and felt that she should conserve her strength for the day's outing; she was selfishly keeping Céleste with her. Olivier had not sent down word at all. He had apparently taken it for granted that he would receive service in his room. Anna was inclined to be querulous again.

"I don't believe Mrs. Fontaine ever takes any exercise. At least she never seems to. If she got more fresh air she wouldn't feel so tired. And I think it's dreadful, Breck, for a young

girl in her teens, perfectly healthy, to get the habit of breakfasting in bed. The more I see of the way Céleste's brought
up, the less I think of it. Why, she isn't encouraged to make
the slightest effort, to take the initiative in anything! And as
for a *man* having breakfast in his room——"

"You really wouldn't call Olivier Fontaine a man, would
you? He's just a spoiled simp!"

Anna immediately rose to the defense of Olivier. She was
disappointed because she had not been called upon to defend
her virtue during the course of her little expedition the night
before. But she was more and more intrigued by the handsome
Creole all the time, and she was still hopeful that eventually
he would betray the ardor which she was confident she had
not failed to arouse. After all, there was another whole day,
and another evening still before them. If Breck had not so
stupidly joined them the night before, just when she thought
Olivier was showing signs of incipient gallantry, probably by
now she might have had more reason for satisfaction. She
was still reproving Breck for the slighting way in which he had
referred to a guest under their roof, when Roscoe came out
on the piazza with a disturbing announcement.

"I done took Mr. Olivier's breakfast up to his room, Mis'
Breckenridge, lak you tole me. But ain't nobody dere."

"Nobody there! Of course there's somebody there! Don't
stand like that, Roscoe, just saying something stupid and
looking at us vacantly."

"You went into the room, didn't you, Roscoe, after you
knocked on the door and didn't get any answer?" Breck inquired patiently.

"Yassah, Mr. Breck. And I done look in the bathroom,
too. But wasn't nobody dere."

"Why, there must——"

"That's all right, Roscoe. We don't need you any more
just now. You'd better go back to Mr. Olivier's room in half
an hour and try again. And half an hour after that, if he isn't
there the first time. And so on. Of course we want to be
sure he gets a good breakfast. But when you finally find him
you don't need to say you've been there before."

"No sah, Mr. Breck."

The respectfulness of Roscoe's manner did not entirely
compensate to Anna for the slight smirk which she saw on his
face as he left the piazza. She looked from him to Breck with
puzzled annoyance.

"You act as if you knew exactly what had happened. If you do, you might clarify this mystery for me."

"I think I do know, and I think Roscoe does, too. But I didn't want to talk about it before him. I'm afraid Olivier's indulging in a time-honored form of diversion on plantations, Anna."

"I haven't any idea what you're talking about."

"You didn't happen to notice Olivier looking at Lute Saturday night, did you?"

"Lute? You mean the girl I got in to help with the barbecue?"

"Yes. I wouldn't get her in again, if I were you, Anna. I meant to suggest that to you anyway. I'm rather grateful to Olivier for giving me such a plausible pretext."

"But surely you're not intimating——"

"I'm not intimating anything. And I certainly don't want to begin the day by trying to discuss the most cancerous problem of the South. Let's drop it, Anna. And for your own sake, I suggest that you don't try to question Olivier too closely when he does show up."

Anna opened her lips again and then pressed them together firmly. Her indignation was almost uncontrollable. Her pride would not permit her to believe that Olivier, who had been so indifferent to her own receptivity to attention, should have hastened away from her side to accept the advances of a mulattress. But her reason would not allow her to believe anything else, now that Breck had done what she asked in "clarifying the mystery." She was seething inside, but she managed to maintain the appearance of calm until she had quieted herself enough to speak in a detached way.

"How early do we have to leave for this fish fry of yours?" she asked, with the condescension which always annoyed Breck even more than her sharpness.

"It isn't my fish fry, as you know. It's the Randolphs'. They asked us to be on hand around noon."

"That's going to make an awfully long day, isn't it?"

"I suppose it's all in the way you look at it. If you enjoy that sort of thing, it's possible to put in a good deal of time at a picnic without having the hours drag."

He went out again as soon as he had finished breakfast, inventing small tasks with which to busy himself. He had hardly slept at all, and he was very jumpy; the hours were certainly dragging for him. Until he could see Céleste, until he could be sure that she would greet him this morning without reserve or self-consciousness, and until he saw her mother, and found no reproof in Mrs. Fontaine's manner, he knew that he would have no rest. He did not go back into the house until the last possible moment, and while he was changing his clothes, Roscoe knocked on the library door and told him that he had visitors.

"Dere's a Mr. de Gruy from St. Martinville here to see you, Mr. Breck. He's got another gentleman with him, a Mr. de Hauterive."

"You mean my father's old friend, who used to come here to visit when I was a little boy?"

"Yassuh. Dat's de same one."

"Tell him I'll be right out. Tell him I hope he and his friend will spend the night. And by the way, tell Mrs. Fontaine as well as Mrs. Breckenridge that he's here. He's a cousin of hers. She'll want to know."

Breck was naturally tidy, but now he could not seem to find anything he wanted to put on. It took him some time to dress. When he finally reached the drawing room, though Anna was nowhere to be seen, Mrs. Fontaine had the situation graciously in hand, and to Breck's enormous relief, she greeted him with her usual affectionate kiss. She and Céleste, whose manner was also natural and cordial, were making agreeable conversation with the two visitors, and coffee was already being served. Breck was genuinely glad to see Allain de Gruy, less because he had a pleasing personal recollection of the man than because de Gruy represented a living link with Andy Breckenridge. Breck greeted his guests heartily.

"Well, this certainly does seem like old times! I can't tell you how glad I am you dropped in on us, Mr. de Gruy. My wife will be down in a minute, I'm sure. Meanwhile, I know you've had a delightful surprise in finding your cousin here. Isn't your sister with you? I remember her very well, too."

"No. Myrthé didn't come on this trip. But Omer de Hauterive here is her husband. Perhaps you didn't know that she married——"

"No, I'd forgotten that, if I ever did know it. But I do remember how you all used to tease her because she went into such ecstasies over the Splendida plumbing. You must tell her it's all just as it was when she was here the last time, and bring her with you the next time to see for herself. I'm delighted to have you here, too, Mr. de Hauterive. Of course you'll both stay overnight with us. And would you care to come to a fish fry with us? We're just starting out."

"So Estelle's been telling me. I've been having quite a little visit with Estelle. It's years since I've seen her, but it might have been yesterday if it weren't for this great girl who's grown up while I had my back turned. Why, yes, Breck, we'd be glad to spend the night. We were rather hoping you'd ask us to. We had to come to Plaquemine on business, so we thought we'd drop down here, too. We got a rig at the livery stable. I've had some of the best times of my life at Splendida, and it's good to be back here again and to see it looking finer than ever. There isn't a place on the river that can touch it— And so you're off to a fish fry? Is that part of the political program I hear you're mapping out? Aiming to be a delegate to the Constitutional Convention, eh?"

"News must travel faster in Louisiana than it used to. Well, I don't suppose it does any harm to get around among people at such gatherings. But as a matter of fact, I like them anyway, and——"

"And I wanted to go," Céleste broke in. "I've never been to a fish fry, Mr. de Gruy. I wanted to see what it was like."

"That's right. Make Breck show you a good time. But you ought to have a beau. A pretty girl like you oughtn't to have to depend on an old married man like Breck."

"I do have a beau, of course, Mr. de Gruy. He was here, too, but he had to go back to New Orleans last evening. I like Breck better anyway. And I don't see what you mean by calling him old. I don't call a man really old myself until he gets to be thirty, and Breck is only twenty-eight."

In the midst of the merriment which followed this generous statement, Anna came into the room, and there was a new round of introductions followed by a detailed discussion of arrangements for getting to the fish fry. There were still very few automobiles in the vicinity, and the side roads were even worse than the river road; therefore, Breck had suggested the use of one or more of the old carriages at Splendida, which this would be an opportune occasion to bring out again. But Anna had been adamant, and as usual had planned to go by car. The advent of two extra guests, tactlessly arriving in a horse-drawn vehicle, besides coming unheralded, complicated a situation which she had vainly thought she had well in hand at last. But it was finally decided to keep the hired hack for the day and use the motors, too, and the enlarged party set off.

The grove was already fairly well filled when they reached it. Wood fires had been lighted in low-built fireplaces, and Negro women, wearing clean calico dresses and bright *tignons*, were nursing the flames with solicitude while they waited for the fish to be brought in. Some of them were chanting as they worked, in a rich husky singsong, and others were circulating among the guests, proffering the strong thick coffee which it had been their first task to prepare. The male guests were lounging about on the ground or sitting on fallen logs, smoking cigars, swapping stories and giving a general effect of large leisure and genial contentment. A few of the women were equally idle; they sat on camp stools, fanning themselves, their stiffly starched white muslins forming fans, too; and when Anna, introduced by Mrs. Randolph, joined the group, they were intently discussing a church bazaar for which they were preparing. After Anna's arrival, however, their remarks became more intermittent, and were chiefly centered on obstetrics, lingering illnesses, and recent bereavements. Céleste and her mother had not sat down with them. After pleasantly acknowledging their presentation, they had gone on with Mrs. Randolph to mingle with another group, more actively engaged. The women in this were making *ayoli* with a good deal of friendly argument as to how much garlic should go into it. Céleste watched this preparation eagerly.

"It looks delicious," she said. "It smells good, too. Could I help? Did you ever see anyone make *ayoli* before, Mamma?"

"Yes, *chère*. When I used to visit the de Gruys as a young girl. But that was a long time ago. I am glad of the opportunity of enjoying the tartare sauce of the bayous again. And I also should like to help in its preparation."

She smiled, and the local ladies smiled back to her. She had caused none of the constraint that had paralyzed the group on which Anna had descended. Presently she and Céleste were stirring and sampling with the others, and helping to assemble the contributions, which had been added, as a matter of courtesy, to the ample supplies brought by the Randolphs. A fine linen tablecloth was unknotted and spread out, disclosing loaf after loaf of fresh crisp bread. How good this was going to taste with the fried fish, Céleste exclaimed, and the local ladies looked at her gratefully. She lifted the cover of a well-packed ice-cream freezer, and saw that it was filled with frozen cream cheese; this also elicited an exclamation of delight. A second freezer proved more disappointing; it had nothing in it but cracked ice, which was to go into drinks later on. Anna, resentful both of the silence which her own stiffness had created and of the ease with which the Fontaines had fitted into the picture, left the fanners, who immediately resumed their discussion of the bazaar, and joined the *ayoli* makers herself. She could perfectly well have brought some thermos jars, she said, looking at the second ice-cream freezer with condescension: but her husband had discouraged it. He had said that everything would be supplied. However, in spite of his protests, she had brought along an English tea basket, one that Cross had made to order for her. Personally, she disliked paper and wooden utensils at a picnic, as she was sure most ladies did; and this basket was fully equipped with nice agateware plates and aluminum cutlery and neat little fringed napkins. Mrs. Coutourier, the wife of the cotton gin owner, and self-appointed chief of the *ayoli* makers, who did not propose to submit to any encroachments on her authority, had been wondering what to do about Anna. Now she seized upon her chance to put the Yankee in her place.

"Mrs. Randolph always brings china and linen and silver from Nottaways Plantation, Mrs. Breckenridge," she said severely. "Of course it was very kind of you to think of the tea basket. But we don't ever use paper plates and cups or wooden forks and spoons at our fish fries. We wouldn't think of such a thing, us."

It did not seem to Anna that the picnic was starting off very well. She was thankful to see that the black boys had begun coming into the grove, because she knew this meant that lunch would soon be really under way, and after that she could think up some kind of excuse for going home early; that is, if these queer people did not start playing charades, or giving recitations, or something of that sort, which she had begun to fear was possible. The black boys looked very dirty to her, and their mules, all wet around the withers, even worse; she shuddered to think of the condition of the fish in those coarse, bulging sacks, slung on either side of the saddles. Of course it would be fresh, since it had been caught that very morning; Breck had explained to her that the boys were sent out into the swamps at dawn to get it, on the day of a fish fry; but she did not like to think of the conditions under which it had been caught or carried. The very names of these horrid little local fish were repugnant to her—bream and gaspergou and goggle-eye. *Goggle-eye!* Now if they had only been invited to some nice cool club-house to eat cold Penobscot Bay salmon and broiled live lobster and clam chowder, in select surroundings, that would have been different. She hoped that not many fish fries would be indicated for Breck's political advancment. Surely he could get beyond that point presently. There was no denying, of course, that the Randolphs were gentlefolk. But as for most of their guests——!

These benighted beings were either unaware of her malaise or unconcerned by it. The Negro women who had been tending the little fires and pouring coffee had now fallen upon the fish and were cleaning it, before Anna's very eyes. One of them, going down to the bayou's bank carrying a tin dish piled high with offal, had started back with a scream; a moccasin had writhed out of the water and snatched greedily at the refuse. Anna had seen the dreadful creature quite clear-ly, and was convulsed with shudders. But no one sympathized with her; the other picnickers seemed to accept the possible presence of moccasins quite calmly. The fish was sizzling in the iron skillets now, after being dipped in cornmeal and liberally salted; the crackling sound it made as it was turned formed an obbligato to the buzz of conversation which had become more centralized as the scattered groups gathered together, and masculine and feminine voices blended. Indeed, the first of it was already being passed on Mrs. Randolph's porcelain plates, and everyone, Anna observed with chagrin, was supplied with silverware and a large monogrammed linen napkin. The sauce was circulating, too, and Mrs. Cou-tourier, with an air of triumph, was receiving compliments about her judgment regarding the garlic. The long loaves of crisp bread were broken into segments, and the *ayoli* was sopped up with these. It reminded Anna of the way she had seen very bourgeois French people eat, at small coastal resorts in Brittany. There was nothing to go with the fish except the sauce and the fresh bread and the frozen cream cheese. But there was a good deal to drink—more and more coffee, more and more wine, more and more whisky. On such a hot day, Anna thought some nice cold lemonade would have been much more appropriate. But there was no lemonade.

After luncheon was over, the guests began to stroll down

to the edge of the bayou to wash their hands. Much as she hated the feeling of hers, greasy from the fried cornmeal and the *ayoli*, Anna could not forget the moccasin; so she wet one of her disregarded fringed napkins in the ice that still floated around in the freezer that had held the cream cheese, and moistened her fingers with that. Even if it had not been for the memory of the moccasins, she would not have enjoyed going down to the banks of the bayou, because everyone who did so made such silly jokes about being primitive, washing in that way. Anna hated jokes of this type. She noticed that Olivier did not go down to the bayou bank either, and she edged over to the place where he was standing, and expressed her general sensation of disgust, feeling sure that he would share it. She had been wanting to do this for some time, but Olivier had always been one of a group, up to then, though he had sat still most of the time. He had not moved about freely like Breck and Mr. Randolph, or like his mother and sister. Now at last he was standing alone. Anna seized upon her opportunity, as avidly as Mrs. Coutourier had done.

"I'm afraid you're not enjoying yourself any more than I am," she said solicitously. "I can't see what people think is so funny in joking about being primitive. It *is* primitive. Much too primitive to make me feel like laughing. And coming right on top of the barbecue——"

"I suppose the idea was to show us all the sylvan pleasures of a plantation life," Olivier said, civilly enough. But Anna noticed that he shrugged his shoulders slightly as he spoke.

"*Breck's* idea," she said, emphasizing her husband's name. "But tonight we'll return to civilized ways. We're giving a dinner that I really think you'll find very enjoyable. For all the nicest planation people. None—none of these townsfolk." She dismissed their fellow-guests with a word and a gesture, confident that Olivier shared her opinion of them. "Can't we sit down and keep each other company?" she inquired. "We seem to be such congenial spirits! And I'm afraid there's going to be some sort of an entertainment. That generally goes with a picnic of this sort, doesn't it?"

Olivier, shrugging his shoulders slightly again, agreed that it probably did, and asked her, rather diffidently, where she would like to sit. They were hardly ensconced on the settee which she indicated when her worst fears were realized. With almost no urging, Mrs. Coutourier embarked on a recitation in Cajun dialect of which Anna could not follow a single word. It went on and on, and when it was finally finished, the gratified performer was persuaded, again with very little difficulty, to give a lengthy encore. Four young men, all local merchants and all great friends, were equally obliging about a group of popular songs; it appeared that they were informally banded together in a quartette, and that they could be counted on for music on almost any occasion. They rendered *You Made Me Think You Cared for Me, The Trail of the Lonesome Pine* and *Peg o' My Heart* with a great deal of feeling, though occasionally a little off key, accompanying themselves on mandolins and guitars. When this contribution came to an end, again after several encores, Mrs. Randolph said that they would have some more music by and by, but that meantime they would play Truth and Consequences. This was a game which represented to Anna the very essence of peurility. She could not bring herself to take part in it, and she hoped her attitude about it would be evident. But nobody seemed to notice her attitude, nearly everyone else concentrating on the game, though while it was going on she noticed that Breck wandered around, speaking first to Mrs. Fontaine, then to Céleste, and then to Mr. Randolph. When the first fervor of Truth and Consequences began to wear off a little, Mrs. Randolph rose and made another announcement.

"We are fortunate in having a very talented young musician here with us this afternoon. I did not like to take advantage of Miss Fontaine's good nature by importuning her. But I have just learned from Mr. Breckenridge that she will be glad to sing. I think you have all had the pleasure of meeting her already, so she needs no formal presentation. Ladies and gentlemen, Miss Marie Céleste Fontaine."

The applause that followed this announcement was exceedingly hearty. Evidently the assembled company, to which Céleste had been a complete stranger only that morning, had already accepted her with eagerness. She curtsied, charmingly and unaffectedly, and turning towards the quartette, asked if one of its members would lend her his instrument. The four young merchants sprang forward simultaneously. She accepted, with a murmur of thanks, the first of the mandolins that had been actually thrust into her hands, seated herself on one of the fallen logs and crossed her knees. Anna had always considered that such a movement was exceedingly vulgar, and she was amazed that Marie Céleste should be guilty of it, or that her mother would permit such an exhibition. But reluctantly she was obliged to confess to herself that Marie Céleste looked anything but vulgar, as she sat on the fallen log with her chestnut-colored curls wreathing her face, and her white skirts spread out around her; she looked modest and graceful and altogether lovely. She strummed for a moment, aimlessly, on her borrowed mandolin. Then she glanced appealingly up at Breck, who was standing beside the log, emanating unconcealed pleasure in the success of his little maneuver.

"What shall I sing for them, Breck?" she asked, as if his choice and his decision were of supreme importance.

"Well, of course you must sing them *Toutes mes cannes sont brulées, Marianne* and *En avant, Grenadiers*. But I hope you'll sing that plantation song you picked up at Splendida, too."

"*I'm A-thinkin' of Yo', Honey?* But I don't know that very well. I never heard it until day before yesterday."

"Try it, anyway. I think you can do it."

"Then if everyone will join in the chorus—I wouldn't be afraid to try, if they'd do that."

Everyone was delighted at the suggestion. With the quartette to drown out deficiencies of lesser singers, *I'm A-thinkin' of Yo', Honey* became a rollicking success. When Céleste switched back into the Creole songs that were more familiar to her, the general enthusiasm grew even more intense. The grenadiers marched and the sugar cane burned to full and resounding accompaniment. When at last Céleste stopped, the cries of encore were again persistent and universal. Once more she looked appealing up at Breck.

"Couldn't you sing one or two spirituals before you stop?" he asked. "I believe, if you did, the darkies would sing with you, too. I don't think they quite dared when you began, even though *I'm A-thinking of Yo', Honey* is their own song. But they're more at their ease now. You've put everyone at ease, Céleste, you've made everyone happy."

The words were spoken almost in a whisper. Anna could not hear them from where she sat. But she herself spoke to Olivier, rather acidly.

"Your sister really has a very good voice, hasn't she? But I didn't realize she sang in public."

Olivier shrugged his shoulders again. "Céleste's singing is

one of Mamma's little manias," he said satirically. "It seems that she wanted to sing herself, when she was younger, and first her parents, and then later my father, discouraged her. When Céleste showed the same strange predilection, Mamma was determined that no one should discourage *her*. But I think she carries her indulgence almost too far. Letting Céleste sing at a fish fry is putting her in the same category as that horrible quartette."

"I think you're absolutely right, Olivier. I don't understand Madame Fontaine's attitude myself. I'm sure if I had a daughter——"

She spoke smugly. But in her heart she knew that no amount of smug speaking would put Céleste in the same category as the jovial young merchants. There was something transcendently rare about Céleste. She sang *"We'll Understand It Better By and By* and *I'm Going to Tell God All My Troubles* and Breck had been right; the Negroes began to sing with her too now, the chorus swelled to greater and greater harmony and richness. Then there was a hush, as if they were all waiting some supreme song which would be hers alone. She stopped strumming her mandolin, then laid it quietly aside and rose. She did not look towards Breck for guidance this time. She looked straight into the skies and sang:

> *"Ave Maria,*
> *Toi qui fus mère sur cette terre*
> *Tu souffris comme nous:*
> *Tu partageas nos chaînes,*
> *Allège nos peines;*
> *Vois, nous sommes tous,*
> *Nous sommes tous à tes genoux.*
> *Sainte Marie, Sainte Marie, Marie,*
> *Viens sécher nos larmes,*
> *Viens sécher nos larmes.*
> *Dans nos alarmes implore,*
> *Implore ton Fils pour nous.*
> *Amen."*

Céleste's song brought the picnic to a natural conclusion. Everyone in the grove felt that anything after that would be an anticlimax. Her fellow-guests told her how much her singing had meant to them and said good-bye to Mr. and Mrs. Randolph, almost in the same breath. Anna was especially precipitate in her departure, but in her case it was not because she was greatly stirred. It was because the rooms for the two unexpected guests, whom Breck had invited to spend the night without consulting her, would have to be inspected to make sure no detail of perfection was lacking in their appointments; the seating plan for the formal dinner would also have to be completely rearranged. In her haste to return to the house, she entirely forgot the wistful little hope Céleste had expressed to visit the "one-man church." But Breck had not forgotten it.

"Suppose you take Olivier in the runabout with you, Anna," he suggested, "and let me go with Aunt Estelle and Céleste in the big car. Mr. de Hauterive and Mr. de Gruy will excuse us, I'm sure, and go back in their buggy. Since you're in a hurry to get home, and Céleste wants to stop, and will have to make up for it, you're the two with whom the time element counts most at this juncture."

Nothing could have seemed more suitable to Anna than this arrangement. For once, Breck had succeeded in pleasing her very much. She departed, at the wheel of the runabout, which she handled as capably as she did everything else, with Olivier sitting rather stiffly beside her and Mrs. Fontaine looking rather thoughtfully after her. Allain de Gruy also expressed himself as delighted; he didn't care about tearing through the countryside at twenty-five miles an hour, he said; he liked to jog along. Almost everyone in his part of the country still used buggies—in fact, there were merchants he could mention who wouldn't give credit to anyone who came bounding up to their stores in automobiles; they were sure such flighty characters must be undependable. Omer de Hauterive preferred buggies, too, and walked over to the one they had hired without more ado. But just before they climbed into it, Allain made a suggestion.

"I've been watching you today, Breck, and I'd say you had the makings of a good mixer. I don't see why you shouldn't succeed along the lines you hope to. But you want to look ahead. You don't want to stick around in your own parish all the time. You want to make acquaintances all over the state. Now I believe if you'd come down to the Teche Country and go to Lafayette and Abbeville besides—"

"There's nothing I'd like better. But I don't know anyone down there, Mr. de Gruy. I wouldn't have the least idea how to start."

"You know me, don't you? And you know Omer de Haute-rive, too, now. We can both help you, and we'd be glad to. If I'm not mistaken, Odilon Dupré is going to take a party down to the clubhouse on Vermilion Bay next week, or the week after, for a little fishing. I'm sure he'd be glad to have you go along. Anyway, I'll speak to him about it and let you know."

"It sounds grand. But I wouldn't want to intrude."

"Don't you worry about that, don't you worry about that. You'll find everyone will be delighted to have you along, and you'll meet some pretty powerful politicians, though they may not look that way to you, when you first see them."

Allain de Gruy had grown quite portly with the passage of time, but he managed to climb nimbly into his buggy, and he imparted an air of coyness to the farewell flourish of his hat as he drove off. "*Au 'voir,* Estelle!" he called to his cousin. "Céleste, I still think you ought to have that beau along. Of course a church is a church, but if you did a little love-making in one, it wouldn't be the first time such a thing's happened. Well, don't get these ladies back late to dinner, Breck. I can tell from the look of your wife's back hair she wouldn't be too pleased if you did. No disparagement, no disparagement. Anna's a very fine woman, and a very efficient one, too; anyone with half an eye could see that. Good luck to you!"

He was off, jauntily and jokingly, as he had always liked to be. Mrs. Fontaine looked after him with a sad little smile.

"Mr. de Gruy didn't say anything to hurt your feelings, did he, Mamma?"

"No, *chère*. But he did bring back certain memories— Shall we be on our way, then, to see this little church in which you are so interested, for some reason, and for which Breck has so kindly made the time to take us?"

They found it without difficulty, a little outside of the village, facing the river. It was clapboarded and painted gray, and it stood not far from the road, in plain sight of this. A short path, bordered by rose bushes in full bloom, led up to it. Some of the roses were red, and a pomegranate tree towered over them; but those that clustered around the bell, which was suspended from a little frame at the side of the little chapel, were snow-white. Their arrival was happily timed. A bent old woman, wearing a gray sunbonnet and a faded calico dress, had just begun to ring the bell when they caught sight of the church and stopped. She looked up in surprise at the arrival of a motorcar, and her face was revealed as brown and wrinkled, the mouth sunken between nose and chin for lack of teeth, the outline of the cheeks sharp. But her eyes were not unfriendly. She spoke with a marked Italian accent.

"You cumma to see our church? You Catholics?"

Mrs. Fontaine and Céleste answered quickly in the affirmative. Breck, thinking that silence was probably his most tactful weapon, made no direct answer. But he asked the old woman if he could not ring the bell for her.

"No, that's aw right. The others, they be here pretty soon. Cumma in, cumma in, if you want to. I lighta the candles."

"May I help? I'd like to. I've always wanted to light candles on an altar. But in New Orleans I've never had a chance."

Céleste had gone into the little church, looking eagerly around her. It was not much larger than a good-sized closet; the two weatherbeaten benches outside bore witness to its inadequacy to hold even a handful of worshippers who habitually gathered there. There were streamers of crinkled paper hanging on the walls, two gilt-framed chromos representing Saint Anthony and the Blessed Margaret Mary, and a miniature copy of the Sistine Madonna done in crewelwork. The flowers on the altar were all made of paper, in spite of the abundance that bloomed outside, and a variety of small crucifixes, placed with no apparent plan, were scattered among them. A plaster statue of the Virgin and Child, robed in blue and white and wearing silver crowns, stood in a glass-covered niche back of the altar. There were vigil lights as well as candles standing on it, and as Céleste helped the gaunt old bell ringer to light these, the Italian went on questioning her.

"You froma New Orleans? That true?"

"Yes. That's true. But my mother and brother and I are spending the week end at Splendida."

The name seemed to mean nothing to the Italian. But she looked at Céleste intently.

"You marry with thatta fellah you with, no?"

"No. He's married already. He's just a friend."

The answer did not seem satisfactory. The old woman asked another question.

"If he-a married already, why not his wife cumma?"

"She wasn't as interested as I was in your little votive church. It was built as a thank offering, wasn't it?"

"Yes. Why fellah's wife not interested?"

"She was in a hurry. She has a great many guests coming to dinner. She had to go home."

The old woman sniffed, suspiciously. The vigil lights and candles were all lighted now, and Céleste, who was already on her knees, opened her handbag and took out her purse and her rosary. Unclasping the purse, she drew forth a dollar bill and gave it to the Italian.

"Will you burn some lights here for me?"

"They only costa five cents."

"Well, you can burn twenty of them, then."

The old woman turned the dollar bill over in her hand, uncomprehendingly. Her eyes were fixed on the rosary.

"You gotta beautiful beads, little lady."

"Would you like them? I should be very glad to give them to you. Then after this, when you say the rosary and light the candles, perhaps you'll think of me."

The Italian did not listen to the latter part of the speech. But she heard the first part and held out her gnarled hand eagerly for the rosary, fearful lest Céleste might change her mind before the beads could be clutched and tucked away. The other women who had paused outside to gossip for a few minutes came into the chapel, too, now. There were six or eight of them, two or three old and wrinkled like the bell ringer, the others young and buxom. The young women had heavy braids of black hair wound sleekly around their heads, red cheeks and full bosoms. Two of them had brought dark-eyed little girls with them wearing frilly dresses and small gold rings in their pierced ears. Mrs. Fontaine had entered the chapel at the same time with the others, and as she knelt herself, she put her arm, kindly, around the little girl who was nearest to her and asked the child her name.

"Olivia Messalina," the little girl whispered shyly.

"I am very glad that you have come here, with your mother, to pray during Mary's month, Olivia. That is what my little girl is doing with me—the one who is kneeling at the foot of the altar beside the old lady who rang the bell. She is older than you, but she is my little girl just the same."

The child's dark, heavily fringed eyes looked into Mrs. Fontaine's uncomprehendingly. But she was conscious of the kindness that she saw there. When the strange lady began to pray out loud, she began, too.

"Hail Mary, full of Grace, the Lord is with Thee——"

Breck, still standing outside, still feeling slightly ill at ease, looked in through the open door. If there had been one other man there, or even one small boy, he might have gone in. But the unrelieved femininity of the little group added to the sensation of strangeness given by the unfamiliar service and the foreign ways and speech of the worshippers. He did not realize at first that the words to which he was listening were, in meaning at least, the same that Céleste had sung, such a short time before, in the grove. But in her kneeling figure he saw something mystical, something prescient, something that moved him as he had never been moved before. She had gone bareheaded to the picnic, and now she had taken a white scarf and put it over her bright hair, so that she would not be uncovered in the church. She looks like a bride, he said to himself, veiled like that. And then he thought again, no, a bride would not hide her face so completely or bend her body so low; she might be rapt, but she would not be remote. What was it, then, that Céleste looked like? And why did he think, as he saw her kneeling, of the line in the letter she had written him? "No matter who dies that I care for, I shall always wear white."

Because he could not bear to look at her any longer, he walked over to the bush by the bell and began to pick the white roses. When she came out, with a strange, shining look on her face, he found he could not speak to her either. But he held out the flowers, and she took them.

CHAPTER 18

THE INVITATION to join the fishing party at Vermilion Bay had come opportunely. Breck's first feeling that once he was settled at Splendida he would never want to leave it had undergone a change. He was very restless after the Fontaines' visit, and none of the peaceful pursuits he had formerly enjoyed so much satisfied him any more. He multiplied his activities, both on the plantation and in the parish, and though these resulted in healthful physical fatigue, still they did not suffice to occupy his mind or to soothe his spirit. He kept searching for new ways of doing both. It seemed to him that a temporary absence from the round in which he was growing stale, and the scenes where he visualized Céleste at every turn, might be both a safeguard and a solution.

While riding the crops, it had struck him that some of the fences needed repair, but as they still stood and held, and as so many other matters claimed his attention, he had said nothing to Marcy Yates about this one. On the eve of his departure, however, he spoke to the overseer on the subject, and found that Yates, like himself, had failed to say or do anything about this only because there had been so much else to say and do. Now that Breck had referred to it first, the overseer made a frank declaration.

"The fences are in bad shape, Mr. Breck. I've kept them patched up as well as I could. But they're old. Cypress doesn't last forever. It rots, like everything else, in this climate."

"Then you think they need to be replaced rather than mended?"

"Yes. That's one of the reasons I haven't said anything. There's a good many miles of fencing on this place, Mr. Breck. It would run into tall money to replace it, even if you did it with your own cypress, and I've heard you say you didn't want to cut any of that. But you ought to use barbed wire. That's the modern method."

"And how much would the barbed wire cost, do you think?"

Yates produced from his pocket a small soiled notebook with a stubby pencil attached to it, and began to do careful and rather painful figuring. As he went along, he enumerated, under his breath, the parts of the plantation which most obviously requiring refencing—the mule pasture, the nearest headlands, and the boundary between quarters and fields. Finally he looked up and hesitantly named a sum that was as staggering to Breck as it was to him.

"I can't lay my hands on that much ready money, Yates, just now. I guess it will have to be cypress after all."

"All right, Mr. Breck. Of course you understand we'd have to get out the lumber first and then have it sawed and set up. The work couldn't be finished before fall unless we got in extra hands. I can't take the men out of the fields until the crops have been laid by."

"That's all true enough—and I suppose you could get the barbed wire right away, from Plaquemine, and that a couple of men could get it into place pretty quickly."

"That's right, Mr. Breck, and we could put up fences with

only three strands of wire now. That would do for the present and we could add the other one later on."

"I'll think it over and let you know before I leave for Abbeville."

He did think about it, intermittently, all the rest of the day, and at suppertime it was still on his mind. Anna, who was in a relaxed and agreeable mood after a day spent in supervising "improvements," which she herself had instigated, offered him a penny for his thoughts.

It would take more than a penny to pay for these thoughts," he said rather ruefully. "I've found out that we need new fences. The old ones are so rotten that they're not worth mending any more. And Yates thinks they ought to be replaced with barbed wire instead of cypress."

"Well, of course, everyone uses barbed wire in New England nowadays," Anna said conclusively. It was evident that Yates had gone up in her estimation because of his pronouncement. "Why don't you get it, Breck?"

"For the same reason I haven't got a good many other things, Anna. Barbed wire is expensive."

"You know I told you I'd be very glad——"

"Yes, I know you did, and I appreciate it. But you're doing a good deal, as it is. I don't think I ought to let you undertake the fencing on top of everything else."

If only he hadn't let her squander that money on the storehouse, he said to himself! That was all bound to be wasted, whereas the new fences would have represented a sound investment. And for the same sum— And if only he didn't feel it dishonorable, as well as humiliating, to accept money from her for any purpose, now that he was in love with Céleste! He pushed back his chair, with an impatient movement, and lighted a cigarette. Anna spoke to him reprovingly, robbing her generous gesture of all graciousness.

"You know I'd rather you didn't smoke at the table, Breck. I keep telling you. I'm sure it's bad for you to smoke so much anyway. But I'd be very pleased to buy the barbed wire. I'll speak to Yates about it in the morning."

He wanted to ask her to let him speak to Yates himself, and not to reveal that it was her money instead of his that was making the barbed wire possible. But, after all, that was something else he couldn't do. Not under all the circumstances. He put out his cigarette and thanked her.

The barbed wire was bought the next day. The following morning, before Breck left to take the ten o'clock train at Donaldsonville, he went out with Marcy Yates to watch the men starting work on the new fencing. It gave him a queer aching feeling to see the old cypress, which had already been pulled up and wrenched off, lying on the ground. It had served its purpose a long time, and now it would be good for nothing but kindling, gone in a night. There were holes, too, where the old posts had stood, gaping and vacant. They made hungry mouths in the rich earth. Well, it could not be helped. Soon they would be filled with the new posts which were already being cut, and when he got back from Vermilion Bay, the wire would be stretched between them. But he must warn Drew to leave the barbed wire alone. He could not have the child getting all scratched up while he, himself, was not there to watch him.

Drew promised solemnly that he would not touch the barbed wire and asked if he could ride to the Donaldsonville station with his father. Breck said yes, so Drew and two of the puppies went along. Anna, who was now much preoccupied with the hospital, had said good-bye briskly, immediately after breakfast, and had left the house before her husband. She did not resent his impending absence; in fact, Breck gathered that she rather welcomed it, since it would give her a chance to continue her "improvements" without suggestions or supervision. He had stopped worrying because she had bought the barbed wire. But he found it difficult, during the course of his journey, to dismiss the vision of Drew from his mind. The boy had stuck to him like a little burr ever since he had found out that Breck was going away; and at the last moment he had clung to his father so hard that it had been almost impossible for Breck to free himself without hurting the child. Then he had stood on the station platform, waving the big red handkerchief that he kept for the steamboats, his lips unquivering because they were bitten, his head tossed so far back that the tears in his eyes were invisible. But Breck knew that the tears were there, just the same, and the knowledge went with him on the long tedious train trip, which was just the type that Anna most despised.

As the crow flew, the distance between Donaldsonville and Abbeville was comparatively short, but the Atchafalaya swamp made this region impassable, and Breck had to take a roundabout route, changing at Thibodaux from a local on the Texas and Pacific to a local on the Southern Pacific. As he had a four-hour wait at Thibodaux, he went to see the Prices at Acadia Plantation. They were pleasant people, relatives of the Gays at St. Louis Plantation. He had telephoned them beforehand, so Edward Price met him at the station and took him to Acadia for dinner, driving him late in the afternoon to Shriever. This eliminated another bothersome change and a tiresome wait; but still he did not get into New Iberia, where he was to spend the night with Allain de Gruy, until nine in the evening.

He found that Omer de Hauterive, who had apparently begun his celebration betimes, had arrived before him, and was already installed at his brother-in-law's house. Allain had never married, his attitude towards matrimony being exactly the opposite from his eager sister's; but his sugar interests, not to mention his lottery interests, had, like Andy Breckenridge's, been profitable, and he had left his ancestral home at St. Martinville, and bought himself a fine old piece of property which had come on the market just about the time he was beginning to feel that family ties could sometimes be a little too confining for a convivial bachelor. Though the house was in the center of the town, a high hedge of bamboo screened it so effectively from the street that it was hidden from the main thoroughfare; and once inside the grounds, the illusion of remoteness and secrecy was complete. The lawns were ample and attractive, with large magnolia trees rising on one side of the house and a maze of rose bushes spread out on the other; and a little walk, shaded by more bamboo, led to the bayou. The style of construction was typical of the region, the rectangular house being built of mellow brick, with outdoor staircases connecting the upper and lower galleries. There was room in it for as many congenial spirits as Allain cared to gather about him, which was usually a good many; and in addition to the house, there was a small pavilion near the bayou where it was pleasant to have drinks served when the mosquitoes were not too thick.

Unfortunately they proved to be so, on the night of Breck's arrival. The three men were driven indoors by them, and sat in the gun room, swapping stories and having more drinks, until Breck, confessing rather shamefacedly than he was tired, took the initiative in suggesting that perhaps they had better turn in. The room to which he was assigned was big and bare, the bed shrouded in netting, the furniture sparse; but it gave an effect of coolness and space, rather than of emptiness and gloom, as he had first feared that it might. A "small black" was brought to his bedside, as if by instinct, when he was just beginning to stir the next morning; and the servant who set it down beside him said that Mr. Allain would be expecting him for breakfast in the pavilion at ten-thirty. The wind had shifted; the mosquitoes would not trouble the gentlemen now. Breck enjoyed the alfresco meal enormously, though Omer de Hauterive, who by this time was looking very much the worse for wear, did it scant justice; and when they had finished, it was already time to take the twelve-thirty train for Abbeville.

Two other members of the fishing party were waiting to meet them at the station in Abbeville, and hearty greetings, in which Breck felt himself included through courtesy rather than through cordiality, took place between them and the brothers-in-law. He sized the strangers up as he stood a little apart, after the introductions making them known to him as Mr. Clement Pérez and Dr. Placide Anconi had taken place. Mr. Pérez wore his black hair brushed back from his high forehead in a stiff pompadour and had a bluish chin. He was very brisk in his manner, and was clad in what was apparently the local version of the latest style in outing toggery. Breck understood that he was the highly successful manufacturer of a certain chili sauce known as "Dash-o-Fire," and felt sure he must be prominent in Rotarian circles. Dr. Anconi, the parish coroner, was a tall rangy man with a bald head and a sandy mustache. After the first greetings he looked rather vaguely into the distance, while Mr. Pérez waxed more and more voluble. Breck could well understand that the coroner might find it difficult to get in a word edgewise; but at last he did break in with the announcement that Bob Broussard and Dan O'Meara were over in the bar at the Verandah Hotel, and that perhaps it might be just as well to join them for a couple of drinks before it was time to shove off. Dr. Anconi reminded the others that Odilon Dupré was already aboard the *U. S. Boy,* fussing around among the chicken coops and sputtering at King. He would be more fussy than ever if they were late——

"Is the Broussard you mention the one who's the Congressman from this district?" Breck inquired with interest.

"Yes. He got here in the nick of time to go with us. The special session has just adjourned. He's done good work at it, made some fine speeches on the sugar situation. I don't need to tell you that's a live issue here. But if Bob hadn't been along, it's pretty certain some other Broussard would have been. They're as thick as blackberries around here and they're all related. And every other man who isn't a Broussard is a Mouton— Well, shall we be getting along?"

They drifted towards the hotel, the coroner silent again after his one long speech, the manufacturer still talking volubly. The bar, a long tunnel-shaped room, dim with a false coolness, was well filled, and Mr. O'Meara and Mr. Broussard, who had betaken themselves to a secluded corner of it, were not instantly discovered, because so many other boon companions had already surrounded them, and these companions seemed loath to part with them. When they were finally detached from their bar cronies, they wandered agreeably, though rather indirectly, towards the shrimp lugger tied up at the crowded wharf not far from the center of the town, where high teetering black buggies were hitched in a long row and the spires of a red brick church rose reassuringly over a scene that was already peaceful to the point of desuetude. Mr. Broussard and his friend Mr. O'Meara stopped to speak to other acquaintances and to do one or two last-minute errands which seemed to become increasingly important to them the more they were reminded that they should be on their way. It was after three o'clock when they were finally shepherded about the *U. S. Boy,* which glistened with a coat of fresh white paint and was adorned with a broad blue stripe; and Breck instantly saw that Dr. Anconi had been right in predicting that their tardiness would be annoying. Their host, Mr. Odilon Dupré, an officer of the Abbeville Bank, short, paunchy and clean-shaven, wearing a white linen suit and a rosebud in his buttonhole, was standing watchfully on the open foredeck, with an expression of ill-concealed impatience on his ruddy countenance. He could not forebear from reproving his guests as he greeted them.

"Dan, you specie of animal, you never were on time, no, for anything in your life. Don't you know we got to get down-river before good dark, if King's to get started on

the supper? Eh, *là-bas*, Bob, it's good you're back, yes. But
I guess you been getting plenty of bad habits too, in that
thief den at that Capitol— Doc, I been thinking with all
your experience you could keep these boys in line. But you
got a better hand with the dead than the not-so-quick.
Thanks for sending down that case of 'Dash-o-Fire,' Clem.
I'm surprised you didn't forget it, like you usually do. Mr.
Breckenridge, welcome to my yacht. That's just my little
joke, you understand! Allain did good, him, suggesting you
should come along, I'd know you any place, yes, for Andy
Breckenridge's boy. I suppose you hear that plenty of times.
All of us along the bayou were good friends of his."

"I believe he had friends in every part of the country, sir.
It's a great privilege for me to keep meeting more and more
of them."

"Well, make yourself at home. Don't stand on ceremony.
Coffee's most ready now. But I want to point out my little
dwelling to you as we go by it. The grounds slope right
down to the bayou, so you'll be able to have a good look.
I'm sorry the camellias have gone by. I got more varities of
camellias on my grounds than any man in Vermilion Parish."

Breck murmured something appropriate and stood attentively watching for the "little dwelling." He expressed his
appreciation of its ornamental grounds as the *U. S. Boy*
chugged slowly by it, by several other residences which evidently belonged to "prominent citizens" and by a large
sugar and rice warehouse. Gradually the houses became less
pretentious and further apart, and instead of being surrounded by shaded lawns, they stood in the midst of flourish-
ing little vegetable gardens. Later on there were only shacks,
with pirogues tied to their planked piers, black moss curing
on the fences and pink shrimp spread on the flat roofs to
dry. The landscape was changing, too. At Abbeville the
bayou flowed between steep banks, and the black water was
dotted with floating pads of hyacinth and abundantly
shaded with live oaks and pecan trees. But soon the only
oaks were those which sprang so surprisingly from the
chênières, the queer shell mounds that rose, reef-like,
from the swamps; there were these, and thickets of wax
myrtle, clumps of reeds, and saw grass. They were getting
nearer and nearer to the Gulf.

Breck had continued to stand on the deck, watching this
change of landscape, partly because he was genuinely in-

trigued by it, and partly because none of the other men had made any special efforts to draw him away. There were two others already abroad, reinforcing Mr. Dupré, when the rest of the party arrived, but Breck heard their names so indistinctly that he was not sure of these, and their personalities registered no more definitely; he gathered that they were planters, like Allain de Gruy and Omer de Hauterive, but even this was not quite clear. They consumed coffee, murmured that it was too much trouble to get out the ice to go in anything else, and made jokes which were unintelligible to Breck. Eventually one of them drifted over to Breck and asked a question or two.

"Glad to hear you're back at Splendida, Mr. Breckenridge. It used to be one of the finest plantations in Louisiana. How many acres have you got planted in cane?"

"Nearly two hundred, and about the same amount in corn. Only half that much in cotton."

"You'll probably find it's wisest to concentrate on the sugar—I knew your father, and you look a lot like him. Do they call you Andy, too?"

"No, there couldn't be but one Andy Breckenridge. I'm Breck. And my little boy's Drew."

"You've got a boy, then? I've got three of them."

"I wish I had."

The planter nodded and sauntered off to drink more coffee and make more jokes. Breck did not feel hurt by his casual reception, but he was a little puzzled by it. He wondered if he had made a mistake in taking de Gruy's invitation quite so literally. The shrimp lugger was too small to allow for much isolation. Several of the men had now settled down for naps under the heavy red canvas that was stretched over the deck to shade the hatch covers; others, seated on campstools, engaged in conversation which was apparently more or less confidential. Breck moved back towards the pilothouse to give the sleepers more room and to avoid the appearance of eavesdropping. As the coroner was also there, Breck approached him and asked a few questions himself.

"I must have been aboard a shrimp lugger before, when I was a boy, but if I have, I've forgotten it. What's the pulley for that's attached to the mast?"

"It's to raise the trawl when that gets too heavy to lift by hand. You noticed the trawlnet with the boards back there, didn't you?"

"I'm afraid I didn't."

Breck glanced in the direction which Dr. Anconi indicated. The net was very black from the tar in which it had been dipped. It rose in an untidy heap, topped by the heavy trawl boards.

"Well, of course, it's all strange to you yet. But you'll begin to notice these things, instinctively, before long."

"I hope so."

Mr. Dupré came bustling up at this point. He wanted the doctor to look over the fine stock of provisions he had brought along. He thought perhaps Breck would like to see them, too. There was one thing he could promise: his guests would never go hungry. Breck was quite ready to agree with the banker as he surveyed the supplies. He had taken the earlier reference to "fussing among the chicken coops" as a figure of speech. Now he saw that there actually was a large crate of live broilers aboard, not to mention a basket of shrimps, a sack of oysters, several demijohns of wine and a case of whisky.

"And I've a dozen fine counts, too, sprawling around in a basket," Mr. Dupré announced with expanding pride, gratified by Breck's obvious admiration.

"Counts?"

"Yes. Diamondback terrapin. The female of the species, you know. There isn't a more succulent dish in the world than a fine stew made of counts."

"I shouldn't suppose that there could be. I can hardly wait to eat it."

Mr. Dupré was visibly delighted with Breck's attitude as an appreciative guest, and by the time the clubhouse was reached, Breck himself was conscious that word must have mysteriously gone around that he seemed to be a pretty good fellow—though, of course, no match for his father—for the atmosphere became noticeably more genial. The clubhouse itself gave him another surprise, however. It was merely a weather-beaten shack on stilts, containing a bare living room and a dingy dormitory. There was a crude kitchen in the back and a rickety gallery in the front of it. Mr. Dupré explained to Breck that he did not think it worth while to fix the clubhouse up, as a hurricane might come along at any time and make kindling wood out of it.

Personally, Breck felt that the kindling wood stage, even without the help of a hurricane, was not far distant.

The ice, which was too much trouble to get out aboard the lugger, was produced the instant the clubhouse had been reached, and while King, the slovenly but cheery black boy, prepared supper, the men had several rounds of drinks. The liquor was excellent, and so, as Breck presently discovered, was the food. A table in the center of the living room was covered with a piece of oilcloth, somewhat the worse for wear, and onto this King presently dumped a large mound of shrimp, setting a bowl of *sauce piquante* down beside it. After that the table became more and more cluttered as dish after dish and bottle after bottle were brought there. The men drank copiously and ate prodigiously and rather uncouthly, growing increasingly jovial and loquacious as the meal progressed. Breck no longer felt that they were shutting him out, but several of them spoke English with a strong Cajun phraseology which was at times hard for him to follow, and one of the planters did not speak English at all. Breck gathered that the coroner was the scholar of the group; he quoted Descartes and Verlaine without affectation, and his erudition was evidently much respected by his less learned companions. An occasional smutty story, coarse rather than obscene, interlarded the desultory remarks about local politics, which no one seemed either to make, or take, very seriously; the only positions for which possible candidates were suggested were those of sheriff and district attorney, and opinions did not become controversial. An argument concerning the best available recipe for court bouillon grew far more heated. There was not only a decided difference of opinion as to whether it should be made of sheepshead or redfish, but two men, whose voices were eventually drowned out by one which was even more aggressive, continued to mutter for some time beneath their breath, one to the effect that he, himself, was a past master in the preparation of this delicacy, and the other that no one could touch his wife when it came to making it. Mr. Broussard, a thickset, swarthy man, was rather silent, somewhat to Breck's surprise. He had to be pressed before he outlined, with brevity and considerable shrewdness, the main features of the Wilson-Underwood Tariff Bill, and the position of the American Cane Growers Association; he disclaimed any special credit for his own speech on the sugar situation, and he resisted all efforts to draw him into a discussion about "Peck's Bad Boy" and the other Washington scandals. As the questions grew more and more insistent and ribald, especially on the part of his friend Mr. O'Meara, he simply sat and chuckled.

When dinner was over, and the grinning black boy had cleared away the table, except for the glasses, the men began to play poker. There was an occasional call for more liquor and for another "small black." But for the most part the men were intent on their game. When they stopped playing, considerably after midnight, they tumbled off to bed in the dormitory, some of them still in their underclothes, the banter, which took the place of formal good nights, gradually trailing off into silence. The next morning they began where they had left off the night before. The decks of cards were picked up again, the "small blacks" put in a periodic appearance, the plates piled with oysters and chicken and terrapin were brought in by the grinning black boy. About noon Breck, whose cardplaying was limited to bridge, and who was finding time hanging a little heavily on his hands, asked Allain de Gruy a puzzled question.

"I thought this was a fishing party. All the fish I've seen is what we brought with us."

"Eh? What? Oh, don't let that bother you! After all, you called that party we went to on Bayou Goula a fish fry, didn't you? And all you, or any of the other guests did, was to sit around in a grove and wait until one bunch of niggers came in from the swamps with their sacks full, and another bunch cooked the catch. But don't get impatient. About the middle of the afternoon Doc will go fishing, and if you don't make the mistake of suggesting it yourself, he may take you with him. He really does like to fish, and he's taken a liking for you. Of course, he knew your father— He's a queer old boy. You heard him reeling off all that philosophy and poetry last night, didn't you? He's always reading a book, or quoting from one, when he isn't sitting at the end of a line. But his patients like him. We all do."

Breck agreed that the coroner was likeable and awaited developments, still feeling rather puzzled and rather lost. He would have enjoyed reading himself, but there were no books in the camp. However, he discovered that Mr. Broussard's modesty, which precluded him from discussing his own speech on the sugar situation, had not prevented him from bringing along a copy of the *Congressional Record* containing it, which he had left lying in a fairly conspicuous place. Breck picked it up, primarily because he was thankful to get hold of anything with which he could pass the time. But once he had started, he read with increasing interest.

. . . I have long contended in this House that the destruction of the domestic sugar industry in this country will lead us back into conditions which existed long ago, when there was no domestic industry, and permit the refiners operating along the coast of the Atlantic Ocean, the Gulf, and the Pacific to dominate the American sugar market. It is the policy of the refiners of the country to destroy the domestic production, when they will again dominate this market. . . .

They have absorbed the Cuban crop, they have absorbed the Hawaiian crop, they have absorbed the Porto Rican crop, and after they have done that, and they have no further competitors in continental United States, and after, with your assistance, they shall have destroyed the beet sugar in the West and the cane sugar in the South, the price of sugar will rise, boosted by the refiners, as it was when they secured Hawaiian reciprocity. . . .

What will become of this trade of Hawaii? I will tell you what will become of it. There are 80,000 Japanese in Hawaii today. The moment you reduce this duty to the extent of making it impossible for any but the most favored plantations to continue, the moment you reduce it to the extent that these people must reduce the cost of production in order to be able to compete against the world on this market, that minute the American white man in Hawaii will move away from there and come back to his native country and engage in some other pursuit. What is left? The Jap is not going back to Japan. He is getting an outpost in the Pacific, 3,000 miles closer to the United States than before.

He will be a dominating influence; he will become the sole laborer. And do not make a mistake about it. The Japs understand the industry. They developed the sugar industry in Formosa after the Jap-Chinese war. They have sent men down to my State to learn from the Agricultural College that furnishes the sugar chemists the world over today—sent men down there, as I know personally, to learn that industry. And instead of continuing importers of sugar, they are preparing, according to our consular reports, to become exporters of sugar. . . .

Breck had never thought of the situation in this light before. Above all, he had never thought of the Japanese in connection with it. He wished he could discuss the matter with Mr. Broussard, for whose sagacity and shrewdness his respect was rapidly rising. But Mr. Broussard, like his friend Mr. O'Meara, was deep in the poker game; and this was not interrupted until a Gargantuan dinner, which was more or less a continuation of the equally immense breakfast, was shoved onto the table by King. As in the case of the previous meals, the provender which had been brought along on the lugger furnished its sole source of supply, and after it had been devoured, most of the men went to sleep from sheer repletion. But to Breck's relief, Dr. Anconi was not among these. He lounged out on the gallery, where Breck was standing, looking helplessly towards the blue waters of the bay which had so oddly been designated as Vermilion, and without taking his pipe from between his lips, made a casual statement and asked a casual question.

"I thought I'd try my luck for a while. Would you care to go with me?"

"Thank you. I'd like to very much."

"All right. Suppose we get some bait and a couple of poles."

The coroner spoke literally. He did not use a rod and reel, or offer them to Breck; his pole was merely a long cane, and for bait he had a can of shrimps embedded in ice. He accepted Breck's offer to do the rowing, and sat back in the stern until they reached a shallow spot where some barbed wire was stretched between lines of fence posts, strung, with apparent aimlessness, along the waters of the Gulf. Dr. Anconi motioned to Breck to stop rowing.

"This is an oyster lease. We'll fish off the edge of it."

"It's strange to see barbed wire on a place like this. But I'm beginning to think it's ubiquitous. I expect to see it all over my own plantation when I get back there. I've just begun replacing the old cypress fencing with it."

"Is that so? Well, I imagine you'll find it more practical. But no doubt you hated to see the old cypress go."

"Yes, Dr. Anconi, I did. I've got a lot of sentiment for Splendida. I wish nothing about it ever had to be changed. I'd like to see it stay just as it was when my father and grandfather had it."

"We all feel that way about the places we love, if they're

inherited. But we can't keep them unchanged, for all our longing.

> 'The old order changeth, yielding place to new,
> And God fulfills Himself in many ways,
> Lest one good custom should corrupt the world.' "

"How can a good custom corrupt? I've always wondered, whenever I've heard that."

The coroner did not immediately answer. He had finished baiting his line, and now cast it out, settling himself comfortably and pulling away at his pipe. Breck found the silence companionable, and made no effort to break it himself. He was confident that Dr. Anconi's answer would be worth waiting for, and when it finally came, he was not disappointed.

"Webster states that 'corrupt implies a loss of original soundness.' So the word can be applied to either good or evil and to a custom or a system as well as to a place or a man. We mustn't try to go deeply into all that this afternoon. We've come out to fish, not to argue. But speaking of corruption, there's a rumor going around that you want to get into local politics, with a view towards going further in the future."

"The rumor's true."

"If you don't mind my asking, is there any special reason why you want to do it?"

"Several. They're still more or less entangled though. I don't know that I could make them clear to you."

"If you'd care to try, I'd be glad to listen."

"Well, there's one branch of our family—the one in Kentucky—that's done quite well in politics. I don't see why the Louisiana branch shouldn't, too."

"Is the Louisiana branch a very big one? I don't seem to have heard much about it."

"No, it's very small. But I have a son. I think the world of him. And I have a notion that he'd be better off, someday, if I did something definite with my life, instead of just drifting as I've done so far."

"That's a sound enough theory in itself, but it doesn't explain why the direction in which you want to drift is towards politics."

"If I were representing my parish I'd have to live in it, most of the time anyway. I was gone from Louisiana fourteen years. I don't want anything like that to happen again, either to me or to Drew."

"You're not obliged to leave it, are you, for any reason?"

"Not theoretically. But practically, I might be. My wife's a Bostonian. It took me a long time to persuade her to come down here. And she didn't especially like New Orleans after we got there. But she likes Splendida better. She might be satisfied to stay there if there were a definite reason for it. She's very busy already making improvements. It was she who supplied the barbed wire. And the political plan appeals to her. She'd enjoy Washington very much. Meanwhile, she might enjoy Baton Rouge. She takes an interest in public questions herself. She and a Mrs. Cutler have some sort of reform movement thought up that they want to work out through a woman's committee. She's a staunch supporter of equal suffrage, too, and now she's just joined a new welfare organization called the Consumer's League. I think that if I were holding office—that is, if she felt perhaps I'd be in a position to advance some of her own schemes——"

Dr. Anconi's rod twitched violently. With no finesse he hauled back on the cane, and flopped a glistening, yellow-mouthed fish into the skiff.

"Well, a nice speckled trout, for a starter, isn't so bad," he observed as he put a fresh shrimp on his hook and cast out once more.

"Is that what it's called here?" inquired Breck. "It's what they call a weakfish up North. They're very good."

" 'A rose by any other name—' But back to the political bee that's buzzing in your bonnet. You mean your reasons are all selfish, like most politicians'? You haven't got a reform bug in your bonnet?"

Breck was embarrassed to feel himself flushing. "Yes, I have that, too. It sounds conceited when you try to put it into words. But I feel I ought to have something to contribute to politics. I don't have to work for a living. I have some money—between us, my wife and I have a good deal. And I've had a good education—the best possible."

"What do you call the best possible?"

"Why—Groton—Harvard—summer school at several European universities. I didn't take a postgraduate course because I married so young. But I studied briefly at Bonn and Grenoble and Madrid——"

He paused, stopped by an uncomfortable sensation that in spite of Dr. Anconi's courteously blank expression, the coroner was inwardly smiling. Breck had to force himself to go on.

"And I do believe in this reform movement that's sweeping over Louisiana. Now that Behrman's grip on the country parishes has been broken, I think if the better element of the state will only keep behind Hall and support him solidly, that the old abuses will all disappear. I think it's the beginning of a new era, the best there's ever been in politics. I want to have a part in the redemption of my native state. I love Louisiana and——"

This time Dr. Anconi snatched in a croaker, but absently, and without interrupting the thread of the discussion.

"I'm afraid you have an aggravated case of youth, Breck. I thought so as soon as I looked at you. Now I'm sure of it. You've got another handicap, too. I keep hearing everyone saying how much you look like your father, and of course you do. But he had a saving streak of coarseness in him you haven't got. You're sensitive. You'll get hurt. You're storing up sorrow and disappointment for yourself. You haven't his gift of bravado, either. Well, it can't be helped. If you want to go ahead you'll have it to do, and your father's friends will have to get behind you. But don't forget that I warned you."

"I don't want my father's friends to feel they *have* to help me, Dr. Anconi, just because——"

"There you go, doing exactly what I knew you would. Your skin's about as thick as tissue paper. And men who go into this game need to have thick hides. You believe that a cleansing wave of reform has swept over Louisiana and that politics are about to become whiter than snow. Well, wait until you get to Baton Rouge and see what you think then. You'll find that the crusaders and the for-sale apes are cut out of the same piece of cloth. You'll find the man in the next seat to you will vote for the betterment of mankind if you'll vote to reorganize the Courts so that his second cousin can have a three-thousand-dollar job. It will look to you like a pretty sordid bit of barter."

"You make me feel as if I ought to give up the idea entirely, Dr. Anconi, and——"

"I'm not trying to make you feel that way. I'm only trying to open your eyes, so that you won't go into all this like a blind kitten. Well, we won't talk about reform any more now. I want to hear more about your wife, and about that little boy you set such store by. I'll just give you the classic advice for success in state politics and then we'll change the subject: 'In South Louisiana you must go to Mass Sunday morning and play poker with the boys the rest of the day. In North Louisiana you must go to a Baptist or a Methodist Church Sunday morning and to prayer meeting Wednesday night, and never take a drink except behind the barn. In Central Louisiana it doesn't matter what you do, because you're up a tree anyway!' "

Breck managed to laugh, his chagrin swallowed up in amusement. Without warning, Dr. Anconi began to struggle with his cane, and after quite a tussle, landed an eight-pound redfish. He regarded it with an expresssion in which triumph and anxiety were almost equally blended.

"We'll have to go on fishing now until one of us gets a sheepshead," he said. "If we don't, Odilon will take this to make court bouillon, and Clem will sit around bitterly complaining that if he only had a sheepshead, he could make a better one. I can't risk having my evening spoiled like that. Throw out your line, Breck, and try again. And by the way, speaking of playing poker with the boys—you'd better learn to do that. Bridge is all right in Boston. But you're in Louisiana now, and you say you want to stay here. The only place bridge counts for much yet in these parts is among Miss Evie Noble's devotees, as your wife may have told you."

Breck succeeded in catching a sheepshead in the next hour, and returned to the camp in fairly good spirits. The poker game was still going on when he and the coroner got back there, but the men were beginning to show signs of wear. None of them had shaved that day, and bathing had been neither mentioned nor practiced. The next morning Breck thought he detected incipient restiveness under conditions which had previously represented a beatific state of masculine slackness; and though the poker game was resumed, it was slower in getting started than it had been before. About noon it suddenly seemed not to stop, but to disintegrate. There was no signal and no discussion. But the real purpose of the fishing trip was decisively, though tardily, revealed. Odilon Dupré announced that they must select a delegate for the Constitutional Convention who would favor a revision of the Napoleonic Code, so that trust funds could be established in Louisiana. He mentioned several sad cases of magnates who had been prepared to bring sound money into the state and keep on spending it after they had settled there, only to betake themselves and their fortunes to Florida, Mississippi and other inferior places when they learned more about Louisiana laws. The other men listened to his pronouncement respectfully. But when he had finished it, they all turned, as if simultaneously impelled, towards Dr. Anconi.

"Who did you have in mind for a delegate, Doc?" Clement Pérez inquired.

The coroner appeared to meditate, puffing away at his pipe in silence for some minutes. At last he answered as if, after pondering the question for a long time, he had been suddenly vouchsafed a revelation from on high.

"Claude Martin wouldn't be a bad man," he suggested.

There was a murmur of approval that was more or less general. But Mr. Dupré did not join in it. Instead, he protested, in much the same manner that he had fussed among the chicken coops—pompously but entirely without dignity.

"I don't know that Claude would do, Placide. You know I have confidence, me, in your judgment generally. But I sounded him out on the matter of trust funds, and he said——"

The coroner raised a languid hand. "It's a warm day, Odilon. Don't let's try to go into everything Claude said. He's quite a talker, we all know that. I'm not sure whether you can sell him on the idea of the trust funds or not. It's a good idea, as far as it goes, so I hope you can. But whether you can or not, he's got to be the delegate from this parish to the Constitutional Convention. Because, if he isn't, he'll run for clerk of court at the next election, and he'll get elected. Then we'll have a new candidate for sheriff and a new candidate for district attorney, too. In other words, we'll have a fight on our hands. If you want that, well and good. But I don't believe you do. I don't believe you want to upset the whole bandwagon just for the sake of your own little red applecart. That's right, isn't it?"

"But I tell you frankly, Placide, unless we can get the Code modified——"

"I said that's right, isn't it?"

For a moment Odilon Dupré glared at his friend. Then

he glanced around the circle. But none of the men met his eye in a knowing way. Mr. Broussard and his friend Mr. O'Meara, Mr. Pérez, Allain de Gruy and Omer de Hauterive, not to mention the two planters whose names Breck had never yet learned, were all gazing attentively at Dr. Anconi and nodding their heads.

Breck knew that Claude Martin was as good as elected already. He also knew that he himself could count on going as a delegate to the Constitutional Convention.

He found the trip back to Splendida even more tedious than he had found the trip out. The fishing party did not get back to Abbeville until late in the afternoon, and as there was no train for New Iberia until the following morning, he gratefully accepted an invitation from Dr. Anconi to spend the night at the coroner's house, instead of going to the Verandah Hotel, which de Gruy and de Hauterive preferred to do, Mr. Dupré's hospitality being exhausted for the time being and all the other men going their separate ways. Dr. Anconi was ready to go on talking about politics, and Breck was ready to listen. He learned more about personalities than he had in the more general conversation which had taken place before. The names of J. Y. Sanders and Ruffin Pleasant became familiar to him for the first time, and he listened respectfully, though dazedly, while Dr. Anconi told him that John Parker, who was so crazy about Theodore Roosevelt that he didn't know which way he was up, would be Governor of Louisiana one of these days. It did not seem to him within the realm of possibility that Louisiana could "go progressive," that a Bull Mooser could carry the state. But his confidence in the coroner's judgment was increasing fast. He willingly sat up more than half of another night, but the next morning he was very tired, and disposed to be silent going back to New Iberia. He would really have preferred not to stop there a second time, but the train was a little late, so with only ten minutes in which to make his connection for Shriever, he missed it, and was forced to accept de Gruy's hospitality again, this time for twenty-four hours. He had already promised the Prices that he would stop again at Acadia, and he found them even more friendly and congenial than he had before. But he was eager to get home now, and instead of the anticipation which had buoyed him up before, he had a let-down feeling which he could not shake off. This was intensified when he found no one at the Donaldsonville station to meet him. He had wired Anna, as he was always careful to do on the occasion of his rare absences, telling her when she might expect him; but he knew the telegraph system was by no means foolproof. He tried the telephone in the public booth of the waiting room, but got no answer to his call. Vaguely alarmed, he went to the livery stable and hired a hack.

The delay put him back further than he expected. Dusk was already falling when he reached the entrance gates of Splendida. But it was still plenty light enough for him to catch sight of something which brought his heart, with a sudden leap, into his throat, and made his hands turn cold. There was a row of little stakes driven into the ground, and at either end of them a pile of underbrush that had been cut away.

The house seemed to be deserted as he entered it. There was nothing especially sinister about that. Anna was not ordinarily in her study at this hour, and she had ceased to struggle against letting the servants drift off to their own quarters for a short snooze in the afternoon. It was not really dark inside yet, either, so the fact that there were no lights in the vestibule or the drawing room had no special significance. Breck snapped them on, absently, as he went along, wondering why the lack of them should have worried him. But when he reached the rear of the long hall, he heard a strange sound coming from Drew's bedroom. It would have been sobbing if it had not been storming. Drew was raging at something, but beneath the rage there was some form of fear; and Drew, as he himself had boasted and as far as his father knew, was not afraid of anything. Breck opened the door abruptly and strode into the room.

Nana was on her knees in front of the dresser, emptying its contents into a large open suitcase. As she took each garment from its drawer, Drew was attempting to seize it and replace it. The Englishwoman's mouth was set in a hard line and she was not speaking at all. Drew was screaming at her and striking at her.

"I'm not going away, I tell you. I won't let you and Mother take me away. I'm going to stay here with Daddy. You and she can get to hell out of here if you want to, you old hybrid whore, but I'm going to stay at Splendida."

"What is the meaning of all this?" Breck asked sternly.

Drew loosened his hold on the shirt he had been trying to take away from Nana and ran to his father. Nana folded the shirt neatly, put it in the suitcase, and reached for another, her mouth still tight.

"Mother's going away from Splendida, Daddy. She's upstairs, packing too, and Mehitabel is helping her. She says I've got to go with her. And she told Rufus he had to go, so he's run away and hidden where she can't find him. Roscoe would've been glad to go, so he could see Rose, but she won't take him. So now he's hiding with Rufus, because he's mad. I'd have run away, too, if I hadn't wanted to be here when you got home. I didn't want you to have hard work finding me. You're not going to let Mother take me away, are you, Daddy?"

"Certainly not. Nana, stop packing those clothes—I think you heard me."

"I've had instructions from Mrs. Breckenridge, sir, and——"

"Well, now you're having instructions from me. If you don't obey them, I think you'll be sorry."

"I told you so, you old——"

"Be quiet, Drew. You know I've forbidden you to say that. Stop screaming and listen to me. There's something I want you to do."

"All right, Daddy."

"Go straight out of this house. Go over to Mr. Yates' house and stay there until I come for you. Don't rush and don't stop. Just walk over there quietly. Tell Mr. Yates I sent you. Tell him I said you weren't to leave there on any account, with anybody. He won't let anyone take you away if you tell him that. You don't need to be frightened any more."

"I'm not, Daddy. It was only because you weren't here and——"

"I'm here now. Go along, Drew."

"I'm going, Daddy."

Breck did not bother to speak to Nana again. He left her still kneeling in front of the dresser, though she had stopped putting clothes into the suitcase. He did not know whether she would resume her work as soon as he went out of the room, and he did not care. He left it as abruptly as he had entered it and went quickly up the stairs. He noticed, as men will notice small things at big moments, that there were no lozenges of light on them. The sun was overcast as it set and it did not shine through the great colored window. The main passage upstairs seemed very long, as he traversed it. But when he reached the door of Anna's room, he did not neglect to knock on it. It was only when he received no answer, though he could hear her moving around inside, that he turned the handle and walked in, speaking to her maid before he spoke to her.

"You may leave the room, Mehitabel," he said coldly. The girl was not stubborn like Nana, and it was evident that she was as frightened as Drew. She scurried out like a frightened rabbit. When she had gone he asked Anna the same question he had asked Drew, in the same stern voice.

"What is the meaning of all this?"

"You know as well as I do. You know that there isn't a woman in the world who would stay with her husband, if she had any pride, after he deceived her the way you've deceived me."

"I am afraid I don't follow you, Anna."

"You don't *follow* me? Well, I'll help you to follow me. You didn't see any stakes driven into the ground, in a long line, as you came in, I suppose. Or any underbrush that had been cut away and put in piles? Or any marks of blazing on the trees?"

"Yes. I saw them. But that still doesn't explain why you should start a mutiny among the servants and scare Drew half out of his senses."

"You know what those stakes and those blazes mean, don't you?"

"I'm afraid they mean that my efforts to prevent the removal of the levee haven't been successful. I'm afraid it's going to be set back a few hundred feet."

"You talk as if that didn't amount to anything at all. You talk as if you didn't know that meant the beginning of the end for this plantation."

"If I talk that way it's because it doesn't amount to anything. You're the one who's talking wildly. I'm not. It's fantastic for you to say that moving a levee a few hundred feet means the beginning of the end for a plantation of ten thousand acres, where the house is almost a quarter of a mile from the river."

"Perhaps you'd better talk to the men who were here today instead of talking to me. Or perhaps you'd better listen to them. They've explained what's happened already, which you never did. They've explained what's going to happen hereafter."

"The reason I didn't try to explain what has happened already was because I was sure you wouldn't understand. And I can see I was right. You don't understand. And no one but God Almighty knows what's going to happen hereafter."

"You thought I wouldn't understand! But you understood. And still you let me go on spending money, squandering it! I might as well have thrown it in the river. That's what I did do, practically."

"I did try to stop you, Anna. I said I thought perhaps we'd better wait and build a new storehouse instead of trying to repair the old one. Yates told you so, too. But you were determined to do things your own way. As you always are."

"And so, because you think I'm headstrong and unreasonable, you let me go ahead and——"

"I'm more than willing to say I'm sorry for letting you squander money, if that's what you want me to do, Anna. And I can make the money up to you, if that'll help any."

"Oh, you can make the money up to me! Don't you suppose I know you're overdrawn at the bank just as well as you know it yourself? If you make the money up to me, it'll be by selling securities or something else, the way you've done over and over before, to try to make up for other reckless spending. It's been your own before this. But it's mine this time."

"I am sorry that should make so much difference to you. And I'm sorry, as I've kept trying to make clear, that your pride's been hurt. But that doesn't mean I've willfully deceived you. It only means that I've put off telling you something unpleasant until I thought there was a propitious time for it. I reckoned wrong. I didn't think the army engineers would come while I was gone. In fact, I didn't think they'd come at all this year. And I thought before another year I could explain——"

"You could expain! You would have explained that before long this house would be swallowed up by the river, I suppose? I know you better than that, Breck! You never would have said a word if you hadn't got caught! You thought perhaps you could skin through a tight place, the way your father was always skinning through tight places.

But you're not as smart as he was. Or as strong! You're a weakling, you're a procrastinator, you're a——"

"You don't suppose you've had anything to do with making me one, do you, Anna?"

"As if I could make anything of you, one way or another! As if I hadn't tried! But I'm through trying. I'm through with you. I'm leaving you."

"Very well. Of course I'm extremely sorry. But I shan't try to stop you."

"You're not extremely sorry. If it weren't for needing my money, you'd be glad to get rid of me. You'd be glad to marry some woman who would simply sit around and adore you and sleep with you every night and have a baby every year and——"

"And believe in me and encourage me and inspire me. Yes. I'd be glad to know what it would be like to be married to a woman of that sort. But I never shall. I can't stop you from leaving me, but I can stop you from divorcing me. Because you haven't any grounds for a divorce. And I've got a child to consider. I don't intend to let you ruin his life as well as mine."

"Ruin his life! As if I'd ruin his life! I'll give him every advantage. I'll see that he has the best surroundings——"

"Drew's staying with me, Anna. You can go yourself. I can't stop you, I shan't try to stop you. But if you try to take Drew, you'll get into trouble."

"*I'll* get into trouble! I'd like to see myself getting into trouble! I'd like to see you prevent me from taking my own child!"

"He's my own child, too. He means a hundred times more to me than he ever did to you or ever will. If you don't believe I'll prevent you from taking him, try it and find out. Because I'll do it. By force, if necessary."

While she stood hurling accusations at him, facing him furiously, Anna had not stopped to heed the warning note that had been in Breck's controlled voice ever since he entered the room. It was a new note, one she had never heard there before, and she did not instantly recognized it. But she could not help recognizing it now. For the first time she looked at him, still furiously, but with a queer quiver of the same fear that Mehitabel had felt when she scuttled out of the room. But she was confident that she did not show this, as she made a withering retort.

"So you're threatening me now, are you? And do you suppose that if you did use force, you could continue to keep Drew then? Don't you know that then it would be the easiest thing in the world for me to get a divorce for cruel and abusive treatment?"

"You'd have to convince the court first that you really had been cruelly and abusively treated, and why. And I'd have a chance to tell my side of the story. I could say that you had deserted me without cause, and that you had tried to take my child away from me. Also that you had refused for years to live with me as my wife. Which I would tell, if it came to a showdown. But I don't intend that it shall."

He came a step closer to her. Involuntarily she recoiled. He smiled, in a way that was neither pleasant nor merry.

"Don't be so frightened. I'm neither going to throttle you nor beat you," he said. He did not realize it, but if anyone who had known his father had heard him speaking at that moment, his voice would have been a great shock. For it was Andy's voice now, and not Breck's. "I've told you I'm sorry, Anna, for having seemed to deceive you. I know I did it wrongly, but I didn't do it willfully or from any of the motives you've imagined. If you'll believe me and forgive me, I give you my word of honor that I'll never keep anything you ought to know from you again, no matter how much it costs me to tell it to you. We'll never speak of this scene again. We'll go on as if it had never happened. I believe we could go on pretty well. I believe I'd do better and better by you all the time if you'd give me a chance. But if you won't, if nothing I can say seems worth listening to, I'll let you go without raising any sort of a rumpus about that. It's easy enough to say you were called North by illness in your family, or that you couldn't stand the heat of a Southern summer yourself, or something of that sort. That'll be enough to say for the present. Later on we can think of something else. We can agree on it. And I'll bring Drew to see you. But you can't have him without me, and you can't take him away from me. He's all I've got left in the world that matters. I'm going to keep him."

He was very close to her now, so close that their shoulders were almost touching as they faced each other, their eyes almost level with each other, and so near that they should have seen straight through to each other's souls. For an instant, meeting that direct look, feeling that presence which had so mysteriously increased in stature and magnetism, Anna wavered. But her pride, which had already brought her to such a sorry pass, prevented her from listening either to her reason or to her heart.

"You always could talk, when you made up your mind to it, Breck," she said scornfully. "I used to believe you, too. But I don't any more. You've disappointed me and deceived me too many times. I'll leave Drew with you tonight, rather than prolong this scene, as you call it. But I'm leaving you tonight. And someday I'll get Drew back."

PART VI

The Shotgun House

Spring, 1913

CHAPTER 19

ANNA FOUND the drive to New Orleans tiring, endless, and completely shorn of dramatic effect.

In abandoning herself to anger and hurling defiance at Breck, she had entirely forgotten the disadvantages of trying to leave Splendida by motor late in the afternoon. Since Rufus and Roscoe were both in hiding and she had not the remotest idea where to find them, she would be obliged to drive herself, if she went, and she would have to travel all night, in the darkness, over the worst roads she had ever seen, in order to reach her destination. If she had trouble with the car on the way, or if she ran into any mud holes, she would have to draw up by the roadside and wait for daylight, or else strike out alone on foot for help which might or might not be forthcoming. Remembering the number of blowouts which had delayed her and Breck on the way North, the thought was not reassuring. An alternative would be to stop at Old Hickory or Beau Séjour or some other plantation along the way. But under the circumstances this was unthinkable. The people who owned these places were all friends of Breck's, who had accepted her only because of him, which was galling enough in itself, but who would unconsciously ask awkward questions, which, at the moment, would be infinitely worse. She had just come to the humiliating conclusion that it would be practical, even though unimpressive, to postpone her departure until morning, when there was a knock at the door, and upon flinging it open, she saw Rufus, the chauffeur, standing there.

"Mr. Breck says yo' wants to go to town, Mis' Breckenridge," he said politely. "I done brought de car up to de do'. Is yo' bags ready to tote down?"

She could hardly believe that she was confronted by the same Negro who had slunk away from her two hours earlier, looking slovenly, sullen and scared, his defiance of her orders none the less definite because it was muttered under his breath. Rufus was now scrubbed and shaved and dressed in a spotless uniform; his legs were encased in puttees, his cap was in his hand. What was more, his manner was not only civil, but deferential, as became a servant speaking to the chatelaine of a great house. It did not soothe Anna to gather that it was Breck who had brought about this startling change. But between permitting Rufus to drive her and spending another night at Splendida, there was no possible choice.

"You may take the big ones," she said, attempting to speak imperiously and aloofly, but feeling, even as she did so, that Rufus was undeceived and unimpressed. "And you may send Mehitabel back to me. She will have the smaller ones ready to go down in a few minutes and she can bring those herself. You do not need to come up again."

Rufus bowed, assembled the suitcases capably, and vanished. The door had hardly closed behind him when Mehitabel reappeared. Her looks and manner had also undergone a transformation. She had on a neat jacket over her black uniform, and her kinky hair was tightly braided up under a trim hat. She was carrying a tea tray and she murmured that Mr. Breck had told her he was sure Mrs. Breckenridge would want a little something to eat and drink before she started out. While Anna consumed the tea and sandwiches Mehitabel moved quietly about, closing the dresser drawers, smoothing the bedspread, and putting the last trifles into Anna's fitted travelling case. Then she held her mistress's coat for her and stood back for her to pass through the door. At the foot of the stairs, Breck was waiting.

"Roscoe is going with you too, Anna," he said pleasantly. "He's confessed that he's missed Rose very much, and that he's been wishing he could 'get to see her.' This seems a good time for him to go. Perhaps later they can come back here together. But I don't want you to be shorthanded.

It's always easier to manage with a reduced staff in the country than it is in town. Don't worry about Nana. I'll make all the proper arrangements for her tomorrow. Meanwhile, I've wired the Pullman Company to reserve a drawing room on the New Orleans Limited for you tomorrow night, or the night after, if they're all tied up for tomorrow. But I don't believe they will be. I think I've put the matter urgently enough so that one will miraculously be discovered. And I've telephoned the Alpientes, saying that if you had a breakdown or anything, you might barge in on them at Rimini. They're not wishing you any sort of hard luck, but they'd be perfectly delighted to see you. I've told them you've had disturbing news about your mother's health, and that you wouldn't be in the mood for much visiting if you did stop. They were most sympathetic and said they understood perfectly. I telephoned Rose, too, so that she'll have the lights on and your bed turned down and everything in general readiness for you on Prytania Street, in case you do get through all right, as I believe you will. I'll tell Drew good-bye for you. He must be out around the place somewhere, for he certainly isn't anywhere in the house or garden. I've looked, and I don't think you ought to wait any longer. It will be dark pretty soon. Well, my dear, I hope you'll find things in Boston better than you expect. You make a good connection in New York, so you'll be there almost before you know it. Let me know if there's anything more I can do to be of service."

She was actually in the car, moving slowly down the driveway, before she was fully aware of all that had happened. But nothing could obscure her realization of the adroitness with which Breck had engineered their parting. She had never encouraged him to kiss her in the presence of their servants, so their leave-taking had looked no more formal than it always did, and there was certainly nothing about it that bespoke strain or estrangement. To all appearances he was completely the courteous and solicitous husband, facilitating the departure of a wife who had been called away for some urgent reason, but who, for an undisclosed though equally urgent reason, was not at liberty to accompany her. In the fading light, Anna glanced surreptitiously at Mehitabel, who was sitting beside her in the rear, and at Rufus and Roscoe on the front seat. Their faces still retained the somewhat blank, but completely respectful expressions that these had assumed from the moment Breck had taken the situation in hand. If he had deliberately stamped these on their countenances, the imprint could not have been more unmistakable. And still Anna did not know how far the three were deceived. She could not wholly stifle the feeling that underneath the surface civility there were smirks and sneers.

As the car rounded the last curve of the driveway, she could not suppress a momentary pang. She had never seen the grove when it looked more beautiful than it did in this pearly evening light. There was a glow on the leaves of the live oaks that made them lustrous, and the garlanding moss gave the illusion of being violet instead of gray. How could she leave such an enchanted glen of her own accord? But while she asked herself the question, she remembered that within a few short weeks this graceful curve would be gone, this stately avenue would be truncated and torn up. If she must remember it—and she knew she would never succeed in forgetting it—there would be some compensation in re-membering it like this, instead of as it would look after these army engineers had done their multilating work. There might be something in the memory of this beauty which would soften her scorn of Breck's cowardice and Breck's deception, though of course she would always think of him as a coward and a deceiver, not as a temporizer and a placator, as he had pled with her to do. How, indeed, could anything ever be more deceitful than the manner in which he had parted from her!

The road seemed even rougher by night than it had by day, though this time there were no breakdowns. Anna noted, with relief, the passage beyond every plantation where they might have been obliged to seek shelter. When they went by Rimini she was encouraged to hope that they might actually get into New Orleans that night, and they did. But mean-while there were the unrelieved monotony and the everlasting jolting to endure; these went on and on, until she felt they would never have any end. Along with other unwelcome thoughts, came the remembrance of Breck's pleasant and in-formative remarks about indigenous birds and batture dwell-ers and colonial plantation architecture, during the drive North; there was nothing of the sort to while away the time now. And it did not seem to her as if Rufus could be watch-ing for the rough places as carefully as Breck always did. But when she complained that she was shaken to pieces, Rufus said in the same civil, expressionless way in which he had spoken all the evening, that he was very sorry, that he could not see them in the dark: would Mrs. Breckenridge like him to drive more slowly? No, she answered irritably, of course she did not want him to do that. After all, if they were to get to New Orleans before morning they must make some sort of time; he did not seem to realize that this was an emergency. Rufus said yes, Mrs. Breckenridge, with such extreme politeness that she felt as if he had rebuked her for her own deception, though of course that was entirely different from Breck's. Then he went on driving fast, hitting more and more ruts and bounding over more and more thank-you-ma'ams.

The lighted house, on Prytania Street, loomed up like a haven of rest when at last they drew up to it. Like the grove, it seemed to have taken on new beauty. The encircling garden had grown more luxuriant during the weeks Anna had spent in the country; the roses were in full bloom now, the oleanders, the ligustrum, the pittosporum; the magnolias were just beginning to unfold in perfumed profusion on the tall trees, and the walk from the gate to the gallery was bordered with candytuft, marigold and sweet William. Her absence had afforded an occasion to have the façade repainted, and now it actually glistened, as if it were sheathed in snow; the black ironwork was etched against it with extreme distinctness and infinite delicacy. There was no imminent disfigurement here, no indication of impending decay; instead there was every conceivable manifestation of care, order and prosperity, and all were sublimated by the essential beauty and balminess of the South. Regretfully she realized that she could think of nothing that could resign her to the memory of this, when she was back in Boston, in that gloomy house on Beacon Hill that stood flush to the sidewalk, without a shrub or a flower or a blade of grass to soften the severity of its bleak lines.

She succeeded in dismissing the unwelcome realization of this, at least partly, because she was so tired by this time that she could no longer think clearly about anything. Rose had prepared a tray for her, even more dainty and appetizing than the tea tray she had demolished at Splendida, and Mehitabel brought it to her upstairs sitting room. She was too exhausted to eat much, but she ate a little, and then sank wearily and thankfully into her inviting bed. When she woke again, and looked at her watch, she was horrified to see that it was after eleven o'clock. It would be ridiculous to breakfast in the dining room at noon, and it would be as late as that before she would be bathed and dressed and get through the tedious process which she called "doing" her hair; there was a great deal of it, long and straight, and in addition to the hundred strokes which she meticulously gave it herself every day, because she did not consider Mehitabel "thorough" enough, she spent at least fifteen minutes braiding it and putting it into place. She rang for Mehitabel and told her that she would have another tray upstairs, and that this would serve as breakfast and lunch both. She felt that this represented a definite slackening of standards, all around. But after all, it would only be this once, and she did not know what else to do.

She did not know what to do either when she had finished her composite meal, and a long empty afternoon stretched out aridly in front of her. A telephone message had been waiting for her from the Pullman Company saying that her drawing room was reserved; but her train did not leave until eight in the evening and that was still endless hours away. Her first impulse had been to call up Mrs. Cutler, to discuss the progress of their committee for the reformation of Storyville and the enfranchisement of Louisiana's unrecognized female citizens; she had also thought that possibly there might be an opportune meeting of the Consumer's League, and that if there were, she could attend that. But on second thought, she recalled that if she were leaving her husband she would necessarily be obliged to abandon the program for the betterment of his native state; any approach to Mrs. Cutler would henceforth be handicapped by complications. A call on Mrs. Fontaine, or the acquaintances Anna had made through her, would only end in equal awkwardness. She would have to find something to read, and sit in the house until train time.

But there was nothing in the house which she especially enjoyed reading. The *Boston Transcript* and the *Atlantic Monthly* were now being sent to her at Splendida, so there were no copies of these in the house, and she had not accustomed herself to New Orleans newspapers or Southern periodicals. She read, without interest, in the *Daily Picayune*, that Lafayette had been the scene of another fire, that treaty problems were developing in connection with the Alien Land Bill, and that the Montenegrins had agreed to leave Scutari in the hands of the "Powers." A headline announcing that the Honorable Josephus Daniels was visiting the New Orleans Naval Station, and that various receptions and banquets had been planned in his honor, intrigued her but grieved her: here was another celebrity whom the Fontaines instead of the Breckenridges were to take a prominent part in entertaining! The *Item's* headlines displeased her still more:

WILL OPEN RESCUE HOME FOR GIRLS SOON
REDLIGHT PROBE STARTLING

PLAN TO SAVE WOMEN OF THE UNDERWORLD AS IS DONE IN 20 OTHER CITIES OF THE U.S.

MANY HELD HERE IN BONDAGE, IS CHARGE

MRS. M. BOVELL, NOTED SOCIAL WORKER, COMING SOON TO LAUNCH VICE FIGHT AND TELL OF 50,000 RESCUES

AIM TO GIVE GIRL CHANCE

Following an astonishing investigation and crusade in the "redlight district," extending over a period of six months, the Salvation Army will establish in New Orleans within two months a home for women of the underworld.

With the opening of the women's home, according to Staff Captain L. Allison Coe, Tuesday, will be begun the most aggressive campaign ever undertaken in any city to reach girls and women who are held in bondage in the "district," and who are there by unfortunate circumstances and not through their own free will.

The aim of the home will be to give these women and girls a chance to start anew and "make good" and win back their position in life. The home will teach them to be dressmakers, stenographers, bookkeepers, nurses, and homes or positions will be provided for them. The home will be in charge of women workers of the Salvation Army, according to Captain Coe, and there will be six women inspectors who will watch for cases needing attention.

Captain Coe says scores of girls are being held in the resorts because of "debts to the resort keepers," and this one thing he proposes to break up——

Why should the Salvation Army "butt in," Anna asked herself resentfully, just when she and Mrs. Cutler were getting everything so well started, without alien interference? Inevitably this organization would detract from the one she herself had visualized. Not that it would really make much difference, now that she was going away. But it was all very disappointing and it seemed very unjust.

She turned a page, hoping to find something that would

make more agreeable reading. Instead, she found another feature that roused her wrath:

BLAME MEN FOR WHAT WOMEN WEAR

"IT'S REFORM MOTHERS MUST BRING ABOUT"

ORLEANIANS SCOFF AT CAPELLE'S NEW "LAW"

Representative Capelle, of Cincinnati, Ohio, who has kicked up considerable excitement in the feminine world by advocating a law to prohibit women wearing translucent gowns, transparent stockings and low-necked dresses, doesn't seem to have made just exactly what you'd call a hit among the women of New Orleans.

Mrs. E. J. Graham, member of the Era Club, said Mr. Capelle was evidently a very young man or hadn't taken on much experience; for otherwise he would have had sense enough to know that the men of the country are responsible for the risqué dresses women wear.

Mrs. Sake Meehan, another prominent club and society woman in the city, backed this up with the declaration that a wave of morality is now sweeping over the country which would bring women back to the modest dress of other days if it were not for the desire "to please the man." And finally, Miss Bertha Ruffman, of the St. Charles Hotel, said that in her own personal experience mothers were dressing their girls in transparent blouses, translucent skirt and stockings that are nothing but gauze because they know that, if they do not, their daughters will be social wallflowers— very pretty perhaps, and clever and accomplished, but all out of the running alongside the girl who dresses risqué.

Miss Ruffman believes that the style in women's dress is simply an outgrowth of the entire "frivolity and immorality of the day." If men are frivolous, careless and immoral, women will be so— and if there are tendencies that way among the men, the women are bound to copy them for their own self-protection. That is the whole matter in a nutshell. Women are dressing the way they dress because men are getting more frivolous in their "hours of ease." Moreover, we have come to copy these insidious French fashions to the point where I believe some women who call themselves perfectly respectable would wear tights with lace trimmings if the fashion papers said that style was really a Parisian rage.

Several other prominent club and society women in the city echoed the sentiment. None could be found who believed that Capelle's bill will sober up woman in the matter of dress.

"It's just as I've kept telling Breck," Anna said to herself as she threw down the paper. "There's hardly a woman in the city, with the exception of Mrs. Cutler and the group that's establishing the local branch of the Consumer's

League, who has any serious purpose in life. I don't believe Mrs. Fontaine, whom Breck thinks is so wonderful, ever concerned herself for a moment for the betterment of her sex!"

A slight cough, sounding on the threshold of the door, caused her to look up from her paper. Roscoe and Rose were standing there together, and though there was some slight abashment in their manner, they were nevertheless looking at her and at each other with satisfied smirks. She had never liked either of them, but aside from his stubbornness in regard to answering the doorbell late at night, Roscoe was a very good butler, and Rose, without any qualifications whatsoever, was quite the best cook in New Orleans. Anna had never found it expedient to treat them too disdainfully, and Roscoe's recent fit of sullenness and insubordination had been a warning to her not to antagonize him again. She made an effort to speak pleasantly.

"Did you want something, Rose? Is there anything you need to speak to me about, Roscoe?"

"Yass'm. Us'n thinks us would like to get married by the Book."

"Well, I'm very glad to hear it. I'm thankful you've listened to my advice at last. I've kept telling you that it's very wrong to live the way you've been doing."

"Yass'm. Us'n thought likely you and Mr. Breck would give us our weddin' and our clo'es. Rose, she's allus hankered after a white satin dress and a veil with orange blossoms on it, and I ain't got no white gloves and no new black suit."

"But, Roscoe, Rose couldn't wear a white satin dress and a veil with orange blossoms now! You and she've been living together for years and years! You've got four or five children."

"Yass'm. We done thought de chillun would be bridesmaids, and pages, and Rose, she allus wanted a veil with orange blossoms——"

"Why, Rose, don't you know that veils are only worn by——"

She could not bring herself to say the word virgin; it was embarrassing to her except in an ecclesiastical connection. But Rose did not seem to be in the least embarrassed. She looked very coy and very pleased as she contemplated the veil and the orange blossoms. Anna tried another line of attack.

"You know I'm leaving for Boston tonight. You know I've been called away because my mother's very ill. I couldn't possibly do anything about giving you a wedding just now."

"Yass'm. But us'n thought us could have it when you come back. If you would give us the money for our clo'es today, us'n could buy them while you was gone. Us'n would need about a hundred dollars."

"I haven't got a hundred dollars in the house beyond what I'll need for traveling expenses. And the banks are closed now, for the day. You'll have to be reasonable about this wedding. I'm sure that later on Mr. Breckenridge will be glad to see that you have a nice, quiet, suitable ceremony. But I can't do anything about it today. I'm very sorry, but you've asked for something that's very inconvenient and very inappropriate, too. I think I ought to tell you so."

She picked up her paper again, as a signal to Roscoe and Rose that they were dismissed. They continued to linger for a few minutes on the threshold, talking to each other in hushed and disappointed voices, and she rattled the paper, hoping they would take the hint and go away. Eventually they did so. She had found the interlude upsetting, and now her impulse to call up Mrs. Cutler, and hear her echoed expressions of indignation about the intrusion of the Salvation Army, grew stronger and stronger. But the obstacles to this course of action remained unchanged. Anna tried to read again, opening a package of books which had just come to her from Lauriat's, where she kept a standing order. She leafed through *The Land of the Spirit* by Thomas Nelson Page and *The Flirt* by Booth Tarkington, but she did this with decreasing rather than with mounting interest. By mid-afternoon she was looking at the clock every fifteen minutes. Then she had a sudden inspiration.

She had always wanted to see the shotgun house where Olivier Fontaine lived. From the moment his mother had spoken to her about it, she had been intrigued by the description. Mrs. Fontaine had never followed up her first casual suggestion that someday she would take Anna there; but after all, there was no reason why Anna should not go there by herself. Only the evil-minded could imagine that it would be improper for a married woman of unimpeachable character, in her later twenties, to drop in briefly on a charming boy who kept an unpretentious, but attractive, bachelor establishment, in which she was interested architecturally.

Besides, no one would know about it anyway. She would be gone from New Orleans in a few hours—and perhaps she might tell Olivier the truth about her departure. She was sure he would be sympathetic if he knew she was leaving Breck and why. Latins, that is Latins of the upper class, had so much sensibility. Yes, she was sure she could count on Olivier's understanding, and her departure would not seem half so flat or half so pointless, once she had dramatized it for him.

She had a moment of concern when the thought struck her that Olivier might have no telephone, and that if she did not find his address in the telephone book, it would be embarrassing to call up his mother's house and ask. Of course she would not necessarily have to give her name. She could say that she was an old friend, just passing through the city with her husband, and that they were trying, on the spur of the moment, to get in touch with Mr. Fontaine. But even if the servant answered the telephone, it might be necessary to attach some sort of a name to her inquiry. And though she could say she was Mrs. James Brown or Mrs. John Smith, or something of the sort, easily enough, that would not necessarily prove convincing, if Mrs. Fontaine, herself, or that pert little Marie Céleste, happened to take the call, instead of a servant. Olivier had been away from New Orleans very little, except to go to Europe; his mother and sister knew all his school and college friends, and he was not old enough to number many married couples among them, in any case. But fortunately her fears proved unfounded. Olivier's number and street address were both duly listed in the telephone book. Anna smoothed her already smooth hair, put on her hat and gloves, picked up her purse and started down the stairs. As she reached the lower hallway, she met Rufus.

"Ah was jus' comin' to ask yo' if yo' didn't want I should take yo' for a little ride, Mis' Breckenridge. It's such a mighty pretty day, it's too bad to stay cooped up like yo' is."

"I am going for a little ride, Rufus. But I'll drive myself."

"Ah'd be mighty pleased to drive yo', Mis' Breckenridge. Mr. Breck done tol' me——"

"Never mind what Mr. Breckenridge told you. I'm going to drive myself this afternoon."

"Yass'm. Ah'll bring the car right around."

Rufus was still smooth, still civil in his manner; and still, underneath it, Anna knew there was a sneer and a smirk. Her anger, which had been engulfed in weariness and tedium, flamed up again with the sensation that he gave her. But it subsided as she drove along. It was indeed an unusually "pretty" day. The foliage, though still fresh, had become full; the city was a bower of verdure. In the gardens that she passed she could see groups of women, in light dresses, seated with their sewing. There were handsome turnouts in the streets, for the elite of New Orleans still clung to its carriages, in spite of the encroachments of the motorcar; other women, also wearing light dresses, and carrying little parasols, were riding about in open victorias behind high-stepping horses and coachmen in smart livery. Huge cotton-clad colored women were wheeling perambulators from which pampered babies, done up to their ears in fine starched frills, looked curiously out on a world that seemed a very pleasant place to them. Older children were rolling hoops and skipping rope and twisting pinwheels, the little girls wearing the characteristic bonnets that were an adaptation of the Norman coiffe and full short frocks, the little boys white piqué sailor suits with broad blue collars and knotted silk ties. The itinerant venders were abroad, too—the fruit carts from which angular odd-looking Negroes descended languidly to dispense multicolored wares, while the horse and driver slowly proceeded, the pushcarts where "snowballs" made of crushed ice and thick bright syrup were mixed as they were sold. The manifold aspects of a city given over to gracious living and carefree enjoyment had never been more manifest to Anna or more inescapable than on this perfect spring day.

It took her some time to find Olivier Fontaine's house. She was not familiar with the section of the city in which it was located and she had to stop and ask her way several times. The street-corner loafers of whom she made her inquiries were almost unbelievably stupid, and when they did not reply vaguely, they were apt to reply leeringly. She felt first irritated and then insulted, stopped inquiring, and lost her sense of direction. It was later than she had intended when she reached her destination. The numbers marking the houses were small and inconspicuously placed, as she had discovered was usually the case in New Orleans, and she rang the doorbell of two, mistaking them for Olivier's, before she found the right one; in both cases, the householders who came to the door looked at her curiously as they directed her further. When she finally arrived, to her considerable surprise, Olivier opened the door himself. His personal answer to her summons took her somewhat aback. It was hard for her to speak casually and naturally in the face of his blank look. But she made a determined effort.

"Why, good evening, Olivier! I didn't expect—that is, I thought of course your housekeeper would come to the door and tell me whether you were here or not. I'm delighted to find that you are. I simply couldn't resist the temptation of coming to see your lovely little house any longer. Your mother told me, the first time I called on her, that she knew I'd enjoy it, and I can tell that it's charming, just from the first glimpse. And I'm doubly glad to have that, because unfortunately I'm going away tonight and I don't know when I'll be back. You see——"

She was still undecided whether it would be better to begin with the fiction that her mother was ill and that she had been sent for, and then gradually work around to the subject of Breck and his deception, or to take the plunge at once. She played for time, while waiting for Olivier to make the next move. It was not as hospitable a one as she had hoped.

"You are going away tonight?" he echoed, in a voice that was not regretful and not even curious. "But you came to the city unexpectedly, did you not, on some slight errand? I am sorry that you did not let me know beforehand that I might expect the honor of a visit from you, Mrs. Breckenridge. I should have tried to receive you more adequately than I can at present."

She had urged him several times to call her Anna, and he had always bowed, and said he would not have her feel, for the world, that he was presumptuous, and then, in the next breath had called her Mrs. Breckenridge again. She would have liked to believe that this was really because of respect. But she was afraid that his underlying reason was much like the servants', in addressing her with the same formality; he did not feel she belonged, and he would not give the satisfaction of acting as if he did. But she could not take up the subject advantageously again, while she stood on the gallery, where anyone might see her, waiting for him to invite her to enter his house.

"I didn't expect a formal reception," she said with an attempt at a laugh tinged with coyness. "Just the welcome you'd give to any warm friend, Olivier. What a sweet little gallery this is! It looks almost as if it had been designed to go on a toy house. And I understand the little drawing room is a gem, too, done all in maple. Let me see—it was my mother-in-law who furnished it, wasn't it? The fabulous Andy's first wife, Anne Forrestal, who was apparently a sweet little soul, not the gorgeous Aurore he married later on, who was your aunt. I have the hardest work keeping all these Southern relationships straight! But yes, I'm sure I'm right. My father-in-law bought it for Anne to give to some poor relation and she did the decorating herself. You know she had New England affiliations too, just as I have— In fact I've always known the Northern branch of the Forrestal family very well. Probably she chose maple on account of her Puritan taste. It was almost unique in the South during a rosewood and black-walnut period, wasn't it?"

"I must confess I have not given the matter much thought. I have never seen anything remarkable about the maple. But the original furnishings are unchanged, largely because it has seemed futile to give myself the trouble of redecorating, in a simple bachelor establishment. If you are really interested in them, by all means come in and take a brief look at them. I must warn you again, however, that I am unprepared to give you a suitable reception. In fact, there has unfortunately never been a time when I could receive you less suitably. My housekeeper has been ailing. She has kept complaining of headache and yesterday she was nauseated. This morning she was worse, and after she had served my lunch, she had a chill and collapsed. Then she crawled rather miserably to bed. That is how I happened to open the door for you myself. In fact, when you rang, I thought you were probably the doctor. I have sent for him."

"For Dr. Beal?" Anna inquired, beginning to waver between continued curiosity and tardy discretion.

"No, unfortunately I could not reach John Beal. This man is a comparative stranger, named Breaux. He lives in this vicinity. That is why I called him. I thought he could get here quickly. But he seems to be unaccountably delayed."

"Then I will come in, just for a minute, since you are good enough to ask me. But I won't stay, of course, since you have sickness in the house—that is, unless I could be of some service?"

She had a sudden vision of herself as a ministering angel,

earning the gratitude and admiration of Olivier by the efficiency and devotion of her ministrations to the stricken housekeeper. Unfortunately, he did not seem to share this dream.

"I think perhaps it would be better if you did not go to her room. Naturally I suppose there is nothing serious the matter with her. But one never knows, with these mulattoes. They have not the slightest knowledge of hygiene, as you may imagine, and they are very careless in their habits. Indeed, Mrs. Breckenridge, I hesitate to let you have even a glimpse of my unregulated ménage, when you are such a remarkable housekeeper yourself."

Whatever the true source of his hesitation might be, the hesitation itself was certainly unconcealed. But Anna had no idea of retreating now. As he reluctantly drew back to let her pass, she swept into the little drawing room with the satisfaction peculiar to a woman who has feared that she might be thwarted and who has finally gained her point.

"You shouldn't disparage your house like that. Why, it's charming, just as I knew it would be! You have no idea how glad I am that I came." Olivier bowed in his characteristic stiff and distant fashion, without indicating that he shared this gladness, and Anna went on, "Especially as I do not know when I shall have another chance to see it. You are mistaken in supposing that I have merely come down from the country on a trifling errand. I'm on my way to Boston."

"Indeed? But that is very interesting. Your train leaves early in the evening, doesn't it?"

His eyes moved mechanically towards a small clock that stood on the mantelpiece. Anna saw the movement, but she disregarded its significance.

"No, not until eight o'clock. I have plenty of time."

"Indeed?" Olivier said again. "I was under the impression that the northbound train left at seven-thirty."

"That's the express on the Queen and Crescent route. I am going on the New Orleans Limited of the Louisiana and Nashville."

"Yes? But I am sure you like to get organized and settled before the disagreeable swaying and jerking begins. Many ladies find the effects of those so unpleasant. My dear mother always makes it a point to retire before the train starts."

"I've never been trainsick. I'm a very good traveller. I've never been seasick either."

"Indeed?" Olivier said for the third time. "You are very fortunate, are you not? Excuse me. I think I hear the telephone ringing. I was expecting a rather important call. I am so sorry that I must answer it myself, since poor Lulu cannot do so."

The telephone was in a rear room, probably Olivier's bedroom, Anna thought, as she watched him out of sight. It was certainly ringing very insistently, as if the person at the other end of the line had no idea of being put off with "no answer" from the operator. Anna would have scorned the idea of eavesdropping. Nevertheless, there was not another sound in the house to trouble the silence and she had nothing with which to occupy herself; then presently the realization that Olivier was deliberately lowering his voice, and that he was speaking in very rapid French, piqued her curiosity. Since he obviously did not wish to have her hear, or understand, what he was saying, there must be something intriguingly secret about it. She sat very still, alert and attentive, and presently she began to catch fragments of the smothered phrases.

"*Ecoute, je suis désolé, complètement désolé. J'y serai, aussitôt que possible. Mais ce n'est pas ma faute. Lulu est très souffrante, j'attends le médecin. Comment? Aussi? Gravement? Voyons, Laure, ne pleure pas. Je croix que tu te tourmentes pour rien.*"

She could not piece the sense of it together. But evidently Olivier was expected somewhere, and evidently someone besides Lulu, with whom he was concerned, was sick or in trouble. *Laure!* Why, Laure was the girl they had seen on St. Joseph's Eve with Octave Fontaine! Octave's illegitimate daughter! Olivier's cousin, "on the wrong side of the blanket!" An octoroon—no not an octoroon, for Laure was only one-sixteenth colored. What did you call a girl who was only one-sixteenth colored? And why was Olivier talking to her now, in terms of fond and anxious intimacy, and awaiting a message from her, when, that other time, he had acted as if he did not know her? Anna decided that there was only one interpretation to put on his behavior. It seemed to her insufferable that Olivier should willingly entangle himself with an octoroon—well, whatever it was a girl like Laure should be called—when he had shown himself so indifferent to the cultivated companionship of a wom-

an like herself. In a way it was even more of an affront than
the assignation with Lute, which might be regarded as a
sign of a violent but momentary aberration, and as such
forgivable though lamentable. This was evidently an established relationship. It was really shocking. She would show
him exactly how she felt about it when he returned. Or
perhaps it would be better still not to await his return. He
seemed to be talking on and on, and again she heard him
say "Laure," and afterwards *"chère,"* coupled with the
comforting phrase *"Voyons, voyons ne pleure pas!"*

Anna rose, with dignity, and moved across the little drawing room. There was really nothing very remarkable about
it after all, or about the house—a long, narrow graceless
structure, shaped something like a New England shed. She
did not see why Orleanians made such a fuss about this
type of architecture, merely because it was unique. Certainly she did not care if she never saw a shotgun house
again. Or Olivier Fontaine either, after the way he had acted.
Why, she had never had a chance to tell him that she was
leaving Breck and why! He had kept saying indeed, and
looking at the clock, and giving her the feeling of an in-
truder when she had honored him with a visit. She would
leave at once, while Olivier was still talking to Laure Dupuy.

"Good evening. I'm sorry to have walked in so unceremoniously. But I've rung the doorbell several times and no
one has answered. I'm Dr. Breaux. I understand you have
a very sick woman in the house. This is Mrs. Fontaine, I presume?"

"No, this is Mrs.— I'm an old friend of the Fontaines.
I happened to be in the neighborhood so I dropped in to do
an errand. I didn't know there was sickness in the house.
I'm just leaving. Mr. Fontaine's on the telephone. I'm sure
he'll be here in a minute."

"Perhaps you'd better not leave right away, Mrs.—? I
don't think I caught your name. Well, it doesn't matter.
But perhaps you'd better come with me to the patient's room.
I won't take you into it, but if she's as sick as Mr. Fontaine
seems to think, I may need help. I'm sure you'll be glad to
assist in any way you can, as an old friend of the family.
And sometimes minutes count at a time like this."

Anna had changed her mind about wishing to be a ministering angel. But the doctor seemed to have no idea of permitting her to elude him. Taking her by the arm, he propelled
her down the narrow hallway, past the room where Olivier

was still talking intently on the telephone, through the tiny dining room and the kitchen at the rear of the house, and towards the servant's room. On the threshold he permitted her to pause while he went on in, but Anna had the feeling that he would reach out and detain her if she tried to escape. She could see Lulu quite plainly. The sick woman was lying on her back, looking vacantly in the direction of the ceiling, and she did not move or turn as the doctor approached the bed. She was a heavy middle-aged woman, and she had quite evidently "collapsed," as Olivier had said, after striving to serve him as long as she could, and before miserably "crawling into bed." The room was not dirty, but it was untidy. The clothes Lulu had taken off were flung carelessly over the back of the only chair in the room, and the bed had evidently not been freshly made up since she was taken sick. Her face was flushed, her eyes injected, and her expression anxious. When Dr. Breaux spoke to her, she answered him in a vague way, as if she were confused or stupefied, rather than delirious. He removed the clothes from the chair to a small chest and sat down beside her, feeling her pulse and listening to her respiration. When he took the thermometer from her mouth, he looked grave.

"What's the matter with her?" Anna asked, for the sake of saying something. She felt no special sympathy for the stricken woman. The whole episode had become more and more revolting to her, and she was determined to get away as quickly as possible. But the doctor seemed equally determined that she should remain, and under all the circumstances, she could not actually run.

"I don't know yet. Her expression's not unsuggestive of pneumonia. But I think it's more likely that she has typhoid fever or malaria."

"Typhoid fever!"

"I said I wasn't sure yet. I haven't finished examining her. Stand over there in the corner, will you, Mrs.— I still don't know your name. Well, it doesn't matter. But you're cutting off some of my light, there in the doorway."

He was peeling back the dingy nightgown from the sick woman's shoulders. As her breasts were exposed, Anna saw that there were small salmon-colored spots on them, varying in size from a pinhead to a pea. Dr. Breaux looked searchingly at the spots, and then hoisting the patient up, began to examine her back and upper arms. As he laid her down, replacing her nightdress, his lips tightened.

"Do you know now what's the matter with her?" Anna asked sharply.

"I'm still not sure. It's too soon to be sure. But I can tell you right away that it's very serious. Very serious indeed."

Anna turned and looked past him to the doorway, feeling as if she were suffocating. But she was not alone with the doctor and Lulu any longer. Tardily, Olivier had finished his telephoning, and hearing voices, had come to the rear of the house. He stood at the entrance, fear and loathing battling with each other on his weak, handsome face. The doctor rose and confronted him.

"There are fourteen cases of bubonic plague in the city," he said shortly. "I think we've got a fifteenth here. Anyway, I'll have to quarantine the house for seven days and set a guard outside it. It's superfluous to tell you that no one can go out of it during that time."

CHAPTER 20

BRECK'S FIRST act, on the morning after Anna's departure, was to dismiss Nana. He paid her a month's wages in advance, supplied her with enough additional cash to cover Pullman transportation to Boston, and gave her a good reference for experience and reliability. Then he drove her to the White Castle station himself, so that she could take the "Ferriday local" which Anna had disdained, and which left there at seven fifty-nine in the morning. He conversed with her very pleasantly along the way. He was sure Mrs. Breckenridge would be glad to help her get a good situation on the North Shore that summer, he said. He fully appreciated the excellent care she had always taken of Drew. But now that Drew was getting to be such a big boy, and in some ways such a headstrong one, he really felt the child would be better off under a man's supervision than a woman's. Drew had slept in a cot in his father's room the night before, and the arrangement had been mutually satisfactory. He had to be driven to the bathtub, of course, like most small boys, but Breck would undertake to do that, and Drew really did not need much help with dressing any more—Breck shook hands with Nana, helped her with her bags, and charged a rubicund conductor to take good care of her. As she watched him until the train took her from his sight, Nana felt more respect for him than she ever had before.

With Nana out of the way and Dew on his hands, Breck's next move was to reorganize his somewhat demoralized household. His efforts met with a slight setback. He suggested to Shoog that Valina, the most personable of her minions, might act as waitress, temporarily, since he could manage, for the moment, without a butler. Shoog shifted her vast weight from one foot to the other and shook her head, looking very much subdued.

" 'Lina ain't here dis mornin', Mr. Breck. She ain't feelin' so pert."

"I'm sorry. But we can get along today without anyone, and she'll probably be all right by tomorrow, don't you think so?"

"Ah's afraid not, Mr. Breck. Her husban' done beat her up, real bad."

"Why, I thought Sam was a very good boy! I didn't know he was ever unkind to her!"

"Yas, suh. No, suh. But you see she was cotched in adultery, Mr. Breck."

Breck, striving to suppress a smile, admitted that even a good-natured nigger like Sam might be roused to wrath by the carelessness of Valina's behavior. He suggested Susie, another minion.

"She done had a baby yestiddy, Mr. Breck."

"A baby! Well, that is news! I didn't even know she was married yet, or that she'd 'taken up' with anyone."

"No, suh. She ain't. Susie done have three babies, so far, and none of them ain't had no pappy."

Smiling again at this biological phenomenon, Breck asked Shoog to make some suggestion herself.

"I done hear de bishop's granddaughter would like to come back to live at Splendida, Mr. Breck."

"The bishop's granddaughter!"

"Yas, suh. You know our preacher, what was raised here hisself, he done got to be bishop a while back."

"*Got* to be bishop! How did he get to be bishop?"

"He jes' natcherly riz, Mr. Breck. But seems like his family ain't rested easy since dey all left. Jezebel, she's hankerin' to be back here before soon."

"Do you mean to say the bishop, as you call him, let his own granddaughter be named Jezebel?"

"Yassuh. He done say he thought it would be a warnin' to

her. He say dere wasn't a woman livin' so triflin' she wouldn't want more'n her skull an' her hands an' her feet left to be buried."

"So you think I could count on Jezebel not to get cotched in adultery or to give birth to a baby that didn't have any father?"

"Yassuh. I'm most sure you could."

Before the day was over, Jezebel was installed and had begun her duties, under Shoog's competent supervision. Breck saw no reason for being dissatisfied with her. He did not try to replace Rufus or Mehitabel, for he liked to drive himself, and there was certainly no occasion to employ a lady's maid in a place where there was no lady. He decided to consider his household staff complete and devote his attention to the engineers.

There were five of them on the grounds now, a chief of party, an instrumentman, a rodman, and two chainmen, and they had a "likely" colored boy with them to help them drive the stakes. After staking the center line of the new levee, the surveying party had cross-sectioned the area to be occupied by it, at one-hundred-foot intervals; they now desired to discuss with the owner the acreage of the property which would be thrown out on the water side of the levee and the rental value of the ground which would be occupied by the contractor's camp. There was very little trouble in reaching an amicable agreement on both these points. Breck bore the engineers no personal ill will, for they were all courteous and likeable, and the rodman, a dark, striking student from Tulane, advancing himself by the means of a summer job, had unusual grace of bearing and such a distinctive way of expressing himself that Breck found him actually appealing. By a fortuitous chance, the district engineer happened to have reached this point on the river, going south in the course of his bimonthly inspection trip. The engineers signalled his steamer, the *General Newton,* and she drew up at the Splendida landing. With great heartiness the inspector invited Breck to come aboard, and the genial captain, Joe Pierce, second the invitation with equal cordiality. Breck accepted the invitation with the same eagerness that he had accepted the one to go on the fishing trip to Vermilion Bay, thankful for the prospect of the robust male companionship, the excellent fare, and the rather Rabelaisian stories that it offered. If anything, he enjoyed the engineers more than he had the pseudo-fishermen and the practical politicians. They were at one and the same time more direct and more cultured, and their cook, unaccountably named Jap, was much more of a character than the slatternly black boy at the camp. Jap stuttered badly, and the men delighted in drawing him out; but there was no one, Captain Pierce told Breck, who could cook a chop on the hot lid of a stove as well as Jap could. Having put this proud boast to the test, Breck thoroughly agreed with Captain Joe, and said that he hesitated, after such a sample, to suggest that they should all come back to Splendida with him for supper. But the engineers showed no hesitation in following this suggestion, and an evening which would otherwise have stretched rather emptily out in front of Breck was filled with unexpected good cheer. Drew ate at the table with the others, and the men drew pictures for him. They showed him, on a diagram dotted with matches to represent stakes, just how they intended to change the levee, and on another diagram, just why this had been necessary, by indicating the rate of recession on the bank, the river side tow, the water-surface elevation at low-river stage and the under-surface slope. When Drew went to bed, his father found that he had placed these diagrams on a table beside him and that he was studying them intently.

"This is going to keep us safe at Splendida, isn't it, Daddy? That's what it's meant for?"

"Yes, Drew, that's what it's meant for, and that's what it's going to do."

"I'm very glad, Daddy. I'm very happy about it. Because I wouldn't want anything to happen to Splendida, and now I understand that it won't. Of course we'll be sorry to see them shovel away the pretty clover grass, but more grass will grow, won't it? Next year we'll hardly know the difference."

"You're right, Drew. More grass will grow, and next year we'll hardly know the difference. And Splendida'll be safe, just as you say. I'm glad you're happy about it."

"Aren't you happy about it, too? Of course I understand that you must have been sorry, at first, to think that some of the land has to be shovelled away, just as I'm sorry about the clover. But then Captain Joe explained it all in such a nice way, when he said the lives and safety of hundreds of people and the security of the banks mustn't be jep—what was that queer word he used, Daddy?"

"Jeopardized. He said they mustn't be jeopardized to save one man's pride, and he was right. Yes, I'm happy about it, too, Drew. I wasn't at first. But I am now. Especially as you are."

"It was interesting, wasn't it, hearing Captain Joe talk about the tax on cotton? When I see our own cotton being baled, next fall, I'll do what he told me to. I'll pretend I can see a dollar bill pinned on every bale. I didn't understand everything he said about the tax, but I know it's just the same as if there were a dollar bill pinned on every bale in Louisiana, and that that gives somebody up in Baton Rouge enough money to keep the levee safe."

"That's right, Drew."

"But I don't understand about the under-water slopes and different kinds of carry and——"

"You will by and by. Perhaps Captain Joe will talk to you about it some more tomorrow. Good night, Drew. I have to go back to my guests."

Breck had told the truth. He was really beginning to be reconciled, though he had not let Drew know, when he said Splendida was safe now, that this meant the reconstructed levee should protect it from the changing course of the river for ten years, and that after that, it might be necessary to set it back again. Ten years! In ten years Drew would be only seventeen. And the next time the levee was set back, it would have to be far enough to insure safety for twenty years. This was to be the new rule, Captain Joe had said, and it meant that by the time Drew was thirty-seven, the driveway would be almost gone, there would be only the fringe of the grove left around the garden. And after that——

But somehow he succeeded in ceasing to think what would happen after that. There was always a chance that the river might swing to the other side, or that new methods of control would be discovered. Anyhow, by the time Drew was thirty-seven, he would have packed many years of joy on the place into his life already, and would have learned how to pack many more. His children should be half grown by that time, his wife a gracious matron. And after all, a short allee and a pleasant garden were as much as most plantation houses could boast. What if the grove did go?

Having successfully stuck to this line of thought, Breck was able to pass the next day pleasantly and constructively continuing his conferences with the engineers, devouring more of Jap's lid-grilled chops and dispensing adequate hospitality in return. Drew, clutching his diagrams, had sub-

stituted the personable young rodman for his father as a
questionnaire victim; and the handsome youth had stood up
under this so buoyantly that Breck's liking for him was
further increased. He went to bed, replete with good food,
and tired, yet tingling from physical exertion; for a few
moments he lay contentedly awake, chuckling again to himself over Jap's stuttering and Captain Joe's stories. He was
sorry that the inspector and Captain Joe both had quite so
much to say about the high water further North. At Colum-
bus, Kentucky, the residents had been obliged to flee to the
hills as the flood swept through the city, and the captain
had kept telling him that at Ponte Coupée it looked, for a
while, as if the river might rise above the floodmarks of
1912. But they had admitted, when Breck pressed them,
that later it had receded, and that now they were looking
for no immediate trouble. He successfully tried to attach no
undue importance to their subsequent statement that the relief might be only temporary, and that general warnings had
been sent out, and dwelt on the pleasanter topics they had
discussed. Then he turned over and fell into a deep and
dreamless sleep from which he arose completely refreshed.
But while he and Drew were breakfasting in a leisurely way
on the piazza, he was called in with the announcement that
New Orleans wanted him on the telephone.

"Did you say I was at breakfast, Jezebel?"

"Yassuh. But de operator done say it's urgent. She done
say yo' shofer had to speak to yo' befo' soon."

Rufus, like most of the other darkies, hated and feared the
telephone and never used it if he could possibly help it.
Breck jumped up and went into the library.

"Yes, this is Mr. Breckenridge speaking," he said, picking
up the receiver. "Yes— Yes— Hello, Rufus! What's the
matter?"

"Mis' Breckenridge went out yesterday afternoon, suh, and
she never did come back to the house."

"You mean you took her straight to the train?"

"No, suh. I didn't take her nowheres. She went out by
herself."

"Are you sure she didn't decide to drive North instead of
taking the train? Or to stay with a friend for a day or two
before she started?"

"No, suh. Her bags is all here. And she done tell Mehitabel,
before she went out, she'd be back for dinner, sure."

"But she must have had her license with her, and that has

her address on it. If there'd been an accident, the police would have called up the house."

"Yassuh. Dat's what Roscoe say and Rose say. Unless she done drive de car into de ribber."

Having unbosomed himself of this cheerful theory, Rufus waited for his master to develop it. Breck shouted back at him sharply.

"Of course she didn't drive the car into the river! Have you telephoned the hospitals?"

"I done go to all of 'em, Mr. Breck. She ain't in any of 'em. Does you want I should foam de police?"

"No, not just yet. I'll come straight down to New Orleans. I'll start immediately. I really don't believe anything serious has happened to Mrs. Breckenridge. But you did right to telephone me, Rufus. Don't try to do anything else until I get there."

"No, suh, Mr. Breck."

Breck hung up the receiver, aghast at his own lack of anxiety. He had complete faith in Anna's ability to look out for herself, no matter how uncomfortable or unhappy she made other persons in the process. And then he felt a little forking flame, evil and venomous as a viper's tongue, creeping along the edges of his consciousness. If something *had* happened to Anna—if there *had* been a serious accident—why, then he would not be bound to her any longer! Fatality for her would mean freedom for him. And if he were liberated——

He rose hastily, more and more horrified at his own involuntary reaction. He was only halfway across the floor, when the telephone rang again. This time he found it hard to hold the receiver or to control his voice.

"Yes, this is Mr. Breckenridge speaking—Mrs. Marcel Fontaine? Yes, Aunt Estelle— Yes, I can hear you perfectly— Why, of course, I'd be glad to, if you want me to. As a matter of fact, I was thinking of starting anyway. There isn't anything wrong, is there? I mean, you and Céleste are all right, aren't you? That's good. And—you haven't any other bad news, for me, have you?— No, there's no special reason why I should think you had, only naturally I wasn't expecting you to call me. The morning train's left already, so I'll drive. It's raining, but not hard. I think I can get into town sooner than if I waited for the afternoon train. It's been running late these last few days."

He was puzzled, but he was no more anxious than before.

Mrs. Fontaine was extremely noncommittal; all she said was that she would like to see him at once, if she possibly could. But she assured him that both she and Céleste were perfectly well and that there was nothing else, at the moment, which need cause him concern. Only she thought the sooner he could get to New Orleans——

All the servants had their own bells, distinguishable by the different sounds, which hung in a line against the wall in their gallery. He rang the one that summoned Shoog and had a suitcase half filled before she came lumbering in to the "bachelor bedroom" in response to his summons.

"Rufus has telephoned me that he thinks I ought to start for New Orleans right away, Shoog. And so has Mrs. Fontain. The two calls came almost together. Tell one of the boys to bring my car around to the front. And send Master Drew in here to me. I'll give him his choice between coming with me or staying here, just as he prefers."

Drew asked only one question: Was Mother in New Orleans? When Breck said that she was, Drew instantly stated that he would prefer to remain on the plantation, and Breck did not urge him. He had complete confidence in Shoog's ability to take good care of Drew until he returned. He swung rapidly down the driveway, noting that the engineers were getting along fairly fast with their work. When he struck the road, he was surprised to find that it was already rather muddy. He had not realized that there had been so much rain during the night, and looking up at the sky, he saw that the clouds were still low, though there was only a drizzle at the moment, and he made better time than he had dared to hope. When he reached New Orleans, he went straight to Mrs. Fontaine's house. Emile, the butler who had been instructed never to forget his cherry cordial, was evidently awaiting him. The front door flew open instantly.

"Rest yo' hat, suh? Miss Estelle's waitin' fo' yo' upstairs. But Miss Céleste thought maybe you'd step into the drawin' room for a minute before you went up, if you wasn't in too big a hurry, Mr. Breck."

"Thanks, Emile. No, I'm not in too big a hurry."

He parted the curtains and went into the dim drawing room. Evidently Céleste had been watching for him, too, for she was standing by the window. But as he went forward, so did she. This time he held out his arms and she threw herself into them. The movement was so spontaneous, and so mutual, that he could not tell whether he had claimed the embrace or she had invited it. But it did not matter. Nothing mattered except that he was holding her against his heart, and that she wanted him to keep her there. It was only after a long time that he felt her stirring a little, as if she felt impelled to speak to him and found she could not do so while his lips were pressed so close to hers. He raised his head, without releasing her in any other way, and listened for her whisper.

"Breck—darling—you won't ever let anyone separate us, will you?"

"Separate us? After this?"

"I'm afraid someone will try to. I'm afraid something dreadful is going to happen."

"There's nothing to be afraid of any more. I won't let anything happen. How could I when you've come to me this way?"

"I don't know. But I know I ought not to have come. I forgot for a moment that you were married. I only remembered that I've waited and waited for you, and that at last you were here."

"If it hadn't been right for you to come to me, you wouldn't have done it. You couldn't do anything that wasn't right. It would be impossible for you. Keep on forgetting that I'm married. Let's both forget it for a little while. Then by and by, when we remember again, we can decide what to do about it. I'm sure there must be something— Darling, it breaks my heart to think you've waited and waited before I came. If I'd dared to hope you'd let me, I'd have come long ago. You know that, don't you?"

"Yes, I know that."

"Then why didn't you send for me? How could I tell it wasn't Walter you wanted?"

"It ought to have been easy for you to tell that, just by instinct. I never wanted Walter. He knows that."

"Have you told him so?"

"Yes, I've told him so, but he knew it anyway. He must be better at guessing than you are. And he's been wonderful about it. But I couldn't send for you. I had to wait. I didn't send for you this time. It was Mamma who sent. And for a very grave reason. So you mustn't keep *her* waiting any longer. You must go upstairs and see her right away. But I had to see you before you saw her. I was afraid that if I didn't——"

"Dearest, I've told you there's nothing to be afraid of. I think your mother will understand. I think she'll help us."

"She might, if it weren't for Olivier. She wouldn't help anyone if it meant sacrificing Olivier, not even me. She loves me, Breck, but I'm only her daughter, her little girl. She thinks I'm a child still, she believes that if I'm unhappy I'll get over it. But Olivier is her first-born, her only son."

"I don't know what you're talking about, darling. I don't believe you do either. Olivier doesn't enter into this at all. Of course, he's your brother, I'll try to like him for your sake, but otherwise I don't care much about him. I never have. And Anna doesn't enter into it either. She's left me, Céleste, she's left me of her own free will. I'll tell you all about it after I've talked with your mother. And she hasn't lived with me as my wife for years. She doesn't want me, she hasn't ever, really. She wants a divorce. And I'll let her have it. I've been hesitating, on account of Drew, but I'm not going to hesitate any longer. Think what it would mean to him to have you for a mother instead of her! Why, he wouldn't even come to New Orleans with me when he found she was here. I've left him on the plantation with Shoog. He isn't afraid of anything else in the world, but he's afraid of his own mother."

"Oh, Breck, darling, how terrible—how terrible! But you still don't know what you're saying, you still don't understand."

"I understand that you love me and so nothing else makes any difference. I've loved you for a long time already. And no matter what you say, I believe your mother'll help us. There's a special reason why I think so. Kiss me again, darling, and then I will go up, before she begins to wonder where I am, before she sends someone to get me or comes herself. We mustn't let anyone see us like this, in each other's arms, not yet. Give me one more kiss, darling, and then go into the music room and sing while I'm upstairs. I'll listen for you. I'll be able to hear you, and I'll keep thinking about these few minutes we've had together, while I'm talking to your mother, and of all the lifetime together that's still ahead of us. I want you to keep thinking about it, too, while you sing. Because we belong to each other, Marie Céleste. We always have. We always will. There isn't any power on earth that can keep us apart now. This is stronger than anything except death and destruction."

It was true, he told himself repeatedly as he went up the stairs, still tingling with the ecstasy of that rapt embrace. Céleste had already begun to play; her music went with him, encouraging and exalting him. Anna and the scrape she had got herself into, whatever it was—Olivier—Estelle Fontaine —even Drew—none of them mattered any more compared to Marie Céleste. He had told himself this, once before, in the silent grove at Splendida. Then he had permitted himself to be silenced and frustrated by the appeal her mother had made to his sympathy and his chivalry. He could hardly have done otherwise then, when they were both guests in his house, when Estelle Fontaine had told him so touchingly that she trusted him, and Céleste had shown him that she did. But what a fool he had been not to snatch at his freedom when Anna gave him the chance! This was the folly he must now abjure, the mistake he must find some way of mending.

He made no sound as he went up. Like the rest of the floors, the stairs were thickly carpeted; that was why his footsteps were inaudible. Still, the hush in the house did not seem natural to him, any more than it had at Splendida, and the hallway was so dark that he had to grope his way along. When he reached the head of the stairs, he hesitated for a minute. He had not been on the upper story since the week after his father died, and he told himself that he really did not remember which way he ought to turn. As a matter of fact, he remembered perfectly, for he knew that everything must be unchanged here, as it was below. But he was groping for an excuse, as he had groped in the dark, to postpone the impending interview. He wanted to cling to every remnant of the rapture which Céleste's embrace had given him.

While he hesitated he heard Céleste singing the song she had learned on the plantation, the only song that he had ever known her to sing in English, except spirituals. It seemed almost uncannily apt at the moment:

> "I'm a-thinkin' of you, honey,
>   Thinkin' 'case I love you so,
>   An' my heart keeps thumpin' an' a-thumpin'
>   As I hoe down row after row."

The words came to him clearly through the silent house and he stopped to listen to them. Then he heard Mrs. Fontaine calling him. Her voice was soft and gentle, as it always was. But, like Céleste's song, it came to him with almost startling clarity, and there was an alien note in it, imperious and impatient.

"I am waiting for you, my dear boy. Here, at the left."

That would be the large upstairs sitting room, adjoining her bedroom, less massively furnished than the apartments downstairs, and slightly less formal in character, but hardly any lighter, and still more cluttered with bric-a-brac, family photographs, sofa cushions and screens. Breck went towards it slowly, and saw that Mrs. Fontaine had also come forward to meet him, and even before he bent his head to kiss her, he noticed how shockingly she had changed and aged. Her hair was still dressed with faultless artistry, her figure still encased in black of molded perfection, her face still calm and gentle. But her eyes betrayed her. He knew that she had been weeping, for the fine powder which blended so smoothly with her skin concealed neither the swollen lids nor the dark rings beneath them, and the careful control of her speech was obviously studied and regulated.

"I am thankful that you have come. But what caused the delay? I heard Emile admit you some moments ago. And I had told him that he was to bring you upstairs at once."

"Yes, but Céleste had told him that she would like to speak to me for a moment first. So of course I went into the drawing room to see her. I wasn't there very long. I hope it doesn't matter."

"I hope not, Breck."

Her words were heavy with sadness. He tried to disregard the significance of them.

"I'm sorry if I've displeased you, Aunt Estelle, by seeming to disregard your instructions. I didn't meant to. And suppose we don't lose any more time, if you think we've lost too much already. Tell me why you wanted to see me. Has it something to do with Anna?"

"Yes. It has a great deal to do with Anna."

"What's happened to her?"

"Nothing has happened to her. That is, she is neither dead nor injured nor lost."

"I didn't think for a moment that she was. Rufus telephoned, just before you did. He said she had taken the car out yesterday afternoon and that she hadn't come back. He was worried. But I wasn't."

Mrs. Fontaine sat down on a fragile French sofa, and motioned Breck to a seat facing her. She bit her lips, so slightly that the motion would have escaped anyone watching her less intently than Breck, and then pressed them with a delicate black-bordered handkerchief, as if to erase any mark that her teeth might have made.

"Since you've told me that she isn't dead or injured or lost, suppose you tell me just what she has done with herself, Aunt Estelle. We'll understand each other better if you do tell me that, first of all, won't we?"

"No. I think there are one or two other things I must say to you first. Or rather, one or two other questions I must ask you. And it isn't easy for me to speak, Breck. I must break a very long silence to do so."

"I thought it was you who were in a hurry. I'm not. I've come to New Orleans on purpose to see you and to find out about Anna. Since I know she hasn't come to any harm, I've nothing on earth to do but to sit here as long as you'd like to have me. Please take all the time you want to. And please don't tell me anything that's painful for you to say."

"I must. I must. So that you'll understand."

"Perhaps I understand part of what you feel you have to tell me, better than you think I do, already. May I go into your bedroom for a minute?"

"Why, yes, of course. But you are bewildering me now, Breck."

"I won't for long."

He rose, pushing back the petit-point chair in which he had been sitting, with a gesture of ill-concealed impatience. It seemed to him preposterious that a conversation vitally affecting the lives and happiness of several persons should have a setting that was so stilted and artificial. If he could have talked to her in the garden, it would have been infinitely easier. But it helped to hear Céleste, whose voice still came to him clearly, and who was now singing *Toutes mes cannes sont brulées, Marianne.* He walked straight to Mrs. Fontaine's dresser, and came back to her sitting room carrying the jeweled mirror in his hand.

"Anna saw this, that first night we came to dinner, when you brought her upstairs to powder her nose. She told me about it, because she admired it so much. In fact, she coveted it. She wanted me to give her one just like it. I didn't, but I could have easily enough—that is, as far as the design goes. I don't know where I'd have found the cash, just now, for fifty two-carat diamonds. But I have the original sketch for this mirror, made by Schooler. I found it among my father's papers."

"Then you did know. You've known ever since Anna told you about the mirror."

"That he loved you? Yes, of course. I've known it longer than that. At least, I've felt it. I knew he loved somebody whom he didn't marry, because he told me so himself. I wrote you that just after he died. And I've always been so fond of you myself that I couldn't help feeling there was some special bond between us. A very strong one. And there is, Aunt Estelle. Because since I went with you to the cemetery at Splendida, I've been certain that you loved him too. Why didn't you marry him?"

"I was afraid, Breck. He dazzled me and—and enraptured me, but he frightened me, too. He had extraordinary magnetism, I don't need to tell you that, and extraordinary force. It was the force I was afraid of. That and the scandal. There were all sorts of strange rumors——"

"You let the Lottery cheat you out of a lifetime of happiness? If you did, I should think probably that was one of the worst results it ever had!"

"Not just the Lottery. There was the ractrack, too, you know; there was gambling, there was dissipation."

"I don't know just what you mean by dissipation. I never saw my father drunk, and I never heard him make a lewd remark."

"No, but that was because he could drink untold amounts without showing it, and because he said things in such a charming, brilliant way that their suggestiveness was smothered— And then he was an atheist."

"He wasn't anything of the sort. He encouraged my stepmother to go to church and very often he went with her. Both my little half sisters were baptized with his entire approval. The clergy was always made welcome at his house, from Cardinal Gibbons down, and there wasn't one among them who didn't delight in coming there. Any number of his friends were priests—your brother Auguste, for instance."

"Breck, please don't speak to me so abruptly. It isn't like you. I'm not trying to argue with you, or say anything derogatory to your father. I know how you adored him. But I am trying to make you understand. It was only—afterwards —that his attitude towards the Church softened."

"Well, wouldn't it have softened 'afterwards' as you call it, if you'd married him, instead of Aunt Aurore? I should think it would have. I should think he might even have become a Catholic himself."

"That's what he tried to tell me, the last time I talked to him. But I didn't believe him. He alarmed me very much that day. He made violent love to me. And he was violent in other ways, too. He held my arms so hard that he left red marks on them. I'd heard—mysterious things about him, you see, and this violence frightened me most of all. I'd never been kissed, I'd never been touched by a man. And this recklessness and ruthlessness were so alarming that they were almost horrifying."

"I see. You were so frightened by the passion of a man you did love, that it didn't occur to you that a man you didn't love might make a hell on earth for you, if you were married to him!"

He spoke with unconcealed scorn. As he did so, Marie Céleste's voice rang clearly through the house again, softening his taunt:

"Le coeur de ma mie est petit, tout petit, petit;
J'en ai l'âme ravie. Mon amour le remplit."

Mrs. Fontaine walked over to the door and closed it, as if she were trying to shut out the song. Breck saw that she found it hard to bear. When she came back to the sofa where she had been sitting, her eyes were overflowing, and he reproached himself for having spoken so harshly. She wiped her tears away, quietly, as she had wiped her lips a few minutes before, and when she answered him the effort she made to keep her voice from trembling was surprisingly successful.

"I've scorned myself for a good many years, Breck," she said sadly. "I've had to live with the knowledge that I cheated not only your father and myself, but my husband too, hard as I tried to make everything up to him. Do you have to remind me, at this tragic time, of my cowardice and duplicity?"

"I'm sorry, Aunt Estelle. I didn't mean to make you feel so badly, and I'd never think of you as cowardly or deceitful. But I do feel I have a right to say that the mistakes of one generation shouldn't be repeated in the next. After what you've admitted, I don't see how you can logically raise any objections to a marriage between Céleste and myself."

He knew she had realized that this was coming, and that she was not unprepared for it. Yet she seemed to brace herself against the silly sofa, which offered such inadequate support.

"In witholding my love from your father, I was unable

to give it elsewhere. That is what I meant when I said I had cheated. But this tragic lack of liberality was untouched by dishonor. I never saw Andy Breckenridge alone from the day my betrothal to Marcel Fontaine was officially announced. I never saw him at all if I could help it. I faithfully kept every vow I made, Breck, and I believe that he did, too. I am certain that you also believe it. Therefore, it should not be necessary for me to remind you that you are also a man of honor. And you are married already. You are not free to marry Céleste or even to speak of love to her, as I am afraid you have done already."

"I understand the way you feel, but I don't consider that I've done anything dishonorable in telling Céleste that I love her or telling you that I want to marry her. I don't want to offend your sensibilities, Aunt Estelle, but I think you might as well know first as last that Anna and I have been estranged for a long time. When she left Splendida she left for good, and she told me she wanted a divorce. It was she who brought about the estrangement. In fact, she insisted upon it. At first I was terribly hurt, terribly isolated by it. But finally I got used to it. And I've never—consoled myself for it. That's the euphonious phrase, isn't it? But I don't see why I should live like a hermit all the rest of my life. I'm only twenty-nine now. I've got a long way to go."

"I think you may find Anna more reasonable after this, Breck, and more docile. I'm very sure that you will."

"But good God, I don't want Anna any more! I haven't wanted her in a long time! A man doesn't go on forever wanting a woman who's treated him the way she's treated me. I want Céleste. And she wants me. You know that, you've known it almost as long as I've known that you loved my father. What's the use of all this beating about the bush?"

"You will understand better, Breck, when you know what *has* happened to Anna."

"Well, tell me, by all means. I suggested it before, but you wanted to wait. Now perhaps if you do tell me it'll clear the way to talking about Céleste."

"Nothing will clear the way to talking about Céleste, as you persist in doing. I see that I must go on reminding you of factors that you either willfully or stubbornly ignore. Céleste is naturally very devout, and, the Church is adamant about such marriages as you rashly suggest. She may have listened to you for a little while, because she is very young and very inexperienced and you have swept her off her feet. But she will not do so for long. When the error of her ways is pointed out to her, she will never consent to what you intend asking of her."

"I've asked her already, and she has consented. If you don't believe me, send for her and see what she says herself."

"I shall send for her a little later, and then I shall prove to you that you are wrong. But first I will tell you what has happened to Anna. When she went out yesterday afternoon, she drove herself, because she did not wish Rufus to know where she was going. She had a good reason for not wishing him to know."

"You're not suggesting that Anna was keeping an assignation, are you, Aunt Estelle?"

His lips twisted in a wry smile as he asked the question. Even at a moment as desperate as this, there was something humorous to him in the idea that anyone might suspect Anna of an intrigue. But the lines of sadness in Mrs. Fontaine's face deepened as she answered.

"No, I am not suggesting that she was keeping an assignation. But only because that presupposes an appointment, made as a result of mutual ardor and mutual eagerness. The man she went to see was wholly unprepared for her coming, and most reluctant to receive her."

"The man she went to see! What man?"

"She went to Olivier's house, Breck."

For a moment he stared at her incredulously. Then as he started to speak, she interrupted him.

"Please let me go on, Breck, now that I have begun. You have prided yourself, I know, that you discovered my secret. You have felt that it would be a strong weapon in your hand. But when you were putting together the pieces of a long-lost romance, you entirely overlooked a present passion that affects you even more intimately."

"You mean that Anna and Olivier are in love with each other? Why, it's absurd! She's years older than he is, almost as old as I am. What's more, she's as strait-laced as a Methodist minister and as frigid as an iceberg!"

"I did not say they were in love with *each other*. Olivier is entirely indifferent to Anna. In fact, he took an instinctive dislike to her the first day he saw her, and this dislike has deepened into something very close to aversion. But she was drawn to him as instantaneously as he was repelled by her. I noticed this immediately, and it is not as phenomenal an occurrence as you seem to imagine. Women of thirty, or thereabouts, are not infrequently attracted by very young men, and the danger that this may happen is all the greater if they are either unmarried or estranged from their husbands and unconsciously yearning for union. Very often, the greater the prude, the greater the eventual indiscretion, and the colder the nature, the more calamitous its melting. None of this is any secret to me, in spite of the secluded life I have lived. Surely it cannot be a surprise to you."

Breck continued to sit staring at her incredulously. But he managed to answer before Mrs. Fontaine spoke scoffingly again.

"I'll have to admit that you have surprised me very much. But you suggested yourself that perhaps we'd better get down to cases. So let's grant I've been blind as a bat and let it go at that. You say Anna went to Olivier's house yesterday afternoon. Are you trying to tell me that's where she still is?"

"Yes, Breck, that is where she still is."

Breck laughed again, in the same wry way that he had laughed before.

"In that case, I think even you would admit I have grounds for divorce, Aunt Estelle."

"Naming my son as a corespondent? *Céleste's brother?* What sort of a foundation for a happy marriage would that make, even if there were no question of religion?" It was she who was speaking scornfully now, and Breck, with a sinking heart, realized that he had no ready retort for her scorn. She saw her advantage, and went on rapidly, "You do not need to have me tell you, Breck, how a Creole mother feels about her only son. You do not need to have me say that much as I loved your father—much as I love you, too—you would never darken my door again if you brought disgrace in any form to Olivier. Even if he deserved it. And he does not. He has not dishonored your wife, though it will be a miracle if she has not injured him irreparably."

"You've reminded me how Creole mothers feel. Perhaps I might tell you a few enlightening facts about the habits of Creole bachelors—or any other bachelors, for that matter."

"It is entirely unnecessary. How unnecessary you can judge for yourself when I tell you that the reason Anna is still in Olivier's house is because it has been quarantined for bubonic plague."

"*Quarantined for bubonic plague!*"

"You see I had more than one surprise in store for you.

Olivier's housekeeper has been ailing for several days. He had just summoned a physician when Anna made her inopportune call. Unfortunately he could not reach John Beal. I cannot help feeling that if he could have, there might have been some escape from this disastrous situation. There are doctors who believe that since bubonic plague is a disease transmitted by rodents, the detention of individuals is not effective in itself and that even indefinite detention would have no value. If I am not mistaken, John Beal subscribes to this school of thought. But Dr. Breaux, who is in charge of the case, is more conservative in his ideas. The usual seven-day quarantine has been placed on the house, and a guard has been set in front of it to prevent anyone except the doctor from entering it, and anyone at all from leaving it."

"For seven days!"

"That is the period prescribed by Louisiana law. Meanwhile a nurse has been installed and every proper precaution has been taken. The housekeeper has been isolated, and since she has survived so far, there is every reason to hope for her life. Olivier and Anna have both been inoculated and a strong disinfectant has been scattered through the house. Of course, I shall not feel entirely easy until the quarantine is lifted. But somehow I am not afraid of danger from disease for either Olivier or Anna. It is the other dangers that I am thinking more about."

Loathingly but inescapably, Breck had begun to think about them, too. This time he made no effort to prevent Mrs. Fontaine from going on.

"It is not the fact that Anna has been obliged to stay in Olivier's house that will be so damaging to her, Breck, under the circumstances. It is the fact that she went there in the first place. If she had never gone, she would never have been detained. No matter how careful we all are, it may be impossible to keep her adventure a secret. Her car is still parked in front of the house."

"I didn't think of the car," Breck muttered.

"There are many matters you have not thought of, Breck— Have you thought of the effect of all this on your little son, for instance?"

"I've thought of the effect of having Anna take him away from me. You haven't given me much time to tell you what's been happening to me, Aunt Estelle. Anna left Splendida in a fit of rage day before yesterday because she thought I'd deceived her about the levee. It's got to be moved. It was because she was angry about that, that she threatened to divorce me. And I told her I'd prevent her, on account of Drew. But afterwards I changed my mind about that, too, as you know. I began to feel I didn't care how I got my freedom as long as I did get it. I figured I could always get Drew back, even if I lost him for a little while, which wasn't likely. I didn't realize how easy Anna'd make it for me to divorce her. She's done that now, no matter what you say. I won't need to name Olivier, publicly, as a corespondent. I can see that would be very upsetting to you and—and Céleste. But I can hold the episode over Anna's head just the same, if she tries to take Drew away from me, or trouble me in any way. I can threaten her with exposure if she doesn't give me a right of way, so that I can marry Céleste."

"Do you honestly believe, after all I've told you, that Anna has been unfaithful to you, Breck?"

"Perhaps not. But only because Olivier didn't want her. If he had, there's no doubt at all in my mind what would have happened."

"And do you think it will be any easier for Anna, Breck, when she comes out of quarantine, to realize that she has gone unmolested for seven days and seven nights, not only because disease in a horrible form was in the house and death stalking it, but because a man she desired did not desire her in return?"

"I don't suppose it will. But I'm past caring what's going to make life easy for Anna any more. I'm thinking about my own happiness now. Mine and Céleste's. Send for Céleste. This is the second time I've asked you if you wouldn't. Ask her if she doesn't want to marry me, on any terms. You'll get a shock yourself."

"Very well. I will send for Céleste. But before I do so, there is one thing more I must tell you. There is another situation in which I must solicit your help, with the hope that you will be less hardhearted than you have been about this one."

The closed door had not sufficed to shut out Céleste's singing. It kept floating up through the open window. Now she began to sing "Breck's own song":

"Je suis la délaissée
Qui pleure nuit et jour
Celui qui m'a trompée

Etait mon seul amour.

J'avais seize ans à peine,
Belle comme une fleur,
Il a fallu qu'il vienne
Empoisonner mon coeur."

Breck felt, in his turn, that he had heard almost more than he could stand. "I don't mean to be hardhearted," he said, more gently than he had spoken before. "But I don't intend to let you terrorize me, the way you were terrorized yourself. I don't believe you'd have been afraid of my father if someone hadn't put the idea into your head. Your parents, I suppose. I can imagine what they thought of him, just from seeing them, when I was a little boy. I haven't forgotten how grim they could be. Well, I'm not going to let anything like that happen a second time. If you'll just keep clear about that, I'm willing to do anything—in reason. What is this other situation?"

"My brother-in-law, Octave Fontaine, is very ill also. He and—and Laure's mother. You told me once to let you know if Laure were ever in great trouble. She is in great trouble now."

"You mean there is plague in that house, too?"

"I am afraid so. Yes, certainly, it is the plague. And Laure's father and mother are much more desperately ill than Olivier's housekeeper."

"Did Laure let you know about this herself?"

"No, Laure has never approached me herself. Olivier told me, when he telephoned me about the other."

"And how did Olivier know?"

"Laure had approached him. Or rather, she was expecting a visit from him, so she telephoned him, partly out of anxiety because he was late in arriving, and partly to tell him that it probably would be safer, in any case, that he should not come. Since then, that house has been quarantined also."

"She was expecting a visit from Olivier! So he makes a practice of visiting Laure! Another custom carried down from one generation to another!"

Breck had jumped up, furiously. Mrs. Fontaine rose, too, and laid a trembling hand on his arm.

"Don't look at me like that, Breck! Don't dare to speak to me like that! How can you compare the two?"

"I'll wager Laure's as good a girl as Céleste! Or that she's meant to be and wanted to be! If she isn't, it's because her own father hasn't protected her, because her own cousin didn't respect her! I'm sick of the standards of these Southern men who——"

"And aren't you a Southern man yourself, Breck? Isn't that what you have always gloried in being? What has happened to your own standards? You are ready to denounce your wife for a crime she hasn't committed, to sully your son's memory of his mother, to estrange an innocent girl from her family, and deprive her of her Faith, in order to satisfy your own passion!"

"Good God, you talk as if I'd disgraced Anna and seduced Céleste! Anna's disgraced me! Céleste's in love with me! And while we stand here talking, getting nowhere, poor little Laure is down there in that charnel house all alone. I'm going to her. I'll get past the guard some way. I'm not afraid of plague or anything else. And when I find out from her what Olivier has done to her already, and what he means to do, I'll tell you whether he can go scot-free or not, as far as Anna is concerned!"

CHAPTER 21

CÉLESTE WAS still sitting at the piano when Breck pushed open the door of the music room. He knew that she had remained there because that was where he had asked her to stay, and again the consciousness of her touching compliance pierced him poignantly, as it had done so many times before. But he was afraid she had been crying, or, if not, that she had struggled so hard to maintain her self-control that the effort had cost her far more than easy tears. She had ceased to sing, and her hands were resting lightly on the keys, striking only stray chords. When she saw him, she rose, with a little cry of gladness and relief, and for the second time that day cast herself into his outstretched arms. He kissed her, not passionately and lingeringly this time, but quietly and gently. Then, with his face still pressed against hers, he spoke to her in a soothing way.

"Darling, it was sweet of you to stay here all this time. I could hear you singing, while I was talking to your mother, and I can't tell you how much it meant to me. But it breaks my heart to see you so sad. I can't bear to have you cry."

"I didn't cry, Breck. And I kept on singing, as long as I could. But I was so worried——"

"Don't worry. I'll admit that things are in an awful mess. But we'll find a way to straighten them out, somehow."

"Wasn't I right, though? Didn't you find that Mamma wanted to shield and save Olivier more than she wanted to do anything else, that she'd sacrifice anyone for him?"

"Yes, you were right about that. But I'm not sure it won't be our trump card, after all. Because Olivier needs to be shielded in more ways than one, dearest. And I don't think she'll risk having him ruined in one way to save him in another."

"I don't understand what you mean, Breck."

"No, and I haven't time to tell you now. I've got to leave you, darling, without wasting another minute. Because there's someone who needs me even more than you do, just now."

"Is it Laure?"

"Yes, it's Laure. Her father and mother are both dying. I'm afraid she's all alone."

"I'm afraid so, too, Breck. You see, I was near the telephone when Olivier talked to Mamma. I heard everything he said."

"Then you do understand, don't you, Céleste, that I've got to go to her?"

"Yes, I understand. And I want you to. But I'm afraid to have you, just the same."

"I'll come back as soon as I can, you know that. And I'll be thinking of you every moment while I'm gone."

"I'll be thinking of you, too, Breck. And praying for you. For—for us. And for poor little Laure."

"That's right. Pray for us all. And keep on singing for me. And don't forget that you're not to let anyone frighten you or coerce you or trap you. I'm not too certain that no one will try. But if that happens, keep saying to yourself, 'I belong to Breck now. I don't owe obedience to anyone else, and I won't promise it. I believe he was telling the truth when he said "Nothing can separate us but death and destruction." I'll never marry any other man. I'll wait for him to come back to me, patiently and courageously. I know he won't fail me, and I won't fail him. Never, never, never.'"

"I promise you, Breck. I promise you all that."

She went with him as far as the front door. He had half

expected that her mother, who must certainly have known that he would go to her again, might come downstairs and intercept their farewell. But the hallway still gave the same weird effect of unnatural stillness and vacancy as when he had entered it. He parted from Céleste tenderly, and went out of the house without looking back.

He noticed now the mired condition of his car. It was strange that he should, he thought, when his bewildered brain was full of so much more that was disturbing. But again he realized that the rains of the night before must have been far heavier than he had noticed. There had been bad rains already that spring: a cyclonic storm had struck Provençal, wrecking the village and killing four persons, while scores had been injured in near-by places. At that time the damage, financially speaking, had come to about five million dollars in Louisiana and to several thousand in New Orleans alone, where streets had been deluged, traffic stopped, and houses struck by lightning, though no one had been killed. Iberville Parish had suffered comparatively little then, but the dissaster had given a pretext for a mass meeting at White Castle, at which the current levee system had been denounced, and the Atchafalaya Board called upon for protection. Breck had attended the meeting, and spoken at it, in support of the Newland Bill, promulgating "unit treatment of the Mississippi drainage basin problem and the utilization of all wise means of water handling, stream control, flood prevention and navigation maintenance." Afterwards, he had signed a resolution appealing to the members of the Board to bear the expense of the guards and inspectors placed on the levees. But he had done this because it was obviously part of the political plan which he was so carefully working out, and not because he permitted himself to believe that his own parish was in any real danger, or that one plan for its protection was basically better than another.

In the great floods of the previous year, when thirty thousand persons had been made homeless and ten million dollars' worth of property destroyed, the Iberville losses had been heavy. The levee had broken in front of Torras, at the extreme north of Pointe Coupée, endangering the richest and most extensive sugar region in Louisiana. All railroad communication had been cut off, since the Frisco had been washed out for miles, the water flooding the land on the east bank and being up to the base of the levee on the west bank. Conditions resulting from the flood reached an acute stage in the

Fordoche and Grosse Tête sections. Water covered all of the country north of the Frisco tracks, and the east bank of Grosse Tête was inundated. Below Livonia, as far as Grosse Tête, the west bank had held except for a small crevasse at Grimmers; this was only about twenty feet wide, but it sufficed to flood Woodley and Vernalia Plantations. Heavy rains and thunderstorms further south made the condition of the country there still more terrible. Many planters in the vicinity of Plaquemine and White Castle abandoned their field work and built additional levees around their plantations, and one hundred and seventy-five men were rushed to old Hickory levee, where a weak spot developed. Union and Homestead Plantations, which, like St. Louis, belonged to the Gays, were soon half under water, and a few days later, so was Myrtle Grove, belonging to the Wilberts, where there was another break in the levee. All in all, more than half of the crops of Iberville Parish were destroyed by the backwaters of the Torras crevasse, and there had been much other damage and unrelieved danger besides.

Breck knew all this as well as he knew his own name. He had not only heard it discussed over and over again, he had seen the results of it with his own eyes. But because he desired to accept it he subscribed to the truth of the proverb that lightning never struck twice in the same place; what was true of lightning should be true of floods.

He kept repeating this to himself as he drove on towards Octave Fontaine's house. But the repetition did not give him as much reassurance as he felt it should. His tumultuous thoughts about Anna and Olivier, Céleste and Laure, became further complicated by thoughts of Drew. Everyone on the plantation loved the child, everyone would watch him and safeguard him as far as possible. But Drew was hard to handle, for anyone except his father. If the water were really rising, he would want to watch it, and he would rush off, if Shoog's back, or Marcy's, were turned for a single instant. Breck suddenly remembered that he had not seen a newspaper that day, and now he jerked his car to a stop in front of a drugstore and went in to buy one. The headlines were not as alarming as he had feared they might be, in a moment of panic, but they were not reassuring either:

RAINS IN UPPER VALLEY CAUSE OF RISE
VIGILANT WATCH KEPT ON RIVER

POINTE COUPEE SECTION ENDANGERED
SAND BOIL PUTS HOLE IN LEVEE
IRVINE CALLS FOR HELP
TWO MEETINGS ON LEVEES CALLED

There was a news item stating that the Mississippi River had already fallen at Memphis, Helena and Vicksburg, that it was stationary at Arkansas City, still high at Natchez, higher at Baton Rouge, and higher still at Donaldsonville.

Further on a notice of the Texas and Pacific Railroad caught Breck's eye:

Due to high water in the Atchafalaya River at Melville it is necessary to keep the drawbridge at that point open for a few days, during which time Passenger Trains Nos. 59, Leaving for New Orleans at 6:35 a.m. and 54, Arriving at New Orleans 9:20 p.m. will detour via Eunice Branch and Bunkie.

ALL OTHER THROUGH PASSENGER TRAINS
TEMPORARILY DISCONTINUED

Nos. 55, Leaving New Orleans 4:25 p.m. and 56, Arriving New Orleans 11:45 a.m., will operate between New Orleans and Addis on regular schedule. Freight service will be maintained, detouring via Eunice and Bunkie.

He glanced at his watch. It was after six already. Obviously, he could not get out of New Orleans that night in any case, but he could still telephone to the plantation unless the lines were already down—another disturbing thought. He went into the drugstore booth, and put in a call; after a delay that seemed endless, he heard Drew, himself, at the other end of the wire. The telephone had a fascination for him, as for most children, and apparently he had rushed to answer it before anyone else could get there.

"Drew?— Hello there, are you all right?"

"Yes, Daddy. I'm lonesome, but I'm all right. When are you coming back?"

"Tomorow night. I'd come tomorrow morning, but the early train's been cancelled, because the river's so high in some places. Is it high at Splendida?"

"Yes, Daddy. There are guards all along the levee. And the men have been putting up sandbags. I've been watching them."

"I'd rather you stayed away from the river, Drew."

"But, Daddy, I stay right beside Mr. Yates. And he says

that tonight the river'll be a beautiful sight. There will be fla—flam——"

"Flambeaux. You see I was right, Drew. You ought to have had that French governess."

He was determined that his fear should not show in his voice. But the jest fell flat before it left his lips. It could not possibly carry over the poor connection.

"The river roars, Daddy. It doesn't sound like a river. It sounds like a dragon. The wind roars, too. Like some other kind of a monster. I like to listen to them. It's exciting."

"Drew, if you'll promise me to stay in the house until I reach there tomorrow night, I'll get you anything you'd like to have, as a reward."

"Will you get me a baby brother, Daddy? Or even a sister?"

"I told you I'd get you anything!— Do you promise?"

"Yes, Daddy. I'm sorry not to see the flambeaux and the lovely light they give, but I promise."

Breck climbed into his car again, and drove on, rapidly and abstractedly, in the direction of Octave Fontaine's house, unable to think clearly and connectedly about any one thing, and also unable to think calmly about the problems that were confronting him as a whole. If he left Laure in her extremity, her whole life might be altered by his desertion. If he did not strike his hard bargain with Olivier now, there would be endless complications to his conquest of Céleste. If he did not go to Drew, and the levee did break—no, unquestionably, he must go to Drew. The next day, by train. But since the morning local had been discontinued he could not leave until mid-afternoon, and that gave him nearly twenty-four hours in which to operate. If it were not for the cursed quarantine, much might be done in twenty-four hours.

As he got out of his car, he saw a priest coming slowly down the steps, and in spite of the man's bent head, he recognized Auguste Fontaine. In his confused and desperate state, he had entirely forgotten Octave's elder brother, though he knew, in a vague way, that Auguste had defied public opinion and had calmly accepted malicious criticism and even censure so severe that it had precluded his clerical advancement, in preference to alienation from his erring brother. A wave of immense relief surged through Breck's troubled mind. If Auguste were intelligent and resourceful, as well as scholarly and saintly—and Breck was inclined to believe that he was—the priest would be a mainstay and a comfort to Laure, whatever happened. The very sight of him simplified one problem and lightened one burden.

"Good evening, Father," he said respectfully. "I don't know whether you remember me or not, for it's a long time since I've seen you. But you used to know me well when I was a boy. I'm Andrew Breckenridge."

Father Fontaine glanced up quickly, and Breck instantly saw that his face had a stricken look. But he held out his hand with an attempt at a smile.

"Of course, Breck, of course. It is a long time. But I should have known you anywhere by your resemblance to your father. My poor brother often spoke to me about you. He was very fond of you. And you have been a good friend to him and his always, I know."

"Is he better, Father?"

The priest shook his head, sorrowfully. "My brother is dead, Breck," he said in a sad, tired voice. "He and Camille, too. I have been here all day, giving what consolation and help I could, and finally administered the last rites. Now the undertaker is there. I cannot do anything more at the moment. And I am badly needed elsewhere. Though I shall come back, of course, later."

"Father, I don't need to tell you how terribly sorry I am. I know how much you cared for Uncle Octave. And I know how much he cared for you, too. But if you go away now, doesn't that leave poor little Laure all alone while the undertaker's ghastly work is being done?"

"No, or of course I shouldn't be going. There's a very faithful maid, who's been here for years. Perhaps you remember her, for she's the same one who was with the family when you were a boy. And there's a good nurse. She's been tireless, too. And Mrs. Avery."

"Mrs. Avery! You don't mean Walter Avery's mother!"

"Yes, I do. Walter Avery's mother is here. It seems that Walter tried to see Laure, two days ago, and when he found he couldn't, and why, he asked his mother to go to her. I succeeded in having her admitted. She is a very great lady, Breck, and a very brave one. Laure could not possibly be in better hands."

"I don't see how she could. But I'm more and more confused. How does it happen that Mrs. Avery, who's a very great lady, as you say——"

"Perhaps we're not using the term in quite the same sense. And perhaps you are forgetting that she is not a Southerner by birth, and that, therefore, certain prejudices, which we will not name, are not bred in her bones, as they are in ours. I will talk this all over with you later, if you like, and try to make you understand as much as I understand myself. But we must not stay here on the banquette indefinitely now. I am urgently needed elsewhere, as I told you. And you—were you about to try to get into my poor brother's house, when you met me?"

"Yes. If I could get past the guard. And if the undertaker's there, that ought to be easy. I could always say I was his assistant. But now that I've met you and that I know Laure's all right—at least as far as she can be—I'd like to talk to you first, Father, if I could."

It had suddenly occurred to Breck that Auguste Fontaine might help him as well as Laure, that he might help them all, as no one else would or could. A priest who would stand by his brother as Father Fontaine had stood by Octave, would stand by other members of his family also. He would not judge, he would not condemn; he would understand everything, he would know a great deal—how Olivier could be coerced, how Céleste could be comforted, even perhaps how Breck himself might be set free——

"If you wish to see Laure, I believe, with you, that this is the best time for you to slip in, and as I have told you twice already, I am needed elsewhere at the moment," Father Fontaine reminded him. "I shall come back here, of course, tomorrow morning, to conduct the funeral. That must take place within twenty-four hours, and it cannot be held in the Church. That is forbidden by law, as I believe you know, after death from the plague. And no one but the nearest relatives is allowed to attend. The services will be very brief and bare, and very sad. After we leave the cemetery I must come back here with Laure to make sure that she eats and rests. But later on in the day I might be able to talk with you."

"I must go back north tomorrow, Father. The morning train's been cancelled, but there's one in the middle of the afternoon and I've got to take it. The river's rising fast. I've left my little boy on the plantation with no one to look after him but the servants and I must go back to him. I started south as soon as Aunt Estelle sent for me, but I can't stay. It would be different if Drew had his mother with him. Perhaps you haven't heard—my wife is quarantined in Olivier Fontaine's house."

Without answering, the priest looked at Breck searchingly

and noncommittally. Then he glanced away again, without giving any direct answer.

"If your little boy is alone, under conditions which may become perilous, of course he must be your first concern," he said at last, very quietly. "I have been so preoccupied with the plague and with other personal problems that I have read almost nothing about the floods. I will make some inquiries myself this evening, and in the morning I will tell you whatever I have been able to learn from sources of my own. But now I have to go. I know you realize that unless the matter were urgent, I should not be leaving my poor brother's house at this time. Shall I speak to the guard first? He knows me and has confidence in me."

"Yes, Father, if you will."

The priest had said nothing that was not kind and reasonable, yet Breck, after his one uplifted moment, felt baffled and reproved. As he crossed the little gallery, the undertaker came out of the house with a spray of immortelles tied with streamers of black ribbon and hung them on the door. Breck thought, with a shudder, of the floating crepe that had hung on his own front door after the wreck of the *Bourgogne*, and for a moment he recoiled, feeling as if he could not go on. The undertaker, however, seemed to be exuding satisfaction.

"I have the caskets in the parlor. The corpses will be placed in them as soon as I've finished the process of disinfection. Then the caskets will be sealed. Perhaps you'd rather not see them until they are. Or would you like to have a look at them now? They're the handsomest we could get, under the circumstances."

"No, I don't want to see them. I want to see Miss Dupuy. Where shall I go?"

"You're a relative, of course?"

"Yes, of course."

Breck spoke shortly. The undertaker continued to talk with the unctuousness of his kind.

"I'm sorry, sir, if I've offended you. We always try to be considerate of the bereaved. Our hearts ache with sympathy for them. But the rules are very strict, and if we don't obey them we get into trouble. We can't afford to do that. We have to earn our living, like everyone else."

"I've always understood you made a damn good one."

Breck was sorry, the instant he had spoken so rudely, but not quite sorry enough to stop and apologize. He walked on

through the hallway, trying to control his shuddering as he
went past the closed door of Octave Fontaine's bedroom.
He knew the house well. It was situated in the same quarter
as Olivier's and was not unlike this in style, but it was newer
and less true to type, and a "camel-back" addition had been
built in the rear, giving it a partial second story and extra
space. The dining room was deserted. In the kitchen, the
maid, whom he did remember, was seated with her face hidden in her hands, rocking back and forth and sobbing. He
went over to her and laid his hand on her shoulder.

"Don't cry, Solange," he said kindly. "It's sad, terribly sad,
all this, but you must keep up your courage so that you can
help Mademoiselle Laure. She's going to need you more than
ever now. Is she upstairs? Do you think I could see her? And
Madame Avery? I'd like to speak to her, too, if I could. I
suppose the nurse is—busy just now."

Solange took down her hands, and still sobbing, pitifully
wiped her eyes and blew her nose on the corner of her apron.
"Oh, Monsieur Breck! Thank God you have come! Monsieur
Octave, he loved you so! And poor Madame, whom all these
spiteful people would never call Madame——"

"I know, Solange, but they can't hurt her any more now.
Or him either. Try to think of that. Try to think that they
are not suffering any longer, that they're at peace— And try
to answer my questions, too, if you can."

"Yes, Monsieur Breck. The nurse is—busy, as you say. I
think that Madame Avery is resting a little, at last. There,
Monsieur, is a woman who has been like an angel sent
straight from heaven! And Mademoiselle Laure is supposed
to be resting, too. She's lying on her bed. However, I know
very well she is weeping and not resting. Shall I go and tell
her you're here?"

"Yes, please, Solange. Tell her I'll wait for her in the dining room."

She came to him almost instantly. As she entered the room,
he was startled again to see how closely she resembled
Céleste. She was a few years the elder, and her life had always been shadowed, instead of carefree; but Céleste had
developed so rapidly, after love had touched her, and had already suffered so much because of it, that she had spanned
the differences and distances which had previously divided
her from her cousin. Even the costly composure in Laure's
face, so much more tragic than tears, was like the look Breck
had seen in Céleste's face, only an hour or so earlier, as she

sat at the piano, no longer able to play and sing, but still quiet and controlled. When he went towards Laure, however, she held out her hand warningly, instead of casting herself into his arms, as Céleste had done.

"Don't try to touch me, please, Breck. I suppose it's safe. Every precaution has been taken. But I'd feel easier if you didn't."

"Then I won't. I won't do anything that will worry you, dear. But I had to come."

"I knew you'd come. I never doubted it. I knew I could count on you for comfort."

"How can I comfort you best, Laure?"

"You've done it, just by coming."

"There must be something else."

She shook her head. "No, there isn't. Let's sit down, shall we? I'm a little tired. It'll be easier to talk if we sit down."

They sat down on opposite sides of the round dining-room table, in two of the high straight dining-room chairs. Breck felt stiff and uncomfortable, more uncomfortable than he had been while he was standing. But he knew that Laure must be exhausted, and that unless he were seated, she would stand, too. She went on talking to him, quietly.

"Everything's been done, really, Breck. Everything that could be. I can always remember that, thankfully. There hasn't been any suffering which could be avoided. We've had a good doctor and a good nurse. The very best. Solange hasn't had a thought for herself. And Uncle Auguste——"

"I met him, as I was coming in."

"Then he told you that Mrs. Avery was here, and that he'd managed to get her in?"

"Yes. That must have meant more to you, in a way, than anything else."

"It meant a great deal. But a letter I had from Walter meant still more."

"Would you like to tell me what was in it?"

"Yes. I'm going to tell you. He wrote and asked me to marry him. Not here. Of course, we couldn't be married here. But he said his mother'd take me to France, or any place I'd care to go, where a marriage between us would be legal, and that he'd come there, too."

"I hope you're going to say yes."

"I can't."

"Why not, Laure?"

"Because he didn't write that letter out of love. He wrote

it out of sympathy and—and chivalry. He doesn't love me.
He loves Céleste. I thought you knew that."

"I think he must care for you very much, Laure."

"No. He doesn't. Not that way. He cares the way you do.
If you'd been free, I believe you'd have done the same
thing."

She looked directly at him with her great clear eyes and
Breck instantly realized, with a pang of shame, that what she
was saying would have been true up to the time that he, himself, fell in love with Céleste, but that it was true no longer.
He was humiliated by the knowledge that Walter Avery, who
was free, and who was favorably regarded by Céleste's family, had shown greater chivalry than he could have shown
himself. But Laure was unconscious of his shame. She was
conscious only of his kindness.

"But I'd have had to say no to you, just as I've said it to
Walter. Not only because of the way he feels and you feel.
Because of the way I feel. Do you remember that when I
was a child, you used to say I reminded you of a little sister
you'd lost, though I didn't look like her? You treated me then
as if you'd been my big brother, a very tender, indulgent
brother I've always thought of you as one. I don't think of
Walter quite so fondly, but it's the same sort of thinking.
There isn't any way of explaining, in English, how I feel. I
have to say it in French. *Je ne t'aime pas avec amour.*"

"Perhaps by and by you'd find you could love Walter that
way, Laure. After you got over the shock of your grief and
all. It would be the best thing in the world for you if you
could."

"Of course, I know that. But I can't, I never shall. It hasn't
anything to do with my grief. It's because I love someone
else."

So I wasn't mistaken, Breck said to himself, shuddering
again. It's that skunk, Olivier, who's going to do just what
his uncle and his great-uncle did before him. Unless he's
done it already— He looked at Laure across the dining-room
table, and saw that her gaze was still clear and direct, that
there was no shame or evasion in it, and again he, himself,
felt shamed.

"If Olivier would write me a letter, Breck, like Walter's, or
if he'd say the same thing to me——"

But Olivier never will, Laure, and you know it. He did
not speak the words, but he was sure she was aware of them
just the same. You know that marriage has never been in

Olivier's mind when he's been here, that he's waited for his chance to catch you unawares, or to coax and cajole and de- ceive you. You've never given him the chance yet, that's clear enough, thank God. But now that you're going to be all alone, now that your very grief will weaken you——

"It would be hard to say no then, Breck. But I've had to, just the same. I couldn't make an exile or—or a pariah out of Olivier. Not when I love him so. I couldn't live with the knowledge that someday there would be pages torn out of a registry, so that my children shouldn't learn—that when my daughters were old enough to marry, every suitor they had would get anonymous letters, saying they were tainted——"

"That wouldn't happen, Laure, if you went and lived some- where else."

This time he had been able to speak. He knew that what he said was true enough, just as everything she said had been true enough. But he also knew that it did not matter how true it was because Olivier would never ask her.

"I said I couldn't make an exile out of him," Laure an- swered sadly. "This is the only place he's ever lived, the only place he ever could live contentedly. He's never been sepa- rated from his family; he never could be without feeling as if he'd been torn asunder himself. Even if I could make him happy for a little while, away from here, it wouldn't last long. He'd be homesick. He'd be lonely. He'd be sorry he'd married me. He'd reproach me. He might even taunt me. I couldn't bear that, Breck."

For the first time, her eyes filled with tears, her lips began to tremble. Breck leaned across the table and tried to take her hand. She drew back, shaking her head.

"No," she said. "I said no before, Breck. I meant it. I don't want you to touch me. Not just on account of contagion. On account of—I don't think I could bear it, if you touched me tenderly, just now. Do you remember the first time you came here, when I went to sleep in your arms, and you carried me to my bed? I've always remembered that, I always shall. I want to remember you the way you were then and myself the way I was then. A little girl, very happy, very sheltered. But I'm grateful to you for coming, more grateful than you'll ever know. And I'm glad I've had a chance to talk with you, too. Because there won't ever be another."

"Laure, you're exhausted, you're completely overwrought and beside yourself. Of course there'll be another chance. There'll be dozens of them. Why shouldn't there be?"

"I'll tell you. I'll tell you what I'm going to do."

She rose, and walked across the room. Rising too, and following her, Breck saw that she was looking up at the picture which hung above the mantelpiece: the same portrait which had fascinated him when he was a boy, and which represented a beautiful girl with big black eyes and soft lustrous hair, wearing a low-cut green bodice and a white ruffled skirt.

"You know who that is, don't you, Breck?" Laure asked, steadily.

"Yes, dear. It's your grandmother. She must have been very lovely. I've always thought that was one of the most beautiful portraits I ever saw in my life."

"I'm glad, Breck. Because I want you to have that picture. I want to give it to you."

"Laure, you know that I'd be very proud to own it. But I wouldn't rob you of it for anything in the world."

"You wouldn't be robbing me of it. You'd be taking care of it for me. And that would mean a great deal to me. Because I couldn't keep it anyhow."

"Why not?"

"I'm going to tell you. I said I was going to tell you. You know where Théophile Fontaine met my grandmother, don't you, Breck?"

"I think so. I'm not sure."

"Don't lie to me, Breck. You know he met her at a quadroon ball. You know she was taken there by her mother on purpose so that some rich young Creole would see her and make her his mistress. You know that her bodice wasn't cut like that by accident, that it was meant to show that lovely creamy surface of her skin. You know she had to wear some kind of a turban, even though she disguised it with jewels and flowers, and some kind of a red shawl, even though she reduced it to a little gauzy scarf. You know those were her hallmarks. You know she was a quadroon."

"I know that she was beautiful and that Théophile Fontaine loved her," Breck said stubbornly.

"Very well. We won't argue about it. But you know where the quadroon balls were held, don't you, Breck?"

"I believe it was in the old Orleans Theatre. But I've heard that denied, too."

"There's no use in denying it. But perhaps you don't know what the building's used for now."

"No, I don't. I've never been interested in finding out."

"It's used for a convent. A convent for colored nuns."

"A convent for colored nuns?"

"Yes. They teach little children and care for the destitute and sick. They use the old ballroom for their assembly room. You go up to it by the same staircase that the girls used to mount with their mothers, when they were taken there to be shown. It's a broad, graceful staircase, with a magnificent mahogany banister. I've often thought how the girls' hands must have looked, Breck, against that banister, as they went up the stairs. Some of them must have gripped it hard, because they were frightened. Their knuckles would have shown white against it then, even if there were that telltale little line of blue around their nails. And some of them must have tapped it in time to the music they could hear, floating down to them. Those were the joyous ones, so eager to know what love was like that they could hardly wait for it. And others must have just let their fingers slide over the banister, list-lessly, wondering whether anything in the world mattered, since their own mothers——"

"Let's not talk about it, Laure. You've made me see it all, but I'd rather not see it."

"But I want you to see it. As it was then—and as it is now. With the nuns' plain shoes tapping quietly over the floor, instead of the dancing slippers, and the nuns' beads clicking, instead of the dancers' fans. I want you to look up over the doorway, too, and study the inscription that's there."

"What is the inscription, Laure?"

"'I have chosen rather to be an abject in the House of the Lord than to dwell in the Temple with sinners.'"

She was still looking at him steadfastly and more intently than before, and again he was seized with the shuddering which had kept shaking him ever since he had entered the house. He tried, and tried without success, to keep his voice as steady as hers.

"I don't think I ever heard about that inscription, Laure. Or if I did, I'd forgotten. But I don't see what difference it makes whether I had or not."

"It may make a difference to you someday, Breck. Because I *have* chosen. I'm going to enter that convent. I'm not ashamed of my heritage. But I'm not going to pass it on to someone who might be, to someone who might suffer for it. As I have. As my mother did. As I've seen her suffer, for years, a thousand times more than she did with the dreadful illness that caused her death. If the sins of the fathers have got to be visited upon the third and the fourth generation, I'll try to atone for them. But no child of mine shall ever atone for me."

A slight cough sounded from the doorway. Breck, turning abruptly, saw the undertaker standing there, his long moist hands rubbing against each other, the unctuous expression of his face blending with a bland smile.

"I don't like to interrupt," he said smoothly. "But I have everything in order in the parlor, Miss Dupuy. I think it looks very creditable under all the circumstances. But I'd like to have you come now and tell me whether the arrangement is satisfactory to you. I have another professional call to make this evening, and since the services here are to be to-morrow morning— Thank you. I was sure you would understand."

CHAPTER 22

BRECK WENT down the steps with his head reeling. He had not eaten anything since breakfasttime, which could account in part for his vertigo, but he did not realize it. As far as that went, he did not realize how long he had fasted. On the difficult drive south, hounded with the urgency of Mrs. Fontaine's summons, he had not stopped long enough to snatch so much as a sandwich, and he naturally had not thought of food either in her house or in her brother-in-law's. He did not think of it now. He was still hounded by urgency, this time of the conviction that he must get back to Splendida. But he could not start until the next afternoon, and he could not stay with Laure any longer. She would not let him. She would not listen to anything he tried to say, or say anything further to him. On the very day of her parents' death, he could not harass her or argue with her. Later on, of course, he would try to argue with her. He knew that she could not do anything irrevocable instantly. Even if she could not be dissuaded from entering the convent, he believed, without knowing much about it, that she would have to undergo a long novitiate, and that while this was in progress, she would not be wholly inaccessible. He also believed that when she had recovered from the series of emotional shocks which had been dealt her with such merciless rapidity, she might listen to reason. Besides, she would not be leaving her own home for several days, at the very least, and probably before those had passed, he could get back from the plantation. Meanwhile, Mrs. Avery would be with her and Mrs. Avery was sure to be a wise and temperate counsellor.

Since he could not stay with Laure or leave for Splendida, he must find something else to do with himself. It was regrettable that Father Fontaine had put him off so uncompromisingly; a conference with the priest would have given him an interlude of invigoration and enlightenment. He knew that he would not be able to sleep, and it was unthinkable that he should spend all the empty hours that still remained before traintime in his own silent shrouded house. He knew he must not try to see Céleste again until he could say something definite and comforting to her and something authoritative to her mother; and he would not be in a position to do that until—with lightning swiftness a clear thought darted through his confused brain. If he could contrive to get into one quarantined house, he should be able to contrive to get into another; and if he could get into Olivier's, he could talk both with that wretched weakling and with Anna. He leapt into his car and started the engine. Then, turning a sharp corner, he drove rapidly in the direction of Kerlerec Street.

He had never been to Olivier's house, but he felt sure he would recognize it when he saw it and he was not mistaken. It was outstanding for its trimness among its shabby surroundings, as it had been when Estelle Lenoir had gone to meet his father there, more than twenty years before. Its high hedge and closed shutters gave it a secret look, oddly at variance with its gleaming paint and inviting gallery. The guard, who was seated in the gallery, had slumped down in his seat, half asleep; his task was obviously tedious and distasteful. He half roused himself when Breck went to the door and rang, but only to swear under his breath when he saw that the new arrival was not his relief. However, Breck decided it was safest to forestall any latent opposition which might arise. As there was no car except Anna's parked carriage waiting outside, he decided that the first lie upon which he happened to hit was a fairly safe one.

"I've come in Dr. Breaux's place," he said tersely. "The doctor may be able to get here himself later on, but he doesn't feel sure of it, there's so much sickness now in the city. So it seemed best for me to take over his evening call."

The guard muttered something almost inaudible about wishing someone would take over his work, that he wasn't supposed to stay on duty forever. Then he lapsed into semi-consciousness again. At the same moment the door was opened by Anna.

Breck's first sensation in looking at her was one of sardonic amusement. He had never before seen her when she was not meticulously turned out; now her dress was stained, her hair was awry, and there was a smudge on her cheek. She stared at Breck incredulously for a moment and then she threw her arms around his neck and clung to him.

"Oh, Breck, how wonderful of you to come! How did you get here? I never was so glad to see anyone in my life."

"Look out, Anna. I'm supposed to be Dr. Breaux's assistant. I think the guard is practically comatose. He's been on duty so long he's groggy with sleep. But let's get the door closed, before we try to talk."

He freed himself, not roughly, but impersonally, and shut the door. Then he folded his arms and continued to look at her, half fearing and half hoping that he was going to burst out laughing.

"What on earth have you been doing with yourself?" he managed to inquire, more or less objectively.

"Oh, Breck, I've had to do all sorts of things! Cook and clean and——"

"I'm afraid in that case everyone must have gone pretty hungry. I never knew you to make so much as piece of toast. And as for cleaning, you've always enjoyed seeing your servants slave, but I don't believe you ever dusted off the piano yourself."

"Of course you're right, Breck. I never did. That's what's made it all so terribly hard. But the nurse is one of that kind who won't lift her finger to help, stiff as a poker and pert and inconsiderate. And the doctor keeps saying that, naturally, since I'm such an old friend of the family, I must be glad to help out in any way I can. I've telephoned Mrs. Cutler to ask if she wouldn't use her influence with the health department to get me out, and when she found out where I was she simply froze up."

"Why didn't you telephone the servants? You gave them a bad scare."

"Oh, Breck, I couldn't. The telephone's where everyone can hear it. I didn't want Olivier and the nurse and the doc-tor— But I did try to telephone you today. The more I thought about everything during the night— Oh, Breck, please don't stand there with your arms folded like that! Come into the drawing room and sit down and let me explain everything to you. You don't know what a relief it is to see you and to have someone to talk to. I'm sorry I'm such a sight, but I didn't have so much as a comb with me——"

"I left Splendida early this morning. Mrs. Fontaine and Roscoe got me all right. I'm afraid the idea of appealing to me came to you a little tardily. I also might remind you that there's a good old English proverb which runs 'Never explain. Your friends don't need it, and your enemies don't believe it anyway.' I don't know whether you consider me your friend or your enemy at this juncture, but it doesn't matter. I know all about this mess you're in, and how you happened to get into it, too."

"Why, of course, I consider that you're my friend! How can you say such a thing? You're my husband!"

"As I recall it, your own attitude wasn't especially friendly when you left Splendida three days ago. Indeed, unless I've had a complete mental breakdown, you told me then that you wanted to get rid of me as your husband."

"Breck, I didn't say that seriously, you know I didn't. I was angry about the levee, and when I get angry I often say things I don't mean. But I do understand now that you had a good reason for not telling me, that you weren't deceiving me needlessly and pointlessly. I'm—I'm sorry I spoke to you as I did, Breck."

"You mean you've changed your mind about wanting to leave me?"

"I tell you I never——"

"Why don't you tell me the truth, Anna?"

"I— Yes, I have changed my mind."

"Well, that's unfortunate, under all the circumstances. Because I've changed mine, too."

"I haven't the slightest idea what you're talking about."

"I'm trying to tell you that I'm perfectly willing you should get a divorce. I can see that it's futile for us to try to go on together. And I'll be reasonable about Drew. As I've thought the matter over, I've realized that I wasn't before. I'm willing to let you have him for part of each year. That is, if he's willing to go to you. He wasn't willing to come to New Orleans with me when he knew you were here. You must have said some things to him you didn't mean, too, before you left Splendida. I've never seen him frightened before. But we'll put the matter up to him fairly and squarely. I think I'd better keep him until the divorce is final, but the process won't take long, if you go out West. Of course you'll want to talk the matter over with your father first, but I believe he'll advise you that the courts might make it more uncomfortable for you in Massachusetts than they would in Nevada. And Reno is said to be a very pleasant city."

"Breck, you don't sound like yourself, talking this way. I can't think what's come over you. I keep telling you——"

"I hoped it wouldn't be necessary for me to call your attention to the fact that you've complicated the situation a little since we last saw each other. We can't cope with it merely by saying that you've changed your mind or that I've changed my mind. I believe your behavior has been a little —unusual, shall we say? I also believe it's normal for a husband to be slightly resentful under the current circumstances. I thought you'd compliment me on my generosity in letting you get a divorce instead of getting one myself."

"But, Breck, I haven't done anything wrong! You know I haven't! You know I couldn't help——"

"I know you couldn't help the quarantine. It must have been very annoying and very awkward for you. But you didn't need to come here in the first place. I'm afraid you'd have hard work making a judge believe that your motives in doing that were purely platonic."

"But they were! They were! It was just that I was so bored, waiting for the train with nothing to do, and I thought of Olivier——"

"He must have been very much touched. Where is he, by the way?"

"I suppose he's asleep. He sleeps most of the time. Or least he stays in his bedroom with the door locked. He's the most awful cad I ever knew in my life."

"It took you quite a while to find that out, didn't it, Anna? But at least he's showing defensive instincts. If he's keeping his door locked, he must be absolutely desperate, and you must have been even more aggressive than I thought. It's unusual, to say the least, for a man to go to quite such lengths."

"Breck, don't—don't talk to me like that! If you knew how awful this had all been—how humiliated I am—how tired —how——"

She had begun to cry. There was no chair in the narrow

hallway where they were still standing, and she leaned for support against the framework of the door leading into the little drawing room, sobbing bitterly. It was as extraordinary to Breck to see her unpoised as to see her untidy. He no longer felt like laughing, but neither did he feel in the least sorry for her. He felt only a sort of detached disgust, augmented by the contrast of her self-abandonment to the control which he had seen both Céleste and Laure exercise that same day. But at last he spoke to her.

"There were a few things I meant to say to Olivier, as well as to yourself, when I came here. Of course, the really dramatic thing to do would be to go into the drawing room and fire a shot, in the hope that it would hit him. But there's always the chance it might hit the nurse or the invalid instead. I should think that would have been a disadvantage from the beginning in these shotgun houses. It's all very well to have said that a shot fired in the front would go straight through to the rear. But I should think you would have had to plant your victim first."

Anna, still sobbing, did not answer. Breck gathered that at the moment she did not care very much whether Olivier were shot or not. She had told the truth when she said she was completely exhausted and humiliated past all endurance.

"But I guess it wouldn't do any good to shoot him," Breck went on. "I mean, it wouldn't help any in another situation that needs straightening out. I don't get Olivier's fascination myself. But I'm willing to grant that he must have it. You're the second woman I've seen this evening whose life's been ruined by him, though he wasn't interested in ruining you and didn't succeed in ruining the other one. No, we won't go into that now. But if you really think you've had enough of Olivier and would like to leave here, I believe I could get you away. I think the guard's in a state of coma, as I said before. I don't think he'd even notice if I took you out with me. We can make a dash for my car and I'll drive you up to Prytania Street. You can take a bath and brush your hair a hundred strokes, and get into a bed someone else has turned down, and eat a supper someone else has cooked. When you've done all that, you'll feel a lot better. I think you'll have a good sleep. But I suggest that even if you do feel bored tomorrow, you stay in the house until train time. Rufus will drive you to the station. And by the way, you needn't bother to explain to the servants where you've been or what you've been doing all this time. They'll be curious, of course, and a little disappointed to find that their own theory to the effect that you'd driven your car into the river was incorrect. But I'll tell them, in the morning, that you've been visiting a friend, and that's the sober truth. They won't expect any details from me. They know me too well."

Anna's sobs had gradually begun to subside while Breck talked. But she had nothing with which to wipe her eyes or her nose. Breck gave her his handkerchief.

"Here, take this," he said. "I'll go out and have a look at the guard— Yes, he's sleeping quietly, just as I thought. Come on, Anna, this is your best chance."

He wished he did not keep thinking about Anna, the next day, on the train. She had recovered her self-control, during the drive to Prytania Street, but she was still dirty and dishevelled when she reached the front door of her husband's house. He knew how much she must be dreading to have anyone see her in such a state. Transiently, he felt sufficiently sorry for her to shield her.

"You never did succeed in training Roscoe, Anna," he said as they drew up at the entrance. "I still have to let myself in with a latchkey, after what he considers normal working hours. Go on upstairs and get into the tub. I'll bring you something on a tray."

She was in bed when he took it to her. Objectively, as he had regarded her all the evening, he saw that she was looking very lovely. There was a softness about her which was as alien as her earlier dishevelment. Her abundant hair was parted smoothly in the middle and hung in two long flexible braids over her breasts. Her fair skin was clear and smooth. She had on a fine linen nightgown, delicately embroidered, that smelt of lavender, and in spite of the heat, everything about her was fresh and fragrant. As she held out her arms to take the tray from him, the sleeves fell away from them, showing them soft and white.

"Breck," she said appealingly. "I meant it when I said I was sorry. I'll prove it to you in every way I can. *Every* way. Won't you—won't you stay with me while I eat my supper?— And afterwards?"

"I'll be right in the next room while you eat your supper. I want to get off a letter. If you need anything else you can call me. I'll be glad to get it for you. Then I'll take the tray back to the kitchen. After that I think I'd better say good night to you. We both need to get some sleep. I judge you haven't had much the last three nights, and I've got a hard day ahead of me tomorrow. I don't think I've mentioned to you that Octave Fontaine and Camille Dupuy have both died of the plague. I've got to go to their funeral and after that I want to have a talk with Auguste Fontaine. Then I'll take the afternoon train north. I'd take the morning one, funeral or no funeral, but it's been discontinued. The highroad's completely under water, so I'll have to leave the car here, and of course a boat isn't to be considered while a train makes better time."

"Are you afraid of a flood?"

"I'm not afraid of it, except on Drew's account. But there is one."

"Then I think I ought to come back with you, Breck. I want to."

He shook his head. "The trouble with things that have been said, Anna, is that they can't be unsaid. And things that are done can't be undone. And no one can go back over a road that's once been travelled. We all have to stop, or detour or go forward. I'm going forward now, and I hope you are, too. It was you who decided we weren't to go forward together. You've been trying to tell me that for a good many years. Three nights ago you succeeded. There honestly isn't anything more we can say to each other."

She had not eaten very much of her supper, after all, he remembered, as the train lurched slowly along. But he had left the tray with her while he wrote not only one letter, but two. The first was addressed to Mrs. Fontaine.

Dear Aunt Estelle:

I've been to both Uncle Octave's house and Olivier's since I saw you. As you know by now, there was nothing I could do at the former. Probably Uncle Auguste told you that he met me there, when I was going in and he was coming out. I don't know why I didn't guess that he was on his way to see you. I must have been pretty dumb not to think of that right away. But I thought of it afterwards.

I have a pretty good hunch what you and he said to each other, and there's nothing I can do about that at the moment either, though I'm going to try to see Uncle Auguste after the funeral tomorrow. And as soon as the flood's over, I'll be back to see you. Meanwhile, it may interest you to know that Olivier's entirely safe. Laure's going into a convent and Anna's going back to Boston. I don't see why I should bother to do anything or say anything to Olivier under those circumstances.

Probably you'll think a convent is a good place for Laure. But I can't help believing you'd feel differently about it if she were your daughter instead of your niece. I know how carefully you've planned for Céleste's debut and for her reign at Carnival. Well, I hope she'll get more out of it than you did out of yours under similar circumstances. And you can count on me not to disrupt any of your plans for her pleasure, and not to complicate next winter for her in any way. I won't be back on the scene until later. And I won't even give her a mirror to remember me by in the meantime. I have confidence that she'll remember me anyway, and that she'll wait for me until I'm free.

This letter isn't meant to sound bitter or resentful, for I've always loved you very much and I do still. But I love Céleste more, and until I'm convinced that you'll give her and me the chance for happiness that you and my father lost, I'm afraid there's bound to be some strain between us. But I hope it won't be too long-drawn-out, and that later on you can forget it ever existed. I know I can.

Good night, Aunt Estelle, and thanks again for everything you did for me when I was a boy, and for going to the cemetery with me at Splendida. I'll never forget the goodness you've shown me, as long as I live, and I'll always be sorry you weren't my second mother when I was growing up. But I hope you'll be my mother still.

Always affectionately yours,

Breck

The other letter was shorter, but it took him longer to write. In fact, it took him so long, that he called out to Anna in the course of writing it, to know if there were anything else she would like. She replied that there was not, that he had thought of everything, and that the supper was delicious.

My little darling—my own sweet Céleste:

This has been a dreadful day, except for the happy moments I spent with you, and I'm not going to try to tell you now about everything that's happened. Perhaps I'll never tell you. It wouldn't do any special good for you to know. But if it's the last thing I ever say, I'm going to tell you that I

*love you, that I'm holding your promise close to my heart
tonight, as I would hold you if I only could.*

*I have to go away tomorrow, to my little boy. I know you'd
be the first to say I ought to go to him. I'm afraid the flood's
very bad, darling. I'm afraid Drew is in danger. There, I've
said it to you. I couldn't say it to anyone else. But there's
nothing I couldn't say to you, because I love you so.*

           Yours, till death and destruction,

                     Breck

He took the letters out to the mailbox when he carried
Anna's tray down. It was then he saw how little she had
eaten, though he did not think about it until afterwards. Her
light was still on when he went upstairs, and he thought he
heard her calling, but he was not sure, and he did not go
back to her room. The next morning he saw that a small
envelope, of the type in which she usually carried her visiting cards, had been slipped under his door. He picked it up
and opened it. There was only one sentence on the tiny piece
of paper inside.

Please give me another chance.

He tore it into infinitesimal pieces and threw these in the
scrap basket.

He tried to read the papers as the train lurched along. The
news was anything but reassuring.

    FIGHT FOR PRESERVATION OF LEVEES
    CONTINUES TO BE STRENUOUS ONE

    ARMY OF TOILERS IS STILL HOLDING
    RIVER IN BANK AT REMY

    FLOOD IS FOUGHT BY FITFUL FLAME

  WATCH FIRES BURN DIMLY ALONG LEVEE AT
REMY—STAMPEDE OCCURS DURING HOURS OF
    NIGHT WHILE HEAVY RAIN FALLS

    HERCULEAN LABORS DONE BY MANY

        SECTION BY SECTION
        OLD LEVEE SLOUGHS
        INTO MISSISSIPPI

      WOMEN SHOW BRAVERY

(Special to the *Item*)
Lutcher, La.

. . . The cave-in grew steadily hour by hour. Almost every 15 minutes there would come a sullen roar and a section of the levee would slough off into the river. The thin line of green sod which stretched between the river and the roughly constructed bulwark of sandbags steadily diminished until at dawn only a strip one foot wide was left of what had once been a levee with a 12-foot base and 6-foot topping.

The scene in the cold gray dawn was one of despair. Only those who live with the fear of the river in their heart, can appreciate the sensations of the determined men who worked throughout the entire night.

Hungry, thirsty, weary, they were, but ever adding one more bit of earth, one more shovelful of gravel, one more sack of sand to the frail bulwark, which they were directing in the darkness to check the angry river's sullen greed. Below the threatened crevasse there were a number of tents. In them slept all the awakened women and children of the men in the vicinity. These frailer ones in the leaky tents withstood the driving rain and the chill of the air before the dawn without a murmur.

Stumbling through the darkness on sacks which slipped beneath their feet, two newspapermen came upon a woman who stood dejectedly at the door of one of the shaky white canvas structures. She wept silently and asked, "Has it gone any more yet?" "Yes," said one of the men. "It is still sloughing." The woman turned away. Her sobs became louder; she stumbled and stooped beneath the tent flap and grasped a child in her arms. "Wake up, wake up, dear," she said. "We may have to go at any minute."

They might have to go at any minute! What was true at Lutcher and the near-by hamlet of Rémy could also be true of Splendida! Sloughing in one section of the levee could mean sloughing in another, even though the sections were on opposite sides of the river. If the conditions were really as bad as the *Item* indicated, he might not be able to get any further north than Vacherie, and there would still be nearly fifty intervening miles between that point and his home. As far as that went, he might not be able to get as far as Vacherie, itself. The next time the conductor went through the car, Breck stopped him and spoke to him.

"I'm Andrew Breckenridge of Splendida. My plantation's between Donaldsonville and White Castle and——"

"Yes, sir. I know. I used to know your father."

For once Breck had no desire to discuss his father or anyone's acquaintance with Andy. He spoke with unusual brusqueness.

"I've got to reach there tonight, come hell or high water. That's not a saying, it's a fact. I've got a boy of my own now, and he's alone there with the servants. Is the train going to get through?"

"It's too soon to say, sir. I can probably tell you when we get as far as Edgard. But I can tell you this already: It'll be the last one leaving New Orleans until the water goes down."

"What about rescue ships?"

"I've heard that the *Baton Rouge* has been sent out. You might be able to get aboard her, somewhere along the line."

"I'll have to get aboard her, if the train doesn't go through."

The conductor, looking kindly and sympathetic but non-committal, went on down the aisle, stopped at almost every step by other anxious passengers who were seeking information and to whom he could give none. Breck tossed his newspaper aside. After all, what good did it do to look at it? He only grew more frantic with every line he read. And no matter how much he read, he kept thinking about Anna——

"Please give me another chance!"— As if he had not given her one chance after another, for eight years now! And still she seemed to expect that he would go on indefinitely, giving her more! And not only Anna, herself, but others as well. He was still raging over the futility of his talk with Father Fontaine—with the futility of the whole dreadful day.

He had gone to the ghastly double funeral, and after leaving the cemetery, he had returned to Laure's house with her, riding in the same carriage with her. He had tried to talk with her again. But she was adamant. They had said everything there was to say to each other the day before, she told him. She would rather not see him at all again, at present, if he did not mind. Of course, after her novitiate had actually begun, he could come to the convent, if he cared to. There were certain hours on certain days when visitors were permitted. But he must promise her beforehand that he would not say anything which could possibly hurt the feelings of anyone who might overhear their conversation, and they were almost sure to be overheard. Did he really want the portrait of her grandmother? Well, should she send it to Prytania Street or to Splendida? Very well. She would attend to that within a day or two. But she hoped he would excuse her now so that she could go and lie down. She was really very tired——

He sat in the little parlor for a few minutes after she had left him. It had the stiff cold look that a room takes on, almost human in quality, after a funeral. The furniture was still pushed back against the walls, there was a vacant place

in front of the fireplace where the caskets had stood, and a
few crushed leaves and wisps of fern on the floor. There was
a stale smell of scented flowers and death in the air. Breck
sat looking straight ahead of him at nothing, trying to think
what he could say to Father Fontaine which would be more
effective than what he had said to Laure, and while he was
still sitting there, Mrs. Avery came in and sat down beside
him. He noticed that she had her hat on and that her purse
and gloves were in her hand.

"I thought perhaps you'd drive me home, Breck," she said
gently. "Laure feels she'd like to be alone now, so I'm going.
I know I'm leaving her in good hands with Solange."

"I hoped you'd stay on for a few days."

Mrs. Avery shook her head, smiling rather sadly. "I've a
son and a daughter, you know, Breck, not to mention a husband. And I've been here several days already. I'm needed
more at home now. Besides, Laure won't be here long herself. I think she's planning to have a talk with the Mother
Superior of the Holy Family tomorrow. Father Fontaine's
paved the way for her already. I don't think there'll be any
delay about her admission as a postulant."

"It sickens me to think of her in that convent. Why, I suppose some of those nuns are as black as Solange! And
Laure's as white as——"

"As Céleste? You mean she *looks* as white as Céleste. But
she isn't, no matter how hard any of us try to pretend.
There's no use talking about it any more, as I think Laure's
told you herself. If it isn't convenient for you to take me
home, Breck, I'll telephone for a hack."

Of course Breck had to say it would be perfectly convenient for him to take her home. He saw her safely to her
house on Coliseum Square and then went on to the rectory
of the Church of Our Lady of Mercies. The parlor there
had a personality, too, as distinct as that of the parlor in
Octave Fontaine's house. But this was like the personality of
all rectory parlors in which Breck had ever been: the draperies were dingy, shutting out the light, the lamps had
shades made of leaded glass and were placed on crocheted
mats, the pictures represented the Pope, the local Archbishop
and the Sacred Heart, and there were artificial flowers in a
vase made of pressed glass. Breck had always wondered why
the greater the profusion of natural flowers growing in a lo-
cality, the greater should be the determination of many persons living there to use paper flowers. He also wondered why

the Catholic Church, which set so much store by beauty, and distributed it with such prodigality in its temples, did not extend it with more lavishness to the homes of its pastors. He felt that almost any outsider seeking succor and counsel would be repelled and intimidated to start with by his surroundings. His repugnance and abashment were intensified after Father Fontaine had entered the room. Breck tried to make allowances, to remember that the priest had buried his own brother that very day. Still, the man's air was one of severity rather than of sadness and it did not encourage Breck to bring up a difficult subject.

"I've come to talk to you, Uncle Auguste, about two things that matter to me a great deal."

"I am ready to listen to you now, Breck, and I shall be glad to help you if I can. But I must warn you in advance not to expect too much of me."

"Couldn't you prevent Laure from going into that colored convent?"

"I doubt it. There are no apparent impediments. She is of age. She has no one dependent on her, and she feels very sure she has a vocation. Of course, if she shows herself inadaptable to the rule of the order during the course of her novitiate she might be dismissed."

"She won't prove inadaptable to the rule. You know that as well as I do. But you also know she hasn't any more of a vocation than I have. You know she's going into that convent merely because——"

"I think the reasons which impel her are between her and her own conscience, Breck. Or rather, between her and God. I do not think that any man, not even a priest, has a right to question her sincerity when she gives them."

"You mean you won't so much as try to stop her?"

"If you choose to put it as bluntly as that, no."

"Then I'm afraid you won't help me about anything else either."

"I've already told you, Breck, that I don't know whether I can or not, until you tell me what you want me to do."

"I want you to make it possible for me to marry Céleste."

The priest's lips tightened a little. Then he spoke in an absolutely expressionless voice.

"It is not within my power to make such a thing possible. It shouldn't be necessary for me to remind you that you are married already."

"My wife wants a divorce."

"Are you sure?"

If only he didn't keep hearing Anna say "Please give me another chance, Breck!" Her voice seemed to penetrate the bare, dingy parlor now. But he hardened his own voice with his heart.

"She told me so herself, three days ago. I don't know that I'll gain anything, in the long run, by lying to you, so I'll admit that she seems to have changed her mind since then. But changes of mind on her part are apt to be only temporary. However, I'll put the matter differently, if you prefer, and say I want a divorce. I'm willing to let Anna get it, for the sake of appearances. I don't care to have the name of my son's mother publicly smirched. And as long as he's Aunt Estelle's son and Céleste's brother, I'll try to restrain my natural impulse to put an end to Olivier's chances of complicating life for any more women. But there's going to be a divorce, on one ground or another. And as soon as I'm free, I'm going to marry Céleste."

"I think my sister-in-law has already reminded you that the Church does not recognize divorce. Though as far as that goes, you should not have needed a reminder. You are not an ignorant man, and you were brought up under Catholic influences, to a large extent."

"I escaped from them when I was fourteen. And since then I've learned that they played a very large part in preventing my father from marrying the woman he really loved. You can't expect me to be enthusiastic about them, under those circumstances."

"Perhaps not. But you might add to your resolution not to harm Céleste's brother, the resolution not to disparage the memory of mine who married her mother."

"I'm sorry, Uncle Auguste. But I'm completely shot to pieces. And you're all so set against me——"

Andy Breckenridge would never have spoken like that, Breck knew. He would never have pleaded, nor cringed, nor apologized. But Breck was not another Andy. Only his son.

"We're not all set against you, Breck. The Fontaines have always been very fond of you. I have heard you say yourself that they treated you as one of their own from the time your father married into the family. I shall always be more grateful to you for the kindness you have shown my poor brother, Octave, than you will ever know. And I am sensible of the respect and affection you have always shown my sister-in-law, though you did not include my brother Marcel in it. But you are causing her great grief now."

"She's causing me great grief."

"She has no choice. How can she consent to your proposal? It is an outrageous proposal, as you know very well yourself. And because you have made it, I'm afraid you'll have a great deal to answer for, as far as Céleste, herself, is concerned."

"I don't know what you mean."

"I will tell you. I talked with her last night. I'm sure you have already guessed that I was on my way to my sister-in-law's house when you met me. She and I talked to Céleste, together and separately. Céleste has always been the most docile and dutiful of daughters. She has a naturally sweet and gentle nature as well as a joyous one, and——"

"That's another thing you don't need to tell me. And now you've made that gentle little girl unhappy! I hope to heaven you have to answer for it someday!"

"You are the one who has brought about her unhappiness, Breck, at least indirectly. She is not trying to defy the authority of the Church, she does not want to do that. As a matter of fact, she desires to seek all the consolation which religion can give her in her present hour of trial. But she is sure there is some way out of the difficulties now confronting her because you have told her it is so. And therefore she feels that, while she is waiting for you to show her what this is, she would rather remain in retirement and seclusion. She has asked my sister-in-law to excuse her from a formal presentation to society next year. She is willing to go abroad, she is willing to continue her studies and actually eager to pursue her musical education. But she says she could not possibly undertake to dance when her heart is heavy or to see other young men in a social way when she would be thinking of you all the time. She has already written to Walter Avery and several other highly eligible suitors asking them not to call on her any more. I should never have believed that such a child as she appears could show such unalterable resolution. I understand that she has even gone so far as to pack away, this morning, all the pretty dresses she bought a short time ago, which were designed for her debut."

In spite of himself, Breck felt his heart leaping at the thought of Céleste's ultimatum. This was the sort of devotion of which he had dreamed, of which no one but her could be capable. He saw her, exquisite and remote, withdrawn from the very sight of all other men until he could come to claim her, and the vision gave him new determination and new hope.

"I do not need to tell you what a blow this is to my sister-in-law," Father Fontaine went on. "Of course it is a truism that every Orleanian mother sees a future Carnival Queen when she leans over the cradle of her baby daughter. But in my sister-in-law's case there has been an added factor. There were—complications to her own debut, as you hinted a few minutes ago. She's counted, for many years, on experiencing, vicariously, the happiness she, herself, missed. Through Céleste."

Father Fontaine paused, but Breck did not help him out by answering. The priest was obliged to go on.

"I went to Estelle's house for a few minutes again this morning, Breck, after we left the cemetery. I knew you were going home with Laure, you see, so I was sure there would be time for me to have another conference with my sister-in-law before you reached the rectory. She had received the letter you wrote her last night. She read parts of it to me. In that, you said you would not do anything to interfere with her plans for Céleste. But you have. Not intentionally, I know that. However, the result is just the same. And Estelle ventures to suggest, with my approval, that since your wishes have so much weight with Céleste, you should write the child a letter—not the letter of a lover, of course, but of an affectionate friend, saying you hope she will reconsider, that she will carry out her mother's plans for her as these were originally made."

"I wrote Céleste a letter last night, too. She didn't show you hers, did she?"

"No. And of course there has been no effort made to force her confidence."

Breck laughed. Andy's laugh, the one that Estelle had always dreaded to hear. Then he rose.

"Oh, of course not. And probably it's just as well. Because the letter I wrote her was lover-like. Intensely so. Any letter I wrote her would be. I am her lover. Don't look so startled. Not in fact. But in thought. Just as she's already my wife in her thoughts. I shan't intrude on them by telling her what she ought to do. She knows. Better than anybody else could possibly know. I approve of her position. I'm greatly touched and highly honored by it. I'll try to be worthy of it."

He did not put out his hand. He had ceased to think of Father Fontaine as his uncle, or even as his friend. He was bitter through and through. Except towards Céleste. Towards Céleste and towards Drew, to whom he was going now. Thank God, it was almost train time.

"Good-bye, Father," he said formally. "I hope you'll pray for me, if we don't see each other very soon again. I may need it. But not any more than some others will. So don't forget them either, in your prayers."

Father Fontaine put his hand on Breck's reluctant arm. "I shan't, Breck. I shan't forget or neglect to pray for you or any of the others. Estelle and Céleste and Anna and little Drew. I'm sorry to have you feel like this, as we part. I don't think hardly of you, though you believe I do, from the way I've had to talk to you. And I hope you won't always think hardly of me. If you live long enough, you may find out that the attitude of the Church isn't as harsh and unreasonable as you think it is, just now. There's a finality about marriage, in many of its phases, that's humanly inescapable. After a man and a woman have been joined together by God's authority, and have become one flesh, only God, Himself, can really separate them, no matter what poor benighted human beings may believe, or teach, or practice to the contrary. I'm not telling you this dogmatically. I'm telling it to you almost sorrowfully, in a way. Because I've seen it bring about suffering before. But there's no escaping any eternal truth, no matter how much anguish is interwoven with it."

The interview had been painful enough without having it brought to a close on such a note as this. Breck wished that he had never gone near Father Fontaine, and since this conference had brought no assuagement with it, he knew there was no other that would. It still did not occur to him to rest or to eat. He went straight from the rectory to the station. After all, he might as well go there as anywhere else. Certainly he was not going back to the Prytania Street house, to encounter Anna and have her ask him again for another chance. He wanted to telephone Splendida, but he could do that from a public booth again. That is, if he could telephone at all. But this time he found he could not. The operator told him she was afraid the lines to the north were all down. Yes, she would keep on trying but she was almost sure it was no use. In spite of what she said, he hounded her, until it was time to get on the train. And after that there was nothing to do but read those horrible head-lines, and ask the conductor questions which he either could not or would not answer, and think about Drew alone at Splendida, and Céleste alone at her silent piano, and Anna alone on her way to Boston——

The train was stopping. It was almost dark already and Breck could not see anything very clearly when he looked out of the window. He got up and walked down the aisle to the platform. Then he saw that they had reached Edgard. He was tempted to get off the train, and try to find out something for himself there, but he realized that the stop would be very brief, and he could not take any chances of being left behind. He called down from the platform to several passers-by, but they went hurrying on, without an-swering him. Some of them were talking excitedly, and he could catch a stray sentence or two—"A bad break above here"—"Rising at the rate of about eight inches an hour"—"Don't know yet how much loss of life"—The friendly conductor swung himself back onto the platform while Breck was still straining his ears and trying to quiet the pounding of his heart.

"I've been talking to the engineer," the conductor said. "He knew your father, too. And I've told him about that little boy of yours. It's a risk, but we're going to try to send the train on through the water, Mr. Breckenridge, and beat the flood if we can. Some of the track's submerged already. But we think we can get as far as Donaldsonville anyway. And maybe you can hire a hack there."

"What's that I heard about a bad break further north? And some loss of life?"

"The loss of life is way up at Torras. That is, if there really has been any. The report isn't confirmed. I don't know just where the bad break is."

"It was the Torras break that caused all the damage to the south last year."

"Yes, but that isn't likely to happen a second time. I don't think conditions are anywhere nearly as bad as they were last year."

Breck was not sure the conductor was telling him the truth, but there was nothing he could do about it. He could hardly keep his feet as he lurched back to his seat, clutching the tops of other seats filled with frightened passengers, as he went. Most of these passengers were too terrorized to speak, but occasionally a woman screamed and a man tried to smother her shriek or soothe her, and occasionally a baby wailed, and its mother tried to comfort it. The oil lamps suspended from the ceiling swayed back and forth, the flame in them first flickering and then plunging. The train had begun to rock like a skiff in a stormy sea. As it swung slowly forward over the submerged track, there was a sullen sound of swishing which went on and on. Breck thought the conductor was avoiding him now, but he got up and made his way towards the man again.

"How much of the track is under water?"

"I can't say for certain. Maybe ten miles of it."

"It doesn't seem to me that we're making any headway at all."

"In the last flood, three flatcars and a caboose overturned on a train that was trying to make headway too fast. It wouldn't do you much good, Mr. Breckenridge, if that should happen to us."

Breck went back to his seat and tried to pray. It was only a few hours since he had told Father Fontaine, jeeringly, that the priest had better pray for him. Now he yearned to pray himself, and found he could not. He had gone to church as a boy, he had even been confirmed while he was at Groton; but that was only because Dr. Peabody, the headmaster, had more or less expected it, only because it was what most of his classmates were doing. He had never felt any real urge towards worship or towards prayer. He did not think of worship now. But he passionately desired to pray. And he did not know how to begin, or how to end, or what to petition at any part of a prayer. He thought of Céleste's prayer, embodied in Gounod's superb music which she had sung in the grove at Bayou Goula:

> "Ave Maria—
> Tu partageas nos chaînes
> Allège nos peines;—
> Dans nos alarmes implore,
> Implore ton Fils pour nous.
> Amen."

Yes, that was beautiful and profound and touching. But it was a woman's song, addressed to a woman, not a man's cry addressed to the Divinity. What was it someone—he could not remember who—had said? "Half of Christendom worships a Jew and the other half a Jewess?" Or course that did not mean it was necessarily the men who worshipped Christ and women who worshipped Mary. It meant to differentiate between Protestants and Catholics, and at that, he had heard Catholics explaining every carefully that they worshipped only God, that the rest was veneration or devotion or adoration—something like that. But whatever it was, it did not seem to him at this moment that the "Ave Maria" was his prayer, either as Céleste had sung it in the grove or as she had murmured it in the little chapel afterwards. Then what might be? Did a man bargain with his God? Did he say, "If You will grant me this one boon, I will never ask another? If You will save my child for me, if You will take me to him tonight, I will do anything that You ask of me in return?" But he was not ready to say that, even now. He was not ready to give up his love or to be reconciled with his wife. And could a man bargain with the Almighty? He was not sure. He did not suppose so. He hoped so——

The train had pulled slowly into Donaldsonville at last. The people around him were gathering up their packages and their children and making for the door. The faces of the men and women going past him were a queer gray color, for the most part; one of the women was weeping now, and one was laughing hysterically. The husband of the weeping woman looked sheepish and ashamed; he was pretending not to notice her grief. The husband of the laughing woman was trying to quiet her, as he shepherded her down the aisle; but her outcry and her laughter grew louder and louder. Breck gripped his suitcase and tried to get to the door faster than the others. Without shoving and pushing the frightened women, who still did not believe in their safety, he could not do so. He had to wait his turn.

He had no better luck in getting definite information on the platform at Donaldsonville than he had had at Edgard. There was very little light. It was hard for him to see where he was going, and the forms and faces of other men eluded him. He passed some Negroes who were unloading lumber and sacks, and tried to question them. They stared at him for a moment, almost as if they had not heard him, and then they muttered something about a crevasse and went on with their work. When he pressed them, angrily, to answer him, they allowed that they really did not know anything about it. Breck strode forward into the station and found the stationmaster, entrenched behind his little wicket, busy with his ticker. Breck shouted at him.

"Has there been a crevasse? Do you know where? For God's sake, don't stare at me like that! I can't stand having anyone else stare and stare and not speak! Tell me something!"

The stationmaster lifted his head. He was a tired-looking man, drab and gray before his time. "Yes," he said slowly. "I got word over the ticker, me, that there's been a crevasse north of here. But I don't know where, not exactly. I'd be glad to tell you if I did."

"Haven't you any idea?"

"It must have been somewhere near White Castle. But I don't know just how near."

Breck plunged out of the station and made for the livery stable. The owner was very loath to let him take a horse and buggy. He did not know, either, exactly where the crevasse had occurred, but it was somewhere this side of White Castle. He did not recognize Breck at first. He said he couldn't risk a big loss, just then. Breck, identifying himself, opened his billfold and drew out its contents. There was not as much in it as he had supposed there would be. There never was. He had some blank checks with him, but he had an idea his account at the bank was overdrawn, as usual. It didn't matter. He started to write a check.

"That's all right, Mr. Breckenridge. I'm sorry I didn't know you right off. Of course you're welcome to the horse and buggy. You can pay me any time. I hope you get through all right."

He started off through the mud. It was not very thick at first—not more than ankle deep, he thought, judging from the clop-clop made by the horse's hoofs as he went through it. But presently the clopping changed to splashing. Breck jerked at the reins, turning the horse away from the road and towards the levee. He did not dare to use a whip for fear the horse might rear and upset the buggy. But to his breathless relief, the buggy spanned the narrow ditch in safety, without sinking into the mire, and jolted across. The next instant the horse was scrambling and struggling up the bank, while Breck braced himself and tried to keep his balance as the buggy swayed. Then it righted itself again, and they were off along the top of the levee.

The sky was still overcast, though it had ceased to rain, but the river seemed to generate a luminosity all its own.

As his eyes grew accustomed to the darkness, Breck could
see it clearly, plunging and foaming and billowing towards
the sea. It was very high. The crest of the current was rising
almost to the level on which he was riding. Its height affected him first, and most, after its uncanny radiance. But
there was a noise that arrested him too, a queer gurgle, that
sounded like a superman choking to death. That he knew
came from the crevasse, somewhere ahead of him in the darkness, where the river had burst its man-made limits, and
was pouring itself out with elemental force.

He drove on, looking at the luminosity, listening to the
gurgle. The horse floundered from time to time, but it stag-
gered forward. The buggy was fairly steady. But Breck knew
it would not take him much further. He knew he must find
some kind of a boat. His best chance was that someone
whose house was already submerged had taken one, in seeking shelter on the levee, and that he might meet such a
man. The thought became a hope and the hope a prayer,
though that was formless, for he still had not hit upon a
way he could pray. Then almost before he knew what had
happened, the thought and the hope and the prayer became a
reality. A group of Negroes were huddled together, directly
in his pathway. It was a marvel that he had not run them
down, before he saw them. They were clinging to each other
and to their pirogues. There were three pirogues—enough so
that they could give up one, and still get away, if they had
to. They had not come together, but they could leave together.
He reined in the exhausted horse, which needed no compul-
sion to stop, and spoke to them.

"It's a bad night, boys, for all of us. Where did you come
from?"

"We's from Homewood, boss. Our quo'ters is all under
water. But us'n got away all right."

Homewood! That was one of the Hébert plantations,
nearly five miles below Splendida. He had a long way to go
yet. But he saw now how it could be done.

"I've got to get to Splendida. Do you know where the
crevasse is?"

"Yassuh. It's right close to there."

"I was afraid so. I'll leave this horse and buggy with
you. They belong to Mr. Vandry of Donaldsonville. You'll
get them back to him as soon as you can, won't you?"

"Yassuh, Mr. Breck, we sho' will."

They had recognized him already, before he spoke of

Splendida, before he was out of the buggy. Gratefully, he felt their sympathy and solicitude enfolding him. He did not ask them if they would lend him one of their pirogues. He knew that they not only expected him to take one, but that they wanted him to take one. However, the man who knelt down to steady it as he got into it asked him an anxious question.

"You done handled a pirogue before, isn't you, Mr. Breck? You's not afeared? You don't want one of us should come with you?"

"Don't worry about me. I used to handle one a lot as a boy and I've been out in one a few times this spring. Meanwhile I've done a lot of paddling in canoes and shells, up North. I can get along all right. I'm not afraid."

"Yassuh, Mr. Breck. Us'll look after dis here hoss and buggy. Us'n knows you'll get through to Mr. Drew all right."

Breck had told the truth. He felt no fear whatsoever as he stepped into the pirogue and squatted down in it, and his self-confidence was wholly justified. Like most New Englanders living near the sea, or in the lake regions, he was used to handling all kinds of craft, and he had not become Captain of his 'Varsity Crew at Harvard without having specialized training and thorough experience added to natural aptitude. He did not underestimate the trickiness of a pirogue, far greater than that of any ordinary canoe, which had been balanced and refined by the arts of a civilization more advanced than the one which the pirogue still embodied; but he felt confident that he could handle this, and the confidence gave him the first exhilaration which he had felt since he started on his dreadful journey. He was his own master again now, not a helpless prisoner in a train crawling over a submerged track, or the desperate driver of a floundering horse. A sense of power and freedom swept over him, and with the awareness of these came a return of the triumphant conviction that he could not only rescue Drew but win Céleste, in spite of every obstacle. On the train he had been trammelled by the thoughts of his wife. Now, in his liberation, his thoughts soared to his beloved. Above the sound of the river he seemed to hear her singing—not the "Délaissée" which had saddened him or the "Ave" which had mystified him, but those lilting songs of love whose meaning she guessed only by instinct, a meaning which, all in good time, he would

teach her in its entirety. *Its entirety!* What did a priest know
about passion? How could a church frustrate fulfillment? He
would prove the futility of their preaching to them yet!

Still exalted, still confident and triumphant, he paddled
up through the easier water along the levee, listening intently to the sound that the river made, since sound, rather
than sight, would have to guide him for the next few miles.
He did not hear the gurgle any more. Instead he heard
the roar of which Drew had spoken to him the day before
over the telephone—the menacing roar of a monster unleashed. And above the roar he could hear a gigantic
splash, too, and knew that the undermined hill of the
levee had toppled and tumbled into a flood. In the swell
of the water around him he felt the force of the unseen
current plunging through gashed barriers somewhere ahead.
But he forged along, still keeping in the shadow of the
levee, unfrightened and unthwarted.

He was not only listening now, he was watching. If he
could see, through the darkness, the outline of the allee
of oaks leading to the house, he could follow it. He felt
the current catch him, and sweep him back, faster than he
could battle against it. But at the same instant he saw the
outline of the house, itself. It was luminous against the sky,
in the same way that the river had been luminous against
the earth. He knew he could not be far from the quarters
then, and he believed he could force his way to them.
Feeling himself in the grip of the current, he still did not
fear it. He had kept the pirogue on an even keel so far.
He would have to keep on doing that, or he would capsize.
But there was no reason why he should not keep on. The
water was choked with flotsam that went hurtling by him
in the darkness, poles and planks to judge by the half-
caught glimpses. But he could see the quarters now, and
the big shadow of the mule barn beyond. He could feel
the slackening of the current. Soon he would be through
the worst of it. The rest would be easy. It was only a matter of minutes before he would reach Drew.

He could not understand what it was that suddenly
caught him across the chest. His legs were free, they had
shot ahead of him as the pirogue slid out from under
him. But his body was first pinioned and then entangled.
All at once he remembered. The barbed wire. The new
barbed wire, which, in thinking of everything else, he had
forgotten until then. The pirogue had slipped between the

lower strand of it and the upper and then sped on. But he himself was ensnared by it. In the same instant that he knew this, the prayer which all day had eluded him came clearly to him at last: "God, give me one more chance!" It was the prayer that was still on his lips as he fell backwards into the water.

PART VII

"Anywhere from a Bayou"

June to September, 1935

CHAPTER 23

STELLA FONTAINE sat on the cluttered wharf in Abbeville, swinging her bare legs over the edge of the wooden pier as she alertly watched the bayou and asked herself, for the hundredth time, if it were possible, after all, that something might happen in such a dump as this.

She and her grandmother, Mrs. Marcel Fontaine, with whom she lived in New Orleans, were making a long, leisurely visit near St. Martinville, at Bois Fleuri Plantation, which was the home of Mrs. Fontaine's cousins, Mr. and Mrs. Omer de Hauterive. The de Hauterives were a conservative couple who had clung to the original spelling of their name though all their relatives had now adopted the abbreviated form of Dauterive. But this conservatism was fated to end with them since they were elderly—"doddering," Stella expressed it—and they had no children, for Mrs. de Hauterive, nee Myrthé de Gruy, had married after all hope of fruitfulness was past—so late, indeed, that matrimony, itself, had long been an elusive state, and Stella's scornful opinion was that Cousin Myrthé had accepted Cousin Omer only so that "she would not go to her grave wondering." Cousin Myrthé had a brother, Allain de Gruy, who had a nice house in New Iberia and thought he was quite a gay old dog. He was at Bois Fleuri a good deal, and was always ragging Stella; scornfully again, she thought his line was about as fast as a St. Bernard's gait.

Of course, it was Drew Breckenridge who was supposed to supply the line. Stella knew this and so did Drew, and each was aware that the other knew it, which was possibly the main reason that Drew seldom said anything Stella thought worth listening to, and that even when he did, she stubbornly ignored it. Of course, he had class no end, and charm. More than all the other men she knew, or ever had known, put together. But Stella was sick of class and charm. She felt surfeited with them and smothered by them, and that was why she was out looking for something else. She had decided long before that Drew Breckenridge was a total loss, as far as she was concerned. She wished she, herself, had thought up the old story about a Harvard man: that you could always tell one, but you could not tell him much. It expressed her sentiment succinctly, and she liked to add that if he had been to Groton before going to Harvard, you could not tell him anything at all. Someone had told her another story, less hackneyed, about a tombstone in an ancient Connecticut cemetery, that had just one line on it for an epitaph: "He went to Harvard."

Well, that was Drew, as far as Stella was concerned. Except that Harvard, and even Harvard and Groton, were not the half of it. He had spent a whole winter in Washington when he was in his teens, after an attack of typhoid fever, and that had affected him, too. Some relative of his from Kentucky, who was in the Senate, had taken a great shine to him; he had been in and out of the Capitol and the White House and all the rest of those great cold-looking buildings, just like that. And after graduating from Harvard, he had gone to the Beaux-Arts in Paris and won all sorts of fancy prizes, and everyone had said he was going to become a great architect. But he hadn't. He hadn't become great in any way, only more and more different. Stella didn't see why he ever bothered to come back to Louisiana at all—why he didn't go on living with his mother on Beacon Hill in Boston instead of on Splendida Plantation and in the big white house on Prytania Street, a few blocks from Grannie Fontaine's. But Stella, for all her scorn, was constrained to be just. She knew Drew Breckenridge had come back to Louisiana because he loved it better than any other place in the world, just like his father and his grandfather, and she also knew that there were a great many Louisianians who loved Drew Brecken-ridge. Her own grandmother thought the sun rose and set on his head.

Drew, who was also visiting at Bois Fleuri, might have come over to Abbeville himself that afternoon, Stella re-flected, shaking back her mop of bright brown curls and swinging her bare legs faster than before. He could have taken her out on the town while Cousin Omer and Cousin Allain were rambling on and on about Louisiana politics with that funny old Dr. Anconi they had come to consult. There was something to do with a young Cajun lawyer who was in the State Legislature, who had done so well during his first term in the House that they thought they might run him for the Senate. This Cajun was anti-Long, and they had not quite decided, themselves, whether they were going to be anti- or pro-Long that summer; apparently IT DEPENDED— They said it depended, and then they stopped, so Stella never found out on what exactly. Not that she cared. But Cousin Omer and Cousin Allain had wanted to come over to Abbeville, and Drew, instead of offering to drive them in that classy Cadillac of his, had murmured something about riding horseback that after-noon. So Stella, who was almost desperate at the prospect of sitting aimlessly on the gallery at Bois Fleuri for an-other long, hot summer afternoon, had said she would be very pleased to go to Abbeville herself, and wouldn't they ride over in her Chrysler? The two elderly men had ac-cepted her invitation with alacrity, of which they had re-pented before they were halfway down the driveway of Bois Fleuri; for Stella was a speed demon, and though she conscientiously tried to slow down to sixty every now and then, when they implored her to do so, this did not represent a normal rate of speed for her, and she kept forgetting to hold herself to it. Besides, she dodged a turtle that was crawling quietly across the road only by swerving so sharply to the side that the Chrysler rocked, and killed a snake which was also traversing the highway, by the simple process of beating its swift dart towards safety by a swifter dart of her own. By the time she had brought her car to a sudden stop in front of Dr. Anconi's door, both her passengers were convinced that they were far more likely to require his services in his capacity of coroner than in his capacity of mentor.

They climbed out of the car, thankful for even a momentary respite, and went into the house, which was low and white and deep-set among the crape myrtles. Presently they came out again, bringing Dr. Anconi with them. He was completely bald, and had a white mustache which probably had once been sandy, and a decided stoop which kept him from looking as tall as he really was, and that was very tall, indeed. He said he would get in with them and drive over to Raoul's office. He spoke agreeably to Stella, and she was surprised to find that there was something rather likeable about this queer old codger. He directed her to a stark-looking, red-brick building that stood wedged into the middle of a block, with a drugstore on the ground floor, and a separate door on the side, flanked by a black sign lettered in fading silver with the words: RAOUL BIENVENU, ATTORNEY AT LAW. The building was not hard to find, as it was the only one in the block that was two stories high. The three old men got out of the car and opened the second door, disclosing a very dusty wooden stairway, which they laboriously climbed, leaving Stella sitting outside alone in the glare. She thought they might at least have asked her to go in with them. She was mildly interested in finding out what Raoul Bienvenu's office looked like, if only for the sake of something to do, though if it were no more snappy than his sign, she did not know whether it was worth the trouble, at that.

Fortunately, she did not have long to wait. Her passengers soon came down the rickety stairway, almost as painfully as they had mounted it, with the information that Raoul was not in his office—only Amédée Pérez, with whom he shared it.

"Is that his partner? Couldn't he help you?" Stella inquired, trying to sound polite, though actually not caring about all this.

"No, he's a rice broker," Dr. Anconi answered. "He and Raoul have always been good friends. They went through grade school and high school here in Abbeville together. Afterwards Raoul got a scholarship and went to L. S. U. and Amédée stayed here. But they kept close, just the same. When Raoul got ready to hang out his shingle, he asked Amédée to share his office. Of course, it wasn't wholly altruism; it was also sound economics. I think we'll drop around to Reveillon's Restaurant, Miss Stella, and see if Raoul isn't there having a small black. Just take the first turn to the left and then go straight ahead until I tell you to stop."

Stella, greatly surprised and reluctantly impressed by Dr. Anconi's easy use of such words as altruism and economics, followed his directions obediently and discharged her passengers once more, this time in front of a small restaurant with an upper gallery supported by slim iron columns at the gutter's edge, so that an oasis of shade held out an elusive promise of coolness. Again her wait was a short one. But only Dr. Anconi came out to report the lack of developments.

"Raoul isn't here, either," he said. "Reveillon thinks he may be at home, though. Would you feel like driving up to his house and finding out? We thought we'd have a small black ourselves, while we waited."

Privately, Stella thought Dr. Anconi might have suggested that perhaps she, herself, would like a small black, though, as a matter of fact, she would greatly have preferred a "coke," and decided to buy one at the Esso Station on the corner, where she wanted to go, anyway. Still, she could not help liking the old codger, and she did not mind riding around.

"Sure, I'll be glad to go," she said. "How do I get there?"

"Drive up three blocks and turn to the left. Then go straight ahead until you come to a big pecan tree. After that you bear right until you see a wooden fence that——"

"It sounds something like a treasure hunt to me."

"I'll be glad to go with you, if you think you can't find it. Or Reveillon will send his boy."

"What do you take me for? A deaf-mute or a blind man? Of course I can find it, or ask my way. So long!"

"If that's your attitude, I shall expect you to come back with your shield or on it, young lady."

Stella was good at ferreting out unfamiliar places under any circumstances, and this time she was spurred to success by the challenge of this queer old coroner who used long words and lapsed into classical quotations with such extraordinary ease. Nevertheless, when she reached the fantastic little house on the edge of the town, which, from its location, seemed to be the right one, she was baffled. It must have been nondescript to begin with, but various additions, all apparently aimless, branched out from it without any attempt at balance and uniformity. It certainly did not look to Stella like the sort of house in which a rising young attorney, sufficiently up-and-coming to have got to the Legislature and to merit consideration for advancement, would be likely to live. A dun-colored cow was tethered in the yard, munching the long grass contentedly, and an enormous vegetable garden extended, in amplitude and abundance, on either side of the bizarre building. In this garden, a billowy little woman, with her hair screwed into a tight knot on the top of her head, was industriously weeding. She looked up as Stella got out of the car and approached her, and Stella saw that her round olive-tinted face, while rather flat, seemed literally to exude contentment and well-being. Small turquoise earrings dangled from her pierced ears, and she wore a gold band, so wide that it came almost halfway up to the knuckle, on the fourth finger of her left hand. Her calico dress was about the same color of gray as the nondescript house.

"Good afternoon," Stella said pleasantly. "Could you tell me whether Mr. Raoul Bienvenu lives here?"

The industrious gardener did not instantly answer, though she nodded and continued to look at Stella in a friendly way. After a moment Stella guessed that, though she had mentioned a name which was familiar to this funny little fat woman, the rest of the question had been unintelligible. She repeated it in French, and the gardener, beaming broadly by this time, nodded more vigorously and answered in broad Cajun, which Stella, in her turn, had a little difficulty in following. She was obliged to ask her informant to repeat more slowly what the latter had first said rapidly and excitely: that yes, indeed, this was Raoul's home, but that he was away for the day, over on Chênière-au-Tigre. There was no telling what time he would be back. One never knew, with Raoul. If the young lady would care to wait——

"I'm sorry. I couldn't do that. I came over from St. Martinville with some gentlemen who are very eager to see him—Mr. de Gruy and Mr. de Hauterive. They're at Reveillon's Restaurant now, drinking small blacks and talking to Dr. Anconi. If Mr. Bienvenu should happen to come back, within the next hour or so, would you be kind enough to tell him that they'd be very happy if he'd join them there?"

"Assuredly, Mademoiselle. As soon as my son comes back, I will give him your message. But I am sorry that you are so pressed for time. Would you not have a small black yourself, or something cold? It is a very warm day."

Stella was still thirsty, and she did not really feel pressed for time. She willingly followed Mrs. Bienvenu into the front room of the nondescript little house, where her hostess threw open the door with pride. It was unlike any room Stella had ever seen before. In the center of it was a round table adorned with paper flowers rising from a pressed-glass vase, and over the mantelpiece was a tasselled "throw" which matched the curtain hanging at the open entrance into the room beyond, where a large iron bed, painted pea-green and surmounted by a picture of the Sacred Heart, pre-empted practically all the space. The furnishings of the parlor were as heterogeneous as the additions to the house, but Stella had a general impression of rockers, tidies, golden oak and pressed plush. Among the chromos of religious character, which hung on the walls, were various family photographs in heavy frames, outstanding among which there were two very presentable brides, two equally presentable first communicants, and two pictures of the same young man—one as he appeared in cap and gown, the other as he appeared in cadet uniform. This young man bore a vague resemblance to the likenesses of certain early Normans, that Stella had seen in prints and portraits when she had visited her relatives near Lisieux —a wiry, purposeful type whose small features were strong. She kept glancing towards the photographs while she drank her coffee and chatted with her hostess, and each time she looked she saw something more arresting than when she had looked the time before.

When she finally left, although she went back to the center of town at a snail's pace, for her, she missed several turns, because she was pondering much more seriously than was her habit, and she had a one-track mind; she could not think about Mrs. Bienvenu and the Bienvenu house and the Bienvenu garden and watch where she was going, all at once. The episode which had just occurred was so alien to anything in her previous experience that it absorbed her completely. In a vague way, she had always known that there were people who lived like the Bienvenus, instead of like the Fontaines and the Breckenridges and the de Gruys and the de Hauterives, but since she had never seen the way they lived, the remarks she had heard about it lacked the illusion of reality. Now that she had seen it, the fact which emerged most vividly from her

jumbled impressions was not that it was an unpleasant way
to live, but that Mrs. Bienvenu was devotedly attached to
her husband and inordinately proud of her children, and
that all her interests, and, indeed, her whole life, were
centered in them. During the course of their brief visit
together, she had told Stella a great deal about her husband
and her children, apparently less because she was aware of
any necessity for conversational amenities than because
her pride and devotion were such that she could not keep
them to herself. Mr. Bienvenu, it seemed, owned five shrimp
luggers, renting out on shares the four he did not run
himself, and he also owned an iceboat which gathered
shrimp from the other fishermen, for delivery at the can-
nery. Evidently, his financial status was extremely sound,
according to the Bienvenus' standard of prosperity. When
Mrs. Bienvenu spoke of her eldest son, she inferred that he
could have gone to college, like Raoul, if he had really
wanted to; but he had been going with a girl, and he was in
a hurry to get work, when he finished high school. Now
he was captain of one of the seine crews, and between
seasons he did some trapping and gathered moss, which
was dried and used commercially. The two eldest girls
were married; one of them lived at Gueydan, where her
husband was foreman in a rice mill; the other one lived
in New Orleans, on Annunciation Street; her husband was
a streetcar conductor. Mrs. Bienvenu, who at this point in
the conversation had already gleaned that Stella, herself,
came from New Orleans, said that perhaps the young lady
knew them—Mr. and Mrs. Patrick Shea.

No, Stella had said, she didn't, but she hoped she would
have the pleasure of meeting them sometime. She said it
not only politely but sincerely. She was beginning to like
Mrs. Bienvenu very much, and she also cannily divined
that the more interest she evinced in the captain of the
seine crew and the wives of the factory foreman and the
streetcar conductor, the more Mrs. Bienvenu was likely to
tell her about Raoul, who came next after Mrs. Patrick
Shea. Such a smart boy, his mother said. Valedictorian
when he graduated from high school! Winner of a scholarship awarded by Lawyer Broussard, who was a local member of the Legislature then, though, of course, the young
lady would understand—Mrs. Bienvenu said this with a
knowing look—that Dr. Anconi had actually had a good
deal to do with it. Raoul had been in the cadet corps at

L. S. U., and the colonel of the cadets had asked him to his own house, a very fine one, right often. He was in a fraternity, too, with house parties before the dances. Afterwards, when he studied law, he had been in the same group with Mr. Henry Sevier and Mr. George Perrault and such gentlemen as that; Raoul had been to their houses, too. Mr. Bienvenu had told his wife that perhaps, when Raoul came back to Abbeville to practice, he wouldn't care to live with the old folks; he'd want a fine new house of his own. But she had been sure it wouldn't be like that. Of course, if there had been a girl, as there was in the case of her eldest son, they'd have set up housekeeping for themselves. But not in a fine house—not to start with. Raoul was too smart for that. He knew as much about money as his father did, and how handy a savings-bank account could be. He'd start small. But sound——

There were two girls younger than Raoul, but Mrs. Bienvenu seemed to sense that her visitor would find details concerning them an anticlimax, after hearing about the valedictorian who had been a cadet officer and a frequent visitor at Mr. Henry Sevier's. So she did not press Stella to stay when the girl rose to go, though she did say she hoped the young lady would come back sometime. And Stella answered, again sincerely as well as politely, that she would be glad to, and would Mrs. Bienvenu be sure to remember to tell her son, when he did come in, that Dr. Anconi and Mr. de Gruy and Mr. de Hauterive were waiting for him in Reveillon's Restaurant——

It was not so much because of what Mrs. Bienvenu had told her that Stella kept missing the turns on her way back to the center of town. It was because of the way it had been told. That pride. That joyous, bursting pride. Stella tried to think how long it was since she had seen her own mother. She couldn't remember. Then she tried to think how long it was since her mother had written to her. She couldn't remember that either. This was late June. Well, she thought there had been one letter since the Pilgrimage. Of course, during the Pilgrimage, no one in Natchez wrote any letters. Stella wouldn't have expected that. Particularly from anyone as active in the Pilgrimage as her mother. But that had been over in April, and she was almost sure there had been one letter since, a short one——

Naturally, there was no special reason why her mother

should have been proud of her, when it came to that. She had never won any scholarships, or been valedictorian, or anything of the sort. She had just lived along with her grandmother, doing the same things as the other girls she knew in New Orleans, and not much else. Her father and mother had been married about the time the United States entered the World War. She had heard—it was the sort of thing you always did hear—that her father had hoped his marriage would save him from the selective draft, and that it hadn't. He had never gone to France, he had never fought, gallantly and desperately, in the War to End All Wars, but he had got as far as Camp Beauregard and there he had died, ingloriously, of influenza, before Stella was born. Mrs. Marcel Fontaine had treated her widowed daughter-in-law with the utmost tenderness, so Stella had always heard. (That was one good thing Stella had heard, anyway!) She had urged Bessie Rose to come and live with her in her big cream-colored house on Prytania Street. But Bessie Rose had not wanted to do that. She had wanted to go back to her own family, the Reniers, in Natchez. And presently she had wanted to marry the boy she had liked better than Olivier Fontaine all along, and who came out of the war unscratched, though he had been to France, though he had fought gallantly and desperately. He had been very nice about Olivier Fontaine's baby, Stella, too. He had said he would be glad to have her. But Bessie Rose, herself, had not wanted Stella. She had not wanted to keep anything that would remind her of her first marriage. Not the name, nor the money, nor the position, nor the baby. She had been glad to turn Stella over to Olivier's mother, and start life all over again.

Of course, now that she had been happily married for a number of years, now that her second husband was no longer the dazzling hero that had become her bridegroom, now that their children were beginning to grow up and were not taking so much of her time, she might have wanted Stella back again, after all, if it had not been for the Spring Pilgrimages. But she had become one of the prime movers in the exploitation of Natchez as the embodiment of anti-bellum culture and charm. Her own home, Myrtle Grove, was always on the tour; her own daughters were always in the tableaux and the Confederate Ball. She, herself, wearing crinolines, cameos and other unmistakable symbols of dear dead days, was a smiling chatelaine during the weeks apportioned to tourists, and, wearing serviceable sports cloths, a driving executive during the months when the preparations for these tourists were being made. Her time was already taken, her strength was already taxed; she could not complicate the one or burden the other by introducing an extra daughter on the already crowded scene——

Stella sighed, and then swore, partly because she was ashamed of the sigh and partly because she saw that she had taken another wrong turn. A moment before, she had been in front of the school run by the Sisters of Mount Carmel. With conflicting emotions, she had stopped to stare at the cross formed by the stained glass over the door in the rambling white building, and at the miniature statues, set in grottos of greenery and separated by the width of the walk, of the Virgin holding the Holy Child and of Saint Joseph, the Virgin's Most Chaste Spouse. Now she was in front of a small, white clapboarded house with green shutters, that had a sign beside the front door which read: HOT BREAD DAILY. She could smell the bread, which was so fresh and fragrant that it made her very hungry, and she was tempted to go in and buy some. But she would never get back to Reveillon's Restaurant at this rate. And then, suddenly, she decided she would not go back to the restaurant anyway. She could just see Dr. Anconi sauntering out of it and finding her alone. She could just hear him saying, "So you didn't come back with the shield after all?" She didn't want to hear anything like that just now. She had heard enough for one afternoon. She would just go down to the wharf and sit there. If Dr. Anconi and Cousin Omer and Cousin Allain didn't have enough sense to look for her after a while, that was just too bad. If they couldn't find her, that was their hard luck. Besides— Mrs. Bienvenu had said that her son had gone to Chênière-au-Tigre. There was only one way to get to Chênière-au-Tigre, and that was in a boat. In this case, the boat would probably be a shrimp lugger, because if Mr. Bienvenu had five of those, Raoul ought to be able to borrow one whenever he needed it, and since he had such sound financial ideas, he would doubtless do that, instead of keeping one of his own. Then, there was just one place to land from a shrimp lugger or any other kind of boat, and that was at this wharf. If there was any justice at all in the world, which Stella was often inclined to doubt, Raoul Bienvenu would come back from Chêière-au-Tigre before Dr. Anconi and Cousin Omer and Cousin Allain found her. She ought to be able to recognize him readily from his pictures in the cadet uniform and the cap and gown. She would hail him and tell him that she was waiting for him, and why. And he would go with her to Reveillon's Restaurant and she could make a triumphant entry there, instead of a crestfallen one. It was a grand idea. She would believe it was true when she saw it worked.

She parked her car among the high black-topped buggies that were hitched along the main street near the short rough road sloping down to the wharf, and went and sat down on the edge of the pier, dangling her bare legs over it and thinking some more. She did not mean to be critical of her mother. Her mother had been given a raw deal when she got Olivier Fontaine in the first place, and then she had had one bad jolt after another in the short time she had been married to him. Of course, Grannie worshipped her only son's memory and never spoke of him to this day except in a hushed voice, with great emotion, as a victim and a hero. But various tales had filtered through to Stella, as such tales had a way of doing. The worst one, the one she had never succeeded in forgetting for more than a few days at a time, centered around an episode which had occurred just after the young couple's return from their honeymoon. They were staying temporarily in a little house on Kerlerec Street, that Grannie owned, while they were looking for something more suitable, and Lute, the "high-yellow" girl who had been Olivier Fontaine's maid for some time —supplementing the services of the elderly Lulu, who claimed she had never got her strength back after she had been smitten with bubonic plague—had brought morning coffee to their bedside, according to the immemorial custom of the country. But when she had set down the little silver tray with the precious porcelain on it, instead of respectfully retiring, she had stood at the foot of the bed, giggling helplessly. Bessie Rose had been bewildered as well as shocked, and Olivier had rapped out a sharp order and asked a curt question.

"Behave yourself, Lute! What in time ails you?"

Lute had gone on giggling for a moment, apparently unable to stop. Then, retreating towards the door as she spoke, she had dealt her deadly blow.

"Ain't nothin', Mr. Olivier, 'ceptin' it seems so funny to see you in bed with a white lady."

Of course, Bessie Rose had not told this story to her daughter herself. But she had told it to one or two other persons in defending her course when she remarried so shortly after Olivier Fontaine's death. And these persons, in due course, had told one or two others, in strictest confidence, and so on and so on, and that was how it had come to Stella. All her life she had gone with her grandmother to visit her father's tomb in Métairie Cemetery at regular intervals, and, on All Saints' Day and on the anniversaries of his birth and his death, she had helped to decorate it with flowers. She, herself, had never said a word about him that could mar her grandmother's memory of him. But she had always known that her father had been a cad as well as a coward, and the knowledge had bitten deep into her sturdy little soul.

She heard some kind of a craft coming close to the wharf and looked up to see if it could be the lugger for which she was waiting. But it was a gasolene boat with big steel drums strung across the deck, and it did not stop; it went on to the oil dock, where the Negroes who manned it rolled the big drums ashore, chanting as they worked. Then a young Cajun went by in a pirogue that was piled high with black moss, and she watched him with fascination, marvelling at the skill with which he balanced himself and his load. She had always wanted to go out in a pirogue herself, and she had hoped that this summer there might be a chance, but she could not even talk about it, as long as Drew stayed at Bois Fleuri. It was dreadful for Drew to know that his father had been drowned, trying to reach him, in a pirogue, under the impression that he was in danger, when all the time he had been quite safe. The crevasse in which Drew's father had lost his life had hardly damaged the big house at Splendida at all; this was still magnificent, though, of course, the grounds were no longer what they had been, now that the levee had been moved back three times. The plantation was not as productive as it had been in the lifetime of Drew's father and grandfather, either. There was no cotton grown there any more, and only about half as much cane as in the early days. But Drew did not care much. That is, Stella did not think he did. After all, why should he, when oil was gushing out at the rate it was on other property he had inherited, which his poor father had thought was worthless? Drew Breckenridge was a very rich man—one of the richest men in Louisiana —and one of the least sentimental. As long as he had more money than he knew how to spend, why should he care whether it came from oil or sugar? Mrs. Fontaine had asked this question herself, in speaking to Stella about Drew's immense fortune, though as far as that went, Mrs. Fontaine *was* inclined to be sentimental.

Stella was genuinely attached to her grandmother, but, still, she could not help wishing that there were not such constant strain between them—that she was not always on the defensive. It wore her down, arguing with Grannie all the time, and she knew it wore Grannie down, too. There was not just that tiresome subject of Drew Breckenridge. There was also the subject of her singing. She wanted to go to Paris and study for the stage, but Grannie had collapsed when Stella talked to her about Mary Garden and her spectacular success at the Opéra Comique, which was exactly the sort of success Stella thought she would like to achieve herself. Of course, she was ready to admit that she did not know all the details about Mary Garden's rise to fame, but those she did know were inspiring and provocative to her. She thought Grannie might at least take her to Paris and let her try to make the Opéra Comique. But though Grannie was perfectly willing to go on taking her to Paris, which she had been doing ever since Stella was a small child, it was just to go to the Louvre and to Worth's, the way it always had been. If that was all there was to it, Stella would rather go over the Lake to the Pass, where most of her friends went, in the summertime, and where it was fun to fool around with the crowd, swimming and sailing.

Even the question of clothes was a constant source of dissension. Take today, for instance. Grannie thought that, if Stella were going to drive her Cousin Allain and her Cousin Omer to Abbeville on an important political errand, she ought to wear a "costume suitable for the afternoon." Well, cripes, that was all right in principle. The only trouble was that Grannie's idea of a suitable afternoon costume for a June day began with a longish print dress, worn over a slip and a bra and a girdle and step-ins, and it also included such items as long silk stockings, gloves and shoes made of white doeskin, a large hat and a matching handbag. Stella's idea of a suitable afternoon costume on such a day began and ended with slacks, or shorts, and sneakers. Some of her shorts were made with detachable, knee-length skirts that buttoned around her waist at the belt-line of the blouse, and after a terrific struggle, she had finally compromised on one of these and on socks as well as sneakers. But just because Grannie had made such a fuss about it all and had acted as if she, Stella, had no idea of decency, she had taken off her skirt and socks and flung them into the back of the car while she was waiting for Dr. Anconi and Cousin Omer and Cousin Allain outside of Raoul Bienvenu's office in the stark little red-brick building. She did not feel particularly proud because she had done so. Indeed, she had half a mind to put them on again now. But they were all rumpled up, and messy. She would be a perfect sight in them. Besides, it was a lot cooler this way. If anything could be called cool in Abbeville on an afternoon in late June.

The afternoon was getting on. She wondered if those poor old boys had failed to find her, after all—if they'd been bothered because she'd left them in the lurch. When you came right down to it, there was no real reason why a girl should be a bad sport herself, just because her mother had been a quitter and her father had been a cad and a coward, especially when her grandmother was actually something pretty fine. If you could only take it on the chin when you and she did not see things in the same way, instead of raising an unholy row about it. And you ought not to cheat, either, by taking off part of your clothes when she wasn't looking. Stella stopped swinging her legs and jumped up. She had decided to go back to the car and get out the skirt and the socks and put them on again, even if they were a mess. She would feel better about it. And none of the old boys, except possibly Dr. Anconi, would ever notice whether she was clean or dirty.

But she did not get to the car parked among the buggies, after all, because, just as she stood up, she saw the shrimp lugger she had been waiting for. At least, she was almost certain this was the one. The young man who was at the wheel had on a very good-looking straw hat, instead of being bareheaded like the other men who had gone by, and a spotless seersucker suit instead of a faded blue shirt and still more faded khaki trousers. And he had the strong, purposeful look of the boy in the photographs at Mrs.

Bienvenu's house, and of the early Normans in the prints and portraits near Lisieux. He shut off the motor expertly and coasted smoothly up to the dock. The black boy on the bow of the lugger snubbed the line around the piling, and the young man in seersucker stepped swiftly ashore.

"Hello!" Stella said, without wasting any time on superfluous amenities. The young man from the shrimp lugger had the air of being very brisk about everything he did. She did not want him to escape her by the simple process of tearing across the wharf before she had even had a chance to find out who he was.

"Hello, yourself!" said the young man. He answered her without apparent surprise, much less resentment. Indeed, he sounded fairly cordial, not to say responsive. Well, perhaps he was used to being picked up. After all, he was far from bad-looking, and he had been to the Abbeville High School and to L. S. U. Stella did not quite know what the technique was in those places, but there was one thing on which she already would have been willing to bet her bottom dollar: it was different from at Groton and at Harvard.

"Your name isn't Raoul Bienvenu, by any chance, is it?" she inquired, still without superfluous delay.

"By some chance, it is. Would that happen to be of interest to you?"

"Not a bit. But it's of interest to three old boys who've been all around Robin Hood's barn looking for you. I finally told them I'd find you for them."

"Mighty white of you. Who are these three old boys?"

"Two of them are cousins of mine, Omer de Hauterive and Allain de Gruy. I drove them down from St. Martinville in my car. And then they went into a huddle with a queer old bird named Dr. Anconi, who spouts Shakespeare, or something of the sort, whenever he speaks to you. They say it all depends, but they've more or less decided they want you to run for the State Senate. Would that be of any interest to *you?*"

"Yes, young lady, it would. Considerable interest."

"But they want to pump you about it first. To find out whether you're going to be pro-Long or anti-Long. So for that noble purpose, I took them first to your office, and you weren't there. And then to Reveillon's Restaurant, and you weren't there. And then, while they sat and consumed small blacks, they sent me out to your house to look for you, and you weren't there. But I had a nice visit with your mother."

"Oh, you did, did you?"

"Yes. And she told me you'd gone to Chênière-au-Tigre. She didn't say why."

"I didn't tell her why. I didn't think it was necessary. But I'll tell you, since you seem to think it's germane to the subject. I went there to take a deposition in a suit over an oil case."

"I don't know what you mean by 'germane to the subject.' But I figured the only way you could get to Chênière-au-Tigre, or back from there, was in a boat. So I came down here to the wharf and waited for you. I figured if I had any kind of a break at all, you wouldn't be able to get away from me."

Raoul Bienvenu laughed out loud, revealing two rows of amazingly white teeth. When he stopped laughing, he looked at her with increasing attention.

"I'm not so sure I want to get away from you," he said eventually. "What made you think I would?"

"I didn't think about it at all. That is, as far as you and I were concerned. If you ask me, I think you've got a lot of nerve to imagine I would."

"I have got a lot of nerve. Well, where do we go from here?"

"To Reveillon's Restaurant. What happens to your boat?"

"Oh, the boy takes care of that. Unless you'd like to go for a ride in it first."

"I would not. I'd like to have you climb into my car this minute. When I've delivered you to Dr. Anconi, I'll fade out of the picture again. It never seems to occur to these old boys that, while they're talking about Huey Long and drinking small blacks, I might like to be doing something myself. If there is anything to do in Abbeville."

"We do all the usual things here."

"What do you mean, 'the usual things'?"

"If you don't know, I'll have to show you the next time you drop around this way. Which I hope will be fairly soon. Meanwhile, let's get this conference over. When the political decks are cleared, we can get on to the next case on the docket. Do you drive, or do I?"

"I do. After all, it's my car."

"You mean you have a car here. But so have I. You

could leave yours here and come in mine. That vintage Ford, over at the left."

They had been scrambling up the rough slope as they talked, and now they had reached the main street, where the high-topped buggies were hitched close to each other, the dejected-looking horses drooping between the shafts. The "vintage Ford" and Stella's smart Chrysler were the only automobiles parked among them. Stella went steadily on to the Chrysler, and Raoul did not argue with her about it. But when he got in beside her, he saw the discarded skirt and socks lying on the floor in the back, and asked another amused question.

"You don't do a strip-tease act on the side, along with your other benevolent acts to old gentlemen, do you?"

"I do not. Or any of the other 'usual things' to which you so delicately referred. It might save trouble for both of us if you got that through your head right away."

"I get it. I also gather that you don't mind breaking the law about speed limits, whatever you think of a fast line. We'll be at Reveillon's Restaurant in about half a second, at this rate. Would it be asking too much if I suggested I'd like to know your name before we got there? Merely, of course, so I can give you a credit line when I hail Dr. Anconi?"

"It's Stella Fontaine. And while you're giving me that credit line, you might also tell him for me that I hope he'll believe me now when I say I always come in with the shield. Never mind what I mean. Just tell him."

She brought her car to a stop as smooth as it was quick. Then, with her characteristic gesture, she shook back her mop of curls and faced him.

"Such a privilege to have met you," she said. "I'm sorry I can't give you something to remember me by."

Raoul Bienvenu got out of the car and lifted one hand in a casual farewell.

"If I thought our separation would be prolonged," he said, "I'd take along the skirt and socks for a souvenir. After all, I'd only have to snatch at them to get them. But I'm not anticipating a lengthy parting. I'm sure another conference, concerning senatorial prospects, will be called for tomorrow evening, at Bois Fleuri. That's where you're staying, isn't it? I'll be seeing you then and there, around suppertime."

CHAPTER 24

THE DINNER at Bois Fleuri, on the night of the political conference, was very good indeed, but it was very long and, in Stella's opinion, very dull.

First there was a gumbo which was a meal in itself. Then there was a jambalaya which, after all, had so many of the same ingredients—shrimps and rice and so on—that she could not see the sense of having both at the same meal, even if both had not been so filling. After that there were stuffed crabs and roast duck with numerous vegetables, and a salad which brought forth a long dissertation from Dr. Anconi. With a courtly inclination of the head, he told Mrs. de Hauterive that it was a relief to find a lady still living who understood the true meaning of the term. Recently it had been his misfortune to sit at several tables where his hostess had served concoctions of marshmallows and nuts and dates, marinated in mayonnaise, topped with whipped cream, and rising in mounds on slices of pineapple, and these she had designated as salad. Whereas it was still true, as it always had been, that a real salad was inevitably green—unless you counted an occasional touch of tomato—and that a good dressing could be made only when you had a spendthrift for oil, a miser for vinegar, a sage for salt, a connoisseur for pepper, and a crazy man to mix them all together. Obviously, he said, Mrs. de Hauterive had been fortunate in assembling all these unseen helpers, not to mention the one who had rubbed the bowl with exactly the right amount of garlic and the dependable person who had never drenched the wooden serving bowl and spoon in scalding water, so that the benefit of previous dressings which had soaked into their substance had not been lost. Dr. Anconi was still talking about salads and all that they should and should not mean when the chocolate soufflé was brought in, and he had not really exhausted the subject when the coffee and brandy made their appearance. Coffee and brandy took a long time to drink, too, as Stella knew all too well from past experience. The guests would put sugar into their spoons and pour brandy over it, light it, and watch this mixture caramelize under the little blue flame before they stirred it very slowly into the coffee, itself. And then they would sip and sip. And have some more. And start all over again.

Stella had hoped the political discussion would begin while they were still at the table, not because she was interested in hearing it, but because the sooner it began, the sooner it would be finished. Besides Dr. Anconi and Raoul Bienvenu, who had come over from Abbeville in the vintage Ford, there were several other guests: the president of the Abbeville Bank, Mr. Odilon Dupré, a fussy fat little man who had brought his wife, equally fat and fussy, along with him, and Mr. Clement Pérez, the very rich manufacturer of "Dash-O-Fire," who looked like an aging brigand, and who had brought his daughter, a faded and spineless spinster. Stella gathered he had labored under the delusion that she and this daughter were more or less contemporaries, whereas Miss Pérez was actually old enough to be her mother. But anyway, with six interested men at the table, not counting Drew Breckenridge, she thought quite a little progress should be made. She did not suppose Drew Breckenridge was really interested, though she had to admit she had seldom seen him in better form, and all the other men except Raoul Bienvenu, who, naturally, was too young to be able to say anything of the sort, kept telling him they had known his father and evincing great pleasure in his company; so his presence was no drawback, at least. As a matter of fact, a pretty good beginning was made when Mr. Dupré said that of course they should all support the opponent of the man Long picked for Governor Allen's successor, and the other men said that depended, just as Cousin Omer and Cousin Allain and Dr. Anconi had kept saying the day before. They got a little further than "that depended" this time. Dr. Anconi reminded Mr. Dupré that if Long's candidate won and they were on record as having opposed him, there would be no appropriations for highways for Vermilion Parish, and none of them would have any voice in the appointment of even a deputy sheriff or a schoolteacher. The appropriations and appointments were pretty important, Dr. Anconi reminded Mr. Dupré. And if, after they had wrangled and wrangled, all the anti-Long forces had been able to produce in the way of a candidate was a sacrificial lamb, the way they had in the last election, then it might be better to play ball with Long, after all. On the other hand, if the anti-Long forces found a real race horse——

This was quite interesting, after all, Stella decided, besides having the merit of advancing the conference. But, unfortunately, Cousin Myrthé did not seem to find it intriguing, nor did she seem to care whether the conference were advanced or not. She shook her finger playfully at Dr. Anconi and asked him what good he thought it would do to praise her salad if he spoiled their enjoyment of it, after all, by talking politics. She and Mrs. Dupré and Miss Pérez were not interested in sacrificial lambs and real race horses. They wanted to talk about the next Delphian program and the engagement of Sylvia Melancon to that Yankee oilman. As for Mrs. Fontaine and Stella, who were complete outsiders, it was imposing on them to go on and on like this.

Dr. Anconi inclined his head again, this time in the direction of Mrs. Fontaine as well as Mrs. de Hauterive, and the conversation at once turned on the Delphian program and the young L. S. U. professor who was to edify them on the Elizabethan drama. Mrs. Fontaine did not take a very large part in it. She looked lovely, she smiled graciously, she spoke charmingly; Stella had never known her grandmother to fail in doing all these things, and she did not believe that anyone else at the table had noticed that Grannie was not only quiet, which was her way, but rather withdrawn and very watchful. Grannie kept looking at Drew, who, Stella thought again, had never been in better form, and then at Raoul Bienvenu. Stella could not help looking from one to the other herself. They did not look in the least alike, except that they both had black hair. Drew was at least half a head the taller of the two and much the better-built; he carried himself better, too. He had bright blue eyes, instead of flecked brown ones like Raoul, and high handsome color, instead of olive-tinted cheeks. Then, there was the same marked difference in the shape of their hands and in the way they used them. Moreover, Drew was dressed in beautifully tailored pongee which, Stella knew, had been bought in London, and he wore his clothes casually, as he always did, while Raoul had on spotless white duck, shiny with starch, which had ready-made written all over it and which he wore more self-consciously than he had his seersucker; there was something about him that reminded Stella of a little boy who had got all slicked up for an important birthday party and who was afraid he might spill something on himself before he got through with the ice cream. And yet, in spite of all these points of dissimilarity between the two, Stella felt there were qualities which they shared. Magnetism? Was that the word? Yes, they both had magnetism. She knew that Drew had it, even though he did not make her feel it quite enough; and Raoul made her feel it a little too much. And what was that other word? Virility? Yes, that was it. They were neither of them sissies or softies. They both would love a girl hard, if they loved her at all. They both had what it took. Stella wondered if Mrs. Fontaine, who had known that for a long time about Drew, was finding it out about Raoul.

She had been careful not to tell her grandmother anything which could have been upsetting about the expedition of the day before—only that it had been so late before Raoul Bienvenu, the young lawyer Cousin Omer and Cousin Allain had gone to Abbeville to see, got back from Chênière-au-Tigre that they did not have much time for a conference then, so they had asked him to come to supper at Bois Fleuri the next night, instead. She had not said anything about the cluttered wharf where she had sat, without any skirt or socks on, swinging her legs over the edge of the dock, or about the nondescript little house with queer excrescences, set down in the middle of a huge vegetable garden, or about Mrs. Bienvenu and her calico dress and her turquoise earrings. She would have liked to tell Grannie about all this. She had come back to Bois Fleuri simply bursting with the need to talk to someone about the grand time she had had, after all, and how and why. But she had known it would not do. So she had gone to bed early and thought about it for a long while, instead, before she fell asleep.

In spite of her discreet silence, however, Grannie must have guessed something, for here she was, looking from Raoul to Drew and back again with veiled but troubled eyes. And when dinner was finally over, coffee and all, and the men, including Drew, who seemed quite pleased when the others asked him to join them, in spite of the local character of their meeting, had gone out on the front gallery to talk, Mrs. Fontaine took her needle point and withdrew to a distant corner of the parlor, a long way from the bridge table around which the other women had gathered. At least she had stayed by while Cousin Myrthé showed off her new mirror, the round one with the gold knobs on it, to Mrs. Dupré and Miss Pérez, and had put in just the right tactful word about its merits, at just the right moment, though Grannie knew as well as Stella—much better when you came down to it—that a mirror of that sort had no logical place in Cousin Myrthé's drawing room. But after that she had said she did not want to disturb their game—as if she had ever disturbed anyone!—and had stitched away on the chair seat, which was one of a set she was making for Stella's trousseau, as if the wedding were going to take place the next week, and as if all the chairs in the house of the man she hoped Stella would marry did not have priceless coverings already. That was because she was disturbed herself and did not want to show it, as Stella knew perfectly well. She had hardly touched the needle point before, in all the weary weeks they had already been at Bois Fleuri.

Stella could not think of anything much worse than an evening of bridge with Mrs. Dupré and Miss Pérez and Cousin Myrthé. She, herself, played a very snappy game, preferably for fairly high stakes and in mixed society; she hated the casual absent-mindedness which usually accompanied moneyless, feminine bridge—the viewpoint that no one could be expected to keep track of five-spots and that it really didn't matter if you forgot that the queen of diamonds had been played. She also hated the endless chatter, sinking from time to time into sordid gossip, that inevitably formed a running accompaniment to a game of this sort. She had always thought it was probably at a bridge table that the story of Lute, helplessly giggling as she stood beside the bridal bed of Olivier Fontaine and Bessie Rose, had first been repeated.

Well, there was no help for it, any more than there was for so many other things, so she must go through with it as well as she could. As she took her seat opposite Miss Pérez, whom she had drawn for a partner, she caught a sentence or two drifting in from the front gallery— "Well, boys, it boils down to this: do we want to buck him, or do we want to go along with him?"— "I don't know whether you've been back in Louisiana long enough to realize it or not, Mr. Breckenridge, but some of the parishes will be anti-Long, even if there's a corpse for a candidate. Caddo, St. Landry, the Felicianas, East Baton Rouge, De Soto, Iberville—that's yours, isn't it? Perhaps you'd like to try——"

There, she had caught herself just in time; she had been

on the point of revoking. She was a great one to criticize other people's bridge! But there had been something about the way Raoul Bienvenu had said "even if there's a corpse for a candidate" that had made her listen in spite of herself.

"I still don't see any sense in offering up Vermilion," someone on the front gallery was saying now. Stella was not sure who it was this time. That was Dr. Anconi's philosophy; so much, she had already gleaned. But she did not think it was his voice. Mr. Pérez' perhaps. While she was wondering, she was aware of Mr. Pérez' daughter glaring at her across the bridge table.

"I'm terribly sorry," Stella said. "I seem to have lost track of the bidding."

"Mrs. De Gruy opened with one club. I went to three hearts and Mrs. Dupré, to three spades. We're waiting for you."

"A small slam in hearts."

"Oh, Miss Stella, how *could* you? When I have to play it!"

"I think I've got it here for you. After all, you did give me a jump bid, and I have four hearts myself and a singleton ace of spades."

The small slam was there, no doubt of that. But Miss Pérez would probably miss it. Stella sat back in her seat, trying to give the impression that she was watching attentively and, at the same time, really trying to listen to the voices on the gallery.

"The leaders of those anti-Long parishes have just held a caucus in New Orleans, Mr. Breckenridge. Huey claims those Old Regulars hatched a plot to murder him. Of course, his claim doesn't amount to anything, even though he did say there were dictaphones hidden in the hotel room. If as many as five people get together anywhere, he always says there's a plot!"— "I'd like to know what would happen to this state if someone did shoot the son of a bitch."— "I can tell you what would happen. A Long man would be elected then for sure, because the only issue would be martyrdom————"

"Perhaps you could have made it, Miss Stella. But I couldn't. You see the clubs—after all, Mrs. de Gruy did open with one club. And my jump bid wasn't intended to signal for a slam—just to show general strength."

"I'm sorry. It's my fault, of course. I'll be more careful next time."

If only she could smoke a cigarette! That would help while she waited for some tidbit of gossip to be finished before the others picked up their cards, and while she sat back, as dummy, watching Miss Pérez missing every obvious chance of making her bid and listening, herself, to the fragments floating in from the front gallery.

"The people of Louisiana are going to remember Long's first great speech years after they've forgotten Bryan's 'Cross of Gold' and Theodore Roosevelt's 'Armageddon,' " Dr. Anconi was saying. "Why, in one short week it overturned the political structure of an entire state and became the focal point in the most spectacular campaign of this generation. I can quote it to you word for word, though I doubt if a single one of you needs to have me: 'We have more food in this country, more corn and wheat and beans and meal and meat, than we could eat up in two years if we never plowed another furrow or fattened another shote—and yet people are hungry and starving. We have more cotton and wool and leather than we could wear out in two years if we never raised another boll of cotton, sheared another sheep or tanned another hide—and yet people are ragged and naked. We have more houses than ever before in this country's history, and more of them are unoccupied than ever before—and yet people are homeless.' It's because Long can make speeches like that, and do it the way he does, that he's got and kept his strangle hold. Don't forget that, or anything that it means."

Certainly, she, herself, would never forget it, Stella thought, after hearing Dr. Anconi declaim it in that way. It had given her a big thrill, and a queer one—just as queer, in its way, as some of those other queer thrills that were making her so jumpy. Perhaps a cigarette would have helped. Not that there was any good reason why she should be jumpy. But she was. She wanted to go out on the front gallery herself. She didn't see any reason why a girl shouldn't sit in on a political discussion. She wondered what would happen if she simply laid down her cards and walked out on the front gallery and said, "I'm terribly intrigued by all this you're talking about, and I can only hear about a third of it, in the drawing room. Do you mind if I stay here? I won't interrupt or anything. I just want to listen." But she could see the way Dr. Anconi would look at her if she did that. And Drew. And Raoul Bienvenu.

"I really don't believe we'd better start another rubber.

I'm sure you all know the old saying that you can start one five minutes before eleven but not at five minutes after. If you do, it drags on for the rest of the night, with everyone scoring above the line. It's fortunate we weren't playing for money, isn't it? You'd have lost a lot, Stella. But then I don't suppose a young girl like you takes such a scientific game as bridge seriously. Estelle, do come over and join us! You don't have to finish that chair cover tonight, do you?"

While Mrs. de Gruy was speaking, Mrs. Fontaine folded up her work and came across the room, moving with the same composure and grace that her carriage had revealed when she was a young girl. Stella, suddenly jumping up and smoothing down the frills of her lemon-colored organdy, pulled out her own chair for her grandmother.

"Sit here, Grannie, do, and make up for all my sins of omission and commission. I've been the world's worst tonight. If the rest of you don't mind, I think I'll go out on the rear gallery and get a breath of air. It *is* hot, isn't it? And I seem to have picked up a headache somewhere."

"I'm afraid you sat bareheaded out in the hot sun too long yesterday, *chère*. If you'd only have worn a hat, as I suggested——"

There it was again, that eternal wrangle that never ended! And she couldn't explain that if she had worn a dozen hats, it wouldn't have made any difference. She couldn't say that the real trouble was that she hated everything about her life, from the fact that her father had been a coward and a cad and her mother a quitter to the fact that she couldn't be an opera singer, and that she was supposed to fall in love with a man she didn't want and who didn't want her. Yes, and now on top of all this, like the straw that broke the camel's back, was the fact that she did want to talk to Raoul Bienvenu, and he was out on the front gallery, answering, when Drew asked him, "Isn't this all rather venal?", "Oh, no, it's just what we learn to take in our stride."

Her grandmother did not try to stop her when she went through the center hall to the rear gallery. Mrs. Fontaine would have considered it an insult to her granddaughter to infer that she had the least idea of meeting anyone there, and besides, the conversation on the front gallery had at no time been more heated and intense than it was at this very moment. Stella did not suppose that Grannie believed in the headache, though, as a matter of fact, she did have one; but it was quite possible that Grannie did suspect the cigarette.

Stella had never lied about smoking, and, strictly speaking, she had never smoked surreptitiously; but knowing how offensive it was to Mrs. Fontaine to see her with a cigarette in her mouth, she tried to be reasonably tactful—to smoke mostly when Grannie was not around. And she did not care about smoking all the time, anyway—a package a day, more or less, the way some of the other girls she knew did. It was just that every now and then—and this was one of the times.

It was pleasant on the rear gallery—quiet and quite cool, considering that this was late June. In the soft light Stella could see the peaceful cows resting among the pecan trees, and beyond, the twisting, effulgent bayou. Stella inhaled the smoke from her cigarette and the scent that stole up from the garden with equal gratitude for both. A light breeze brought the scent to her insidiously. The crape myrtle was at the height of its bloom. Its massed loveliness was all around her. And the butterfly lilies looked chalk-white in this queer light. Too white for reality. Was any of this real? Some bullbats were singing raucously, and the sound grated against her jangled nerves. Then she heard a single mockingbird, drowsy at first and afterwards, for no reason at all, bursting into full-throated jubilance. It was at the same moment that she heard Raoul Bienvenu coming up behind her.

"After the severe way you spoke to me yesterday, I don't know whether it's safe for me to come out here or not. But it seems to be indicated."

"I don't get you. What do you mean, 'indicated'?"

"I know what you think I mean. I know that you're sure, in spite of all your noble efforts to repress me, that I'm going to grab at you, after all, and say, 'What about a little necking?' I'm sorry to disappoint you, if you weren't telling me the truth when you said you didn't go in for that sort of thing. But, as a matter of fact, I didn't come out here to make the obvious suggestion. I came out because it seemed to be tactful for me to withdraw from the conference about this point, and there didn't seem any place to go except the rear gallery. I could tell, from the way your grandmother looked at me during supper, that I'd be about as welcome in the drawing room as poison ivy."

"My grandmother looked at you in the same lovely way she looks at everybody."

"Oh, yeah?"

"Besides, if you think it would burn her up to have you

come into the drawing room, how do you think she'd feel about having you come out here?"

"I think we'd better pass that up for the moment. Especially, as I've kept trying to tell you, in spite of the affront such a statement must be to your vanity, the reason I came out here was to give the rest of the crowd a chance to decide whether they really want to run me for the State Senate. Of course, I know they like what I've done in the House, or they wouldn't have anything of the sort in mind. But what they've got in mind isn't necessarily conclusive. They've been talking, in a general way, about getting a campaign started—scheduling a series of trips through Iberia and Vermilion, with speeches and barbecues and so on. I thought it would be a little more gracious if I got out out of the way while they were getting down to cases."

"I see."

"But, of course, I might not have been quite so gracious if I hadn't been pretty sure they would decide to run me. I'd have stayed in the scrap and fought tooth and nail for the chance. Because I'd like very much to get into the State Senate. It's one step nearer the United States Senate."

"Is that where you really want to go?"

"Yes. By and by. I'm not in any great hurry. Just at present Louisiana looks pretty good to me. More specifically, Vermilion Parish. More specifically still, the rear gallery of Bois Fleuri, looking out on Bayou Teche. I'll admit, now that you've been so nice to me, that there was a secondary reason for my gracious withdrawal. I did want to see you again and I thought you might be out here, by this time."

"I don't see why you should have thought that."

"Well, I figured that the sort of bridge game you'd have to play inside would get under your skin, sooner or later. And that eventually you'd want to smoke a cigarette without having someone look at you, while you did it, as if you'd been the malefactor who led Mary Magdalene astray. And I also figured that in spite of everything you said, you wouldn't really mind seeing me again, and that this would be about the best place, all things considered. Was I wrong?"

"About which?"

"About any of it."

"Well, the bridge was pretty lousy. And I don't know that I could have brought up a swell line like that you just got off about Mary Magdalene. No, I'm damned sure I couldn't have. But that was the way I did feel."

"You're coming along nicely. You're two-thirds through already. But there's no reason why you should balk at the third answer."

"All right. The third answer is yes, I did want to see you again. Yes, I did think this might be the best place, all things considered."

"That's the girl. Now come clean. Tell the truth, the whole truth and nothing but the truth."

"I don't get you this time, Raoul, really. You work too fast for me."

"All right. If you don't get me, I'll have to show you. And mighty quick, too. I have to work fast. I haven't any choice. Because I've got to get back to the conference before the old boys in there change their minds after they get everything all settled, and you've got to get back to the drawing room before Grandma knows for sure that you've fallen for a common Cajun. Instead of just guessing it, the way she does now. Turn your face around, Stella."

Instinctively she hesitated. Something protective and primitive kept her, momentarily, from looking at him. But presently something still deeper, something still more essential, forced her to do so. When his kiss came down, hard and hot, on her mouth, she was ready for it. Then she knew that it was not only his kiss that she wanted, but everything. Everything for which he might ask, everything he might take without asking, everything she had to give, everything there was in life. It couldn't come too soon——

"Listen," he was saying. The kiss was over, leaving her so stabbed with ecstasy that she did not know when it had ended. "I do have to go back. So do you. If I don't, I'll lose my big chance. If you don't, you'll give yourself away. We can't either of us afford to do that. Not now. By and by it won't matter. You go back to the drawing room, and don't you dare look at me when you say good night, either. Just nod vaguely in my direction. But I'll come back here next Saturday night. That is, I'll come next Saturday unless something important turns up in the meanwhile that I need to do then. You'll have to get used to things like that. They happen all the time. But I'll let you know if I can't get here Saturday, and I'll come as soon as I can, anyway. In the vintage Ford. We'll go to a dance or something. Maybe just something. But if there's a party at Odd Fellows' Hall, with a prize waltz, we'll go to that, and if there's a *fais dodo*, we'll go to that. And anyway, we'll have time to talk. We'll have a chance to find out more about each other than we know now. Not that any of it matters too much, because we know the main thing. But it may come in handy, just the same. After a girl and a fellow have decided that they want to marry each other, they might just as well learn each other's middle names, too."

CHAPTER 25

STELLA HAD never before realized that a handy, common-place instrument like the telephone could suddenly embody both a temptation and a menace.

It was a temptation, because she was obliged to steel herself a dozen times a day from going to it and calling Raoul Bienvenu on her own initiative. There were thousands of things she wanted to tell him and to have him tell her, and though, of course, this could not all be done over the telephone, the groundwork could be laid for the questions that would be asked and the answers that would be made, when they next met face to face. Besides, it would mean a great deal merely to hear his voice, which was so gay and so resonant and so assured. But she had always despised girls who gave men the idea they were chasing after them, and she knew, without being told, that there was no surer way to convey this idea than to keep telephoning them. Besides, a chance remark of Drew's had given her a wholesome warning. Mrs. Fontaine had asked him, in Stella's hearing, if he did not think Julia Beal, a pale pious young woman who had made her debut several years before, was not a very fine girl, and he had said, oh, yes, but still she was the sort that called you up by Tuesday. This had given Stella a new sidelight on Julia's character, for she never would have supposed that Julia was bold enough to call up any man at any time, least of all Drew Breckenridge by Tuesday. But the information had supplied an additional check to her own natural impetuosity.

On the other hand, the telephone had become a menace, because every time it did ring, she was sure she would find that Raoul was calling her to say he could not take her out Saturday evening, after all. She kept listening for it, and when she found the call that came through was not for her, she felt a sharp pang of despair because she had not heard from him, and a great surge of hope because, since she had not, everything might still be all right about Saturday. There were no extensions to the telephone at Bois Fleuri—only one instrument very publicly placed in the hall. She sat on the rear gallery, where Raoul had come out and kissed her, listening for it, resolved to act very nonchalant and very much surprised when someone came and told her that Mr. Bienvenu of Abbeville wanted to speak to her, yet devoured with fear lest she might not have any opportunity to stage such a deceitful act.

She watched the mails with the same alertness with which she listened for the telephone, snatching up the letters as soon as they were brought in to see if there would be one among them with an Abbeville postmark. She thought it would be very natural, as well as very suitable, if Raoul would write to her and tell her that he loved her. He had not taken time to tell her when he came out on the rear gallery. He had merely made her admit she had fallen for him, and then he had grabbed hold of her, and after that he had said he would be back the next Saturday unless something else came up before then. Of course, there had been that one line about two persons deciding they wanted to marry each other and incidentally finding out each other's middle names, too. That was something to tie to. Enough. When men were driven to mention the word marriage, right off the bat, they were hard hit themselves, because they would really prefer to say everything else first, and that last, if at all. Stella had already gleaned that much from the conversation of her elders during the course of her brief but observant life. So she knew, without being told, that Raoul did love her. But she wanted to be told, just the same.

At the end of five days, in the course of which she had done nothing but listen for the telephone and watch for the mails, both vainly, she had grown so edgy that she was afraid not only her grandmother, but Drew Breckenridge, was beginning to notice that something was wrong with her. Mrs. Fontaine had made no further remarks about the expedition to Abbeville and none at all about the political conference which had been held at Bois Fleuri. But Stella knew, from her manner, that she was disturbed and that, sooner or later, this disturbance would take some unwelcome form, such as a suggestion that they had better return to New Orleans, with a very plausible pretext for doing so. Drew Breckenridge did not act in the least disturbed, but several times Stella caught him looking at her with veiled amusement, and she thought his ironic expression indicated that he suspected something. She had reached the point where she was almost ready to ask him to tell her, for the luvamike, what was eating him, when he astonished her by asking her to go for a ride with him.

"I thought I might trot over to Breaux Bridge this afternoon and see the characteristic old cottages there—the ones with the *garçonnières* on the top stories, and the separate staircase leading up to them. I believe some sort of an adaptation could be made of them, for town architecture. You haven't taken very much exercise these last few days. I should think you'd be tired of sitting on the rear gallery smoking cigarettes and staring into space. It isn't as if you cared for light literature or fine needlework. I'd be glad to have you come along, if you'd care to."

"I don't see why you bother to go and look at the Breaux Bridge cottages. You know you'll never adapt them or anything else to city architecture. You're too lazy. I don't believe you've darkened the door of your office for a year."

"I don't think a young lady who hasn't been further away from the drawing room than the rear gallery for the greater part of a week better talk to anyone else about being lazy. But do just as you like. I thought I'd enjoy celebrating the Glorious Fourth in some way, and there doesn't seem to be anything special going on in the vicinity except a barbecue enlivened by an oration from the sheriff. The prospect of such a treat as this left me absolutely unmoved. So I'm leaving about three for a ride and asking Mrs. de Gruy to have some supper saved for me, because I don't know exactly when I'll get home. Sometimes these exploring expeditions take longer than you think. As I said, I'd be glad to have you go with me on this one. Unless there's some special reason for all this watchful waiting of yours."

"What gives you the idea I'm doing any watchful waiting?"

"I don't know. But I've got it. You might tell me whether it is unfounded. Or not, just as you like."

"Drew Breckenridge, I think you're the most exasperating man I ever knew in my life. You'll get into trouble with some girl, someday, if you go on baiting and badgering every one you meet."

"I doubt it. It isn't as easy to get a rise out of most girls as it is out of you, Stella."

"Oh, for the luvamike! Three o'clock, did you say?"

She was still very loath to leave the rear gallery, but the mail was already in, unproductive again, and the telephone had not rung once all day. After all, she could not spend the rest of her life waiting around for Raoul Bienvenu to write to her or to call her up. It would serve him right if she *was* out when he did call. The thought buoyed her up while she went to get into riding breeches and a soft shirt. But the buoyancy did not last long. After all, it would not do her any good to serve Raoul right if she were going to be utterly miserable in the process herself.

Drew was waiting for her with the horses at the stile when she went down the walk between the beautiful ivy-wreathed trees which the first owner of Bois Fleuri had planted two hundred years earlier. He inquired, in that smooth way of his that simply prickled with sarcasm, whether he might have the honor of helping her mount, and after casting one glance at him, which she knew was not as annihilating as she would have liked to make it, she sprang easily into her saddle un-aided and started down the driveway at a smart clip. She would not speak to Drew at all, she decided, not once, the whole afternoon, unless he stopped baiting her and badgering her. Those were exactly the right words to describe what he did. And he was wrong when he said it was easier to get a rise out of her than out of most girls. There wasn't a girl living who wouldn't be burned up by the way he acted. She would show him just how insufferable she thought he was, and it would serve him right. But she had hardly reached her lofty decision about silence and example, when she saw an unmistakable car tearing up the driveway towards them. It was the vintage Ford. She reined in her horse quickly and turned to Drew almost apologetically.

"I'm sorry, Drew, but I don't think I can go to ride with you, after all. I think I have a caller and you see——"

"Oh, then of course— Good afternoon, Mr. Bienvenu. How are you?"

Raoul swung the car to the side of the driveway, jerked it to a stop, and leapt out of it, slamming the decrepit door. He appeared to reach the two riders in one bound.

"Good afternoon, Mr. Breckenridge," he said civilly. "Hello, Stella!— I don't want to interrupt your ride. I can't stay but a second. I just stopped by to say that I can't get here Saturday, after all. I'm on my way to Baton Rouge now. Huey Long called another special session of the Legislature at noon today."

"Huey Long? I thought Oscar Allen was governor."

"The hand was the hand of Oscar, but the voice was the voice of Huey. The session's called for eight o'clock tonight. That's the way Huey does. I haven't any more than enough time to get there and find out what's on the fire. I tried to telephone you, but something was the matter with the line. And I didn't want you to think I'd let you down."

"How long will the special session last?"

She could not make her voice sound natural. There was no use in trying. She was desperately disappointed about Saturday. But that was not the worst of it. She couldn't get off her horse, when Raoul had said he wasn't going to stop but a second; she couldn't show him how glad she was to see him, even if it were for just a second, when there sat Drew, looking first at her and then at Raoul in that suave noncommittal way of his which, she knew, was concealing more condescension and more satire. She couldn't have a kiss, she couldn't hear Raoul say he loved her, she couldn't have anything or hear anything. She didn't believe there had ever been a girl in the whole world who had had such rotten luck. If she had waited on the rear gallery just fifteen minutes longer, at least Raoul might have——

"Probably four days," Raoul was saying. She could not call his voice casual, exactly, because it was too intense. But certainly it betrayed none of the wretchedness and frustration which were devouring her; it sounded as if he were eager to be on his way to take part in a fight, and as if he considered his call on her as incidental as it was brief. "That's the length of time these sessions usually last. This is the fifth one that's been called like this since last November."

"But what *happens* at these special sessions?"

"Well, tonight forty or fifty bills will be introduced. All of them by the same man. That's Eddie Burke of New Orleans. The assistant attorney general will walk over and give them to him with Burke's name already on them. He'll send them up to the desk by a pageboy and that's all he'll know about what's in them. The rules will be suspended, so that the bills can all be referred to committee tonight, too. The Ways and Means Committee. No matter what they're about. Then, tomorrow morning the Committee will meet at nine and Long will be there. He'll take the top bill away from the chairman

—that's Eddie Burke again—and say, 'This is a good bill. It's to help the schools,' or something like that. It doesn't matter what. Nothing else. The bill won't be read; it won't be discussed. But the Committee will instantly give a favorable report on it, eleven members voting for it and two against it. I'll be one of the two voting against it."

"But if it's going to be passed anyway, what good does it do for you to go all the way to Baton Rouge to vote against it?"

"Oh, for God's sake, Stella!"

A pang went through her, deeper than those sharp thrusts which had pierced her as she sat waiting at the telephone. She knew that she had asked something which revealed almost unbelievable ignorance, and that she was being rebuked, like a stupid child. She saw Raoul glance impatiently from her to Drew, and then she saw the two men's eyes meet in a look of understanding. But she also saw, to her amazement, that there was nothing satirical about Drew's expression now —that it was kindly as well as comprehending. Then Raoul turned to her again.

"I can't stop to explain the political setup of this state, here and now, Stella. After all, the middle of the driveway on a hot afternoon isn't a very propitious place, and, as I have already told you, I'm in a frightful hurry now. But I'll try to explain as much as I can to you the next time I see you. I'll stop in on my way back from Baton Rouge, anyway. I'll wire or telephone when that'll be. Don't sit around waiting for me."

"Will you write to me in the meantime?"

She knew she ought not to say that, but she simply could not help it. The words were wrung from her by some force which she did not understand and with which she could not grapple. She dreaded to look at the two men, for fear she would see their eyes meeting again in a glance of masculine superiority and understanding. Yet she could not help doing that, either. And when she did, she saw that this time Drew was gazing straight ahead of him, as if he were intent on something at the other end of the driveway, and that Raoul was gazing straight at her, kissing her with his eyes, though he still spoke in a way that was brisk to the point of brusqueness.

"I'll try. But I don't have much time to myself. The Capitol's a madhouse and so is the lobby of the Heidelberg Hotel—that's where I'll be staying, by the way. Then, after I get to my room, there are generally two or three people there, drinking and jawing until all hours. I'm not much of a letter writer, either. But I'll try. So long, Stella. Good-bye, Mr. Breckenridge."

"Good-bye," Stella and Drew said together.

Raoul wrenched the door of his car open again, and turned it around, with almost incredible speed and no apparent difficulty, on the narrow driveway. Then the vintage Ford went scurrying out of sight, leaving a cloud of dust and a smell of gasolene in its wake. Stella sat very still on her horse. She was no longer impelled to look at Drew. She did not dare to. She knew that, if Drew badgered and baited her now, she would burst out crying. But Drew, after also sitting very still for a minute, did something entirely unexpected. He brought his horse close to hers, and then he leaned over and laid one of his hands over her hands, firmly and quietly and with infinite friendliness and tenderness.

"Would it help at all if you should tell me about it, Stella?" he asked.

Though she was so terribly in love with Raoul Bienvenu, she was nearer, in that moment, to loving Drew Breckenridge than she had ever been before in her life.

The next morning, while she was still loitering at the breakfast table, Drew came in with a sheaf of papers under his arm. Mrs. Fontaine always took coffee in bed, and Mr. and Mrs. de Gruy had both left the dining room. Drew spread the papers out on the table in front of her.

"I don't suppose you've ever really read a paper in your life," he said. "I know what Aunt Estelle's views are on the subject of shielding young girls from the sordid and sensational contents of the vulgar press. But now that you're interested in a rising young legislator, you might as well learn to follow his career through the easiest medium. I rode over to St. Martinville and got these for you."

"Oh, Drew, that was swell of you! Did you—was there any mail?"

"Listen, give that poor boy a break, as you say yourself. He didn't get to Baton Rouge until last evening. Then he had to go straight to a session of the House. He's at a committee meeting now. And someone is after him about something every minute of the day and most of the night, besides. He can't even eat or sleep in peace. He tried to tell you that himself yesterday. You'll get a letter sooner or later. It may not be very long and it may not sound very loving, but it'll come. Maybe tomorrow. Maybe the next day. Meanwhile, read these, and I'll get you some more this afternoon."

"Is there something about Raoul in them?"

"I didn't go through them with a magnifying glass to see. I thought you'd enjoy making a possible great discovery yourself. The roll calls on the most important bills get printed and, of course, his name will appear, when those come out, in the column headed: AGAINST. I don't know whether he'll do anything that'll make him hit the headlines or not. I rather doubt it, at least for the present. There's no doubt that he will by and by, though. I think you've picked a winner, Stella— What would you say to a little coffee for the tired horseman who brought the good news from Ghent to Aix?"

"Oh, Drew, I'm sorry! I supposed you'd had it before you started."

"You supposed right, too. But I could do with another cup now, while we look these over together."

He spread them out on the table between them. He had brought the bulldog editions of the *Times Picayune* and the *Tribune,* which were already in from New Orleans, the *Lafayette Daily Advertiser* and the *Baton Rouge Morning Advocate.* He and Stella looked at the headlines first:

SENATOR ACTS TO "PROTECT"
RELIEF CASH FROM POLITICS

LONG'S BILLS SEIZE ALL CITY'S TAXES
EMPOWER POLICE, FIRE BOARDS TO BORROW
FIX PENALTY FOR MISUSE OF RELIEF FUNDS

ORLEANS IN TWO PARTS,
UNLIKE GAUL IN 3,
LONG SAYS

LONG WIRES PRESIDENT
HE SEEKS TO CARRY OUT PROGRAM
PREVENTING MISUSE OF
MONEY APPROPRIATED
FOR RELIEF

ENTIRE PROGRAM GIVEN
COMMITTEE'S APPROVAL
IN LESS THAN AN HOUR

MEASURES PUT THROUGH AT SPEEDY RATE

TODAY WITH SENATOR DIRECTING ACTIVITIES
AND COMMENTING ON PLANS

FAR-REACHING
LOUISIANA "DICTATOR"
MOVES SEEN. GOVERNMENTAL EMPLOYE
MEASURE AND SCHOOL BILL ARE ON
LIST OFFERED BY LONG

"Why is 'protect' put in quotes, Drew?"

"Because there's nothing really protective about any of this. The term's used sarcastically. Read the first paragraph in George Vandervoort's article."

" 'Senator Huey P. Long celebrated Independence Day by convening Louisiana's Legislature in extraordinary session . . . for the principal purpose of stripping the city of New Orleans of the last vestige of local self-government.' "

Stella read it aloud. Then her eyes caught another caption further down in the column, and she read another paragraph:

" 'COPIES NOT AVAILABLE

Copies of the bill introduced . . . were not available. . . . While the bills were read only by title, the purport of many of them was obtained from various sources.' "

"That was what Raoul was trying to tell us, wasn't it, Drew? That hardly anyone would even know what was in the bills?"

"Yes. He'll tell you lots of things if you'll give him time. But the better you understand them—the fewer questions you have to ask—the better he'll be pleased. Read the text of the telegram Long sent to Roosevelt that's given in the *Tribune*."

" 'I am drafting an act, which a friend and political ally will introduce in tonight's session of the Legislature, to send to jail any person who may promise or threaten to use funds of the United States relief agencies for the purpose of affecting anyone's political attitude. Always in the vanguard for liberation and lofty ideals, Louisiana's leadership, in transforming your enunciation into law, will no doubt gladden your heart. I would thank you to wire the Legislature urging favorable action on this legislation, which will insure its enactment. Even though you should not wire, I shall none the less battle for your principle to the limit of my ability.' "

"Do you think the President will wire Senator Long, Drew?"

"I do not. Haven't you heard anything about the feud between those two?"

"No. Tell me."

He told her, simply but fully. She listened to him with rapt attention. Mrs. Fontaine, passing by the door of the dining room and seeing the two heads, one covered with crisp black hair, the other with tangled chestnut curls, bent so close to each other, smiled to herself and decided that perhaps everything was shaping for the best, after all. She suggested to Myrthé de Hauterive that orders should be given not to clear the table until after Drew and Stella had left the dining room. Myrthé gave the order, greatly thrilled herself.

When Drew went into St. Martinville to get the afternoon papers from New Orleans, *The Item* and *The States,* Stella went with him. This time Stella held up the fluttering sheets, so that he could see them as he steered the Cadillac slowly along.

SENATOR TO NULLIFY
POLITICAL EFFECTS
OF P. W. A. FUNDS IN STATE;
WILL HURL VENGEANCE
AGAINST STANLEY

"Who's Stanley, Drew?"

"The district attorney. He's fought Long from the beginning. Just like Raoul, only, of course, he's been able to do it on a bigger scale."

"Why haven't you been fighting him, too, Drew?"

"I hoped you wouldn't ask me that question."

"Why?"

"Because the answer doesn't do me any credit. I ought to have gone into politics long ago. The chance was there for me, ready-made. Those same old boys you've just met—

Anconi, Pérez, Dupré—were all ready to back my father in anything and everything he wanted. He was going to start by going as a delegate to the Constitutional Convention in 1913. And then he was drowned, as you know. That was just a few months before the Convention was held. Well, when I came back to Louisiana, five years ago, Anconi and all the others came over to Splendida to see me. I was glad enough to see them. But I wasn't ready to take off my shirt and get to work. If I had been, a good many things in this state might have been different."

"Couldn't you go to work now?"

"I might. I may. But Raoul's got a head start on me now. In lots of ways." He smiled whimsically. "As you're finding out, I'm rather a laggard," he said, "in politics as well as in love. The old Breckenridge stock is rapidly running to seed. Now my grandfather—and even my father— But putting politics aside, I thought, for once anyway, it might be rather original of a Breckenridge not to be a cradle snatcher. And then comes along young Lochinvar from out of the West, in a vintage Ford instead of on a trusty steed, and does the swiftest cradle snatching I've ever seen, right under my very eyes."

"He didn't come in a vintage Ford first, Drew. He came in a shrimp lugger. And it wasn't under your very eyes. That was the afternoon you wouldn't go to Abbeville."

"Another example of the way I've neglected both my obvious and my golden opportunities."

"But you don't mind, do you, Drew? I mean, you didn't really want to marry me yourself. You know you didn't."

"I didn't want to marry anybody, Stella. I still don't want to. I saw the mess my father made of his marriage. I was only seven when he was drowned and yet I'll never forget his wretchedness to the day I die myself. God! I think he was the most unhappy man I ever saw! And I know all about my grandfather's marriage—both of them, as far as that goes. I made up my mind, a long time ago, that I wasn't going to get caught, like my father, or cheated, like my grandfather. So I'm very grateful to you, my dear, for falling in love with someone else before your grandmother got really worried because I didn't propose to you. She had it all so nicely planned, I'd have hated to disappoint her. In fact, I'd have hated it so much that I might have taken the line of least resistance, after all, as I have about so many other things. You've saved me from a great deal."

"You're terribly unflattering, Drew."

"I could be just the opposite very easily. Now that I'm getting better acquainted with you, without any ulterior motive attached to the acquaintance, I'm beginning to find you quite an engaging young lady. Here, we didn't come out to talk this way. We came out to discuss politics. Let's get back to them, so you won't need an interpreter when Raoul's first letter comes in. There may be parts of it you'd be just as glad not to have me see. Listen, this editorial in *The Item* is good:

" 'Mr. Long assembles his so-called Legislature in its sixth extra session—or is it the eighth, ninth or tenth?— to receive some new dictation from him, doubtless to the further harassment of those he doesn't like, and the further sapping of self-government.

His designs have not been revealed to a suffering public, as this is written. Neither are they known to his willing servants in the Legislature. But they will doubtless appear in the news columns of this edition.

Whatever they are, nobody doubts that the revelations will be briskly adopted as handed down from on high.

The Dictator oddly chose the anniversary of the Declaration of American Independence for his latest performance in this line.

The Declaration of Independence is not a long document. It can be found in most encyclopaedias and books of American history. Louisianians should take a look at it.

They will find in it a statement of many, many grievances inflicted by a British king on his American subjects which were singularly like those that Mr. Long is imposing on the once-free people of Louisiana.' "

Drew and Stella read papers and talked politics all the rest of the afternoon and most of the evening. Raoul's first letter came the next day. It was written on official stationery, with a print of the silo-shaped Capitol rising on the side and, underneath, the words: Raoul Bienvenu, Vermilion Parish. The very sight of the envelope gave Stella a tremendous thrill, and the sheets of cheap bond paper inside, covered with heavy black writing that looked as if it had been dashed off at top speed with a soft pencil in the midst of various interruptions, were infinitely more exciting. Besides, the letter, itself, was longer than Drew had led her to hope, and it was satisfying in other ways as well, though, technically, it was not much more lover-like than Drew had said it would be. Stella thought it was the most wonderful letter she had ever received in her life.

Hello there!

We started off last night in a blaze of glory. I mean this literally. The session opened not only with fireworks but firecrackers. A whole pack of them was set off on one desk. Presently they were exploding on all the desks and in every corner. It sounded like machine-gun fire. Finally some one called out "All aboard," and the session was called to order for prayer while some of the crackers were still going off. That's what you'd call real reverence, isn't it?

I was wrong about the number of bills. There were only 26 introduced instead of 40 or 50. One of them puts all municipal employees of every character in every city, town and village of the state under a state-controlled and state-appointed "Civil Service Commission." No public employee of any Louisiana community can receive or retain his post without the warrant from this Commission.

Another law takes the right to collect its own taxes away from New Orleans, turning this duty over to the State Tax Collector. Still another makes it a penitentiary offense to use Federal funds or Federal jobs to seek to influence Louisiana voting. But an amendment one of our boys introduced to extend this to a similar use of state jobs or state funds was voted down 56 to 17.

I'm sorry I snapped at you when you asked me what the use was in voting, or even going to Baton Rouge at all, when I knew my vote couldn't do any good. Of course, you can't be expected to understand those things by intuition. The most obvious is that what my record shows now is also what is going to count in making it possible to pile up bigger and better records later on. But it's still more important that I, myself, should be able to feel that I've fought the incubus that's crushing out freedom in this state every step of the way. It's been a losing fight, but that isn't what matters most. What matters most is that I haven't given in. I don't mind playing politics where little things are concerned. I do it all the time, just like Dr. Anconi does. But it's different where big things are concerned. And didn't Disraeli, or someone like that, say that no politician should ever forget one with God can form a majority?

Look, this isn't the kind of letter I meant to write you at all. But there's an ungodly racket going on around me, and three men are trying to talk to me all at once. I'll do better when I see you. Which ought to be about Tuesday. So long!

R. B.

P. S. How did you happen to fall for me with the great Breckenridge available? He's a regular fellow and don't you ever get the idea that he isn't. I don't see. But then, I'm still too stunned to think straight about any of it. I'll confess to you now that I didn't suppose I had a prayer of getting that kiss, when I asked you to turn your face around. Have you got a lot more where that came from?

On Tuesday, the eighth, another letter came in. It was briefer than the first, but still better.

Dearest Stella: (That's the way I really ought to start in, isn't it?)

Let me be the first to tell you that a great and glorious speed record has been set in the history of legislation. The Senate Finance Committee has "considered" and favorably reported all 26 bills, one at a time, in a total of 20 minutes; just enough time to read the titles at top speed and take a vote on each. Now that this has been done, I don't know of anything that Huey will think needs to detain us here. He has begun to designate himself as Roosevelt's "aide and ambassador," so doubtless he feels he should give the President the benefit of his invaluable presence in Washington, now that he's smashed the last vestige of self-rule in Louisiana. I believe he'll shove off by plane within the next hour or two. That means you'll be seeing me almost as soon as you get this. I don't know of a dance anywhere in the middle of the week that we can go to, but we can go to the movies, or out along the bayou, just as you prefer. Me, I'd like the bayou. Don't forget I'm a fisherman's son. The water's my natural element. The law only came along later.

But after all, it isn't the order you get things in that counts. You're the latest development in my life, but you're the biggest.

I'm afraid I forgot to say it before, but I love you a lot, and I hope I'll always be able to make you happy.

Yours,

Raoul

It was after she had read this letter four or five times that Stella decided to speak to her grandmother. She knocked at Mrs. Fontaine's door, and, with her usual directness, went straight to the point.

"May I come in, Grannie? I want to see you."

"Certainly, *chère*. You know I'm always delighted to have you come to me."

"Well, I don't know. You may not be, when I tell you what I've come to say this time."

"I cannot imagine that you would ever have anything to say that would be upsetting, Stella. You are naturally very considerate."

She made room for Stella on the chaise longue where she was lying, moving aside her slender feet and indicating, with an affectionate gesture, that she wanted the girl to sit down beside her.

"I do try to be, Grannie," Stella said earnestly. "I'm glad you realize that. But still, you know we don't always agree. And I'm quite sure we're not going to this time— Do you remember Raoul Bienvenu, the young lawyer from Abbeville who came to dinner a week ago Saturday?"

Mrs. Fontaine lay very still for a moment before she answered. Then she spoke with a calmness that was obviously artificial.

"Yes, Stella. I remember him."

"He came out on the rear gallery for a few moments while the political conference the other men were holding was going on. Something came up that made him think it would be tactful if he left the conference for a short period. And I had gone out there to have a smoke. You know I left the drawing room to recover from that lou— from that dreadful bridge game. So we happened to see each other out there, and we had quite an interesting talk. Of course, I had seen him the day before, in Abbeville."

"Yes, Stella."

"Well, he said something about coming back to take me out to a dance that next Saturday night, if nothing more important came up in the meantime. But something more important did come up. Huey Long called a special session of the Legislature and Raoul Bienvenu had to go. He stopped in on his way to Baton Rouge to tell me. Drew and I were just starting out for a ride and met him in the driveway, so he didn't come up to the house. But I've had two letters from him since. I think he'll be here this afternoon or to-night."

"Of course, you are old enough to receive callers now, Stella, though with Drew here——"

"Drew's being here doesn't make a particle of difference, Grannie dear. And Raoul isn't coming here to call. He's coming to take me out. So that we'll have a chance to talk."

"But surely you could talk as much as you chose on one of the galleries or in the drawing room!"

"No, we couldn't, Grannie. That's just the point. When two people want to talk to each other, *really*, they don't like to have other people coming and going around them all the time and interrupting them when they are right in the middle of important sentences by offering them drinks, or saying, 'Are you related to the family by the same name in St. Martinville?' Or anything like that. They like to be alone. That is, alone with each other. They like to *feel* alone with each other."

"But, *chère*, how can you possibly have anything of importance to say to this young man? No doubt his legal attainments and his political progress are very commendable. Indeed, I have gathered that your Cousin Allain and your Cousin Omer think well of him on both those counts. But neither the position of a rural lawyer nor a local legislator carries any cachet with it. And you have had almost no chance to judge his personality. You have seen him only three times. Very briefly, if I understood you correctly, each time."

"Yes, Grannie, you did understand me correctly. But each of those three times was important. Especially the second one."

"Stella, I shall have to confess that you are disturbing me very much, after all. Are you trying to tell me that you imagine you are seriously attracted to this young Cajun?"

"No, Grannie. I mean, I don't imagine it. I know I am. It doesn't necessarily take long to find out a thing like that. Does it?"

Mrs. Fontaine made no direct answer. When she did speak, the veneer which constituted her composure showed signs of cracking.

"I shall not forbid you to receive Mr. Bienvenu, Stella, since apparently you have already agreed to do so. But I must ask you to see him in this house, and not to go with him, or meet him elsewhere. I feel very strongly about this."

"So do I, Grannie. Very strongly."

"You mean that you would go with him against my expressed wishes?"

"Yes, Grannie. I'm sorry, but that's just what I should do, if you expressed any such wishes. I hoped you wouldn't, when you heard how important it was to me. And I didn't want to do it on the sly. But I'm going to do it anyway."

"Stella, surely you wouldn't——"

"Grannie, you don't want to lose your granddaughter as well as your daughter, do you?"

Mrs. Fontaine pressed her lips together and looked away without answering. For years it had been understood that Marie Céleste's name should never be mentioned. Stella leaned forward and took her grandmother's hand.

"Grannie, I didn't mean to hurt you; I didn't want to say anything you would think was cruel. Raoul isn't going to be drowned and I'm not going to become a Carmelite. But you might lose me just the same, if you tried to come between us. And then you and I would both be terribly unhappy. We'd miss each other. We need each other. But just now I need Raoul more than anyone else in the world, even you. If I had to make a choice, that would be the way I'd make it. And it would be the right choice, too. If you don't believe me, ask Drew."

"Ask Drew?"

"Yes. He knows all about it, and he approves very highly. I'll see if I can't find him. If I can, I'll ask him to come and talk to you. Maybe you'll feel better when he's done that. Anyway, I'm going down on the front gallery to watch for Raoul."

CHAPTER 26

THIS TIME her wait was a short one. She had hardly settled herself in the swinging seat, with the supply of newspapers that Drew had brought her that morning, when the vintage Ford came bucking into sight. She ran down the steps and across the yard to the stile, jumping from the further side of this into the driveway. Raoul had barely time to put on the brake, before she was in beside him.

"Oh, Raoul, I'm so glad to see you! I'm so thankful you're here! Let's get away quick before anyone stops us!"

"But, hell! What makes you think anyone is going to try to stop us?"

"I just do, that's all. And I couldn't bear it, if it happened."

"All right. Where do you want to go?"

"Out on the bayou, just as you said. I'd rather do that, too, than go to the movies. Can you manage a pirogue?"

"I can, but I'm not going to tonight. A pirogue is the trickiest thing on earth, except perhaps a girl. I never try to attend to both at the same time, and tonight I want to attend to you. Besides, the bayou's about the most public place we could possibly choose. I want to see you alone, and I thought that was your idea, too. I said we'd go *along* the bayou, not *on* it. Do you care which direction we take? If you don't, I've got a place in mind."

"I'd like to go there, wherever it is."

"All right. But I think first, though, we might better go to De la Houssaye's Restaurant in New Iberia and snatch us some supper. Otherwise, we'll both be starving to death before the evening's over. But right now———"

They were nearing the end of the driveway. He swung the car to the side of the road, in the swift easy way he had, and shut off the engine. Stella looked at him inquiringly.

"What are you going to do here?"

"I thought I'd kiss you, if you don't mind. After all, we're out of sight, both from the house and the highway. I don't know that we'll find another place as propitious until we get to the grove where we're going. That's a good many miles from here. And what with supper coming in between, and everything, it'll be quite a while before we get there."

He put his arm around her. It encircled her easily, as if it were meant to fit around her waist, and this time she lifted her face without the asking and leaned back, grateful for support. How could she resist an embrace which encompassed her so naturally and so inevitably? *Why should she?* She felt as if, from the beginning of time, she had been waiting for it and preparing for it. As it became less tender and more urgent, her strength seemed to flow from her, but this did not matter, because she was engulfed by Raoul's. His strength and his love, the love she no longer needed to have him put in words———

But afterwards, when she was no longer in his arms, she wanted to hear his voice and he was silent. He had started the car and was driving rapidly along again. She waited eagerly and then anxiously for him to say something to her. When he did not, when he continued to keep staring straight ahead of him with a strange, tense expression around his mouth, while he drove faster and faster, she finally spoke, almost timidly, herself.

"Drew brought me all the papers, Raoul, beginning with the morning of the fifth. He showed me how to read them. I never had read a newspaper before, that is, not really. But Drew said I'd have to learn to follow the career of a rising young legislator, through them—that it would be the easiest way. He's been awfully kind. He knows all about us. He asked me if it would help, to tell him, the other afternoon when we all met in the driveway. And it did. I hope you don't mind."

"No, I don't mind. But your grandmother is going to mind a lot, Stella."

"I've told her, too. Yes, she did mind. She tried to make me promise I wouldn't come out with you today. That's why I wanted to get off so quickly. I was afraid she'd find some way to stop us, just as I told you."

"Perhaps it would have been just as well if she had."

"Oh, Raoul, how can you say such a thing!"

"Because it's true. You don't know yet what you're letting yourself in for, falling for a fellow like me."

"What am I letting myself in for?"

"Loneliness. Uncertainty. Insecurity. Disillusionment. Misunderstanding."

"I don't think we'll ever misunderstand each other, Raoul."

"No, we won't misunderstand each other. That is, I hope we won't, though we can't be sure. But everyone else is going to misunderstand us. Except a few regular fellows like Drew Breckenridge, perhaps. It'll wear us both down, being misunderstood the way we will be. It'll make me mad and it'll make you unhappy. You'll fight against it, just as I will, but you'll be heartsick while you're doing it. And I won't be around to help you."

"Couldn't we—couldn't we get married now? Then you would be around to help me."

"No, I wouldn't. I'd be away half the time, going to special sessions that Huey calls, and chasing votes from one end of the parish to the other. And, of course, we couldn't get married now. Do you think I'd take you to Abbeville, and let you start light housekeeping in a tenement over a drug-store, which is all I've got to offer you at the moment?"

"I wouldn't mind."

"You think you wouldn't, because you haven't the first idea of what it would be like. But you'd find out pretty damn quick and it would be an awful shock to you. You'd mind when you woke up and found yourself with breakfast to get on a two-burner stove you didn't know how to handle, and dishes piling up in a small iron sink faster than you could wash them, and towels and shaving things all over a messy bathroom, with no one but yourself to pick it up, and a man's clothes strewn from one end to the other of a bedroom you couldn't call your own."

"That would be only part of it. And besides, none of that would last long. I could learn to handle the stove and wash the dishes. You seem to take it for granted I'm a complete nitwit. And I wouldn't mind tidying up a messy bathroom. I don't believe it would be any worse to see a man's shaving things around than the spilled powder and crumpled Kleenex and the wet stockings and the towels stained with rouge you have to see if you share a bathroom with another girl. You know I could learn, and you know I wouldn't mind learning. You're only saying all this to discourage me."

"I'm only trying to make you face facts. Incidentally, you have a great way of leaving part of a question un-answered, or ignoring part of a comment."

"No, I haven't. I answered all of your question the other night, when I got around to it. And I'll take up the last part of your comment now. I wouldn't mind having a man's clothes strewn from one end of the bedroom to the other, if they were your clothes. And I wouldn't mind not being able to call it mine. I'd be very proud and very happy to call it ours."

"Well, that's very nice of you. But maybe we'd better postpone our bedroom conversation until a little later in the evening. We seem to be just about at De la Houssaye's Restaurant."

Stella had thought it would be great fun, having supper with Raoul at a restaurant, when he first suggested it. Though it was true that what she really wanted was to get off alone with him, she did not mind too much waiting to do that, once she knew she had made good her escape from Bois Fleuri. She visualized a little table for two in a secluded corner, almost as a preview of the table which they would have in their own little home, with Raoul facing her across it, not so far away that they couldn't reach out and take each other's hands, or lean over and kiss each other, whenever they felt like it. She thought they might manage some handholding, even at De la Houssaye's Restaurant. But they were not inside the door, before a big burly man came up to them, hailing Raoul very heartily, saying, what the hell, and asking the details of everything that had just happened at the special session in Baton Rouge. Raoul gave them to him, standing on the steps, and he apparently forgot all about Stella while he was doing it, for it was only very tardily that he presented the man to her as Mr. Martin Tassin, a very good friend of his, who owned the service station on the corner and went in for real estate on the side.

Mr. Tassin nodded vaguely in Stella's direction and said he was pleased to meet her, and then he went straight on talking about Huey Long's typically spectacular arrival from Washington by airplane, accompanied by five bodyguards, just fifteen minutes before the special session began, and about the swell speech Mason Spencer had made, and about the bill depriving the district attorney of Orleans Parish of the right to name a single assistant or other employe in his office. While Raoul was still talking with Mr. Tassin about all this, three other men came up and hailed Raoul with just as much heartiness as the firstcomer. They did not seem to see Stella at all, for they insisted that Raoul must come in and have supper with them, and again he, himself, apparently remembered her rather tardily, for it was not until he had accepted their invitation that he said, oh, he had Miss Stella Fontaine of New Orleans along and of course she'd have supper with them, too. The men echoed, oh, of course, but Stella thought the heartiness in their voices fell away quite noticeably as they said it, and after they had installed her at a table for six in the very center of the room, because that was under the big ceiling fan, they went over to the bar to get a drink. Evidently the bartender was also a friend of Raoul's, for he, too, hailed the young lawyer very heartily and said everything was on the house and what would they have and what about Mason Spencer's speech?

Raoul came back to the table for a minute and told Stella she could come over to the bar, too, if she liked. But she flushed a little and said no, she didn't know why exactly, but she had always hated the way a girl looked, standing in front of a bar with a lot of men around, or even without any men around; she would rather stay where she was; she didn't mind waiting. Raoul nodded approvingly and said, that was all right; he had always hated to see a girl at a bar, too; only he hadn't wanted her to feel left out in the cold; he would bring her whatever she'd like to drink while she was waiting for him to come back, which he would as soon as he could. What about a Sazerac? She flushed again, more deeply this time, and said she'd like a glass of wine very much, with the crabmeat, when they got to it, but that she'd never had a Sazerac and that, if he didn't mind, she'd just sit and smoke. He nodded again, still more approvingly, and then he put his arm across the back of her chair in a way that made her feel almost as if he had put it around *her* again, and whispered to her.

"I don't believe it was such a hot idea of mine to come here, after all. I was just thinking what a relief it was to be away from that bunch of trained seals, snapping fish off their noses, up at Baton Rouge, and having you to myself. Then I had to run into this bunch. But it can't be helped now. You don't mind, do you, Stella?"

"No, I don't mind," she said valiantly. She wouldn't have been able to speak with such valiance if it hadn't been for his arm around the back of her chair.

"You're a nice, cheerful little liar," he whispered back. "I hand it to you, Stella."

It was because he had praised her, instead of rebuking her as he had done the week before, that she found the courage to carry on through supper the way she did. Raoul went back to the bar, and, while he was there with the other men, having another drink and talking about the possible ouster of Mayor Walmsley, she shifted her seat to the head of the table. When they finally all came back, after a third drink, she was installed there with the air of a youthful but serene and capable hostess. It was she, from then on, who indicated to the waitress that a plate should be changed or a glass filled, and who directed and controlled the progress of the meal generally. Several of the group were rather high by this time; evidently the three drinks they had taken did not represent the beginning of their evening's libations. And they were hardly settled, when they were joined by one more congenial spirit, who was even worse for wear. A rumor that Raoul was at the restaurant had reached Allain de Gruy, whose house, which gave such an illusion of remoteness and seclusion, was actually almost next door. He had not heard about Stella, and he burst into raucous laughter when he saw her, and made a jocose remark which would never have passed his lips if he had been sober. Stella flushed again, but she answered him without any reference to his inexcusable vulgarity and with the same complete courtesy and composure with which she had ignored the hilarity of the others.

"We're just starting supper, Cousin Allain," she said. "Why don't you take the place at the foot of the table—the one that's still vacant? You see I haven't any host, and I think it would be so suitable if you'd act as one for me. That would make this a real family party. Thank you— Mr. Tassin, when Cousin Allain came in you were talking about the repeal of the law giving the state charge of the W. P. A. funds. Now that we're all nicely settled, won't you go on?"

Mr. Tassin went on, feeling a little shamed and considerably sobered by the episode which had just taken place. Damn it, that must have been hard on a young girl like this—a young lady, he would say. Her presence here in their midst was not quite clear to him yet, but he was ready to tell the world that wherever she was, and no matter why, she would be able to manage. He resumed his discussion of the diversion of the W. P. A. funds, and the other men joined in. Stella did not try to obtrude on the conversation at all, but every now and then she made a brief remark which showed that she was following it with interest and, for the most part, with at least partial understanding. She saw Raoul looking at her with pleasure when she quietly called the waitress's attention to the fact that Mr. Tassin needed some more butter, and with unconcealed pride when she commented on the item in Governor Allen's message saying that the session was called to enact legislation not only on certain specified measures but also on "any other object which might be especially enumerated in any supplemental proclamation which I might send to the legislature during the said session."

"That would have made it possible to bring up *anything* additional Huey Long wanted brought up, wouldn't it?" she said. "I thought it was terribly clever, when I read it. I thought the editorial on 'Back to Bondage' in the *Times Picayune* this morning was very good, too. Didn't you, Mr. Tassin?"

Mr. Tassin, giving her the tribute of real attention, admitted that the editorial in question had escaped his notice, and Stella, inwardly quaking but outwardly still quite collected, gave him the gist of it. After that, the going grew easier and easier all the time. She found herself talking about Mason Spencer's speech herself, unself-consciously and earnestly, along with all the others; she liked the line that ran, "Before the sap goes down this fall, everyone of these bills will be declared unconstitutional by some high court." She could not help feeling that there was something prophetic about this, she said.

"I had the same feeling in April," Raoul broke in, "when he spoke against the bill giving Long the sole right to appoint all the future polling commissioners. Of course, it's something just to see a huge man like that heave himself to his feet and lumber over to a microphone. It gives anything he says the effect of a pronouncement, from the outset, and this becomes more and more marked as he goes on. This time he said with dreadful distinctness, 'When this ugly bill is boiled down in its own juices, it disfranchises the white people of Louisiana. I am not gifted with second sight, nor did I see a spot of blood on the moon last night. *But I can see blood on the marble floors of this Capitol, for if you ride this thing through it will travel with the white horse of death.* In the pitiful story of Esau, the Bible teaches us that it is possible for a man to sell his own birthright. But the gravestones on a thousand battlefields teach you that you cannot sell the birthright of another white man.' I'll never forget the silence that came before the applause when Mason Spencer stopped. It was as if the galleries had not only heard the words he spoke, but as if they had seen his great fingers writing in giant letters at the same time, and as if the crowds were still looking at those letters of flame on the immense blank wall. Of course, almost the next moment, the bill was passed by a big majority and became a law. But I tell you my own blood ran cold for the next hour. It still does when I think about the incident."

Aside from the thrill that Raoul's recital gave her, which was very great in itself, a warm glow of gratitude suffused Stella because he had told the men who were listening to them that he had the same feeling she did and because he gave her story significance by telling a similar one. Now that he had filled her with self-confidence, she redoubled her efforts to deal competently with the supper party, and her success became more and more marked. And as a crowning triumphal touch, she managed to convey the impression that

she was eager to have them linger over their small blacks
and their brandy, instead of betraying any sign of her inner
restiveness before they had swallowed their ice cream, as
she kept fearing she might do. It was Raoul who spoke the
word that finally brought the gathering to a close, just as
she had kept hoping it would be, holding fast to the hope
even amidst waves of despair.

"Stella and I were on our way to Jeanerette when we met
you. We were just going to snatch a sandwich here and then
cruise along. If we don't get started, it will be too late for
us to see anyone by the time we get there. So I'm afraid we'll
have to be off."

"Nonsense! You're all coming over to my house now.
We'll have a few drinks in the pavilion. I'll telephone your
grandmother that you're staying with me, Stella, or you can
telephone, yourself, just as you like. You'd better get to bed
before it gets much later. The rest of us will probably make
a night of it."

She was not quite sure just what she ought to say. Perhaps
that would be what Raoul would want her to do—to spend
the night at Cousin Allain's and go to bed so that she would
be out of the way, now that he had met these men. He cut in
quickly, answering for her and slipping his arm through hers
as he did so.

"The rest of you can make a night of it if you want to.
But I've got to get on to Jeanerette. I'm counting on Stella to
keep me company, and her grandmother's counting on me
to get her back to Bois Fleuri at something like a reasonable
hour. I'm sure Stella isn't going to let me down, and I'm
not going to let Mrs. Fontaine down. But I'm sorry we have
to hurry off like this. It's been great seeing you all. Hasn't it,
Stella?"

"Yes. I've enjoyed every minute of it."

How could she help playing up to him when he included
her like that? She didn't want to help it. She wanted to do
her share; she would have wanted to, even if that would
have meant starting back to Bois Fleuri, after all—even if
this had been all there was to the evening. She had conscientiously kept her eyes away from the big clock hanging
so conspicuously on the wall; she had tried not to listen to
its ticking. But she knew that they had been at De la Houssaye's Restaurant for a long time, that it was getting late,
and that Raoul had to be up very early in the morning. It
was also true that, if she weren't home by a reasonable time,

her grandmother would worry—that is, more than she was worrying anyway. So Stella had been thinking that perhaps it would be better if they did go right back to Bois Fleuri. She had been thinking that perhaps she, herself, ought to suggest it. And now Raoul had taken everything out of her hands. She didn't have to make any decision herself. She wasn't going to be cheated out of that precious time with him, after all. They were safely back in the car again by themselves, they were speeding south, and Raoul was looking at her with affectionate approval, not tempered by discretion, as the pride and pleasure he had revealed in the restaurant had been, but open and glad and uncontrolled.

"Well, you certainly have all the makings of a politician's wife, and then some. You can give as much credit to Drew Breckenridge as you like. I'm not begrudging him any that's coming to him. But he couldn't have taught you if you hadn't been an apt pupil. It makes me feel like thirty cents to think how I called you down, that day in the driveway. I'll say it again, Stella: I have to hand it to you. You were simply swell all through supper. Everyone of those men will be your friend for life now. And what's more, they'll be mine too— You're not tired, are you?"

"No. Why?"

"Because, no matter what your grandmother's counting on, we're going to be pretty late getting home, after wasting all that time. Well, it wasn't wasted; it was darned well spent. But it's gone right on fugiting, just the same."

"Are we really going to Jeanerette?"

"Almost. At least, that was my idea. There's a plantation this side of there, where the house has burned down. The place has been deserted quite a long time. But the road through the allee is still passable, and leads to another one that goes along by the bayou—one that used to connect the warehouse with the quarters. There's a grove on the landside of it and it's very pleasant there. I thought we could get out and sit under the oaks. That is, if you'd like to."

"Yes, I'd like to."

She tried to say it quietly. She tried to suppress the tumult that was bursting the bounds of her heart and penetrating to the uttermost parts of her being. But though she could still control her voice, she could not control the inner turmoil. When Raoul spoke to her again, she knew she might as well stop trying, since by now the very sound of his voice sent little forking flames all through her. When next he touched her, she knew these flames would almost consume her.

"You look lovely, Stella," he was saying earnestly. "I never thought much about yellow, as a color, until I saw you wearing it. I'd thought of blue and green and rose and violet, but not yellow. I've always liked that line of Israel ben Moses that says blue is not merely a color; it is a mystery. Now I'm going to paraphrase him and say yellow's not only a color; it is a glory. It's *your* color—bright and warm and very, very vital. You wear it a lot, don't you?"

"Yes, I wear it a lot. I'll wear it all the time, if you want me to."

"If you did that, perhaps it wouldn't seem quite so wonderful to me. But I'd like a chance to find out." He was speaking less earnestly, and he laughed a little and fingered a fold of her skirt. She could feel his hand against her knee, through the light fabric, as he did it, and the forking flame leapt and spread, as she had known it would, though his touch, now, was almost as light as his voice.

"Do you know this is actually the first time I've seen you fully clothed?" he asked almost teasingly. "We're rather reversing the usual order of things, that way. First I see you in shorts and sneakers. Very little left to the imagination. Next I see you in an evening dress where all the material there was to spare had evidently been used up in the skirt. Next I see you in a shirt and breeches. Very boyish at first glance. Considerably less so, if you look a little closer. Well, now, here we are alone at last, as they say in the movies, and you're wearing shoes and stockings and a real dress and everything. That is, I suppose there's everything."

"Yes, there is."

"Well, I don't think you have on any too much, Stella. I think perhaps it's better this way for now."

"I want it to be just as you want it."

"I know you do, honey. You're wonderful about everything. But you don't wholly see my side yet. I've got to try to make you."

She waited, expecting him to talk about it right away. Instead, he asked a question that seemed to her wholly irrelevant.

"Is there anything that means a lot to you, Stella? Not about being in love. I understand how you feel about that. But in the sense politics do to me. I haven't had a chance to find out yet. That was one of the things I thought you might tell me tonight, besides your middle name."

"My middle name's Lenoir. Officially I am Estelle Lenoir Fontaine Second. I'm Grannie's namesake, you see— Yes, there is something I care about. I don't know whether I care as much as you do about politics, but I think so. It's music."

"What kind of music?"

"All kinds. But especially I like to sing. I've been begging Grannie for years to let me study for opera."

"The opera! Can you sing well enough for that?"

"I think I could, if I were taught."

"Will you sing for me? After we get into the allee?"

"Yes. What do you want me to sing?"

"Anything you like."

"But I want it to be what you'd like, just as I do about everything."

"I don't know enough about music to choose, Stella. You'll have to help me learn about that, just as you're learning about politics."

"Would you like me to sing the song from *Louise*—the one Mary Garden sang in her first great hit?"

"Yes, very much."

They had reached the old allee of oaks which had once led to the great house of a proud plantation. Now the place was full of shadows and silences. The house was gone; the road was rough with ruts. They went down through the trees slowly and without speaking. When they were out of sight and hearing of the highway, Raoul stopped the car.

"Sing to me now, honey," he said.

Stella clasped her hands tightly together in her lap. Somewhere, deep within her, a fervent little prayer took form and finish as it rose and merged into the first bars of her soaring song. "Please, God, let him love my singing! It's part of me and I want him to love all of me. And this is the song that seems made on purpose for me to sing to him. It says what I've been trying to tell him and haven't known how. Please, God!" That was what she was saying inside, with all her heart and soul. But the impassioned words that poured from her lips were different:

> *"Depuis le jour où je me suis donnée*
> *Toute fleurie semble ma destinée!*
> *Je crois rêver sous un ciel de féerie,*

L'âme encore grisée de ton premier baiser!"

The song came to an end. Stella sat still, her hands still tightly clasped in her lap. It seemed an eternity before Raoul spoke to her. She was beginning to be afraid she had failed. Then he did speak, and his voice was so husky that she knew the reason he had not spoken before was because he could not.

"I should think you could sing," he said. The words, as he pronounced them, did not seem inadequate. They told her everything she needed to know. But after a moment he cleared his throat and went on with mounting vehemence, "God! What a song! What a *voice!* Stella, you've got something there. There isn't anything you won't be able to do with it!"

"Grannie won't let me do anything with it. And besides, now——"

"Besides, now—— You've got to do something with it. We've got to think."

He switched on the engine again and started the car. The shadows and silences still enveloped them. The road was still very rough, but as they neared the end of it, they saw a glow coming gradually over the water, which spread and crept in among the oaks. Then a lighted steamer swung into sight above them on the bayou. It was not noisy, but it made a cheerful, purposeful sound as it swept along, and laughter drifted down from its deck. A boy was playing a banjo, and someone else was singing. Evidently the people aboard it were happy, and there were surprisingly many of them. Their forms seemed to detach themselves from the form of the ship, as it came along, and to rush forward, in friendliness and understanding, to meet the watchers on the shore. Raoul got out of the car and held out his arms to Stella. When he had lifted her down, he continued to stand with them around her, holding her close. But his eyes were still on the boat. He did not speak to her until it was almost past them.

"Look," he said at last. "That was the river boat for New Orleans. It started from New Iberia, on this bayou, the Bayou Teche. But most of its passengers didn't start there. They started from little places, on little bayous. They took small luggers and even pirogues to get to it. Now they'll go on Bayou Teche to Berwick Bay and Morgan City, and from there through the canals to Bayou Lafourche and Lockport. When they get to New Orleans, they can still go on, if they want to. They can go across the Gulf to the West Indies, to Mexico and Central America and South America. They can go on and on, as far as they like. There'll always be another boat, a bigger and better one, that will take them further. Do you understand, Stella? *You can go anywhere in the world from a bayou!"*

He drew her still closer to him. "I'm glad that boat came by just now," he said. "It helps me to tell you what I've been trying to explain. Men and boats are alike somehow. I've always thought so. I've always felt that boats were alive. Well, men like me, who come from very humble beginnings —from very little places—can build on their beginnings; they can go to bigger and bigger places. And by and by they reach the point where they can go anywhere in the world. I've just begun to build; I've just begun to go places. But some day——"

He looked away from her again, down the bayou. The radiance released from the river boat, which had overspread the water and crept among the oaks, was fading fast. Presently there would be only the shadows and the silences again.

"I know the way you feel," he said. "I know you want to build with me. I know you want to go with me. And I want to have you. You don't know how much. You think you do, but you don't. And I've got to save you all I can. I've let you in for enough already. So I can't save you from much. But I can save you from some. Of what you'd rush into if I'd only let you."

"Won't you let me rush into anything, Raoul?"

"I've already let you rush into an engagement. That is, I suppose we are engaged. Aren't we?"

"I—I hope so."

"All right. I hope so, too. So we are. You can tell the world we are, if you want to. I'm going to tell a few people myself, right away. My father and mother, for instance, because it wouldn't be fair to them if I didn't, and for a very different reason, Allain de Gruy. I told you there would be misunderstandings that would make me mad. I thought, for a minute this evening, that I should probably kill him right where he sat, and it's just as well not to risk anything like that again. I haven't anyone else on my mind to tell at the moment. But the more people you tell, the better I think it will be. When everyone knows, it will give you a chance to find out whether you can stand hearing your friends in New

Orleans say, '*My dear*, have you heard about Stella Fontaine? She's fallen for a common Cajun from Abbeville. His father's just barely able to read and write. His sister's married to a streetcar conductor and lives on Annunciation Street. If she marries him, she'll be cut off from everyone in her own crowd, and she'll be so poor she'll have to do every bit of her own work. Can you feature that? When she might have had Drew Breckenridge, after all, if she'd only played her cards right. And, of course, her grandmother's heart is broken.' It will be, too, you know, Stella. And then they'll go on talking about me. 'He doesn't know anyone we know; he's never done anything we've done; he's never been anywhere we've been——' "

"But he's going further than any of them! You said yourself, Raoul, that you could go anywhere in the world from a bayou!"

"Yes, I did, and it's true. So when I've gone a little further, when you're a little older, when we've found out how much I can do and how much you can take— Well, if you feel the same way then as you do now, we'll be married. With a fair chance, by that time, of living happily ever after. Which we haven't got yet."

"And what are we going to do in the meantime?"

Again he looked away from her, out towards the bayou. "Well, that isn't going to be so good. But it won't be unbearable. I think you'll find, tomorrow morning, that your grandmother has decided she'd better take you back to New Orleans. And I think you'd better go, without making too much fuss. It won't mean you'll never see me if you do. I get down there fairly often myself. To submit briefs and try cases before the Supreme Court. Sometimes I stay with my sister, but usually I stay at the Monteleone, because that's nearer the Court House. It won't be hard for us to meet from time to time. In fact, your grandmother may think it's a good deal too easy. In which case, she'll probably suggest taking you to Europe and letting you study for the opera, after all. If she does, I think you'd better do that, too. Not just on account of your singing, though that's more important than ever, now that we're engaged, and don't you get the idea that it isn't. But on account of us, too. I think you'd better find out whether this engagement of ours can stand the test of time and separation as well as the test of ridicule and heartbreak."

"Oh, Raoul, you're making it terribly hard for me! You're not giving me any comfort at all!"

"I tell you, I'm trying to make you face facts. But I think, perhaps, you've faced about enough for one night. I think we've talked enough for a while, too."

"You mean that now you're going to take me home?"

Her voice was piteous with entreaty. He answered her very slowly.

"Yes, that's what I mean. Before I start making violent love to you."

"But I thought you brought me here on purpose to make violent love to me! And I want you to!"

"I know you want me to, and I did bring you out here on purpose. That is, I started out that way. I thought, when I had my arms around you, at Bois Fleuri, that the next time— Well, I guess you know. I didn't think we ought to get married, for a long while, but I didn't see, then, why we shouldn't get all the joy we could out of each other, while we were waiting. It was a pretty poor line of reasoning, one that doesn't do any more credit to a lawyer than it does to a lover. I stopped reasoning that way at suppertime. I knew, when I saw you sitting at that table, with all those men around you, that it couldn't be the way I planned it at first. Because I cared too much; because I was too proud of you; because you were too grand a person. You weren't just a girl I was out to get any longer. You were my partner and my mate and my good angel all in one."

"I don't know that I can go on being all that. I don't know that I wouldn't rather have all the joy we can get, when we can get it."

"Yes, you can. No, you wouldn't. Listen, Stella. Do you remember what I wrote you about the record—that it didn't matter so much about little things, but that where big things were concerned you had to keep it clear? Not just so it would show for other people to see. But so that a man could live at peace with himself. That goes for a girl, too. This is the biggest thing that's ever happened to either of us —the biggest thing that ever will happen. Don't you think we'll both be glad, by and by, if we can keep the record clear? It'll be hard tonight, for me to take you home— now. It'll be hard for you to go. But don't you believe that some day——"

He dropped his arms. He and Stella stood facing each other in the shadows and the silences, barely able to see each other's face, but still looking straight into each other's souls.

"It's for you to choose, though, Stella," he said steadily.

She drew a deep breath. "No," she said. "It isn't. You've chosen. And you're right. I still want it to be the way you want it. Even more than I did when I thought you wanted it the other way. But, Raoul—we can still kiss each other, anyway, can't we?"

He laughed. It was a joyous laugh, snapping the tension between them, dispelling the hopelessness that threatened them. He put his arms around her again.

"You bet we can," he said. "And how——"

This time her strength did not stream away from her as he held her. It surged up within her, giving her confidence that in the difficult years which lay ahead, it would continue to rise to greater heights, in clarity and beauty and sustaining power.

CHAPTER 27

STELLA FELT no pleasurable thrill of anticipation as she dressed for the dinner dance which followed the skipperette races taking place on the seventh and eighth of September. This was not due to any lack of interest in yachting or any lack of knowledge about it either; all her life she had been in and out of boats; she had the same natural aptitude for handling them as her second cousin, Gail Rutledge, who, like his father and grandfather before him, had won trophy after trophy and championships which dated from the old gaff-rigged twenty-one-footers to the newest one-design gulf class. In fact, she, herself, had just finished first in one of the skipperette races, sailing Gail's *Undine III*. Having qualified as a victor, she was to be an honor guest at the dinner dance for which she was dressing, and she was also on the skipperette committee, both for the regatta and for the dinner dance, itself. But everything about the coming celebration seemed to her dull, flat, stale and unprofitable because she was going to it with Gail and not with Raoul.

Raoul had expected to be there. He had come to New Orleans twice, since she had left Bois Fleuri, to file applications for writs with the Supreme Court, just as he had predicted, and they had had lots of fun together. She was proud to be seen with him. He was increasingly attractive-looking, for, though he had not copied Drew's clothes, they had apparently given him excellent ideas about his own, which he had been quick to adopt. She had assumed that he would have to count his pennies when he took her out on the town, and she had felt no resentment or disappointment over this prospect; she knew she would be happy, wherever they went together and whatever they did, merely in being with him. But she could not help feeling gratified as well as surprised, to find that he knew how to order a meal in such a way that it commanded a headwaiter's respect, that he tipped liberally for good service, and that he chose delightful places to which to take her, and never gave the slightest indication of being either stingy or straitened after they got there. They had been to the Court of the Two Sisters to dine and dance, and to La Lune to listen to the Mexican singers, and to Frank Swanson's in Bucktown to eat boiled crabs, and they had driven out to the Pakenham ruins, in the vintage Ford. They had talked to each other about everything under the sun, including Raoul's political prospects and Stella's career as a singer, and the long low white house, with grounds sloping down to the river, that they would have in Abbeville, and what they would name their first three children. Raoul even joked with Stella about having a "buggy" wedding, and Stella even told Raoul about her Aunt Marie Céleste, who was a Carmelite and whose name was never mentioned, and about her mother and the Natchez Pilgrimage, and about her father and Lute; and after she had done this, she felt as if a smarting seal had been lifted from her lips and as if a tight band had been released from her heart. She believed there could never be anything, after this, as long as she lived, that she would not be able to tell to him, and that he would always give her full understanding and sustaining sympathy.

Besides taking her out, Raoul came to the big cream-colored house on Prytania Street, not as freely and informally as Stella would have liked, to be sure, but still, without being forbidden and without having to do it on the sly. Mrs. Fontaine had not invited him to drop in at any time for meals or given him a general sense of welcome, as Stella had hungrily hoped against hope that her grandmother might do, after all; she had not consented to announcing an engagement or even acknowledging an engagement, though she did countenance an acquaintance; and her natural sweetness of disposition had not stayed her from keeping Stella continually conscious of how completely her own projects had been upset and her own heart's desires thwarted. The plans for Stella's debut the following winter had already gone far past the tentative stage. Mrs. Fontaine had been practically assured that Stella would be Queen of the Pacifici and a Maid in the Courts of both Oberon and Comus, and it was definitely arranged that she was to be presented at the Harlequin Ball and to appear in the Attican Club tableaux. It would be very embarrassing now for Mrs. Fontaine to tell the Captains of the Pacifici and the other "Krewes" that Stella was not coming out that next winter, after all, but going to Paris to study music, especially after saying to so many persons that she did not approve of Stella's operatic aspirations. Besides, Mrs. Fontaine had never swerved from the comforting conviction that, before the end of another winter, "everything would be settled" between Drew and Stella, and that a splendid wedding would bring the season to a spectacular finish. It was a crushing blow to find that this vision had been dissipated like a mirage.

Stella was still perfectly willing to make her debut according to schedule, so Mrs. Fontaine was not entirely consistent in her complaint that, of course, now it must be put off, and that they must go abroad indefinitely. Stella had also conscientiously tried to put the best possible face she could on their departure, saying she thought it was wonderful of Grannie to give in about her singing, and that she was sure the next few years in Paris would mean everything in the world to her future. But her own courageous and co-operative stand had been largely nullified by her grandmother's attitude, and, though she had been respectful and restrained in everything she had said and done, the tension connected with doing this and, at the same time, declining to be swerved from her commitment to Raoul had told on her nerves and on the cheerfulness of her general outlook towards life more than she would have been willing to admit.

It was not just because Raoul was so reassuring and satisfying and stimulating in every way that she felt badly about not going to the party with him, either, or even because Gail was a second cousin and a curiously immature and unexciting person, anyway, that she was disappointed about going

with him, instead. It was also because she knew that Gail
really preferred fooling around with their Darcoa cousins,
Clarinda and Amelina and Franchot, the grandchildren of
Narcisse Fontaine, who were still just kids, and with the
Darcoas' great friend, Patty Forrestal, who was just a kid,
too. Gail was actually older than Stella, when it came to
that, but it was Patty Forrestal, whose family had just moved
back to New Orleans after a long absence, whom he liked to
take sailing, and whom he would have taken to parties, too,
if she had been old enough. Stella did not have anything
against Patty, who also had a flair for boats, and who had
made an excellent showing in the annual Junior Regatta.
She was really a very nice kid, simple and sincere, and a
good-looking one, too, in her own way, which was a way
that had fair skin, so tanned that it was darker than her fine-
spun yellow hair, and a face that was very grave, except when
she smiled suddenly and showed a surprising little dimple
at the lower side of her mouth. But she was just a leggy little girl, twelve or so—the same age as Amelina Darcoa, who
was younger than her sister Clarinda and her brother Franchot and ages younger than Gail Rutledge. Stella thought it
was silly for Gail to have such infantile tastes, and she had
half a mind to tell him so before the party was over. In her
edgy state, it would be a relief to say something disagreeable
to somebody. That is, not really, but at least momentarily.

Gail was a last resort, as far as this dinner dance at the
Yacht Club was concerned. When Raoul had tardily telephoned that he could not come down for it, after all, because
Huey Long had called another special session of the Legislature and he, himself, had got to tear back to Baton Rouge,
Stella, trying to keep her disappointment out of her voice,
had called up Drew Breckenridge, who was back in town,
too. In fact, Drew had been capturing trophies himself, for
though he was not boat-crazy like Gail, he was good at handling boats, as he was about everything else, and he had just
won two fish-class races in the Lipton Cup Series. Stella did
not in the least mind asking Drew to take her to the dinner
dance, because she knew he would understand her request
perfectly, and that, as he had no "entangling alliances," as
he, himself, liked to put it, he would be glad to take her,
under ordinary conditions. Indeed, the regret in his voice,
when he told her he could not, sounded very sincere.

"I'm tremendously sorry, Stella. I thought of course you
were all fixed with Raoul. This is the second bad break

you've had, with one of those damnable sessions of Huey's, isn't it? But I'm all tied up. I'm going as Julia Beal's guest. The group at her table is a good deal older than your crowd, and it's more or less centering around Harold and Evelyn Baird. They're just back from their wedding trip around the world. You know they've been gone almost a year, and everyone's entertaining for them. I didn't understand, when I accepted Julia's invitation, that I was to be her escort as well as her guest. But she indicated so unmistakably that she didn't know how she was going to get out to the Yacht Club, that there didn't seem to be anything else to do but fall in with her indirect suggestion."

"I don't see why you're such an easy mark for Julia Beal, Drew. If there ever was a spineless female, she's one. And you certainly have plenty of backbone yourself."

"The backbone may be there, but nothing seems to stiffen it. You know what I told you about following the line of least resistance."

"Well, as long as you don't wake up some morning and find yourself married to her."

"*That* I won't do, I promise you. And I'm terribly sorry about tomorrow night. Shall I call up one of my cronies? I know at least a dozen men who would jump at the chance of taking you."

"Oh, I'm not that badly off! I've got a good crowd together for my table, too, and Gail Rutledge will take me. He asked me in the beginning. Maybe prompted by his mother, who was maybe prompted by my grandmother, but anyway he asked me. I haven't anything against Gail, and he's a decent enough dancer as well as a crack sailor. But I know that after the races are over, he'd really rather get away from the clubhouse and go to the Darcoas' or the Forrestals', and play tiddlywinks or something, with Clarinda and Patty."

"You don't mean my kid cousin, Patty, from Boston?"

"She did live in Boston for a while. Is she your cousin? Oh, I suppose she is—at least her grandmother and yours were cousins, weren't they? She's related to Gail in some remote way, too, on the Rutledge side of the family—even more remote than mine on the Fontaine side of the family. Well, she is nice for twelve, or whatever she is, but I wish Gail would grow up and act his age. I'm going to ask him if he's begun to shave yet."

"Don't put on airs, just because you ensnared a he-man who needs to shave twice a day. Well, I'll be seeing you at the Yacht Club, anyway. And what about coming up to Splendida for a few days this next week? We could get in some riding, and that might be fun, for a change, after all this sailing. Incidentally, it's a very easy run from there to Baton Rouge, in case you took a fancy to have a look-see at the special session. I wouldn't mind doing it myself. I'd be glad to go up there with you any time, if you'd like to."

"Can a duck swim? That's a very noble thought of yours, Drew. I'll see what I can do with Grannie. She's really in a terrible hurry to push off to Europe. The house is half-closed already, and at least six of the necessary fifteen trunks are packed. But since it's you— Well, so long. I'm sorry I said what I did about Julia. I'm a great one to talk, when I did the very same thing I'm blaming her for."

"No, you didn't. You asked. She hinted. Between a girl who asks and a girl who hints, give me the first every time. But as I've had to abandon all hope as far as you're concerned——"

"Oh, Drew, shut up, for the luvamike!"

After this conversation, what with no time left and everything, there was nothing for Stella to do but go to the party with Gail, which was what Mrs. Fontaine had thought from the beginning that Stella should do. She had not forbidden Stella to invite Raoul, but her disapproval of the invitation had been as unconcealed as her relief later on, when the message came through saying he could not get down to New Orleans, after all—her relief and her unspoken implication that, since this was the second time within two months that Stella had found Raoul undependable, she would probably soon discover for herself that undependability was a characteristic of his. Stella resented the implication. She had already decided that the only kind of man who really intrigued her would always be so busy that seeing him might well be a matter of catch-as-catch-can, but that, even so, this would be infinitely more satisfactory than having a man constantly under foot who could think of nothing else to do with himself except to hang around her, and whom nobody else needed. Take Drew, for instance. Of course, there were plenty of people who wanted Drew—that simp, Julia, for instance, and a dozen other girls Stella could think of, and they would have wanted him if he had not had a cent to his name, instead of having an immense fortune; but his own diffidence and lassitude were the very qualities which made Stella feel she did not want him herself, in spite of all his charm. She wanted someone who had the same fierce zest for living and loving that she had herself, someone who was a bear for work and a glutton for good times, and someone to whom obstacles were only something to shove aside, a goal something towards which you raced, and a victory something you fought for and then grasped hard with both hands and hugged to your heart. In a word, she wanted Raoul.

Nevertheless, she felt more and more friendly toward Drew—more and more grateful to him all the time. It was Drew who, as a member of the Yacht Club, had given the necessary O. K. to her choice of Raoul, a non-member, as a guest at the skipperette supper dance, and, what was still more important, it was only because Drew had been so staunchly her ally—because he had supported her in her earnest appeal, supplemented by an adroit suggestion of his own—that Mrs. Fontaine had consented to receive Raoul and had given him the chance, for which he, himself, had also asked, to put the current case before her in his own way.

Stella had offered to withdraw during the interview, but both her grandmother and Raoul had preferred to have her remain, and she had felt her heart bursting with pride at the dignity, comparable to his antagonist's own, with which Raoul had met her. He hoped Mrs. Fontaine would believe, he said, that there had been no deliberate intention on his part of precipitating a situation of which Stella's grandmother would disapprove. He and Stella had fallen in love with each other at first sight; the second time he saw her he had told her he wanted to marry her, and she had given him to understand she would be glad to do so. But force of circumstances had made it impossible for him to speak to Mrs. Fontaine about it at the time. Though he was sorry she was not willing to countenance an engagement, the fact remained that this already existed, and that, therefore, it could only be broken by mutual consent, on his part and Stella's, which was lacking. However, he thought it would be a very good idea for Stella to go to Europe and study singing, while he tried to forge ahead in politics, and he agreed with Mrs. Fontaine that there should and could be no question of an immediate marriage. He had told Stella that from the beginning, too. But this was only because—again he must ask Mrs. Fontaine to believe him—he could not provide for Stella properly at the moment, though he was sure he would be

able to do so within a reasonable length of time. He had
some money in the savings bank and some more—not much,
but some—in sound securities, and he had a good law practice. It had brought him in, the year before, about three
thousand. He thought that when he was earning as much as
four thousand, which ought to be within a year or two, he
would be justified in buying a little house, in which Stella
could be comfortable, on some kind of a finance plan, and,
of course, he would take out life insurance in her name right
away. It did not seem to occur to him that Stella might have
money of her own from her father's estate, and that eventually she would have a good deal more from her grandmother's,
or if the idea did occur to him, he brushed it aside as neg-
ligible, after the manner of a man who not only desires and
expects to support his wife but insists on doing so. Stella,
herself, started to speak at this juncture—to tell him how
very well off she was—and she saw her grandmother's lips
part, as if Mrs. Fontaine felt reluctantly impelled to reveal
something of the same sort. But Raoul went straight on talking about other things, and the moment passed when it would
have been suitable for Stella to speak of money.

He and Stella would have to live in or near Abbeville,
Raoul said next, because otherwise he could not build up
the law practice which had already begun, or continue to
represent Vermilion Parish in the Legislature, which he
hoped to be able to keep on doing until he could go to Washington, another contingency which he seemed to regard as
neither improbable nor distant. Though, of course, it would
be a great change for her after New Orleans, he did not believe Stella would really mind living in a small and quiet
place, because there were so many things which he and she
both enjoyed that they could do together in the country, and
because he had so many friends who would be pleased to
contribute in every possible way to making her life a pleasant one. Besides, she could get into New Orleans fairly often,
coming with him on his legal trips, and by and by, as he had
said, he hoped that they would get to Washington. He did
not think there was anything in his record, either personal or
professional, which should make Mrs. Fontaine feel he had
no right to ask a girl like Stella to marry him, but he would
be glad to have Mrs. Fontaine talk with Dr. Anconi or Mr.
de Hauterive about him, if she would like to do so, or to put
any questions which occurred to her direct to him. He had
told his own parents that he was engaged, and to whom,

and while feeling, like Mrs. Fontaine, that there were some obstacles to overcome—though these were not the same ones she had in mind—they were sure they would be very fond of Stella, and they would also do everything in their power to make her happy. Of course, Stella had met his mother, accidentally, already, but he would like very much to take her to see both his parents before she left for Europe, if Mrs. Fontaine did not object. If she did, that was something else for which they could wait; his father and mother would understand. He had not told anyone else about the engagement except Mr. de Gruy who had behaved and spoken in a way which he, Raoul, considered offensive, considering that Stella was his future wife. The fact that Mr. de Gruy was a relative of Stella's had made a bad matter worse instead of better, in Raoul's opinion. But Mr. de Gruy had now apologized, and Raoul did not think there would be any more trouble in that quarter. He did not wish or propose to have any trouble in any quarter.

Mrs. Fontaine brought the interview to a close courteously and competently, though Stella suspected that inwardly she was a good deal shaken by it. She appreciated the candor with which Mr. Bienvenu had spoken, she said, and she hoped he would believe that she, in turn, was sincere when she said she did not for a moment suppose there was anything to his discredit, either personally or professionally. But she did feel that perhaps Stella, who was still very young, had been temporarily swept off her feet and did not really know her own mind, and that, therefore, it would be better not to assume, too hastily, that she would be happy in a sphere very different from any to which she had been accustomed or for which she had been prepared. Mrs. Fontaine did not think it would be best for Stella to go to Abbeville to see Mr. Bienvenu's parents at present, since that would certainly seem to indicate an official engagement, but she would consent to his request that he might call on Stella when he came to New Orleans; it would not be long, in any case, before she and Stella would be leaving for Europe to stay indefinitely. Mrs. Fontaine hoped that Mr. Bienvenu would not feel that she was unduly severe and unyielding. She knew that at least they were agreed on one point: Stella's happiness must be their first consideration and they must both do all they could to safeguard it.

The interview ended without awkwardness, if without warmth, and Mrs. Fontaine voiced no objection when Stella and Raoul immediately went out of the house together for some undisclosed destination, which, as a matter of fact, was Bucktown, of which she would not have approved at all, and where they probably would not have gone if she had only unbent a little and made them feel a little gladder that they were going to respect her wishes. Later on, after Raoul had gone back to Abbeville, Stella waited rather wistfully for her grandmother to make some comment on the conference, but none was forthcoming. She wanted to hear Mrs. Fontaine admit that Raoul's bearing and behavior had done him great credit and that perhaps, after all——

But Mrs Fontaine did not mention Raoul's name; she did not ask whether he had finished his legal business before the Supreme Court or inquire when he was next likely to come to New Orleans; she did not say she was sure he would get to Washington in time and that probably he would do very well in Congress. She still had not said a single one of these things when Stella, herself, revealed that she had invited him to the dinner dance after the skipperette races, and that Raoul had accepted. And then there had been that telephone call saying he couldn't come, after all—that he would try to see her the next week, instead—and all the next day, Mrs. Fontaine's unspoken inference that things would always be that way, that Stella would always find Raoul undependable——

Stella stepped out of her shower and into the soft yellow dress which she had thought Raoul would admire so much, with very little intervening ceremony. She had been wet to the skin when she got home, for a stiff wind had been blowing all day, so she had dropped her drenched slacks and sneakers to the floor of her bathroom, and had sat soaking luxuriously in a bubble-bath of rose geranium before turning on the cold spray. Now there was not much time left. As usual, she had left everything till the last minute. She had not packed the old-fashioned costume—a long flounced white dress which had belonged to Mrs. Fontaine when she was a girl—that she was to wear in the song and dance skit part of the celebration that night. She had to get this dress, and all the fussy things that went with it, into a suitcase. Julie had already let it out six inches around the waist, because before that Stella could not get into it, slim as she was. Cripes, what a lot of doodabs girls had worn when Grannie was young! Stella did not see how they had so much as breathed, let alone moved.

Gail was already honking the horn outside as she tore down the stairs, carrying the suitcase herself. She had not stopped to ring for Emile and ask him to take it for her, but she did stop long enough to call out to her grandmother, who was sitting alone in the dim drawing room, as usual at this hour, to tell her that, by the way, Drew wanted them to go up to Splendida the next day, and how about it? She had been so busy, with the races and all, that she had forgotten to say anything before. Mrs. Fontaine replied quietly that she would be very glad to go to Splendida with Stella, and that she hoped Stella would tell Drew so, with her love, when she saw him at the Yacht Club. Stella said all right, that was swell, and banged the front door after her, shouting to Gail as she went down the walk to come and help her with the darned old suitcase, for the luvamike.

They did not say a great deal to each other as they drove out to the club. Gail told Stella he was glad she had come in first with the *Undine III*, but that, of course, if he had not supposed she would, he would not have loaned it to her; and Stella thanked him for his generous spirit and said that, in that case, she was doubly thankful she had not let him down. Then Gail said he understood she was not coming out at the Harlequin Ball, after all, and he thought she might have told him before he took so much trouble about the matter, in his capacity as captain. This annoyed Stella still more, so she retorted she didn't know he had graduated into the captain class, even in the Harlequins, and, therefore, she had not dreamed he was taking any trouble; she supposed he was still sitting at home playing checkers with Patty Forrestal. Then she remembered that Drew had told her not to be sarcastic just because she had a real he-man of her own now and she was sorry she had snapped at Gail, but there was nothing she could do about it, because he was immovably sulky all the rest of the way out to the Southern Yacht Club.

The old yellow-clapboarded clubhouse, rising up over the water, looked very pretty when they went into it. Of course, it was always attractive, what with the big showcases full of silver cups and the old maritime prints on the walls, and the bar in the shape of a ship's bow, with a mast and lanterns at the back, and life preservers forming a frieze all around, painted with the names of her friends' yachts—the *Jade* and the *Windjammer* and the *Spike* and the *Sunshine* and the *Bonne Fortune* and the *Porte-Bonheur* and all the rest of them. But in addition to all this, there were decorations of palms and smilax from one end of the clubhouse to the other, and in the big ballroom giant posters had been fastened on the wall, painted to represent the different boats which had won in the regatta and the girls who had sailed them. Stella had a momentary thrill when she saw the poster of the *Undine III* and the picture of herself, with her curls blowing out behind her in the wind, as she sat at the tiller. But the picture of Gail standing beside her looked very stodgy to her. She knew it was fair that there should be a picture of him, because he was the owner, but still, she did not think he added anything to the scene, and presently she went out onto the gallery to see if her table was all right, and found that her guests were already there, waiting for her. A stiff breeze was still blowing, and it whipped up the soft skirt of her yellow chiffon dress, so that she had to hold it down with her hands. One of the boys in her party made a joking remark about her knees, and she turned on him furiously. Then she was sorry again, just as she had been in the car when she spoke sarcastically to Gail. But she could not help thinking how differently the same remark would have sounded if Raoul had made it—that it seemed natural and amusing and cozy when he talked to her like that; and, anyway, he had a right to. This made a still greater difference, because the fresh boob who had spoken to her did not, and if Raoul were there and she could go out on the pier with him between dances, and maybe even during dances, the whole evening would be different.

Julia Beal's party, a large one, was already assembled at the table next to Stella's, so Stella went over to speak to Drew for a moment, to tell him it would be all right about Splendida. He was acting as host for Julia, sitting at the foot of the big round table, and Mrs. Harold Baird, the beautiful bride everyone was talking about, who had been Evelyn Denis before her marriage, was sitting at his right, because Julia's party was being given in her honor. Stella had thought Evelyn Denis was the most wonderful-looking girl in New Orleans, ever since she had seen her presiding at a tea table, wearing a hostess dress of burnt-orange velvet, girdled in emerald green, which would have looked fantastic on anyone else, but which transfigured Evelyn into the sort of mediaeval chatelaine depicted on superb tapestries and stained-glass windows. She did not think so much of her in other ways, however, and now, as she leaned over to speak briefly to Drew, she had the first uncomfortable feeling, as far as he was concerned, that she had had in weeks. She felt as if Drew were also very much aware of Evelyn's beauty—so superconscious of it, indeed, that he did not want anything to interrupt his enjoyment of it, not even a swift word with an old friend. Of course Drew said he was delighted, and thanked Stella for relieving his suspense, but just the same, in spite of his flawless manner, she knew he would rather have had her wait to tell him later in the evening, when he came to dance with her, after Evelyn had broken the spell herself by getting up to dance with someone else. Stella had grown so fond of Drew that she hated to think Evelyn's beauty could create even the smallest sort of strain or estrangement between them. But after all, she did not have much time to brood over that at the moment, because Rusk Patalia's syncopated band, which played the best jazz in New Orleans, had already begun to tune up, and she had not so much as swallowed her soup.

Besides, not counting in Rusk Patalia, it was a rackety party, anyway, not conducive to serious thought. Paper caps were going off and rattles jingling and bells ringing. When seven hundred people were snapping paper caps and jingling rattles and ringing bells, you did well if you could concentrate on the song you were going to sing pretty soon in the old-fashioned skit, and on the few graceful words you would have to say into the loud-speaker when the Commodore gave you your cup, and so on. Especially, if all the time you were thinking terribly hard about your boy-friend and the fact that he wasn't there with you.

But in spite of Stella's problems, Evelyn and her beauty intruded themselves on her notice very soon again, after all. For the minute Rusk Patalia's band really got into action, Stella saw that Drew was on his feet and that Evelyn was, too, before anyone else at their table or any other had moved. They danced off together, laughing into each other's eyes and forgetting, apparently, all about Julia, with whom Drew, according to an unwritten law, should have had the first dance, not to mention Harold Baird, with whom, according to much more solidly established custom, Evelyn should have had it. Stella felt uncomfortable again, for it was the first time she had seen a side of Drew—not to mention a side of Evelyn—about which she had heard a good deal of gossip, but in which she had never taken much stock. The sight helped her to understand why she had never fallen in

love with him herself, because it revealed—on top of the
lassitude and diffidence she had discovered already—a lack
of singleheartedness which, for her, would be an absolute
essential in any man to whom she gave her heart. There
were certain masculine crudities, none of which Drew possessed, which would not trouble her beyond a certain point,
nor would she repine because she would never receive the
small attentions and the flattering tributes which Drew
would give, as a matter of course, to any woman upon whom
he looked with favor. She was sure, for instance, that Raoul
would never put a fresh rose on her breakfast tray, according to the traditional habit of the Breckenridge men. In fact,
she was sure there would never be any breakfast tray to put
a rose on, unless she were seriously ill, because he would
take it for granted that she would get up and eat breakfast
with him and, moreover, prepare it for him, until he was
much better off financially than he was at this moment. He
would not remember her birthday or the anniversary of their
marriage or any of those dates so dear to a feminine heart.
He would keep on being forgetful, too, about telling her
that he loved her, and he would always expect her to understand when he left her or did not come to her in the first
place or was preoccupied when he was with her.

But she believed she could endure all this, because she
had already learned it was better to know that a man loved
her than to hear him say that he did, and to have him honor
her in great ways instead of having him compliment her in
small ones. With this knowledge, his stubbornness should
never irritate her and his ambition should never appall her
and his force should never frighten her. But she would demand, as she would give, complete emotional integrity as
well as great emotional intensity. She had never analyzed
any of this before but, involuntarily, she did so now, in
the midst of the din and confusion. It did not add to her
happiness, however, as far as Drew and Evelyn were concerned. She turned her head away, so that she would not
see them laughing into each other's eyes as they danced very
close together; then, just as Gail signalled to her that they
ought to be up and about it themselves, one of the waiters
came and told her she was wanted on the telephone—that
Baton Rouge was calling. Gail spoke to her almost crossly.

"You can't go to the telephone now, Stella. You know it's
way over on the other side of the lounge, and the Commo-

dore will be starting to give out the cups any minute. You'll have to be on hand to take yours."

"I've got to take this call, whether I take the cup or not. Let me go, Gail."

She tried to shake him off. He clung to her doggedly.

"You don't suppose I'm going to let you strike out by yourself, do you, since you insist on going? If you stalked out on me, right at the beginning of a dance like that, everyone would think we'd had a quarrel or something."

"Oh, for the luvamike! Come along then! But you don't need to stand with your ear glued to the outside of the booth, when we get there."

"But, darn it all, who *is* there up in Baton Rouge who could be calling you and making you feel it was this important? I've never heard——"

"The number of things you've never heard is simply appalling, Gail. If you must know, though Grannie would much rather you didn't, that call is bound to be from my fiancé. His name is Raoul Bienvenu, and he's a representative from Vermilion Parish. Drew O.K.'d an invitation for him and he was coming here tonight, but Huey Long called the 'steenth extra session within a year, so then he couldn't. I don't know why he's calling me in the middle of a dance, when he knows that's where I am, but you can bet your bottom dollar it isn't just for instance. That isn't Raoul's way. You'd better hurry, if you want to keep up with me. I'm not crawling to that telephone. I'm sprinting."

That, Gail thought, was putting it mildly. It seemed to him that Stella was fairly flying across acres of slippery floor, dragging him after her, since he would not let her go without him, and whipping out personal insults and shocking news items as she sped along. *Stella engaged!* To a Cajun from Vermilion Parish! So that, was why Aunt Estelle was hurrying her off to Europe; that was why the Captain of the Harlequin Ball—not to mention the Captains of the Pacifici, Oberon and Comus—had been put to so much needless trouble. That was why Stella had snapped at him about playing checkers with Patty Forrestal and why she was making him conspicuous at the Yacht Club now. He had heard a lot, from his own grandmother, nee Clarisse Fontaine, of how Stella's grandmother, nee Estelle Lenoir, had acted up in her youth about Andy Breckenridge, and from his father, Napier Rutledge Junior, of how Stella's aunt, Marie Céleste, had immured herself in a Carmelite convent because Andrew

Breckenridge the Second had been tragically drowned. And he had assumed, like everyone else he knew, that, in this generation, everything was to be put to rights by a well-arranged marriage between Stella and Drew. And here was Stella acting up herself, and not about a Breckenridge, at that, but about a Cajun. It was upsetting; it was unsporting; it was alarming——

Stella had finally shaken herself free from him; she had gone into the telephone booth and banged the door after her, just as she had banged the front door of her house a couple of hours earlier. Gail did not stand with his ear glued to the telephone booth, but he was near enough to it to see her face brighten as she picked up the receiver and to hear the gladness in her voice as she excitedly answered. Then the expression changed to one of horror, though the excitement grew. She cried out once, in unbelieving agitation. After that she listened intently, asking only a few tense, terse questions from the fragments of which Gail could make neither rhyme nor reason. Then she hung up the receiver, and Gail saw her fumbling hastily in her handbag for a coin. Presently she was on the wire again, this time doing nearly all the talking herself, still excitedly, still tensely and tersely. When she came out of the booth at last, she started straight down the corridor towards the lobby at the same flying pace with which she had crossed it before, so that Gail had to catch hold of her arm to keep up with her. And again she whipped out her words in short, sharp, alarming sentences.

"Huey Long's been shot. In the Capitol corridor, between the House and Senate. By a Dr. Weiss. Who's already been polished off by Huey's bodyguard. Huey's in a bad way himself. Raoul was in the corridor. He saw it all happen. He thinks he was the first person to get to a telephone. He told me to call up a reporter he likes, here in New Orleans, on the chance this man hadn't got the news yet. He hadn't. He'd been out at his farm all day, giving a barbecue, and he'd gone to bed, dead tired, with a big dose of barbital inside him, to get some sleep. He'd been asleep just ten minutes when I called him. Now he says he'll be lucky if he gets to bed again before Wednesday. But he was terribly grateful to me. He said he could write a story about Huey, for the bulldog edition of his paper, and be on his way to Baton Rouge within two hours. I wish him luck.

Meanwhile I'm to do a little swift reporting myself. Raoul wants me to."

They had reached the small cubbyhole of the club secretary in their mad dash back to the ballroom. Stella stopped and hailed that long-suffering and thunderstruck functionary.

"Huey Long's just been shot," she said. "He's probably dying. I've had an official message from Baton Rouge. Representative Bienvenu, of Vermilion Parish, who telephoned me, thought you'd probably want it announced over the loudspeaker in the ballroom." She spoke proudly, after the manner of a trusted messenger to whom an important task has been confided and who is eager to show that the confidence is well placed. Then suddenly she shuddered, putting her hand to her face with a swift panicky gesture. "The blood!" she said. " 'The bright red blood on the polished marble!' It was prophetic, after all."

CHAPTER 28

THE DRIZZLING rain which had been falling all day, and which had made the drive from New Orleans to Splendida even duller and more disagreeable than usual, had developed into a downpour which, in turn, was causing an abnormal amount of interference on the radio. Stella, impatiently twisting one dial after the other in a vain effort to get a clear connection with Baton Rouge, felt as if the grating and crackling caused by the static, and the intermittent reception which was all she could secure, constituted the last straw in the bothersome burdens of the day. She was just about ready to throw the instrument across the floor, to see if that would make her feel any better, when Drew walked into the library and, by his inopportune arrival, automatically prevented any such puerile act.

"Why, hello, Stella!" he said amiably. "I didn't know you were in here. Is anything wrong? Somehow you don't seem to radiate that calm contentment I like to see on the countenances of my guests."

"If you said I looked mad through and through, you'd be a damned sight nearer the truth. Because I am. I've had a hellish time ever since I got up this morning. And now I can't get a thing on this blasted radio. I'd like to smash it into smithereens. In fact, I probably should have, if you hadn't come in just when you did. Incidentally, I'm not in the way here, by any chance, am I?"

The words were hardly out of her mouth before she divined that she had hit upon an uncomfortable truth. The reason that Drew had come into the library was to make sure that it was empty, prior to inviting someone else into it. If her intuition was correct, she was very much in the way. And there was not another radio anywhere in this great hulking house. With characteristic feminine inconsistency, she raged at the prospect of being separated from the instrument which, a moment earlier, she had been ready to destroy. If Drew drove her out of the library, so that he could get Evelyn into it, under the pretext of showing her the Audubon books and the Shakespeare folios, Stella, herself, would be thwarted still further in her effort to keep in touch, indirectly at least, with Raoul and everything that was important to him.

Her worst fears, however, proved entirely groundless. Drew did not betray any intention of driving her from the room. In a leisurely way, he poured out two drinks from a decanter on the desk, offered one to Stella, took the other himself, and sat down, lighting a cigarette as he did so.

"Believe it or not, libraries are still occasionally used to read in," he said, with the slight sarcasm she disliked so much. "Moreover, I'm very fond of reading, which will probably surprise you still more. One of the bad habits I picked up in Boston, from the Forbes and Forrestal families. I thought I might indulge this peculiar taste for a little while before dinner, as everyone else seems to have drifted off. I suspect a few supplementary naps, though no one came to life until noon, as far as I've been able to find out. That was quite a party last night, wasn't it, Stella?" And incidentally, you were quite the heroine of it, with your dramatic announcement about Huey Long. Well, I've complimented you on that, in my poor way, already. I think it was about three when I did so the last time, wasn't it? Keeping Rusk Patalia on for an extra hour seemed like a good idea when it was put into action. But along about one p. m. I think there were those who regretted it. Not to mention regretting those last three or four drinks which the extra hour gave the guests a chance to consume. I have a notion you and I were about the only persons who left the Southern Yacht Club anything like sober."

"You're not very complimentary to gentle Julia and the beautiful bride."

"Oh, Julia ought never to stray beyond the limits of a single coke! Anything more and anything else are too much for her. As for the beautiful bride, hers was just a champagne sparkle—remarkably becoming, too, which was a good deal more than you could say for the load her husband was carrying— Well, now to get back to the place where we started: another point you overlooked is that this particular library connects with a bachelor's bedroom, and that he does have to go in there, every now and then, to get a clean handkerchief or something of the sort."

"I'd forgotten about that, Drew. I really had."

This was true enough. She had forgotten about it. But now that Drew had jogged her memory, the reminder made her uncomfortable again. The library was in a remote wing at the rear of the house, beyond the staircase hall; it connected with Drew's bedroom, but it connected with nothing else except some of that famous "first plumbing," which was still unchanged, and its own little gallery. And in spite of all he had said about the use of the library and the somnolent state of his guests, Stella felt more and more convinced that Drew had meant to bring Evelyn to this cultural retreat.

"Would you like me to see what I can do with the refractory radio?" he inquired, still pleasantly and unhurriedly. "I'm fairly good at tinkering with such things as a rule. Or better still—why not let me call up Raoul and see if he couldn't run down here and spend the night, and give us the news firsthand? I think he'd be a great addition to the house party. When I said that everyone had erred on the side of overcelebration last night—or rather this morning—I might have added that, since then, everyone's drinks have certainly died on them. I don't blame you for being bored. Let's get hold of Louisiana's leading live wire, shall we?"

"Oh, Drew, that would be swell of you! I didn't have nerve enough to ask you if you wouldn't, but I've been dying to have you! Because you see I thought we could get up to Baton Rouge today, after what you said about being glad to take me any time. And then we were so late in leaving New Orleans and everything, and there were so many more people along than I thought you meant when you said we'd get in some riding and so on——"

She stopped abruptly, ashamed of her impetuosity. Again, what she said was true enough, but it was also inexcusably tactless. The reason they had left New Orleans late was because of the hang-overs to which Drew had so lightly referred, but which, as Stella was well aware, had been pretty bad in several cases. Poor Julia, whom Drew was driving up himself—doubtless because of another "indirect suggestion"—had not been able to lift her head until noon; Evelyn had not been able to get Harold from his bed without a struggle either. As for the size of the house party, it had been augmented not only by Julia and by Walter Avery—who had also shown up at the Southern Yacht Club after a long absence from New Orleans—but also by the Bairds, at the last moment. Drew's guest list, however, was certainly his own affair, and she had been entirely unjustified in expecting that he meant to devote the better part of the week exclusively to her.

It was a relief to hear Drew talking agreeably to a succession of telephone operators. Was the first operator quite sure that Mr. Bienvenu could not be reached at the Capitol? Oh—so the special session had adjourned at one-fifteen p. m.? Well, what about the committee rooms? Mr. Bienvenu did not seem to be in any of those either? Then, would the second operator please connect him with the Heidelberg Hotel?— Since Mr. Bienvenu's room did not answer, Drew said, still pleasantly, to a third operator, would she be kind enough to have him paged in the lobby?— All right. He would leave his number. As soon as Mr. Bienvenu came in, would she please have him call Mr. Breckenridge at Splendida Plantation? It was urgent. Very urgent.

"I'm afraid your boy-friend doesn't have much leisure to sit around doing nothing but wait for a telephone to ring, like some privileged persons I might mention," Drew said, replacing the receiver. "He's probably in a huddle, with some of his closest cronies, trying to map out a plan of action to follow through after Huey dies. I suppose the man is going to die. They wouldn't have operated except as a last resort. I've sent to White Castle for the afternoon papers. Meanwhile, let's try the radio again."

If Evelyn really is waiting for Drew to come back to the parlor, or wherever she is, and report that the coast is clear, she must be mad enough to chew nails by this time, Stella thought, wondering if she ought to be self-sacrificing and leave the library of her own accord now. But after all, the message from Raoul ought to come through at any minute, and Drew still did not act as if he expected her to go.

"I'm sorry you've been having a hellish time all day," he said sympathetically. That habit he had of shifting quickly from satire to solicitude was very disarming, Stella reflected, by no means for the first time. "It makes me feel surer than ever that I must have fallen down somewhere, as a host. I did have to wait for Julia to recover this morning, as I know you realize. And I didn't dream you really cared about riding with me alone, or there wouldn't have been so many people here. You'll have to come back, or stay after the others are gone, just as you'd rather, and we'll still fix that up. Then I didn't quite take in that you wanted to get to Baton Rouge today. I thought any day would do. It was before Huey's little accident that we discussed the visit, and that does change the picture. But we'll try to make the great and glorious capital tomorrow. I'm almost sure we can. And I'm sorry for all my sins of omission and commission. Did anything else happen to make you feel badly, that I couldn't help?"

"No. You're a wonderful host, Drew, and I'm a horrid little cat. I do think Walter Avery's tiresome, though. Three times last night he called me into the private dining room where he was gambling with the rest of the rocking-chair fleet. I thought it was disgusting to see those men squatting around on the floor, with a big pile of money between them, and to hear them calling out, 'Come seven! Come eleven! Come peritonitis!' while they rattled the dice and threw them. Of course, I feel just the same way about Huey Long that the rest of you do. But it was pretty raw. And today Walter's kept telling me about it, as if it were a great joke and as if I hadn't already seen and heard it all. You don't suppose he's in his dotage, do you?"

"Well, he is on the shady side of forty. And he was in his cups last night. He still isn't wholly out of them. But he's a good fellow. And my father was very fond of him. Though they were both in love with the same girl. When you can say that, you've said a good deal. If I were in love with a girl, I'm sure I'd want to murder anyone else who looked at her. Not that I ever was or ever intend to be. It's certain I'm not in love with you, isn't it? Because I like Raoul very much myself. Here, let's try that radio again while we're waiting to get him."

Drew leaned over and began turning the dials. The sputtering sounds recommenced. I wonder if he wants to murder Harold Baird, Stella thought, watching him. He doesn't act as if he did. He acts as if he were contemptuous of Harold, but not as if he hated him. I don't suppose, when he talks about being in love with a *girl*, he means someone who's married already, and who's had three or four affairs besides. Because Evelyn has had affairs. Everyone in New Orleans knows that. Why, she was slated for Queen of Carnival, one year, and her name was withdrawn.

There had been a great stir and a great scandal. Evelyn weathered it insolently and well, because that was her way, and her engagement to Harold Baird, who had an unassailable position, even if he was an awful souse, and had all kinds of money, had been triumphantly announced not long afterwards. And now she was going to have another affair, though she had been married so short a time that people still talked about her as a bride. "It's disgusting; it's revolting," Stella said to herself. "I don't see why Drew, who's such a corker in so many ways, isn't repelled by her instead of being fascinated——"

The sputtering sounds had stopped. Under Drew's skillful ministrations, the reception had become clear. ". . . Only members of the family and close friends are at the hospital," the broadcaster was saying unctuously, "among them Dr. George Long, who arrived from Oklahoma today. Pay no attention to the newspaper headlines, which are making Senator Long's condition appear much worse than it is. We have talked only a short while ago to Senator Noe, who gave blood to Huey Long in one of the transfusions, and he assures us Senator Long is doing as well as can be expected. Meanwhile the Legislature is preparing to carry out the program of laws which were introduced Sunday night, while messages of sympathy are pouring in from every part of the United States. All traffic has been detoured from the road leading past the Lady of the Lake Sanitarium grounds, except for official cars——"

The telephone rang sharply across the stereotyped monotone. Stella switched off the radio as Drew picked up the receiver.

"Hello! Oh, hello, Raoul. How's everything going? Still alive, eh? Well, if they've sent for oxygen— Listen! I've got a very discontented guest here at my house. I'm at my wit's end to know what to do with her. I wonder if you couldn't help me out——"

Stella snatched the receiver out of Drew's hand. "You make me sick and tired," she said savagely. "No, I wasn't talking to you, Raoul. I was talking to Drew— Can't you come down tonight? Drew says he'd be glad to have you. Oh, yes, he has his points, but still— Well, I wish you could, but if you really can't, we'd love to have you tomorrow, instead. Only we thought we might come to Baton Rouge tomorrow. Oh, it isn't—" She turned from the telephone and spoke to Drew again, far less savagely this time. "Raoul says the House isn't going to be in session tomorrow. He says there was almost no debate—that the session was very listless. The thirty-nine administration-approved measures are passed and sent to the Senate already, so the House has adjourned until Wednesday. He'll be free and he'll be glad to come down here then, if that's all right, and have us go up there Wednesday, instead. Here, you'd better talk to him yourself."

The receiver changed hands several times. The two men spoke briefly together, and to the point. Stella kept breaking in. She wanted to talk on and on. She paid no attention to Drew, who was murmuring something silly about sending him into bankruptcy with toll charges. But she had no choice when Raoul said, rather brusquely, "Listen, couldn't you say all that tomorrow morning just as well? I'm talking from one of the booths in the lobby, and I'm in an awful hurry." Of course, Drew had heard, and she hated to have him know that Raoul's rebuke on the driveway of Bois Bleuri did not constitute an isolated case. She shook back her curls, ready to say something defensive. But Drew was already speaking, satirically again.

"Well, that seems to be that. I hope I've redeemed myself as a host, partially at least. I can see that this old house has too few modern conveniences though. You'll find an extra radio and an extension telephone in your own room when we get back from Baton Rouge. I hope you'll enjoy using them. And I hope you don't mind if I add that perhaps they'll help you to remember that libraries, especially libraries connected with bachelor's bedrooms, should be quiet retreats primarily reserved for reading."

"He is getting me out of the way, after all. I was right from the beginning," Stella said to herself as she left the library and went in search of her grandmother. "He has spoiled my whole visit by bringing Evelyn here, though I couldn't tell him that. I had to blame it all on poor old Walter. Of course, Julia doesn't count. She's too neutral, too negative, though she doesn't belong to Splendida either. It wasn't meant for women like her any more than it was meant for women like Evelyn. If Drew fills it with women like these, it won't deserve to be called Splendida any more——"

She was still preoccupied with this thought as she passed into the entrance hall. Through the door, framed in rainbow-colored glass, which opened onto the main portico, the levee confronted her, rising abruptly only a few hundred yards from the house. The grove, which had once been a glade of mystic loveliness, according to all accounts, was completely gone; the sweeping length of the allee had been cut in half; even the trees that were left seemed truncated. The overgrown garden, still intact as to size, had lost most of its effectiveness, partly for lack of a proper approach and partly because it had an unkempt, uncherished look, as if no one who loved it nurtured it any more. The house was beginning to have a similar look, Stella reflected. For all its magnificence, there was something shoddy about it. Its great rooms seemed mouldy and musty to her; its splendor was growing stale. This was not for lack of money, as Stella knew very well. It was for lack of care, not only the kind of care that kept things clean and tidy but also the kind of care that kept them sound and sweet. There had been no worthy successors to Shoog, indoors, or to Marcy Yates, outdoors. There was only a foreman instead of an overseer in the fields, and though Jezebel, the "Bishop's" granddaughter, had stayed on and had always done the best she could, she, herself, had not proved prolific like her predecessor. Having no brood of her own which she could rule, she had been obliged to rely on the undependable assistance of Valina, Susie and their offspring, and the results were somewhat sketchy. The situation might had been different if Drew had only taken it over. Or if he had asked his mother to come back and take up the reins of government which he held in so slack a hand. Or, best of all, if he had tightened the slack reins and looked after his plantation himself, which he certainly had time to do, since he did nothing else. But Drew thought, as he spoke, slightingly of Splendida. The next time the levee was moved back, he said, it would be practically at his doorstep, and someday he would come there and find the portico covered with water, and that would be the end, for not long afterwards there would be nothing left of it except some mutilated columns rising above an eddying pool. He supposed he must take the furnishings and paintings and ornaments away before this happened, but there was still plenty of time for that. Meanwhile, what was the sense in bothering about a place which was already doomed? He would get what use and what amusement out of it he could, as long as it lasted. When it went, he would find another which he could use, and where he could amuse himself——

Mrs. Fontaine was nowhere to be found in the house. Having searched the parlor, drawing room and reception room, which, in their deserted state, looked more decadent than she had ever seen them, Stella went upstairs and entered the huge state chamber where Drew always installed her grandmother; it was possible that Mrs. Fontaine might be there resting, like the others, before dinner. But this room was empty, too. Stella went downstairs again and through the gardens, finding them even more rank and tangled, as she sauntered up and down the unweeded paths, than they had looked from the portico. Finally she remembered the little cemetery on the other side of the house. She retraced her steps, traversed the famous arbor without an instant's sentimental stop and, pushing back the clusters of white flowers that hung over it, unlatched the gate to the graveyard.

Mrs. Fontaine was sitting on one of the horizontal tombs raised above the surface of the ground by a little pedestal. It was so gray and moss-grown that it gave the effect of having always been a part of its ancient surroundings—of merging naturally into the earth in which it was embedded. But the great alabaster chalice towards which she was gazing was white and shining and translucent; it seemed both to receive and to give forth light. She did not hear Stella's step behind her and she looked up in bewilderment tinged with formless fear when the girl leaned over and kissed her.

"Did I startle you, Grannie dear? I didn't mean to. I've been looking everywhere for you. I've made some plans, tentatively, for tomorrow and the day after, and I want to know if they're all right. Drew offered, before we came up here, to drive me to Baton Rouge from Splendida, so that I could sit in at a special session of the Legislature. He's just been talking to Raoul Bienvenu on the telephone. I have, too, but it was Drew's idea to call him, and he and Raoul made all the arrangements. The House isn't in session tomorrow, so Drew invited Raoul here."

"I see. Well, of course, *chère*, Drew has a right to ask anyone here that he likes. I shall not offer any objection to such a visit."

"Thanks, Grannie. Then we'd all start out together early the next morning. Julia and Walter and the Bairds are going, too. Of course, we'd love to have you come with us, if you'd enjoy it. In that case, we'd take two cars. Otherwise, we'll all go together in Drew's big Cadillac. Raoul says the roads are very crowded already, with people pouring into the capital from all over the state. Capitalists and politicians and journalists and lumbermen and fishermen and trappers and farmers. It must be a great sight."

"Yes, I can understand that. And it is natural that you should wish to see it, *chère*. I have no objections to such a trip as you propose either. But I do not care to make it myself. I should prefer a quiet day here alone." As she said, "here," Mrs. Fonatine looked towards the alabaster chalice again, and Stella knew her grandmother would spend the "quiet" day in the cemetery. "Besides," Mrs. Fontaine went on, "I can see that it will be much better if you all go in one car. And you will all keep together, of course, after you get to Baton Rouge."

"Yes, of course, Grannie."

She said it sincerely and joyously. She was grateful for her grandmother's softened mood, which she rightly laid to the memories Mrs. Fontaine's surroundings had evoked. And she was happy because Raoul was coming to see her, because they could linger in the arbor and wander through the gardens together. She was so glowing with gladness that she welcomed a chance to prove that he and she could be trusted to keep the promise they had made to respect her grandmother's wishes. But Tuesday turned out to be another trying day. Raoul telephoned very early to say that Huey Long had died about four that morning, and in consequence the whole place was in a turmoil; he could not possibly leave. He spoke brusquely, as he had the night before, and Stella, who had been so sure she would not mind because he would always expect her to understand when he acted like this, found that she did mind, after all, now that it had happened twice in succession so close together. Then there had been the necessity of explaining to her grandmother that Raoul was not coming, and the inevitability of meeting, once again, the unspoken inference that he would always be undependable. It had been Sunday when he failed to come to New Orleans; now it was only Tuesday, and he had failed to come to Splendida. Finally she gave up trying to explain and went off for a ride by herself. It was still raining, and the others all preferred to stay in the house and play bridge. They urged her to stay with them and cut in, which was what the three men were planning to do. But she was sure that if she did, Drew would somehow contrive to be cut out at the same time as Evelyn and take her off to the library. If Stella were not there, Evelyn would have to stay in the game all the time. Stella extracted a malign satisfaction from this thought as she struck off in the downpour.

The evening was as dull as the day, and the next morning did not begin much better. It was still raining, and no one was in especially good spirits on the trip to Baton Rouge. The start had been too early to make for geniality; the roads were so crowded that driving was difficult; then there was a long wait to get across the ferry. From the ferry to the Capitol they progressed "by inches," as Evelyn rather peevishly put it, and when they finally reached the State House, Raoul was not waiting for them by the hostess's desk in the bizarre lobby, as he had said he would be, nor had he left any message for them. They argued for a few moments as to whether they should wait themselves, or whether they should try to find him, and at last, still with some division of opinion, they adopted the latter plan. They were just passing the elevator, which slid open smoothly with a metallic click, when he came hurrying towards them.

"Why, hello! I'd almost given you up," he said. "I waited at the desk nearly half an hour, and then I had to rush off to see a man who'd been waiting for me, too. I'd figured that after I got you all settled I'd be free for a while. Well, come along now. I'm taking you into the Chamber with me, Stella. Will you wait here for me until I get the others into the gallery?"

"Yes, of course. I'd be glad to wait."

Her brief answer was a triumph in understatement. She had not known until then that Raoul could take her onto the floor of the House with him, that every representative had the right to install, at will, one chair beside his own, and that hers would be waiting for her by Raoul's. He had places, good places, saved for the others in the gallery. But he took it for granted that she would stay with him.

So did the Bairds and Julia and Walter and Drew, as soon as Raoul indicated this. In her joyous surprise she did not remember, for more than a moment, that this would separate her from the others. She realized only that it would keep her close to Raoul.

She had thought, at De la Houssaye's Restaurant in New Iberia, that her heart would burst with pride as she sat at the head of the table, surrounded by Raoul's friends whom she was helping him to entertain. But it was nothing to the pride she felt now as she went into the huge ornate Chamber, at his side, with his fingers under her elbow. They were placed there, naturally enough, to guide her in the unfamiliar direction, and they rested there lightly. No one looking at her could have thought that they formed a pretext for a caress. But there was no touch of his so fleeting or so casual that it had not become a caress to her by now, and though this was her own secret to hug to her heart, everything about his general bearing towards her told its own story: The way he held open the bronze gate for her, nodding to the doorkeeper, as they passed, a friendly nod seeming to say, "This is my girl, Ben. She's a peach, isn't she?" The way he pronounced her name when some other man stopped him or he stopped some other man— there were no words too hurried to include her in them. The way he looked up towards the gallery, lifting his hand to salute Drew and the others, giving her a little nudge so that she would do the same and calling her attention to the coatless, red-necked individual who sat directly behind Drew, staring open-mouthed at the unaccustomed magnificence with which he was surrounded. The way Raoul pulled out the chair which was hers, beside his, and smiled at her when he sat down and then leaned over, whispering to her. "That's Allen Ellender in the speaker's chair. Arthur Provost is standing beside him—the one in white linen. Isom Guillory, the floor leader, is back of Provost—he's lost without his whip-cracking job, now that everything's so tame. And over there, those two big men are Mason Spencer and George Perrault, talking to Norman Bauer. Those are the three they call the dynamite squad. They've led what opposition there's been to Huey. Perhaps you'd like to meet Mason Spencer. You know it was his speech that made such an impression on you."

"Yes, I remember. I'd be awfully thrilled to meet him." Mr. Spencer caught Raoul's eye, smiled, and came lumber-

ing over towards them with evident friendliness. But just
then the speaker rapped with his gavel, and Raoul muttered
that a divine blessing would now be invoked on all the
nonsense which was about to be set in motion. Stella was a
little disappointed because she had not actually met Mr.
Spencer before the session began, but this disappointment
was swallowed up in exultation at the feeling that there was
not a single man in the House, noticing her at Raoul's side, in
her fresh yellow dress and big white hat, who had not more
or less sized up the situation and who did not know that
Raoul was proud to have a chance to show her off. She
thought of the intrigue which was so imminent between
Drew and Evelyn—of how they would have to scheme and
sneak and lie to hide their feeling for each other from the
world, instead of proclaiming it openly and gladly—and she
forgot, just as Raoul had forgotten, that her grandmother
had said there should be nothing which would give the
appearance of making their engagement official or even intimating that there was an engagement.

The general setting and her own prominent place on the
scene were much more thrilling to Stella than the proceedings, themselves. The House began its session by adopting a
resolution providing for the selection of a burial site on
the Capitol grounds for Long and a concurrent resolution
providing for the attendance of the Legislature at Long's
funeral. It unanimously adopted a measure killing the "small
loan business" in Louisiana. It returned bill No. 27 to the
calendar. Raoul whispered to her that this was similar to bill
No. 1, and had merely been put in so that if No. 1, which
required a two-thirds vote, were defeated, No. 27, which
required only a majority vote, could be passed instead;
No.1 was a bill providing for the removal of Judge Pavy, the
father-in-law of the man who had killed Huey Long, from
the 13th to the 15th judicial district. While he was trying to clarify the reasons for this, a page came up to her and
handed her a note. She looked at it with surprise, thinking
there must be some mistake. Then she recognized Drew's
handwriting and opened it.

Dear Stella—she read.

*The King James Version being a required subject at Har-
vard, I remember some parts of it pretty well. You might
do worse than to choose the book of Esther for your bedtime reading tonight. (I'll see that there's a Bible in your*

*room along with the radio and the extension telephone!)
The story was recalled to my own alleged mind by the sight
of you sitting by Raoul. Especially the line about the person
"whom the king delighteth to honor."*

*Well, this is just leading up to the remark that I'm sure
Raoul (not to mention your own sweet self) would prefer
a tête-à-tête luncheon to one with a crowd, so don't
bother to try to rejoin us after the session closes. Say we
meet at the Heidelberg around five instead.*

*With all due respect to Queen Esther,
Her unworthy subject,
Andrew Breckenridge III.*

"What's Drew Breckenridge said to upset you?" Raoul inquired under his breath.

Stella could feel herself flushing. It was probably inevitable that Raoul should have guessed it was Drew who had
sent her the note; he might easily have seen Drew scribbling
it and summoning a page. But she wished he had not asked
her what Drew had written her, which was practically the
same thing as asking her to show him the note. This was
partly because she had always regarded letters as possessions that were so completely private and personal that
she had never expected to share them with anyone, and it
had not previously occurred to her that Raoul might expect
her to share hers with him. But it was also because she
thought, in one way, it would seem conceited of her to
show such a letter about herself, and because, in another, it
would seem as if she had something to conceal if she did
not. For the first time it occurred to her that Raoul might
be jealous as well as possessive, that though he was as
nearly perfect as anyone possibly could be, he had the
faults of his virtues no less than the virtues of his faults, like
everyone else, and that she might find it hard to put up with
these, after all. Now he noticed the flush, and the tone of
his voice when he spoke to her next confirmed her fears.

"I asked you, what's Drew Breckenridge written you that's
upset you so?" he inquired inexorably.

She handed him the note, her flush deepening as she did
so. Then she glanced up at the gallery. Involuntarily, she
was aware of the coatless, red-necked man again; he was now
staring open-mouthed at the automatic signal lights which
registered the voting. She also saw Drew's eyes resting on
her with unconcealed amusement; the expression of his

face revealed complete comprehension of her embarrassment
and the reasons for it, and it did not make her feel any
better to realize that he, himself, would never have insisted
upon reading a note which another man had written
to anyone in whom he was interested. Raoul, taking in the
contents of the troublesome missive quickly, gave a short
laugh as he handed it back to her.

"Is that all?" he said tersely. There was a new note in
his voice, one curiously like relief. "Well, there's another
well-known passage to the effect that the devil can quote
Scripture to his purpose. I'm not sure Drew Breckenridge
isn't saying one word for us and two for himself. I
shouldn't be surprised if somehow, in the shuffle, he and the
fair Evelyn got separated from her stupid souse of a husband and the modest maiden who's so piously bent on becoming the next Mrs. Breckenridge and thereby bringing
about the rake's reform."

"Oh, had you noticed all that, too?"

"What do you take me for? Well, our luncheon won't be
much of a tête-à-tête. If we can get into the Capitol
Cafeteria with a shoehorn, we'll be lucky. If we can't, we'll
try to fight our way through to the Coffee Shoppe at the
Heidelberg. Or just pick up a stray sandwich somewhere.
Though if you really want to see the lying-in-state, we'd
better not leave the Capitol. But I may have to leave you,
part of the time. I've got an awful lot to do today. And
you see I counted on having the others look after you,
from lunchtime on."

He did not sound disagreeable. But he did sound preoccupied. Stella knew, as soon as he spoke, that though he
had been proud to take her with him into the Chamber—
though he had experienced great satisfaction in having her
sit beside him there and showing her off to his colleagues
—he had expected this public tribute to mark the end of
their association that day. He did not want to spend the
rest of it showing attentions to a girl, even though this girl
was herself; he wanted to spend it with men, getting things
done. After her brief hour of triumph, it was doubly hard
for her to feel that she was in the way and that there was
nothing she could do about it. Because she was hurt, she
answered defensively.

"You don't have to stay with me at all, if you don't want
to."

"Don't be such a little fool. It isn't a question of what

I want to do, it's a question of what I've got to do. Come on and act your age, or the age you ought to be if you're going around with me. I keep forgetting you're nothing but a spoiled kid."

It was almost midnight when Stella went slowly up the steps of Splendida. There was a light burning in the portico and another in the entrance hall. But the drawing rooms were dark and deserted, and only the musty smell, which she hated, intensified by the prolonged rain, stole forth to meet her. She put out the lights and crept quietly along. She had been disappointed at first, because no one had waited up for her, but she had changed her mind about this already. It was just the principal of the thing, the feeling that it would have helped if someone had wanted to wait up for her which would have comforted her. She did not really want to see anyone. She was so utterly exhausted, so wretchedly heartsick, that she thought she would scream if she did. When she heard subdued voices and light laughter as she passed by the library, she quickened her dragging footsteps and went up the winding staircase in a wild spurt, obsessed with the fear that Drew and Evelyn might discover her presence before she could get out of sound and hearing.

She entered her own room breathlessly, but here she found a certain measure of solace. Her bed was turned down invitingly, her fresh nightgown lay across it, and there was a rosy-shaded lamp burning beside it. On the center table was a tray attractively set with covered procelain dishes and shining thermos jars. She was very hungry, for she had not had any supper, but the sight of the gleaming tub beyond the bathroom door was even more alluring than the sight of the appetizing food. She would shed her soiled sticky clothes and have a lovely bubble-bath, and then she would eat and eat and afterwards she would sleep and sleep, and in the morning she would feel better again. The very thought of the bath and the supper, the very sight of the bed, had made her feel better already. But she had just stepped out of the last encumbering garment when the door between her grandmother's room and her own opened slowly, and Mrs. Fontaine came towards her in the dim light.

"Put on a dressing gown, Stella, and come here. I want to talk to you."

In all her life Stella had never seen her grandmother uncontrolled, and it was very seldom that she had lost her own temper with Mrs. Fontaine. As a child, she had never been spanked, or even scolded, like the other children she knew; she had been lapped in unfailing indulgence and perpetual loving-kindness, and she had returned devotion for devotion. Later on, when strain had come between the two because each was self-willed and neither could bridge the half century's difference in view-point which divided them, Mrs. Fonatine had always glossed over her own immobility with surface gentleness and suavity, and Stella had nearly always been tolerably temperate. Now, as Mrs. Fontaine entered her room and spoke to her, she saw that her grandmother was not only very angry but that she was also making no effort to mask or curb her anger, and the storm which had been swelling in Stella's own breast broke with precipitous fury. But as she snatched up a dressing gown and wrapped it hurriedly around her, force of habit still impelled her to listen before she spoke.

"Stella, I am very much displeased with you and I think I have cause to be. I trusted you, supposing I was safe in doing this, and you have shown me that you are unworthy of my trust. So is the young man in whom I have had no confidence from the beginning."

"Grannie, you can say what you like about me, though I don't think I've done anything to deserve what you've just said. But you haven't any right to speak about Raoul like that. If you weren't prejudiced and snobbish and narrow-minded, you wouldn't have distrusted him until he gave you some reason to. And he's never done that."

"He has done it today. And so have you."

"No, he hasn't, and neither have I. I haven't the least idea what you're talking about."

"Stella, you have. You know that when I consented to this trip you have just taken, it was with the distinct understanding that the group in which you went would remain together."

"Well, it wasn't my fault that the others went streaking off to lunch without me. I didn't suggest it. I didn't think of such a thing. I thought of course we would all have lunch together, until Drew sent me a silly note, full of obscure Biblical quotations and stuff like that. I couldn't even make out what he was driving at, when I first read it. But gradually I gathered that he wanted——"

No, I mustn't say that, she said to herself, biting the words back just in time. No matter how unjust Grannie is, no matter how hurt I am, I haven't any right to be a tattle-tale. I won't put myself on a level with those women who gossiped about my father and Lute while they picked up their cards and licked up their cocktails. If Grannie hasn't noticed how Drew and Evelyn are acting, I mustn't give them away. Even if she has noticed, I must pretend she's mistaken. But she won't notice, she won't even think about them, because she's too busy thinking about Raoul and me——

"How could Drew *send* you a note, Stella, if you and he were together?"

"Why, we weren't together just then. I was on the floor of the House with Raoul. Each representative is allowed one seat for a guest. But only one. So Raoul put the others in the front row of the gallery. He had splendid seats saved for them."

"You sat with Raoul Bienvenu on the floor of the House? Publicly, as a person to whom he was showing special attention? When you knew how I would feel about such a procedure, considering that I had declined to permit you to visit his parents?"

"I didn't think how you'd feel about it, Grannie, honestly I didn't. I forgot everything in the world, I guess, I was so pleased that he asked me and so proud that he wanted me."

"So pleased and so proud to be made conspicuous——"

"He wasn't making me conspicuous, not in the way you're inferring. He never would. He was honoring me very much. If you don't understand that, there's no use in trying to explain it to you. Besides, you've made up your mind about it already. I can tell from the way you talk you knew where I sat before I ever came into this room."

"Yes, I knew. Evelyn Baird told me. But I thought possibly you might have something to say in self-defense."

"No, I haven't anything to say in self-defense. I don't think I've done anything that calls for self-defense. But I'd rather not talk about it, anyway, since you're determined to let a bitch like Evelyn Baird make you believe something was sordid, when I'm telling you it was wonderful."

She swung around savagely, bent on escape, past caring now what she said about Evelyn or anyone else. With incredible swiftness, her grandmother stepped in front of her.

"You will apologize, Stella, for using such a word in my

presence, and in reference to a beautiful bride, the daughter of one of my oldest friends."

"I'll apologize for using the word in your presence, if you can't take it, and I don't suppose you can. But I shan't apologize for applying it to Evelyn. If it ever fitted a girl in New Orleans, it fits her."

"Instead of slandering an innocent young married woman, I think you had better tell me what you did after you left the House of Representatives, and why you failed to rejoin your friends in the lobby of the Hotel Heidelberg, at the time agreed. I still don't know that."

"Well, I'll tell you, since your friend Evelyn couldn't. I had lunch in the Capitol Cafeteria, and nearly had the breath squeezed out of my body. It was about as public as a ball park, and ten times as painful. After that we just wandered around the Capitol. We went into the Senate and the Supreme Court Chamber and some of the committee rooms and up to the top of the tower. I got awfully tired, walking and walking, so finally we just sat around. We had to sit somewhere while we were waiting to see the lying-in-state."

"And I suppose all these places were also as public as a ball park?"

"Just about. People were coming in and out of them all the time. You don't seem to realize that twenty thousand persons were in that Capitol today. And flowers kept coming in by truckoads, too, with all the commotion that caused. By the time the lying-in-state began, there were enough wreaths to reach to the ceiling of Memorial Hall, all around the room, and to line all the aisles besides."

"I take it that Mr. Bienvenu was not personally arranging the flowers and that the twenty thousand person were not all trying to talk to him."

"Of course he wasn't arranging the flowers. But it did seem as if thousands of people were trying to talk to him. Reporters kept dashing up to ask questions, and frantic colleagues wanted to confer with him, and queer-looking constituents and clients from all over Vermilion Parish began to appear on the scene, and finally that weird old Dr. Anconi from Abbeville, with two or three of his usual cronies. They and Raoul went into a huddle together, in spite of the hubbub all around them, and completely forgot about me for a while. There was nothing for me to do but sit and stare out of the window at the cars that were going round and round the Capitol—old rattletraps covered with mud and snappy little sport roadsters and huge sleek limousines all jumbled in together. I never saw such thousands of cars in my life or so many different kinds. I looked at them until I got dizzy, and then I looked at the men who were digging Huey's grave and the crowd that was gathered around them, and that wasn't a very cheerful sight either. Anyway, my eyes ached almost as badly as my feet by that time."

"And did Dr. Anconi continued to talk to Mr. Bienvenu all the afternoon?"

"Almost. And if you like, I'll tell you what the sole topic of conversation was between Raoul and me afterwards. Or rather, what his sole topic of conversation was, because he did all the talking. It was that everything was fixed for him to run for the State Senate now, and that the sooner I got off to Europe, where I wouldn't distract his mind during the campaign, the better it would be. Or words to that effect. I hope you're satisfied now."

"No, I'm not satisfied now. I still don't know why you didn't rejoin your group—why you weren't at the Hotel Heidelberg at five o'clock."

"If you'd only gone with us today, as I asked you to, you'd know why. You'd have seen for yourself what the streets in Baton Rouge were like, how they were blocked, how they were swarming. The sidewalks were worse than Canal Street on Madri Gras, and special trains kept coming in every five minutes, disgorging more people. And everywhere you turned there were soldiers who wouldn't let you go up here or down there until you identified yourself. I've never even dreamed of anything like it. We couldn't *get* from the Capitol to the Heidelberg Hotel by five o'clock. No one, caught the way we were, could have done it in that length of time. And when we did get there, we had to fight our way through the lobby, just as we had fought it through the cafeteria and through the streets. My clothes were half torn off me. I must be black and blue from one end of me to the other. And my group, as you call it, wasn't anywhere around. I looked and looked and waited, and so did Raoul. And finally I found out that Drew had left a note for me at the desk, saying they were starting back to Splendida without me, that Julia had a backache and Evelyn had a headache, and that they all knew Raoul would jump at the chance of bringing me back, anyway. Like hell he did! He had a committee meeting on for the evening, and he had to send word he couldn't be there and go back to the Capitol to get his car out of the parking space, walking all the way over again in the pouring rain, through the mob we had just got out of. Then after we got into the car, I didn't think we'd ever get to the ferry landing or on the boat or off it again. Motors were blocked for miles on both sides of the river. And finally Raoul had to buck the worst crowd there ever was anywhere in the world for thirty miles to land me at home, with the prospect of doing the same thing all the way back to Baton Rouge, another thirty miles, afterwards! If you think he made love to me when he was all hot and bothered about the committee meeting, and foaming at the mouth about the crowd on top of that, you're terribly mistaken. Why, he even forgot to kiss me good-bye!"

The oversight, when it happened, had been a bitter blow after a series of bitter blows. Now, as Stella spoke of it, her hurt pride and her unappeased yearning both surged up within her uncontrollably. She lashed out at her grandmother, exulting, despite her overwhelming weariness, in the chance to wound in her turn.

"I wish I'd stayed in Baton Rouge," she said desperately. "I wish I'd gone to Raoul's room. That would have been much the easiest way out for both of us. I mean his bedroom, where we could have locked the door. If I'd done that, and stayed there, you and I wouldn't have had this scene, at least not now, when I'm so tired I can't see straight, and when I haven't got anything worth saying to tell you, anyway. We might have had it tomorrow, but by then I'd have got my bearings, and I would have had something to tell you, that is, if I'd felt like it. If I'd stayed in Raoul's room overnight, it would have put an end to all this damned endless talk about campaigns and careers and everything else. Because he would have gone to his committee meeting and got that off his mind, and everything all straightened out about his career, but after he came back, we'd have gone to bed together. He'd have forgotten that he ought not to make violent love to me, if I'd been right there in his room, just the way I forgot you didn't want me to be seen with him. He wouldn't have talked with me about keeping the record clear, and all that, the way he did the night we went to Jeanerette together. And you thought you couldn't *trust* him! You don't know how much you can trust him! You don't know a real man when you see one, or if you ever did, you've forgotten! But I don't believe there's any man, no matter how trustworthy he is, if the girl he wants is right in his room, and wants him, too, so much she thinks she'll die, and it's dark and still and secret and they put their arms around each other, who wouldn't——"

"Stella, my child—my dear child—you mustn't say these dreadful things— You mustn't think of them— You must stop——"

The anger was all gone from Mrs. Fontaine's voice. In it there was unbelief, there was shock, there was fear; but these had completely engulfed her helpless and bewildered rage. Now, aghast at the torrent she had, herself, unleashed, she tried with equal helplessness and with ever mounting horror to stem it. Stella shook off her trembling arm.

"Dreadful! They're not dreadful! The reason you think they are is because you married the wrong man. You didn't dare find out for yourself that they aren't, in the only way there is to find out! In the arms of the man you love! And still, if you could, you'd make me do the same thing you did. If I did that, then I would have hideous memories all my life, just the way you have." She sobbed once, sharply, and went on. "But if I'd only stayed with Raoul—if I only belonged to him by now—everything would be all right. Because probably I'd have thought, pretty soon, that I was going to have a baby, and then Raoul would have married me right away. He'd have been crazy to, campaign or no campaign! And I could have gone home with him, to Abbeville! We could have had a long low white house without waiting, because he wouldn't have minded using my money either, once we were really married. We could have lived in peace without having anyone interfere with us and loved each other a lot and been ever so happy. And now, when we both tried to do right, when we were both trustworthy, whether it looked that way or not, I've got to go away and leave him! While Evelyn goes right on being a bitch without any bother at all! But I've got to be a singer, because I was silly enough to say that was what I wanted, and a social success, because you're silly enough to want me to be. All right then, I will! I'll show you! I'll show Raoul! I'll show the world! If he can go anywhere from a bayou, I can go anywhere from a stuffy old Victorian house. But I'll never forgive you, Grannie, for what you've said to me and what you've done to me tonight, never, as long as I live!"

PART VIII

The Raised Cottage

Spring, 1940

CHAPTER 29

EVELYN BAIRD had always given noisy, flashy luncheons—
"loud" in every sense of the word. But it seemed to Drew
Breckenridge that the one she gave at the Métairie Golf
Club, the first Sunday in Lent, was the noisiest and flashiest
he had ever attended.

Drew, like everyone else, thought of these functions as
Evelyn's parties, though, of course, her husband, Harold, was
the host, nominally at least. Harold had never had much
strength of character, however, or, as Drew reflected contemptuously, he would not have married Evelyn in the first
place, much less indulged her every whim and condoned her
every folly. He must have known her for what she was from
the beginning, and an acquiescent cuckold was bound to be
a weakling and deserved his degradation. Harold had not
seemed dissolute as a boy. His habits would easily have
borne comparison with those of his friends, and his personality was much more pleasing than theirs, taken by and large.
He had been lazy and inconsequential, but he had been good-
natured and generous; he was agreeable and attractive. But
now, seated at the end of a long, disordered table which
was littered with dishes of melting ice cream and overflowing ash trays and drooping flowers, between two smartly-
dressed, artificially-colored young women whose natural propensity to scream had been intensified by excitement, drink,

and the determination to drown each other out, he looked almost loutish. His fine high color was empurpled; his bright blue eyes were dull; his silence, more or less enforced by the chatter which engulfed him, was broken by occasional meaningless laughter, or by a story as smutty as it was ill-timed. Drew, unconcerned that he might conceivably have contributed to the gradual and tragic disintegration of Harold's character, looked away from the sad spectacle presented by his host, lest his own scorn should be too scathingly evident.

It seemed to him that Evelyn would never give the signal to rise. He was placed at her right, and they had hardly been seated when she had slipped her foot against one of his. When he did not instantly enfold it with the other, pressing it gently between the two, she wriggled a little, and somehow the movement filled him with disgust, though the touch of Evelyn's slim, silk-shod little feet had long been provocative and thrilling. He had withdrawn and had managed to retain his aloofness all through the tedious meal, with its succession of unimaginative courses, rendered tasteless by the number of Sazeracs that had been consumed before lunch, and superfluous to start with, because everyone had eaten a late and hearty Sunday breakfast. He found the endless rehash of Carnival events—now, thank God, over and done with!—excessively dull, and the agitated discussion about Sam Jones, the new "reform" candidate for governor, roused only ironic memories. He remembered all too well that the Constitutional Convention to which his father would have gone in 1913, if Breck had not been drowned, had been called by a "reform" governor, Luther Hall, whom the state had regarded as a savior because he had broken the strangle hold of Martin Behrman; but after the first wave of exhilaration had subsided, Louisiana had sunk deeper into degradation than ever before. It was extremely doubtful whether Sam Jones could smash the "Long machine" which was the bloated legacy the Kingfish had left to his heirs and henchmen. But supposing Jones did, what then? Would history fail to repeat itself within a year or two? Drew did not believe so. He thought that corruption, like Carnival, was in the blood of Louisianians from the best to the worst of them. His own included——

His expression retained its customary suavity, but it was tinged with more and more skepticism as he continued to listen, and the realization that Evelyn was punishing him for his aloofness by forcing him to sit indefinitely at her side annoyed him excessively. He was almost ready to affront her unpardonably by asking to be excused on the ground of a pressing engagement elsewhere, when one of the smart, screaming young women, sitting beside Harold, delivered him from this temptation. She looked at the large diamond wrist watch gleaming against the beautifully-cut sleeve closing with fine little buttons around her white, beringed hand and gave a piercing shriek.

"My dear, how *horrible!* Do you know it's long after four already? And I was supposed to be at Mathilde's, way down on Esplanade, by quarter of. Well, it's all your fault, Evelyn! It's practically impossible to tear oneself away from your parties."

"You take the words out of my mouth, Corinne," Drew remarked suavely.

He was safely on his feet at last. Evelyn had perforce risen to accept the farewell embrace of her dear friend, Corinne, who had flung her arms around her hostess's neck with a violence which suggested an indefinite and intolerable separation. By the time Evelyn had extricated herself from Corinne, she was seized on the other side by a second guest who had been similarly startled to discover the time and who was equally intense in her manner of parting. Evelyn was almost smothered in silver fox furs, *Shocking* scent and prolonged kisses which were bestowed like a barrage, with a little exclamation between each. After that the party seemed to stampede. Nobody even listened to Evelyn's vehement protests.

"Why I took it for granted you were all going to stay for bridge and cocktails! I'm sure I made that clear! I did hear about Mathilde's party, but for some reason she didn't include Harold and me, so I thought she was having a different crowd this time—those Northerners Walter Avery's had around during Carnival, and people like that. Later on I thought we would go over to the house for supper. Everything's ready— Harold, you expected everyone to stay, didn't you? Or almost everyone?"

"Well, I thought Drew probably would, anyhow," Harold said, and laughed loudly and aimlessly, as he had been laughing at intervals throughout luncheon.

The laughter, like the leave-taking, became general. Harold's retort was accepted as a good joke; no one took it seriously, partly because no one took anything Harold said seriously any more and partly because everyone was already too

preoccupied with departure. But two bright spots of color
blazed suddenly on Evelyn's smooth, white face, high on
the cheekbones, under her languishing eyes. Somehow she
had controlled her fury over Drew's *double-entendre*, because she knew that if she revealed her anger, she would
lose him for good and all, instead of losing him temporarily,
as she was beginning to fear that she had. But she struck
out now, heedlessly, at Harold.

"Shut up, you swine!" she said in a savage whisper. Then
she turned appealingly in the direction of the place where,
a few moments before, Drew had been standing. But he was
not there any longer, and reluctantly she remembered that
she had heard him murmuring something about being in a
hurry, too, while she had been engulfed in Corinne's embrace. She could not count on him to get Harold home inconspicuously and into his own room where he would sleep
soundly for the next few hours, leaving her free. She could
not count on Drew for anything any more. And later on,
though her guests had taken Harold's vile remark so lightly
when he made it, they would think of it again, less lightly,
and talk about it among themselves—"Of course, he can't
be responsible. I saw him take five drinks before lunch myself. There's no knowing how many he'd taken that I didn't
see."—"Well, I don't know, maybe Harold's suspicious of
something. I have been, myself, for quite a while. You know
what Evelyn is!"—"Yes, and you know what Drew Breckenridge is, too. Whom will he go out after next, I wonder?"

That was the bitterest blow of all. If Drew was indeed
tired of her, it was because he was already intrigued by the
idea of a new chase and a fresh conquest. She ought to
know— The reason she, herself, had stolen him so easily
from Julia Beal was because he was tired of Julia, of her
dull righteousness and her fierce virginity. But Evelyn, herself, had given Drew no reason to tire of her. At least, none
that she could think of. Passionately, she tried to remember
what she could have done or left undone to deserve Drew's
desertion. But it was hard to think at the Golf Club in the
middle of a Sunday afternoon, when she had to sign the
checks paying for the drinks and the luncheon, indicate what
disposal she wanted made of the wilted flowers, and get her
drunken husband home.

Unlike Evelyn and Harold, Drew had been invited to Mathilde Villeré's party, and he had really intended to go there

when he left the golf club, though he said nothing about this invitation and decided to take a circuitous route. He did not want to ask Corinne Lane to go with him or to arrive so soon after she did that she would wonder why he had not done so and, with her usual lack of delicacy, publicly inquire. He was driving himself, for the invaluable Louis, generally regarded by Drew's acquaintances as an affectation in any case, was seldom pressed into service as a chauffeur except in the evening, and as Drew switched on his engine, he thought vaguely of going out further into the country and dropping in, unheralded, at one or two of the many plantation houses within easy reach, where his arrival would be hailed with delight, or even going as far as Splendida. Momentarily, a wave of nostalgia engulfed him; but with bitter realism, he knew it was not Splendida as he would see it today for which he longed so intolerably at times. It was the Splendida of his childhood, when he watched the fishermen on the batture and the steamboats on the river, when he rode his pony through the fresh white clover and tagged at his father's heels along the rows of sugar cane, humming in unison with their people who worked there, *We'll Understand It Better By and By*. He had thought this was true then, for his understanding of the place, like his love of the place, had grown day by day while he watched with eager eyes the unfolding miracle of a plantation's production and listened with alert ears to the patient and enlightening answers that were given to all his questions.

But the promise of the spiritual had been a false one. In his cynical maturity, he did not understand better than he had as a trustful child. He could not understand, nor could anyone, why the relentless river had ravaged his land again, so that the allee, like the grove, was now swallowed up, leaving only the overgrown garden around the house and bringing nearer and nearer the day which he, himself, had foretold, when he would go there and find water eddying around the portico. He could not understand, nor could anyone he knew in Louisiana—whatever the swivel-chair "experts" in Washington might think they understood—why he should have been told to destroy a quarter of the crops on the land he had left. Acres and acres of "over-quota" cane had been ordered burned. He could still smell the acrid odor that had been wafted towards him and still feel the smouldering fires that had confronted him when he looked out over his fields the previous fall; he could still see the blackened stalks bereft of their gracile leaves. The extinction of so much rich life had deepened the depression and strengthened the cynicism which had so long engulfed him. Not that the money he had lost mattered much to him; his oil wells were gushing with greater and greater quantities of "black gold" all the time. But it had mattered to many other men who were dependent on their parity payments. How was anyone to understand the justice of that? And when it came to justice, what would be meted out to a nation which deliberately destroyed good food in times of plenty when the inevitable time of want came again?

Drew had been driving aimlessly out on the Airline Highway as he thought of all of this, and now, with equal aimlessness, he turned his car towards town again. Of course, he could always go to the Fontaines', and there were many duller places to spend a Sunday afternoon. Mrs. Fontaine, to whom he was genuinely devoted, never failed to give him so warm a welcome that it "touched even his black heart," as he was fond of saying; and Stella invariably managed to gather around her, in an effortless way, the most attractive examples of the city's gilded youth and a good many stimulating specimens of a slightly older and more sophisticated order, so that there was always a gay heterogeneous group at the house. She was unquestionably the outstanding debutante of the season, or of any season Drew could remember. She had developed amazingly during her years abroad, and her musical achievements were only a small part of this development; the entire Continental experience had broadened her horizon in every way, and there was not one of Drew's own feminine contemporaries who could compete with her in culture and charm. Well as he had known her all her life, there were moments when he actually had difficulty in believing that the poised and accomplished and fascinating young woman who was now Stella Fontaine was the same person as the tumultuous, refractory, passionate child who only a few years earlier had beaten her shining, willful head against the stone wall of her grandmother's opposition to her heart's desire and the equally immovable bulwark of her beloved's resistance to her urgency and impetuosity.

She had certainly turned the tables on both since then. At the end of two years, Mrs. Fontaine would have been only too glad to bring her back from Europe; Raoul Bienvenu would have made almost any concession in order to marry her. But it was Stella, herself, by then, who proved immovable. She was already singing small parts at the Opéra Comique, for her success from the beginning had been phenomenal, and she did not mean to leave Paris until she was singing big ones. If her grandmother wanted to return to New Orleans without her, she would understand perfectly; she would secure another suitable chaperone and stay on in the charming little apartment on the Ile de la Cité, where she was so agreeably established; she controlled her own income now; she could do as she pleased. If Raoul wanted to break the engagement, she would understand that, too. She still loved him, for none of the other suitors, of whom there were many, who had besieged her in the meantime had made any dent on her now unimpressionable heart. She would still be glad to marry him some day, but she no longer felt it was a matter of immediacy. She had stood aside once, so that he could pursue his career; it was only fair that he should stand aside now, so that she could pursue hers.

Stella had won all along the line. Mrs. Fontaine had stayed on in Paris, wistfully but resignedly. Raoul had gone back to Louisiana alone after losing one of the few cases he had ever plead, in the course of a trip to Europe which he had visualized as ending in a wedding journey but which had led to lonely leave-taking instead. And one by one, the big parts had come Stella's way. At last there was a night when she sang the supreme song in *Louise,* not among the shadows of a ruined allee, but on a great stage, facing a brilliant amphitheatre packed to the last inch of standing room. Raoul had crossed the Atlantic a second time to hear her sing. But after the opera was over, there was a champagne supper in the director's quarters, and a dozen men were clustering around the prima donna, clamoring for the privilege of taking her home. She had laughed lightly at all of them including Raoul and, in the end, she had slipped away from all of them, under the wing of the faithful Julie, through a side door. She had gone back to a bedroom which she could still "call her own," and where no disorderly masculine possessions were strewn around to clutter its gracious feminine perfection.

It had taken a second World War to bring her back. She could not steel herself, after this broke out, against her grandmother's piteous entreaties to start for home before it was too late or against the desperation in the cables raining in from Raoul, telling her that he would have no rest until he saw with his own eyes that she was safe. She had reached

New Orleans in the early fall of 1939 with no tale of terror or hardship to tell, but with trunkloads of beautiful clothes which she had somehow managed to bring with her, while other travellers were recklessly abandoning their baggage on the disordered piers of France, and with packing cases full of beautiful possessions with which she transformed her own quarters in the cream-colored house on Prytania Street. What was more significant still, she slipped with apparent ease back into the life which she had led before, never showing off her singing, never bragging about her successes, never seeking or claiming any of the limelight which shone so inescapably upon her, and managing to retain a certain unassailable simplicity in the face of everything that contributed to destroy this. But the less she claimed for herself, the more others accorded her. Her pre-eminence as a Carnival Queen formed a small part in her pattern of conquest. Young and old alike found her delightful. There were, apparently, no limits to the "infinite variety of her charm."

Mrs. Fontaine watched her carry off the honors of the season with the feeling that there were only two flaws in this picture, but that these were grave ones. The first was Stella's still unshaken determination to marry Raoul Bienvenu, since he had waited for her, and the second was the detachment in her attitude, though this was still restrained and respectful, which showed she had spoken the truth when she said she would never forgive her grandmother for what had been said and done at Splendida. For Raoul, there were perhaps more and graver flaws in the picture. With all that Stella had gained, something had gone out of her, too—some essential gladness, some spontaneity of self-surrender, which once he might have rapturously imprisoned for himself but which he now feared he might never recapture. She had been loyal in spite of her procrastination; she was affectionate in spite of her aloofness; she was generous though she was no longer prodigal. The perfection of any part she would play as a politician's wife would exceed the perfection of any part she had acted on the stage. Her engagement, though still officially unannounced, was an open secret, and Raoul came constantly to the Prytania Street house, sometimes alone, sometimes with the men whom he wanted and needed to see in New Orleans. It provided an impressive as well as a convenient meeting place and Stella was an impeccable hostess. She had a special gift for putting shy and uncouth men at their ease and for giving elderly men the impression that the importance of a youthful gathering was immeasurably enhanced by their presence. Raoul was not unmindful of the advantages of all this, any more than he was ungrateful for Stella's loyalty or unmoved by her loveliness. But, still, he yearned to hear her say again, ardently and unreservedly, "I want everything to be just as you want it"—to hear her sing her supreme song for him alone. But it was he, himself, who had once suppressed the saying; it was he, himself, who had silenced the song. He wondered with increasing anxiety whether he would ever be enabled to listen to either again.

Some of this Drew only divined. Some of it he knew, having seen it with his own eyes and heard it with his own ears. For some of it, as in the case of Harold's downfall, he knew he was himself responsible, but the knowledge did not leave him as untroubled as it did regarding Evelyn's sottish husband. If he had not left Stella in the Capitol at Baton Rouge, or even if he had waited for her in the Heidelberg Hotel afterwards, he knew that she might have retained that vital confidence and gladness without which everything else she had gained profited her so little. It was that dreadful day when Huey Long had lain in state which marked the change in her character; until then she had been strong enough and courageous enough to bear the limitations both of Raoul's devotion and of her grandmother's understanding. But she had been too immature and too inexperienced to bear alone the impact of all that had overwhelmed her then. A steadfast friend could certainly have helped her and probably could have saved her. She had believed that she possessed this friend in Drew, and he had failed her also, for no better reason than that he was infatuated with a woman whom he knew, even then, was worthless. It was not the fact that she had gone to Europe which had changed her; it was the desperation and disillusionment with which she had gone. He had a great deal to answer for as far as Stella was concerned, and some day he would have to do it. But not today. Not now. He was still seeking to find escape from reality, not to add further responsibilities to his life——

He had continued to drive aimlessly towards town as he thought about Stella, and he was still going in the general direction of her house, though this had ceased to be even a considered objective, when he turned into St. Charles Avenue. But before he had gone many more blocks, he suddenly knew what he wanted to do, wondering, as the swift realization came to him, why he had not known it all along; and presently he brought his car to a stop in front of the long walk, bordered by azaleas, which led to a "raised cottage" belonging to distant kinsfolk of his grandmother, of whom he had once seen a good deal but whom he had neglected for an indefinite period.

It was really a charming place, he reflected, as he walked slowly towards the house, glancing about him as he went, with an appreciation sharpened because the tranquil beauty which he now beheld presented so striking a contrast to the vulgar pandemonium from which he had just escaped. Here nothing was out of harmony; nothing was out of balance; the effect was one of complete repose and unassailable refinement. Large magnolia trees were scattered over the lush law in such a way that they gave the illusion of a grove rather than a row, although there were only eight or ten of them altogether; and beyond them were two or three ivy-wreathed hackberry trees, which had such a bad name as "banquette breakers" because their strong roots persistently pushed up through the pavements; the slight unevenness of the walk here and there might be blamed on these. But they gave so exquisite an effect of sheltering grace that it was easy to understand why a householder would put up with the slight inconvenience they caused. Beyond the azaleas, on either side of the high steps leading up to the main entrance, rose two guardian palms, and smaller ones, mingled with the shrubbery, almost concealed the lower gallery and the dimly lighted windows on the ground floor. This, Drew remembered now, was separately rented to some Northern family which took no part in the life of the community. But a lantern hanging outside the front door cast its friendly beams on the beautiful Corinthian columns supporting the upper gallery, making the panels of the door and the fluting of the columns seem all the whiter by comparison with the surrounding darkness. Early as it was, the long curtains inside had already been drawn; the rooms Drew faced looked, from without, even more untenanted than the quarters below. But he was not deceived; he knew the custom of the country which decreed that curtains be drawn before darkness fell, both to insure complete privacy and to keep out the cold from the imperfectly heated houses; and he could, moreover, hear a reassuring murmur of voices in the distance. He pushed the bell and waited with confidence and without impatience for someone to answer it, continuing his appraisal of his surroundings with an expert eye.

How misleading the term "cottage" as applied to a house of this type must be to an outsider, he reflected, and, as far as that went, how misleading was such a house, itself, seen at a distance! From the street, even from the walk, it really did look like a cottage, with unobtrusive dormers above the Corinthian columns. It was only when you began to climb the steps that you realized the height of that concealed ground floor, only when you stood on the iron-railed upper gallery and glanced at those long curtained windows that you recognized the far greater height of this main floor "raised," in truth, above the secluded one supporting it. The rooms beyond the front door must be fifteen feet high at least, and if he remembered rightly, there were three on either side of the immense central hall dividing them. When you added to these the ones on the ground floor and the four chambers served by dormers above, the house began to take on the proportions of a mansion rather than a cottage!

These details were intriguing to Drew in spite of his life-long familiarity with them. Shamefully as he had neglected his chosen profession of architecture, he understood and appreciated beautiful building in all its forms quite as well as he appreciated and understood beautiful women in all theirs. For all that, he could not be content to stand outside the front door indefinitely, as he now seemed fated to do. His second ring, like his first, had remained unanswered; nowhere was there a sound of footsteps indicating that someone was on the way to let him in. He raised the brass knocker, which at first he had been disposed to regard as ornamental rather than useful, and knocked vigorously. Almost instantly he heard a near-by door inside open and close, and immediately afterwards the front door, itself, was flung open; the light from the lantern, streaming like a beacon into the shadowy hall with its dim landscape paper and its superb screens, fell full on the bright hair and candid face of Patty Forrestal.

She drew back a little, giving a small smothered exclamation of surprise as she did so. Then she held out her hand, and Drew saw that she was wearing a diamond bracelet, beautiful in itself but incongruous with the short and simple dress made of natural-colored wool which she had on.

"Why, Mr. Breckenridge!" she exclaimed. "How nice of you to call! I do hope you haven't been waiting long."

"It didn't seem long. I stood here and admired your charming house. But after a time I decided something must be the matter."

"The doorbell's out of order," Patty said apologetically. "It generally is. I'm afraid our visitors don't get the right sort of reception." She thought of Mrs. Fontaine's perfectly appointed house, where the servants were always on duty and everything ran on greased wheels, and hoped that Drew Breckenridge, who probably often dropped in to see Stella, was not making mental comparisons also. "Mother'll be awfully pleased to see you, though," Patty went on. "She was saying, just the other day, that she hadn't laid eyes on you in a long time, and that you were a great favorite of hers, when you were a boy. She's in the drawing room with some friends —Aunt Lula and Mrs. Fay, and one or two others. I poured tea for them, and then I went into the library with the boys, because they wanted a fifth, for rummy. You'll go in to see mother first, won't you?"

"Yes, I suppose so. But I'm not in any immediate hurry. Let's just stand here for a minute and talk by ourselves."

He smiled engagingly as he made the suggestion. Patty fell in with it readily enough, making two in her turn.

"Of course, I'd enjoy that very much. But perhaps, after a while, you'd like to play cards, too. We can switch to some other game. And we'd like very much to have you stay for supper, if you aren't too busy. We get it ourselves, Sunday nights. But it's fun, puttering around in the pantry——"

She stopped abruptly. Her momentary embarrassment had vanished so swiftly that she felt almost immediately as if she were talking to an old friend. She supposed she ought to feel in awe of the famous Andrew Breckenridge, and, instead of that, she felt completely at ease with him. She could not remember that her feelings in regard to anyone had ever changed so fast before, except once, and that had been on the night of the Jubilee Ball of the Pacifici, when she had received her initial call-out. The same feeling of release had delivered her then, and there had been no renewal of strain in her subsequent dances with the same masker that night. No, nor at the later balls of Momus and Comus in the dances with a certain masker whose height, carriage, manner, voice and effect upon her had so closely resembled those of her first gallant. She had easily divined, in spite of his varied disguises, that all these engaging tributes belonged to the same man. His *voice!* Why this was the very first thing she had noticed, because it had such a different quality from that of the voices to which she was accustomed—smoother and richer, and yet tinged with some alien element of the

North. In a flash, she realized why she had not only looked at Andrew Breckenridge with attention but listened to him with attention, every time she had seen him lately: at the Sunday breakfast which Walter Avery had given in the Mystery Room at Antoine's in honor of his New York guest; at the midnight supper for the Queen of Comus, where she had unexpectedly been placed in an advantageous seat facing the golden head table; at the Boston Club on Carnival Day, when she had gone there with Gail to see the Carnival Court.

Drew Breckenridge had spoken to her courteously but casually on all these festive occasions, as he had always spoken to her whenever they met, from the time she was a little girl; but he had not paused to talk with her or given any sign that he thought of her now except as a little girl. He had been with the Villerés at Antoine's, with the Fontaines at the Queen's supper party, and with the Bairds at the Boston Club, and each time he had remained close to his own group. But it had been hard for Patty to keep her eyes from straying in his direction, and involuntarily she had strained her ears to hear what he was saying. She had even begun to watch for him, unconsciously, at the functions where he did not appear: at Mrs. Baldwin's house, for instance, where, according to the immemorial custom of her family, they had all gone to watch the parade of Rex pass by, and exult when the great golden chariot of the King halted in front of the gate. Mrs. Baldwin, like all former Carnival Queens, flew the royal purple, green and gold banner from her flagstaff that day, and it was her proud privilege to welcome Rex and proffer him refreshments in the course of his progress.

Patty, for the first time, had been allowed to handle the great silver loving cup filled with champagne which Mr. Baldwin carried down to the float, climbing the ladder which had previously been placed there to reach its eminence and proffering the precious beaker to the merry monarch. But even this honor had not compensated for her vague feeling of disappointment, and later she had asked Mathilde Villeré, as nonchalantly as she could, whether Drew Breckenridge was not coming to the Baldwins' luncheon. Why no, Mathilde had answered, looking at Patty with unconcealed astonishment; he was on the committee at the Boston Club; of course, he would not have a free moment. Why no, of course not, Patty had echoed, feeling slightly snubbed. But she had continued to watch for him just the same, and later, when she had caught a glimpse of him on her way to the Bounders, she had been inexplicably pleased. Yes, and now that she thought of it, he *had* shown her one special mark of favor: when the band began to play the Carnival song, *If Ever I Cease to Love,* as the King and Queen advanced towards the luncheon table, in the ceremonial march which formed part of the celebration at the Boston Club, Drew had caught her gaze as it rested on him and had raised the glass of champagne he was drinking, smiling at her with such directness that the toast became personal in its import. She had blushed deeply and painfully and glanced covertly around her to see if the salutation had been noticed by others as well as herself. But everyone else was absorbed in acclaiming the Queen, and when Patty had summoned the courage to look at Drew again, he was apparently pre-occupied, too. So she had not dared to attach much importance to the episode afterwards. But now——

"If I stayed, could I help you make the cocoa?" Drew Breckenridge was inquiring in that rich, alien voice, interrupting her startled train of thought. It was as fantastic to him as it was to her that he should put her such a simple question. This was the first time that he had ever asked a young girl if he might help her with some homely task, or wanted to help her. And yet, the words were hardly out of his mouth before they ceased to seem fantastic. Patty had first roused his sympathy and admiration; then, in turn, she had amused and touched and charmed and thrilled him. But this was not only because she was ingenuous and responsive and lovely; it was also because she was sincere and straightforward and courageous. He had learned to evaluate these qualities better than when he had first been conscious of them in Stella five years earlier. His appreciation of Stella, like his knowledge of her need for him, had come too late. But he had not made the same mistake with Patty, and he knew that, whatever his relationship with her was to be, there would be many homely things, and even many hard things, that they would need to do together and that they would be willing and glad to do together. They would reach great heights if the fates were auspicious, for there was a spirituality about Patty, too, as far surpassing Stella's earthiness as Stella's loyalty surpassed Evelyn's inconstancy. But they would not always stay on the heights and see into the heavens; they would tread the rough plain and descend the tortuous depths while they shared the bread of life with each other.

"Why of course," she said cordially, breaking in on a train of thought, in her turn. There was still some surprise in her voice, but not much, and there was no hesitation. Apparently, she accepted it as logical that he should want to help her. "Only the pantry is rather messy," she went on, in explanation rather than apology, "and there are ants in it."

"There is nothing on earth so barren-looking as a neat pantry," Drew remarked encouragingly. "And a Southern house wouldn't be complete without ants, would it? Any more than it would be complete without a gallery around it and magnolia trees in front of it? Of course we talk more about the galleries and magnolias than we do about the ants—to outsiders, anyway, and strangers. But you and I belong here, so we don't need to pretend. What's more, we're more or less related. Which reminds me—you don't call your other male cousins Mr. So-and-So, do you? Gail Rutledge, for instance?"

"Oh no! But Gail really is my cousin. That is, his Aunt Clementine married my——"

"Patty, don't let's try to go into all that just now. It's too complicated. I'll take your word for it that he really is your cousin, if you'll take my word for it that I am, too. In fact, I never dreamed of calling your mother anything but Aunt Eleanor when I was a boy. I'm sorry to say I haven't seen much of her since then, so I haven't called her anything. But I'm going to see more of her in the future."

"I don't seem to remember——"

"Because you were just a huge-eyed baby then—a very pleasant baby, but rather on the sober side. Only, when you did smile, there was a darling little dimple right near your lower lip, on your chin—a little to the left. Come over here to the light and let me see if it's still there. You'll have to tilt your head up a little. You don't mind, do you?"

It would have made her self-conscious to have walked over to a light on purpose for inspection, not to mention tilting up her head so that this inspection could be closer, if anyone else had asked her to do it, but it seemed entirely natural to do both at the request of Drew Breckenridge. Almost instantly, however, Patty realized that he was not referring to the light or the tilt when he asked her if she minded. He was referring to the fact that he had lifted his hands and very gently framed her face with them, raising it until her eyes were almost on a level with his own. But she did not mind that either. He looked down at her, and she returned his gaze steadfastly. But she did not smile. Somehow it seemed too solemn a moment. Drew must have thought so, too, for he did not refer to the dimple again. Instead, he spoke suddenly and sincerely, forgetful of the adroit evasions and smooth phrases of which he was such a past master. And he said something very strange and very wonderful.

"I love you, Patty. I love you dearly. It means everything in the world to me to have you look at me like that. Promise me you'll never look at me in any other way."

It was hard for Patty, after that, to open the door of the drawing room, where her mother and her Aunt Lula and Mrs. Fay were sitting, and to say, trying hard to keep her voice quiet and casual, that she was bringing in Drew Breckenridge, who had come to call. She knew exactly what would happen when she did. There would be a great deal of astonishment at Drew Breckenridge's appearance, and this astonishment would reveal itself in various ways. Her mother would nervously press tea upon Drew, though the tea by this time would be quite cold and terribly strong and bitter, and ask Patty to please go and see if she could not find some more little cakes, because she had never *dreamt* she and Aunt Lula and Mrs. Fay would have eaten all there were on the tray; and Patty would know there was no use in looking, because the boys had devoured all those Roberta had left in the pantry when she went out for the afternoon. Aunt Lula, who could talk more rapidly and steadily than any other woman in New Orleans, which was saying a great deal, would begin to draw in her breath in the middle of every sentence, as if she had been running hard or had a stitch in her side, and then she would forget what the first part of the sentence had been about and start all over again on some other subject. She always did this when she became very much excited, and she would be terribly excited about Drew. Mrs. Fay would not say very much, since Aunt Lula would not give her a chance, but, because she resented this enforced silence, she would watch like a cat every movement Drew made and hang on his every word. Then the next day when she started out immediately after breakfast on her next round of visits, she would tell her friends, with whom she drank black coffee and ate little sweet cakes in midmorning, that Drew Breckenridge had come to call at the

Forrestals, of *all places*, when she, herself, was there Sunday afternoon. He might have known that Eleanor Forrestal did not make a practice of receiving gentlemen informally, since her husband's death, but preferred to confine her own little circle to ladies, except, of course, for her son's special friends. But Drew was *years older* than Richard and Vincent and Ffoulke and could not conceivably be coming to see any of them, so *why* should he have been at the Forrestals' when, naturally, *Patty* Forrestal was the last girl in New Orleans he would ever care about seeing——

It was because she knew exactly how all this would be that Patty did not want to go into the pleasant fire-lit drawing room with the closed curtains. Even the thought of the ancestral portraits on the wall was oppressive to her. They seemed so much alive, those men and women, looking out from their gold frames at the furniture and ornaments they, themselves, had owned and the room where they, themselves, had sat and at their descendants surrounded by the ornaments and the furniture and inhabiting the room. Patty was proud of her ancestors, like any Orleanian, but she felt they would not approve of Drew's call if they knew about it, and she was seized with the uncanny feeling that they did. There was one picture, in particular, of a woman with brown hair and brown eyes, wearing a low-necked, brown-velvet dress which blended with these and a silken scarf which matched her creamy skin. This picture had always been a favorite of Patty's, not because it had been painted by Sully and was therefore very valuable and important, but because she loved the soft tones of the canvas and the tranquil look of the woman—her bearing even more than her beauty—her composure even more than her elegance. These were the very qualities which made Patty want to avoid the painted presence now; she was sure this gracious ancestress of hers had never been confused or inadequate. And she, herself, was both—yet after all, what did it matter, she thought with a great wave of relief, since Drew loved her and had told her so? Her discomfiture melted away as she began to glow at the secret realization of Mrs. Fay's mistake. And when Drew had held her face between his hands for a few moments and had told her again that he loved her, even more tenderly and convincingly than he had said it before, he released her in the same lingering way that the masker at the ball had released her every time he danced with her. Then Drew said that of course he had come to see her, and only her, as if he had divined her anxiety and were putting it to rest, but that they must go in and talk with her mother and her mother's callers for a little while, because that was the right thing to do under the circumstances, and after that he thought that probably they had better play rummy, or some such game, with the boys for a little while, too, because that was also right and natural under the circumstances. But later on, when they had made the cocoa together in the untidy pantry and sprayed Flit on the ants and eaten supper and stacked the dishes for Roberta to wash the next morning, why then he did not believe anyone would object, or even notice very much, if he and she lagged behind a little and ended by staying in the octagonal morning room together.

"It's all right to sit in the morning room in the evening, isn't it, Patty?"

"I suppose so. I never did sit there in the evening, but I don't see why we couldn't. We could start the custom."

"Would you like to?"

"Yes. Very much."

"Then we'll do it."

Her hand was already on the knob of the drawing-room door when he checked her, putting his fingers lightly on her wrist and bending over to look at it in somewhat the same searching way that he had looked into her eyes, but less gravely.

"That's a pretty bracelet you've got on, Patty."

"Yes, isn't it?"

"Mind telling me where you got it?"

"Not at all. A masker at the Pacifici Ball gave it to me."

"Oh, I see. Are you wearing it all the time?"

"Yes. I like it very much. It's the first favor I got. I was afraid I wasn't going to get any, and then suddenly I had this beautiful present. It wasn't only my first favor, it was the first present I ever had from a man."

"Not really?"

"Yes, really. Except from Gail, of course. And he doesn't count."

"Doesn't he?"

"Oh no!"

"You relieve my mind enormously. But didn't you get other favors after this?"

"Yes, lots of them. But those didn't count either. It was this one that counted. You don't mind having me wear it, do you?"

Something in her voice made him look up. This time she was smiling, and the dimple at the left of her lower lip dented her chin. He laughed, enchanted.

"I'm delighted to have you wear it," he said. "I've always thought a bracelet was perfect for a first present. It prepares the hand for a ring."

It was not until he had gone, hours later, that Patty remembered her bracelet was a counterpart of the one she had seen Evelyn Baird hiding and realized that, since Drew Breckenridge and the mysterious masker were identical, it was Drew who had given Evelyn her bracelet, too.

CHAPTER 30

THE UNPREDICTABLE Orleanian weather had turned warm overnight, and Louis, alertly answering Drew's morning ring, suggested that his master might like to breakfast on the upper gallery. The suggestion seemed an excellent one to Drew, though he never sat there without remembering how his father had yearned to use it and how his mother had suppressed the desire. However, the afterglow of his visit with Patty had been too radiant for nostalgia to overwhelm him a second time within twenty-four hours, and he savored to the full the strong steaming coffee and the waffles covered with *cuite* which Félicie, his cook, prepared so inimitably. As he ate, he glanced at the headlines. Nearly all of them were about the gubernatorial campaign, and he read them without either undue interest or undue earnestness.

SQUARE DEAL FOR
ALL, JONES AIM

LITTLE BUSINESSMAN AND OIL
PEOPLE TO BE TREATED RIGHT,
CANDIDATE SAYS

TREND TO JONES
FROM OVER STATE

CAMPAIGN MANAGERS REPORT
MANY NEW SUPPORTERS

The same old story, Drew said to himself ironically, turning from his paper to his correspondence: "Man never is but always to be blest." He began opening those letters which, from the envelopes, appeared to offer something of interest or import, after having cast the others aside. Often he read to Louis extracts from the intriguing letters, jestingly remarking that he might as well do this in the first place as to be haunted by the thought that Louis investigated them later on for himself. But this morning Drew did not jest with Louis. He read his mail without comment, and when he had finished his breakfast, he sat relaxed in the sunshine, his long legs stretched out in front of him, a cigarette between his slim fingers and the pleased little smile which was so characteristic hovering around his handsome mouth. It was unexpectedly agreeable to stay there thinking about Patty at his leisure for a little while before he called her up or went to buy her a present. Not that he intended to delay very long——

As he pondered, he heard both the telephone and the doorbell ringing in the distance and Louis' prompt response to the simultaneous summons. Then presently Louis reappeared on the upper gallery, carrying a note on a silver salver.

"This just came for you, Mr. Drew," Louis said respectfully, hitching up first one shoulder and then the other, according to an incurable habit he had, and then thrusting his hands out of his cuffs. He presented the salver to Drew but, at the same time, cast a reproachful glance at the unshared letters. Then he put the salver down and began to pick up the dishes with a practiced hand. "And Mrs. Baird just foamed," he went on in a smooth way. He made no noise with the dishes, and his voice, as usual, was soft. "I told her you wasn't up, and she said she'd call you back in about an hour, 'less you was to call her before then. Is there anything else just now, Mr. Drew?"

"No, not just now," Drew answered rather absently—he had already opened the note and, catching a glimpse of the engraved address, was plunging into it—"except that if Mrs. Baird should telephone again, before I have a chance to call her, you can tell her that I'm still asleep."

"Yes, Mr. Drew," Louis remarked, hitching his shoulders and thrusting out his arms again. Then he picked up the last dish without the slightest change of expression and retired unobtrusively from the gallery.

Drew, deep in his letter, paid no attention to Louis' departure. The pleased smile continued to play around his lips while he read.

Dear Drew:

I am not quite sure whether you intended to come to see me today or not. Of course I know you must be very busy, with campaign work on top of office work, like all the other men; but I thought from something you said last night that you did mean to come. So this is just a little note to tell you that I should be especially glad to have you, if you could spare the time, because I should like to talk to you seriously about something very important as soon as it would be convenient for you to have me. I had planned to go sailing with Gail late this afternoon, but I can give that up, if teatime is the best hour for you to call. I really think perhaps it would be, from my standpoint anyway, because mother is going to tea with Aunt Lula today, after the Causerie du Lundi, *and the boys don't get home until after six on account of baseball practice. You see I rather wanted this talk to be confidential.*

Affectionately yours,
Patricia Anne Forrestal

P. S. I did have a lovely time with you yesterday.

Drew went into his study, ringing for Louis a second time as he crossed the room. "I want you to take a note to Mrs. Forrestal's house for me, Louis," he said, without looking up from his desk. "I'll have it ready for you in a minute. And then I want you to bring the car around. I may go downtown before you get back." He addressed an envelope, took a sheet of paper from a brass rack, and wrote rapidly.

Dearest Patty:

Thank you for your delightful note. Of course I meant to come to see you today. Indeed, I was on the point of telephoning to ask if I might come this morning, when your missive arrived. But now I see clearly that afternoon would be the best time. I shall be at your house around three unless I hear from you within the next hour that this would be too early, and I shall count on you to let Gail know before then that you won't be free to go sailing or do anything else with him this afternoon. Incidentally, you don't go sailing with him often, or regularly, do you? Because I was hoping that you'd go riding with me often, or even regularly, this spring, and I'm afraid you won't have time to do both. But we can discuss that, and various other matters, in the course of our confidential talk, to which I am looking forward with great eagerness.

Devotedly yours,

Drew

P. S. I had a lovely time with you yesterday, too, in fact, the best time I ever had in my life. But I believe there are lots of better times ahead of us.

The telephone rang again. Louis, who was standing by the door of the study hitching his shoulders and waiting for Andrew to finish writing, instantly started towards it. But Drew held up his hand and reached for the instrument on the desk himself.

"That's all right, Louis, I'll take it," he said. "Here's the note— You can run along— Oh, hello, Evelyn. Yes, I did sleep late. I was a little on the languid side this morning. I'm afraid something at your luncheon must have disagreed with me. Yes, I'm feeling better now. In fact, I'm just on the point of going downtown. Why, I thought I might go to the office for a little while— Well, if no one does recognize me there, I'll refresh a few memories, whether I accomplish anything else or not, and I might at that. You never can tell— Oh, sometime later in the week. Yes, I'll call you. No, I couldn't say exactly when just now."

He hung up the receiver, sat looking ahead of him rather absently for a minute, and then rose and crossed the study, opening a door on the further side of it. Beyond a small entry were the rooms which had been his mother's and which had always remained unchanged and untenanted since her departure. It was a long time since Drew had entered them, but he did so now, frowning a little as he advanced. After all these years they were still more suggestive of Beacon Hill than of the Garden District. At a period when twin beds were the exception rather than the rule for a conjugal chamber, Anna Breckenridge had insisted upon their installation and use. They still stood, narrow and white and austere, their slim posts unsoftened by any overhanging draperies; a bedside table, where a volume of Emerson's *Essays* and the *Oxford Book of Verse* lay beside a Bible, separated them from each other. The lowboy and the highboy, the ladder-backed chairs and the small sewing table, which completed the furnishings of the room, matched the beds in type. They were all authentic Hepplewhite, elegant and restrained, but still, they lacked some essential quality. Jewel-colored rugs or draperies and upholstery of gay flowered chintz might have redeemed them, but there was a gray carpet on the floor, curtains of cream-colored net at the windows, and a complete absence of padded furniture. The dressing room on one side of the bedroom—Anna would never have called it a boudoir—and the library—she never would have called it a sitting room—on the other were equally neutral and equally uninspiring.

Drew shook his head, his smile growing a little bitter, and then continued his tour of inspection to include the guest rooms, where it became mocking. These were as flamboyant as his mother's were subdued—furnished in the most fussy French style with frills and furbelows, bric-a-brac and *bibelots*. The chaise longues were piled high with little pillows; the lace counterpanes were overlaid with billowing puffs. Porcelain figurines of shepherdesses, milkmaids, flute players, Pierrots and cupids were scattered prodigally over the mantelpieces, whatnots, and insecure little gate-legged tables. The colored prints on the walls depicted various aspects of sophisticated and libidinous love-making; the close air was suggestive of stale scent. No wonder his mother had gone to the other extreme, Drew thought, jerking back a dusty brocade curtain and flinging up a window; no wonder she had always declined to install any member of the Forbes family in this suite. It was a legacy of Aurore Fontaine's flamboyant taste and of the gaudy period to which she belonged; every evidence of it should have been destroyed long before.

"This place makes me think of the old saying among the Splendida Negroes that there's always a strange smell in a bachelor's house," Andrew said to himself grimly. "Perhaps that's what Stella's always hated at Splendida. Anyway, I must get some fresh air in here whatever I do. And I might offer all these mementos of luxurious living to Evelyn— or send them to a junk shop— Either gesture would be appropriate." He had given almost no thought to his house since he could remember, beyond his own quarters. These had also been kept as his father and grandfather had used them, except that, over the mantel in the study, where there

had once been a Troye painting, there was a portrait of a
beautiful dark girl wearing a low-cut, green bodice and a
full flounced skirt. The portrait had been brought to the house
on the same day that Breck had met his untimely death,
and for a long time it had been stored in the attic. Years
later, when Drew had found it and the note that was packed
with it, he had put the portrait where he could see it every
day, and he had answered the note by going to call at the
Convent of the Holy Family. When he left there, he had
asked Sister Mary Dolores, who received him, whether he
might come again. She had shaken her head and said no,
not unless there was some very special reason. But he had told
her where the portrait of her grandmother had been placed,
and he knew that she was glad.

Perhaps, if a young and lovely girl came to this house
to live, she would resent seeing the portrait of Sister Mary
Dolores' grandmother hanging over the mantel in his study.
Perhaps it would be better to change that, as so many other
things must be changed. She might prefer a portrait of
Anne Forrestal—weird how the same names ran through
families!—or even of Aurore Fontaine in that place. It was
conceivable that she might not object to a portrait of Anna
Forbes. She would have to be consulted. He was obsessed
with the thought of the unfitness of the house to receive
anyone who was young and lovely. Suppose—just suppose—
that a bride might come there to live, a girl to whom the
refinements of cultured and ordered living would be essential,
but who would thrive and develop only in an atmosphere
where cleanliness was combined with charm and sunshine
with splendor. It would take time and thought to create
such an atmosphere in the neglected habitation where there
had hitherto been so little happiness, despite its elegance,
and where so many warring elements had striven against
each other. He would have to put a great deal of both into
the problem before the shining white house with the delicate black balconies could become a dwelling place of love
and light.

He was still turning the problem over in his mind when
he stopped in at a florist's and did one or two other errands,
but later in the morning it was driven temporarily from his
mind. As Evelyn had predicted, his unheralded descent upon
his office was the occasion of considerable astonishment, not
to say consternation. It was literally true that the receptionist, a new one, did not recognize him as he entered the outer

office and she made a polite but determined effort to prevent him from going any further. His personal secretary, Ruby Compton, looked up with considerable confusion when he went into his private office, and the formidable array of cosmetics which she was busily applying to her natural complexion did not suffice to conceal the blush which overspread her face as she jumped to her feet, upsetting a jar of base cream and spilling a box of powder as she did so.

"Why, Mr. Breckenridge!" she gasped. "I didn't have the least idea you were coming in this morning."

"So I see," Drew remarked a little dryly. But he did not speak harshly, and he picked up the jar of cream and the box of powder and handed them to Ruby, his mouth unsmiling but his eyes amused. "Perhaps I ought to have telephoned and warned you. I didn't realize you were using this office as a beauty shoppe—that's what they're called nowadays, isn't it? Never mind, Ruby, it's quite all right. Any interesting or important mail this morning?"

"I haven't opened the mail yet, Mr. Breckenridge. You see, I wasn't expecting you and——"

"And you've been very busy achieving that schoolgirl complexion and the skin you love to touch, and so on. Well, Ruby, I appreciate the importance of good grooming for the career girl and I'd be the last to interfere with it. But I still think perhaps it might be a good plan for your individual efforts in that direction to be completed before eleven-forty in the morning. Such a schedule would leave a little more time for the pursuit of the career itself."

"Yes, Mr. Breckenridge. I promise you it won't happen again."

"Not in my office, anyway."

Drew was smiling now, very pleasantly, and the look of amusement had not left his eyes. But Ruby understood him perfectly just the same and watched him with some inner qualms while he sat down at his desk and began to open his mail himself, and she hastily assembled the offending cosmetics and stowed them away in a deep drawer. Drew tossed two or three circulars into the scrap basket, laid two or three bills carefully to one side, and read two or three letters almost at a glance before putting them in a pile near the bills. Then he opened one which he read and reread with evident care and interest before looking up from it to meet Ruby's alert and anxious eyes.

"Next time you must put mascara all the way around, or

not any of the way," he said, still speaking whimsically. "The present half-and-half effect is really too startling for me to stand. And those shadows *were* made with a pencil, weren't they? I ask because they suggest the final stages of tuberculosis. Well, you relieve my mind very much, Ruby. Do you happen to know whether Mr. Villeré is in yet?"

"He's been in, Mr. Breckenridge. But I think he's gone for lunch now, at the Louisiana Club."

"My arrival seems to be very inopportune all around— too early for my secretary and too late for my junior partner. The luncheon hour must have been shoved ahead since I was last downtown. I thought I might consult Mr. Villeré about this letter I've just been reading. But, after all, I believe I'm capable of handling it without his advice. You haven't forgotten all your shorthand while I've been gone, have you, Ruby?"

"No, Mr. Breckenridge."

"All right. I'm going to dictate my answer right away."

Ruby picked up her notebook and pencil, thankful that her employer's attention had been diverted from herself at last. He began to dictate rapidly.

"My dear Mrs. Fauntleroy:

I found your letter of the 5th awaiting me at my office when I reached here this morning after a temporary absence. I greatly regret the delay in acknowledging it.

I am also distressed to learn that the security of your charming old house, Ruth's Repose, has been jeopardized by the change in the river's course. I have always felt it was one of the most attractive places of its type in Louisiana, and its destruction would seem to me both an historical and an architectural disaster. I can also understand that it would lose some of its sentimental value and much of its material value for you if it were separated from its original setting. But I do not think you should consider the verdict of the other architects you have consulted as final. I admit that the knowledge I have of the structure is superficial. But still, I believe it would be possible to demolish the house and rebuild it in or near town, as you suggest. Of course, the location of a lot large enough to do justice to a house of its size might present a problem. But I know an old gardener in Métairie who might be persuaded to sell his pecan orchard, and this would be admirably suited for your purpose. If you are willing, I will approach him on the subject.

Should the answer be favorable, I should like to spend a day at Ruth's Repose inspecting its structure carefully. I believe that after I have looked it over, I shall be able to report that the building can be taken apart and the frames crated and moved to another site. The new house would then be built of the old brick but backed with hollow tile.

Needless to say, I feel much complimented at the confidence which caused you to consult me, and I hope very much that I may be of service to you.

With kindest regards, my dear Mrs. Fauntleroy, I am
                    Very sincerely yours,
                            Andrew Breckenridge"

Ruby waited a minute and then, as Drew said nothing more, she turned to her typewriter and began to tap out the letter carefully, so that she would not soil or break the ends of the nails which she had just finished lacquering to a shade that went well with her name. Drew tore open another letter.

Mr. Andrew Breckenridge,
Queen and Crescent Building,
New Orleans, Louisiana.

Dear Sir:

I have recently purchased a large tract of land north of Nashville Avenue with the purpose of developing it as a new subdivision.

I am asking several firms to submit drawings which would be suitable for two-family houses within the $10,000 to $15,000 price bracket and which would also embody some characteristics of simple Creole architecture. I would appreciate it if you would let me know, at your earliest convenience, whether you would be interested in considering an undertaking of this sort.

Hoping for a prompt and favorable reply,
                    Very truly yours,
                            Ernesto Braggio

Drew read this letter with great attention, also. But he did not immediately turn to Ruby to dictate a reply. Instead, he pulled a piece of paper towards him and began to sketch, slowly at first and then with increasing rapidity. Presently the house in the sketch began to assume the aspect of one of the Breaux Bridge cottages in modified form, the staircase leading to the attic *garçonnière* providing the entrance for the upper part of a duplex. He was just starting a second sketch when the telephone rang. Ruby answered it with alacrity.

"Aileen says Mrs. Cutler is in the outer office. She wants very much to see you. She says it's tremendously important."

"Aileen? Mrs. Cutler?" Drew inquired vaguely, putting down his sketch with reluctance.

"Aileen is the new receptionist. She came during your 'temporary absence,'" Ruby replied demurely, unable to refrain from such easy vengeance. "And Mrs. Cutler is chairman of the Women's Council. She's an old friend of your mother's, too, isn't she, Mr. Breckenridge?"

"Lord, so she is! Well, tell her to come in."

Mrs. Cutler gave him no chance to change his mind. She charged into his office grimly and gracelessly, seized a chair before Drew could offer her one, and seated himself midway between his desk and the door, as if to preclude any possibility of escape on his part. But once safely ensconced, she made a few critical remarks of a general character, according to a lifetime habit of hers, instead of plunging straight into her subject.

"I'm very much relieved to find you in at last, Andrew. I have been here several times before, during normal business hours, and I have always been told either that you had not come in yet or that you had left for the day or that you were not expected at all. It is beyond my comprehension how you run an office that way."

"'There are more things in heaven and earth, Horatio—'" Drew began absently and pleasantly.

"What did you say, Andrew?" Mrs. Cutler inquired sharply.

"It's just a quotation from Hamlet, Mrs. Cutler. The rest of it runs, 'than are dreamt of in your philosophy.'"

"I didn't come here to discuss Hamlet, Andrew," Mrs. Cutler said with increased severity.

"The error is wholly mine. Won't you have a cigarette while you tell me what you did come to discuss?"

"I never smoke, Andrew. Nor drink."

"Nor pet, I am sure," Drew said smilingly but softly.

"What did you say?" Mrs. Cutler inquired sharply again. Then deciding not to press the point, she went on. "How is your dear mother? With all her admirable qualities, she is, nevertheless, a very poor correspondent. It is a long time since I have heard from her."

"It's a long time since I've heard from her myself, but I believe she's very well. I'm sure some member of the Forbes family would telephone me, collect, if she weren't. They're a very thrifty lot, and I never knew one of them to lose an opportunity of driving my own extravagant habits home to me— Speaking of extravagance, you didn't come to ask me for a campaign contribution, by any chance, did you?"

"Yes, Andrew, of course I did. The Women's Council has never needed money more than it does now. We have put you down for a thousand dollars."

"But my mother, who's such a good friend of yours, wouldn't approve of that at all. She doesn't think I ought to spend a thousand dollars on anything."

"I'm sure she would, if she only knew how urgent the need is. This is a real crisis, Andrew. It isn't like the Community Chest or something of the sort, that you can give to any time. Why don't you persuade your mother to come and make you a visit? Then she would see the situation for herself, and there would still be time for her to do a great deal to help us before the run-off on the twentieth."

"I'm afraid she hasn't registered in Louisiana lately. But then, I understand that a number of other earnest ladies neglected to do so and found their best efforts thwarted in consequence."

Drew was smiling again in the way so many women found irresistible and that Mrs. Cutler found excessively annoying. But he was reaching for his checkbook at the same time, and even Mrs. Cutler realized that when a man is so engaged, it is generally not the best moment to antagonize him.

"I'm making this out for fifteen hundred, Mrs. Cutler. Do you think that will see you through all right?"

"I think you've shown a very proper realization of the crisis, Andrew. If Sam Jones doesn't win the gubernatorial election, I don't know what will happen to Louisiana! Why, at present, there are legislators on every payroll of the state. The Conservation Department and State University scandals are not even half told. The Levee Board bond-issue deal is robbing us of half a million dollars more. Nobody knows how much hot-oil thievery is going on——"

"I realize that this is all very serious, but, unfortunately, we've always had political scandals in Louisiana and I'm afraid we always will."

"Not if Mr. Jones is elected. He's promised us every possible reform. No more deadheads on the payrolls, civil service for all state employees, depoliticalization of all the boards, no more sales tax to lay up slush funds and graft— Oh, it will be a real reform this time, and a lasting one!"

"I see. Well, that's all very encouraging. And exactly what is the Women's Council doing to bring this millennium about?"

"Well, for one thing, helping to get the ghosts off the registration rolls and getting people to meetings and to the polls. Why, at the first primary some of the ladies were at the polls from five o'clock on as watchers, giving out sample ballots, driving their cars to bring in voters who would stand by our cause. Besides, of course, opening their houses for parlor meetings, and serving sandwiches and hot drinks and——"

Mrs. Cutler, having once warmed to her subject, found it difficult to relinquish this. Drew decided that she must lunch even earlier than Ursin Villeré or that there must be something about her political zeal which rendered her impervious to the pangs of hunger. At last, unable to endure these any longer himself, he asked her if she would do him the honor of lunching with him at Antoine's and she accepted the invitation with alacrity. He excused himself long enough to read through the letter he had written Mrs. Fauntleroy and to sign it. Then he put Ernesto Braggio's letter with his own sketches into his pocket and held open the door of his private office for Mrs. Cutler, explaining briefly to Ruby as he did so that he would not be back that afternoon because of an important uptown engagement, but that she might expect him at nine-thirty the next morning. As he escorted his guest down the outside corridor, the open transom enabled him to hear Ruby unburdening her troubled mind to Aileen.

"Say, can you feature that? He comes and stays two whole hours, when he hasn't been near the place in two months. Or maybe it's three. I've lost track. And me just halfway putting on that new Tangerine 'Allure' when he breaks in on me! Listen, something tells me things have got to be different, beginning tomorrow, sister——"

It was soon evident to Drew that politics had not, after all, rendered Mrs. Cutler impervious to the pangs of hunger.

She did full justice to the shrimp aspic, *pigeons paradis* and *soufflé surprise* that Drew ordered. He had hard work to keep his eyes off the big clock at the rear of the room as Mrs. Cutler ate on and on to the running accompaniment of more political comment.

At last, however, deliverance came from an unexpected quarter: several other members of Mrs. Cutler's committee were lunching in the Mystery Room, and when they discovered her, they urged her to join them for *café brûlot.* They did hope Mr. Breckenridge would understand and forgive them for tearing his luncheon guest away from him. It was so important that they should confer with her.

Without too much difficulty, Drew made the matter of his forgiveness clear, signed his check, and overtipped his waiter upon the assurance of this functionary that he always offered a special prayer at the Carmelite Chapel in behalf of generous patrons. Then, stopping for the briefest sort of word with the proprietor, his old friend, Roy Alciatore, Drew hurried out of the restaurant.

His first instinct had been to telephone Patty's house when he found that he would be delayed, but he feared that his call might be answered by Mrs. Forrestal instead of her daughter, and he gathered that Patty had not, in this instance, confided her plans to her mother. So he made no attempt to explain his tardiness beforehand, and as he went up the walk towards the raised cottage, he found himself stricken by the sudden fear that Patty might greet him with a rebuke, as Evelyn had so often done. He could not understand why it should matter much if she did—why it seemed so essential to him that she should always be gay and friendly and unreproachful. But it was as if a load had been lifted from his breast when the door was flung open for him by Patty, herself, again, before he was halfway up the steps. It was evident that his reception had been carefully planned and his coming eagerly awaited. There was no long delay because of a decrepit bell this time, and, instead of the nondescript wool, Patty was wearing a crisp blue silk with frills of white organdy edging the round neck and elbow sleeves. Drew realized it was exactly the sort of dress Patty would choose for "best," and he was delighted that she had put it on in his honor.

"I've been watching for you," she said joyously. "I'll always try to watch for you, so that you won't ever have to wait again— Oh, Drew! It was sweet of you to send me those lovely flowers! I never saw roses exactly like them before—barely tinged with color, and still so warm-looking! I've put them in my grandfather's whiskey glass—the one with the chiselled hunting scenes on it. I thought that was appropriate for a present from you, because you love horses so. They do look lovely, though usually I'm not a bit good at arranging flowers. Come quickly and see them!"

She seized his outstretched hands and drew him into the study, where he caught a glimpse of the roses rising amidst their glossy leaves from a crystal beaker that stood on a battered desk. Then, unexpectedly, Patty threw her arms around his neck and kissed him gladly and quickly and spontaneously, like a child. "I don't know how else to thank you," she said, still speaking joyously. "And you said we were cousins. But perhaps we're not 'kissing cousins'— Perhaps there would have been a better way."

"There couldn't be any better way," Drew said gravely. She had taken him so completely by surprise that the kiss was over and she had dropped her arms before he could draw her more closely to him or kiss her in return. Now he framed her face with his hands and looked steadily into her eyes, as he had done the day before. "We're not kissing *cousins*," he said slowly, stressing the last word. "But, of course, we're going to kiss each other. I haven't dared to hope it would be so soon, because I want a great deal more than just the '*privilège du cousin.*' Now that you've kissed me, though, you must let me kiss you, too, the way I do want to."

Momentarily he waited, giving her a chance to slip away from him if she were startled or shocked. But she did not stir, and he bent his head until his lips touched her brow, slowly moving his hands from her face until they first slid over her shoulders and then rested lightly on her waist before they encircled it. Still she did not stir, and his lips, like his hands, moved slowly downwards, touching her eyelids and her cheeks and, last of all, seeking her mouth. Briefly, he felt her catch her breath, not as if in fear, but as if in unexpected rapture. Then, unresistingly, she received his kiss, her acquiescence a touching token of the response she longed but lacked the knowledge to make.

He released her slowly and caressingly, as he had always done when he was dancing with her, and looked at her searchingly again to see if she would be troubled or bewildered now that he had set his seal so irrevocably upon her. Instead, her expression of trustfulness had only deepened, and there was a new look, almost of adoration, in her eyes. He knew that if he embraced her again, her groping instinct and wakened senses would help her, this time, to return his kiss. But still he did not dare to go too fast.

"Suppose we sit down," he said, trying to speak quietly. "You said in your sweet little note that you wanted to talk to me, confidentially, and I want very much to have you. But first I want to tell you something myself. I told you yesterday that I loved you, but that was only half of what I wanted to say. Now that you've let me kiss you, I can say the other half. I do love you dearly, more than I ever loved anyone in my life before, more than I thought I ever could love anyone. And so, more than anything else in the world, I want to have you for my wife."

He paused and, again, he heard the slight, ecstatic intake of breath which was in itself an answer. He pressed the hand which he had continued to hold.

"I won't hurry you, if you'll just give me a promise," he said gently. "Don't you think you could promise that sometime you'll marry me, Patty? Not right away, if you'd rather not, but sometime."

"Yes. That is, I'm not sure, but I think so. Because I love you dearly, too. I didn't know I could love anyone so much either. I loved you a lot before you kissed me, and now—" She stopped, the look of adoration deepening in her eyes.

"Patty, if you look at me like that and speak to me like that, I'll keep right on kissing you, over and over again, whether you promise to marry me or not. I won't be able to help it."

"Well, of course, I hope you will kiss me over and over again, but don't you want me to answer you first?"

"Yes, I do want you to answer me first. I want your promise most of all and first of all."

"I'd like to promise. When a girl loves a man, she wants to do whatever he asks her to, doesn't she?" Patty said, speaking with wonder. "But I've got to be sure first what everything means. I don't understand all that's happened very well yet, it's come with such a rush. I didn't think two weeks ago, that anyone would ever want to marry me, I was such a failure. And that *you* should want to—" The expression in her voice, like the look in her eyes, was adoring.

"Patty darling, you never were a failure. The failures were

the stupid sheep who followed a blind leader in pursuit of just one kind of a girl—and you're not that kind, thank God! They didn't have the brains to realize how perfect you are. But I'm afraid the leaders won't be so blind or the sheep so stupid for very long. I've seen signs of a change already. Pretty soon someone will be trying to snatch you away from me. That's why I'm trying to hurry you into an engagement. I can't bear the thought of losing you, now that I've found you."

"You won't lose me. I will promise you that. I promise that I'll never marry anyone else. I—I couldn't. But because there's so much I don't understand, I'm not sure I ought to promise to marry you."

"What is it that you don't understand, Patty?"

"That's what I wanted to talk to you about. I don't understand about this bracelet."

She began to turn it slowly around on her wrist, while Drew looked at her without answering. So there's no way out, he thought, watching her. I'll have to come clean, or she won't give me a chance. I haven't got more than that at best, and if I lie to her, I'll lose that. I'd like to lie to her, because if I don't, I'll hurt her so. At the very beginning, when she's so happy. It wouldn't be so bad, if it hadn't come so soon. But I don't see how I can lie to Patty. I'm afraid I'll be trapped into telling her the truth. The whole, hideous, revolting truth——

"There's no reason why we shouldn't tell each other everything, is there, Drew?" he heard Patty asking. "I mean, it would be all right for me to explain why I'm troubled about the bracelet."

"Yes, darling. You must tell me about everything that puzzles you and troubles you."

"I'm very glad you think it would be all right. Because I hope that when I have told you, you'll make me understand that it was very silly of me to worry. And then we could be engaged; then I could promise to marry you."

She did not ask a question; she made a statement. Drew Breckenridge, who had never been conscious of inadequacy in the presence of a woman before, felt his complete helplessness now.

"It's this way, Drew," Patty went on. "I sat beside that beautiful Mrs. Baird in the call-out section of the Pacifici Ball. I couldn't help looking at her all the time, because she *is* so beautiful. And that's how I happened to see her stuffing something back into a box, that looked like a diamond bracelet. She acted as if she were afraid someone would see it. Of course, I looked away very quickly when I realized this, but I think she knew I had noticed it. Because after that she acted angry as well as frightened. Especially after I had a call-out myself. That's what puzzled me in the first place. I couldn't understand why Mrs. Baird should want to hide her bracelet—why she didn't put it on proudly. And I can't understand why she should be angry with me. Can you?"

"I think so. Naturally, it's harder for me to try to explain Mrs. Baird's feelings and actions to you than it would be to explain my own. But I'm afraid she wasn't proud when she received the bracelet as a favor; I'm afraid that for some reason she was ashamed. And I'm afraid she was angry with you because you received one like hers."

"Yes, but I still don't understand. Why should she be ashamed; why should she mind if I had a bracelet like hers?"

"Patty dear, you know there are some things a man mustn't say about a woman—about any woman—to another. But Evelyn Baird's husband isn't a member of the Pacifici. So the masker who gave her the bracelet must have been—well, an admirer. And lovely young ladies, who are already married, don't ordinarily accept jewelry except from their husbands. In fact, ordinarily other men don't offer it to them, not even at Carnival Balls. And when it is done, it's done—furtively. It isn't done openly. It couldn't be. That would account for the shame and the stealth. And a woman who would accept a diamond bracelet from—an admirer, would naturally be upset if she thought he had given one just like it to another partner. That might account for the anger. Because the second gift would suggest to her that she might have a rival, wouldn't it? Someone with whom she couldn't compete. The rival might be far lovelier, in every way, than she was herself."

"Drew, I'm getting more and more mixed up. I did know what you just told me, of course, about young ladies who were married, and the sort of presents they accept. I'm not— I do understand about some things. But when I got a bracelet exactly like Mrs. Braid's, I thought, of course, it must be paste. Because I didn't think a masker would give away two bracelets, exactly alike, to different girls unless they were. It wouldn't be a compliment to either one if he did. It wouldn't be becoming in a gentleman. Why should he do such a thing?"

"I'm not sure, darling. Perhaps for no special reason. Or perhaps just because he was in an unnaturally daring mood. There's always a spirit of deviltry abroad at Carnivaltime. You know that, too."

"Drew, we're not getting anywhere at all like this. You said we could tell each other everything—that we didn't need to pretend. I know you were the masker who gave me my bracelet. Every time I've seen you this last fortnight I've felt there was a tie between us. And then last night I knew. Because I felt so natural and so happy with you, and because you thrilled me so. No one ever made me feel like that before. And it wasn't until after you'd said good night and left, that I remembered—if you gave me my bracelet, you must have given Mrs. Baird hers, too."

"That doesn't necessarily follow, does it? The similarity between the two bracelets might have been accidental. Or you may merely have thought they were alike. You didn't really have a good look at Mrs. Baird's, did you?"

"Drew, you're not going to lie to me, are you?"

She was looking at him for the first time with fear in her face. He recaptured the hand which she had drawn away.

"Don't look at me like that, Patty. I told you last night that I wouldn't be able to bear it if you looked at me except as you did then. And please try to forgive me, even if you don't understand."

"I can't forgive you if you lie to me."

"I won't lie to you. I wouldn't have dreamed of lying to you except to keep you from being hurt."

"It won't hurt me to have you tell me the truth. That is, I hope it won't. Anyway, it won't hurt me as much as it would to have you lie to me. There's something else that's puzzling me, and I'll tell you right away what it is, because then you can explain everything together. If the bracelets were paste, why then of course there was no reason why you shouldn't have given away any number of them. But in that case, why did you say that you always liked a bracelet for a first gift—that it prepared the hand for a ring? Imitation jewelry wouldn't do that—or any kind of an imitation——"

Her lower lip had begun to tremble a little. Drew leaned forward, trying to take Patty in his arms and overwhelmed with longing to smooth away the quivering with a caress. To his horror, he felt her flinch.

"You mustn't kiss me again, Drew, until you've told me. Are the bracelets made of rhinestones?"

"No, they're made of diamonds. Don't talk about imitations, Patty. Don't even think about them. You'll break my heart and yours, too, if you do. There's nothing false— there's no kind of sham—in anything I've given you or in anything about my feeling for you."

"But you gave the first diamond bracelet to Mrs. Baird!"

"Yes. I'm terribly sorry, terribly ashamed. But I did give it to her."

"And the bracelets are alike—a pair. You must have meant to give them both to her."

"Yes, I did. I bought them for her."

"Why?"

"You must know why, Patty. You say you understand about some things. And you say you couldn't keep your eyes off Evelyn Baird yourself. Well, how do you suppose a man might feel about her? I haven't been able to keep my eyes off her—or my hands off her—for a long time. But I hate the very sight of her now. I wouldn't touch her with a ten-foot pole."

"Does—does she care about you?"

"If you call that kind of feeling caring, I suppose she does."

"What else would you call it?"

"Lust. It's an ugly word, Patty. I hope you'll never make me say it again."

"And that—that sort of feeling was what you had for her, too, wasn't it, before you began to hate her?"

"Yes."

"Is—is it anything like the feeling you have for me?"

"Good God, no!"

"And still you gave me a bracelet you meant to give her? You—you quarrelled with her, or something, and afterwards, to spite her, you asked me to dance and then——"

"No, Patty, it wasn't like that. I swear it wasn't. But Evelyn did see you looking at her bracelet, and she spoke to me about it, because she was frightened, just as you guessed. She was mean and hateful about you. She said you 'stared' at her, she said you would 'tattle,' and that did make me angry, Patty. Because I knew you never would look at anyone in a prying way, or betray any kind of secret, consciously. It simply isn't in your make-up. So I answered her rather sharply, I'm afraid, and she began to make fun of you because no one had asked you to dance. And I felt sorry for you. I decided that I'd give you a rush, that I'd see to it you were the belle of the ball before it was over."

"You felt *sorry* for me! The only reason you asked me to dance was because you were *sorry* for me!"

"That was the reason I asked you the first time, Patty. But before the dance was over, I was entranced with you. And before Carnival was over, I was in love with you. Don't you remember what I did on Madri Gras at the Boston Club?"

"Yes, I remember. But it was just a gay gesture, just a Carnival catchword!"

"No, it wasn't, Patty. It was a public tribute. I was saluting you for everyone to see. If you'd let me tell the whole world tonight that you'd promised to marry me, I'd be the happiest man alive. *If Ever I Cease to Love* isn't a Carnival catchword for me—not any more. It's a pledge. A pledge I'll keep to my dying day."

Again he leaned forward, trying to take her in his arms. She did not instantly repulse him, but there was none of the joyousness in her response which had so thrilled him before. Instead, he presently felt her trying to free herself, and he could not hold her against her will. He could not stop her either, when she unfastened the bracelet and handed it to him.

"I can't wear it any more. You know that, Drew," she said. She spoke steadily, as she had all along except for that one instant when her lips trembled over the word "imitation." But the joyousness was gone from her voice as well as from her manner, now. "I was very pleased with it and very proud to wear it. But that was before I understood. I think I do understand everything. I believe you when you tell me that you didn't give it to me out of spite, or because you were sorry for me. I'm glad I can believe you. I'm grateful to you for telling me the truth. For I do love you. I love you with all my heart and soul. But I couldn't wear something you bought for someone else, no matter how much I loved you. I would always feel that it belonged to —to the other person, and as if you did. I could only wear something you bought on purpose for me. And I'm not ready to do that right away. Not after what you've told me. Please don't ask me to. Don't tell me you've bought something for me already—that you've brought it with you today, meaning to give it to me. I couldn't bear it. And don't ask me to promise you anything either. Because I'd have to say no, after all. And it's awfully hard, Drew, for a girl to say no to a man she loves."

CHAPTER 31

PATTY DID not go to the door with Drew, as she had the day before when she said good-bye to him. She sat very still after she had told him that it was hard for a girl to say no to the man she loved, with her bare brown hands clasped in her lap and her head bent, so that he could not see the tears on her lashes or the quivering of her lips. But he did not need to see them to know what they were like. He sat still himself for a moment, holding the bracelet she had given back to him. Then he slipped it quietly into his pocket and rose, putting his hand gently on her bowed shoulder.

"Patty," he said. "Patty." Again he was overwhelmed by the sense of his own inadequacy. There was no suavity that could prevail against such sincerity as she had shown, no apology that could atone for her hurt, no declaration of love that would not be an affront to her touching confession of love. But he knew he must leave her now, and he could not do this without saying something. "I love you with all my heart and soul, too," he said at last. "I've said that already, but I have to say it again. And as long as you've told me that you love me, too, and promised me that you'll never marry anyone else, I'm not going to let you say no to me for long. I don't mean that I'm going to hurry you or harass you. I'm going away now, and I won't try to see you again for a day or two at least, until we've both had a chance to think over all that this means to us. Then I'm going to ask you to let me talk to you again. I won't try to touch you, if you don't want to have me, and I won't importune you in any way. But you'll let me talk to you, won't you, Patty?"

"There isn't anything more for us to say."

"Not now. But there will be. When you've thought it over you'll find that there will be. I won't come until you realize that, too, but I want you to promise me that when you do, you'll let me know. Couldn't you promise that much, Patty?"

Her answer was so long in coming that he felt as if she were never going to make it. But at last she nodded her head slightly without speaking.

"Thank you," he said, still very quietly. "That's all I'm going to ask you to do—just now. I did buy you a present today, Patty. I did bring it with me. I hoped you'd let me give it to you before I left. I wanted to put it on your hand myself, to see it there, so that I could remember how it looked after I had gone. But I understand why you can't let me. I understand that this bracelet you've given back to me wasn't the proper preparation for it, though I didn't mean to affront you when I told you yesterday that it was. I understand now that the preparation for giving you a ring has got to be a great deal longer and a great deal harder than I realized at first. But don't forget, darling, while I'm trying to make this preparation, that the ring is waiting for you, that it's yours, that it never was meant for anyone else and never could be. Will you remember that? Could you promise me that one thing more, after all?"

There was another long silence. But this time Patty did answer him, though her voice was so low that he could hardly hear her.

"Yes," she said. "Yes, I can promise that one thing more. I won't forget that you're keeping the ring for me. And I'll go on hoping, too, that some day I can wear it. But if you don't mind, Drew, I'd rather you went away now. Without talking to me any more, or making me talk to you. I'm terribly tired, somehow. And I'm afraid I'm going to cry. I'd rather be alone."

"I'm going, darling. I feel dreadfully that I've exhausted you and that I've made you unhappy. I know that I have, though. And I know it won't do any good to keep on saying, over and over again, that I'm sorry. I'll have to show you that, not say it to you."

He moved his hand from her shoulder to her hair and let it slide slowly down again. Then he bent over and kissed the white part that divided the shining waves from each other.

"God bless you," he said. "Try not to grieve any more than you can help. I'm not worth all this grief from you. But I'll make it up to you yet. Good-bye, Patty."

"Good-bye, Drew," she said without looking at him.

He closed the library door after him as he went out, leaving her shut in with the grief which he had caused and which he could not assuage. It hurt almost unbearably to leave her like that. He, himself, felt that he could not see anyone or speak to anyone at that moment. But as he opened the front door, he came face to face with Patty's mother, who had just returned from the *Causerie du Lundi,* full of culture and gossip and satisfaction, and who was fumbling in her handbag for her key. She looked up at him in unconcealed amazement.

"Why, *Drew!*" she exclaimed. "Have you been here to call *again?* Wasn't it just yesterday——"

"Yes, Aunt Eleanor, it was just yesterday. But I have been here again."

"Did Patty give you some tea? I'm terribly afraid she wasn't prepared, unless you told her you were coming, and I don't suppose you did. You see everything gets eaten up on Sunday, and unless we know we're going to have company, usually Roberta——"

"It's quite all right, Aunt Eleanor. I didn't come to have tea. I came to ask Patty to marry me."

Mrs. Forrestal dropped the handbag with which she was fumbling though, since Drew had flung the door open, she had no further need for her latchkey. Drew picked up the bag and handed it to her with more apparent *sangfroid* than he actually felt.

"She's declined. And very properly, under all the circumstances. Of course, I hope to persuade her to change her mind, by and by. But there's nothing more I can say to her just now. And if you don't mind my doing it, I'd like to suggest that you didn't say anything to her at the moment either. She's rather upset. It's all my fault and I'm feeling a good deal cut up myself to think that I have upset her. So I hope nobody else will. But I'd like you to know that I want her for my wife. I'd like everyone to know it, for that matter. But under the circumstances, you're probably the only person I shall tell at present, and I don't believe she'll tell anybody. If the boys tease her, I shall beat them all to a pulp. You might pass on that much news. Good-bye, Aunt Eleanor."

He nodded and ran down the steps, his manner still cool and casual despite the inner tumult which possessed him. He was sorry that he was saddled with a car. He would have liked to stride through the streets for miles and miles until he was too tired to think of Patty sitting with her brown hands clenched together and her bright head bent. But he knew that even if he could walk to the end of the world, this would not be far enough to obscure the vision of Patty looking as she had when he left her. Less poignantly, but more practically, he knew he could not indefinitely leave his car parked in front of the Forrestals' house. He swung into it and drove down Saint Charles Avenue at a pace which would have landed anyone else in the police station. When he got out of it in front of his own house, he slammed the door with such vehemence that Louis, who was waiting for him in the front hall, heard him before he started up the walk.

Although Louis was by no means as undependable in his ideas of attendance as Roscoe had been, it was not usual for him to be alertly awaiting his master's arrival. If Drew's thoughts had not been centered elsewhere, he probably would have expressed some mildly satirical surprise at seeing Louis in the front hall. As it was, he started past him with only a curt nod. Louis detained him.

"You have a caller, Mr. Drew."

"You shouldn't have let a caller in. You'll have to say I can't see anyone this evening."

"I'm sorry, Mr. Drew, but she brushed right past me. It's Mrs. Baird."

"What in hell——"

"I couldn't help it, Mr. Drew."

The frequent and profuse employment of profane language did not happen to be among Drew's many failings. But he swore now. Then he flung open the drawing-room door, only to find this apartment empty. Louis forestalled his next inquiry.

"She went straight upstairs, sir, to the study. I couldn't help that either."

Drew went rapidly up the stairs himself, still swearing. But by the time he had reached the study, he had collected himself and cooled off. It was just as well. The first glance at Evelyn revealed that she was in a state of intense excitement which had been either caused or increased by violent rage. A different type of woman would have been hysterical, and still another would have been bitterly weeping. But Evelyn was neither stunned nor sorrowful; she was furious. Her obvious anger had the effect of calming Drew, at least outwardly.

"Well, Evelyn," he said coldly. "You certainly have given me a very great surprise. I thought we agreed, in the beginning, that this was one of the things that wasn't to happen."

"I don't care what we agreed. Everything's changed now. And I could tell from the way you spoke to me over the telephone this morning that you hadn't the slightest idea of coming to see me right away. 'Oh, some time later in the week!' You needn't attempt to deny it."

"I shouldn't dream of denying it. It's perfectly true. But I would still suggest that you might have waited for me to come to your house, even if I didn't get there until the latter part of the week, instead of forcing your way into mine."

"You'd better not be so insulting about it. If you want to know, I shan't be at my house the latter part of the week. Or rather, at Harold's house. He's asked me to leave it."

"Really? Well, I wouldn't take such a remark too seriously, if I were you. Harold was rather the worse for wear yesterday. That is, rather worse than usual. Probably he's got a bad hang-over, if he hasn't already started on another binge. And I shouldn't think you'd be exactly soothing to a man, Evelyn, when he was in either of those conditions, if you don't mind having me say so."

"I mind very much. I think it's despicable, under the circumstances. But you haven't given me a chance to tell you what those are yet."

"I beg your pardon. I am all attention."

"Harold hasn't got a hang-over today, and he hasn't started on a new binge either. He's cold sober. What's more, he's sent me a formal letter, through Narcisse Fontaine, whom he has engaged as a lawyer, asking me to leave the house, before he gets back to it tonight. He's going to bring action to divorce me."

"Are you telling me the truth, Evelyn?"

"Of course I'm telling you the truth. I *have* left the house. There wasn't anything else that I could do. I've tried, over and over again, to reach you by telephone and I couldn't. I don't know where you've been, but evidently you found a very complete hideaway."

Drew made no direct answer. Instead, he glanced towards the chairs on either side of the fireplace.

"Since you've come to discuss something as serious as a divorce, perhaps we'd better sit down."

"I think that's a very good idea, though it entered your

mind a little tardily to express it. And I still don't see why we need to sit across the room from each other."

"Not across the room. Just across the hearth. That really gives a rather homelike touch to the conversation— So Harold is suggesting divorcing you? I assume you've made the logical countersuggestion that he let you divorce him, instead?"

"Of course I have. That is, Father made it for me. He went to see Narcisse Fontaine as soon as I told him what had happened. Fortunately, I did get in touch with Father at once. He tried to see Harold, too, but Harold had told the receptionist at his office not to let anyone in, and not to put anyone through on the telephone. And Narcisse said that his client would absolutely decline to consider any such proposition. Evidently, he felt sure beforehand that I would suggest it. He's determined to sue me for divorce on the ground of adultery. He's going to allege that I've been unfaithful to him, specifying dates and giving names."

"Either Harold must be better at deduction than I thought he was, or more observant."

"You beastly cad! How dare you say anything like that to me?"

"Why shouldn't I dare? If Harold actually has been keeping track of your actions, he won't have the least trouble in specifying dates and giving names. I notice you don't say giving a name. But I gather, from your attitude, that Harold intends to name me as a corespondent, if not as *the* corespondent. Under the circumstances, to use your own phrase, I should think coming here was about the unwisest thing you could possibly have done. And I should think the sooner you were out of this house, and in your father's, the better it would be for all concerned. I don't believe it was such a good idea to sit down after all. I believe you'd better let me ring for Louis to see you downstairs."

"Don't you touch that bell! Don't you stir out of this room until I have said everything I've come to say or you'll be sorry."

"I'm sorry already, extremely sorry. For more reasons than you know. But I'm not in a position to defend the suit, unfortunately, so there's nothing I can do about it. I thought I'd always been pretty discreet about our little affair, Evelyn, except at the very beginning, and that's so long ago everyone's forgotten what was happening then, except Stella, perhaps. But someone must have given Harold a hint. Perhaps you did, yourself. I wouldn't put it past you to tell him that if he didn't stop drinking, you'd leave him—that there were plenty of other people who would be glad to have you. One person in particular."

"Well, suppose I did say something of that sort to him?"

"If you did, that's something else again that's extremely unfortunate. Because I'm not glad to have you. In fact, I wouldn't have you, in the way you've got in mind, for anything on earth."

"You—you——"

"I wouldn't start calling names, if I were you, Evelyn. If my memory isn't playing me tricks. I called you one, when you were about four years old. I didn't know what it meant then, but I do now. And unfortunately, it describes you perfectly, and always has. If Harold didn't know what you were when he married you, he was about the only man in New Orleans who didn't. And I believe he did. I believe he wanted you enough to marry you anyway, the poor fool. But not many men are such fools as Harold is. I'm a fool myself, but not that much of a fool."

This time Evelyn spat out the epithet that Drew had previously forestalled and followed it with a stream of abuse. Drew made no effort to stop her. He did not speak to her again until she paused for lack of breath.

"Now that you've got that out of your system, perhaps you'll feel better," he said calmly. "Someday I think I'll have to tell my mother what you called her. Considering her type, it really has its amusing side. As far as I'm concerned, you haven't hurt my feelings in the least. But you haven't done your own cause any good. Because, when you began your recent declamation, I was about to suggest that if there were anything I could do, financially speaking, to make things any easier for you, I'd be very glad to. I always believe in paying for everything in the coin of the realm, and I know what the coin of your realm is. The sum I had in mind was two hundred thousand dollars. But I don't believe you'd want to accept as much as that from such a low species of humanity as you've just labelled me and my parents, so I've changed my mind. However, if a hundred thousand would make life look any rosier to you, I'll have that amount settled on you, after your divorce. I'll see that it's done tactfully, so that you won't be embarrassed by it, the next time you undertake a little casual diversion. You might find another man who's as big a fool as Harold, after all. Who knows? If you can, I wouldn't want anything from the dear dead past to rise up and hit you in the face. On the contrary, I'd wish you the best of luck. Just to prove it to you, I'd like to make you a parting present."

He reached into his pocket and drew out the bracelet which only an hour or so earlier Patty had put into his hands. Then, with a strange expression on his face, he offered it to Evelyn.

"Through a very grave error," he said, "I failed to give you this bracelet before. It's the mate to the one I did give you on the night of the Pacifici Ball. I intended to give this to you then, too, and I should have, because, of course, I bought them both for you. Of course, I meant them both for you. It's a little late, I know, to offer this to you now. But I think you'd better take it. For your own sake and mine, too. I know you want to get everything out of me that you can, and I don't blame you. I'll try to meet you more than half-way except on one point. But I happen to have a different feeling about the terms of our parting than you have. I don't want to be left with anything that was meant for you, or that was connected with you, either on my hands or in my life."

After Evelyn had gone Drew dressed with his usual care for a dinner at the French Consulate General and went to it, as he had agreed a fortnight earlier to do. During the next few weeks, when all New Orleans began to seethe with the scandal of the impending divorce between the Bairds, several of his fellow guests found occasion to remark to each other that they had ever found him more delightful company or seen him when he seemed to be taking life more exuberantly than in the course of this dinner. If they had seen his face when at last he was at home again that night in his father's study, the tenor of their remarks might have been very different—if they had seen that or the letter which Patty Forrestal received the following morning.

Dearest Patty:

I have no right to call you that, but I'm going to, once more, for this is the last letter I shall ever write to you.

I felt I couldn't bear it today, when you told me that you wouldn't marry me. But now I'm thankful you did; if you hadn't, I should have had to come back to you tomorrow, and tell you that I couldn't marry you. Because, unless some-thing can be done to stop it, and I don't think anything can, a man you and I both know, here in New Orleans, will very shortly sue his wife for divorce, naming me as corespond-ent. Within a week or two probably nearly everyone you'll meet will be talking about this terrible scandal, for which I am responsible. And don't make any mistake. This won't be idle, malicious gossip. I am responsible. I've done every-thing this man will accuse me of having done, and more. And worse, too.

Of course I had no right to ask you to marry me when I had a record like this. It may be a partial excuse to say that I didn't suppose the man in question would ever take the attitude and the action he has, and that's also true. I didn't suppose he would. I didn't suppose that if your name were linked with mine, as my future wife, it would also be linked with a sordid, smutty story that would be on everyone's lips. I had the effrontery to think it would only be linked with a great fortune I wanted you to share and a great position I wanted you to adorn, and with a man who isn't great but who has been called "the great catch of New Orleans," whom you've not "caught," as others have vulgarly tried to do, but enraptured and uplifted and who in time you might have also transformed. It's too late now to hope for that, because of my own folly and my degradation. But not through any failure of yours. You could have done it, Patty, and I know you would have.

I want to tell you that the bracelet is no longer in my pos-session. Don't ever think of it again, if you can help it. But if you can't help it, then try to forgive me for offering it to you. I wouldn't have done it if I had known how much you were going to mean to me or—do I dare say this?—how much I was going to mean to you. For, knowing that you love me, and how unworthy I am of your love and how impossible it is for me to accept it, makes all this hardest of all.

I want to tell you also this last time, that there'll never be anyone else for me as long as I live. But you're very young, and I know that there's at least one other man, much more worthy of you than I am, who loves you dearly, who'd do everything in his power to make you happy, and who hasn't any reason to be ashamed when he looks you in the face. Look back into his, Patty, as soon as you can, and try to find happiness there. The more quickly you forget about me, the better off you'll be. And I want you to have "every good and perfect gift" life has to offer, because I love you so.

> *Eternally yours,*
>
> *Drew.*

CHAPTER 32

SINCE THE Ball of the Pacifici Mrs. Marcel Fontaine had failed very fast. She had known, at the time of it, that her triumphant appearance had also represented her ultimate effort. For the first few days after its occurrence neither Julie nor Stella remonstrated with her when she said she felt unequal to rising or, without saying anything, had gone no further from her bed than her chaise longue, and neither one had suggested calling in Dr. Beal. But when a fortnight had gone by, and her listlessness and languor seemed to increase rather than diminish, Julie spoke anxiously to Stella, and Stella, in turn, spoke to her grandmother.

"Grannie, dear, I hate to see you like this. Isn't there anything I could do to help you take heart?"

Mrs. Fontaine smiled faintly. "I'm afraid not, *chère*, not any more. I did take heart, as you call it, for the ball. But now there's no special reason why I should try to do it any more."

"You're not grieving over what I said to you, the night of the ball, about my own plans, are you?"

"No, Stella, at least not willfully, or even consciously. I have accepted them as inevitable."

"Well, Grannie, I don't know that they are. I've been wondering whether to tell you or not."

Stella picked up the diamond-studded mirror which lay on the little table beside her grandmother's chaise longue and began to turn it over in her hands without looking at it. Her grandmother, though slightly startled, waited with apparent composure for her to go on.

"You know I almost never sing at a party," Stella said at last. "But the other night I did, at the little dinner Walter Avery gave. That attractive friend of his from New York, Sandra Hastings, who went to the Pacifici Ball with him, is still here, and he keeps on entertaining for her. She seems to be more or less digging herself in. Some people are saying that she's in love with Walter. I don't believe so. I believe she's merely in love with New Orleans. But good old Walter certainly likes her very much, so, personally, I should think it was all to the good if she did fall for him. However, that's beyond the point. I started to say that she's quite a musician herself, and apparently she's on the inside track with the powers that be at the Metropolitan. She asked me, after I stopped singing, if I'd be interested in having an audition there."

"And what did you tell her?"

"I told her I would be, very much."

"And have you told this to Raoul, too?"

"Yes. I told him when he was here on Sunday."

"With an indication that if you went to New York, with favorable results, you might postpone announcing your engagement, after all? And that a postponement of this announcement might mean a postponement of your marriage, too?"

"Yes. I don't think I put it to him too baldly. But I'm sure he understood that was what I meant. After all, if you've postponed a marriage for over five years, another year or two don't matter much, do you think so, Grannie?"

Stella spoke lightly. But she laid down the mirror and looked at her grandmother with attention as she asked the question. Mrs. Fontaine's answer was guarded.

"I should say that depended on circumstances, Stella. In the present situation, if I may say so, I should not think you were justified in asking Raoul to wait much longer for you. It seems to me that he has been remarkably patient."

"I haven't asked him to wait any longer for me, Grannie. I suggested that perhaps he wouldn't want to. I made it very easy for him to withdraw from the engagement, and he won't. So as long as he feels that way, I don't think I ought to break it either. I do want to be fair. And I'm willing to stay engaged, unofficially. But I may as well admit I don't especially want to get married. The nearer we come to June, the less I want to."

"And I thought you wanted to so much that I have been waiting for the right moment to tell you that I should not object, after all, if you did so sooner than you originally planned! The wedding would have to be a quiet one, because I do not feel equal to giving you a large one now. But I should be willing—in fact, I may say I should be glad—to have it take place at any time."

"It's very kind of you to say so, Grannie. I'll tell Raoul you suggested it. I'm sure he'll be pleased and touched. But I'll also have to tell him that I wouldn't let you go ahead with your plans. Not because I wouldn't be satisfied with a quiet wedding—I'd rather have it quiet, if I were going to have one at all. But I dread the thought of any kind of a wedding. Not just the wedding, itself, of course. Everything that it stands for. Everything that comes afterwards. I'm sorry, but it's so."

She rose and turned away. Her grandmother knew that Stella did not want the expression on her face to be seen just at that moment and answered still more guardedly than before.

"I am sorry, too, Stella. You never expected to hear me say this, and I must confess that I never expected to do so. You know that I greatly disapproved of your engagement at first. I made that very plain—too plain, I am afraid, as I look back on it. But I am obliged to confess that Raoul has roused me to greater and greater respect all the time. I must say he has behaved extremely well."

"Yes, Grannie, he has. Extremely well. He's a grand person. That's why it's so sad that I don't care for him the way I used to—that I don't really want to have a part in his life any more. I've tried to make myself believe that I did; I've tried to make everyone else believe so. But that's been done out of loyalty. It hasn't been done out of love—not for a long time."

"He probably has a great future, Stella."

"Yes, I know. But I haven't helped to build it, the way I thought I was going to. Raoul's always been self-sufficient and he always will be. He can have a great future without me. I might help a little, here and there, along the way, but I'd never be essential to his political progress, and I certainly ought not to marry him for what I'd get out of it, when I haven't given anything to it. Besides, I can have a future of my own, without him. Without—without love."

"Do you want a future without love, Stella?"

"I've been in love, and I've found out that it hurts. I don't want to get hurt all over again. You know the old proverb about the burnt child and the fire. Well, we won't talk about it any more. Probably nothing will come of this audition idea, anyway. I just thought I ought to let you know how things are, that's all. I'm sorry, but I have to go out now. There's a rehearsal on for the spring fiesta. Is there anything

I can do for you before I go? Or is there anyone you'd like to see?"

Mrs. Fontaine looked through the long window into the garden almost as if she expected to see that someone was waiting for her there. Stella, following her gaze, felt a queer quiver go through her.

"There is nothing you can do for me, darling," her grandmother said at last. "But there is someone I want very much to see. And I believe I shall, before so very long."

"If you talk that way, I'll send for Dr. Beal."

"I have always liked John Beal. I have always felt he was my friend. But I don't need a doctor, Stella. I should prefer that you would not summon him until I tell you to. In fact, I must ask you not to do so."

Mrs. Fontaine would not even look at her mail. Stella, in the brief intervals between the parties to which she, herself, went, reminded her occasionally that there must be invitations among the unopened letters, and Mrs. Fontaine, admitting that this was so, told her granddaughter to look at them and acknowledge them, declining them all. Stella protested, at first vehemently but gradually with less violence. She was beginning to feel annoyed with her grandmother, and because she did not wish to betray this annoyance, she stayed with Mrs. Fontaine less and less. But she thought about her with more concern than she liked to admit, and one day she mentioned her to Patty Forrestal, who happened to sit beside her at an Orléans Club luncheon.

"You haven't got any old people in your family, have you, Patty?"

"No, not here in New Orleans. I wish we did have. I like old people."

"Maybe you'd like my grandmother, then."

"Why I do! I always have. That is, I've never had a chance to know her very well, but she's always been awfully kind to me, and I've always thought she was a magnificent old lady, just as everyone says."

"The magnificence seems to be a little dimmed lately. I'm worried about her. I know she's worried about me, too, and there's nothing I can do to help it. And now I'm afraid she's begun to worry about Drew Breckenridge, too. She's always been very fond of him. And he certainly is in hot water now. Did you ever know anything to cause so much scandal as this affair of his with Evelyn Baird?"

"No, never. It seems a shame, too, just at this time, when he was beginning to take some interest in his profession and in public affairs, at last. Mrs. Fauntleroy is perfectly delighted because he's told her he's sure he can move Ruth's Repose for her, and Mrs. Cutler's going all over town, bragging about the contribution he gave her for the work of the Women's Council."

"I think he's pulled off a real coup with Ruth's Repose. But it seems to me he was just an easy mark when he let Mrs. Cutler bulldoze him into giving her all that money."

"I don't believe she bulldozed him. I think he enjoyed giving it to her. He's very generous."

"You mean he's terribly extravagant. It seems to be in the blood. All the men in that family squander money."

"Did you say your grandmother specially likes Drew Breckenridge, Stella?"

"Well, you probably know she was in love with his grandfather."

"No, I didn't."

"Why, I thought everyone knew that! They had a thwarted love affair after his first wife, Anne Forrestal, died. She was kin to you in some way, wasn't she? And didn't you know about Drew's father, Breck, as they call him, and my Aunt Marie Céleste either?"

"But I thought your Aunt Marie Céleste was a nun!"

"She is now. But naturally, she wasn't born a nun. She and Drew's father fell in love with each other, too. He was married already, though, to a Boston girl, named Anna Forbes. And then he was killed in a crevasse. Aunt Céleste left Grannie's house for a convent the day after his funeral, and never went back to it. She belongs to a cloistered order. Grannie's never even seen her since she took the veil."

"Oh— No, I hadn't heard about that either. It's terribly sad, isn't it? And I suppose Mrs. Fontaine thought that if you and Drew——"

"Yes, just like in storybooks. But I had other interests, and so did he. Not that they've done us much good, in either case."

The girl on Stella's other side spoke to her just then about some new aspect of the impending Baird divorce, even more spectacular than anything she had heard up to that time. This girl had gleaned that Mrs. Baird was going to bring a countersuit, charging her husband with habitual drunkenness and cruel and abusive treatment. The details were all very lurid, and Stella listened to them with attention. She was so engrossed that she did not have a chance to say anything more to Patty, nor did she pay any particular attention to the thoughtful expression on Patty's face when they met while they were bidding their hostess good-bye. She, herself, was going on to a bridge party from the luncheon, but Patty, who did not play bridge and who avoided teas whenever she could, had nothing on her calendar before a dinner at the Patio Royal. When she left the Orléans Club, instead of walking up Saint Charles Avenue, she walked down it and presently took a cross street over to Prytania.

Emile answered the doorbell at Mrs. Fontaine's house. He was getting to be an old man, but Mrs. Fontaine still found him adequate for her needs, and she had turned a deaf ear to Stella's suggestion that he might be pensioned off and a younger and sprightlier servant installed in his stead. He justified Mrs. Fontaine's good opinion of him this time. Instead of telling the pleasant young lady who confronted him with a smile that Miss Estelle was right poorly and could not receive anyone, he ushered Patty into the dim drawing room, still completely unchanged, and went laboriously up the long stairway to announce her.

"Miss Patty Forrestal done come to see you, Miss Estelle. She waitin' in de drawin' room."

"Didn't you tell her I couldn't see her, Emile?"

"No'm. I figured you'd like to see her. She's a mighty nice lookin' young lady, and she brung a sweet pretty little bunch of flowers with her. I ast her, should I put 'em in water, and she said no, she wanted to give 'em to you yourself."

"Very well. Since you've let her in, I suppose I'll have to permit her to come up."

"Yes'm. I thought so, Miss Estelle."

It was never necessary for Mrs. Fontaine to "fancy up," like so many of her contemporaries, before she admitted a visitor to her room. Her hair was still always exquisitely dressed; her skin had kept on growing softer and whiter with age; her figure, even when unsheathed by the corsets to which she still clung, was as elegant as it had been at the height of her bloom. The lace-trimmed negligee she had on, the light coverlet which lay over her feet, were both the last word in daintiness and chic. She looked up with her inimitable smile as her visitor came towards the chaise longue.

"Why Patty, *chère*, how very kind of you to come to see me! I don't understand how you could find time to wedge in a call on an old lady. I know from Stella's schedule how crowded yours must be. And you brought me some flowers, too—pansies for thoughts!"

"Stella told me you weren't well. So I was very glad to come to see you. But I didn't do it just to be kind. It wouldn't be honest to let you suppose that."

"Then why did you come, *chère?*"

"I thought, from something else Stella said, that perhaps you'd let me talk to you about Drew Breckenridge."

Mrs. Fontaine gave a smothered exclamation, so slight that Patty hardly heard her. She looked at the girl searchingly. But she spoke to her very kindly.

"Why should you want to talk to me about Drew Breckenridge, Patty?"

"Because I love him."

Again there was a smothered exclamation, and this time Patty heard it. She also noticed the shaking of Mrs. Fontaine's fragile, ring-laden hands, though she could not be sure how much of this was due to the infirmity of old age and how much to sudden emotion. She leaned forward in her chair, clasping her own hands and speaking with great earnestness.

"I ought to have put it differently. I ought to have said because we love each other. Of course, if I loved him, and he did not care for me, that would be different. I would never let him know that I cared, if I could help it. But he does love me. He told me so. He asked me to marry him."

"If Drew Breckenridge asked you to marry him, Patty, you may be very sure he loves you. I doubt if he ever asked anyone else."

"Yes, I am sure. But I made a very great mistake. I didn't accept Drew when he asked me to marry him. I didn't feel as though he really belonged to me—that is, not wholly. I thought he belonged partly to someone else and I wasn't willing to share him. But now I know the other didn't matter. I know that if he and I love each other, that's all that counts."

This time there was no possible doubt as to why Mrs. Fontaine's hands shook so. Patty knew that, unconsciously, she had struck very deep. She came closer to the chaise longue and leaned over it.

"I'm sorry if I hurt your feelings, saying that. I didn't mean to. I only said it because I don't see how you can help me if I don't tell you the truth."

"I can't, my child. And there was no reason why you should not have said what you did. You could not know that someone said the same thing to me, a great many years ago. But, unfortunately, I didn't realize its truth. You should be thankful that you do."

"I am thankful. And I'm thankful Drew loves me and wants to marry me. I want to marry him. I want to tell him so. But now he won't listen. He won't come to see me; he won't answer my letters. Now that——"

"There, there, my dear, I know. You don't need to tell me. I've been hearing, all these last weeks. And listening, sick at heart. But I hadn't heard about you. I didn't know——"

"There hadn't been time for anyone to know. Except my mother. Drew told her right away. Before he heard what Mr. Baird was going to do. And mother found out soon afterwards. So now she thinks I ought not to marry him. And I love my mother. I've always tried to be a good daughter—to do what she wanted to have me. But I'm going to marry Drew, no matter what my mother thinks. And I believe if I could see him, everything would be all right. It's so hard to make a person you love understand in a letter. So, since he won't come to see me, I don't see anything to do but to go to see him. Only I can't go to his house alone. I can't do anything that would make Drew think I was cheap."

She was afraid she was going to cry as she had never cried but once before in her life, which was the day Drew had left her, taking his unbestowed gift away with him. But this time she was not alone with her grief. She was with someone who understood it and shared it.

"Drew Breckenridge will never think you are cheap, Patty. But you are quite right. You should not go to his house alone. That is, unless there is no other way at all. And of course there is. I am right, am I not, in supposing you hoped I'd go there with you?"

"Yes, Mrs. Fontaine. If you're well enough. If it wouldn't be too much of a strain."

"It will not be too much of a strain. Or if it were, what would that matter now?"

She said the last sentence so softly that Patty hardly heard her. But Patty had heard the part that mattered. She knelt down beside the chaise longue and buried her face on Mrs. Fontaine's breast.

Afterwards, though what happened was very hard, this was not because Mrs. Fontaine did not do everything in her power to make it easier, and without her help, most of it would have been impossible. The old lady had not even risen from her chaise longue, before starting to help. When at last she released the girl from her feeble, kindly arms, she picked up the telephone that stood on the little table beside her and called a number with the quickness of long familiarity.

"Louis? This is Mrs. Fontaine speaking. Has Mr. Drew come back from his office yet? Oh— I'm very glad. Because I should especially like to talk to him if it would be convenient for him to have me. —— Drew, this is Aunt Estelle. Oh, no, you have been misinformed. Not ill, only indolent. But I am shaking off my sloth. Indeed, I have telephoned to ask if you wouldn't let me celebrate my recovery by coming to call on you. —— No, not this time. I'd really rather call on you. I've been shut in so long, that a little outing is just what I need. —— Well, in about half an hour, if that is agreeable to you. —— Thank you, *cher*. *Au revoir*."

"Do you have a car here of your own, Patty, or shall I order mine?" she asked, quietly replacing the receiver.

"I'm afraid you'll have to order yours. I don't have a car of my own. I walked here. We're not at all rich, you know, Mrs. Fontaine. That's another thing I've got to face. That people will say I want Drew for his money."

"It is perfectly convenient for me to order my car. I only thought that if you were driving, it would be a pleasure for me to have you take me. I believe you would drive a car very well, and Drew will certainly see to it that you have one. Do not worry about what people are going to say, if it is not true. That is something else I learned too late and that I hope you may learn in time. Now go into my sitting room, *chère*, while Julie is helping me to dress. I shall be with you in a few minutes."

It was not easy to sit still while Mrs. Fontaine dressed, and Patty could not believe it took her only a few minutes to do so. She kept looking up at the ornate little gilt clock that stood on the mantelpiece, for she had never seen the hands of any clock move so slowly. Her heart was beating very fast, there was a choking sensation in her throat, and her brown hands were growing colder instant by instant. Suppose Drew were angry when he saw her? She did not believe she could bear seeing him angry, any more than he

could bear seeing her mistrustful. Mrs. Fontaine had not told
him that she was bringing anyone with her. He might feel
Patty had acted deceitfully in coming. He might refuse to
talk to her when she did reach his house. He had refused
once already when they had met by chance at a party and
she had manoeuvred to speak to him privately. He had said
that until the Baird divorce was over he could not and would
not see her or speak to her in any way and that there was
no telling how long the proceedings might last. Thirty days
must elapse from the time Harold Baird had asked Evelyn
Baird to leave his house before the case was actually filed;
there was the possibility of a countersuit and of endless
other technical delays. He did not propose to deny the
charges. They were true. That was all there was to it. But
neither did he propose to have Patty involved, even indirectly, in such sordid degradation. He would not have
come to the party if he had supposed she would be there.
He had thought it was for an older group. He must beg her
to excuse him——

"I'm afraid the time has seemed long to you, *chère*.
But I have really shown myself very sprightly, for an old
lady. Shall we go on now? Oh—and I thought, if it would
be agreeable to you, I would leave you in the car for a
little, while I first went in to see Drew alone. The time
will drag then again, I know. But I believe it will be the
best way."

It was even harder, waiting alone in the car with nothing
at all to do, than it had been to wait in Mrs. Fontaine's
sitting room, watching the hands of the little gilt clock.
Patty looked up at the white façade of the beautiful house
in front of her, gleaming in the afternoon sunshine, and
thought of the things she had heard people say about it:
that long ago it had been likened to a snowy satin dress
trimmed with exquisite lace, such as a queen might wear,
and that the simile had stuck. Yes, she could see how people
might say that about it and keep on saying it from one
generation to another. But she remembered that other saying,
too, that it was a house in which no one had ever been
really happy. Andy Breckenridge had not been happy in it
for all his arrogance and his display, or poor futile Breck,
and now Drew, willful and cynical— But if she were living
with him, Patty thought, she would make Drew happy somehow; she would restore his faith and his illusions. She would
try to take the curse off the house. Or if that were not

possible, there must be another house somewhere, a smaller, simpler house, where they could be happy. She tried to think of other houses she had seen as she went around the city—of one which she could visualize as being right for her and Drew.

She looked away from the shining façade of the house where no one had ever been happy and thought of a great many others, none of which seemed to be right either. Then suddenly she thought of just one more, and on that her thoughts dwelt hopefully. It was a little house on Kerlerec Street, that stood out among its surroundings because these were dingy and shabby, while the little house she had in mind was always bright, as if it had just been painted, and the high hedge around it was always green and trim, as if it were faithfully watered and had just been clipped, and the banquette looked as if it had just been scrubbed. But the little house was empty; its shutters were always closed. She did not know who owned it. Evidently, no one who wanted to live there. Perhaps she and Drew could buy it. It couldn't cost much either to buy it or to run it. She could do her own work in it. They needn't see any of the people who had thrown mud at Drew and who would like to throw it at her. Besides, if they lived in a little house liked that, quietly and simply, no one could say she had married Drew for his money——

"Aunt Estelle wants you to come in, Patty. Will you, to please her, for a few minutes?"

Drew was standing at the door of Mrs. Fontaine's ponderous black limousine, which Emile had hastened to open. She had been thinking so hard about the little house on Kerlerec Street that she had not heard him come down the walk or across the banquette. Her heart gave a quick leap of joy when she heard his voice, but instantly it stood still again. For she saw that he was not smiling, that his face was very stern, and that there was nothing warming or welcoming in his words. He did not say, "I want you to come in," and he did not act as if he did. He acted as if he were obliged to invite her, because Mrs. Fontaine had asked this of him as a favor, and Mrs. Fontaine was a magnificent old lady to whom no one could deny a boon, least of all the son of Breck and the grandson of Andy Breckenridge. It was very hard for Patty to get out of the car when Drew looked at her like that and spoke to her like that. The voice of her hurt pride whispered to her insidiously. "Tell him you're sorry, but you can't. Say you're in a hurry, that you're going somewhere else, that you were just waiting for a minute while Mrs. Fontaine——" For a moment she looked at Drew without moving or without answering. But this was only because she was determined not to let him know how hurt she was, and she found she could not instantly gather her forces; she knew all along that this was not the time to listen to the voice of hurt pride. She remembered hearing Stella say once, very bitterly, that a single moment could be too long for a girl to do this instead of listening to the mandates of love. Patty did not know the details of Stella's reasons for this remark, but she knew it had something to do with Raoul Bienvenu and with the indefinite postponement of Stella's marriage to him. Patty did not intend to have anything like this happen, as far as she and Drew were concerned, and when she finally did manage to speak, it was quietly and naturally.

"Thank you. I'd like to very much. You know I've never seen your house. And I've heard, over and over again, that it's the most beautiful house in New Orleans."

"Then you've heard wrong. It's a whited sepulchre."

Someone has said that about it, too, she thought, and hurt him. I mustn't pay any attention to that either. She got out of the car without seeming to notice the hand he offered her, because she knew he was holding it out for Emile to see and not because he really wanted to help her or to feel her fingers inside of his. As she walked up the path beside him, she spoke of the beauty of his camellias, which were at the height of their bloom, as any courteous caller might have done, and not of her joy in seeing him again, as his beloved, when she had been defeated again and again in trying to do so. She did not feel any joy. Only dogged determination.

"Was it your idea to go over the house? I'd be glad to show it to you, if that's what you want."

"No. That wasn't my idea. That isn't what I want. I'd like to go wherever Mrs. Fontaine is, please."

"She's upstairs in my study. I'll take you there."

He went ahead of her up the wonderful circular staircase. She had been told the truth: this was the most beautiful house in New Orleans. She was aware of the panelled walls, the splendid somber paintings and the jewel-colored carpets, as she went along. And then Drew stood back for her to enter the door of his study, where the walls were lined with wonderful books, and she saw Mrs. Fontaine sitting in a big chair near the fireplace, underneath the portrait of a lovely dark girl wearing a green bodice and a white frilled skirt.

"Patty has come in, Aunt Estelle, as you wished. What would you like to have her do next?"

"It isn't a question of what I'd like her to do next, Drew. It's a question of what I'd like you to do next. She's done her part. Which is what very few young girls would be honest enough to do, in her place. What one I knew very well failed to do."

"I'm sorry to be obliged to remind you again, Aunt Estelle, that the cases you have in mind aren't comparable. Andy Breckenridge was never involved in a sordid scandal."

"He might have been involved in dozens of them: on the race track, in the Lottery, at every gaming table in the city. But he was adroit enough to slip through them all unscathed. The only reason he was never involved in a scandal affecting a woman was because the one women he really desired was not the kind that scandal ever touches. Only tragedy."

"Very well. I don't propose to have any more tragedy either. If you're bound to discuss that, we might talk about my father, instead of my grandfather, for a change. About him and another seventeen-year-old girl, whose name, as I recall it, was Marie Céleste. There was enough tragedy in that case to last for a long time."

"I am not bound to talk about tragedy, Drew. But, like you, I do not propose to have any more of it occur, if I can help it. I, too, am thinking of another seventeen-year-old girl, whose name was indeed Marie Céleste, when I ask you to listen to Patty. And of still another, who was also seventeen when you and I both failed her. Let us show more wisdom in Patty's case than we did in Stella's, Drew."

She saw that, for the first time, she had scored. A changed look came into Drew's face, and he answered a little less harshly.

"Very well. I'll listen to her."

Mrs. Fontaine turned from Drew, who was facing her on foot from the further side of the fireplace, to Patty, who was still standing near the door, just inside the threshold. It had not seemed possible to come any further.

"Would you rather I went into the next room, *chère*, while you talk to Drew?"

"No, Mrs. Fontaine. I'd rather you stayed. I haven't anything to say to him that I wouldn't be proud to have you hear."

It was after she said this that Patty found she could come across the room, after all. She walked over to the chair where Mrs. Fontaine was sitting and put her arm over the back of it. She was grateful for the nearness and the support. But she stood up straight and she looked unflinchingly at Drew while she spoke to him.

"Drew," she said, and stopped, because after all it was very hard to say this before a third person. "I love you very much. And I know you love me, too, or I shouldn't be here. I wouldn't intrude on you when you've made it plain that you don't want to see me or have me come into your home. But I think Mrs. Fontaine is right and that you're wrong. I think you're the one who is going to repeat a mistake and prolong a tragedy if you don't listen to me. And I'm not going to let you, if I can help it."

"I've said I'd listen to you. I am listening."

"I want you to do more than listen to me, Drew. I won't ask you to talk to me, that is, not the way I'm talking to you. But I do want you to answer me when I ask you a question. Won't you do that much?"

"Yes, I'll do that much."

"I'm not mistaken in believing you love me, am I? You haven't got over loving me, just within a few weeks, have you? I want you to tell me the truth. If you have got over loving me, I want to know it. And then I'd go right away and not bother you any more."

"No, I haven't got over loving you. But everything else has changed since then, Patty. If you weren't so young—if you weren't so inexperienced—you'd realize that."

He had said something voluntarily to her at last. And he had spoken more like himself when he said it; he was beginning to look more like himself as he met her unflinching gaze.

"I realize that some things have changed. But I believe they're unimportant compared to the thing that hasn't. I don't see why we should let them ruin our lives. I'm not too young and inexperienced to know that it isn't safe to let little things choke big ones. That's what Stella did. I wouldn't say so if Mrs. Fontaine hadn't spoken of her first. But it's true. I've heard Stella say so myself. And it's kept her for years from getting married."

"It isn't a little thing, Patty, for a man to be named as

corespondent in a suit for adultery. And it isn't a little thing for a girl like you to have anything to do with such a man. This is another time when cases aren't comparable. If I had a record like Raoul Bienvenu's, I'd have a right to ask you to marry me, and you wouldn't have any reason to refuse, if you loved me."

"You thought it was all right to ask me to marry you a few weeks ago, didn't you? You're the same man, aren't you, that you were then? The only difference is that now more people know what you've done. I should think I'd be the person to whom knowing it would matter most. It mattered a good deal to me at first. I told you that. But now it doesn't matter so much. It's behind you. It's behind me. I don't feel any longer as if you were only partly mine. I feel as if you were all mine. I'd be glad to tell the whole world I feel that way, if you'd let me, just as you said you'd like to tell the whole world that you wanted to marry me."

"You mustn't tell the whole world, Patty! You mustn't tell anyone!"

"All right. I won't tell anyone, if you'd rather I didn't. I just want you to understand *I'd be glad to*. But you and I will *know*. The knowledge will comfort and sustain us, while we're waiting for each other. I understand that you couldn't marry me, or even be publicly engaged to me, while this trial is going on. But I'll be glad to wait until it's over. Because, you see, I feel just the same way, about being your wife, that you said you did. I want it more than anything else in the world."

"Patty, you don't know what you're saying."

"I do know what I'm saying! I'm not a child; I'm not a fool. Don't speak to me as if I were. I do know what it would mean to be your wife. *I do want it more than anything else in the world!*"

She had taken her hand off the back of Mrs. Fontaine's chair. She did not need its support any longer or the support which the nearness to Mrs. Fontaine had given her. She went up to Drew and put her hands on his arms.

"Give me the ring you bought for me, that I wouldn't let you give to me before," she said. "I want the present that was bought on purpose for me. I won't wear it on my left hand. You needn't be afraid I'll give in, if I'm teased about it, and tell who gave it to me. It'll be our secret. It'll mean a lot to me, sharing a secret with you, until we can get married. I'd like to see you in the meantime, too. I don't see why I shouldn't. I don't see why you couldn't ask your mother to come back and live with you for a while. I think you'd find she'd be willing to come, if you told her you needed her and why. I think she's had enough of tragedy, too, and its consequences. If she were here we could see each other openly, once in a while, at this house, besides the times we happen to meet elsewhere. Not hole-in-the-corner meetings. I couldn't do that, and I know you wouldn't want to. Not imposing on Mrs. Fontaine again. Neither of us would want to keep on doing that. Not making love to each other either, because you think that isn't best. But we'd say 'Hello, Drew!' and 'Hello, Pat!' when we happened to run into each other at the Country Club, for instance. We'd sing it out, freely and joyously, so that everyone around would hear us. We'd dance with each other once or twice, too, when we met at parties. Not a lot. I should think we could ride together once in a while, too, the way you said we would. Of course, I'd go sailing with Gail, too. But all the time you'd know it didn't count. Not the way the things you and I would do together counted. Because you'd see your ring on my finger whenever you looked at me—because you'd know what it meant to have it there, for you and for me both. Give it to me, Drew, so I can have it on when I go out of this house!"

All the time she had been talking to him, she had gone on gripping his arms hard with her strong little brown hands. Now she dropped them and then put her own arms around his neck and pulled his face down to hers. When she felt the first force of his kiss, no longer reluctant, no longer hesitant, and the urgent pressure of his breast against hers, she gave one little glad cry. After that she could not cry out because he had silenced her. Neither one of them was aware of Mrs. Fontaine quietly leaving the room and closing the door behind her.

CHAPTER 33

Of her three brothers-in-law, Auguste Fontaine was the one to whom Mrs. Marcel Fontaine had always felt closest and whom she had seen most frequently, once she had outgrown her girlish awe of his priestly profession. She had never liked Octave from the time he was a boy, and though she would not have confessed this even to herself, she was not altogether sorry when his connection with Camille Dupuy definitely removed him from her orbit. Even after his tragic death her aversion for him continued in the form of a grudge against his daughter, which she knew was unchristian, but which she tried to persuade herself was not illogical: if Laure had not fallen in love with Olivier, she might have married Walter Avery; if she had married Walter Avery, she would not have inopportunely entered the Convent of The Holy Family; and if she had not done this exactly when she did, perhaps Marie Céleste would not instantly have thought of going further still by becoming a Carmelite. The only serious strain which ever existed between herself and Auguste had been caused by the difference in their respective attitudes towards the vocations of the two cousins who had simultaneously become nuns for reasons which were certainly akin to each other even though they were not identical and which Father Fontaine considered good and sufficient in both cases while Mrs. Marcel Fontaine did not.

Eventually they had tacitly agreed that the subject should not be mentioned between them any more, and it was not, even during that period after the Pacifici Ball when Father Fontaine came daily to his sister-in-law's room to celebrate Mass and give her Holy Communion. But once, just as he was leaving, she called him back and surprised him very much by telling him she would like to see his younger brother, Narcisse, sometime later that same day, if it was convenient, and if not, the next day. He knew that when she was a young girl, she had always spoken of Narcisse as a "sweet child," the way they all did, and that she had shown the same tenderness in her attitude towards him that Marcel had. Carmen de Alpiente, whom Narcisse had married, was a favorite of hers, too, and their daughter, Carmelita, who later married Francisco Darcoa, was a frequent visitor at her house until Marie Céleste had left it for the cloister. After that she had seen less of Narcisse and his family, which was not surprising, for she had seen less of everybody. Indeed, for weeks at a time she had not seen any of the Fontaines except Auguste, and the old habits of intimacy had never been renewed. Stella's interests all centered in an entirely different group, and it was her friends and Raoul's, not her grandmother's relatives by marriage, who filled the house. Father Fontaine would not have been surprised to hear that it was a year at least since his younger brother had been there, and now that it was so necessary for Estelle to conserve her strength, he did not see how any useful purpose would be served by her tiring herself with a visit which could represent nothing but the vagary of a fragile and elderly woman. It was all very well for her to talk about being indolent. Auguste knew that she was ill.

"Narcisse is unusually busy these days, Estelle. I happen to know that he has a number of especially important cases on his hands. And you are very far from strong, no matter what you say. Why don't you wait until he is less occupied and you are in better health?"

"Because I do not feel it wise to wait for such a time. I feel it is best for me to see Narcisse now. Of course, if you do not care to give him my message, I can telephone him myself."

"If you make a point of it, Estelle, naturally I shall give him your message."

He, himself, telephoned his sister-in-law later in the day that Narcisse was very much pleased that she wanted to see him and that he would come to her house straight from his office, probably about five. When he arrived, he found that she already had two callers, one of whom, at least, he would have preferred not to see at this juncture: Drew Breckenridge's mother, who since her husband's death had called herself Mrs. Anna Forbes Breckenridge in order to avoid confusion between her name and her son's and who had unaccountably returned to New Orleans after an absence of more than twenty-five years. The other was that little Forrestal girl, Patty, who, everybody had said at the beginning of the season, was going to be such a failure as a debutante and who since then had unaccountably become such a success.

Narcisse regarded them both appraisingly as he accepted the coffee his sister-in-law offered him. Anna Breckenridge was handsomer at middle age than she had been as a young woman, he reflected. Not that she had been bad looking then, but she had been totally lacking in charm. Now she certainly presented a very distinguished appearance, in an austere way. He wondered if she would go in for causes again, as she had done so prematurely before. The political campaign which was raging at that moment should certainly be right down her alley. It was too bad Louisiana was no longer her legal residence—or was she planning to claim it again as such? It really was none of his affair, and he did not know why he should give it even a passing thought. But, in a way, he could not help feeling it was unfortunate that she should have chosen to visit her son just now. The proceedings in which he was about to be involved would certainly be very repugnant to her, and on the other hand, the air of respectability, not to say dignity, which she would lend to her son's discredited household would not do anything to help Narcisse Fontaine's own client.

His glance shifted from Anna Breckenridge to Patty Forrestal, and again he felt vaguely disquieted without knowing why he should. She had always been a nice girl; everyone in New Orleans said so. But she was also surprisingly attractive, and until lately he had not heard anyone say that. He had never realized before that there could be something so arresting about fine tanned skin in connection with golden hair. Now, brown eyes *were* effective with golden hair. That he had always known; and Patty had those, too—eyes that were almost disconcertingly clear and candid, and a long smooth bob nearly down to her shoulders, that showed the rich, shining quality of what was literally a "crown of glory." Then, there was a profile of extraordinary purity. That was a word you couldn't use lightly, but you did use it almost instinctively in connection with her. And a brow that was pure and grave. But at the lower left of her mouth was a little dimple that kept coming into play when you would least expect it, and you began to watch for it. You looked at her limbs, too—long and tapering off to slender feet and into brown hands that looked extraordinarily strong for all their slimness. And you looked at her body, which was long and slim, too, though not in a boyish way; Narcisse Fontaine could have sworn that her breasts were beautiful, though the white blouse she had on was so cut that they could not be seen. Modest. That was another old-fashioned word you didn't use lightly or easily but that you thought of instinctively with this girl. She was very modestly dressed, as well as very becomingly dressed, in the same kind of clothes, generally speaking, that Mrs. Breckenridge was wearing—tailored and simple—except that Mrs. Breckenridge's were obviously much the more expensive and Patty's very much the less severe. The two would approve of each other's clothes, though, as they would probably approve of each other in many other ways. Narcisse could not help wondering how they had happened to meet so soon and to get well enough acquainted to make calls together. It seemed strange to associate Patty Forrestal with any Breckenridge.

Narcisse was enabled to ponder all these details, because the volubility of Anna Breckenridge prevented him from taking any immediate part in the conversation himself. He had been right in assuming that the current political situation would absorb her. She had just come from a meeting at which Mrs. Cutler had presided, and she was so roused by a recital of the abuses perpetrated during the aftermath of Huey Long's regime that she insisted on enumerating these for Mrs. Fontaine's benefit, though Narcisse could see that they were very wearing to his sister-in-law. It was Patty Forrestal who finally took advantage of a slight break in the diatribe to signal tactfully to Anna Breckenridge that perhaps they were tiring the invalid and to put the hint into effect by rising herself before the other visitor could embark on a fresh phase of Louisiana's wrongs.

"I'm sorry we have to leave now," she was saying, bending over to kiss his sister-in-law. "Mrs. Breckenridge and I are going to the Symphony this evening, and I have to rush home and dress first. Not that it takes me long to get up Saint Charles Avenue now that I have my cute roadster, but I don't want to run too close to the wind. I'll drop in sometime tomorrow, probably just before lunch. I'm sailing in the afternoon."

Oh, yes, Narcisse Fontaine remembered vaguely, this was the girl his grandnephew, Gail Rutledge, had always cared about. Well, now that he had a good chance to look her over, he was afraid poor Gail would have a run for his money, even if she were going sailing with the boy.

"I'm so glad to have seen you, Mr. Fontaine. Your grandson and granddaughters are such great friends of mine, I've always wished I could meet you, too, sometime. It's nice to have wishes fulfilled, isn't it?"

She held out one of those slim brown hands, and, as Narcisse had expected, he found there was greath strength in its clasp. But what an amazing ring she was wearing! He had never seen a star sapphire of such size, or of such brilliancy and beauty. The diamonds that surrounded it were magnificent in themselves. If she had had it on the other hand, he would have taken it for granted that it was an engagement ring. But not many young men in New Orleans could give a girl a ring like that, who would have the taste to choose it combined with the money to pay for it. Certainly Gail

Rutledge would have neither the one nor the other. Offhand, he could think of only one man who would have both, and that was Drew Breckenridge. But Drew Breckenridge and this girl! It would be appalling, if it were true. Fortunately, it was impossible.

"Good-bye, *chère*," his sister-in-law was saying. "I shall be looking forward to your visit, and you know that any hour you can come would be convenient for me. That is one of the great advantages in being a quasi invalid—there are no conflicting engagements to confuse a tired mind! But as soon as I feel a little stronger, I am going to ask you to take me out for a ride in that new car of yours. I have already told you I was sure you would drive one beautifully, and I am so glad you have a 'cute roadster' all your own— Anna, it seems like old times to have you for a neighbor again! Shall I send you some vetivert to put on the shelves of your armoires, as I did before?"

"I'd like very much to have you, Mrs. Fontaine. But you look rather mischievous as you say that. I'm afraid someone must have told you the mistake I made about it the first time."

They were gone, with kisses and smiles, to the vague relief of Narcisse. He had been a rosy, chubby, cheery child, and the rosiness and chubbiness had lasted; so had the cheeriness, to a remarkable degree. He did not like to have anything upset it, however. Octave had enjoyed a good fight, Auguste took an austere pleasure in minor martyrdoms, and Marcel had always contrived to pretend that everything about life was urbane, elegant and delightful. Narcisse had neither the tastes of Octave and Auguste nor the talents of Marcel. He enjoyed comfort and joviality, but he was not able to achieve and sustain them without some reluctant effort on his part. He made an effort now to speak to his sister-in-law with great sprightliness.

"Well, I see you have been having very pleasant visitors, Estelle. No doubt it is good for you, if it does not tire you too much. But somehow, it is a surprise for me to find you on terms of such intimacy both with Mrs. Breckenridge and with *cette petite* Forrestal, who is, incidentally, much more charming than I was prepared to find her. I do not wonder Gail is so intrigued. What are his chances, should you say?"

"Extremely slight. I believe that dear Patty is on her way to becoming what Amelina and Clarinda quaintly call 'the number-one glamor girl' of New Orleans, succeeding Stella in that role. Have they not said something of the sort to you also? Naturally I doubly appreciate the thoughtfulness and unselfishness she shows in spending so much time with me, since I know in what great demand she is. I had forgotten that young company could be so stimulating."

"But surely Stella——"

"Stella is a dear girl and I love her. She is my own grand-daughter, and is cast in the same mold that I am. I can understand that. But I can admire a finer one still more."

Mrs. Fontaine smiled, and picking up the jewelled mirror which lay on the little table beside her, began to toy with it.

"I am happy to see you, too, Narcisse. We have drifted too far apart these last years. I hope you will try to come here often in the next weeks, and bring your family with you. But today I wanted to see you alone, professionally. I desire to make a few slight changes in my will. Probably all that would be necessary would be to add a codicil."

"I shall be glad to give you any advice I can, of course, Estelle. Tell me about these changes you have in mind."

"I should like to make two bequests outside the family. First, I should like to leave this mirror I am holding in my hand to Patty Forrestal."

"That mirror! But it does not require a codicil to dispose of a trifle like that. A simple memorandum would be enough. Neither your granddaughter nor any of your grandnieces could possibly object to having you give a mere Carnival favor to anyone you chose."

"I am afraid you are not entirely accurate in describing this mirror as a mere Carnival favor, Narcisse."

"Why, I was one of the little chefs of the Twelfth Night Revels the night you received it! It was given you in one of the first call-outs—by Marcel, I suppose. Otherwise, why should you have treasured a bauble like that all this time? Yes, Clarisse was the Queen and you were one of the Maids. I remember it all as well as if it had been yesterday."

"And so do I, Narcisse. But it was not Marcel who gave me the mirror. I danced with him in the second call-out, and he gave me a *bonbonnière*. It was Andy Breckenridge who gave me this mirror. And those brilliants which surround it are not rhinestones, as you seem to suppose. They are diamonds."

"*Diamonds!* Of that size!"

"Yes. You say you remember those scenes as well as

though they had occurred yesterday. Then you must also remember that Andy Breckenridge was given to doing everything in a very lavish way."

"But if those are diamonds, then that mirror is worth——"

"Yes, it is worth a small fortune in itself. Of course, this might not have been discovered after my death, since it has not been discovered during my lifetime. On the other hand, it might have. And then perhaps there would have been a slight awkwardness if there were only a memorandum stating that I wished to give this small fortune to Patty Forrestal, instead of my own kith and kin."

The round and rosy countenance of Narcisse Fontaine had become more and more troubled as his sister-in-law talked to him. She continued calmly, still fingering the mirror.

"As a matter of fact, it does not happen to be on account of its monetary value that I wish to give this to Patty," she said. "I have reason to believe that Patty will never be poor. My reasons are symbolic—sentimental, if you like. I wish the bequest to be worded in this way: 'I leave my diamond-studded silver mirror to Patricia Anne Forrestal because I believe that she will have the courage to face the future in it. I, myself, have been able only to look at the past, through bitter tears.' "

"But, Estelle, you can't make a bequest like that!"

"Do you mean it would not be legal?"

"It can be legalized, of course. But there are other reasons——"

"The other reasons seem unimportant to me now, Narcisse. I shall count on you to see that this bequest is drawn up in proper form. As for the second legacy, I wish to leave my property on Kerlerec Street—the small shotgun house that I own there, where Olivier lived for a short time—to Drew Breckenridge. I wish it to be made in a certain manner also: 'To Andrew Breckenridge, the third of his name, from his devoted friend, Estelle Lenoir Fontaine, with the hope that he may find in this house, with his beloved, the joy which his grandfather was denied.' "

"Estelle, it would create a scandal throughout New Orleans if you carried out any such purpose as this."

"And is scandal here anything so new, Narcisse? I should not have said so. Nor should I think that a harmless old lady, whose life had caused none, could create any after her death. Find some way to make the bequests privately, if that would be better. But make them."

"The only thing you could do would be to present the mirror to Patty Forrestal and the house to Drew Breckenridge during your lifetime, with any comment you choose. They would then be donations *inter vivos,* not legacies. And some of the scandal could be avoided."

Narcisse Fontaine rose and began to pace the room restlessly. He poured himself another cup of coffee, then set down the cup and came back to his sister-in-law's side.

"I suppose it is useless to try to change this *idée fixe* you have about the mirror, Estelle," he said. "But I do hope you will listen to reason about the house. You have probably heard that Harold Baird has placed his divorce suit, which is very shortly to be tried, in my hands. I do not need to point out to you that it would be very awkward for me, while I am acting as his attorney, if you presented a valuable piece of property to the man he is naming as corespondent, especially with such a statement as you have in mind."

"Harold Baird! Why, I had forgotten about him! How sad it is to see the change time makes in some men, Narcisse! Now you, yourself, are as you were when I first knew you— so cheerful, so kindly, so charming. But poor Harold— He was a pleasant little boy, too! And now he takes this crass and vulgar action!"

"No man with any self-respect would endure what Harold Baird's wife has done to him, Estelle."

"No man with any self-respect would have married a girl who would make him such a wife, in the first place. But I am sorry to see his degradation take the form it has now— of hurting the innocent when he has so long condoned the guilty."

"I'm afraid I do not follow you, Estelle."

"Why, Evelyn will not be hurt by this divorce! She will probably have some huge sum of money settled upon her, as soon as it is over, and go to the Riviera, or some such place, and marry a Roumanian prince, or some such person, who will be delighted with her fortune and entirely unconcerned as to her character. No, not the Riviera, of course, with this war going on. I am getting very forgetful in my old age. But to Palm Beach, perhaps. I am sure there must be Roumanian princes, or their equivalent, at Palm Beach. Then there is always Hollywood. Evelyn is very beautiful. She might make quite a sensation in Hollywood, either on the screen herself, though she is a little past the best age for that, or by becoming some handsome actor's fifth wife."

"Estelle, this is a very peculiar train of thought for you to be pursuing."

"I know. I am just a wandering old woman. But in my senile state, it seems to me that Harold Baird is pursuing a very peculiar train of thought himself. It would hurt Evelyn so much more if he would simply get a separation from her. Then she wouldn't have any huge sum of money settled on her. Then she wouldn't be free to marry a Roumanian prince. But possibly Harold desires to remarry himself. If he does, if he has given Evelyn any cause for complaint, except because of his intemperance——"

"He has not," Narcisse said almost sharply. "There has been no question of another woman in Mr. Baird's case. Women have never been his weakness. And now he is so disillusioned, so embittered——"

"Ah! Then I should certainly think a separation would be his best solution, at least for the present, if he is bent on humiliating his wife. Not that this is ever the act of a gentleman or a Christian. And it seems to me most unjust that an innocent young girl like Patty Forrestal should suffer for what a *déclassée* like Evelyn has done, instead of Evelyn, herself."

"I don't follow you, Estelle," Narcisse said, speaking sharply again.

"I told you I was beginning to be a garrulous old woman. I am afraid I came very close to betraying a confidence. Perhaps it would be better if I did not try to talk any more today. Thank you for coming to see me, Narcisse. I will follow your advice. I will give the mirror to Patty the next time I see her, and the house to Drew the next time I see him. Perhaps I can make the two presentations simultaneously. It sometimes happens that Drew and Patty get here together. There, there! Bring Carmen and Carmelita to see me, won't you, Narcisse? And tell Harold Baird I should like to see him sometime, too. I am sincere in saying I was very fond of him when he was a little boy. And now I shall probably not have so many more occasions to visit with my old friends. Oh, only on account of indolence, of course! *Au revoir*, Narcisse. And thank you again for coming."

Raoul Bienvenu saw Mrs. Fontaine on the same day that Narcisse paid her his troubled visit. Stella, who was not expecting him, had gone to an all-day barn dance "over the lake," and when Emile told him she was not at home, Raoul asked the old butler if her grandmother would receive him, instead. Emile hesitated; with the intuition of his race, he knew that Mr. Narcisse had wearied Miss Estelle and he felt that her strength should not be taxed any further. But like most other persons, Emile found it hard to deny Raoul Bienvenu anything for which he asked; he had grown steadily more persuasive, as well as steadily more personable, with the passage of years.

"She's po'ly, Mr. Raoul, mighty po'ly. I don't rightly know ought I to tell her you's here."

"Tell her, Emile, but say that if she doesn't feel equal to seeing me, I'll wait downstairs until Miss Stella gets back."

"Yassah. I don't think Miss Stella was figurin' on gettin' back till mighty late, though. She done told me not to sit up for her."

Raoul nodded without answering, and Emile left him standing in the dim drawing room and climbed the long stairway in his usual laborious fashion. But presently he came back with the announcement that Miss Estelle would be very pleased to see Mr. Raoul—that she hoped he would stay for dinner with her. She was not quite equal to coming down to the dining room, though; if he would not find it dull to have it in her sitting room—he was to let Emile know.

"I'd be delighted. Only I don't want to tire her too much."

"I reckon poor Miss Estelle tired most all de time, Mr. Raoul. But she gets lonesome, too, come ebenin', and dat's worse dan de tiredness."

Of course, she must be lonesome, Raoul thought as he went up the stairs in his turn. Stella was in such constant demand that she was very seldom in the house, and when she was, it was always full of company; there could not be many hours when she would be free to sit with her grandmother in the twilight. Well, she was the success of the season, and that was what her grandmother had wanted, just as he, Raoul, had wanted a long engagement; and now, in both cases, their heart's desire had turned to Dead Sea fruit. But they should not blame Stella for that. She had plead, pitifully enough, for her own heart's desire, and they had denied her; she had retaliated only in giving them what they said was theirs.

It was nearly two weeks since Raoul had seen Mrs. Fontaine, and he was shocked to see the change that these had made in her. She would be elegant, he knew, even in her shroud, but he felt as if the shadow of its folds were already touching her. It was strange that Stella had not seen it or, at any event, that she had not spoken of it, but he had often heard that a change was less noticeable to those who saw it every day than to those who observed it only intermittently. Because he shrank from showing how shocked he was, he tried to greet her with a jauntiness which he hoped, rather than believed, was convincing.

"Well, this is a great piece of luck! In my wildest dreams I should never have dared aspire to a tête-à-tête dinner with the Crescent City's perennial Queen!"

He took her hand as he spoke to her and then, on a sudden impulse, leaned over and kissed her. It was the first time he had ever done so, and he felt startled afresh at the uncanny softness of her white cheek. But he saw, with increasing astonishment, that the caress had really pleased her and that she was genuinely glad to see him.

"Now, that is the way you should salute your grandmother," she said almost gaily. "Which reminds me—I have been meaning to ask you, for some time, why you do not call me *Grand'mère?* All the other young men I know call me Aunt Estelle. But you never have, and, after all, it would be much more appropriate——"

"Thank you. I'd be very proud if you'd let me do that. But my presumption, great as it is, never would have carried me that far without permission."

"I do not see why not. It has certainly carried you a long way," Mrs. Fontaine went on, still gaily. "Of course, certain other qualities have gone with it. And when we come to the question of the dinner, it is not often that an old lady like me can command the exclusive company of such a popular bachelor! Stella's loss is certainly my gain. Emile told you, I suppose, that she has gone to some kind of a country dance near Pass Christian. She started off, early this morning, wearing shorts—a costume to which I must confess I have never accustomed myself. Still, she did look very pretty."

"I don't doubt it. I've always liked seeing Stella in shorts myself, perhaps because she was wearing them the first time I met her. I thought then she was the prettiest girl I'd ever seen in my life. I still think so."

"I am sorry you should have missed her."

"Well, I rather think I'll wait for her. I won't keep you up, of course, if she's very late. But I especially wanted to see her tonight. I've had a chance to buy a house that's just the sort she used to say she'd like—long and low and white, with ornamental woodwork over the galleries and quantities of greenery around it, and a garden sloping down to the bayou in the back. I didn't come to new Orleans on legal business this time or to see any of my political pals. I came on purpose to tell her about this house. The purchase proposition was unexpected, or I'd have got in touch with her before I left Abbeville. I've got to give an answer right away."

"I see. And I suppose you hope, if she encourages you to buy this house, that then——"

"Yes, *Grand'mère*. She told me you'd been good enough to suggest that we shouldn't wait until June to get married— that we might do so at any time, as far as you were concerned. And I thought—"

"She also told you about the possible opening at the Metropolitan, didn't she, Raoul?"

"Yes, she told me that, too. And of course I shan't stand in her way. But I can't help believing that if I could only get her to marry me, she'd find out afterwards that the sort of happiness she used to want is still the best kind, after all—that she'd be satisfied if she never sang again, except to me."

"I believe so, too, Raoul. But I do not know how either of us can make Stella believe that now."

"Can't you think of some way that we could, *Grand'mère*? Since we're friends and allies at last, instead of antagonists?"

Of her own accord she took his hand again. He held it between his, hard, as she went on talking to him.

"It is my fault that we were not friends and allies from the beginning, Raoul. I know that now. But I am afraid the knowledge has come too late. Just as the knowledge that Stella wanted to share your struggle as well as your success came too late for you. And I am also afraid that there is still bitterer knowledge in store for you."

"What is it, *Grand'mère*?"

"That Stella cannot give herself up to love any more. The ability to do that does not last, indefinitely, with a woman, if she is thwarted in her first deep desire. She builds up defenses around herself. She couldn't survive if she didn't. And then she isn't strong enough to tear them down again. No matter how hard she tries. Stella has tried. I've watched her trying and it has nearly broken my heart. But she can't. And neither can anyone else."

"I'm going to try once more, anyway, *Grand'mère*."

"I don't know as I ought to disturb you and Mr. Raoul,

Miss Estelle. But dere's a long distance call for Miss Stella. I done told de operator she wasn't in, but central done call back again, and say, effen de party in New York dat wants Miss Stella can't speak to her, she's got to speak to you."

Emile stood in the doorway, apologetic and unhappy. It was evident that he knew this was no moment to break in on his mistress. And yet he had been impelled to do so. Raoul sprang up.

"Why, I didn't hear the telephone ring! I'll go and answer it."

"It does not ring in my room, *cher*. I spare myself that annoyance, by having the bells in the rear of the house. But see, I have an extension here. I will take the call, Emile. You did right to tell me about it."

She picked up the receiver and went on talking in the same quiet gentle way in which she had been talking to Raoul. But the gaiety with which she had greeted him was gone now. A new note, unbelievably and appallingly sad, had crept into her voice.

"This is Mrs. Fontaine speaking. Yes—yes—I can take a message for Miss Stella Fontaine. I will give it to her as soon as she comes in this evening. I'm afraid that will be very late, but I shall be glad—— Oh, yes, Mrs. Hastings—— Yes, Stella did tell me, but I did not understand it would be so soon. I thought you were still in New Orleans—— I see. Then it would be necessary for her to take the train for New York tonight, or if she misses that, the plane tomorrow morning, in order to be there in time—— Yes, I will make reservations on both—— Yes, one of us will call you back."

Mrs. Fontaine put back the receiver slowly. For a moment she did not speak, and Raoul did not try to speak to her either. Then she went on again, in her quiet gentle voice.

"I must ring for Julie, Raoul, and tell her to pack for Stella. And perhaps you will be good enough to call up the station and the airport and see what reservations are available. I am afraid we must postpone our gala little dinner, after all. Neither of us would be in the mood for it now. It seems that Stella's great chance has come sooner than we expected. She can have her audition day after tomorrow, if she can get there for it."

"I'll make the reservations. And I'll take her to the train or the plane, if she wants to go. But I'll tell her about the house on the bayou first. Perhaps she won't go, after all.

Perhaps at the last minute she'll decide to stay. Or perhaps she'll go and come right back."

"Perhaps she will, Raoul. Perhaps she will."

Mrs. Fontaine spoke steadily, as he had spoken. But they both knew as they looked at each other that there was no use in speaking as they had, and still, they shrank from speaking the bitter truth. Raoul was saying to himself, "Now Stella will not marry me this spring, after all," and Mrs. Fontaine was saying to herself, "Now Stella will not be here when I die." But neither one said it aloud.

Stella did not get back in time to catch the *Crescent Limited*. It was long after midnight when the car she was in drew up at the banquette in front of her grandmother's house. She got out quickly, and so did Gail Rutledge, who was at the wheel. But Gail came no further than the gate of the cornstalk fence with her. Raoul had not wanted to startle her when she got back, so he had kept on all the lights in the front drawing room and left the shades up; she could see him moving about as she came up the walk, and when she caught sight of him, she dismissed Gail, in a somewhat summary fashion, with a brief cousinly kiss. Raoul opened the door and called out to her cheerily.

"Hello, there! Did you have a good time?"

"Hello, yourself!— Fine, for the first few hours. But these barnyard parties do have a way of dying on you before they're over, especially if they start as early as this one did. I'd done all the horseback riding and played all the games of chance I wanted to long before sunset. And I'd danced with all the drunks I wanted to long before ten o'clock. But I was with a crowd, so I couldn't do much about it. Why didn't you let me know you were coming over? It would have given me a good excuse for breaking away."

"I didn't know myself until this morning. Then I thought I'd run for luck. I've got a couple of surprises for you. Come on into the drawing room while I tell you about them."

Stella tossed the shaggy sports coat she had been wearing onto a chair in the hall and shook back her curls. They were tumbled, after her long windy ride, and the shorts she had been wearing all day were rumpled. For the first time since Raoul could remember, she did not look like an animated fashion plate. She looked so uncannily like the little girl who had confronted a strange young lawyer on the Abbeville wharf nearly five years earlier that a wild weird hope leapt up in Raoul's heart. He put his arm around her.

"You haven't got a kiss for me, by any chance, have you?" he inquired, managing, with a great effort, to speak dispassionately.

"Of course. What are your two surprises, Raoul? Grannie isn't worse, is she?"

Stella turned her face towards him as she spoke and kissed him, as she finished asking her second question, in much the same way that she had kissed Gail Rutledge five minutes earlier. The wild hope in Raoul's heart died down at the carelessness of the caress. But he answered without either reproachfulness or urgency.

"She doesn't seem to have as much strength as when I last saw her. But I don't believe she's suddenly developed any new or alarming symptoms, if that's what you mean. So don't worry. I wasn't referring to her when I spoke of surprises."

He seated himself in one of the ponderous chairs, drawing Stella down on his knees and keeping his arm lightly around her. She reached for a cigarette from a little box on the end table beside the chair, lighted it, and began to smoke while she waited for him to go on. Neither his nearness nor his undisclosed news seemed to stir her in the least.

"I've found the house I've been waiting so long for, Stella. Exactly the right house for you. It's not new, but it's in perfect condition. One of the rice-mill officials renovated it completely two years ago. And now he's been transferred from Abbeville to Crowley. He wants to sell immediately. In fact, I've got to give him his answer tomorrow. That's why I came tearing down, not to meet anyone myself or get you to entertain anyone. Just to talk to you about this house."

"I've always been delighted to receive your friends here, Raoul, you know that."

"Yes, and you do it wonderfully. I've told you that over and over again and so have they. You've got great gifts, Stella, and that goes for lots of other things besides music. But you suited me as a sweetheart before I knew you were a knockout as a hostess, or that you were a second Jenny Lind, or that you had more cold cash than you knew what to do with. You still do. I like to have you to myself once in a while. In fact, I want you a lot more to myself. I think it's about time."

He drew her closer to him, taking her cigarette gently away from her and kissing her lingeringly, as if he hoped that her lips would grow warm, too, if his own rested long enough against them. Then he began to describe the house to her as he had described it to her grandmother but with more detail: the beautiful proportions, the fine old floors, the undisturbed quaintness, the tranquil charm. There was a big living room facing the garden and the bayou, a big dining room and a big bedroom leading out of it. They could be as quiet there as if they lived in the heart of the country, though the place was only a mile or so from the center of the town. The house was tastefully furnished with authentic antiques, and the man who was moving would be willing to sell the furniture, too, if Stella would like to have it. But Raoul had an idea she might prefer to take down some of the things she had brought back from France. In any event——

"In any event, it was your idea that if you bought this house, we might get married right away, and spend the spring and summer there, while you're campaigning for Congress?"

"Yes. I don't think it'll be a hard campaign, Stella. The Long crowd's through—in my district anyway. Over in the Lake Charles district, next door, they're not even putting up a candidate. And of course I have Dr. Anconi and all his cronies with me. I don't believe I'd have to be away from home a great deal. And naturally, I'd like to have you come with me wherever I went, if it would interest you to do it, and I think it would. We've got plenty of time to take a wedding trip, too, if you like. We could go to Mexico. Or anywhere else you prefer. But at that, I don't believe we'd find a place more beautiful than the bayou at Abbeville in springtime."

"No, I don't suppose we would— What's your other surprise, Raoul?"

He hesitated. It would be so easy not to tell her now, to go on talking about the house until she was really interested, and then to seek the weak place in her armor until he found it. He had her to himself now; he could plead his cause without danger of interruption or interference. And her grandmother was on his side at last, not only as an individual, but as an invalid whose whims must be gratified and

whose frailty must be considered. He could plead her cause
as well as his own. He could beg Stella to have Father Fontaine marry them the first thing the next morning when the
priest came to give Holy Communion to his sister-in-law.
And Stella would consent. That is, if Raoul could make his
plea moving enough and she did not know about the audition——

"You've had a long-distance call."

He was speaking so mechanically that he hardly knew
the words were formed before they left his lips. "Mrs. Hastings telephoned from New York," he went on. "She's arranged for the audition. But you'd have to be there for it
day after tomorrow. I had a compartment tied up for you
on the *Crescent* tonight, but you didn't get here in time to
take it. I've got a seat for you on tomorrow morning's plane,
though. I'll drive you out to the airport. That is, if you
think you want to go."

"If I think I want to go! Why Raoul, you must be crazy,
even to ask such a question!"

She was on her feet, her hair tossed back again, her face
alight, her eyes sparkling. Her apathy, her guardedness, were
completely gone. She was all eagerness, all excitement.

"What time does the plane start? I must hurry and pack.
You don't mind, do you, Raoul? You understand, don't you?
You see this is so terribly important——"

"Julie's packed for you already. You've got plenty of time.
The plane doesn't go until nearly noon. I'll get you there all
right. But don't leave me now, Stella. Please stay with me.
Please listen to me. Please tell me I can go ahead and get
the house. I'm so afraid that if you don't—if I don't——"

"But Raoul, I've got to have some sleep. If I don't, I'll be
exhausted; I won't be able to sing. I've been racketing around
all day and I've got a hard trip ahead of me. I'll be terribly
tired when I get to New York, anyway. And I haven't had
any chance to practice or prepare. It's all come so suddenly.
I want to go upstairs now, and check everything over, to be
sure I've got what I need, and look through my music, and—
But I'll see you in the morning. We can talk on our way out
to the airport."

"You wouldn't marry me in the morning before you leave,
would you, Stella?"

'*Marry* you in the morning! Why how could I?"

"It would be simple enough. Father Fontaine could marry
us here."

"But then you'd expect me to come back, no matter what happened in New York! Then you would go ahead and buy the house! Wouldn't you?"

"It wouldn't be astonishing if I did, would it, honey?"

"No, but you see——"

"I see that I made a great mistake in not seducing you, Stella, five years ago, when you wanted to have me."

He smiled as she spoke, and his tone was whimsical, though the smile was sorry and the whimsicality shot through with sadness. But Stella pounced on his words as if she had been waiting for them, ready to resent them as soon as they were uttered, eager for the opportunity they offered.

"I knew that someday you'd say that to me! I know it's what you've been thinking for a long time already, even though you've never said it before!"

"Stella, I haven't. I've never thought it. I only said it now —well, because I was feeling pretty badly and I had to say something to cover up the way I felt."

"I don't believe you! I know you'll never realize that wasn't the mistake you made. But you made plenty of others. You dropped me and picked me up again whenever you felt like it. You never let me know beforehand whether you were going to exalt me or humiliate me. You made me feel that your career meant more to you than I did. You drove me away from you when I needed you and worshipped you. Those are a few of the mistakes you made, in case you don't know it."

"I do know it. And you ought to know how sorry I am. I've tried hard enough, for five years, to make up for them. So you also ought to know, by this time, that I've always loved you, with all my heart and soul."

"Well, I loved you, too. I loved you enough to stand all that and stick by you. I loved the memory of the little we'd had together enough to want more—at least I did for a long time. And even after I stopped wanting more, I still wanted to be loyal. I still tried to be fair. I've never stopped trying. But now——"

"Stella, don't go away from me, in anger, a second time. It was my fault before. All my fault. But this time it isn't."

"It is! When you talk to me about the great mistake you made, why don't you say it was in not *marrying* me when I wanted to have you? I did want it! And there wasn't anything in the world I could do about it, because you weren't willing."

"Of course I was willing. Of course I was crazy to marry

you, from the moment I laid eyes on you. Why, I told you so, the second time I saw you!"

"You told me you wanted to and then you told me all the reasons why you couldn't. Now you think you can. But you can't. There's nothing in the world you can do about it now, because I'm not willing."

"You don't mean that, Stella. You can't."

"I do. I can. I'm sorry, Raoul, but it's true. I'm not speaking to you in anger now. I was only angry for a minute, and you're right; I shouldn't have been. Forgive me for striking out at you like that when you didn't deserve it. But I don't love you any more. I can't marry you. This is the end."

She sank down suddenly in the big chair, where a few moments before he had held her in his arms, and covered her face with her hands. He could not hear her sobbing, but he saw that her shoulders were shaking, and after a moment he went over and laid his arm firmly across them to steady them. But when she regained her self-control and looked up at him with a face that was calm again, she saw that his had changed, too.

"There," he said. "You *have* wanted to say that for a long time. Now that you've said it, you'll feel better. Don't try to talk about it any more now. I won't try to talk either. There are a few things I might say myself, but I won't. Go to bed and get some sleep. You're right; you do need it. And go ahead to New York. I shan't try to stop you and I won't come back in the morning. I don't see why it's taken me so long to find out that you can't face the music—the real kind, not the opera sham—any better than your grandmother could. But I've found it out now, and I hope you won't be as sorry when you're seventy as she is— Well, I'll put your tickets on the hall table. Emile can drive you to the airport. I'll go back to Abbeville and tell my rice man I don't need his house, after all. Don't worry about that or anything else any longer. But don't make a mistake yourself either. You've told me you wanted this to be the end. So it's going to be. Not just because you say so, but because I do, too."

Mrs. Fontaine gave Patty the mirror the next morning, after Stella had taken the plane for New York. She told the girl what she had meant to put in the legacy.

"I do believe you have the courage to face the future, *chère*. Otherwise, I shouldn't give this to you now. I should keep it until the end, after keeping it for fifty years."

"I can't bear to have you part with it. I can't bear to take it from you, Aunt Estelle."

"Yes, you can, *chère*, because it makes me so happy to know that you have it. It makes me so happy to know you have the courage I lacked and that Stella has lacked. Otherwise, the mirror would have gone to her."

Patty took the mirror in her own hands and turned it. "I don't feel brave all the time, Aunt Estelle," she said in a low voice. "I try to pretend I do, but very often—especially when I haven't seen Drew in several days——"

"When that happens, do what I have told you, my child. Look into the future and see his face framed with yours."

That same afternoon she spoke to Drew about the house and told him what she had meant to say concerning it in the legacy. She knew that he was tremendously touched by her gift. But still, he ventured to argue with her about it, though no one except Drew would have argued with her in those days.

"I'd like to own the little house, Aunt Estelle. I'm grateful to you for giving it to me. But it won't hurt your feelings, will it, if I tell you it isn't the house to which I want to take Patty?"

"Why not, Drew?"

"Because I want to keep her like a queen. Think of the joy I'll have in heaping riches on her. She's never had too many, bless her heart. But she's going to. She's going to have everything."

"She'll think she has that when she has you."

Mrs. Fontaine pressed his hand affectionately and smiled at him, but he saw that she was very tired—that he must not argue with her any more that day. He told her he would be in again the next evening about the same time. But before he got there, Patty called him. He knew there was some emergency when Louis, speaking with great respect, told him that she was on the wire. She had kept the letter of her bargain with him as well as the spirit. She had never met him except by chance, and she had never tried to get in touch with him in any way since she had gone to his house with Mrs. Fontaine. He went very quickly to the telephone.

"Yes, Patty."

"I'm speaking to you from Aunt Estelle's house, Drew. I'm here because she sent word that she wanted to see me. And

Dr. Beal thought I ought to come at once. Now she wants to see you."

"I'm starting."

Patty was waiting for him in the dim drawing room when he entered it. She came forward to meet him.

"I want to speak to you for a minute, Drew, before we go upstairs."

"All right, Patty."

He had not taken her in his arms. He had only raised her right hand with his ring on it and kissed it. Then he had waited.

"I couldn't tell you over the telephone. She does want to see you. She wants to see you and me together. She wants it very much and most of the time she remembers that's what she wants. But every now and then she forgets. Then she asks for just one person."

"Yes, Patty?"

"Andy Breckenridge."

"I see."

"And Dr. Beal thinks, if the next time she did that, you went to her by yourself, she might think you were Andy. You look so much like him, and she wouldn't notice clothes and things like that. Of course, I'd be in the next room, in case she remembered the present. But Dr. Beal thinks if she saw you alone, perhaps——"

"I understand, Patty. I'll go to her with you, if she asks for you and me. But if she asks for Andy, I'll go to her alone."

It was both of them that she asked first. They went to her bedside together and stood near it, holding each other's hands. She seemed satisfied when she saw them. But afterwards, when it was almost night and the room was full of shadows, she asked for Andy, and Drew went to her alone.

"Are you there, Andy?"

"Yes, Estelle."

"I want to take your hand. I want you to help me through these deep waters."

He enfolded her hand with his hands before she could grope for them. Its frailty was shocking to him, and its coldness. He thought of the strength and warmth of Patty's hand which he had held only a few moments before, and it was hard for him to keep his voice steady. But he did.

"Don't be afraid of them, darling. They're really not very

deep. I've been through them myself, you know, and I got through all right. So I know just how to help you."

"Yes. I was sure you would. And I have something to say to you, Andy, while we're going. Something you asked me to say a long time ago."

"I'm listening, darling. Hold my hand hard while you say it."

" 'Andy, I do love you. I'll prove it to you. I will stay with you. I won't let anything stop me or delay our marriage. I'm not afraid of obstacles or scandal or disaster. I'm not afraid of what you'll take from me or of what you'll do to me. I want you for my lover. I'll have you for my husband. Not just for richer; for poorer, too. Not just for better; for worse, too. Not just in health; in sickness, too. Till death do us part.' Only I don't believe, Andy, that death will be a parting, after all."

PART IX

"If Ever I Cease to Love"

Autumn, 1940 to Winter, 1941

CHAPTER 34

IT WAS Saturday afternoon, and Ursin Villeré, Ruby Compton, Aileen Hodges and the rest of the staff had already left the office, but Drew was still seated at his desk, an open checkbook on one side of him, a pile of scratch paper covered with figures on the other. Behind the inkstand, the "Blue Streak" edition of the *Item* was propped up, folded once across, but with the black headlines still plainly visible. They leapt out at him whenever he looked up from his figuring.

He had lunched early and haphazardly, hoping that the quick consumption of a sandwich and a glass of milk might expedite his departure. There was a great deal he wanted to say to Patty that afternoon, and he knew he would need a great deal of time to say it. But he also wanted all the clutter which surrounded him cleared away before he went to her; when it was behind him, it would cease to ride him even thought it still worried him, and he would be able to talk to her more openly and easily.

As he went on working, with this in mind, the realization that he wanted to talk to her not only without haste and without reservation but also without interruption kept growing stronger and stronger. Patty's mother and brothers had an incurable habit of breaking at unpredictable moments into the morning room, which he and Patty had more or less appropriated; it seemed to Drew that if they had deliberately chosen the ones when they would be least welcome, they could not have hit upon them more successfully. In his present mood, he could think of nothing that would suit him less than an attempt at private conversation in the raised cottage. At his house, he and Patty would be safer from intrusion. They generally sat in the study, and his own mother had developed and revealed a surprising amount of tact in dealing with the current situation. Drew had never supposed before that she had it in her. Of course, she regarded Patty with a degree of affection and admiration that he had never known her to lavish on anyone, which all went to prove Patty's perfection, if Drew had needed any further proof of it, which he did not. But even so, both Anna Breckenridge and the ubiquitous Louis had fixed ideas as to the hours when tea and cocktails and dinner should be served from which Drew had never been able to swerve them. No one would burst into the study unannounced. But there were moment when a knock was almost as inopportune as a presence, and, in any case, it presaged an inescapable summons. Drew did not want any sort of intrusion or any sort of summons that afternoon.

He picked up the telephone and called Patty's number. She answered immediately, herself. He had asked her once how she always happened to be on hand when he called her, and she answered, quite simply, that it was because she was generally waiting, hoping to hear from him. He had chided her gently, saying that she ought not to waste her time like that and remembering, not without a pang, how he had teased Stella for hanging on the telephone at Bois Fleuri. Patty only answered, again quite simply, that she thought it was a wonderful way for a girl to spend her time, and after that there did not seem to be anything further to say on the subject——

"Hello, darling. Aren't you worn out, this time, waiting for me?"

"Of course not. I didn't even expect you for an hour or so yet."

"Well, I think it will be just about that long before I can get there. This seems to be a pretty nice afternoon. What would you say to a ride in the country?"

"I'd love it."

"Right. So would I. Is there any special place you'd like to go?"

"Could we go to Splendida?"

"Why, I suppose we could. I hadn't thought of Splendida."

It was true. He had hardly been to Splendida at all that summer, and it had never occurred to him to invite Patty to go there with him. But if they drove up on the Air Line Highway and then made a good connection with the ferry at Donaldsonville, they could get there in a little over two hours. They might even stay for supper there and drive home by moonlight. There was no reason now, as he saw it, why he should not ask Patty openly to his house.

"I think you've got an idea there. I'll telephone Jezebel to expect us. That'll give her time for a 'lick and a promise' at least. But I'm afraid you won't find the place in very good order, Patty."

"I wasn't thinking of looking around in the corners for dust. I thought maybe you'd keep me too busy to do that."

"Patty, you're priceless. Shall I telephone to St. Louis Plantation, too, and see if some of the Gays would come down and have supper with us? Or shall we just picnic by ourselves?"

It was the first time that he had suggested they might do something by themselves, and he heard her catch her breath a little, as she so often did when she was unexpectedly made happy. The trifling habit was the more attractive to him because Patty, on the whole, was so calm, for a young girl; it affected him in the same way as the surprising sight of her dimple. He felt suddenly uplifted himself, even before she replied, in knowing what her answer would be.

"I'm very fond of all the Gays. But I think it would be fun to picnic by ourselves, don't you? Shall I fix some sandwiches and drinks while I'm waiting for you?"

"Oh, I believe Splendida, even in its present depleted state, can provide enough to keep us from going hungry. In an hour or so, then, darling. It may be a little longer."

It was considerably longer. The clutter took more time to clear away than Drew had expected, and the afternoon, though undeniably "nice," was also undeniably hot, even for September. So on his way uptown he stopped at his own house for a quick shower and change. Then, as he went on up Prytania Street, he saw Stella on the gallery of the Fontaine house, and when she waved to him, something impelled him to get out and speak to her.

She was looking very badly, he thought, as he went up to the gallery—terribly thin and pale; the circles around her eyes were far darker and deeper than those of which he had spoken so jestingly to Ruby. Of course, her black clothes enhanced her pallor and her emaciation, and he could not help wondering why she had not chosen to wear white instead. Confronting her, he thought of a letter he had found among his father's papers, which he had read innocently enough, unaware until he had almost reached the end that it was an artless declaration of love. "Mrs. Astor's dress has made a great change in my life. I shall never wear terrible black crepe again, no matter who dies. I shall wear lovely white dresses." So Marie Céleste had written to her beloved, and she had kept her word. Never in the annals of the Carmelites, so Drew had been told, except possibly in the case of the "little" Saint Theresa, had the investiture of a nun taken such a magnificent form as in the case of Marie Céleste. The lilies she would have carried, the laces she would have worn, if she had gone to the altar to meet his father, had been the accoutrements she had chosen when she had immolated herself instead. It was also rumored that there had never been songs so sweet within the cloister as those which she sang, unheard and unheralded except by her own small community. Well, it was a strange world, and women in love, especially Fontaine women in love, were strange creatures. But at that, Drew could understand Marie better than he could her niece. Of course, Stella had gone through a trying period of readjustment since the death of her grandmother, and her broken engagement must have meant a tremendous emotional upheaval, too. Inevitably matters had to come to a head sometime between her and Raoul; they could not drift along forever. But it seemed doubly tragic that a passion which had sprung so spontaneously and irresistibly into being should have been slowly wasted instead of being perpetuated in lasting and vital force. In the last analysis, there had been nothing to prevent the consummation of Stella's love except her own stubborn will. And here she was, looking like "death and destruction" and still hell-bent on a course begun as bravado and continued as requital. If anyone had ever sold a birthright for a mess of red pottage, Stella had done it, whereas Patty had guarded hers as if it had been the Grail and, because of her vigil, had saved from destruction not only herself but also the man she loved.

"I haven't seen you in a long time, Drew," Stella was saying cordially. Her charm of manner, at least, was still unimpaired, in spite of her white face and her black clothes—that same supreme faculty of creating an atmosphere of enchantment, which her grandmother and her aunt had possessed before her, was her own imperishable dower. "Where do you hide yourself?" she went on, giving him her hand. "Or is it just that you are working so hard that you don't do much of anything else?"

"I am. Moving that Fauntleroy house hasn't been as easy as it looked, and I've had some pretty anxious moments, wondering if it was coming out all right. But I think now that it is. And then of course the development of the new subdivision—"

"I've been waiting for a chance to congratulate you on that, Drew. I've been sorrier than ever that I didn't go to see those Breaux Bridge houses with you, now that you've made such a success of adapting them."

"Well, we can still go to see them, if you like. You're not going back to New York for another fortnight or so yet, are you?"

"No. But you certainly haven't got time for long drives into the country, with everything else you're doing."

Drew smiled. "Oh, yes I have. I'm taking Patty on one today."

"That's different. I should have said you haven't time to take me for a long drive into the country."

She accented the word "me" very slightly. Drew continued to look at her smilingly.

"Wrong again. I'd like very much to take you for a long drive into the country. I'll call you up and we'll make a date. But I've got to run along now."

"Good-bye, Drew. Give my love to Patty."

She must be terribly lonely, all by herself in that huge dismal house, he thought as he went on. I wonder if there's anything in the rumor that she's thinking of selling it, and that Walter Avery wants to buy it. If there is, it's probably also true that Walter and Sandra Hastings are going to be married, for Walter would never want that great ark, just for himself. Well, it would make him a very fine place, once it was lightened and modernized, and doubtless Walter, who had been something of a sentimentalist when he was younger, no longer thought of it painfully, in connection with Marie Céleste. A marriage between him and Sandra Hastings would be highly suitable, and the house which had been his first love's home would make a very suitable establishment for him. Certainly, Stella would not need it herself, now that she was to spend practically all her time in New York.

And it would be rather a *beau geste* for her to turn over her house to Sandra, considering that Sandra had engineered that fine contract with the Metropolitan.

He was still thinking about Stella and her fine contract and, not inconsequentially, of Raoul Bienvenu and his triumphant nomination for Congress, when he drew up at the raised cottage. Patty was already standing at the end of the little overgrown walk at the side of the house. She was bareheaded, so that her bright hair was shining in the sun, and she was dressed in sky-blue linen so fresh and clean that Drew was sure it had barely left the capable hands of the faithful Roberta. As she looked hopefully down the street, she saw him, and her face lighted with gladness. He flung open the door of the car and got out.

"I'm afraid I've kept you waiting forever, darling. I simply had to stop and have a shower. And then I stopped to speak to Stella. She was out on her gallery and I didn't like to go right by her."

"Of course not. I'm terribly sorry for Stella, Drew."

"I am, too. But I'd be still sorrier for her if she hadn't insisted on having an archangel, when she could have had a real man. Raoul Bienvenu had all the qualities she claimed she wanted most, but she thought he ought to have all those she wanted less thrown in for good measure, too. Men don't come that way, as you know only too well. Just girls. Or rather, just one girl in the whole world— So you're not going to scold me for keeping you standing here?"

"Why should I? I've told you over and over again that I like to wait for you. Because I always know you're coming."

She slipped her hand naturally into his, and then, also unhesitatingly, she raised her face. Since Drew was taking her to Splendida, to picnic there with her alone, she was sure this meant the time had come when they could kiss each other again, though he had not told her so yet. She was not in the least self-conscious about possible passers-by. Drew put his arm around her.

"How do you always guess exactly what I want you to do, Patty?"

"I suppose because we're close to each other in thought, just as we are in other ways. Is that what you wanted me to do?"

"Why, bless your heart, it's what I've been hoping for all day!"

It was not a long kiss. That could come later, too, Patty

knew now. But it was the kind of kiss, as natural as breathing, which only two persons who loved each other very much could risk exchanging without seeming casual—two persons who did not need the intensity of a passionate embrace to reveal their mutual sympathy and their mutual joy in being with each other. Drew took his arm away from Patty's waist to put it under her elbow as he helped her into the car, and then they shot off up the avenue, exchanging smiling glances but not saying anything more until they had gone quite a long way. Then it was Patty who spoke first.

"I still feel terribly sorry for Stella. I think you're too hard on her. Do you think it would please her if I asked her to be maid of honor at our wedding?"

"It ought to. And I suppose you'd ask her Darcoa cousins to be the bridesmaids?"

"Yes. That's what I had in mind. I thought I might ask Mathilde Villeré, too, if you were planning to ask Ursin, even though she is older."

"A very good idea. It sounds as if you were planning to have a big wedding, Patty."

"Well, I'd like to. Because——"

"Because you're going to show the world we've won through? Or rather, that you've won through? I couldn't have done it without you."

"Of course you could have. But, yes, that's it."

His heart contracted, almost painfully. But it was not the time to speak seriously—not yet. He smiled back at her.

"When's the wedding going to be, Patty?"

"I thought perhaps you were going to tell me that, today."

"I'm going to consult you. What would you think of the latter part of October?"

"I'd think it was wonderful, unless you could make it sooner."

The pain in his heart left him. He laughed, and kissed her again. They were out on the Air Line by this time, but he did not feel, at the moment, that this made any special difference, and neither did she.

"Well, if the engagement is announced next Sunday, we'd have been engaged only a little more than a month, at that, before we get married."

"How can you tell such an awful story? We've been engaged, or as good as engaged, ever since the night of the Pacifici Ball."

"Has it been as good as engaged, Patty?"

"Well, not quite. But I've known it was going to be. And I've told you I enjoy waiting."

"You're not going to have much more chance for that kind of enjoyment, Patty."

She looked up at him with her entrancing smile, her dimple deepening. Then she quickly grew graver.

"But just the same, I'm sure there's some special reason why you set the latter part of October."

"Yes, Patty, there is— Have you read the afternoon paper?"

"Why, yes, sort of. But I don't see——"

"I guess I'll have to teach you to read newspapers, Patty, the way I tried to teach Stella once. No, more successfully I hope. Congress passed the Selective Service Act this morning. The President will probably sign it Monday. And registration's set for October sixteenth."

"Do you have to register for the draft?"

"Yes. One of the numerous things that's troubled me, Patty, has been the thought that I was too old for you—that I didn't have the right to tie you down to—a man twice your age."

"You're not twice my age any longer. I'm eighteen now. And when I'm thirty——"

"Yes, it's possible to be very mathematical about it, I know. But that doesn't help. However, what I started to say was that lately I've been selfishly sorry I wasn't a year older, after all. Because the draft age has been set for twenty-one to thirty-five. Of course I'd have tried for some kind of a commission a little later in any case, if the need of men like me seemed more evident than it does now. But that wouldn't have been until after we'd been married long enough so that parting wouldn't seem quite so hard."

"Don't you believe it gets harder and harder all the time, Drew? That is, in the kind of marriage ours is going to be?"

"I hadn't thought of it that way. Perhaps it does. Well, I have to register October sixteenth, as I said. And I think I ought to register as unmarried. Because it's the unmarried men who are going to be called out first. And I wouldn't want to use our marriage as a pretext to avoid that. Would you, Patty?"

"But if you're called out——"

"Yes. That's what I've known I'd have to tell you today. Along with some other things that are going to be hard telling and hard hearing, too, I'm afraid. That's why I asked you to come out into the country with me, Patty. Not so that we could have a joyous evening together. At least not primarily. But so that no one would intrude on us while I was telling you these hard things and you were listening."

For a moment she sat with her eyes downcast, looking at her clenched hands lying in her lap. It was the same way she had looked at them when she had dismissed him after he had told her the truth about the bracelet, as if she did not want to let him see that there were tears on her lashes. But this time she looked up at him presently again of her own accord and met his eyes steadily.

"You're not going to tell me that we can't have a few weeks together at first, are you, Drew?"

"No. If registration's the middle of October, I wouldn't be called out for a month or so after that, at the very earliest."

"That's all I need to know. As long as I know that, I can stand all the rest."

"I hope so, dearest. But you know I've told you from the beginning this wasn't going to be easy for you."

"I haven't wanted it to be easy. I've wanted it to be wonderful. And it is. It's going to be more so. No matter how soon you have to go off after we're married. No matter what you tell me now. Go on, Drew."

It was harder than he had thought. Patty had always said that there was nothing they could not tell each other, and, in a sense, of course that was true. But he knew he would never get over his revulsion against dragging his sordid past into her shining present. He drove on, silently and slowly, more averse than ever before to speaking of Evelyn to Patty.

"Is it about the Baird divorce?" she, herself, asked quietly at last.

"Yes. Did you know it had gone through?"

"I heard so day before yesterday. I've been waiting for you to say something about it."

"That's what I'm trying to do. I've got to tell you why Evelyn didn't contest it, after all, or bring a countersuit—how it happened to go through with such apparent ease, after all her threats."

"All right. I hoped you would. I knew you would when you thought the time had come to do it."

"The time's come now, Patty."

"Then don't put it off."

"I won't, any longer. The day I asked you to marry me, and that you declined, I found Evelyn at my house when I went home. She was very angry. In fact, she was in a state of uncontrollable fury. She made some very unfortunate remarks. In replying, I did, too. I said that I had thought of settling two hundred thousand dollars on her, if a situation like the present one ever arose, but that under the circumstances I thought a hundred thousand would be plenty."

"But why should you settle anything on her?"

"You've probably heard a sentimental statement to the effect that the woman always pays. Actually, in cases like this, it's the man."

He spoke with unrestrained bitterness. Again Patty's voice was very quiet when she answered him.

"I think I'm beginning to understand. Let's get this over, Drew. You've settled a hundred thousand dollars on Evelyn Baird?"

"No. I've settled two hundred thousand, after all. She decided she could make me do it because I'd been such a fool as to say I'd thought of it. So she finally sent me a message—through Narcisse Fontaine, of course—that if I'd revert to that sum, she'd take it and get out, without making any more trouble. She knows she's through in New Orleans, and she's glad of a chance to start somewhere else. But if I hadn't consented, she'd have made all kinds of trouble. She would have brought a countersuit then, or she'd have take the case to the Supreme Court. It might have been a couple of years before it was cleared up. I meant what I said when I told you I wouldn't marry you until it was. And it wasn't only a question of the time element in that way. It was a question of the scandal that would have been more and more widespread—more and more smutty and slimy as time went on."

"And you paid all this money so that everything would be over quickly and quietly?"

"Yes. That's what it boils down to. Of course, it was extortion. But you don't think I made a mistake in consenting to it, do you, Patty?"

"No. I think you did the very best thing you could. What does giving up money amount to if it makes you feel free to get married?"

"That was the way I reasoned. So I did it. We can get married. In six weeks. And the talk will all die down. That is, the talk about Evelyn and me. It'll be about you and me, instead. And it'll be fulsome instead of dirty. But we can stand that. We can have the big wedding you want. To show the world that we've won through. And we can have a few weeks of complete happiness together. But afterwards——"

"Can't we begin to think about that later on, Drew?"

"No. We've got to think about it now. We got to talk about it now. By now I mean today. But if you'd rather, we won't do it until we get to Splendida."

"I would rather. I think that would be a perfect place to talk about it. We've got one of the things that was hard to tell and hard to hear behind us. And it wasn't unbearable, after all. But now let's just drive for a while. I love to be with you when we don't talk. I think there's something so sweet about a shared silence."

It was already late in the afternoon when they reached Splendida. As they approached it, Drew told Patty how it had looked when he was a boy—how beautiful the grove and the allee had been before the levee was moved back; now there was only the garden left, not much of a garden, either. When his father had taken his mother there, it had still been the most magnificent place in Louisiana, and everyone who saw it had been filled with awe and admiration. But after that, everything had changed; as it was gradually shorn of its glory, people had ceased to admire it. Stella, for instance, had called it mouldy and musty when she was there in the autumn of '35; and now, five years later, it was a good deal mouldier ad mustier than it had been then. Drew was afraid Patty would be terribly disappointed.

"No, I shan't, Drew. I never saw it with the allee and the grove, so it'll look beautiful to me with just the garden. Besides, if the house is mouldy and musty, probably all it needs is a good airing. Why don't we come here for our honeymoon, and keep the doors and windows open and fill it with sunshine all the time? Wouldn't that help?"

"Of course it would help. But you don't want to come to this desolate, deserted place for anything as happy as a honeymoon, do you?"

"It wouldn't be desolate or deserted if we were in it, would it?"

The question seemed unanswerable. And Patty's rapturous exclamation when she first caught sight of the rose-colored façade and creamy pillars, rising above the encircling garden, was so spontaneous that Drew could not doubt that her enthusiasm was genuine. She could not decide where she wanted to go or what she wanted to see first, it was all so wonderful. She was sure that beyond the pillars there must be such grandeur as she had never found in any house. And yet, there was that long brick walk dividing the flower beds in the garden, with a glimpse of a fountain in the distance. Drew would have to decide for her what they should do. But in the end it was Jezebel, appearing in the open doorway, who took the decision out of their hands.

"I has coffee ready for yo' young lady and you, Mr. Drew. I reckoned you'd want it in de parlor right away. Or does de young lady want to fancy up first?"

"This young lady never needs to fancy up, Jezebel. She always looks lovely, because it's natural for her to look that way. But I'll take her upstairs later on myself."

"Yassuh, Mr. Drew."

"And her name is Miss Patty Forrestal, Jezebel. Only presently it's going to be Mrs. Andrew Breckenridge."

"I'se sho'ly pleased to hear dat, Mr. Drew. An' I welcomes you to Splendida, Miss Patty, wif all my heart. I hope you comes here offen and stays long."

Though Jezebel had never achieved the omnipotence of Shoog, the confidence which Shoog, herself, had placed in the "Bishop's" granddaughter had proved increasingly justified with the years. She was as tiny as Shoog had been huge, bent, wrinkled, grizzled and excessively neat; her solemn, blinking eyes were obscured by large moon-like glasses and her gnarled hands had a tendency to shake. But the coffee she brought in was excellent in itself and impeccably presented in well-polished silver; other evidences of her eagerness to please and ability to serve were everywhere evident. There were fresh flowers in all the vases and new candles in all the candlesticks; the hearthstones showed signs of recent scrubbing; the inlaid piano was open. Patty noticed all this, saying indignantly that she could not see how anyone could call such a lovely house mouldly or musty; and Drew, realizing that she really did not see the cracks in the plaster or the scraps of loosened wallpaper, or the frayed edges of the upholstery or the holes in the rugs, did not have the heart to point them out to her. And after all, Jezebel was not to blame for those. She had done the best she could, and while she continued to hover solicitously over the coffee table, Drew could not hurt her feelings, either. When she lifted up the tray to remove it she asked respectfully whether she should serve supper in the dining room or on the piazza.

"Where do you want it, Patty?"

"How can I tell? You keep forgetting I haven't seen the

house, Drew, and I keep telling you I want you to decide."

"All right. I decide for the piazza. That's where my father always liked to eat, and where I've always liked to eat, too. But come on now. I'll show you the house. And don't serve supper anywhere, Jezebel, until I tell you to."

They began a progress through the great rooms, so that Patty could stop and marvel and question as they went along. She stood for a long time before the painting of Laura de' Dianti, listening to the history of the valuable replica with interest, and though she did not mention her own mirror in connection with it, Drew realized that she had been swift to reach her own conclusions. She applauded his choice when they got to the piazza, saying it was delightful there and proving her point by sitting down to look out towards the arbor and the rear lawn before going any further. When she finally was persuaded to leave it and go to the stairway hall, the lozenges of light from the great stained-glass windows entranced her still more, and she bent over them as though playfully trying to imprison them with her hands. After this pleasant pastime the library somehow seemed a little depressing; the gallery shut off the sunshine at the south, and, on the north, the light, even at this benignant time of day, was untinged with any tenderness of twilight; the endless shelves of books, stretching from floor to ceiling, intensified the gloom. But Patty had heard about the Elephant Edition and the Shakespeare folios, and the eagerness with which she asked to see them was not simulated. She was intrigued, too, by the arrangement of this rear wing where the library was situated, with its own gallery and the small secluded bedroom leading out of it.

"This looks like a man's room, Drew. Is it yours?"

"Yes. I've slept here ever since I was a little boy. As long as my father was alive, I slept in a cot beside his bed, the same one that's there now."

"But——"

The bed was unmistakably a Mallard, but it did not have the imposing proportions which usually characterized the great cabinet maker's masterpieces. Patty stopped, the warm color flooding her young face.

"I haven't told you, have I, Patty, that my father and mother weren't happy together——that there was always strain and strife between them? There hasn't been any reason to tell you before, but now that you're coming here to live, you'd learn it in one way or another, and it's better you should hear it from me than from anyone else. They were separated in spirit—and in every other way. I remember when I first found it out myself."

He paused, the memory, which had so long been vague, suddenly vivid. Patty guessed that it was a painful one. She pressed his hand.

"Would it help at all if you should tell me about it, Drew?"

"It might— You see, I never had a live pet until we came to live in the country. My mother thought they were too much trouble. She wouldn't let me have a woolly toy, either, like most children. She thought those were unsanitary. But I did have a little wooden dog I slept with. My father used to worry about it. He was afraid I'd hurt myself on it. One night he came over to my bed while I was groping for it, though half asleep, and he put it back into my hands, so that I wouldn't miss it. Then he said something, really talking to himself, of course. But I heard him. I was awake enough for that. And presently I began to puzzle over what he meant until I figured it out."

"What did he say, Drew?"

"He said, 'Don't worry, old man, I won't take it away from you. I hope you won't have to go on hugging wood forever, though. I hope you'll have more sense than your father and your grandfather. I hope you won't marry while you're still a kid yourself. I hope you'll wait until you know what it's all about.'"

"Then he'd be pleased to know that you have waited, wouldn't he, Drew? He'd think you were just the right age to get married now."

"Yes, he would be pleased. He'd be very happy about you, Patty."

Drew had not been able to tell Patty all that Breck, in his misery, had said that night so long ago; he had not been able to say that the words, 'No matter how you amuse yourself in the meantime' and others with the same significance, had been added afterwards. He had tried, often enough, to justify his liaison with Evelyn on the ground that his father would have taken a bitter satisfaction in it, and though he had pretended this would have been true, he had always known this was not really so. Now he did not need to pretend. He knew that his father would have been very happy about Patty— that she would have represented to him all he hoped his son's wife might embody. By and by, perhaps later that evening, Drew thought he might tell her about a memorandum he had found among Breck's letters. But for the moment he had said enough concerning his father.

"I'll show you my mother's room when we go upstairs," he said, speaking dispassionately again. "Perhaps you'd like it for yours."

"Don't you think she might like it herself when she comes here to visit us? I wouldn't like her to feel that I'd tried to take it away from her. She must be terribly unhappy, Drew, because she failed your father. She must have been unhappy all these years. We ought to try to make her happier if we can."

"I hadn't thought of it in that light. Probably no one but you would have, Patty. All right, then, you can choose any other that you like for yours."

"You mean to say for ours, don't you, Drew? We're not going to be separated—in any way, are we?"

The warm color flooded her face again, but she spoke with the assurance of anticipated happiness, with no trace of either coyness or evasion. Drew's eyes rested on her with adoring wonder.

"I did mean to say for ours, but you're continually getting ahead of me, Patty, because you're so much more honest and so much more generous than any other woman I've ever known."

"Why, I don't do anything except try to show you, all the time, how much I love you! I—we—could manage in this little room off the library, if that seems more homelike to you—if that's where you'd rather stay, Drew."

"No, I wouldn't rather stay there. I'll never sleep in there again. And I'd rather cut off my right hand than let you do it."

The tenderness was all gone from his voice. It sounded horribly harsh. Patty had never heard it when it souded like that before except— She knew now when it was. It sounded like that when he spoke about Evelyn Baird. So Evelyn had been to Splendida, too; she had invaded even this part of Drew's life. Patty had not known that before; she had supposed that here they would escape. But she knew she must not say this. Instead, she went on with her customary quietness. "Then have you any other choice?"

"No. I want to see which yours will be."

His voice was still harsh, for he knew that he had revealed one more chapter of his life which he had hoped she would never see, and the bitterness of the knowledge kept him silent, after his brief reply. Patty was silent, too, but it was still with the quietness of impregnable serenity. After they had mounted the great circular staircase, she went twice through all the beautiful upstairs bedrooms slowly and attentively. But in the end she returned to the great state apartment with the circular dressing room.

"Wasn't this meant——"

"For a bridal chamber? Yes, it was. My grandfather brought your kinswoman, Anne Forrestal, to it. But it's seldom been used since. It's said to be haunted."

"I don't care if it is. I don't believe in ghosts. I think Anne Forrestal must have been a lovely lady. I'd like to be with you where she and Andy were together."

"All right, darling, you shall. If there is a ghost, it's only a very little one, and it goes away if you light a candle. We can always do that. Besides, I think we may have other ways of exorcising it."

He sounded happy again, which made her happy, too, but he did not offer to explain, and she did not ask him, what he meant. Instead, she continued to go around the room, familiarizing herself with everything in it, and then she asked a very different question.

"Will we be coming back to Splendida again before we're married?"

"If you like. Of course, I can only get away on week ends. And next Sunday we'll be announcing our engagement, won't we? But after that——"

"I think, sort of, I'd like to wait and come back the next time when——"

"All right, Patty, that's the way it'll be, then."

"And now I think we ought to go downstairs, don't you, and get those other hard things behind us before we have our supper?"

"Yes, I think we should."

They went out on the portico and sat down on the front steps with their arms around each other. The shadows were slanting from the great columns now and lying in long stretches over the lawn and the garden, and the birds were singing. All the decadence of the place was engulfed in its tranquility and beatitude. For some moments they sat silent, after all, reluctant to break the spell of such enchantment. Then, with resolution, Patty asked still another question.

"Was there something else connected with the draft that you felt you had to say to me, Drew?"

"Yes, indirectly. It didn't have anything to do with registration. But it did have something to do with money."

"Have we got to talk about money again, too?"

"Yes. I'm very sorry, but that's exactly what we've got to do. Because there isn't going to be much for you, after all. You've been assuming, like everyone else, that I was very rich. But you've been robbed in this way, as in so many others, of something which should have been wholly yours."

"No, I haven't either. I haven't been robbed at all. You know I've never wanted your money, and everything else you've given me has been all mine."

"You may not have wanted the money, but I've wanted you to have it and it's your right to have it. I've said a lot about lavishing luxuries on you and that's what I meant to do. Now I know that I can't. Two hundred thousand dollars is a lot of money for anyone to take out of capital suddenly in a lump sum, as things are nowadays. I didn't have it to spare. I've had to sell a lot of sound securities at a sacrifice to do it."

"Let's not talk about the two hundred thousand any more, Drew. I know you'd rather not, and I don't want to either."

"All right. I've got to tell you something else, though. There's been an invasion of salt water on my oil field. It's slight so far. Only one or two wells are affected. But sometimes these invasions spread, and when they do, a good field can be utterly ruined. I don't want to bother you with technicalities, but——"

"You don't need to. I'm sorry about the securities and the oil field, if you're worrying over them, but I'm not."

"That's because you're too young and too inexperienced and too disinterested to know that you ought to. I hate to make you face these disagreeable financial complexities. But I've got to."

"All right, Drew. I'll try to understand. But you've begun to earn money now, so I should think that presently the oil and the securities wouldn't matter so much. You told me yourself that you'd earned a good deal these last six months, more than you ever thought you could."

"That's true enough. But if I should have to go away, I'd automatically stop earning money."

"Go away? You mean if you were drafted?"

"Yes, that's just what I mean."

"I wouldn't need much to live on, would I, Drew?"

"It would depend on how you lived. You know I've wanted you to live surrounded with every luxury."

"Well, couldn't I live here?"

"No, Patty. In the first place, a young girl like you couldn't live on a big place like this all alone, and in the second place, you wouldn't be living in luxury if you did. You wouldn't have enough servants or enough companionship or enough basic comfort of any sort. It gets very cold here in winter. There's no heating plant. The plumbing is archaic. The structure isn't stormproof."

"I don't see why I should mind all that any more than Anne Forrestal did when she lived here."

"Anne Forrestal died," Drew said abruptly. "She probably died for lack of proper comfort and proper care. Her husband was accused of letting her, often enough. The accusation was as cruel as it was unjust—that is, unjust in the sense of inferring that he didn't want and try to care for her. But I'm not going to take any of the same risks. Even if I were willing to, which I'm not, there's another risk you'll understand better, perhaps. The horror I have of it, I mean. The next time there's a flood, Splendida will go. You mustn't be here when that happens. I couldn't stand the fear of that, if I were separated from you. I think you know why."

"Yes, Drew, I do. Of course you couldn't stand it. Well then, we'll have our happiness here at Splendida together this fall and leave it together afterwards. Now let's be very practical about what I'll do next, if you have to go away."

She leaned forward a little, putting her chin in her hand and looking out thoughtfully towards the garden. Her hair, falling forward in glossy sheets of gold, hid her face from Drew. He smoothed it back, trying to tuck it behind her ear. But it would not stay there. Uonconcernedly, Patty extracted a blue ribbon from her slip and fastened it around her head.

"Is that better?"

"Much better. I love your hair, but I love your face still more. Now that you've bound up the golden locks, let me hear the golden thought."

"The thought is that I could stay with your mother. I think she wants to go on living in the Prytania Street house. I think she's happy to be back in Louisiana, and I think she'd be happy to have me with her. I could live with her, if I had to, couldn't I?"

"It would be possible. Of course she'd be very happy to

have you. She's extremely fond of you. But I wouldn't be happy to have you. I don't want you to live in a house my mother directs and finances. I've almost as good a reason for not being willing to have you do that as for not being willing to have you stay on at Splendida alone."

"Well then, I could live in that little house on Kerlerec Street, that Aunt Estelle gave you. It's what I'd really rather do than anything else. It's what I've always wanted to do. I'm glad of the chance to tell you so at last."

"It isn't good enough for you, Patty. It isn't suitable."

"It is good enough. It is suitable. I'd love to live there. I've never been rich; I can manage on very little. It can't cost much for one person to live. I could do all my own work, easily, if I had to. I'm not talented like Stella. I can't sing in opera and entertain politicians and do things like that. But I can cook. And clean. I like to. And——"

"Patty, darling, there's no question of your having to do anything like that! I wouldn't dream of letting you do your own work. There's not the slightest necessity for it. When I told you that we wouldn't be rich, I didn't mean we'd be poverty-stricken. There'll always be enough money for every reasonable necessity."

"Then I don't see what we're talking about. And I think it's time we stopped."

She jumped up, freeing herself from his embrace. As he rose, too, more slowly, she faced him with resolution.

"Listen, Drew," she said. "You told me you'd be sorrier for Stella if she hadn't made the mistake of demanding an archangel when she could have had a real man. I made a mistake myself that might have been pretty costly for both of us when I let your past come between us for a little while; but I'm certainly not going to make the mistake of letting it keep on coming between us. I've accepted the fact that you haven't always been a saint, and I'm delighted to know that you're not a multimillionaire any longer. Instead of talking about the things you've robbed me of and the things you're forcing me to face, I think we'd better talk about the things you've given me and the things you've done for me. Why, Drew, I was just a shy, undeveloped, graceless girl until you transfigured me! Through your presence and your courtesy and your charm! And after you'd done that, you glorified me through your love! I couldn't have anything greater in the world than that! I want you just the way you are and I don't want anyone but you!"

"I am honored beyond all desert and all measure because you feel that way. But don't you want children, too, Patty?" Drew asked very quietly.

His question took her utterly by surprise. For the first time, she answered him stumblingly.

"Why yes! That is, it is natural to want children, isn't it? But I haven't thought much about that, Drew. I'd thought just about you and me."

"Yes, but now I want you to think about the other, too. Because if our marriage is the kind I've hoped and believed it would be, we'll have several children, and we'll have one right away." There was another new note in his voice now, one of yearning, one of appeal. "I know how self-reliant you are, Patty, and I'm proud of you. But we'll need money for them, too. Not just money to feed and clothe them. Money to give them a good home and a good education. There'll be enough, if we're careful. But you'll have to learn to save your resources, so that you'll know what to do if I'm not there to help you. Your resources and your strength. You mustn't squander that either. Because you'll need that, too. A great deal of strength and a great deal of courage."

Suddenly she understood; suddenly she knew what he had thought all along. He had seen her not only as an enamored wife but also as a fostering mother. He had believed from the beginning that, instead of denying him his destiny as his father had been denied, she would beatify his life with her prodigality. And now that he was going away— now that there might be a war—he was torn between the fear that he would burden her with more than she could bear and the fear that he might not leave behind him some part of himself which would still be imperishable whatever happened to him. In her lay all his hopes, not only of happiness but also of survival. She threw her arms around his neck, pressing her face and her breast against his.

"Of course our marriage is going to be the kind you hoped and believed it would be, Drew," she said. "And don't be afraid. I will learn to conserve my resources; I won't squander anything. And I've got lots of courage and lots of strength. Because you've given them to me already, with your love, just as you've given me glory. Just as presently you're going to give me your child!"

CHAPTER 35

Mrs. Forrestal did not understand how Patty could take time to go to a parade, when there was so much to do in preparation for the wedding, with this only three days off. Besides, she felt that Monday evening rather than Wednesday evening would have been the best time for Drew to give his bachelor dinner. She did not actually say that this was because it would have given him and his guests more time to recover from it, before the ceremony; nevertheless, she made her inference so plain that Patty could not help grasping her meaning. But Patty, by this time, had had considerable experience in coping with her mother's inferences about Drew personally and about the situation in general, and she did so with increasing calm as the weeks went by.

"There wouldn't have been any bachelors to go to the dinner, if he'd had it tonight, Mother. They'll all be either watching the Preparedness Parade or marching in it. It's such an exciting prelude to registration tomorrow that none of them wants to miss it." She unwrapped another present as she spoke. There was a fresh delivery of presents every few minutes now, and the doorbell had actually been repaired because Mrs. Forrestal, who was enjoying the arrival of the gifts more than any other aspect of the marriage was unwilling to run the risk of having some valuable offering left outside on the front gallery by a careless driver. "It's another silver shell," Patty went on, lifting the little dish from its tissue-paper wrappings and holding it up for her mother to see.

"It's very handsome," Mrs. Forrestal said, taking it from her daughter and turning it over admiringly. "That makes the twentieth in this style, doesn't it, Patty? Now if you and Drew were only going to entertain at Splendida on the same scale as Andy Breckenridge and Aurore Fontaine, you could use all these elegant ornaments. As it is, I don't see what on earth you're going to do with them. You might as well not have them."

"Oh no! We're very much touched that our friends are so interested in our marriage and so generously disposed towards us. The presents help to prove that. Besides, it's fun just unpacking and arranging them, don't you think so?" She knew very well that her mother did think so, and this knowledge contributed to the calmness with which she still spoke. "And just because we're not going to use them right away, that doesn't mean we never will— Please help me with these plates, will you, Mother? I think they are Capo di Monte, and, of course, that's terribly valuable. I'd feel very badly if I broke one, and I might, if I tried to handle them alone— You know there's never been anything like this Preparedness Parade in New Orleans, even on Mardi Gras. That's why I wouldn't miss seeing it either."

"I wish you wouldn't talk about Mardi Gras, Patty. It makes me unhappy every time you mention it. When I think that you could have been Queen of Carnival——"

"Why, Mother, I didn't realize I'd mentioned it very often! I won't again. But now that we have spoken of it, won't you confess that you think Clarinda will make a much lovelier Carnival Queen than I would have? I feel certain she'll be chosen, and she'll be superb."

"You'd have been superb yourself, Patty. I can't believe that it's only a year since I was worrying for fear you'd be a complete failure. I never saw a girl blossom out the way you suddenly did—never. But that's no reason why you shouldn't have given yourself, and me, the satisfaction of remaining unmarried another season, and showing everyone how far you could outshine Stella Fontaine, once you got started. She followed her grandmother's wishes, whatever else she did and didn't do, and I think you might have followed mine."

"One of the reasons I didn't was because Stella did," Patty said cryptically. " 'I learned about values from her.' "

"I don't know what you're talking about, Patty," Mrs. Forrestal replied, almost peevishly. She was very tired, and the wearier she became, the more cause she felt for dissatisfaction. "I thought Stella was greatly overrated myself. Everyone else would have thought so, too, pretty soon, if you'd only given them a standard of comparison. But instead of that you insist on marrying the first man who asks you, and burying yourself in a ramshackle old house in the country. Of course, it would be different if Drew's affair with Evelyn Baird hadn't become common knowledge and if he hadn't lost so much of his money."

"Drew wasn't the first man who asked me," Patty said, disregarding her mother's final remark and rising as she put the last of the Capo di Monte plates on a shining multicolored pile, "Gail asked me years ago. I thought you knew that. I was only fourteen the first time. Of course I said no. But he kept right on. I had to stop him someway, and Drew was a great help— And I never could have outshone Stella. You only think so because you're my mother and prejudiced. It's just as well I didn't try. She'll always be remembered as the greatest success since her grandmother, and that's saying a good deal. Where is she, by the way? I haven't seen her in two or three hours."

"I think she went for a final fitting on her dress. You've done one good thing, Patty, in getting her to lighten her mourning, and to take it off altogether for one day. I never saw anyone to whom black was so unbecoming. Nobody meeting her for the first time, when she was wearing it, would ever say she was a beauty. I don't see why you had to ask her to come and stay here, though, without consulting me at all. As if we didn't have enough to do for the wedding without having a house guest!"

"But Mother, it was natural for me to ask my maid of honor to stay with me, when she couldn't go to her own house. I mean the one she used to have. It's full of workmen already, remodelling and redecorating. It'll be beautiful when it's all done over. But I liked it the way it was. And I'll never feel as if it really belonged to anyone except Mrs. Fontaine. She was part of it and it was part of her. And part of New Orleans is gone now that she's dead. Besides, it makes me sad to think of Stella without a home. There, I think I hear her now. I'll go and meet her, Mother."

The front door had opened and the telephone had rung simultaneously. Stella, letting herself in with a latchkey and flinging down the latest consignment of presents, which she had garnered from a deliveryman as she came in, signalled that she would catch the call. Patty, who had come out of the littered drawing room at the same moment, began to pick up the presents again and inevitably overheard the conversation, since the telephone was in the hall.

"Yes, this is Mrs. Forrestal's house. No, but Patty's right here. Why, hello, Raoul. I didn't recognize— Oh, I wouldn't have expected you to! Yes, I'm staying here with Patty. Well, I am ordinarily, but I was able to get a few days off. I'm flying both ways and I'll make up for lost time after I get back by working over next week end. Why certainly—" She turned from the telephone, with a burning face, and handed the receiver to Patty. "I'm going up to my room," she said shortly.

"That's Raoul Bienvenu, as you probably gathered. He began by telling me he didn't recognize my voice, and almost the next minute he asked to speak to you, as if there weren't a thing in the world he could say to me. I told you all along he couldn't be trusted to act like a civilized human being, if you and Drew persisted in having him in the wedding party. I know all about his temper. But I didn't suppose we'd have to put up with it for three whole days beforehand. I supposed he'd stay in Abbeville until Wednesday."

Patty, who was already talking over the telephone, shook her head warningly at Stella, trying to indicate she was afraid that Raoul would overhear, and presently Stella, herself, heard Raoul laugh in a way which revealed unmistakably that he had. She went stormily up the stairs, tossed her wraps on the bed, and took off her dress. When Patty rejoined her, she was in her slip, sitting before the dressing table and viciously brushing back her curls, with a mutinous expression on her face.

"You mustn't put your hat on the bed, Stella. The darkies at Splendida say that, if you do, it drives the lovers out of the house."

"I don't care what they say. You don't mean to tell me you believe in those silly old superstitions, do you? Anyhow, you're leaving the house in three days. And I'm damned sure there aren't any other lovers in it."

Patty had noticed that when Stella was angry she lapsed into the phraseology and mannerisms that had been natural to her before she became a sophisticated belle and successful singer. It always surprised her a little when Stella reverted to type in this way, but it had never disturbed her.

"Well, I don't know," she said with a pleasant little laugh. "Richard has begun to make sheep's eyes at Amelina Darcoa. He was tickled almost to death when Drew asked him to be one of the ushers— But you're right. I'm not superstitious. I've deliberately chosen a room at Splendida that's supposed to be haunted. I only told you the old saying because I thought it would amuse you. Incidentally, there's another to the effect that it's bad luck to have three lights in the same room, and you've got those, too— Why, Stella, you needn't snap them all off like that! You can have two or four or six if you want to. It's just three— Are the dresses all right?"

"The other girls had finished their fittings before I got there, and Miss Lilian at Town and Country said they were very much pleased. I'd have preferred some other color, myself. But yellow's logical for this time of year. It goes so well with chrysanthemums. And I like the model. It's really very chic. Your own dress is certainly sweet simplicity, though. I saw that, too."

"I always did like very simple dresses," Patty said agreeably. "I suppose I always shall. And Drew doesn't mind. He thinks they suit me. So as long as he is satisfied, and I am, I don't have to worry about anyone else. Stella—Raoul telephoned to say he thought it would be fun to go to Antoine's after the parade. He wants to give a party himself. He's engaged the 1840 Room. He'd already got in touch with Drew, and Drew thought it was a grand idea. Raoul told me to speak to Richard and see if he wouldn't like to bring Amelina, which of course he would. Raoul has asked Clarinda himself. But he said if you'd like to join us, he was sure that Gail——"

"Oh, Patty, for the luvamike! You always thought yourself that Gail was an awful bore! And now you think I ought to be satisfied when Raoul suggests that as a last resort—just like the night that Huey Long was shot—I might go to a party with Gail!"

"I never thought Gail was an awful bore. I've always liked him very much. It's just that I didn't love him," Patty said patiently. "And the idea of this party must have been a sudden brain storm of Raoul's. You know he does have those, every once in a while. I hadn't heard anything about it until he telephoned. Of course, I knew he was coming up from Abbeville today, because he's marching in the parade, with the unit of Marine Reserves——"

"I didn't knew he belonged to the Marine Reserves," Stella said sharply.

"Why, yes. He has for a long time."

"I don't seem to know any local news. I hadn't heard anything about this frenzy of patriotism and I hadn't heard that Raoul Bienvenu was taking Clarinda Darcoa out on the town."

"I don't think he takes her out very often. I don't believe he has a chance to. She's terribly popular. But you know, yourself, that when a man and a girl are both members of the same wedding party——"

"Well, I'd like to know if I'm not a member of the wedding party, too!"

"Yes, but you're the maid of honor. Ursin Villeré will take you around, because he's the best man. It just happens that he couldn't tonight, though. He's in the parade, too, and he'd already agreed to go off on some kind of a stag party, the same one Walter's going to, before Raoul had his bright idea. Mathilde can't come, either, because she has to go to the dress rehearsal for the *première* at the Little Theatre. So we'll have just an even number without them, and Gail seemed the logical escort for you. Drew and I both thought you wouldn't want to go around with Raoul, Stella—that is, any more than you could help. Not because we didn't think he'd act like a civilized human being. Drew's devoted to him, and I like him very much myself. But we thought there might still be a little strain, though we were awfully pleased when you both consented— Come downstairs as soon as you're dressed, won't you? A lot more presents have come in and I'd be so grateful if you'd help me list them. We're going to have just an early pickup supper. With everything there is to do, getting ready for the wedding, as Mother keeps saying, Roberta couldn't manage anything else. And Walter's coming for us a little after seven. Of course, our seats will be saved for us, but still, he thinks we ought to be early."

Stella did not especially admire Mrs. Forrestal, but still, she felt that Patty's mother was right in saying that it was far-fetched for a bride to attach so much importance to a parade. Stella, herself, could not see anything imperative or inspiring about bolting an early pickup supper and then hurrying down-town, with a middle-aged man who was as good as married al-ready, to crowd in a department-store window for three hours and watch thirty thousand persons march past. On the contrary, she thought it was tedious and bourgeois and senti-mental. She felt this way beforehand, and nothing happened to change her feeling after the parade was actually under way. She was not impressed by the new "jeeps" and reconnaissance cars and 155-millimetre howitzers which Walter pointed out to her with such excitement; and she went on to say, almost sarcastically, that there ought to be a law limiting the number of veterans' societies, or at least the number which could ap-pear in public at the same time: The United Spanish War Veterans, The Disabled American Veterans, The Veterans of the World War of 1917–1918 for America, and the Negro Veterans, not to mention The American Legion, were simply too many to see consecutively, at least for her. When they were followed by endless commercial and political organiza-tions and community clubs and hundreds of high-school kids, it began to be fantastic, that was all there was to it. And if one more band played *God Bless America, My Own Sweet Home* and one more group sang it off key, she was sure she would have hysterics; that song was certainly the epitome of bathos.

After she had expressed herself in this vein three or four times, Walter, in an abrupt lapse from his customary urbanity, asked her to shut up, for God's sake, and let Patty and himself get some enjoyment out of the show, even if she had grown so high-hat after living in Paris and New York that she could extract none. Patty tried, more patiently, to appease the ill-humor which she knew was the cause for Stella's critical attitude.

"It thrills me to think that all those groups want to testify publicly that they believe in preparedness, and that they're willing to support it," she said sturdily. "Most of the clerks and artisans who are marching tonight will be registering for the draft tomorrow morning. This is their way of showing that they're eager to do it, and not reluctant. And even if all those veterans aren't impressive to look at, they're impressive to think about. They are to me, anyway. "Besides," she added almost pleadingly, "you can't say that the National Guard and the Marine and Naval Reserve Units didn't make a wonderful showing. I got an awful catch in my throat watching them."

"I didn't say it. But there weren't many of them compared to all the Knights of Pythias and Rotarians and Kiwanians and Heaven knows what else."

"It isn't just numbers that count. And I enjoyed seeing the Red Cross Unit, too," Patty persisted. "I think it's wonderful that Julia Beal has been appointed vice-chairman of that. She's been working at headquarters faithfully all through the worst heat of the summer, and the chairman says she's a perfect tower of strength. She's seemed awfully happy, too, every time I've seen her. For a while, she was groping, sort of. Now she's found herself, besides doing no end of good."

"Well, I'm glad she's got the idea of being a nun out of her head, anyway. If you've got to choose between the two, I think an office is a better place than a convent for a woman who's been disappointed in love."

"Not that either is as good as the stage," Walter remarked angrily.

Stella turned on him with savageness, but somehow she could not make the biting retort which came readily to her mind, partly because Walter had hit so cruelly close to the truth and partly because she was well aware that she had spoken outrageously, herself, in goading him into such a remark. She knew that in spite of his impending marriage, which was so eminently suitable in every way, Walter had never forgotten Marie Céleste, and that he never would; and while Patty might look like an ingénue, there was actually nothing she did not know about the nonchalant indifference with which Drew Breckenridge had permitted Julia to pursue him, as well as about the unscrupulous covetousness with which he, himself, had pursued Evelyn. Just because Patty could take it was no reason for baiting her; inevitably it must flick her in the raw to keep hearing reminders of his checkered career. A strained silence, which even Patty's disarming good will was not strong enough to break, succeeded Walter's outburst. Nothing more was said until Patty, gathering her forces again, observed that this was the end, wasn't it, and would it be convenient for Walter to take them down to Antoine's before he went on to his stag party?

Walter said it was perfectly convenient—that of course this was what he had expected to do—and Stella felt better when she had escaped from her cramped position at the window and walked across Canal Street and down Royal and then through St. Louis to the famous restaurant. Walter left them, when he had seen them safely to the entrance of the 1840 Room, though the other men had not yet arrived. She had fully expected this and he was not to bother about them any more, Patty said pleasantly; Drew and Gail were both in civilian groups and those had marched last. So Raoul had suggested that he should wait for them at the Louisiana Club, of which he was now an out-of-town member, and that they should all come on to Antoine's together. They would be there presently. Meanwhile, she and Stella and Amelina would have a chance for a nice cozy visit together, for Clarinda and Amelina had arrived just before them. Patty greeted them with affection and at once began telling them about the Capo di Monte plates and other treasures she had received that day.

The place cards had already been put around the table, and Stella surveyed these surreptitiously as she and the other girls took off their wraps and, with the exception of Patty, applied varying degrees of make-up. Raoul, Patty, Drew, Stella, Gail, Amelina, Richard, Clarinda, she read, going from right to left. Well, naturally, Raoul would give Patty the seat of honor, under the circumstances, and also place Drew beside her. And if that silly boy, Richard, who had Patty's coloring and build but not her character, was really already making sheep's eyes at Amelina, at his age, probably Raoul thought it was in keeping with the general atmosphere of love's young dream to give the callow pair a chance to hold hands under the table. But certainly, he might have shifted Clarinda and herself. Certainly, there was no reason why he should proclaim so insolently that he had nothing special to say to her and that it meant nothing to him to have her near him, by putting Clarinda at his left and giving her, Stella, the most meaningless place at the table! Between Drew, whose courtesy to her would not for one moment hide his real absorption in Patty, and Gail, who had never meant anything in any girl's life and probably never would!

Stella jerked out her chair and sat down, taking no part in the gay chatter that was going on around her except to answer in monosyllables whenever one of the other girls spoke to her. She was studying Clarinda with even great attention than she had bestowed on the place cards. None of her cousins had ever loomed very large on her horizon or occupied a very important place in her affections. She had begun by grouping Clarinda and Amelina with Patty as the leggy little girls for whose unsophisticated company Gail showed such a strange predilection, when he might have been diverting himself with his own contemporaries, and she had never really got around to reclassifying them. Now here was Patty about to become the bride of the man who was still regarded as the "great catch" of New Orleans in spite of his philanderings and extravagances, Clarinda slated for Queen of Carnival and revelling in a rush from a Congressional nominee, and even Amelina daringly "dated" by a personable collegian, while Stella, herself, was relegated again to Gail!

To make matters worse, it was easy enough to see why all this had happened. It was all very well to deride the simplicity of Patty's clothes and the artlessness of her outlook, but increasingly, she seemed to emanate a sort of shining glory which was all her own and which a man like Drew would instinctively worship. As for the Darcoa sisters, theirs was an entirely different type: they were both dowered with the dark cloud-like hair, the immense dark eyes, and the warm creamy skin that were an essential part of their Spanish heritage. But while they both gave the effect of graceful gravity, Stella was certain that, though Amelina might be genuinely demure, there were smouldering fires under Clarinda's surface serenity. She had all the arts and all the allure which, a few years earlier, Evelyn Baird had held in such supreme command; but she had, besides, the unassailable dignity which was another essential part of her patrimony. Clarinda would reign splendidly, as Patty had foretold, and there would be countless courtiers among her subjects. Sooner or later she would also seek and secure a great passionate experience, which she would contrive to celebrate sumptuously after safeguarding it sacramentally. But she would never love lightly or kiss casually. Stella extracted a curiously cold comfort from the conviction that Raoul had not touched more than Clarinda's fingertips, because the time had not yet come when Clarinda was ready for superb self-surrender.

Stella's eyes wandered from Clarinda's unconcerned and lovely face to the orchids which she was deftly pinning on her sloping shoulders. There were exquisite corsages in cellophane boxes tied with wide, colored ribbons back of every girl's place card: white for Patty, rainbow colors for the others; and these colors blended with those in the centerpiece. The array of silverware and the coolers of wine in the corners of the room also bespoke entertainment on a lavish scale. So did the room, itself, for that matter. It had been decorated and opened only a few months earlier to mark the centennial celebra ion of the famous restaurant. Portraits of the present proprietor's father and grandfather, Jules and Antoine Alciatore, who had preceded Roy in his supreme rôle of restaurateur, hung on the crimson-covered walls; the mirror above the mantel reflected a bronze clock, and there were bronze statuettes in the corner niches; the sideboard supported a unique duck press, and the overhead light fell from a period chandelier. This room was the special pride of Roy Alciatore, and if Raoul had secured its use almost at a moment's notice, this was a sign less that he now had money to spend freely—though this was abundantly evident—than that he had been admitted to the charmed circle of those whom Mr. Alciatore considered his friends as well as his patrons, just as he had been admitted to the charmed circle which Drew Breckenridge would include in his wedding party. Raoul's political progress was only one phase of his advance along paths which seemed to be broadening and lengthening in every direction and which he seemed to be finding none the less enjoyable because Stella was not treading them with him.

The door at the rear of the room was flung open by a beaming waiter of rubicund countenance, and Raoul, himself, still in uniform, came into the room, followed by Drew, Gail and Richard. Fleetingly, Stella observed the sentient immobility with which Patty waited for Drew to go to her and the glowing gladness that permeated the quietness with which they kissed each other. She, herself, would have been on her feet rushing forward to meet her bridegroom the instant she heard his step. That is, of course, if she had had a bridegroom. Telling herself vehemently that she was thankful she did not—that she would never have submerged her identity in any man's as Patty was submerging hers in Drew's—she began to watch Raoul with the same attentiveness with which she had been watching Clarinda. He was evidently in the best of spirits, for he was laughing and joking when he came in; his color was high and his eyes were bright from air and exercise. He went first to Patty, greeting her with the affection which he would show a valued friend, but also with the deference in which he would never fail towards another friend's wife. Then he went gaily from Clarinda to Amelina, thanking them for coming, saying how glad he was to see that they were already wearing his flowers, apologizing for the necessity of having kept them waiting. Reaching Stella last of all, he remarked that they were all immensely honored by having a prima donna at their little gathering and, seating himself at the head of the table, began to talk about the parade.

"I wonder if Hitler will get the tip we gave him tonight," he said heartily. "I rather doubt it. In the first place, he probably won't hear that we had a celebration to usher in the first peacetime conscription in American history, and that we held it in the same street where we usually go capering around on Mardi Gras. I don't know just who would be likely to tell him. But even if somebody did, he wouldn't take in what it was going to signify to him eventually. He wouldn't see that it was a parade stretching over a hundred and sixty-four years."

"What do you mean, Raoul?" Gail inquired in a polite but puzzled way.

"Why, while I was marching I didn't feel as if I were a mere member of the Tenth Battalion of the Marine Corps Reserve, in a neat dark uniform with red pipings. I felt as if I were one of the Devil Dogs, as the Germans called them when they met the First and Second Divisions. I felt as if there were a lot of other fellows with me besides the ones that I knew. I could almost see and hear that sergeant who turned to his men in the wheat field at Château-Thierry and yelled, 'Come on! Do you so-and-sos want to live forever?' "

"I do see what you mean now," Gail muttered. He sounded

a little embarrassed, but it was only the embarrassment of Anglo-Saxon reserve in the face of Gallic effusiveness. "Of course, I was only in a civilian group, the Y. M. B. C., but——"

"Israel Putnam was only a civilian when he quit his plow and picked up a musket. Lafitte's Baratarians were only civilians when they paddled their pirogues out of the swamp to put in with Andy Jackson at Chalmette. Paul Revere was only a civilian when he drew the copper rivets for the beams of *Old Ironsides* and galloped out of Boston to give the alarm that the British were coming."

"Where did you learn so much history, Raoul?" Stella asked curiously. A hush had fallen over the room that somehow made her uncomfortable. She was determined to break it.

"It does happen to be a required subject at the Abbeville High School. But a queer old bird, named Dr. Anconi, taught me a lot more than I learned there. Maybe you remember him. You met him once."

"Of course I remember him. I met him twice."

"That's right. For the moment I'd forgotten that second time, at Bois Fleuri," Raoul said cheerfully. "Well, he taught me enough so that I knew the girls were getting their innings tonight, too. Take Julia Beal, for instance. She wasn't just the vice-chairman of the local Red Cross. She was Betsy Ross sewing a symbol to keep ragged men steadfast while they left bloody footprints in the snow at Valley Forge. She was Molly Pitcher at Monmouth taking the place of her husband as a cannoneer when he was killed."

"That's the way I felt about Julia myself, Raoul, only I couldn't have put it into words, wonderfully, the way you do," Patty said shyly.

"Of course that's the way you felt. And Stella, just in case *you* felt the Spanish War veterans were a pretty drab, paunchy lot, forget it. Because they were headed by the *Oregon* racing around the Horn. And Dewey was alongside of them, saying quietly, 'You may fire when ready, Gridley.' "

"I didn't feel——" Stella began hotly. But her cheeks were hot again, too. There had never been any use in trying to hide what she felt from Raoul—not from the very first moment. There was no use now.

"And take the music!" he went on. "I can just imagine what you think of *God Bless America*. Well, you didn't happen to hear Shafter's men roaring *There'll Be a Hot Time in the Old Town Tonight*? Or the harsh chorus of *Where Do We*

Go From Here, Boys? echoing from the old stone roads of France? Or even the deep-voiced chant of *From the Halls of Montezuma to the Shores of Tripoli?* Of course, that was the one I heard the clearest myself because it's the Marines' song. I suppose that one of these days I'll be going from Bayou Vermilion to those halls and those shores myself. The sooner the better, too!—Well, now I guess we've had enough history, especially since I don't believe Hitler took the tip, as I said in the beginning. What about a little food?"

The rubicund waiter was already hovering on the threshold with the oysters Foch, fried to a turn, beautifully imbedded in *pâté de foie gras*, and dripping with Madeira sauce. Raoul did not continue to dominate the conversation as these were served and eaten. He began asking Richard about Tulane's prospects for victory in the football game with Rice the following Saturday, and the Darcoas about the meeting which the Junior League was to hold at the country club the following afternoon. He inquired whether Gail was going to the Berlier-Zengaras boxing match and rallied Drew good-naturedly about a bridegroom's natural but lamentable indifference to the new Civil Service Bill and the impending income tax. By the time the *poulet en cocotte* came on, everyone at the table, with the exception of Stella, had taken a lively part in the conversation. She was aware that her silence had not passed unnoticed while all the pleasant chatter was going on. And now Raoul turned to her pointedly.

"This is all mighty interesting, but haven't we had enough of this local talk now? We poor provincials ought to be taking advantage of such a rare chance to hear about life in the great city. Are the lights on Broadway as bright as ever, Stella?"

She accepted the remark as a challenge. "Brighter and brighter all the time," she answered gaily. "There's nothing like them, anywhere else in the world."

"And what about the local girl who made good—the Story of Stella the Star? Go on, tell us; we want to hear——"

"Don't be silly. You know I'm not a star," she answered. speaking in the same sharp way that she had spoken to Patty that afternoon and striking a jarring note in the warm intimacy of the little party. "I practice for hours every day," she went on, instantly chagrined that her far-famed tactfulness should have been so conspicuous by its absence. "I'm slated to understudy several of the top liners in the good rôles I sang in Paris. There's just a chance, too, that I may get Musetta in *La Bohème* or Micaela in *Carmen* before the season's over. But I'm not counting on that. It's more likely that I'll always be cast for the impeccable maid or the sympathetic friend, who has just a few lines to sing. You know the good old standard type. I didn't expect anything else, the first year. But if my contract's renewed——"

"Why, it's sure to be!" Patty exclaimed confidently. "And isn't there a chance that you might come to New Orleans in the spring, when we have our three-day 'season' here?"

"There might be. I hope so. I'll expect you all to turn out in full force if I do come. But I haven't thought that far ahead yet. Of course, I've been busy getting settled. I've found the cunningest little penthouse. It's just what I've always wanted——"

She stopped, uncomfortably conscious of Raoul's eyes resting on her. They looked amused and not regretful, but they reminded her inexorably that it was not a cunning little penthouse perched on the top of a city skyscraper which she had always wanted—that once she had wanted a long low white house in the country, with a garden sloping down to the bayou behind——

"—And an excellent maid," Stella went on. "I don't need but one. I pay her a hundred dollars a month, but she's worth it. She does as much work in one day as any lazy Louisiana nigger does in a week."

"But is she as much fun to have around?" Raoul inquired quizzically. "My new household staff lacks style, but I'm getting a great kick out of it."

"*Your* new household staff!"

"Why, yes. I had to get one, to help me run my new house. I bought that place I told you about last spring, after all. I never meant to go on living in a tenement over a drugstore all my life and that seemed as good a time as any to make the break. Of course, I'll have to be away from Abbeville most of the time, after the first of January, but it's always nice to know there's a home to come back to. I'm going to have a house-warming after election and Patty's going to chaperone it for me. She and Drew have promised to spend a week with me. Too bad you couldn't be here."

Raoul still looked amused, and what was worse, he looked eminently self-satisfied. It was obvious he was pleased with his new establishment and proud of it—obvious that he was delighted with the idea of giving a housewarming, of having a beautiful bride like Patty for his first hostess, and of entertaining his friends in Abbeville with the same lavishness that he was entertaining tonight. No doubt Clarinda would go down for the housewarming, too——

"It's nice of you to think of me. But I've made quite a few friends in New York already. I've been to a lot of night clubs, and to all the smart restaurants——"

"Which, incidentally, can't hold a candle to Antoine's," Raoul said genially. "Oh, here comes the chef-d'oeuvre of the evening. Let's hope it's as good as usual."

While he was speaking, the rubicund waiter, beaming more broadly than ever, brought in an *omelette soufflée*, delicately browned and encircled with the words, "Hail to you, Pat and Drew," executed in snowy meringue. It was put down in front of Patty for her to admire, and afterwards it was served and eaten to the accompaniment of running chatter about wedding plans. It was understood, wasn't it, that the rehearsal was to be the next evening at nine? They were all to come to supper at the raised cottage beforehand. Very informal. Not a feast like this. Only the combination of a restaurant like Antoine's and a host like Raoul could produce that, Patty said smilingly. It had been wonderful. She didn't know how to express her thanks for such a lovely party. But she was afraid she would have to tear herself away from it now. Drew didn't want her to get too tired, and, as her mother kept saying, there was so much to do, getting ready for a wedding——

She was gone, with Drew's arm around her shoulder, confident, joyous, composed. Something radiant went out of the room with her, so that Stella was even more conscious of that unique quality of shining glory than she had been earlier in the evening. Raoul was bending over Clarinda, saying something almost inaudible to her. But it sounded as if they were making arrangements to go dancing somewhere, after the wedding rehearsal— "It won't last long— Why, that's just the edge of the evening."— "All right, let's ask Amelina and Richard to come along, too." At the moment, Amelina and Richard were very busy themselves. Richard was helping Amelina with her little fur jacket and one of the sleeves was turned inside out, so they had to fuss to fix that, and she didn't want to crush the beautiful orchids that Raoul had given her so she had to take those off her dress, and would Richard hold the pin for her just a moment while she found the best place for them on her jacket and——

"The party seems to be over, Stella. Shall I take you home?"

It was Gail who spoke, agreeably, unoriginally, according to his habit. The party was indeed over. And Gail was taking her home.

The next two days went racing by, but Stella, making a fresh effort to be gay and helpful, found herself feeling that they were not going half fast enough—that the time would never come when she would be on the northbound plane, resting after all this merrymaking and confusion, inaccessible to an inopportune telephone, free from photographers, reporters and delivery boys. Stella was completely exhausted by all this hubbub. She could not understand how Patty continued to move through it with happy serenity—how she could still be serene when she came into the long drawing room on her uncle's arm to meet Drew at the improvised altar between the draped windows.

Just before she went downstairs to be married, Patty asked her bridesmaids and her maid of honor to come into her bedroom, so that she could give them each a little present. The presents were small heart-shaped pearl pins, and as Patty fastened each one on its recipient, she kissed the girl to whom she was giving it and said how happy she was to have such a dear friend with her at such a time and how much she hoped Stella and Clarinda and Amelina and Mathilde would think of her and Drew whenever they wore their little ornaments. Of Drew especially, Patty added, with her persistent naïveté, because she would not have been able to buy the pins if he had not told her to charge them, saying that she could pay for them the next month out of the allowance he was going to give her. Patty was wearing a very charming pin herself, made of diamond leaves, that fastened the turnover collar of fine lace with which her dress was finished at the throat. And when Stella complimented her on it, Patty said, yes, she was very happy to have it, partly because it was a pin that Andy Breckenridge had given to Anne Forrestal when they were married and partly because it seemed suitable to wear with her own kind of a wedding dress. The dress, as Stella had remarked before, was simplicity, itself—a long-sleeved white satin that had no other trimming than the little lace collar; and the fine lace veil, which matched this, lay very lightly on Patty's head, like a scarf, because, she said, Drew had told her he did not want her to hide her hair any more than she could help, even with a wedding veil. But somehow Stella knew, when she saw Patty standing there in that simple dress which sheathed her so completely and became her so perfectly, that one reason Patty had wanted a dress like this was because she was saving the greater revelation of herself for Drew—that she wanted only Drew to have it——

Gail took Stella to the airport after the wedding, at which he had played his part very well—better than she had played hers, Stella reflected, with increasing chagrin. But he cared a great deal for Patty, and he could not be glad that she was marrying another man, though he had tried sincerely because he knew this was what would make her happy. Now that the ceremony and reception were over and he did not have to put up a bold front any more, he showed that he felt subdued. But he made conversation, in a conscientious way, just the same.

"I thought it was very effective, arranging the presents in the two octagon rooms, Stella."

"Thanks. I'm glad you did. Because I thought of that."

"And wasn't it lucky that the weather was so perfect? Because if the guests hadn't been able to go out onto the back gallery, I don't know where we'd have put them all, do you?"

"Perhaps if it had rained there wouldn't have been so many people."

"I don't know. Patty has heaps of friends. So has Drew, for that matter. I guess they'd have come to the wedding, anyway."

"I guess they would— Richard has an awful crush on Amelina, hasn't he?"

"Yes, and——"

Gail did not say it, but that was only because he caught himself in the nick of time. He was thinking the same thing Stella was: —and Raoul has an awful crush on Clarinda. Several other guests at the wedding had said it. Stella had heard them laughing and joking about it. One of them had even gone so far as to say that Clarinda would be a great addition to the Congressional set in Washington.

The plane was late, and Stella had to go on and on talking to Gail while she waited for it. But it came roaring in at last, and Stella climbed aboard. She managed, somehow, to undress, bending over so that she would not hit her head on the upper berth that was swung so low, and lay down wearily in the narrow space allotted to her. There was one hard little pillow, which did not mitigate the discomfort of the hard mattress, and one thin little blanket, which did not keep her warm after the plane had climbed into the higher altitudes. She got up and put on her topcoat over her pajamas, and when she lay down again, she found that she had disarranged her coverings and now they would not stay tucked in. After a time, she gave up trying to make them. She lay very still, thinking of Drew and Patty, who were together in the beautiful bridal chamber at Splendida, and of Raoul, who was having harder work making love to Clarinda than he had had when he had told Stella to turn her face around and she had done it, and of the cunning penthouse and the perfect maid and the good parts at the Metropolitan to which she was going back all alone.

CHAPTER 36

As the first year of his marriage to Patty ended and the second swung into full being, Drew Breckenridge thought increasingly of the months which he had spent at Splendida when he was a little boy and which had marked the end of an era.

There was no comparison between the two periods, in abundance and fulfillment. The first had lasted only a single splendid spring; the second had triumphantly rounded out a whole cycle of seasons and significantly begun another. The first had been bounded by the relationship of a fond father and a questing, confiding child; the second was magnified by the union of a man and a woman and by the creation of new life through their love. But each experience was in itself perfect and complete, though Drew could not forget that, the first time, the perfection had been almost as brief as the bloom of the flowers that were broken from their branches to cover Breck's grave—that the completeness had also been a conclusion. How long, Drew asked himself, unable to evade the question, could this present perfection endure? How far away was the end of the road which he and Patty had taken together?

In the beginning, he would have said that nothing could exceed, or equal, the first ecestasy of possession, for it had been achieved and sustained without a single marring moment. Patty was still so touchingly young, so essentially virginal, that Drew had feared no loving-kindness on his part could suffice to avert instinctive resistance to inevitable conquest. But he had underestimated her glad capacity for self-surrender; he had failed to gage the extent of her trust and the scope of her adoration. Instead of the recoil he had dreaded, there was only the sudden intake of breath, which had always been a sign of unexpected happiness. Then she gave herself up to him with confident joy, and all his solicitude was engulfed in exultation.

As time went on, he wondered how he ever could have believed that the consummation of his marriage, or even the unblemished beauty of the rapture that followed this, represented the ultimate experience and expression of love. Patty's prodigality was a wellspring; it renewed itself from his passion. The weeks went by, and each night, as he took her in his arms, she seemed more essential to him than ever before. Each morning, as he beheld her afresh, he marvelled once more at the loveliness which was so wholly his to have and to hold.

It was nearly always he who waked first, and he loved to lie looking at her as she slept, with her bright hair tumbled around her serene face, one slim arm under her head, the other relaxed at her side. Rosy color glowed through the tan of her cheeks, and there was a deep line of demarcation between the warm brown of her throat and the blue-veined whiteness of her breasts. Stella's guess that the restraint of her wedding dress would find its antithesis in other bridal apparel had been a shrewd one; there was something Grecian in spirit as well as style about the diaphanous garments that Patty wore in bed. They were utterly unadorned, snowy as they were sheer, cut in a deep V to the waist and tapering to a narrow strap at the shoulder. When Drew wanted to wake her, he buried his face in the soft flesh revealed by the division of her bodice and kissed her until she nestled nearer to him and flung her arms, still sleepily, around his neck. But she quickened almost instantly. He never needed to ask her if she were ready for love. Her own responsiveness, her own ardor, told him that.

This was why he remembered so well the first time that he felt his urgency might have been importunate. It was not that Patty failed to return his customary caresses. But afterwards, instead of rising gaily to bathe and dress, she lay very still, and soon he saw that she had fallen asleep again. He waited a little while, and then he waked her a second time. But he was instantly sorry he had done so, for he saw that she was struggling against almost overpowering drowsiness.

"I'm so sleepy, Drew," she murmured and cuddled down again on her pillow.

For a few moments he stayed beside her, watching her closely. Then he rose and went down to breakfast without her. When he returned, she was still sleeping profoundly, and, though she was perfectly at peace, he saw that the rosy color was all gone from her face and that there were violet shadows under her eyes. Increasingly disturbed, he drew a chair near the bed and sat there the rest of the morning. It was almost noon when she wakened again. She reached out her arms, as if feeling for him, and then sat up, rubbing her eyes, confused and disturbed.

"Drew," she said appealingly. Then as he came towards her and took her hand in a soothing way, she looked still more bewildered. "Is anything the matter?" she asked. "What made you get up first?"

"Because you're a very lazy lady today. It's twelve o'clock."

"Drew, it can't be! Why didn't you make me get up?"

"You couldn't get up, darling. You were so sleepy you couldn't keep your eyes open. I'm afraid you've been getting overtired."

"Of course I haven't been getting overtired. And now we've lost a whole morning out of our honeymoon that we might have had together!"

"We had the morning together, even though you didn't know it. I haven't left you at all, except to eat my breakfast. And now you're going to have yours in bed. I'll ring for Jezebel. I told her to bring it up when I did."

"But, Drew, I never eat breakfast in bed. I think it's a silly slothful habit, just as your mother does."

"It's as pleasant as it is rare to find a mother-in-law and a daughter-in-law agreeing the way you two do. But you're going to eat breakfast in bed today, no matter what you think of the custom as a habit. Here, let me fix your pillows for you. And I've got a surprise for you. I've just remembered, very tardily I'm afraid, the traditional tribute of a Breckenridge to his bride."

He smiled at her whimsically as he propped her up in bed, hoping that he did not show how worried he was. When Jezebel came in, carefully bearing the tray, Patty saw that a single perfect rose had been laid across the folded napkin of fine embroidered linen.

The coffee was strong and hot, the toast golden brown, the orange juice imbedded in fine ice; and it was all served in a very special set, made of Dresden china, which Anne Forrestal and Andy Breckenridge had brought back with them when they returned from their "Grand Tour." Nothing could have been more tempting or more attractive, and Drew realized that Patty guessed he, himself, had taken a hand in the general arrangement, besides remembering the rose, when he went downstairs to his own breakfast. But though she usually had a healthy appetite, it was evident that the food was repugnant to her. He could see that she was trying very hard to swallow it, conscious that he was watching her. But finally she had to give up the effort.

"I'm sorry. Do you mind very much? I just don't seem to be hungry."

"Do you feel ill, darling? Don't you think I'd better send for a doctor?"

"No, of course not. I have a little headache, that's all. And I'm still sleepy."

She lifted up the rose and, holding it in her hand, lay down and closed her eyes. She was asleep again almost instantly. Drew took away the tray, put it on the small bed at the foot of the four-poster, and rang a second time for Jezebel. She came so quickly that he knew she had not been far away; she must have had some reason or found some pretext for lingering in the linen room or one of the guest chambers. He suspected a pretext, for Jezebel acted as if she had expected this second summons, and she seemed to be peculiarly pleased with it. She was usually very sober, for a Negress, but now there was a smug, secret little smile on her face.

"Miss Patty doesn't want any breakfast, after all, Jezebel. You may take the tray downstairs. I put it on the day bed."

"What for you allus call dat dere a day bed, Mr. Drew? Doesn't you know it are an accouchement bed?"

It was years since he had heard the old-fashioned term or thought of the old-fashioned practice connected with it. Now, as the elderly Negress stood there blinking at him behind her moon-like glasses, with the smug, secret little smile playing around her lips, he remembered that such beds had indeed been an integral part of plantation equipment and that colored midwives had been accustomed to lifting their travailing patients from the great four-posters to these narrow couches during the last dreadful stage of their labor, so that they could be more easily attended, and then lifting them back again after their delivery. Much the same principle was involved as the modern one of having hospital beds and operating tables very narrow, for the convenience of the doctor and nurse, and of taking parturient women to a delivery room; but the old method had inevitably been much cruder, and frequently there had been no physician in attendance. It had been customary to signify that a doctor was needed by placing a flag at the end of the allee, where it could be seen from the river road, a red flag signifying a preference for one, a white flag for another. Passers-by took the tidings of such distress signals to the doctors' houses. The chance was more than even that these might be making the rounds elsewhere, but eventually they came and did the best they could. Nevertheless, all too often everything was over before their arrival. Drew winced at the thought of all the anguish unalleviated by primitive plantation midwifery; and yet, it had been taken more or less for granted, both by the planters, themselves, and by the women who bore their children. These narrow beds, placed crosswise at the foot of the conjugal four-posters, were not there for the purpose of permitting either one of the married pair to sleep alone occasionally, for such separation was unheard-of, or even to rest now and then during normal waking hours: the term, day bed, as Jezebel had just reminded him, was erroneously used, at least for Louisiana. On the contrary, these accouchement couches were kept close at hand because they were so frequently required. Drew had wondered if elderly Chinese really enjoyed keeping coffins in their chambers as much as this time-honored custom was supposed to indicate; now, for the first time, he wondered whether those compliant, prolific wives of the bygone golden era had not sometimes shrunk from the sight of an acessory which represented a rack to them. Hundreds of them, as far as that went, had not been able to survive its torture. Why, it was in this very room——

"Yo' knows, Mr. Drew, dat pore lil Miss Anne died right heah. My own grandmammy caught bof her babies. She come trough somehow with your paw, but she had a mighty hard time. I done heah my grandmammy say it was tree days and tree nights 'fore she could turn dat child a-loose. When de lil girl come, dey wasn't no way of savin' her. She done bleed to def while dey try to get her back in her own bed.

Yassuh. Dem couches is for accouchements. Looks lak we'll be needin' dis one agin, come summer. Don't it, Mr. Drew?"

"Be quiet, Jezebel. suppose Miss Patty weren't sound asleep; suppose she overheard part of what you said. You'd frighten her to death!"

He spoke in a fierce whisper. Of course Patty was sound asleep; of course she could not possibly have overheard. But he ought to have silenced Jezebel sooner, just the same. He raged at himself because he had not. Jezebel, still smiling, picked up the tray and prepared to leave the room.

"Yassuh. No suh. Miss Patty ain't de kind dat frightens easy, Mr. Drew. And she a fine strong young lady. You ain't got nothin' to fret about. She won't be like po' lil Miss Anne. She gwine have a fine big boy for you and she won't die herself, neither. When dey's sleepy, lak dis, at de first, dat's a good sign. It helps dem to get over dere mornin' sickness. Let her sleep, Mr. Drew, all she wants to. Why doesn't you go over to de mill for a while? I done heah King say he needed to see you soon-soon."

Drew did not believe the foreman had said anything of the sort. He, himself, had paid very little attention to the sugar mill up to that time, partly because he had never felt much interest in his crop, since it had been depleted by the quota, and partly because his concern in everything about the moribund plantation, that fall, had been submerged in his passion for Patty. But so far as he could see, the grinding was going on as well as could be expected, and he thought that King, who had so long had a free hand, might resent interference now, in any case. Besides, how could he leave Patty at such a moment as this? If she woke again later on, she might instinctively search for him beside her, as she had done once already that morning. But Jezebel goaded him on.

"I call you right away, Mr. Drew, effen Miss Patty was to waken. She liable to be sleepy lak dis, days, quite a spell. I done tole yo' already sleepin's de best she can do till she over her mornin' sickness. Most always dat lasts weeks; times it lasts monfs. You cain't spend all yo' time dis winter waitin' for Miss Patty to wake up. You got to go 'long about yo' business, same's odder husbans when dey wives is in de fambly way. I tells you she gwine to be all right. She don't even know what ail her, till yet. I ain't agwine tell her, neither. I gwine to yet yo' do dat, now I's told you. I 'spects you never knowed it, neither, Mr. Drew, till I done tole yo'."

Jezebel was fairly swelling with importance and satisfaction. What she said was so. Drew had not immediately connected Patty's overwhelming drowsiness, or even the dark circles around her eyes and her repugnance for food, with possible pregnancy. Of course he had wanted a child more than anything else in the world, except Patty herself. If he had not, he would not have spoken so impellingly to Patty about one on that unforgettable evening when he had first brought her to Splendida. But since his marriage, the thought so long dominant had been dormant; it was Patty, and Patty alone, of whom he had thought. He had chided her gently, because she had told him that he filled her life, that she wanted him exactly as he was, and that she wanted no one but him. And now she had filled his life as he had never dreamed it could be filled. In this fulfillment, he had forgotten everything else, even the consequences which he himself had so eagerly desired and which he had been so determined to precipitate. Now, like many another man before him, he was appalled by the immediacy of the answer to his own most fervent prayer. It was too soon to let maternity and all that this involved deprive him of his own most precious prerogatives, too soon to share Patty with anyone, even his own child, too soon to have her face a second overwhelming experience, to suffer, to endure——

There had been a time when the sugar mill, running at top speed, would have a suited almost any mood he might be in. He had loved its clatter, its heat, its confusion, its rich scents unlike any other scent in the world. All these were part of the creation and fruition which it represented. But it was another sort of creation and fruition which concerned him now. Assured that Patty was still sleeping peacefully and that nothing would induce Jezebel to leave her post in the passage, he left the state bedroom, though still with reluctance, and wandered out of the house into the rear gallery and from there to the arbor. It was warm there, for the sunlight came filtering in through the latticework, just as the moonlight did on mellow nights; Drew felt it was as good a place as any to stay while he waited for Patty to wake and while he tried to decide what to say to her when she did. It was a place with which he had no special associations himself, and yet he had always connected it with love. He could remember hearing old Shoog tell his mother that this was where Andy Breckenridge had "gained" Aurore Fontaine and how puzzled Anna had been by the statement—almost as puzzled as

he had been, himself; and Drew felt sure his father had had
some special feeling about it, too. What this was he did not
know, though he connected it vaguely with Marie Céleste;
after her visit to Splendida, Breck had never gone there again,
so there had been no "gain" in his case. Perhaps, on the contrary, something had happened which had been connected
with tragic loss——

How much more blessed he had been in his love than
either his father or grandfather, Drew thought, absently
watching the changing color of the sunlight as the afternoon
wore on. Louis, who had followed him to Splendida, brought
his lunch to the arbor, hitching up his shoulders and thrusting out his wrists as usual; but the servant's jauntiness was
tempered, his loquaciousness curbed. Drew felt that Louis,
like Jezebel, was aware of the special advent which, by a
curious coincidence, was so close to that sacred season of the
year which marked the Great Advent. But was it, after all,
pure coincidence? Drew had heard it said that an old belief
among the Jews held that life began not in the spring, but
in the autumn. Was the life beginning here now a mystic
sign that the doom of Splendida was not sealed, after all—
that this season, which he had thought would mark its end,
was, in some still undisclosed sense, only its beginning?

The days were short now, and the sun was already very
low. Soon only the horizon would show a rim of gold. Drew
had sat in the arbor all the afternoon, accomplishing nothing. There had been too many idle days in the past, and he
had firmly resolved, the previous spring, that there should
be no more of them. These weeks here with Patty had
marked the exception to his self-set rule of industry, just as
they had marked the reprieve which was all he had dared to
ask from impending fate. But now he must get to work again.
There were more cogent reasons for it than ever before. And
perhaps the reprieve was, after all, a promise——

He heard footsteps coming towards the arbor again, and
this time he recognized them as Patty's. So she had waked
while he sat there dreaming, and she was better, or she
would have sent for him instead of coming to him! He
sprang up, immeasurably relieved, inexpressibly happy. As
she approached, he saw that the color had come back into
her face—enough of it, at least, to allay his anxiety. Her
hair caught the bright rays of the sinking sun. She had on a
soft blue woolen dress, in the shade that she loved to wear
and in which he loved to see her, but for which he had never

found exactly the right word: sky blue, he had called it, and sea blue; but neither of these terms quite fitted. Now he knew what it was. It was the color that the early painters, Filippo Lippi and Fra Angelico, and those other Italian primitives had used for the robes of the Holy Mother and which, for centuries now, had been known as Madonna blue——

"Well, you have had a good sleep!" he called out gaily. The gaiety was not forced. Now that he saw her looking so well, coming towards him so naturally, he could be gay again.

"Yes, I have. And some strong, hot tea. Jezebel brought it to me without my asking, and it was good. I drank it all up and ate some little cakes with it. They were good, too. She said we ought to have champagne for supper. I don't know why, but I thought it was a nice idea. So I told Louis to put some on ice."

"I'm glad you did. It is a nice idea. Jezebel was right."

"It'll be a sort of party, if we have champagne, won't it, Drew?"

"A grand party."

"I ordered it just because it sounded good when she suggested it. But afterwards, I thought it would be especially nice to have a celebration. Because— Well, I was stupid not to think of it this morning, and so were you, darling. But I have heard—I'm sure someone told me that when a girl stayed sleepy, the way I did, and didn't want her breakfast— I mean a girl who was married—it was a sign that she was probably going to have a baby. Haven't you heard that, Drew?"

"I don't know. Yes, I think I have."

"Especially if some other things were not quite as usual with her, either," Patty continued, without self-consciousness. "And they aren't. So don't you believe, Drew, that I am going to have a baby?"

"Yes, darling, I believe you are."

"And you're glad, aren't you? It's what you wanted, isn't it? And it's come so soon, you haven't had time to worry that perhaps I wouldn't. There isn't any chance now that you'll be disappointed. Oh, Drew, I'm so glad myself; I'm so thankful! If you'd been worried—if you'd been disappointed—I couldn't have borne it. Because I love you so! I love you more every hour that I live. I didn't suppose I could, when I married you. I thought you'd glorified me, before. I told you that. But now—now that I'm your wife, now that I'm going to have a baby *because* I'm your wife, I realize I didn't know even the beginning of glory before!"

She threw her arms around his neck with her characteristic gesture of spontaneous ardor. He held her to him, without speaking anything besides her name: "Patty—dearest Patty!" Then he sat down with her in the arbor, still silently, his arms still enfolding her. How could he tell her of his selfishness in wanting her longer to himself? How could he say he was jealous of his own child? How could he speak to her of fear, or remind her of suffering, when she, herself, was so wholly happy? Once again it was she who had shown him a star and led him on a predestined way. He could not do less than go with her.

It had been Patty's hope, from the beginning, that she and Drew might remain at Splendida until after Christmas. This should be feasible, she thought, if they went together to New Orleans regularly in the middle of the week, leaving the plantation early in the morning, spending one night with his mother, and returning to the plantation late the following evening. This would give him two full days at his office, with no separation from her except during business hours, and on Mondays and Fridays he could motor down and back the same day, leaving her behind. After all, it was not as long or as hard a trip as many businessmen living in the so-called "suburbs" of New York and Chicago made regularly; and with their first six weeks at Splendida representing his vacation, in any case, the following six weeks ought not to make too long a period of commuting. Of course, if he found he could not keep up with his work, they could always change their plans; but as far as she could see, nobody bothered much with business over the Thanksgiving, Christmas and New Year's holidays. Drew had agreed to the proposed arrangement, less because he thought, beforehand, that they would really enjoy so protracted a stay in the country than because he wanted to meet her wishes in every possible way and because he knew she was sincere in saying she would be willing to change their plans, if these did not work out well for him. But to his surprise, he, himself, had been supremely satisfied with the quiet coming and going of the days—the seemingly uneventful pattern of life which was actually so much richer and fuller than any he had ever known, and when he first broached the question of departure, this was not prompted by restlessness or inadaptability but by concern.

"It was all very well to talk about motoring regularly back and forth from town and leaving you here by yourself twice a week when you were perfectly all right. It's different now."

"I'm still perfectly all right. I'll admit I don't feel much like motoring, but that feeling isn't going to last long. While it does, you can go without me. I'll just sleep the time away while you're gone."

"And what if, instead of sleeping away, you faint away, as you did yesterday? You certainly gave me the fright of my life that time."

This was perfectly true. He had been so alarmed that he had not yet recovered from the shock of seeing her suddenly lose consciousness. They had been sitting together in the arbor at sunset, which, after their first experiment, they had both decided was a delightful thing to do, and had just risen to go into the house for supper. Then, without the slightest warning, she had slid from his embrace to the ground and had lain there in lax immobility for moments which seemed to him like hours. When she opened her eyes again, she looked a little dazed, but it was evident that she was neither frightened nor hurt, and while he was still kneeling beside her, speaking to her appealingly and anxiously, she sat up again and remarked, in a matter-of-fact way, that someone had told her about this, too, and she had been wondering when it would happen.

"I don't believe I'll do that many times," she answered now. "But after all, if I faint, all I have to do is to lie still until I feel all right again. If it'll make you feel any better, I'll promise not to go out of the house alone."

"It'll make me feel better to have the best obstetrician in New Orleans come here and tell us exactly what you ought to be doing and ought not to be doing. I don't know who that individual is, but probably Dr. Beal can tell us."

"Couldn't Dr. Beal tell us everything we need to know without asking anyone else?"

"Perhaps. He's getting on, though. I'd like someone younger, more modern and scientific."

"But Dr. Beal is so kind and wise. Let's send for him first and see what he says. Then if you aren't satisfied, we can send for someone else besides."

"Patty, dear, it's just that I want you to have the very

best there is, and that I don't want you to have a moment of—discomfort that can be avoided."

He still could not say the word "suffering." Patty said it for him.

"I know, Drew. I know exactly how you feel. You don't need to tell me. But nothing is going to make me suffer as much as seeing you so anxious. I don't believe having babies is as bad as it used to be. I wish you wouldn't keep thinking about Anne Forrestal."

"I'm not thinking about Anne Forrestal."

"Why, Drew, I thought we promised we'd never tell lies to each other! Not even lavender lies!"

She said it so gaily that his panic was assuaged. And the following Sunday, when Dr. Beal came to Splendida, informally and genially, like an old friend rather than a meticulous physician, Drew was still further relieved, for everything the doctor said, after he had examined Patty and talked with her, was reassuring.

"She's as right as rain. I doubt if this morning sickness of hers lasts long. She seems to have it in a very mild form— Now if it showed signs of developing into pernicious vomiting, as it does by this time with some poor girls, my advice to you would be different. And I don't think you need worry about these little attacks of faintness— Those will probably pass pretty soon, too. This drowsiness of hers is a safeguard, as your old colored servant has probably told you. Didn't you ever see a pregnant cat stretched itself out in the sun and sleep and sleep? You may not think the simile is very elegant or romantic, but that's what Patty's doing, in principle. She's storing up reserve strength for herself and her child, too. I'll gladly send another man up here if you like— George Akers is probably the best of the type you have in mind. A little later she ought to be seeing someone regularly—whoever you and she decide you'd like to have it be. But I'd let her have her own way for the present. It's a good way." He smiled and added, "She's a pretty good girl."

"You don't need to tell me that. But she doesn't half grasp what's ahead of her. She can't. I'm not going to let her pay the penalty for her lack of understanding."

"I wouldn't say that Patty lacked understanding," Dr. Beal said a little dryly. "She was very sure she wanted to marry you, wasn't she? And it wasn't for any lack of sizing up a situation which we don't need to discuss, but which would have offended a good many young women past endurance, if it hadn't actually frightened them. You didn't run up against any resistance or hysterics later on, either, did you? Patty's a very clearheaded, healthy-minded girl, with an excellent physique and a fine character. What's more, she's passionately in love with you, and she's proud and pleased because she's conceived a child. When you get a setup like that, you don't need to worry that she's so young pregnancy will wear her down, or that she won't be able to stand a few labor pains. As a matter of fact, her youth is all in her favor. She'll probably have numerous children, all very easily after the first one, and nurse every one of them, and still become more and more beautiful every year. Of course, I don't know how many causes she'll promote, and how much society racketing she'll go in for in the meantime, but I should think you could afford to be pretty philosophical about having your wife let all that go by the side."

"I can. Especially the causes. But I do want her to have one gorgeously gay season, with all the diversions and homage she has a right to. She'd hardly found herself last winter, before I came crashing in. And this winter she'll have to take things quietly, even if we are in town later on. But next year——"

"Next year she could be Queen of Mystic, or of the Atticans, without a doubt, if she'd enjoy it and you'd like to have her. I've always favored the custom of having two or three Carnival Queens pretty young matrons instead of pretty young girls. Patty'd be the youngest and prettiest we've ever had, too."

"I think you have a very good idea there. I'd be delighted if she were chosen, and of course she would."

The prospect was pleasing to Drew out of all proportion to its importance. He dwelt on it with such satisfaction that he permitted the subject of any immediate change of plan to slide for a day or two, and during that interval, Patty calmly took the attitude that there was to be none. He found himself starting for town without her more philosophically than he would have supposed possible, attacking with renewed zest the work which awaited him at the office and driving home through the dusk with eager anticipation of the warm intimacy with which the day would come to a close. He left Splendida about seven, and though Patty waked up enough to kiss him good-bye, he believed her when she told him that, as soon as he had gone, she fell asleep again and frequently slept, off and on, until midafternoon. Then she had her strong tea and got up and went outdoors. When Drew returned after his twelve-hour absence, she was waiting for him in the arbor or on the portico. And after supper they had a fire in the parlor and sat cosily in front of it until they went upstairs, where, in their bedroom, the friendly flames of another fire cast reflections on the white walls long after all the other lights had gone out.

Drew soon discovered that, during his absence, Patty apparently found time to occupy herself with some practical details, in spite of what she described as "her prevailing state of contented somnolence." She asked him one night what he would think of closing all the rooms on the north side of the house, since they did not really need these, and of installing oil burners in the upper and lower halls to supplement the heat from the fireplaces. She thought, with these, they could keep very comfortable, after all, and the heaters would not be unduly expensive; she had secured estimates from a firm in White Castle and had found out that she could make payments, from her allowance, on the installment plan, if the financing could not be managed in any other way.

"Good God, Patty, of course it could! Your allowance is for you to spend on *yourself*. Haven't you spent anything at all yet?"

Oh, yes, she had paid for her bridesmaids' pins promptly, she said, but there was nothing she had wanted for herself so far. How could there be, when she had her trousseau, and when Drew kept giving her presents all the time? But she did think they ought to buy these heaters. It was not as if they were spending much money in other ways. If they had been silly enough to go tearing around on a typical wedding trip, instead of staying in joyous seclusion at Splendida, for instance, they would have used up a great deal more money than the heaters would cost.

Drew checked his impulse to tell her that it was foolish to sink any sum in a house which probably could never be used another year. She was quite right about the economy with which they had been living; he had never seen household bills so small or known that they could be, and the experience of finding a young and pretty woman who could think of nothing she needed or desired for herself, in the course of six weeks, was another novel one for Drew. If she wanted the heaters, she ought to have them. He told her to go ahead with the purchase and watched the process of installation with more admiration and less amusement than he had supposed he would feel. Patty was practical and competent; she took charge of the work capably and with no sign of undue fatigue or worry. When it was completed, with excellent results, she began to ask other questions and make other suggestions about the house.

"If you feel so sure it's only a matter of time before it's going into the river, the way things are now, why don't you move it? You've moved two houses for other people and everyone's saying you've made a huge success of it. Why don't you move our own house and make a huge success of that?"

"The houses I moved had strong structures, Patty. Splendida wasn't built that way. It was built for show, not for endurance. The foundations have had to be reinforced several times already because they weren't solid. The walls are honeycombed with decay. If you looked at the original specifications for them, you'd see that these read 'stucco to *resemble* stone.' The walls aren't really made of stone."

"There's brick under the stucco. Some of it must be all right still."

"Yes, but not enough. And there's another consideration, Patty. The other houses I've moved have been small, comparatively speaking. This one's enormous. It was built by slave labor, I don't need to tell you it couldn't be rebuilt that way. Rebuilding would cost a small fortune. I haven't got the money to put into it. Or the money to put into modern equipment. A hundred years ago, when a man built a house, everything he spent would be for masonry and plastering and woodwork and decorations and items like that. Now a large part of what he spends has to go for lighting and heating and plumbing and other accessories that we think are necessities but that our ancestors never heard of. Of course there's plumbing here, of a sort, but that was the exception and not the rule. And materials, like labor, were cheaper then, too."

"Well, I think it would be fun to save some of the mottled-marble basins and copper tubs. They're quite a curiosity and they still work all right. And we have a new heating plant already."

"Patty, dear, the heating plant cost a few hundred dollars. It would cost thousands and thousands to reconstruct this house, provided that it could be done at all."

"You wouldn't be moving it as far as you did the others, so that part wouldn't cost so much. You'd just be moving it beyond reach of the river. Couldn't you take the materials that are still sound and build a smaller house? One half this size would be big enough. But we could save all its most beautiful features—the portico and the pillars and the piazza and the doorway and the big colored window and the beautiful mantels. And I could make over the draperies and the upholstery. I've been looking at the materials. If the windows were four inches shorter and four inches narrower, I could use all the same curtains. I don't believe the difference in size would ever be noticed, in a smaller house. And if there were half as many chairs and sofas in use, they could all be neatly covered. Let me show you."

She led him over to the windows, and he saw that there were rows of pins already precisely placed in the frayed brocade. Next she indicated two chairs on which she had been experimenting. One, which was in a rather rickety state, had been denuded of its covering, and the tapestry on the other had been neatly patched with this. She pointed to these renovations with pardonable pride. Then, more shyly, she went over to the desk and spread out a rough drawing.

"Wouldn't the house look almost the same, from the outside," she asked, "if all these rooms we have shut off now weren't there at all? That would make six less, to begin with. And in the rear, there could be just a library, without any bedroom back of it— That would mean the library would have the western sun at the rear, instead of being dark and gloomy, the way it is now. And of course there'd be one less room upstairs, too. That makes eight rooms less. The kitchen and the pantries ought to be in the service wing instead of in the basement, but still, the wing could be half its present size, too. Guests don't bring servants with them any more; we've only our own to think of. And we don't need a housekeeper; I can do my own housekeeping. Then, with all the rooms there are left a little smaller— Naturally, this is only a rough plan; I don't know how to draw. I know that the position of the staircase hall would have to be shifted and that there'd be other necessary modifications. But nothing essential would be gone. I've been thinking a lot about it. You know I'm not fast asleep all the time I'm in bed during the daytime. I take a little nap, and then I wake up and think for a while, and then I take another nap, and——"

"You've been doing some pretty tall thinking. That's a very good sketch, for an amateur," Drew said, looking at her in amazement. "That's not an unsound idea of yours, either. If these were only normal times——"

"But don't you think, Drew, that just because they're not, we ought to try to plan so that we can help to bring them back to normal, later on? Because the plantation won't be engulfed by the river, whatever happens. At least, not enough to count, from the point of view of crops. And the country's going to need those crops someday, isn't it? Just because you've been sore about the sugar isn't any sign——"

"Patty, how can I run a plantation in Louisiana if I'm somewhere over on the other side of the world? Just because I haven't been called out yet isn't a sign that I may not be any day."

"If you are, I can run it until you come back. I don't know how, but I can learn. Lots of other women have learned in wartimes. And in other times, too, when—when it was necessary."

He had never known her to evade a direct statement before. The "other times" of which she spoke, as he was well aware, were when young women he and she both knew had been widowed. But "widow" was a word which Patty could not say, for all her courage. Not with the war clouds growing closer all the time. Not yet——

"We'll think about these plans of yours, Patty," Drew said gently. "And talk about them, too, again, if you like. But not now. Come out in the arbor with me now. It seems to me as if you'd learned almost enough, and done almost enough, for one fall!"

She did not argue with him, but he discovered before long that, little by little, she was exploring the plantation in the same quiet, unhurried way that she had explored the house and that, in the course of her rambles, she was familiarizing herself with its usages and its needs and learning some of the myriad details involved in managing crops and stock. One of the aspects of her condition which was curious to them both was that she was apt to feel better and worse on alternate days; on the "bad" days she stayed in bed until late afternoon, making no attempt to struggle against lassitude and nausea. On the "good" days she spent as much time out-of-doors as she could without undue effort. She also spent a certain amount of time in correspondence. She took an almost childlike pleasure in receiving letters and the more unusual correlative pleasure in writing them, and she was very apt to show Drew both the letters she received and the letters she wrote. One of the latter caused him some slight qualms for several reasons, but in the end he decided not to suggest any changes in it, and it was dispatched in its original form.

*Splendida Plantation,
December 14, 1940.*

Dear Raoul:

You told me you would wait to hear from me about a date for your housewarming, because you did not want to intrude on my honeymoon, and I think you've been very patient especially with Christmas coming on and your departure for Washington so near. I do hope you have not been inconvenienced because I have not written you sooner, for I have really had a very good reason. I have not been so well these last few weeks, and I have been waiting to see whether I would be able to take the trip to Abbeville before it would be too late to do you any good. Now I'm afraid I shall not, and I should be very troubled about going back on you by not chaperoning your house party, if I did not feel sure you would be so pleased to hear I am going to have a baby that this would make up to you for your disappointment.

I have not told anyone else yet, and I've thought I wouldn't for a while, because it is such fun for Drew and me to have this sort of a secret. But I think you have a right to know that the reason I'm going back on you is not because I'm naturally undependable, or anything like that, but because I have symptoms which are a little bothersome just now, and which would make me a very poor hostess. I am sure you will have no trouble at all in finding another—Mrs. Darcoa, for instance. That would simplify matters about having Clarinda, which I should think would suit you very well.

Drew's mother, and my family, are coming down to spend Christmas with us, and Richard is bringing Amelina. This will be the first company we have had and we are looking forward to it. Of course, it will be a very quiet party, but if you would feel like joining us, either on Christmas Day or for the week end before or after, we should like very much to have you. Perhaps you and Drew could get in a little quail shooting. It is very good around here, and a friend of Drew's, Mr. James Hymel, who lives at Helvetia Plantation just below us, on the other side of the river, has been urging him to come down for it. Of course, if an especially good sportsman like yourself could go with him, it would be much more fun for

Drew, because he is better at riding than at hunting, just as Gail is better at sailing.

Which reminds me, I wonder if you have heard that Gail was turned down after being called by the Draft Board, when he came up for his physical examination? He felt very badly, especia..y as he was just sort of drifting along this fall, waiting to be called out and hadn't anything special to do. Now he has gone and got himself a job in the testing division at the Higgins Plant and goes dashing over the lake at fabulous speeds. Since he got over his first disappointment, he seems to be quite contented, from what he writes, really more contented than he has been in some time, and I think he may be very useful building ships.

There is not much news to tell you, because Drew and I have been living so very quietly here ever since we were married. We did not even have many callers at first, which I think shows great consideration on the part of our neighbors, but now people are beginning to drop in and we shall drop in on them, too, when I am feeling better. I have not been away from Splendida at all, but since the latter part of November Drew has been going to town five days a week. He has been asked to take over the development of another subdivision, and the adapted Breaux Bridge cottages were so successful that he is trying to think up something that would be equally good. Meanwhile, he is building a Baptist church and a Catholic hospital, which ought to keep him very openminded. He has not been called out yet, as you have probably gathered, and I selfishly have my fingers crossed, hoping it won't happen for a while.

I am very happy staying here all the time, and it is very beautiful here now. There has been a light frost, so the grass has turned a lovely shade of dusty pink, and that and the façade of the house and the sunset at this time of year are all the same color, just as I heard they would be. I never get tired looking at them. I am also very much interested in seeing the Negroes piling up huge stacks of roseau reeds along the levee for their Christmas Eve bonfires. I can hardly wait to see them lighted. Drew says the tall poles in the center make them look like trees, and that when the roseau reeds begin to burn, the joints explode, and give the effect of fireworks. I suppose you've seen them hundreds of times, but I never have and I'm very excited.

I mustn't forget to tell you, either, that there are some flowers blooming in the garden still. The poinsettias are gor-

*geous, and one of the early camellias is just beginning to
bloom. What's more, I can have a bunch of Louis Philippe
roses waiting for you in your room, if you come to visit, as I
hope you will.*

With affectionate regards always, in which Drew joins me,

> *Faithfully your friend,*
> *Patricia Forrestal Breckenridge.*

*P.S. I wrote it all out because it pleases me so much to
see the Breckenridge at the end of it. Don't you think it
looks lovely?*

*P. S. No. 2. I had a letter from Stella this morning, and
she told me all about Walter Avery's wedding to Sandra
Hastings, which was on the ninth. Apparently it was awfully
smart and New Yorkish. Stella also said she had sung a
small part in* Louise *on the eleventh. It seems queer to think
of her doing that, doesn't it, when she sang that little role
so well in Paris? But she seemed pleased because she had
got on the stage for the first time after more than a week of
performances in which she hadn't appeared, and one or
two of the critics mentioned her favorably though briefly.
Of course, the word* DEBUT *appeared beside her name in
the program, and I suppose there is always a thrill for a
singer when that happens, though of course I wouldn't really
know, because I can't sing or do much of anything else. But
anyway, I am going to have a baby, and I am divinely happy.*

P. S. No. 3. I'm sending along the program of Louise *so
you can see it, too. Somehow, I think you might like to.*

> *Patty.*

Raoul's answer to this letter came by return mail. Patty
hastened to show this to Drew, also.

> *Bayou's Edge,*
> *Abbeville, Louisiana,*
> *December 15, 1940.*

*Dear Patricia Forrestal Breckenridge— It does look lovely!—
Thank you for your wonderful letter of the fourteenth.
You certainly gave me all kinds of news, even though you
said you had none, and while I'm sorry to hear of good
old Gail's hard luck, all the rest of the news was good. One
item especially, of course. I'm very touched and pleased to*

be the first you've told about the baby. I'm delighted to share a secret of this sort with you and Drew, and I do congratulate both you and him most warmly. Will you let me be one of his godfathers, if it's a boy? Somehow, I feel sure it will be, and I'd like a lien of some sort on him.

I never should have dreamed of considering you undependable under any circumstances. Don't give the matter of my housewarming another thought. We'll postpone it until next year. I'm busy getting ready to go to Washington, anyway, and I don't believe I want to bother with it. If I'd cared much about it, I'd have written you asking for a highsign, without waiting to hear from you. As for coming to Splendida, I think I ought to spend Christmas with my father and mother; both my married sisters are coming home, so we'll be having quite a family reunion. And I'm afraid I haven't time for bird hunting this year. But I'd like a raincheck on that invitation. Perhaps next December Drew and I can get some in. Meantime, if I find I can run over, just for a few hours, the last week end before I leave, I will. I'd like to get that bunch of Louis Philippe roses you promised me.

In closing, I'm going to get very fresh and beg you not to say there's nothing you know how to do. I'm sincere in telling you I don't know any girl who's done so much, so well. Please believe me, Patty, and go right on the way you've started.

Now give my best to Drew, and let me sign off,
        Yours with admiration and affection,
                Raoul Bienvenu.
Thanks for the program. I was glad to see it.

Patty waited with a rather troubled face for Drew to make some comment as he handed the letter back to her. When he said nothing, she spoke anxiously.

"That was an awfully nice letter. But somehow, I don't think it sounded happy. Do you, Drew?"

"No. Not at all. I'm very sorry for Raoul Bienvenu. It makes me feel guilty to think of him."

"Why, darling?"

"Because he deserves to have all the things I was lucky enough to get. And instead, I have everything and he hasn't anything."

"I'm not sure I know what you mean."

"You will, someday."

Raoul did not come to Splendida, after all, and Patty was very sorry. But she enjoyed her Christmas company, and early in the new year she began to feel much better. Then she motored to New Orleans with Drew once a week, as they had planned originally, and spent the night with his mother. She went regularly to Dr. Beal's office now, and he was pleased with her progress. He said there was no reason why she should not take in some of the Carnival festivities, if she would like to; so she made Drew's mother a more protracted visit and went to the Balls of the Pacifici and to Proteus and Momus and to see the Rex Parade from the balcony of the Boston Club. As she and Drew mounted the beautiful long staircase together on Mardi Gras, she asked a demure question.

"Do you by any chance remember anything special that happened here last year?"

"Of course I do. When the band struck up the Carnival song, a worthless scamp named Drew Breckenridge caught the loveliest girl in the world eyeing him surreptitiously, as if she were trying to identify him with a bold, mysterious masker who had been paying her marked attentions. He was so amazed and delighted at her covert interest that he ventured to lift his glass and toast her. And it wasn't just a gay gesture. It was a public tribute. *If Ever I Cease to Love* wasn't a Carnival catchword for him after that. It became a pledge."

"It became a pledge for her, too, Drew. Not that she really was the loveliest girl in the world, of course. I'm awfully happy that you remembered. I've always been told that was the sort of thing husbands forgot."

"What? With a wife like you? Not this husband! Probably not any Breckenridge husband. Think of the roses on the breakfast trays!"

"Well, you did forget about those for a while."

"Yes, I'm slipping. I know I'm not in the same class with my father and grandfather. But I'll try to do better. And I'm sure the young man in the next generation will combine all the most irresistible qualities of both Andy and Breck."

He slid his arm through hers and squeezed her hand as they went down the length of the great drawing rooms together. They had come early on purpose so that she might get a good seat on the balcony before this began to be crowded. Besides, Drew was on the committee again, and he was needed here, there and everywhere in connection with the visit of the Carnival Court. Ursin Villeré came to summon him almost immediately, and Patty watched him disappear through the long window leading from the balcony to the reception room, with a feeling of immense pride because he was so important and so necessary. Mathilde Villeré and her friend, Barbara Emery, whom Patty liked very much, too, though she did not know her quite so well, were in the seats beside hers, and Julia Beal had taken a day off from her Red Cross work and was directly behind them. Soon they were all chatting gaily together. Had Patty been in New Orleans long enough, Mathilde asked, to realize that this was the gayest season anyone could remember? The year before, Sandra Hastings had pre-empted a lot of limelight because she was almost unique; but this year nearly everyone seemed to have out-of-town guests. There had been nearly as many parties for them as there were for the debutantes: Carnival breakfasts every noon; Carnival dansants at the country club every evening; supper dances at the Patio Royal to round off the day. Really, she was almost dead——

"Go on, Mathilde. You know you just eat it up, like all the rest of us. When we stop celebrating Carnival, Hitler can have New Orleans."

"Oh, Barbara, don't say that!"

Patty and Julia had spoken almost simultaneously. The same appalling thought had struck them both; but Barbara went rattling gaily on.

"Life wouldn't be the same here if we didn't have this insane, absurd, romantic, fabulous interlude every year. The *world* wouldn't be the same. We might do without gumbo and Sazeracs, or the country-club pool, or the Sugar Bowl game, or even Sex-with-a-capital-S, but never without Carnival. It would be like living with our arms and legs lopped off. Carnival is an integral part of us. Is there any other city in the world that would spend half a million dollars every year on a dozen parades and fifty balls? Is there any other city where a man on a float would toss out a pearl necklace and let a crowd scramble for it? Is there any other city in the world where all the most substantial citizens go capering around in costume, and surround the huge sums they spend with secrecy instead of getting credit for them, and ride in buggies when they're too old to get on horses, and even die on the job sometimes, because they aren't willing to miss a trick? Is there——"

"Barbara, I think the first floats are coming. Let's look."

Patty was right. Rex, in all his glory, was swinging into sight. His glittering throne was surmounted by a huge crown. His sceptre shone in the sun. His salutations took an extravagant form. His float was a gleaming pyramid of blue and gold. Immediately behind him came the title car, covered with masses of fluffy pink clouds and adorned with multicolored stars and a crescent moon which announced "Gems from the Arabian Nights" as the theme of the procession. Then twenty of Scheherazade's immortal stories were magnificently brought to life. Hassan opened the forbidden door and saw the white "Bird Damsels" winging about a secret garden and standing in feathered loveliness beside crystal fountains. "The Kingdoms and the People of the Sea," described by Queen Gulnare to King Bedar, were embodied in mermaids swimming idly among coral reefs and strands of seaweed. "The City of Enchanters," shining above its battlements, was reached by a wide stairway at the summit of a winding path bordered by onyx-like stones. On and on they came, float after float, majestically progressing to the swelling sound of music and towering above the tumultuous maskers who thronged the banquettes: harlequins, pierrots, dominos, clowns, skeletons, scarecrows, gigantic rabbits, miniature elephants, houris, ballet dancers, midgets, giants, dragons and all the motley rout, shoving each other about, yelling above each other's outcry, snatching for baubles over each other's head, dancing with each other, kissing each other, cursing each other—the crowds of Mardi Gras——

"Well, I think that was the most superb show we *ever* had!" Barbara spoke triumphantly. The procession which had just passed had been more than a spectacle; it had been a vindication. "Isn't that a symbol of the everlasting human need for release and the everlasting human urge towards a make-believe? We couldn't stand life as it is, if we didn't escape from its serious side once in a while. Carnival is humanity at play, life in a mask— You understand what I was trying to say, now, don't you, Patty?"

"Oh, yes, I understood the first time. But I can't help wondering—can we always escape? Is there always a release? Of course we like to pretend there is, but——"

"Patty darling, you always were a funny little sobersides. And now that you're a dignified young matron——"

"Now that I'm a dignified young matron, I'm going to see if my husband's free to take me home. I've enjoyed seeing the parade very much. But since it's over——"

"Aren't you coming to the ball tonight?"

"Yes, indeed. I wouldn't miss saluting Clarinda in all her glory, when the Courts of Rex and Comus meet. But I think I'd like to rest a little while first, and—and recover. This was overpowering, sort of, don't you think so?"

"No, I thought it was grand. Well, I'll see you in the call-out section. And at the Queen's supper afterwards."

"I'll be in the call-out section. I'm not so sure about the Queen's supper. That does last until all hours, you know."

"But, Patty, you mustn't miss that! Of all things!"

Mrs. Forrestal shared Barbara's viewpoint about the number of festivities her daughter quietly eliminated from her schedule. Patty had taken it for granted that her mother would be very pleased about the baby. She suffered the first real pangs since her marriage when she found that, on the contrary, Mrs. Forrestal was indignant.

"So *that's* why you've stayed in the country all this time and why you're going around in such a halfhearted way now! And next winter you'll be tied down, probably nursing——"

"I hope so. Dr. Beal thinks there's every reason to believe I'll be able to. But, Mother, the reason I stayed in the country was because I love it. And I'm not doing things in a halfhearted way now. I'm having a grand time."

"I don't see how you can say that. You've been to so few parties that probably people will think you haven't been invited to any others. The feeling about Evelyn Baird hasn't died down yet, by any means. It wouldn't be surprising if Drew were more or less ostracized."

Patty looked at her mother levelly, without answering. Mrs. Forrestal should have been warned, but she was not. She went rushing on.

"Supposing the baby came early?"

"I don't see any reason why it should. I'm in very good condition and I'm not taking any foolish chances by getting overtired, as I might, if I did all the things you want me to. But even if it did, there are all kinds of ways of taking care of premature babies nowadays."

"I wasn't talking about having it get along all right. I was talking about what people would say."

"What they would *say?*"

"Nobody ever believes a baby is really premature if it's born before its parents have been married nine months. You must realize that. And you haven't any time at all to spare, from what you've told me."

Patty rose and walked out of the room and then out of the house without answering her mother. Drew knew, when he came home that evening, that something had happened to upset her, because she was so unusually silent, though her manner towards him seemed especially fond. But she had almost nothing to say about her latest call at the raised cottage, and she stubbornly refused to go back there for another. In the end, Drew, himself, extracted a somewhat expurgated account from Mrs. Forrestal as to what had happened, and he spoke his mind to his mother-in-law freely. But he did not venture to talk to Patty about it. He had discovered that the rare anger of a naturally self-controlled girl was far more lasting than the habitual raging of a shrew.

His own mother's reception of the news was very different, and this Patty did pass on to him, partly in the form of comments and partly in the form of questions. Anna Breckenridge was pleased, but she qualified her expressions of pleasure with words of warning.

"Drew's very like his father in some ways, Patty. Don't let him take advantage of you because you're young and inexperienced."

"Take advantage?" Patty inquired more coldly than she had ever spoken to her mother-in-law before.

"His father wanted to have a large family. I'm afraid he does, too."

"Afraid?" inquired Patty, still more coldly.

"I hope you wouldn't consent to having a baby every year or so."

"There isn't any question of 'consenting.' I think the inference is revolting. Drew and I are married to each other and we're in love with each other. What's more, we're both perfectly normal and healthy and we're living together the way it's natural for us both to want to live under all those circumstances. We're going to keep on living that way, as long as we can. So I suppose I will have a baby every year or so, unless Drew has to go to war. It would be natural if we did, wouldn't it? This baby came along because we loved each other so much. And I should think others would come along for the same reason. I hope so, anyway. I think an only child is a tragedy. Suppose Drew had died, as well as his father. You'd have been entirely alone in the world."

"Yes, I'd have been entirely alone in the world."

There was a strange break in Anna's voice. Her daughter-in-law knew that, as it was, she had been very much alone in the world. Patty was sorry she had spoken with such coldness and such vehemence.

"Well, you won't ever be alone any more," she said cheerfully. "Look how Drew and I have kept overrunning this house all winter! And next year we'll be bringing the baby with us. And the year after that, as you say, there'll probably be another. Little Anna, after little Ken, unless Anna comes first. We're going to call the baby Ken, if it's a boy; did Drew tell you? I think that'll be an awfully cute nickname for him, don't you?"

Drew found out about this conversation later on, because Patty referred, tactfully and without insistence, to his parents' estrangement.

"You said, that first day we went to Splendida, that someday you'd tell me more about it—that there was more you wanted to tell me. You said something about a memorandum."

"I do want to tell you more someday. But I don't know where the memorandum is, just now."

"Another lavender lie, Drew?"

He went to his desk, unlocked a drawer, and drew a sheaf of papers from it. Most of them were covered with random notes which had no connection with each other and no formal beginning or ending. There was nothing like a consecutive diary. But some of the notes were dated. One of them was headed, "Splendida Plantation, March 8, 1913." He handed it to Patty silently.

"I could see that Anna was very much impressed with the first sight of Splendida," Patty read. "And I am thankful that at last she has seen something of mine at which she does not look contemptuously. But she did not wait for me to show it to her myself. She rushed on into the house ahead of me, and I followed with Drew, very slowly, because he could manage the steps going up to the portico only one at a time. He was completely overawed, and I wasn't sorry to have him to myself while I explained to him that this was our home, that someday he would direct it to suit himself, and that eventually he would bring his wife to it. Because, of course, Drew must marry in course of time, though I pray that he will not do so too young. But there must be a suitable chatelaine for Splendida and a mother for future Breckenridges. Drew will not have a solitary son, like my father and me, if my hopes for him come true, but a big brood of happy, healthy youngsters. Anna will 'provide' for him, so his heritage will be safe financially; he will have greater freedom and greater authority than I have ever known. But he will have greater happiness, too, for I will give him a groundwork that will mean more to him than his mother's fortune. And his wife will be no fragile girl who cannot survive childbirth, and no unsexed athlete who will not accept abundant maternity."

"Thank you, Drew," Patty said, giving the paper back to him again. "I understand now why you said your father would be pleased with our marriage. Because I can see I really am the sort of girl he hoped you'd marry. I haven't any money of my own to make complications and I'm not fragile, and I'm certainly not unsexed." She laughed so gleefully that Drew could not help smiling, too; he had refrained from showing her the memorandum, because he had feared it might make her nervous, but it was evident that it had done nothing of the sort. "It's very nice to realize that I'm such an honest-to-goodness female, isn't it? And it's useful to me to know why your mother's been so unhappy and so lonely. I hope I won't make any of the same mistakes she did, and I'll try to help her forget hers. Did you really think it would upset me to see that memorandum? After all the gory details Jezebel delights in? And even after hearing Mrs. Cutler run on? Did you know that Louisiana has the highest maternal death rate of any state in the Union, Drew? And the highest infant mortality rate, too? Well, apparently it has. If I'd let statistics prey on my mind, I'd be practically sure already that Ken and I were both doomed. And of course we're not. But I think we've stayed in New Orleans long enough. I'm getting sort of fed up on all this obstetrical conversation. I can tell Jezebel to stop when she begins to bore me instead of intriguing me, but I can't very well do that with Mrs. Cutler or your mother." Patty did not add, "or my mother," but he knew that was uppermost in her mind, that she was still very angry with Mrs. Forrestal, and that she wanted to get away before she displayed this anger or the cause of it to anyone else. "Let's go home, Drew. Let's go to Splendida, where we can be by ourselves and talk about what we want to and do what we want to."

Drew had agreed not to say anything more about leaving Splendida until the time for the spring rains approached. But in March he insisted that they should go to New Orleans and stay at least through May, and he announced emphatically that he would prefer to stay there until after the baby was born. No matter what Patty or anyone else said, he did not like leaving her for twelve hours at a time, and he did not want her so far away from her doctor.

"All right. You've been very sweet, Drew, about letting me have my way, up to now. I think it's time for me to let you have your way. At least partly."

"What do you mean, partly?"

"I think we ought to stay in New Orleans from now on, because that's what you want to do. But I think we ought to live in the shotgun house, because that's what I want to do."

"Good God, Patty! You haven't mentioned the shotgun house in months. I thought you'd forgotten all about it."

"I really have a very good memory. And a very strong will. Perhaps you didn't realize about the memory. But you ought to have realized about the will. You had a pretty stiff warning of what that was like, before you married me."

"You don't really want to go and live in that shabby little house, Patty."

"You tried to tell me I didn't really know what I wanted when I said I was determined to be engaged. If I'd listened to you, I wouldn't have a husband; I wouldn't be expecting a baby."

"Patty, I don't know what on earth to do with you."

"Why, just what you have been doing, right along. Loving me. More and more all the time."

That was unanswerable, like so many of the things she said. He did love her more and more all the time. It was increasingly revealed to him that he could no more compare the deep and intense feeling he had for her now to that primary passion of possession, which he had once believed constituted the ultimate in fulfillment, than he could compare that to the first impulse which had drawn him to her because she was young and sweet and guileless and he was sick of sophistication and artifice and covetousness. And she asked for so little, while she gave so much! Surely, if there were any whim of hers which he could gratify, he could do no less.

"Very well," he said. "I don't even know what sort of order the place is in. I haven't been near it in a long time. But I'll go and see."

"That's sweet of you, Drew. You don't mind if we stay with your mother while we're getting it in order, do you? Because I'd like to go and watch, and make a few suggestions, perhaps."

"You may make suggestions. But I'm going to drive a bargain. If we go to the shotgun house, we're going to stay there. No driving back and forth to Splendida!"

"But why not? It'll be so beautiful here in the spring. I want to see the clover and the thrift and all the other lovely things you've told me about. And week ends you won't be working."

"Yes, I shall, Patty. I've got to work like a dog on that subdivision. Because, if I should be called out, Braggio would be left in the lurch unless we were a good deal further along than we are now. He's such a decent fellow I can't let him down. And I think I've got an idea for an adaptation of those long low white houses in Abbeville, with the pierced woodwork on the galleries, that will work out just as well as the Breaux Bridge cottages did. They'd be two-family houses, too, only instead of having the garçonnière supply the duplex, on the second story, these would be built all on one floor, with two entrances." He took a pencil and began to sketch, while she watched him admiringly. "Raoul's going to help me out on these. I'm going through a number of them that belong to friends of his. You don't mind if I leave you long enough to go to Abbeville, do you, while we're staying with Mother at the Prytania Street house? It's not just a question of letting Braggio down. These adaptations mark a real step forward in my work. Besides, as you know, we need the money."

"Of course I don't mind having you go to Abbeville, or anywhere else you think you need to. But couldn't we go to Splendida together once a month or so?"

"The roads are pretty rough, Patty—that last stretch between there and Donaldsonville. I'd be a good deal happier if you weren't jolting over them."

She did not say anything more on the subject to Drew, but she did refer it to Dr. Beal the next time she went to his office. He looked at her rather oddly, and then he spoke to her, as he was so apt to do, in a friendly rather than a professional way.

"I'll tell you the truth, Patty. I really don't believe it would hurt you in the least to ride over that road. But if Drew thinks it might, you may as well relieve his mind of that worry. Don't you agree with me? After all, he's been pretty lenient about everything you've wanted to do so far, and at the same time you've proved to him and to everyone else that extreme youth and common sense aren't incompatible. You don't want to break your record, or tempt him to, at this stage."

"No, but if the river should rise, and I should never see Splendida again——"

"Isn't that the chance you'd rather take, Patty, than the chance of hurting Drew? After all, as I understand it, there does have to be a last time. And if this winter was as wholly happy as you've led me to believe——"

"You do make me feel like an ungrateful wretch, Dr. Beal, when you talk to me like that."

"I don't mean to. But I don't want to see you go back on your own high standard, either."

She sat very still, as she was so apt to do when she was turning some important question over in her mind. When she spoke, there was a pleading note in her gravity.

"I couldn't bargain with you, could I, Dr. Beal, the way Drew's bargained with me? That is, if I promised I wouldn't badger him about going to Splendida, would you promise me something, too?"

"I will if I can, Patty."

"Promise me you won't tell Drew if I have a hard time when the baby's born. Because I'm afraid, if he hears I have, that afterwards *he*'d be afraid. Then there'd be a change in the way he showed his love towards me. And I couldn't bear that. I want everything to be the way it was when we were first married—the way it is still. I'm very selfish in asking you to promise, Dr. Beal. Because it wouldn't matter if I had a hard time having babies. But it would matter if anything separated me from Drew."

New Orleans had not stopped talking about the singularity of Patty Forrestal's choice in going to live in a shotgun house on Kerlerec Street, when it began to chatter about the extraordinary prospect of seeing and hearing Stella Fontaine in grand opera. The "Met" was slated for a three-day "season" late in April, and Stella was scheduled to appear in *Manon*. This was not by any means the result of luck; by a curious coincidence, she had "made good" in much the same way as her idol, Mary Garden. After twice singing the small part of Irma in *Louise*, she had been preparing to sing it a third time,

when the prima donna had suddenly been taken ill and her
understudy summoned without a moment's warning. Stella
said afterwards that she had literally been shoved onto the
stage, in order to get there in time; but the enormous audience, at least, had no inkling of any haste or confusion
on her part. Cheated of the anticipated treat in hearing a
great singer, it had begun by trying, with halfhearted courtesy, not to make her substitute suffer for its own disappointment. But by the end of the second act, the applause was no
longer polite, it was enthusiastic; when the performance was
over, it took the form of an ovation. Stella had brought to
the part a warmth and a freshness which even the great star's
superb technique could not surpass in effectiveness. What was
more, she had given it an illusion of reality which the great
star had never succeeded in creating. Her contract for
the coming year had been signed within the next week, and
after that there were no more "impeccable maids" or "sympathetic friends" in her repertoire. The coveted parts of
Musetta and Micaela came to her almost automatically;
and now for the spring tour, she was to have a title role, not
as an understudy but in her own right.

The Crescent City prepared to pay her homage with an
exuberance which had marked the reception of no singer
since the fabled days of Jenny Lind. Stella was one of its
own daughters, one of its own Carnival Queens; lavishly as
it was accustomed to entertain, no routine tribute would
suffice in this case. When the special train pulled in at the
L & N Station, there was a brass band from Tulane, there
were delegations with huge sheaves of flowers, there were
photographers and reporters, there were groups from the
Junior League and the Debutantes' Club, there were all
the old servants of the Fontaine family and the Breckenridge
family, and the others with whom Stella had been most closely
associated. Even under Drew's capable escort and with the
brisk assistance of a delighted detachment of police, she had
great difficulty in getting through the crowd to the car which
was to take her to the "big" Breckenridge house; and when
she was installed there, with Agnes, her New York maid, in
quarters for the redecorating of which Anna and Patty had
made her visit a pleasant pretext, it was impossible for her
to snatch a moment to herself unless Agnes stood guard at
the door and firmly declined to make any exception to the
rule of "no telephone calls." The confusion and excitement
which had preceded Patty's wedding were trifling, compared

to the commotion which reigned now. But this time Stella was not exhausted by the hubbub, as she had been before; she was exhilarated and enchanted. Nothing that had happened to her so far had given her such a sense of vindication and triumph, not even her first appearance as Louise, in Paris, not even her precipitate assumption of the same rôle in New York.

As she was singing at only one performance, on the second evening of the "season," there was ample time for all the scheduled entertainments. There was an alfresco luncheon under the giant live oak at the country club, given by Clarinda and Amelina Darcoa, who succeeded in making all their friends green with envy because they had thought of inviting Stella by wire before the others did and because this party was the first at which she appeared after her triumphal return. There was a large dinner at Antoine's, to which the most outstanding state and city functionaries, from the Governor and the Mayor down, gave an official touch by their presence that was quite as pleasing to Stella as the air of importance which was enhanced by the importunities of numerous uninvited guests who crowded around the entrance to the private dining room, craning their necks to get a glimpse of the star and clamoring for autographs. There was also a smaller but even swankier dinner at the "big" Breckenridge house, at which Drew and Patty acted as host and hostess at one table, and Anna and Gail at another. There were other entertainments as well, but these were outstanding, and of the three, the one which the Breckenridges gave, and which brought Stella's visit to a close, was the most memorable of all, because it marked the only occasion on which she consented to sing in private.

It was Patty who persuaded her. All through dinner, Stella, who was sitting at Drew's right and finding him in unusually good form, had, nevertheless, found her attention as well as her gaze wandering to the other end of the table, where Patty sat enthroned in an intricately carved, high-back chair, upholstered in old brocade. "Enthroned" was the right word, Stella thought, for Patty had begun to reveal regnant qualities; Stella had never seen a well-schooled Carnival Queen who emanated more dignity and more graciousness. Her figure was a little fuller than it had been, but anyone uninformed of her condition would not have guessed it; her flowing blue dress was skillfully and exquisitely cut, and though it had the simplicity and restraint of everything

Patty wore in company, it also had the intrinsic elegance achieved only by very fine French dressmakers. It made the more elaborate and extreme dresses at the table, including Stella's own, look tawdry and showy by comparison. Dresses like that cost a great deal of money, as Stella was well aware; apparently, Drew was not stinting Patty on her wardrobe, wherever else he might be economizing; and the little string of pearls she was wearing had a lovely luster, too. But it was her face and her manner, even more than her clothes and her ornaments, that were so arresting to Stella. There was a bloom about her that Stella had never seen before and a radiance more marked than that she had noticed after Patty was assured of Drew's love, but before their marriage. Suddenly Stella knew what had caused this: it did not come from any material source but from her happiness with her husband and her anticipated joy in her child. This was the first time Stella had seen Patty sitting at the head of Drew's table, and involuntarily her thoughts flew back to the first time she, herself, had acted as hostess for Raoul at De la Houssaye's Restaurant in New Iberia. No setting and no circumstances could have been more different than those and the present ones, and yet, she had felt the same pride that Patty was revealing now, and Raoul had looked at her with the same light in his eyes as the light in Drew's when he looked at Patty. Stella remembered what Raoul had said to her afterwards: "I knew, when I saw you sitting at that table, with all those men around you, that it couldn't be the way I planned it at first. Because I cared too much, because I was too proud of you, because you were too grand a person. You weren't just the girl I was out to get any longer. You were my partner and my mate and my good angel, all in one."

What was there, she wondered, that would make a man feel that way, simply because he saw a girl sitting opposite him at a table, sharing in the hospitality he was showing his friends? It seemed a simple and natural thing for her to do, if she loved him. Perhaps it was just because it was so simple and natural, and because she and Raoul had strayed so far from simple, natural things, that estrangement and strife had come between them. Perhaps there was no real reason why she, herself, should not have had, long ago, that bloom which beatified Patty. She was almost on the point of asking Drew what he thought, for she and Drew were very good friends again. She could talk to him about anything, just as she had during that brief but blessed period after she fell in love with Raoul and before he became involved with Evelyn. Drew, too, had gained immeasurably in stature and dignity since she had last seen him; he was worthy of confidence from any woman. He was not an attractive wastrel and an irresistible philanderer any more; without losing any of his charm, he had grown distinguished; he had become a man of parts and of substance. He had done wonders, in every way, for Patty, but Patty had also done wonders for him. Was it not conceivable that she, herself, and Raoul might also have done wonders for each other, if they had gone forward together instead of taking separate roads? The unwelcome question and the inevitable answer suddenly corroded Stella's triumph. She was sorry she was a star; she was sorry she was a feted guest. She would have given anything in the world to jump into a car and tear, at breakneck speed, down to Abbeville and ask Raoul to marry her that very night. But Raoul was not in Abbeville any more; he was in Washington. And he was not in love with her any more; he was in love with Clarinda.

Patty was giving the signal to rise from the table. Louis was standing behind her, drawing out her chair with respect, and her guests were clustering around her as she led the way into the drawing room, telling her how delightful the dinner had been. The other table, which had been laid in the library, had broken up a little sooner; Anna Breckenridge was already waiting for her daughter-in-law to help her serve the coffee. Obviously, there was great harmony between the two, and great affection. Stella saw Patty whisper to her mother-in-law as if consulting her, before she crossed the room again, and saw Anna Breckenridge nod her approval. Then Patty came over to Stella, herself, in her winsome, unassuming way.

"We're all so delighted and so honored in having you with us, Stella," she said, "that we wouldn't impose on you for the world. But if you feel you could sing for us, just once, you know it would be a privilege to hear you, that we would treasure always."

"Of course I will. What do you want me to sing?"

"Well, of course we haven't heard you in *La Bohème* or *Carmen*. If you would sing Musetta's waltz or Micaela's prayer——"

She sang them both, unaffectedly and with great artistry. She was an excellent actress as well as an accomplished singer. She gave gaiety to Musetta, appeal to Micaela. And because there was nothing grudging in her performance, Patty ventured to ask if she would not go on.

"Of course we all heard you in *Manon* last night, Stella. But could you sing *A Paris* or *On l'appelle Manon, elle eut seize ans* for us again?"

"You're forgetting that those are both duets, Patty dear. But I'll sing you another song about a sixteen-year-old girl, if you like. I found it in the collection of my aunt's music, when I was clearing out my house after I sold it."

For a moment she sat striking stray chords, as if she were hesitating for the first time. Then suddenly she sang:

> *"Je suis la délaissée*
> *Qui pleure nuit et jour,*
> *Celui qui m'a trompée*
> *Etait mon seul amour.*
>
> *J'avais seize ans à peine,*
> *Belle comme une fleur.*
> *Il a fallu qu'il vienne*
> *Empoisonner mon coeur."*

A silence followed her singing, that was more eloquent than any applause. When it was finally shattered, another appeal came with it.

"It's a shame to impose on you, Stella, especially after that. But you know we haven't heard your greatest song; we can't visualize you as Louise. If you will just sing *Depuis le jour où je me suis donnée*, we won't importune you any more."

For a moment she did not move from the piano. Then, without abruptness, without ungraciousness, she shut it and rose.

"I'm sorry," she said in a strange voice. "I never sang that but once, except on the stage or at rehearsal. It happened to be a rather special time, that meant a great deal to me. I'll sing anything for you that you like, except that, after I have rested my voice a little. But that's a song I'm never going to sing, from affection, again."

Stella had not remained in New Orleans or returned there. When the spring tour of the "Met" was over, she had gone to spend the summer in Natchez. Now that she was completely alone, she told Patty, in her pleasant bread-and-butter letter, she was determined to put an end to the unnatural estrangement between herself and her mother. Later she wrote that her stepfather had received her with such kindness and that the youngsters were all so lovable, she was sorry she had not gone there immediately after her grandmother's death. It would have saved her from a desolate and solitary summer. She was thankful to think there would be no more of those, and she was finding it much easier to fit into her mother's pattern of life than she had expected. There was a good deal along these same lines, all of it very reassuring to Patty; but Stella never referred to the episode at the dinner, and about this Patty did continue to worry.

Mrs. Forrestal pressed her daughter a number of times for an explanation of Stella's extraordinary conduct, and Patty irritated her mother very much by saying sincerely that she had none to give, adding that she was very, very sorry that inadvertently she had said something which made Stella unhappy. Mrs. Forrestal was greatly irritated. She could not help believing that Patty might have told her something, if she had really wanted to. Mrs. Forrestal had enjoyed Stella's stay in New Orleans very much, not only because she had gone to all the operas and all the parties but also because Patty and Drew had stayed at the big house instead of the shotgun house most of the time, and she was relieved, as she put it, to see them living like white folks again. When they returned to Kerleric Street, after the exigencies of entertaining a celebrity were over, her habitual annoyance increased, and it increased still further when, early in July, the official announcement was made that no more men over twenty-eight would be called out and Drew immediately applied for a commission in the Naval Reserve.

"I should think he would be satisfied to let well enough alone," she said to Patty. "I thought it was a very queer, quixotic idea of his to insist on deferring your wedding so that he could register as an unmarried man. I have lived with my heart in my mouth, all winter, wondering what would happen to you if his number were called. Here you are only eighteen years old now and pregnant and practically penniless——"

Patty burst out laughing. "You have funny ideas what it means to be practically penniless, Mother," she said. "Or else I've given you a wrong impression somehow. I can't begin to spend my allowance from Drew. I mean the personal allowance. I have one to run the house on, too, and I don't spend half of that either. I'm putting money in the savings bank all the time. Drew won't take it back after he has once given it to me. I think he had queer ideas about money, too, before we were married. Because he told me we'd have to be very economical, and what he calls economical seems like the wildest kind of extravagance to me. Apparently, he never heard of anyone living on less than several thousand a month. At least, not anyone he knew well enough so that he was familiar with their financial circumstances. He's simply amazed to find you can be very comfortable on a few hundred. He'd have called that a mere pittance, until I told her it was rich, for most people."

"But if he does have that much money left, after all, what on earth is he doing with it?"

"I haven't asked him, Mother. But I think, from something he said, that he's putting part of it into life insurance, in my name. I don't like to talk about that. So he hasn't said much."

"I should think you'd be very glad to talk about it. Especially now that he's gone into the Navy."

"It's only the Naval Reserve. He heard there were architects needed for special construction work, right here in New Orleans. And he hasn't got his commission yet. I don't see why you say 'especially' the Navy."

"Well, if he gets into the Navy, sooner or later he'll go to sea. And it's all very well to say lightning never strikes twice in the same place, but I believe it does. Over and over again. Perhaps you've forgotten that Drew's grandfather was drowned and his father, too. Perhaps——"

"No, Mother, I haven't forgotten. I've thought of it a good many times. But I don't think Drew has. Not in the way you mean. And even if he had, I don't believe it would have made any difference. If he felt the Naval Reserve was the place he could be the most useful, he'd have tried out for it, anyway. And I wouldn't have said anything to stop him."

Drew was working long hours that summer, even without the awaited commission in the Naval Reserve. The week ends were all devoured by work, as he had predicted, and on weekdays dinner was served later and later at the shotgun house in an effort to meet his convenience. At that, he often telephoned around five that he could not get home for it—that Patty was to have it without him. These protracted absences gave Mrs. Forrestal more opportunities for uninterrupted conferences with her daughter than Patty, herself, would have sought, and she was visiting expansively when one such message came through. She raised her eyebrows questioningly.

"Does this happen often, Patty?"

"Yes. Two or three times a week. I don't see how he stands it. Because he gets up awfully early, too."

"I don't see how *you* stand it."

Mrs. Forrestal had never succeeded in learning anything from experience. The fact that her daughter had walked out of her house once, earlier in the winter, and stayed out of town for weeks, rather than see her, did not warn her now. Patty, who had learned to knit and who was taking great delight in the work, spread the small sweater she was making out on her lap and looked at it admiringly.

"Stand what?" she said at last. "I'm not working sixteen hours a day, like Drew. I'm not working at all. I'm so lazy I'm ashamed of myself. Don't you think this is a darling sweater, Mother?"

"I wasn't speaking of work when I asked you how you stood it. I was speaking of the way you're being neglected. Of course, it was to be expected, all things considered. But the whole town's talking about it."

Patty laughed. Though it was true she believed lightning could strike more than once in the same place, she did not permit her mind to dwell on this thought, or even to entertain it, very often. She was so happy that she did not want to quarrel with anyone, and she was determined not to quarrel with her mother again, if she could help it.

"Mother, if I listened to you, I'd begin to believe that no one in New Orleans ever talked about anyone but Drew and me. It makes me feel terribly important."

"Have you ever telephoned his office to see if he really is there in the evening?"

"No, Mother, I never have. Of course I wouldn't, anyway. But I know he isn't always there. I know he has lots of business out of town. He's been to Abbeville about the model for his new houses two or three times. And he's in Baton Rouge a good deal."

"On politics?"

"Why, no, I don't think so. Drew's never been especially interested in politics. He's very skeptical about reforms. And he has some reason to be, hasn't he? Mrs. Cutler was here just the other day, and she kept complaining about how many of the Jones reforms haven't been made yet."

"But if he doesn't go to Baton Rouge on political business, what *does* he go for?"

"I don't know, Mother. That's another thing I haven't asked him. He's too tired to talk to me when he comes in at night, and I'm too sleepy to talk to him when he leaves in the morning. He'll tell me sooner or later. And it's ever so much more fun to have a man tell you something because he feels like doing it than because you've dragged it out of him. Didn't you ever find that out?"

"You're not inferring, are you, Patty, that I used to drag things out of your father?"

"Why, no," Patty said again. "But I did think, sometimes, that father acted as if he were dying to give you a surprise of some sort, and that you acted as if you wouldn't let him. I used to wonder why you didn't at least pretend to be surprised, it would have pleased him so much. But I suppose you knew best."

Patty's eyes strayed idly from the little sweater on her lap to the small clock on the mantelpiece. Guarded as the glance was, her mother caught it.

"Have you an engagement, Patty? Are you expecting company?"

"Well, sort of. But it's indefinite. Don't go home yet, if you'd rather not."

"Are you looking for anyone I'd be interested in meeting?"

"Not tonight. Perhaps tomorrow night I might introduce a very charming young gentleman to you."

"You don't mean to tell me, Patty Forrestal, that you receive *gentlemen* when Drew is away?"

"But you see, Mother, I never know when Drew is going to be at home. And you said yourself you didn't see how I stood it. I have to amuse myself somehow. You'd think that was all right, anyway, wouldn't you, if I did, provided he were amusing himself somewhere else?"

"No, of course I wouldn't. I can't make you out at all, Patty. I never could. What on earth do you keep staring at that clock for?"

"I didn't know I was staring at it. But I do like to look at it. It's a pretty little clock, don't you think so? Besides, it was one of my wedding presents. Didn't you have a lot of sentiment about your wedding presents, Mother? I think you must have. You enjoyed mine so much."

"Why, yes," Mrs. Forrestal said a little vaguely. "Well, I suppose I had better be going. Your Aunt Lula said she would drop in for a little chat with me later this evening. And Richard is having Amelina to supper *again*. You'd think, in all this heat, and with everything Roberta has to do, that he'd be more considerate. Not that anyone in love ever is."

Patty saw her mother out of the house politely. Then she laughed and looked at the clock again. The next instant she was at the telephone, calling Dr. Beal.

"I'm having pains every five minutes," she announced. "Yes, for about an hour now. Before that they were further apart, just as you told me they would be. I'm all packed; I'll be ready when the ambulance gets here. And isn't it wonderful, Dr. Beal, that Drew's in Baton Rouge?"

Drew, himself, did not think that it had been, when he came in, shortly after midnight, and sensed an unnatural emptiness in the house. The shaded lights were still on in the little drawing room; the perfume of midsummer roses filled it as usual. But the ticking of Patty's pet clock sounded preternaturally loud. Drew had not expected Patty to wait up for him, for he had several times begged her not to do this, but usually he could feel her presence in the place, just the same. This time he could not, and he went hurriedly down the passageway to their bedroom. The pleasant shaded lights and pleasant perfumed flowers were here, too. But Patty was not sleeping peacefully with one arm under her golden head and the other relaxed at her side, as he loved to see her. The four-poster was also empty, and this vacancy held elements of alarm for him. She had said nothing about leaving the house when he telephoned her at five o'clock; there was no reason why she should leave it unless——

Suddenly he saw that there was a pink slip such as she used for scratch paper, pinned to his pillow. He grabbed at it and read it hastily.

Dearest Drew:

I have been having little pains all the afternoon, but I did not say anything about them when you telephoned, because Mother was here, spreading gloom as usual, and I did not want her to overhear me. Now she has gone, I'm glad to say, and the pains are coming pretty fast, so I have sent for the ambulance. I may have made a mistake to do so, because there is nothing worse about any of this so far than a bad stomach-ache, and I am more than ever convinced that many girls make a lot of fuss about nothing. If you want to, you

*might come along to the hospital after you get back from
Baton Rouge, though I'm told the problem of expectant fathers with their first babies is considered the most troublesome with which the staff has to deal, so probably you won't
be very warmly welcomed there. Why not wait until tomorrow morning? By that time Ken and I ought to be all fancied
up ready for you.*

With all my love,
Patty.

Drew thrust the pink slip into his pocket, tore out of the
silent house, and started his car. What a fool, what an unmitigated fool, he had been to leave her! He had banked on
the leeway of another week, and he was trying to make every
minute count in his work; but he might have known that the
coming confinement could not be timed to a minute; he
should have remembered that no accomplishment in the
world could atone for his absence on a night like this. It was
horrible to think that Patty had been in pain for hours and
hours, even before she scribbled the little note, and that there
had been no one with her but two colored servants when she
summoned the ambulance herself and left the house all
alone. And that was about six, while now it was nearly one.
Anything might have happened in the meantime. Anything
probably had. Good God, were there ever any green lights
on this street? Why in hell hadn't he thought of some route
which would have got him to the hospital more quickly?

The receptionist at the information desk surveyed him
with a calmness which would have been disdainful if it had
not been so wholly impersonal. This was Mr. Andrew Breck-
enbridge? Oh, yes. Well, she thought Mrs. Breckenridge had
come in sometime during the late afternoon, but she was not
sure, because she, herself, had come in on the night shift.
She would have to look it up in the files. Yes, that was right.
Mrs. Breckenridge had room 412. She would call the supervisor of the fourth floor. The supervisor said Mrs. Breckenridge was not in her room any longer. Why, in the delivery
room, of course. No, she could not say how long before, or
how long it would still be. Why, no, of course he could not
speak to Dr. Beal. Naturally, Dr. Beal was in the delivery
room, also. What? Oh, would Mr. Breckenridge please take
the 'phone himself? Dr. Beal would speak to him, after all——

"Hello there, Drew. We made good connections. It's all
over."

"All over!" Drew echoed, terror stabbing him through and through like a sharp knife.

"Easy there. Sorry I scared you. I should have said, 'congratulations!' You've got the traditional fine nine-pound boy."

"Well, for God's sake, tell me what's happened to Patty!"

"Why, nothing's happened to her. Everything's been perfectly normal. Anyone but an excited husband would know it couldn't help being, with that girl. Labor a little on the long side, but after all, this is her first baby. The next time she'll take it very quickly and easily. Yes, come up if you like. You'll have to wait in the reception room a few minutes. But then you can go in and see her."

The few minutes seemed to stretch into interminable hours. Drew sat in the dreary little room, thinking of the newborn baby, whose very being was not only the product of his own passion and the proof of his own manhood but his pledge to posterity. From the very first, Patty had understood his yearning for a child and the overwhelming reason for it. Now, through her, the yearning was appeased; the challenge of the future had been met. A great peace suddenly filled Drew's soul, a feeling of infinite confidence and hope. His son, Andrew Breckenridge, the fourth of the name. Who would be a better man than his father, or any of his forebears, not because of them, but because of his mother——

"Well, Drew. You may come in now if you like. Don't stay but a minute, though. Remember Patty's pretty tired. And don't be shocked by her looks. There's not much color in her face yet. After you've seen her, I'll take you down to the nursery and you can have a peek at the most wonderful baby in the world—through glass. You'll get more satisfaction out of him later on."

Dr. Beal spoke cheerily. The nurse at his elbow, starched and impersonal like the receptionist downstairs, bowed to him formally and led the way through an endless passage permeated with the inescapable smell of disinfectants. Her rubber-soled shoes made no sound on the linoleum, but her skirts crackled as she walked. She went on and on. At last she stopped outside a door that was closed instead of being merely screened, and opened it. Then she stood back and Drew went through it alone.

There was so little light in the room that he could see almost nothing at first. But gradually white shapes detached themselves vaguely from dark shadows: a white chest of some sort, a white-clad figure seated in a white chair beside a white

bed on which another white figure was lying. The seated
figure was only another nurse. She was a nonentity, a super-
fluity. But the supine figure was his wife, the mother of his
child. The color was drained from her face, because the
blood had been drained from her body. It was unbearable
that she should have been brought to this pallor and this pros-
tration because of him.

She stirred, ever so slightly, and opened her eyes. His own
were more accustomed to the light now; he could see hers, as
she looked at him, and the clarity and candor that still shone
from their depths. She recognized him and caught her breath.
It was the same ecstatic intake that he had heard when he
first kissed her and, on their wedding night, when she had
yielded herself up so utterly. He saw her smile, the little
dimple beside her mouth suddenly deepening.

"Drew," she whispered. "Have you seen him yet? He's
perfectly beautiful. I know now what I was born for myself,
besides loving you. It was so I could have babies."

The baby, everyone said, was "all Breckenridge." This
meant, primarily, that he had dark hair, fine color and a
strong body, and that his eyes were not merely "kitten blue,"
like most babies', but that, while he was unbelievably young,
they began to show the sparkling quality which had characterized Andy's and Breck's and which still characterized
Drew's. He also began to grin infectiously, as Andy and
Breck had grinned and as Drew still did, at a period in his
life when babies were theoretically too young to smile. Incidentally, it meant that he was demanding and insistent, from
the beginning, that his appetite was insatiable, and that he
grew and gained with a total disregard for statistics and
schedules. Dr. Beal, scrutinizing the chart which reported
his weight, told Patty that he would prefer to have her stay
an extra week in the hospital and that, when she went back
to the shotgun house, he would expect her to do nothing
more active than move from her bed to an easy chair and
back again, for several weeks more.

"But, Dr. Beal, when am I ever going to get back to
Splendida, at this rate?"

"Soon enough, soon enough! I'm not going to have you
climbing over stairs, or tramping over acres, for a while yet,
young lady, or let you go where I can't keep my watchful
eye on you. When a baby tries to devour his mother alive,
the way this one's doing, someone's got to see to it that he

doesn't succeed too well. You're using up a lot of strength, nursing him."

"I don't know any better way of using it."

"Nor I. But, just the same, it means you haven't got any left over. You've been a Trojan so far, Patty. I'm going to urge you again not to go back on your own standard."

"I'll try not to. But you wouldn't think I was really feminine, would you, if I didn't fuss once in a while?"

Occasionally she said much the same thing, in the same jesting way, to Drew. But, as a matter of fact, in spite of her longing for Splendida, she was not restless, either during her prolonged stay at the hospital or in the weeks at the shotgun house that followed. She took an ingenuous enjoyment, not only out of her flowers and her visitors but out of the mere process of adapting herself to baths in bed, a specialized diet and a regular routine of nursing and resting and nursing again. She had pronounced the nightgowns she wore at Splendida "too Grecian" for the hospital and had invested in a new and limitless supply, somewhat less revealing but very lacy and dainty. Her pride in her baby was prodigious, and she manoeuvred to make guests time their visits so that they could see him when he was brought from the nursery instead of "gazing at him through glass from afar," a practice for which she openly expressed her contempt.

"I wish he'd been born in the good old days when all our relatives could crowd around and rock him and kiss him as much as they felt like doing," she said to Drew on one of the occasions when she was indulging in a little feminine fussing.

"I don't," Drew answered rather shortly. He was thinking of the accouchement bed as he spoke and remembering that the days when relatives came crowding around to kiss the baby were also the days before there were anaesthetics and asepsis, when the baby's mother, if she had survived her labor, was by this time frequently suffering from childbed fever. It had been bad enough, in all conscience, as it was, that night he had come back to the shotgun house and found that Patty was not there and to be told at the hospital that "everything was all over" before he had seen her lying stricken and motionless on her narrow white bed. And yet, that had been a night when everything was "normal"—or so he had been told—when she and their child had been safeguarded by all that skill and science could do for them. If it had been the other way— He still could not bear to think of it.

"Well, won't you admit at least that you'll be glad when you

have us both at Splendida, when you and I are not separated
so much of the time any more, and when we can do what
we please with our own baby without having any prunes and
prisms saying, 'I'm very sorry, Mr. Breckenridge, but it's
better that very young infants shouldn't be handled'—'I regret
to remind you, Mr. Breckenridge, that after taking nourishment, it's usually considered wise——' "

"Yes, I'll be just as glad to be through with that phase of it
as you will. But we'll have the worst of that behind us
when I get you back to the shotgun house."

It was a very happy home-coming. Drew had put roses in
all the vases himself and had done the marketing himself, too,
so that everything Patty liked best to eat would be in the
house; he had supervised the waxing of the floors and the
washing of the windows, so that everything would be clean
and shiny the way she liked to have it. He had installed
an attic fan, too, so that she would be cool and comfortable through the rest of the summer heat, and bought various
new electrical gadgets which he thought would amuse her,
whether she actually found them convenient or not. The appreciation which she showed for his thoughtfulness was very
heart-warming; not the least of his efforts and improvements
went unnoticed or unpraised. But her attitude, rewarding as
it was, could not compare with the reward of her presence.
To have her with him again, so delightfully the same and yet
so adorably different, was the epitome of happiness.

He said nothing about Splendida, except to remark, once
or twice, that with his work as it was now, it was really more
convenient for him to be in town, knowing that after he had
told her that, Patty would say nothing more either. The commission in the Naval Reserve had come through; he had been
given the rank of lieutenant commander and was doing special designing and supervising special construction for the
Government, besides directing the greatly enlarged activities
of his own office. It was not until just before the anniversary
of their marriage that he finally asked her how she would
like to take another wedding trip. He had come in late, as
usual, and the baby was having his ten-o'clock feeding when
his father asked the question, having first bent over to kiss the
downy dark head nestled against Patty's white breast and the
other golden head that was instantly lifted in joy at his
approach.

"Another wedding trip? Why, we didn't take one before!
We just went to Splendida."

"Well, that was what I thought you might like to do this time. I bought one of those bassinets today that are built on purpose to fit in the back of cars. I think you'll like it. If you do, we can put Ken in that, and start off Saturday, anytime you say. I've got a free week end, for a wonder. The packing wouldn't be much bother for you, would it, with Louis and Félicie to help you? And when we get to the other end, of course Jezebel will be in her seventh heaven if you'll turn Ken over to her."

"I won't turn him over to anyone," Patty said jealously. The baby, still feeding voraciously, was kneading her breast with his strong little hands as he nursed, and Drew pried a tiny fist loose and thrust one of his long brown fingers between his son's soft pink ones, for the pleasure of feeling these curl confidently and closely around his own. He smiled and nodded as she spoke, thankful that her attitude had made it possible for them to enjoy their child together like this, without interference or intrusion. She had definitely declined to consider the services of a Northern nurse who had been highly recommended to her, and Drew, who had not forgotten Nana, had no regrets on this score, though neither his mother nor his mother-in-law had failed to assure him that it was unheard-of for a young matron in New Orleans to insist on taking charge of her own baby. But Félicie had proved herself as expert and as willing in the nursery as she had always been in the kitchen, and Louis was already Ken's devoted slave; all Patty's orders were faithfully carried out—all her wishes scrupulously observed—the better because she gave them herself instead of relegating them to a strange, white semiservant.

"Well, what do you think of my plan?" Drew asked again. The surfeited baby had reeled away now, the corners of his pink mouth still moist with milk, and Drew picked him up capably and tucked him into his cradle, arranging the coverings over him with a hand that was fast becoming dexterous at such tasks. "Of course, it's just as you say. But I thought it would be rather fun to celebrate our anniversary at Splendida. We might even have this world-beater of ours christened there, and call in the clans."

"I always like your ideas. Let's celebrate the anniversary by ourselves, shall we? And then call in the clans, as you put it, afterwards. If we're going to have a christening, we must send for Raoul. Remember he wanted to be godfather."

"That's so. He did. I believe he'd come down from Washington on purpose. Whom shall we have for the other one?"

"Would you like to have Gail?"

"Very much. And what about a godmother?"

"Well, if Stella could come down from New York——"

They were still discussing the details of the christening when Patty fell asleep. But she brought up the subject again, of her own accord, when they were on their way to Splendida the following Saturday. They did not leave New Orleans until early afternoon, and then they took the drive slowly, revelling in the beauty of the golden autumn day, the pungent smoke from the burning cane leaves, the sweep of sickle-shaped wings as wild doves settled on the road before them, picking up gravel. Ken, having been fed just before their departure, slept peacefully in his cot all the way. Even the jolting transfer on and off the ferry did not disturb him. He still had not stirred when they reached the last stretch of the road, which Drew had condemned as rough but which seemed to Patty smooth and pleasant as they rolled over it. She turned from the levee, at which she had been gazing with the absorption of complete satisfaction in the rediscovery of long-lost beauty, and looked from the right to the left of the road. In a minute now she would see the pillars and porticos of Splendida looming above the tangled garden against the radiant sky.

She watched with growing intensity for them to appear. There was something about Drew's stillness, as he sat beside her quietly driving the car, which seemed to mark a portentous moment. She sat quietly, too, galvanized into immobility comparable to his own. Then, as Drew had known she would, she drew in her breath before she turned once more, this time to look at him with brimming eyes.

The house which she had left six months before was gone. But above the lawns stretching out in great green expanses far behind the garden, another had risen to take its place: a house that had glowing walls and white pillars, like the old Splendida—a dwelling place, as that had been in its best days, of beauty and of light. But a house that was smaller and sturdier, a house that looked like a home a not like a palace, a house so far removed from the rapacious river that it was inconceivable this could so far change its course as to reach this secure haven and these firm hearthstones. Out of the old decadence and decay had come new progress and new soundness; out of impending ruin and loss had come enduring safety and immeasurable gain. No rottenness could ever corrode the foundations of this house. It was built to stand for all time.

CHAPTER 37

GAIL RUTLEDGE, waiting at the airport for the arrival of the *Silver Sleeper* from New York and Washington, paced back and forth with a rather troubled spirit. It had been Stella's plan for some time to take it on this particular Friday night; her schedule at the Metropolitan was now arranged in such a way that it was easier for her to be absent the first part of the following week than the latter part of that week. But Raoul Bienvenu had expected to come sooner and stay longer. A protracted debate on legislation to prevent work stoppages in defense industries held him up, however; it did not culminate in a record vote on a drastic antistrike measure until after he had intended to leave, and his change of plan had been announced to his prospective hosts only by a last-minute wire. After a general conference, they had all agreed that it would seem to attach undue importance to an insignificant coincidence if they wired back that Stella would be on the same plane. But Gail was not sure the decision had been a wise one. If those two got started, he reflected grimly, fur would fly during the entire course of the thousand-mile flight. Neither of them would get any sleep under these circumstances, and it was quite possible they might effectually prevent the other passengers from getting much, either, unless the steward took a firm hand. But it was not easy for anyone to take a firm hand with Raoul. Gail did not think either his fellow godfather or the much publicized godmother would arrive for Ken's christening in that benign frame of mind suitable for sponsors in baptism. However, there was nothing he could do about it and, after all, it was not his funeral.

The plane slid in smoothly, on time to the minute. That, at least, was something to be thankful for. The flight must have been a good one, and so a rough and trying passage had not been added to other complications. Gail was still further reassured when he saw Raoul spring out of the plane the minute the door was flung open, looking very spruce and chipper, and turn to give a helping hand to Stella, who came out more slowly after several other passengers. She was wearing a superb dark mink coat and a small cocky mink hat, and a billowing spray of lemon-colored speckled orchids was pinned to her shoulder. She had all the elegance of the traditional prima donna, with the added chic of the modern young woman whose indestructible freshness is impervious to trying night travel. She handed Raoul a small bag, which might have contained either rare cosmetics in glass bottles or valuable jewelry, or both, from the care with which she had been carrying it herself, and they came up from the runway side by side.

"Hello, Gail!" Raoul said heartily, while Stella favored her cousin with one of her customary casual kisses, leaving a small smear of vermilion on his cold cheek. "Damned white of you to meet us at this ungodly hour."

"That's nothing. I was awfully glad to do it. What kind of a trip did you have?"

"Oh, quite cozy. Stella hadn't gone to bed when I got on, and presently we discovered we were in the same section. When we recovered from our mutual surprise, we had a very stimulating conversation before we retired to the limited privacy of our respective berths."

"I didn't think it was very stimulating," Stella said rather crossly.

"Didn't you? I thought we were getting on very well before we reached the stage of general deshabille. But perhaps that was only because a sleeper plane is one of the places where you might just as well decide to be on friendly terms with your fellow passengers, because it's impossible to be deadly enemies with any degree of dignity. It doesn't matter anyway— Where do we go from here, after we've picked up our bags? Those, besides these crown jewels so trustingly confided to me, I mean."

"We can go straight on to Splendida, if you like, and you can go back to bed as soon as you get there, or take a nap this afternoon. Or Mrs. Breckenridge would be glad to have you come up to the big house. She isn't starting for Splendida herself until after an early lunch."

"What do you say, Stella?"

"I'd rather go straight on to Splendida."

"Well, it's nice to find we're agreed on something so easily. So would I. Now tell me something else: would you rather have the back seat to yourself, so you can curl up and snooze some more, or would you rather have me sit there beside you and continue our conversation where we left off at eleven last night?"

"You and Gail seem to have naps on the brain. I don't want to snooze any more. But of course if you'd rather talk to Gail——"

"Now listen. We've come down here for a christening, not for a sparring match. If I'd preferred to sit on the front seat with Gail, I'd have said so. Or rather, I'd have just climbed in there. Come on."

It was nice of Raoul to settle all these vexatious problems without involving him, Gail thought. Stella had brought six bags of various types and sizes, but uniformly swanky, for her four days' stay, and, since all these would not go into the baggage compartment and still leave any room at all for Raoul's Gladstone and briefcase, Gail soon found himself wedged in beside a hatbox, a shoe box, a dressing case, and an overnight case, not without some passing wonder as to what Stella must have paid for excess baggage. He had brought a thermos of coffee with him, the contents of which they gratefully drank before they left the parking place beside the flowering shrubbery flanking the ornate façade of the main building at the airport. Then they drove along the Lake Front and Pontchartrain Boulevard to the Air Line.

For a few minutes Stella talked in a sprightly way, mostly to Gail, putting her arms over the top of the front seat and resting her face on them. She asked him all sorts of questions about his work in the testing division of the Higgins plant, but gradually the questions came further and further apart, and finally she settled silently back. A few moments later, Raoul spoke in a warning tone to Gail.

"Take it easy, Gail. She's sound asleep. I'm going to put my arm around her, to support her as much as I can. But at that, if she got a bad jolt, it might wake her up."

Gail glanced at his rearview mirror. Stella had sunk down in a position which indicated utter exhaustion. Without Raoul's supporting arm, she certainly would have slumped forward. Either her hat had come off or Raoul, himself, had quietly removed it, so that her head would rest more easily on his shoulder; Gail suspected that the latter had been the case, for the hat was perched on Raoul's knee in a way that indicated appreciation of its value and a desire to safeguard this. Her hair, released by its removal, blew about her face in a mass of chestnut curls, as it had when she was a little girl. She looked very young and very, very tired. Even to Gail, there was something poignant and pitiful in the sight of her. He was not astonished, as he glanced back from time to time, to surprise an expression of great tenderness on Raoul's face, He drove with extreme care, saying nothing more, absorbed with conflicting thoughts. It was not until they turned into the driveway at Splendida that Raoul spoke again.

"I think I can get her out of the car and into the house without waking her. She can't weigh anything at all. From the looks of her, she must be pounds and pounds underweight. Just give some kind of a highsign to Drew, will you, if he comes out on the portico to meet us? I can't, holding her like this. But I think he'll catch on."

Drew and Patty were both on the portico, waiting to welcome them, and they both did catch on. Drew came quickly down the steps and reached into the car.

"Here, let me take her for a minute. It'll be damned hard for you to get out, laden down like that. And you'd be almost sure to wake her."

He lifted her with great care and with the same ease with which he would have picked up a sleeping child. It was true that she weighed very little, and she was completely relaxed. She stirred slightly and murmured, "Raoul," under her breath. Drew smiled.

"Very unflattering to the willing substitute. I think I'd better give her back to you, Raoul. Let's see if we can't get her coat off while we're shifting her. That may rouse her a little more, but I think she'll drop right off again in a minute."

Her lethargy was still so profound that the second transfer was made with the same ease as the first; the removal of her coat was facilitated because she rolled over unresistingly. Raoul asked only one whispered question as he turned to Patty.

"Where shall I take her?"

"Why don't you put her in the bachelor's bedroom? That's where I'd planned to put you, but it's easy enough to shift. Then you won't have to take her over any more stairs."

"I don't mind taking her over the stairs. But, of course, the less we move her around, the less likely we are to wake her up."

Patty nodded, leading the way. In rebuilding Splendida, Drew had derived excellent ideas from the sketches she had drawn, but he had modified them considerably. Instead of eliminating all the rooms on the north side, as she had suggested, he had kept the characteristic long central hallway, reducing it somewhat in scale; on one side of it there were now only a drawing room and dining room, on the other side, only a large, pleasant library, with a square enclosure for the staircase back of it. At the rear, where the original library wing had formerly jutted out, there was a guest room. It was into this room that Patty now led the way, followed by Raoul with Stella in his arms and Louis with the first consignment of bags. As Raoul put Stella carefully down on the bed, Patty gave a quiet order.

"That'll be all, Louis. Miss Stella can ring for the rest of her luggage when she wakes up and wants her coffee. You may serve breakfast for the rest of us right away." Then, as the servant left the room, hitching his shoulders, she said, still very quietly, "Do you think I'd better try to undress her, Raoul? Or shall we just take off her shoes and leave her?"

"I think we might just take off her shoes. There really isn't anything to 'loosen' for girls nowadays, is there, the way you read about in old-fashioned novels? I'm practically sure there isn't, as far as Stella's concerned. Thanks a lot, Patty. I'll just scribble a little note, and stick it here on the bedside table, so she'll see it when she wakes up."

He extracted from his pocket a small pad with a letterhead of the House of Representatives and began to write hastily. Patty, watching the expression on his face as he did so, went out of the room in the same quiet way she had entered it, while he was still writing.

Dear Stella:

I really got quite a kick out of having you go to sleep in my arms on the way up here, and now I am equally pleased to put you to bed in my room. Unfortunately, I am being relegated to yours, upstairs, in order to make this adjustment, which does rob the experience of some of its zest, but still, there's enough left to give me quite a glow. Can't we call an armistice for the next forty-eight hours? I'll be polite if you will. In fact, I'll go so far as to say that I'll be amicable if you will. I'll take my cue from your manner after you emerge from your chaste slumbers. I'm terribly afraid you didn't get as good a rest on the plane as I did, so I hope you'll have one now. Either you're more completely exhausted than's healthy for anyone, or else you must have taken a pretty stiff sedative, which was slow in getting in its lethal work, to

*help you through your plane trip. Either way, somebody
ought to scold you, but I won't—not at present, anyway.*

*I understand that our promises, in the name of our godson,
to renounce the devil and all his works, the vain pomp and
glory of this world, and the sinful desires of the flesh,
don't have to be made until four o'clock this afternoon, so
that ought to give you time for a nap you so disdainfully
denied needing when we left the airport; though it does seem
too bad not to improve the interval of reprieve by getting
a little enjoyment out of the last of the above.*

Yours,
Raoul.

Stella, reluctantly rousing herself several hours later and
catching sight of this missive propped against the thermos
jar, as she sat up, half-dazed and half-startled, read it with
equally conflicting feelings. Its jauntiness, which was so
characteristic of Raoul, unless he was hurried or irritated,
rather annoyed her, and she did not feel sure that its undertone, which was actually more tender than teasing, did not
vex her even more. Did Raoul Bienvenu imagine that, after
all this time, not to mention the way he had treated her, he
could simply crook his little finger and have her fall into his
mouth like a ripe cherry? The idea was preposterous! And
yet, there was something about the letter which made her
smile in spite of herself, something which touched her,
something which gave her "a glow" in her turn. Suddenly,
instead of feeling annoyed, she felt shy, for the first time in
her life. She was willing to be polite and amicable; she could
not restrain a passing pang over the suppressed "desires of
the flesh." But she did not want to see Raoul, or anyone,
right away. She wanted to stay in her room (his room)
alone, and to have some breakfast and a very luxurious
bath and beauty treatment, and to put on fresh underwear
and a lovely dress, and, at intervals during this process, to
reread the letter and try to decide——

Her ring was answered by Jezebel, blinking and beaming, with a pot of coffee which apparently had already been
prepared and with an air of eager receptivity to further
orders. Should she draw Miss Stella's bath soon-soon?
Should she get Louis to tote in the rest of the bags? Wasn't
there some dresses Miss Stella would want pressed? She
could not conceal her disappointment when Stella declined
to get up and join the others for lunch, which was about to

be served. But she brought a second tray to the bedroom, in a manner that was impeccable even though it was downcast, and her spirits rose again as she began unpacking and saw the quantity and quality of Stella's belongings. In spite of her loyal devotion to Patty, she secretly deplored her young mistress's neglect of "fancy fixin's." And here they were, in such abundance as Jezebel had never beheld: perfumes, powders, lotions, laces, lingerie, footwear of every description, cobwebby silk stockings, rich furs, beautiful dresses of all sorts. And the precious stones! Stella flung open her jewel box and recklessly revealed bracelets, pendants, necklaces and brooches, in glittering profusion. There had been no time to pick up half the clothes she had flung over the furniture or any of the jewelry scattered over the dressing table, before a three-quarter chime from the clock in the stairway hall gave warning that there was no time to spare; and she had hardly finished slipping into a creation of golden-brown velvet and hanging a topaz-studded chain around her neck, when there was a knock at the door. Jezebel had finally been obliged to leave her, to help with the preparations for the party, and Stella threw the door open herself, to find Raoul standing on the threshold, looking first at her and then at the scene of costly chaos behind her with unconcealed amusement.

"It's just as well you never did have a man's things cluttering up your room, Stella," he said. "The poor devil wouldn't have had any place to put them. There, I didn't mean to start right out by setting fire to the gunpowder. You look like a million dollars, and probably that's a conservative estimate of the price you paid for that fetching outfit you have on. It's also just as well that you're an heiress in your own right, for even your startling success in the opera wouldn't provide the wherewith to keep up with your tastes. I hope you're rested. We've been sorry not to have you with us, but I realized you were all in, and I explained to the others. Patty wants to know if it will be convenient to come into the drawing room now, though. There are a few details she wants to explain to you before the company comes. It seems you hold the kid until the Bishop takes him to pour cold water over his unoffending little head, and afterwards the pillar of the Church turns him over to me. The Bishop's here already and the kid's been brought downstairs. Gosh, but he really is a world-beater! You never saw such muscle

on a baby. Come along and have a good look at him. You'll
be proud of your godson."

"Wait a second. I have to fish out his present."

"I hope you didn't bring him a mug. I did and I found
he'd had seven given him already."

"Of course I didn't bring him a mug. I brought him a very
beautiful old porringer."

"Well, bring it quick, whatever it is."

She snatched up the tissue-covered package and went
across the staircase hall, through the long passage and
into the drawing room, at Raoul's side. Even in her haste
and confusion, she did not fail to notice how beautiful it all
was. The multicolored window still cast its lozenges of light
on the marble beneath; the painting of Laura de' Dianti still
reigned superbly over the carved marble mantel; the famous
brocaded hangings, the exquisite needle-point upholstery,
looked just as they always had, except that now they were
fresh and whole. What a good idea it had been also to elimi-
nate that superfluous reception room—not to mention the
superfluous parlor and the extra downstairs bedrooms—and
put a new and different library in its place! She would go
there, with Raoul, after the christening was over. That is, if
she did decide——

Its richness had all been retained. But it had none of the
sordid associations she still connected with the old one.
Those had gone, just as Evelyn and Evelyn's power and
presence were gone and just as the decadence and decay
which had threatened the place had been supplanted by new
vitality and unassailable soundness. In this house there was
none of the mouldiness and mustiness she had hated in
the other; it smelled sweet, and sunlight streamed into it
from every side. The radiance which was so essentially
Patty's own had permeated all her surroundings——

The baby was certainly a very fine specimen; Raoul had
not exaggerated his charms. Drew was holding him, with an
ease that was amazing to Stella, as she approached, and Ken
studied her solemnly for a moment, his big blue eyes searching her face with an infantile gaze disconcertingly candid.
He had on an old-fashioned christening dress, beribboned
and beruffled, into which he had obviously been squeezed
with difficulty. Yet it became him. His pink cheeks glowed
and his dark hair clustered in tiny ringlets above the lace
frills. Suddenly he stopped staring and began to kick and

gurgle; then he grinned, engagingly. Drew smiled in his turn.

"He likes you, Stella. Thank God he's never screamed at the sight of strangers. He isn't shy— Well, you'd hardly expect that from a Breckenridge boy! But he has his favorites among the ladies, like his pa and his grandpa before him. Here, take him. You've got to get used to holding him before the ceremony starts. That's why Patty sent for you. Good Lord, not that way!"

As far as she could remember, Stella had never held a baby before. She was not only inept, she was also embarrassed, and embarrassment, like shyness, was a new sensation for her. But in spite of her ineptness and her embarrassment, she experienced an unexpected sensation of joy as Ken, after one more searching look at her, grinned again and settled comfortably down. He fitted into the crook of her arm and the curve of her breast as if he had been meant to lie there, and she learned, for the first time, that it was natural for a woman to hold a baby in her arms, against her breast. As natural as breathing. Just as once it had seemed as natural as breathing to love Raoul. And now she was standing beside him, facing a robed clergyman and an assembled company, and they were about to pronounce some solemn vows together. Not marriage vows, though. And this baby she was holding did not belong to her and Raoul. It belonged to Patty and Drew. She did not have any prospect, or even any hope, of a baby. That part no longer did seem natural.

" 'I demand, therefore: Dost thou, in the name of this child,' " the Bishop was saying solemnly, " 'renounce the devil and all his works—' " Why, those were the lines Raoul had written in his letter. And now she was supposed to make some kind of an answer to them.

It was only because Raoul unobtrusively handed her a Book of Common Prayer, opened at a marked passage, that she was able to make a stumbling response, holding the prayer book rather awkwardly beyond Ken's head. " 'I renounce them all, and by God's help will endeavor—' " She looked ahead, rather desperately. The next response was simpler. Only " 'I do.' " She said it firmly and, after she had done so, realized that her answer, in her own mind, had nothing to do with her belief in all the Articles of the Christian Faith. She had been thinking again— She felt sick and faint. She was afraid she was going to cry. She bit her lip, hard, feeling as if the moment would never come when the Bishop would say, " 'Name this child,' " and take him from her trembling arms. Because her arms *were* trembling. Just as she had seen her grandmother's tremble, despising it as a sign of weakness. The Fontaine women couldn't face the music. Not real music. Only the opera sham——

"Come along. I'm going to get us some champagne. If you and I oughtn't be the first to drink the baby's health, I don't know who should."

So it was over. She hadn't cried; she hadn't fainted. The baptism was finished and Patty was holding the baby now, having proudly taken him from Raoul. The guests were crowding around her and Drew to congratulate them. But Raoul had seen her trembling—he had known how close she was to fainting and weeping—and now he was going to get her some champagne.

"What do you say we go into the library? It's nice and quiet there. This racket is enough to give anyone a headache. I'm surprised that poor kid isn't smothered."

"I— Raoul, do you think anyone would mind very much if I went back to bed?"

"If you went back to bed! Why, you were in bed all the morning! You haven't spoken to any of your fellow guests yet. Of course you can't go back to bed! They'll expect you to sing for them, after the baby's gone upstairs. He's the only one that's going to bed at this party. It'll go on for hours."

While he talked, Raoul was guiding her firmly across the entrance hall to the new library. Almost grimly, he indicated an easy chair by the window and told her to sit there while he went back and got the champagne. When he returned, it was not only with a couple of glasses but also with a bottle imbedded in a silver ice bucket, all neatly arranged on a spacious tray. He set this down on Drew's desk and began to pour the champagne with a lavish hand.

"I'm extremely suspicious about the number of square meals you're consuming regularly," he remarked, handing her a glass. "No girl brought up on Creole cooking ought to be as easy to carry as you are. I could carry you all the way to Abbeville without any trouble at all. I'm not sure I couldn't carry you all the way to Washington. If I didn't happen to know how disgustingly rich you are, I should suspect you were economizing on food to buy clothes."

"Don't be absurd, Raoul."

"Don't be absurd yourself. If you were getting enough to eat and enough exercise and enough fresh air, it would take more than one bad night to knock you out like this. Because I'm paying you the compliment of assuming that you really are knocked out. I don't suppose you're acting this way just because you're a congenital quitter."

Stella put down her glass abruptly. Raoul, without paying any attention to the gesture, immediately refilled it, though it was only half empty.

"Patty told me this morning she didn't know whether she dared ask you to sing or not. She said that of course everyone was dying to hear you, but that she was afraid she inadvertently made you unhappy the last time you sang in her house. Not that you weren't pleasant about it. But it seems that, after various operatic favorites, you sang *Je suis la délaissée.*"

"I did. It was one of my aunt's songs. I found it, among the rest of her music, when——"

"No doubt. But I don't give a damn whether it was one of your aunt's songs or not. It's also the plaint of a jilted maiden. I ought to know. It's a good old Cajun folksong. I've heard it ever since I was a kid. Probably I was sung to sleep with it when I was Ken's age. But I don't ever want to hear you sing it. Don't you dare sing it tonight. Don't you dare gave the impression that you were a jilted maiden, by being too realistic. Because you weren't."

Again Stella put down her glass. This time she did it hard enough so that it rang against the table.

"If I don't sing that tonight, I shan't sing anything."

"You bet your bottom dollar you will. You'll drink the rest of this champagne and then you'll go into the drawing room and sing that aria from *Louise.*"

"Patty didn't have any right to tell you——"

"She had every right to tell me. You don't think she makes a practice of going around betraying confidences, do you? She followed a hunch and it was a good one. So now, instead of wailing to the world about being jilted, go and tell the world you're loved. You don't have to act the part. You know it's true. Therefore you ought to do it even better than when you were trying to pretend it was true, at that New York benefit. And you did a swell job then."

"How do you know what kind of a job I did?"

"Because I was in the opera house when you did it."

She looked at him in bewilderment. His voice was crisp,

almost stern, still. But the look in his eyes belied the tone.

"I don't understand. I didn't know I was going to sing Louise until fifteen minutes before the show began. I thought I was just going to sing Irma."

"Sure. And I flew up from Washington just to hear you sing Irma. I heard you in almost every rôle you sang last winter. It was nearly always possible for me to get away by taking the late afternoon plane and going back at midnight. I didn't bother with baggage or anything like that. I sat in the family circle, where I didn't have to wear dress clothes."

"But if you flew over to New York every time I sang——"

"You guessed it. I cared a lot about hearing you sing. I always have. Just the same, I'm going to tell you the truth about it: I thought if you weren't much of a success—if the glitter wasn't all gold—why then maybe you'd be reconciled to chucking it, after all. I thought that would be the time I might re-enter the picture. So you see, I wouldn't have cared such a hell of a lot if you hadn't been a success. And then you were. Which upset my applecart completely. But now I don't give a damn any more whether you're a success in New York or not. I'm not going to let it upset my applecart either way. And anyhow, you're going to sing for *me* tonight. Come on, Stella. Turn your face around."

She could not do it. Not a second time. She could not go through all that again—the perpetual uncertainty, the chaotic haste, the repeated disappointments, the pain which was half delight, the delight which was almost wholly pain. She had been sure, once before, that she could stand all that, and she had found that she could not. No woman with a modicum of common sense would even try. No woman with a modicum of pride. She remembered the taunt Raoul had flung at her: "Don't make a mistake yourself. This is going to be the end, not just because you say so, but because I do, too." She remembered Clarinda, arrogant and exquisite, meeting Raoul's urgent gaze with smouldering eyes——

"I'm sorry, Raoul. I'm terribly touched, terribly pleased, at what you've just told me. But you said yourself we'd reached the end of the road, more than a year and a half ago, and since then you've fallen in love with someone else."

"*I* said! And what did you say, to goad me into it? Plenty, and you know it. There isn't a man living, worth being called that, who'd take what you handed out to him and come crawling back for more. As for falling in love with someone else, you know damned well I haven't done that either. Clarinda's a very smooth specimen, and I don't deny she's got what it takes to produce a thrill. But I want a girl who can say, the way you used to: 'What the hell, all for love and the world well lost.' Clarinda's as cautious as they come."

"Cautious!"

"Sure. Not just straightforward and singlehearted and guileless, like Patty, so that even such a wolf as Drew used to be couldn't help being touched and uplifted by her downright goodness. But careful not to get caught. Saving herself for the big chance. So that no one could call her damaged goods when it came along."

"Raoul, that's an awful way to talk."

"Well, there you go again, forcing me into saying more than I mean and then blaming me for it. Probably I'd have had an affair with Clarinda if she'd been a shutter girl instead of a blue-blooded debutante. Probably I'd have got a big kick out of it, too. But I never wanted to marry her. I never wanted to marry but one girl in my life, and that's you. I said, turn your face around, Stella."

Stella slept very late again Sunday morning. When she finally did wake, it was only halfway—to a delicious drowsiness shot through with delight. How, she asked herself wonderingly, between waking and sleeping, had she ever lived all these months without Raoul, without his kisses, without his presence, without his strength? Again, as on that far-off evening when she had gone out with him along the bayou, her own strength had seemed to flow from her at first, because it was engulfed in his. But afterwards it had streamed back again with greater and greater force as her rapture mounted. Now her lassitude, her depression, her sense of futility and loneliness were all gone. Suddenly, her drowsiness was all gone, too. She sprang up, eager to shorten the interval between her first full consciousness and the moment that he would take her in his arms again.

As she thrust her feet into her slippers, she saw a scrap of paper lying on the floor near her bed, which had evidently been slipped under the door. It was folded and sealed this time. But she knew it was from Raoul before she tore it open.

Hello, honey!
I hoped, sort of, as Patty would say, that you'd get up and

go to early church with me this morning. Probably I should have mentioned the hope in passing, or even spelled it out for you in words of one syllable, the way I had to when I was trying to avoid admitting that I'd been a damned fool. (And telling you that you had, too.) But I took it for granted that even if we had been (god) parents to an Episcopalian baby yesterday, you'd remember that we, ourselves, are still good(?) Catholics, and that for such "the Holy Days of Obligation are, etc., etc. and every Sunday in the year." (Perhaps you thought I didn't know this. I remember your unflattering astonishment when you found out I knew a little American history.) So I've been to Mass without you, and now, on my return, finding you still in the arms of Morpheus (instead of mine where you ought to be) I'm off quail hunting for the day with Drew, at Jim Hymel's plantation. The hunt is a holdover from last year, and I'd have gone on it anyway, because I wouldn't have wanted to let them down a second time. But I would have liked to see you before I started. However, I'll see you tonight and we'll talk about weddings and things like that. Probably you'll want to be married at the Cathedral in Natchez, so that you can stay at your mother's while you're getting ready, if you can arrange that much leave of absence from New York. (By the way, the general question about leave of absence from New York is one we've got to take up in considerable detail.) Personally, I should think that would be a very pleasant plan. If you don't agree with me, I'm amenable to any reasonable countersuggestion. It being understood, however, that said countersuggestion is to contain no clause indicative of undue delay.

Gail had to start back to New Orleans this morning. A Naval Board is due by plane to check a tank-carrier demonstration. He left good-bye for you. I think Patty, with her usual intuition, has already guessed that we've decided to stop biting off our noses to spite our faces. But in case she hasn't, why don't you tell her sometime in the course of the day. Or wait until I get home tonight, and we'll tell her and Drew together and have a celebration. Just as you'd rather. (You say I'm dictatorial, and here I'm giving you your choice about two things, both in the same letter!) On the chance you prefer the latter plan, I won't say anything to Drew while we're out hunting.

So long, honey. Gosh, aren't you glad we've come to our senses at last?

> *Yours, as ever,*
> *Raoul.*

CHAPTER 38

PATTY, WHO did most things so simply, loved to make a little ceremony out of the coming and going of guests. She always went out on the portico, both to welcome them and to bid them good-bye. The morning after the christening, she was up early to see Gail off, and a little later, she took an affectionate farewell of her mother-in-law and a more formal one of the Bishop. Raoul's early churchgoing did not pass unnoticed, either; and when he and Drew started off for their quail hunting, she turned to him, after kissing Drew, and touched him very much by kissing him also.

"Good hunting," she said. "And good luck of every kind, Raoul. I'm wishing it for you so hard that I think it's bound to come true."

"So it's your wishes that are making it come true, is it? Well, I knew it must be something beyond my own poor powers. A thousand thanks, Patty. I hope you get the world. You certainly have it coming to you." Then, as he got into the car and it started down the driveway, he said feelingly to his host, "You certainly drew a prize. I hope you realize *your* luck."

"I'll say I do."

"Just the same, Patty takes an awful lot of living up to. Perfect for you. Because you can make the grade. I couldn't. I'm not cast in so fine a mold, as Stella's grandmother used to say, and I know it. I've got to have a girl of my calibre."

"If you get one, I'll say she'll be pretty fine, too."

Without pursuing the subject further, they lapsed into comfortable silence. Both were feeling supremely content. Drew had been delighted with the success of the christening the day before. In a sense, it had been a housewarming, for it had marked the first occasion when he and Patty had asked a group of any size to their new home. Its proven adaptability to hospitality, on a scale less extensive and lavish than that of the old Splendida but, nevertheless, ample and gracious, was very gratifying to him. The simple cordiality of Patty's manner never failed to give the effect of ease and charm. The baby had covered himself with glory; he had not so much as whimpered once, but, on the contrary, had seemed to enjoy the proceedings hugely himself. Drew was also immensely pleased because he had just learned that, in accordance with his hopes, Patty had been chosen as the Queen of the Atticans; this choice assured her of the public homage and the festive season which he had so greatly desired for her. On a perfect winter morning, when Drew was out for a fine day's sport, it was logical for him to dwell on such solid sources of satisfaction instead of on the heavy schedule of work, to which he must go back the next day, and all that this work represented.

Raoul was equally content. Like most country-bred men, he found prolonged confinement in any city irksome. He liked to feel the earth under his feet and the wind blowing through his hair—to have a rod or a gun or a tiller in his hands. Washington was a challenge to him, and a symbol. But it did not offer relaxation of any kind, nor did it represent any fundamental standard of living. His stereotyped hotel room was a poor exchange for Bayou's Edge, his colleagues in Congress unstimulating substitutes for such companions as Dr. Anconi and Drew Breckenridge. In so-called society he had not found his feet at all. There were no spacious, hospitable homes in which he was informally and frequently welcomed and where he could enjoy himself wholeheartedly with a pretty girl. His reception at Splendida, the friendship of Drew and Patty, the geniality of the christening party, the prospect of a good day's sport, and, more than all these put together, the knowledge that his separation from Stella was at an end—these made a sum total sustaining and exhilarating enough for any man. He stretched his legs out in front of him and drew great breaths. It was very good to be alive and thirty and beside a great river and in love——

There was a prompt connection at the ferry, and it was only a little after ten when Raoul and Drew pulled up at the Helvetia Plantation store, where their host, Jim Hymel, was waiting for them. He stood in the open doorway, dressed in khaki riding breeches, high boots, a leather windbreaker and a plaid shirt. He was holding his soft hat in his hands, so his sandy hair was uncovered and his ruddy face unshaded; like the others, he was drinking in the crisp air and bright sunshine with supreme contentment. The embrasure against which he was leaning framed the shelves of miscellaneous groceries and drygoods, the wide battered counters and the high old-fashioned desk, which were visible behind him. The pleasant, homely scents of bread, spices, cereals and coffee stole out to meet the smell of the trees and the grass and the earth. Hymel waved a welcome to his guests and then came forward to grip their hands heartily.

"Come on in to the back of the store and have a couple of small blacks before we start out," he said. "Perhaps you'd like something to eat, too."

They fell in with the suggestion of the coffee but declined the offer of food. They were just up from the breakfast table, Raoul said, and what a breakfast! Jim would have no idea, until he had eaten one of Mrs. Breckenridge's breakfasts himself. No, but he could imagine, Jim replied. Well then, perhaps they had better be shoving along. Their belongings had already been taken from them, so they walked out of the back door unencumbered, across the yard to the big barn which had the kennels built up against it. Jim stopped to open three of these, and his dogs came bounding out. They were very lean, fine-drawn for condition, the largest patched and ticked with liver color, the other two lemon and white. As they circled and leapt around him, he proudly expatiated on their various characteristics.

"This scrubby little fellow is Gus, Mr. Bienvenu. He doesn't look like so much, does he? But you'll get a different impression of him before the day's over. He's an Air Pilot's Sam dog. This cute little gyp is a Village Boy bitch. She's smart as they come, too. I'm going to breed Gus to her the next time she's in season, and that ought to be some litter! Drew's name is in the pot for one of the pups already. Mickey here is only thirteen months old. Of course, he hasn't got the finish of the others yet, but after all, we're out for a day's pleasure, not for a field trial. Well, you'll see for yourself. The boys are waiting for us just over yonder."

They walked on through the spacious, unkempt yard, avoiding the rusty bulk of a discarded boiler and several overturned, old-fashioned sugar kettles. Their walk took them towards a ponderous gate, built to accommodate cane trucks, which led to the fields. It swung open, slowly and creakingly, on its great hinges, and Hymel closed it carefully again after letting his guests through. On the other side, three tatterdemalion Negro urchins, whose shining teeth made white bands across their black faces, stood holding the horses already saddled, and the hunters mounted, the black boys wriggling up behind them. Then they were off past the quarters to the first headland, the dogs ignoring the feistes that yelped around the cabins. As they crossed the first drainage canal over a heavy wooden bridge, which, like the gate they had just gone through, was built to accommodate huge cane trucks, the horses' hoofs, drumming against it, made a sound that was almost startling in the stillness; after that, there was no noise as they went on past the nearest stubble field to the next drainage canal. They were riding along the headland now, the horses slowing down to a steady rack, the dogs making wide diagonal casts across the fields. Jim, watching eagerly, shook his head with an air of disappointment.

"I thought we'd pick up a covey just beyond this canal. I know one's been using here. But I guess we've got to keep on— No— Look! Gosh, I don't care whether we get any birds or not now! That's what I came out to see. Lord, what a smasher!"

Gus had been running, head high, tail swinging in circles, his beautiful body a rhythmic ripple of muscles. But even as he gathered himself to clear a ditch in one magnificent leap, he was struck into immobility. One forefoot was still upheld in mid-stride. But for its consuming intensity, his bearing was one of disdain. Queenie, rounding a clump of sumac, caught sight of him and instantly backed his point. Mickey, who had been gaily following the lead of his elders, paused uncertainly and then froze, too.

"Look at him honor! Who says he's not coming along? I tell you that pup's got everything!"

Jim's voice was vibrant with pride. He and his guests had quickly reined in their horses as the dogs had come to a point; now the Negro boys, sliding swiftly from the horses' rumps, ran around to take the bridles as the hunters dismounted. Jim, slightly doubtful of Mickey's staunchness in spite of his satisfaction, kept talking soothingly to the puppy as they walked warily forward a hundred yards or so, while Raoul and Drew joked under their breath about the handicap of not having one leg shorter than the other, so that one would fit the furrow and the other the middle.

"Steady, Mickey! Steady! S-t-e-a-d-y!"

The men had crept cautiously closer to Gus. As they

reached him, fourteen feathered projectiles exploded off the ground. At the same instant, the three hunters fired, and the Negro boys cried out, their cackle of "Kayai! Kayai!" echoing to the sound of the shots. The horses stood impassively by at some distance, idly switching their tails; the detonation had left them unmoved. Gus and Queenie stayed staunch until Jim's order of, "Dead bird! Dead bird! Go get it!" came quietly through. It was not until then that they were off after the game. But Mickey, in a wild frenzy, had already torn away in pursuit of the covey, and Jim's satisfaction in the performance of the others was swallowed up in his chagrin over this disgraceful exhibition.

"Darn that pup! I praised him too soon! I'll have to break him of that right now."

His tone betrayed his vexation, and he began calling Mickey imperiously. The puppy came trotting back with obvious reluctance. He was already prepared for punishment when Jim, breaking off a dry weedstem, began to flail him. The weed had no weight to it, and it was applied with no force; the puppy was not hurt. But his self-esteem suffered a defeat severer than his master's. He crouched, whimpering, at Jim's feet.

Raoul and Drew had already followed Gus and Queenie towards the singles, which they had marked down as the birds settled among the brush of a distant ditch. Jim moved forward more slowly, with the pretext of himself marking the covey carefully. Actually, he was still smarting with chagrin, for Mickey, even more than Gus, was his pet and his pride. Rather moodily, he kept his eyes on the pup, which was now trotting abjectly ahead of him. Then Mickey, himself, came to a sudden stop. But a suspicion that the puppy was false-pointing crossed Jim's disturbed mind. He spoke to Mickey gruffly.

"What you got there? A field lark or a tee-teece, I suppose. Come on, come on! Don't make a fool of yourself again!"

The puppy rolled one eye, half pertly, half appealingly, in the direction of his master. But he did not budge. Still grumbling, Jim strode across the clump of weeds over which Mickey stood guard, prepared to kick nothing more remarkable than a rabbit out of them. Instead, he was greeted with a second explosion as an old cock quail whirred from the thick vegetation. Automatically, Jim raised his gun and fired, bringing down the bird. Then he glanced swiftly at

Mickey. This time the puppy had not moved. With no other bird to rush after, he had known how to hold his ground. He was still standing rigid when Jim bent over to pat him and praise him before telling him to go and get the bird. His voice was ringing with pride again, and Mickey's mien proclaimed his excitement, as the two went on together to join the others.

"Well, maybe I've got a bird dog, after all! Did you see how my pup redeemed himself? That was a darned good point. I guess we've got enough out of that covey now—Better leave the rest of these birds for next year's seed. I'm going to take you across some pretty rough going, now, but one of the overseers says he put up a covey there last week—a new one never shot over till yet."

Raoul and Drew agreed with alacrity. They remounted their horses and rode on, and within the next hour they had put up two more coveys. But the dense growth of underbrush made the pursuit of singles difficult, and eventually they turned back to the headland and followed it to a wide plantation road. They were all hungry by this time, and Raoul, at least, was beginning to feel that, despite the excellence of Patty's breakfast, he had made a mistake in declining the proffer of food at the plantation store. But his regret was mercifully brief. The hunters had hardly turned into the road themselves, when a rickety top buggy came swaying towards them over the ruts. A gaunt old Negro, with hair as grizzled as Jezebel's and only two or three isolated yellow fangs disclosed by his cheerful grin, was holding the reins in an effortless way, for the aged horse which drew the buggy ambled and stumbled along without either curbing or guidance. The driver sat surrounded with thermos jars, demijohns and baskets, and these, when unloaded, proved to contain water which might well have been a little colder, thick syrupy coffee, crusty man-sized sandwiches and fried chicken which was still warm in its wrappings. The hunters seized upon his supplies and, without a moment's delay, sat down on the ditch bank to devour them.

It would have been impossible, Raoul thought, to find food which would taste better to a man or conditions more ideal under which to eat it. The sun was very bright, the bank warm beneath him. This was winter weather of full and mellow perfection, such as few places on earth could offer. It made him proud to think that one of these places was Louisiana. Lighting his pipe, he thought of his colleagues in the House who came from New England, Michigan, the Dakotas; those poor fellows were probably all snowed in by this time. More poignantly, he thought of the men in Europe caught in the maelstrom of a devastating war. The headlines that morning had been terrible. Hundreds and thousands of desperate human beings, torn from the homes and families left unprotected by their absence, were fighting to-day for survival, under conditions of unspeakable horror. But their suffering seemed vague and intangible; the spell which enfolded him with its magic had begun to blind him, partly because of the earth's enchantment and partly because his entire outlook on life had so suddenly changed. The evening before, standing beside Stella with Drew's child in his arms, his heart had been filled with bitterness and jealousy, because it seemed to him that his friend had everything which made existence worth while and which he himself lacked. Since then, he had regained Stella; he had re-captured the promise of the future for himself. Now, sur-rounded by this golden peace, this abundant beauty, he reproached himself for his ingratitude to the Providence which had given him good hunting and good company in a goodly land and which, in the fullness of time, would give him a wife and a son of his own.

"You know, I doubt whether I'd even try to shoot Hitler at this moment, if I saw him coming towards us!" he said, taking his pipe out of his mouth and turning with a laugh towards his companions. "I feel too full of food and sun-shine and good will to want to shoot anyone!"

"Well, I'd shoot him!" Jim exclaimed vehemently. "When I think that one archfiend like that has the power to plunge the whole world into war——"

"We haven't been plunged into it. When I look around me here, it doesn't seem possible that we ever will be."

He put his pipe back in his mouth and continued to gaze around him in supreme contentment. As far as he was con-cerned, he would have been glad to loll on that sunny bank for an hour or so, smoking and snoozing, and then go back to Splendida and Stella. The sport had been tops, but he had had enough of it for one day. He supposed the others would want to go on, though; they had not got their limit yet, by any means. He was relieved when Jim suggested that they should do some dry shooting to see the dogs work, putting up their empty guns; but though this changed the form of the afternoon's sport, it did not shorten it. The shadows were already very long and the sun was rolling over the top of the distant levee when they finally came jogging up to the plantation store again.

"Won't you come on up to the house this time? I'd like nothing better than to have you stay to supper with me."

"Thanks, Jim. If I were still a bachelor, there's nothing I'd enjoy more. But you know how married men are. They still like their day's sport as much as the next one. But when evening comes, they want to get home to supper with the missus, to say nothing of having a romp with the son and heir before he gets tucked into bed."

"Well, compromise then. Come into the store and have a drink, at least. Mr. Bienvenu and I are both bachelors. You've got to consider our feelings, too."

"This time I'm with Drew, Jim. I'm rather in a hurry to get back to Splendida myself."

"Of course, if that's the case, I won't urge you. Here, please take my birds, you two, along with your own. I can always get plenty more. Divide them up at Splendida, with my compliments. Good luck to you both and good night!"

They left him standing with Mickey at his side and Gus and Queenie at his heels. His face was ruddier than ever, now that he had been out in the air all day; his sandy hair was windblown. There was a ruggedness and a homeliness about him that merged naturally into the general plantation picture. Twilight was closing in, and with it came the comfortable evening sounds of the country: the clucking of fowl, the lowing of cattle, the crunching noise made by grazing livestock of all sorts. A flock of *grosbecs,* in flight to their nesting grounds in the swamps, passed swiftly over the hunters' heads; the birds, too, made a sound as they flew, which seemed an integral part of the crepuscule. A slight breeze stirred the draperies of moss waving from the live oaks. On the levee, some Negroes were already beginning to pile up their roseau reeds for the bonfires of another Christmas. A child, sent out after the cows, was calling them home.

"Drew," Raoul began. This was the moment to tell his friend about Stella. There would never be another so beautiful, so propitious.

"Yes? I say, Raoul, did you realize it was six o'clock already? I'm afraid we've missed the ferry I meant to make. It'll be 'good dark' before we get home. And I told Patty we'd get there by 'just dark'."

"Too bad." Raoul was disappointed himself. And now, remembering his promise to Stella that he would say nothing to Drew until he found out whether this would meet her wishes, he felt bound to let the perfect moment pass. But its escape left him curiously let down. "Six o'clock, did you say?" he asked, struggling to rid himself of such senseless depression. "What if we should tune in on Jack Benny? I haven't many rules of life, but one of them is that I have to listen to him Sunday nights, come hell or high water, or even a message from the President."

"Well, that's a simple enough rule to abide by. If you don't want anything more than that, I guess I can act the perfect host, without too much difficulty. I thought, when you started to speak a moment ago, it was about something else. Just a second now——"

Drew clicked a knob, and the lights glowed behind the station indicator. There was a confused hum from the radio. Then it became abruptly vocal.

"—struction of the fleet. It is not yet known how many were killed, but from all accounts the death list will be appallingly heavy, not only among the military and naval personnel but also among the civilian population of Honolulu, as was announced in the first bulletins shortly after noon today, our time——"

"Honolulu? Did he say *Honolulu?* For God's sake, what's happened?"——

"—At seven-thirty this evening a summary of events following the sneak attack on Pearl Harbor will be given," the commentator continued. "In the meantime, please stay tuned to this station, for we will interrupt all programs with news bulletins as these are received."

The commentator's voice trailed off into meaningless music. Drew, pulling over to the side of the road, began to turn the dial with manual tuning. "There must be some station broadcasting news now," he said, reaching out int the void for communication. "We ought to be able to find out——"

"Find out! We've found out enough as it is! I've got to get back to Washington. Whatever else this means or doesn't mean, there'll be a declaration of war tomorrow. I'll have to vote on it. Get this car of yours under way again, Drew. I've just about time to stop by Splendida long enough to change my clothes and pick up my toothbrush, before I start for New Orleans to catch the night plane. Just about time— Look here, I'm taking it for granted you'll get me there."

"Of course I'll get you there. You've all kinds of time. We mustn't let this get *us*, Raoul, any more than we can help. You know what you said, just a few hours ago——"

"Yes, I know what I said a few hours ago, and I know what I'm saying now, too. Damnation, you don't think we have missed that ferry, do you?"

They had not. It was still waiting, with almost human stolidity, beside the rickety wharf as they went dashing up the steep slope of the levee and hurtling down on the other side. The river gave the same impression of inviolable peace as the fields and forests. Its own luminosity still glowed through the smoky purple of dusk, and above the willow scrub of the batture on the further shore, a church steeple pointed towards a sky already pierced with stars. But the ferry, itself, was in a state of unnatural turmoil. The passengers were not lounging apathetically around as they made the crossing, according to their custom. Most of them were chattering excitely as they moved from side to side and from bow to stern, exchanging surmises, voicing denunciations; a few were still incredulous that anything so preposterous as an enemy attack could really have occurred in the United States of America; others, completely overwhelmed, were trying to suppress the first wild surge of panic. Raoul got out of the car and circulated among them, trying to get more definite and complete information than the radio fragments had supplied. Drew remained at the wheel, talking with the ticket collector, whose conversation was interlarded with the stock comment that he had known all the Breckenridges. Neither one was much wiser upon driving up the Donaldsonville ramp than upon embarkation, and neither one was any longer in the mood for talk. The last lap of the ride to Splendida was made in silence.

Patty was waiting for them on the portico when they came up to it. As they saw her standing there, they knew, from the complete serenity of her bearing, that no bad tidings had penetrated to the plantation. She came forward with a smile, extending a hand to each.

"Welcome back! Did you have good hunting? It's been beautiful here."

"Where's Stella?" Raoul inquired abruptly.

"I think she's still lying down. She's been in bed nearly all day. But I hope we can persuade her to get up for supper."

"In bed nearly all day! Is she sick?"

"No, I don't think she's sick. But she does seem rather upset. You didn't have any reason to believe, did you, Raoul, before you started this morning that—well, that you'd displeased her or hurt her feelings in any way? Because last night she seemed so happy. But today——"

Raoul had not waited to hear the end of the sentence. With a profane exclamation, he plunged down the passageway and through the staircase hall. He did pause long enough to knock on Stella's door, but the pause and the knock were both perfunctory. He was already turning the knob before she answered. He was inside the room, standing beside the bed, where she lay propped up on lacy pillows, attired in a filmy dressing gown, before she realized who had burst in upon her so unceremoniously.

"Would you mind telling me what is the meaning of this?" he demanded.

"I think you'd better tell me what you mean yourself. Here it was only last night we got engaged, or re-engaged, or whatever you choose to call it. And this morning, before I'd even seen you, without consulting my wishes in the least, you started off for a day's hunting. You——"

"I'd promised to go hunting before we got re-engaged. Not that I probably wouldn't have gone, anyway. Drew went, didn't he? And if any man was ever in love, he is. Be that as it may, now I'm starting for Washington. In about ten minutes."

"Raoul, you mustn't. You mustn't begin again; leaving me abruptly, staying away from me indefinitely. I can't stand it. Patty can take it, but I can't. Don't ask me to."

"I'll have to stay away from you indefinitely, later on, but I'm not leaving you abruptly now. I'm not asking you to stand that again. I'm asking you to come with me."

"I think you must be stark, raving crazy!"

"The world's stark, raving crazy. The Japanese fleet has attacked Pearl Harbor. We're at war. Not just England or France or Russia any more. The United States. If that doesn't make a crazy world I don't know what does. But I'm still as sane as anyone left in it. Sane enough, anyhow, to know that we'd better marry each other right now, because if we don't, we may never have another chance. It won't be a case this time of your saying it's the end, or my saying it's the end, or any fancy stuff like that. It'll *be* the end. Face it, Stella.

Face the music. Because, before you know it, we'll be facing something a damn sight worse."

"But you said you wanted to get married in the Natchez Cathedral—that you wanted me to go to my mother's and get ready——"

"Yes, I did say so. I still think it would have been a very pleasant plan. But the Japs didn't consult me before they made theirs. Now I think it would be a damned sight better for us to wedge in a few weeks together, before I start off to the other side of the globe, than to spend those weeks *getting ready* to be married. Don't make another mistake, Stella. I probably *will* be sent to the other side of the globe. Because I'm going to get out of Congress, and into the Marine Corps so quick you won't see me for the dust. And after that— Well, you know what I've always said. You can go anywhere in the world from a bayou——"

He took hold of her arms and pulled her into an upright position. "Climb out of that bed and get packed," he said. "I don't mean all this fluff that's cluttering up the room. You can send for that afterwards. I mean something warm and serviceable, a couple of changes— I'm going upstairs to fling my own things into a bag. When I come down again, I want to find you in the hall waiting for me. If you're not, I'll come back in here, and finish for you, whatever stage of dress or undress you're in at that point. Drew's driving us to New Orleans to catch the night plane. He already knows he's driving me. He knows I have to vote on the declaration of war tomorrow. We heard the news over the radio. He doesn't know about you, though, because I promised you I wouldn't tell him until I found out whether you wanted me to or not. But I'll tell him now, while I'm packing. Not that there's much to say. Just— 'Look here, Drew. I'm taking Stella with me. We're going to be married in Washington tomorrow. We know there isn't time left to bother about an announcement or a wedding or anything like that. But we've still got time to get married and to live together for a little while before I'm ordered away. And we're going to.'"

He let go her arms as suddenly as he had seized them. Then he bent over her again and enfolded her in his own.

"Aren't we, honey?" he said.

CHAPTER 39

THE GOLDEN winter weather went on and on. Drew motored back and forth to New Orleans every weekday, for he and Patty were agreed that they wanted to stay at Splendida until after new year. They had not discussed their plans beyond that. Neither one would have said it was because they did not dare to. Both would have insisted that when lives were like theirs, it was happiness enough to live them a day at a time, savoring each to the full.

Patty did not find that time hung heavy on her hands while Drew was gone. She still took care of Ken, almost unassisted. In the morning, before his long midday nap, and in the early evening, after he waked from it, she was very apt to take him with her, in his carriage, while she made the rounds of the plantation. When he slept, she let Jezebel listen for him and did the errands and the bookkeeping which she would have found it hard to accomplish otherwise. She had learned a good deal about crops and livestock since her marriage, and she had begun to develop the dairy, which had never before been a feature at Splendida. With the successful example of the nearby St. Louis Plantation to spur her on, she was planning to sell milk and butter and cream cheese, and she grasped the details which led to such an expansion of industry easily and delightedly. She kept all the plantation accounts now, paid all the hands, supervised all the work. This was not for any lack of interest, willingness or skill on Drew's part. The love for Splendida, which he had felt as a child and which had later cooled to indifference, had been rekindled by the intensity of Patty's feeling for it. But she had insisted, when they first went back there in October, that he could not run the plantation in addition to his office and governmental work, and he had agreed with her. They had not said anything more on that subject either. There had been no suggestion that it was best she should learn to do it while he was still there to help with advice and guidance, so that she would not be utterly inexperienced when she had to do it alone.

She was never idle, yet she was never hurried either. She

rose early and went steadily from one task to another throughout the day. But she always gave the occasional visitor the impression that she was pleased to be interrupted, and when Drew came home at night, he found her relaxed and serene. She did not raise the question of plantation problems unless he did so first; there was no discussion of them over their candlelighted supper table or after they had gone upstairs to the big bedroom where the flames from the open fire flickered in such a friendly way on the white walls. Neither did she speak to him about the war, though she had needed very little "teaching" to read the papers and to listen to the news bulletins on the radio. Instead, she told him about the pleasant happenings of the day: the remarkable progress which Ken was making, the first indication of bloom on the early camellias, the local news which a visiting neighbor had brought in.

Her interest in correspondence was still undiminished, too; she continued to take an almost childlike pleasure in writing and receiving letters and in sharing these with her husband. It was so rarely that she did not do this spontaneously that Drew's suspicions were aroused when an evening came and went without any comments from her on the subject. She sat knitting, without talking at all, while he read aloud to her after supper. This was not unusual, but the fact that she had said almost nothing during supper, itself, was. The big clock in the stairway hall struck ten just as he came to the end of a chapter, and he closed the book and walked over to her chair, putting his arm around her shoulder.

"What's on your mind, Patty?"

"Several things. I've been wondering how to tell you. Usually it's so easy, and this time it isn't."

"Then let's get them behind us. That's what you told me once, and it was good advice."

"I had a letter from the Captain of the Atticans this morning. I'll show it to you."

She went over to her desk, extracted a letter from the neat little pile which lay there, and handed it to Drew. He looked at her questioningly, and then, as she was still silent, took it from its envelope and read it through.

CLUB OF THE ATTICANS
P. O. BOX 972
NEW ORLEANS

Mrs. Andrew Breckenridge
Splendida Plantation
White Castle
Iberville Parish
Louisiana.

Your Majesty:

I am directed by His Majesty, King of the Atticans, to convey tidings of events which have torn his heart asunder and which even his imperial might has been unable to forestall.

Our nation being at war, all loyal subjects of His Majesty will find themselves occupied with other activities and their minds and hearts filled with such thoughts as are not compatible with and will prevent their devotion to the usual entertainment of His Majesty's subjects during the season usually marked by Carnival.

Accordingly, I am instructed to convey these tidings and to say that it has been deemed best for our nation that your subjects be not entertained as usual at that time.

You will, on Christmas morning, be sent the usual certificate and notification by which His Majesty on all occasions advises his consort of his intention to visit his subjects. This certificate should be retained by you as evidence of His Majesty's sincere regret at the untoward circumstances and as a reminder of the glory and happiness which might have been.

You will receive one of the favors which would have been distributed had the usual entertainment been held.

With assurances that your heartbroken subjects will always look upon you as their Queen of 1942, I remain

Loyally yours,
Captain.

"I know you're disappointed, Drew," she said as he replaced the letter in its envelope without comment. "That's why I hated to show you this letter. But I never cared about being a Queen, so I don't mind at all. Except that this means that I never will be, and you wanted to have me. This proves Carnival's over."

"Yes, Carnival's over. And it's only a year ago people were saying that we couldn't stand life as it is, if we didn't escape from its serious side once in a while. Its serious side! What did we know about its serious side then?"

"I suppose we didn't know much. We were still dallying with 'humanity at play, life in a mask.' I suppose we really don't know much yet about its serious side, when it comes to that, do we, Drew? But at least we're not saying any more, as I did hear people saying last year, that when we stopped celebrating Carnival, Hitler could have New Orleans. Of course I know that *was* only a Carnival catchword—that most people speak thoughtlessly at such times, not feelingly as you did about the song. But I shuddered when I heard it."

"Did you, Patty? Then it *must* have taken hold of you! Because I've never known you to shudder at anything!"

He spoke lightly, as he spoke lovingly. Patty smiled back at him.

"Sometimes I shudder inside when you can't see it or feel it. I'm glad I've kept that much from you. Especially as I've managed to conceal so little. But why do you say 'only' a year? Anything can happen in a year. *Everything* happened to us in a year. Don't you remember, when we were going up the steps of the Boston Club last spring, we spoke of how the spring before——"

"Yes, darling, I do remember."

He laid the letter back on the desk. "I wasn't altogether unprepared for this," he said. "I heard a rumor in town today that Carnival was going to be called off. As of course it should be. But I've been unusually busy. I haven't had time to look at a paper. Perhaps the announcement hasn't been made publicly yet, anyway. I heard some kind of a rumor about Raoul, too. Have you heard from him or from Stella?"

"Yes. That was the next thing I meant to tell you. I don't know why that should have been hard, unless— Well, anyway, apparently they're both very pleased about it. He's been given a special commission to do recruiting all through the Cajun country. Two sergeants are going with him, and he's got a schedule, covering about three weeks, that will take him to most of the principal towns in southern Louisiana, and a good many of the smaller ones, too! Recruiting stations will be opened and he'll make speeches and meet people generally, besides being on official duty—not just the boys of draft age, but their fathers and mothers, too. He calls it, 'bringing the Marine Corps to their front doorsteps,' and I can just hear his charming mixture of cajolery and command. He's even going by pirogue through the smaller bayous and the cypress swamps where he can't go any other way. I know he'll do a grand piece of work. I don't know anyone else who could do it so well."

"Nor I. It's right down his alley—dramatic and original and effective. Whoever thought up that assignment was a bright lad."

"And Stella said Raoul would be at home, off and on, while he was filling it. Her letter came from Abbeville. She's at Bayou's Edge already. She's going to stay there until Raoul's ordered away for good. She's keeping open house for all his local friends, Dr. Anconi and the others, and she's having her own family there, piecemeal, over the week ends. Her mother and stepfather and half brothers and sisters have been down from Natchez, to the satisfaction of all concerned—and Father Fontaine and Gail and his parents——"

"And the Darcoas?" Drew inquired a little drily.

"Well, after all, you know Amelina and Richard are going to be married during the holidays, because he's speeded up his courses at Tulane and will finish in February. Then he's going straight into aviation, from last accounts, and Clarinda never did care much for the country."

"I see," Drew said, still drily.

"The 'Met' has been awfully decent to Stella," Patty went on, attacking the subject from a different angle. "She has an indefinite leave of absence. She isn't going back to New York until Raoul does go away. She wants to go back then. She says she knows she wouldn't be able to stand it—having him gone, I mean—if she weren't busy, and she thinks that's the best way for her to be busy at present. But when the season's over, she's going to Abbeville to stay, for the summer anyhow, except while she is making a short visit in Natchez."

"I see. Well, it seems very logical to me all around. By the time the war's over, Raoul will probably be a Brigadier General and afterwards be nominated to the Senate by popular acclaim. We'll have to get him to teach Ken everything about politics I've never been able to learn—because I do want Ken to learn, Patty. I want him to enter public life. After the Senate, I suppose the next step for Raoul might even be the Presidency. Do you believe we could hope that under those circumstances the Chief Executive and the First Lady would condescend to invite an obscure Southern architect and his wife for an occasional week end at the White House?"

"Well, at least Stella said she hoped we could have a week end together now, either here or at Bayou's Edge."

"That would be nice, too. Don't you think so?"

"Yes, very. If you could go to Abbeville with me, Drew, or if you'd surely be here when Stella and Raoul came to Splendida. I don't think I'd want to be with them without you, though."

"What makes you think you would be, Patty?"

"Because there must have been some reason why I couldn't tell you easily about this special assignment of Raoul's. There must have been some reason why I felt you had a new assignment, too. Haven't you, Drew?"

"Yes. I didn't know you'd guessed. I've been waiting for just the right moment to tell you, Patty."

"This is the right moment."

She rose as she spoke. He took her face between his two hands and looked searchingly into her eyes, as he had in the hallway of the raised cottage so long before. She returned his look with the same steadfast gaze that she had then.

"It isn't an assignment that's original or dramatic, like Raoul's, Patty. But I hope in the long run it will be just as effective. Architects are needed in the war. Not just for defense work, in their own country, as they have been until now, but abroad. To build barracks, to build naval bases and air bases, for all kinds of construction in all kinds of places. I've been asked to go. I've said I would."

"Where?"

"I think it'll be somewhere in the British Isles or in one of the British possessions. But I'm not sure yet. Probably I won't be told myself exactly where, before I start."

"When are you starting?"

"Next week. Unless there's some delay about embarkation. And I don't believe there will be."

"I see."

His hands slid slowly from her face to her shoulders, over her arms, and encircled her waist. This, too, was as it had been on that first day so long ago, and again she waited, quiescent and controlled, trustingly accepting the unknown because it came from him.

"This is going to be a long separation, Patty. We've got to face that. It's going to be a long war. It can't end until it's settled the fate of every nation. You understand that, don't you? Because it's raised questions that have to be answered before life can be resumed on any terms, questions involving not merely the existence of states and the tracing of boundaries, but the future of mankind."

"Yes, I understand that."

"So I have to go now, and I have to stay away as long as I can be of any use. But there's no prospect of any immediate fighting, you know. In fact, I probably won't ever see any, I'm sorry to say. I won't have a dashing career, like Raoul. I'll be in the Engineer Corps. What I'll have to do will be to provide and facilitate fighting conditions for other men. And all the transports will be convoyed. It's not often that one will be lost."

This was the moment she would break down, he knew, if she did at all. She was not superstitious. She had proved this by gaily choosing a proverbially haunted room for her bridal chamber, and she had soon exorcised the poor little ghost that wailed there, according to legend, by the presence of her own vigorous and healthy child. She crossed no bridges until she came to them, and then she always managed to do so with superb disregard of the torrents raging beneath them and the hurricanes shaking their structure. She had never spoken to him of his father's fate, or of his grandfather's. Yet he knew, with the same certainty that he knew she loved him, that some irrepressible instinct had instilled in her heart the fear that he might be drowned. He waited for the recoil which seemed to him inevitable, as he had waited once before, and again, instead of feeling this, he heard her joyous intake of breath. It was the same sign, small but unmistakable, that always marked her most exalted moments.

"I'm glad you want to go, Drew. It wouldn't be you if you didn't, and you know what I've always told you: that I didn't want anything about you different—that I wanted you exactly as you were. I'm sure nothing will happen to you. I'm sure you'll be safeguarded. But even if I weren't, I could still say I was glad you were going. You've guessed that I've been thinking about your grandfather and your father, just as I guessed when you kept thinking about Anne Forrestal. Well, I have; I won't deny it. But you've found out that your fears were groundless, and I'm sure that I shall, too. In any case, if the very worst should happen, it wouldn't be futile and wasteful, as it was before. It wouldn't be like the *Bourgogne* and the barbed wire. It would have a meaning and a purpose. Your life has had more meaning and more purpose than your father's or grandfather's did and so would— I mean it would bring the time closer that you just told me about, the time when the fate of every nation will be settled."

"That's what I wanted to hear you say, Patty, more than anything else in the world."

It had been said once, because it had to be, but it was never said again. After that, the simplicity of the things they said to each other was surprising, at least on the surface. But they both knew, though they never voiced the knowledge, that the seeming simplicity had a deep undercurrent. As always, there was harmony between them, and understanding.

"If you don't mind, Patty, I think I'd like to move that painting of Camille Dupuy from my study in the Prytania Street house and put it over the mantel in the library here. After all, this is where you'll be most of the time, and it was a present to my father. I'd like to have you take care of it for me yourself."

"And I'd like to, Drew. I'd thought of it, too. We changed the library so much when we rebuilt the house that I've always thought perhaps a different picture over the mantel———"

"Yes, that's the idea. And sometimes, when you're in New Orleans, you might drop in at the Convent of the Holy Family and ask if Sister Mary Dolores would see you. I know you won't have much money to spare— Which reminds me: don't let me forget that I must talk to you a little more about finances. But perhaps you could give her a little something, once in a while, for her work."

"Of course I can. I'll have money to spare, Drew. Don't worry about that. You don't need to talk to me any more about finances. I have those all very clearly in my mind; everything I ought to save and can afford to spend is nicely budgeted. I'm going to make money on my dairy, too. So that's that. Would you by any chance like to have me go to the Carmelite Convent as well as the Convent of the Holy Family?"

"Very much. The Prioress can't do more than decline to receive you. But, of course, there'd always be a grille and curtains."

"I think perhaps I could make her understand why you wanted to have me go to her, Drew, even through the grille and the curtains. I'll try, anyway."

"By the way, Patty, I've told you, haven't I, that I didn't

enter Ken at Groton the minute he was born? I overlooked it, I was so excited. And since I didn't——"

"Yes, I'd thought of that, too. I thought probably you'd like to have him grow up here. He'd be much better prepared for a public position here later on, if he did. But of course you'll be back long before it's time for him to go away to school——"

"Yes, of course."

"But I won't forget, anyway. I'll always remember he is a Louisiana lad."

"Drew, I thought I'd ask your mother to come and stay with me while you're gone. As my guest. That would have to be understood. This is our house; this is our plantation; and while you're gone, I'm going to run them for you. I'll probably make mistakes as I go along, but I'll learn better in making them. I don't want your mother to try to teach me or to try to help me. But I'd like to have her with me and I think she'd like to come. And perhaps you'd feel easier if there were an older woman here with me. Though I think if, before you went away, you called all our people together, the house servants and the field hands both, and told them——"

"Yes, I meant to do that. On Sunday, after church. You won't have any trouble with our people, Patty. They'll stand by you. But it would be a good idea for you to ask my mother to stay here, some of the time anyway. She'd be very pleased. I'm very pleased that you thought of her. And when you do want or need to go to town for any length of time, there's always the shotgun house where you can be by yourself, if you want to. You were right about that, Patty, as you've been about everything. I'm glad you've got it. I'm glad I can think of you as going there."

"I've an idea, sort of, that I'm going to have another baby, Drew. I've felt faint once or twice, though I haven't fainted away. And I've been a little sleepier than usual, though I haven't been sick. And I'm not quite up with my calendar. You know Dr. Beal said everything would be very easy this time. There'll be some way of sending you word, won't there, when I'm sure?"

"Yes, I'm certain there will be. I don't know whether to say I'm glad or sorry, Patty. It seems so much for you——"

"Why, you're glad of course! What about that 'big brood

of happy, healthy youngsters' we're going to have? And this is only the second! I've been terribly slow getting started. What do you want me to name it, if it's a boy?"

"Patrick, of course."

"And if it's a girl?"

"Patricia Anne. Don't ask foolish questions."

"Don't you think it had better be Anna?"

"No, I don't. Anna can come later. The middle name won't make any difference."

"We'll have to have a lot of girls, Drew. Because I want a Marie Céleste, too, and an Estelle."

"Don't you believe there'll be a priority on Estelle at Bayou's Edge?"

"No, I think that will start right out being Stella. And I don't believe there'll be as many children, Drew, at Bayou's Edge as there will be at Splendida, anyway."

"Perhaps they won't come along quite so soon or so fast. But I'm sure that by and by— Stella isn't as direct as you are, Patty. It takes her longer to find the basic values. But sooner or later she gropes her way towards them."

"Yes, she's very happy now. I've been wondering, Drew, sort of, now that she's facing the future at last, if perhaps I oughtn't to give back the mirror Aunt Estelle gave me. Don't you suppose that's what Aunt Estelle would want me to do?"

"I don't think so, darling. I think Aunt Estelle wanted that mirror to stay in the hands of a girl a Breckenridge loved. That's where it is now. That's where I believe it had better remain."

"All right. I want you to decide. I just wouldn't like to feel I was robbing Stella of anything she ought to have. She's missed so much. I can't get over feeling that it's tragic she and Raoul shouldn't have had months and months together, before he goes away, instead of only a few weeks."

"We can't live other people's lives for them, Patty."

"No, but we have lived our own. Perfectly. Completely."

This was what she said to him again when she went out on the portico with him for the last time. They had agreed, as they had agreed about everything, that she should not go to New Orleans—that they should say good-bye to each other at the plantation, where they could do it without onlookers and without interruptions. The last night had been like all other nights—a night of love, of joy, of close, intense communion. And now this was a morning like other mornings—

fragrant, still, golden. The baby had gurgled as his father tossed him into the air. Then, as Drew hugged him hard for a moment, he made cooing, conversational sounds. Finally, deposited in his little pen, he sat staring solemnly but confidently at his parents. Drew put his arms around Patty.

"I can't say it, darling. Can you?"

"Yes. I can say everything you're thinking. That it's all been perfect. That no two persons have ever loved each other more than you and I have and that we'll love each other that way always. That this isn't good-bye in any sense that counts, because it couldn't be. But— Good-bye, Drew."

She stood at the top of the steps until the car swung out of sight. As he went down the driveway, Drew could see her still standing there in her blue dress, erect and composed, framed by the white columns, the morning sun shining on her golden hair——

After he had gone, she put Ken in his carriage, as she always did at that hour, to take him with her while she made her rounds of the plantation. But when she had passed through the arbor with him, she hesitated for a moment, and then she turned impulsively, not towards the fields but towards the little cemetery. Drew had not spoken to her of going there, he had not asked her to go there with him, and it was a place where she seldom went of her own accord. Now she felt impelled to do so. As she parted the thick growth of shrubbery overhanging the rustic gate, she saw, as somehow she had known she would, that to this one place he had been without her. Fresh flowers banked the chalice of alabaster which was Andy's memorial, and a great mass of them covered Breck's grave. She knelt down between the tombs.

"He meant to have me find them," she whispered. "He meant to have me see them like this, so that I'd keep them like this always. And I will. I won't forget, Drew—anything. God, I'll never forget—anything."

For a moment she went on praying, her head bowed. Then she rose resolutely.

"I'll come here, often, but I won't linger," she said. "I won't stay here among the dead. I won't live with the past." She was speaking aloud now, firmly and freely. "That isn't what Drew meant to have me do. It isn't what God means to have me do, either. I'm going to stay where there's life. I'm going to live for the future. I'm going to help keep it safe and make it beautiful, for Drew and for me and for our children." Unconsciously she had already stopped saying "our child." She knew now that there would be another, that the name, like the land, would endure, and that she would live with them, beside the unconquerable river, in the house which at last had so firm a foundation. Carnival, and all that it stood for, had been swallowed by the war. But these would survive. She lifted her baby from his carriage and pressed him close to her heart. Then, holding him in her arms, she walked out towards the busy dairy and the fertile fields.